DOWNTON ABBEY

THE COMPLETE SCRIPTS

—— • SEASON TWO • ——

A CARNIVAL FILMS/MASTERPIECE CO-PRODUCTION

DOWNTON ABBEY

THE COMPLETE SCRIPTS
• SEASON TWO •

JULIAN FELLOWES

wm
WILLIAM MORROW
An Imprint of HarperCollins*Publishers*

HarperCollins books may be purchased for educational, business, or sales promotional use. For information please e-mail the Special Markets Department at SPsales@harpercollins.com.

FIRST EDITION

Library of Congress Cataloging-in-Publication Data has been applied for.

ISBN 978-0-06-224135-1

14 15 16 17 18   OV/RRD   10 9 8 7 6 5 4 3 2 1

To Emma and Peregrine, *Downton*'s principal inhabitants.

CONTENTS

NOTE: Dotted lines alongside the script text indicate sections of text that were cut from the original script to make the final edited version.

FOREWORD

Season Two of *Downton Abbey* is very different to Season One, and that was entirely deliberate. The year before, when we first began to think about shaping the show, we decided our starting point should be 1912; that is, just before the end of the Old World, but nevertheless in a recognisable place, with railways and cars and telephones and telegrams, which a modern viewer could connect with. Of course, not very many people live like the Crawleys now, but not very many lived like them at the turn of the last century.

By taking 1912 as our opening, if the series did not prove popular, we would be able to end it with the news of the outbreak of the Great War, and that, to a degree, would give us a satisfactory conclusion. However, if there should prove to be a demand for more, then the second season would take place during the First World War, and the third would chart the early years of the 1920s. In other words, the initial three seasons would cover three periods, which, despite happening within a comparatively short space of time, were nevertheless quite distinct from one another. And so the business of finding a new colour for each series didn't really present a problem, because the material was bound to be very different, and that would dictate the tone.

The challenge, naturally, was how to cover the war. In the end, we decided that, just as we had opened Season One with the news of the *Titanic* in order to pinpoint where we were, similarly we would open Season Two on the battlefield, so there would be no mincing about. From the first scene the audience would know the war has begun. The other decision we made was that we would go forward two years into the middle of the fighting. This was partly because, after the declaration of war, as with all wars, there was a kind of slow-burn start-up, when we wanted to begin with a big bang, literally, but it would also mean that all the characters could have war back stories as the series opened; they could have met other people, they could have different experiences or, in the case of Matthew, a fiancée has arrived in the gap since we last saw him. Added to which, we wouldn't have to show them in training for the Army. That had all happened. They could jump out of the screen, like Athena leaping from the head of Zeus, fully formed fighters, caught in the Sturm und Drang of the Battle of the Somme. Anyway, that was the decision.

Of course, this last detail was quite a tall order in itself, but we felt strongly that we had to accompany Matthew to the front, so it was a problem to which we needed a solution. The point was, we felt it would be cheating not to go to the battlefield. The alternative would have been to present it like a Greek tragedy, with everything happening offstage and people coming in and saying, 'It's terrible over there,' but that felt very feeble as an option. In the end, we had a tremendous stroke of luck when someone told us about a chap in Suffolk, Taff Gillingham, who was a great First World War aficionado and who had actually built a field of trenches, where he and his friends would get dressed up in uniforms and race around firing at each other. All of which was a miracle for us, because the cost, if we had not found him, would have been prohibitive. But even with his extraordinary maze of trenches to make the most of, we knew we wanted the core and heart of the show to remain Downton Abbey itself, and so this series was always going to be about a civilian family being plunged into the demands of total war.

The First World War (of course, every time one makes these generalisations there are six experts living in Thetford who write to tell you how wrong you are, but still...) was the first conflict that became a civilian war to any great extent. This was not so much because of German bombing, as it would be in 1940. Rather, it was the sense that the country had to get behind the war effort in a way that they hadn't when their menfolk fought the Boers, or in the Crimea. Those episodes, like wars in the eighteenth century, were generally considered to be happening 'over there', while the First World War happened to every man and woman in the land.

Part of this phenomenon was manifested by many, many landed families volunteering their houses for war work, usually for medical use – not invariably, but usually – and so, for us, that seemed a good template to go with. The houses weren't requisitioned; it wasn't like the second war, when they were commandeered for the services, for ministries and for schools. That wasn't it. In 1914 these people gave their houses over freely.

In fact, in real life, Highclere Castle became a hospital. The Countess of Carnarvon at that time was a brave, adventurous and vivid figure, and she decided that the proper use of the house was as a hospital, and she paid to kit it out. Actually, she was quite a remarkable character and I am sure worthy of her own television show. Born Almina Wombwell, she was in fact the illegitimate daughter of Alfred de Rothschild, who adored her and gave her half a million as a dowry, with plenty more to come – simply colossal sums at that time. However, while Almina did a lot of good, we weren't tempted to imitate the truth, as when Highclere became a hospital the family moved out, and we needed the Crawleys to stay put. So it seemed more sensible to convert it into a convalescent home, and have the Crawleys, like many families who did this, remaining in their house throughout, even if they did have to retreat to a few rooms. That seemed a much better narrative option for us. With them all ensconced in the house, we would go through the war, through the Armistice, and then use the Christmas Special – the first one we had attempted – to bring us into the New Year, that is January 1920, and the dawn of the new age.

As a final note, the reader may notice some discrepancies between the scripts and the finished shows. Sometimes the actor might have altered a line on the day, and not every change is one I would go to the stake to defend, but I think it quite interesting for the audience to be able to compare the two versions. Mainly the differences reflect cut material, some of which is hopefully quite useful to see, as it can shed light on the existing plots and characters. I might as well confess here that these scripts were really too long when they were first written. By the time we got to Season Three I was producing shorter scripts, because I had more or less found the rhythm of how many pages would go into an episode, but in Season Two I hadn't quite got there. ITV allowed us to vary the length of the episodes in an effort to overcome this, and sometimes the shows would run to an hour and ten minutes or an hour and fifteen minutes, but, to be honest, it didn't really work. The main problem was that it allowed one more commercial break, and it seemed to many viewers that they were being swamped with advertisements, so we reverted to the stricter one-hour length for Season Three, which was better.

To reach the required length, as the edit takes shape, Gareth Neame, Liz Trubridge and I discuss what might go and what must stay. Naturally, not all our 'musts' are the same, but it has evolved into a pretty good system and, while there are of course things that I regret, which you will see, nevertheless I am very proud of the programmes we achieved. At any rate, these are the complete scripts of the second series of *Downton Abbey*, which sees our characters face the ultimate test of war. Some are strengthened by the ordeal, a couple are defeated, but all of them are changed.

Julian Fellowes

EPISODE ONE

ACT ONE

1 EXT. TRENCHES. SOMME. NORTHERN FRANCE. DAY. *

The air is full of flashes and the noise of guns. The Somme.
November 1916. Men, covered from head to foot in mud, are
pouring over the side of the trench and slipping and sliding
into its murky, sodden safety. The last figure, as filthy as the
rest, pulls himself back to his feet. It is Matthew Crawley.

> MATTHEW: Is that you, Davis? How are we doing?

A slime-caked individual nods.

> DAVIS: The stretcher bearers are with the boys now.
> Quite a few gone, I'm afraid, sir.
> MATTHEW: Go back to the dug-out. I just want a moment
> with Sergeant Stephens.†

---

* We started in the Somme because it was a great bloodletting, and a massive, hideous event in which many, many men died. In other words, we chose to begin at the deep end as far as the war is concerned, but without yet committing Downton to its role in all this, because we wanted that decision to be reached on screen. I think it was fair enough; the enormity of the casualties coming back built and built and built, and by the end of 1915 people were aghast at the numbers of dead – figures that were reaching into all families up and down the land. High and low, nobody was spared, and it was a shared grief, which is something you don't see all that often, when a whole nation is bound by the same raw emotion. By 1916 I think that was true of the first war.

† I knew that eventually I wanted to use William (the footman from Downton) as Matthew's servant, but it seemed a bit neat to bring him in at the beginning, so we have a good performance from Stephen Ventura, who plays Matthew's initial servant, Davis. I'm always fascinated by how important it is to get good actors to play small parts. As most people making drama know, one line badly delivered in the middle of the scene can kill it dead. In this area, we have been lucky in our casting director, Jill Trevellick, who is meticulous when it comes to casting any part, but one of the bonuses of being a hit show is that people like to be in it. We have also been very fortunate in getting actors like Peter McNeil O'Connor, who played Sergeant Stephens, and other marvellous players in the supporting roles. They were all very talented.

*Matthew walks forward through the cramped and crowded
trench.* A private soldier addresses him as Matthew passes.*

    MAN: Well done, sir.

    MATTHEW: Well done to all of us. Who are you?

He cannot see for the dirt obliterating the man's face.

    MAN: Thompson, sir.

    MATTHEW: Then yes, well done. Sergeant Stephens?

*A man with the stripes of a sergeant ministers to the wounded
who are being loaded onto stretchers. He stands and salutes.*

    STEPHENS: Sir.

    MATTHEW: I want every wounded man taken down the line
    before it starts to get dark. We've bloody well lost
    enough of them for one day.

    2   INT. MATTHEW'S DUG-OUT. FRANCE. DAY.

*Matthew staggers in to find Davis is there before him. A
paraffin lamp burns. His appearance is even more grotesque.
An envelope is on the makeshift desk.*

    MATTHEW: When did this arrive?

Without waiting for an answer, he opens it.

....

* In larger, more splendiferous films about the first war, you see huge
trenches, tremendously wide, but this is quite untrue, because in a wide
trench one grenade would kill thirty people. Only by keeping them narrow,
and by making them dog-legged and zigzag, could an explosion within them
be contained, which, over four years of war, saved many lives. I read
somewhere the complaint that our trenches were too narrow, but they were,
in fact, built by Taff Gillingham to the exact measurements of how the real
trenches were designed. On top of the simple matter of life and death, being
in these trenches made the claustrophobia they must have had to put up with
so vivid. What was it like? Digging caves out of the mud walls to squat in?
And how did they survive the sheer physical discomfort of it all, being
permanently covered in mud, being permanently soaked? It must have
seemed almost beyond endurance. I found all this tremendously interesting,
but also very, very moving. These were men drawn from all walks of life,
many of them used to a high degree of comfort. And yet the complaints – the
public ones, anyway – were astonishingly few.

MATTHEW (CONT'D): Good news. We're to be relieved today
by the Devons. The men can finally get some rest, and
I've got a few days' leave coming to me.
DAVIS: What will you do with them, sir?
MATTHEW: Oh, London first. To remind myself what real food
tastes like. Then north for a couple of days, I suppose.

He gives his servant rather a playful smile.

MATTHEW (CONT'D): Naturally there's a girl I want to see
while I'm there.
DAVIS: So I should hope, sir.

*They chuckle. Davis has managed to wipe his own face and
hands. Matthew now takes off his Sam Browne and hands it to
Davis to clean.*

DAVIS (CONT'D): It's strange, isn't it? To think of our
old lives just going on as before? While we're here. In
this.
MATTHEW: It's more than strange. When I think about my
life at Downton, I feel like Heinrich Schliemann
excavating Troy. Every part of that existence seems like
another world.*

3 INT. HALL. DOWNTON. DAY.

*Not quite. The hall is a hive of activity. Carson is
supervising and the other servants are there as well. A
stage is being erected. A banner spans from gallery to
gallery: 'Help Our Hospital And You Are Helping Our Boys At
The Front'.† Anna is crossing the space with a pretty
newcomer, Ethel Parks, who looks disgruntled.*

....

* I tried to save the line about Schliemann, but I lost, which I think is a bit of a
shame, because one of the things we do in *Downton* is make references to
things that people would have known about at the time, without necessarily
explaining them. Matthew would have heard about Schliemann's excavations
of what he believed to be Troy – 'I have looked upon the face of Agamemnon,'
and all that – and even if we think some of his conclusions historically dubious
today, nevertheless there is nothing dubious about the artefacts he found,
even if the attribution to Agamemnon and Troy is a little bit wobbly. The
point being that it was thought at the time that Schliemann had found Troy,
and so it's absolutely natural that Matthew would make a reference to it. But
in the end, you can't keep everything, and there have been worse casualties.

ANNA: We normally have everything done before the family wakes up, but it's all at sixes and sevens today. I'll go through it with you tomorrow when we're back to normal.
ETHEL: I do know how to run a house.‡

They go into the library.

....

† Now we go to the house because, of course, the public have tuned in so they can see high jinks at Downton Abbey, and we don't want to keep them away too long. First of all, to take the house and its residents into the conflict, we start with a commitment to the soldiers at the front, and a fundraising event, but we do not yet suggest they should make any great sacrifices. This is, if you like, the transitional stage, when the family and the staff realise that they've got to get behind the war effort and do their stuff, but they haven't really accepted the degree to which they can be helpful, because it will disturb their daily lives profoundly. I think it's realistic. They're well intentioned, patriotic, loyal, but not yet quite ready to sacrifice their way of life.

‡ I didn't know, when I wrote this line, that Ethel Parks would be with us for two series. But here is a deliberate writing trick, which is to begin a character with a distinctive attitude, so that instead of Ethel being just another maid – which makes it harder for the actress or actor to define their character – you give them a tool at the start to work with. The good ones – of which Amy Nuttall is certainly one – will immediately build on that. Here we are suggesting the kind of independent spirit that would become much more in evidence as the century wore on. More and more, young people felt they were not born to serve in the same way as their parents had been. They didn't think (or they thought less and less) that their destiny was to spend their lives cleaning a house for someone else. Many working-class girls no longer believed they had to be a drudge until they died. The screen persona of the film actress Joan Crawford – i.e. the shop girl who goes on to have a career or make a great marriage – worked for her because millions of women all over the world were thinking exactly that. She represented a spirit of rebellion and a desire for change, and became a great star on the back of it. Here, Ethel's first line – 'I do know how to run a house' – is a rejection of Anna's authority over her. We, of course, know that Anna is only trying to help, but her helping hand is batted away.

4   INT.   ROBERT'S DRESSING ROOM.   DOWNTON.   DAY.

Robert is getting into a colonel's uniform, helped by
William. A strap has come adrift. William ponders.

ROBERT: It goes under the epaulette.
WILLIAM: I'm sorry, m'lord. If I'd known, I'd have asked
Mr Bates about it before he left for London.*
ROBERT: Because I'll be in uniform a lot of the time in
future.
WILLIAM: Does being Lord Lieutenant mean you're back in
the Army?

This is a sore point for Robert. He shakes his head.

ROBERT: Not exactly. The Lord Loot is responsible for
the Army in the county while the war's on. Manoeuvres,
training, recruitment and, of course, the Territorials.

He gives the footman a wry look.

ROBERT (CONT'D): But no. I'm not back in the Army. It
appears they don't want me.

He half smiles as he says this, but it is very painful.

....

* This is a minor joke, in that a lot of valets and ordinary people didn't know
how uniforms worked, which was a problem when the whole country had to
be militarised. Bates, of course, was Robert's soldier servant in the Boer War,
so he doesn't have any problems with uniforms, but he's away in London at
his mother's funeral. And William, the footman who is acting valet, is
struggling.

Footmen often had to fulfil other roles. It was part of their job. I have
heard people saying, quite mistakenly, 'There were forty footmen here in the
1880s,' but there weren't. What they have discovered is a cupboard with forty
liveries, and they assume that all those liveries were occupied by permanently
employed individuals. In fact, the reason a house had many liveries was to
make a big show if there was a special event. They would then borrow other
people's footmen, just as they re-cast their own valets, to make a great display
of having a seemingly endless line of footmen up a staircase, but it was all
really a piece of aristocratic theatre. That sort of lending a hand, everyone
getting behind the wheel, was part of life in these houses, and part of the job
description. So, here, there's nothing unusual about William pinch-hitting
for Bates while he's away, but William doesn't know his stuff.

WILLIAM: Your lordship, can I ask a question? Only, when
they brought conscription in, I thought I'd be called up
straight away. I'm young and fit…
ROBERT: You could always enlist.
WILLIAM: I would, but it's… difficult.
ROBERT: You know your own mind.
WILLIAM: But when I am called up, I won't be sorry; I'll
be glad.
ROBERT: Just try to be ready. You don't have to be
glad.*

....

* We start two stories here, both of which must have happened many times
in real life. One concerns Robert; the other William. Firstly, Robert is
unhappy about the fact that he is not able to serve. At the very beginning of
the war there was a feeling that only young men should volunteer, and
preferably young, unmarried men. There were exceptions made for career
soldiers, and Robert thinks an exception ought to have been made for him,
because he used to be a career soldier, but the truth is, he's too old. Even in
1916 they wouldn't have been interested in someone of fifty, married,
running an estate. It's silly of him to think they would. But a lot of men
were disappointed. This tale of Robert's frustration will be one of our
running themes.

Today, we are a very peace-orientated generation and one of the hardest
things for us to understand is the response at the announcement of the war in
1914, when every palace in Europe was surrounded by cheering crowds, as
various kings and queens came out onto their balconies and signed their own
death warrants. By contrast, we have inherited the horror of two world
conflicts, and we know the disaster and the social and democratic collapse
that can follow, so we think anything is preferable to war. I can only say it
was different then.

But the other narrative that we begin here is William's reluctance to sign
up. Of course, William should have been a classic enlistee; he's single and
young, after all, but his problem is that he's promised his father not to. His
father is widowed, all his other children are dead – which we learn later – and
so he cannot face the thought of losing William if it can be avoided.
Conscription had only just come in and, obviously, if William is called up
then there's nothing they can do about it. But he will not allow his son to
volunteer. For his part, William feels he's given his word. We get much
deeper into this later, but I like to start a plot with hints and small references
and then let it build.

5 INT. STAIRCASE AND HALL. DOWNTON. DAY.

Followed by Isis, Robert descends into the buzzing hall.*

ROBERT: Morning. I don't suppose there's any news of
Bates?
CARSON: We expect him back any day, m'lord. He wrote to
Anna that they had the funeral last Monday.
ROBERT: William's a good chap, but he isn't Bates when it
comes to uniforms… I may not be a real soldier, but I
think I ought to look like one.

This is said as a joke, but the butler understands.

CARSON: Quite, m'lord. This afternoon, m'lord, will you
be here in time for Branson to meet Lady Mary's train?
ROBERT: Oh, yes. I should be home by four.

The workers behind them drop something and he winces.

ROBERT (CONT'D): They started very early.
CARSON: You said they could, m'lord.
ROBERT: I suppose her ladyship's awake.
CARSON: She's already down, m'lord.
ROBERT: Heavens. Will wonders never cease?†

....

* I have always had rather a battle to get the dog in, although there are strong
arguments involving logic and expense that make it impracticable at times. The
previous dog, Pharaoh, was actually quite difficult, and by this series we had
moved on to another one. I remember saying to someone in the office that I
would have to think of a name for the new dog, and they said, 'Why not just go
on calling it Pharaoh?' I said, 'Well, for a start, Pharaoh was a dog, and this one's
a bitch.' At that point we all realised we needed another name and so she became
Isis. We stayed with the Egyptology theme, because we're filming at Highclere,
home of the man who discovered Tutankhamen's tomb. It's a sort of joke with
the Carnarvons that the dogs in the show will always have Egyptian names.

† I didn't mind this cut. It is explained in the next scene when he says, 'We
don't often see you in here for breakfast,' and the business about Mary's train
gets explained later with Isobel. In that sense, there are some proposed cuts
where you feel strongly, and others where you don't, and this was one I didn't
worry about. I was slightly sorry to lose Cora's comment on Violet arriving
to help with the concert, because I always think we enjoy the ongoing jokes of
the different relationships, and the fact is, Violet is a tiresome mother-in-law,
and Cora is a patient woman. I like Cora to have a chance sometimes to
express what she has to put up with. But she gets her chances.

6 INT. DINING ROOM. DOWNTON. DAY.

*Carson has followed Robert in as the latter helps himself
from the sideboard. Cora is at the table with Sybil.*

ROBERT: We don't often see you in here for breakfast.
CORA: Isobel said she was coming up to help and your
mother threatened to look in. No doubt they would love
it if they found me still in bed.
ROBERT: I don't know what Mama can do.
CORA: What does she always do? Frighten us into
submission.

By this time, Robert is opening letters. He almost gasps.

ROBERT: I don't believe it.
CORA: Please say it's something nice.
ROBERT: Nice? It's absolutely marvellous! General
Robertson's invited me to be Colonel of the North Riding
Volunteers. 'The Lord Lieutenant would be a welcome
addition to their number.' And this is the best bit: 'It
may please you to know that the idea was given to me by
General Haig.'*
CORA: What difference does that make?
ROBERT: Well, if Haig's involved, it means I'm back in
the Army properly… Well, thank you, God.
CORA: How can that be? You were told you weren't wanted
for active service. You can't jump in and out of the
Army like a jack-in-a-box.
ROBERT: I don't see why not. Churchill went back to the
front after the Gallipoli business.† Commanding the

....

* Douglas Haig, Commander-in-Chief of the British Expeditionary Force.

† This is a classic *Downton* reference that we don't explain, but is real. In
fact, it refers to Winston Churchill's decision, as First Lord of the Admiralty,
to land troops on the Gallipoli Peninsula, otherwise known as the
Dardanelles, in April 1915. They were to capture Constantinople and
effectively knock the Ottoman Empire out of the war. In fact, he had
hopelessly underestimated the strength of the Turks, and the Allies sustained
a crushing defeat with the loss of many lives. Churchill was initially
demoted before resigning in November 1915 and leaving for the Western
Front, where he was given command of a battalion of the Royal Scots
Fusiliers. That is what Robert talks about here.

Fusiliers. If he can do it, why shouldn't I? Sybil?
Are you all right?

*Sybil has also been reading a letter. **Now she stands.***

CORA: Sybil, darling?
SYBIL: Excuse me, I think I'll just —

But she doesn't finish as she hurries out. Cora sighs.

CORA: She's had more bad news. Shall I go after her?
ROBERT: Leave her. There's bad news every week now, and
she has to learn how to deal with it. We can't protect
any of them from the war, and we shouldn't try.

*Cora knows this is true. She finishes her cup of coffee.**

7 I/E. MOTOR CAR/DOWNTON VILLAGE. DAY.

*A tattered old poster of Kitchener shouts 'Your Country Needs
You!' Someone has daubed 'RIP' beneath the face, but
respectfully. It is on the side of the Post Office.† Then a
motor car drives past, jumping and grinding its way along the
road. Edith is behind the wheel with Branson next to her.*

....

* Sybil, being the youngest member of the family, is the one who has most
recently come out and had a London season, which we know was two years
before, in 1914. We began the last episode of the first series with the family
coming back from it. As a debutante, she would certainly have known many
of the young men who were fighting and being killed in enormous numbers.
That was the tough bit about being at the home front. People you'd known
all your life, relations, friends, friends of friends – it didn't matter – were
dying all the time for four long years.

† One of my sadnesses, actually, because of the decision to start at the
Somme – which I'm sure was right – was that my wife's great-uncle, Lord
Kitchener, had drowned earlier in 1916, so I couldn't really refer to him in the
action. Initially, when I knew I was covering the first war, I thought I might
involve Kitchener in something, for Emma, naturally, but also because he
was a genuinely giant figure of the day. In the end, all I felt I could do was to
have a tattered poster of Kitchener for Edith to drive past. They did use
Kitchener's posters marked 'RIP' for a while after his death, and it may have
been one of them – either that or an old one – which would have worked,
except that the shot apparently didn't. It should have started on the poster
and then, as the car crossed it, we would go with the car. But the car sort of
jumped, leapt and bucked as it crossed Kitchener's face, until it was quite

BRANSON: We ought to go back. I'm taking his lordship
into Catterick at ten.
EDITH: A bit longer, please. I do think I'm getting
better, don't you?
BRANSON: Up to a point, m'lady.‡

....

Continued from page 10:

clear that the first part of the shot was unusable. So we could only start the
action after the poster had vanished from the frame. I was really sorry about
that, but it wasn't anyone's fault. And we're not like David Lean; we can't
spend three days getting a shot at dawn, and that's just the truth of it.

‡ One of the journeys we go on in this series is with Edith, who had been, in
the first series, essentially a frustrated character, but also rather a meek one.
She may be jealous and hostile where Mary is concerned, writing horrid
letters and things, but on the whole she does what she's told. Like a lot of
those women, I'm afraid, and certainly like several of my great-aunts, in the
pre-war period they just sort of sat there doing occasional good works,
teaching religious instruction in the village school and waiting for some nice
young man with a reasonable acreage to turn up and marry them.

The war changed that. In fact, the role of women would change
fundamentally once the fighting was done, making it quite clear to the
Government, and to the political class generally, that where women's votes
were concerned it was only a matter of time. In 1919 they chose to say that
they were giving women the vote as a reward for their war work, but it was
really that they knew the hour had come for women to be enfranchised, and
they preferred to make concessions and lessen the risk of their losing control
of the situation. I know they started by restricting the vote to women over
thirty who had their own property and so on, and of course people make a big
thing now about the injustice of that. It was unjust, but it was still a huge
step forward, and it was, as the opponents of the bill would call it, the thin
end of the wedge.

In a way, we use Edith to track how more ordinary women felt about
these changes. She is not a firebrand like Sybil, or Lady Constance Lytton in
reality. She is simply a woman trying to get on with her life. And it is just
such women who were most changed by the events of 1914–18. From Tudor
times there were always female freedom fighters who tore up the rule book
and lived their own lives, but what changed in the First World War is that
non-revolutionaries started having different expectations of the future.
Edith is not a rebel, but the war will change her, and she'll end up with
different ambitions. And the first sign of this is that she is determined to
learn to drive, which is where we begin her story.

She grinds the gears again.

> BRANSON (CONT'D): If you could just get the clutch right
> down to the floor.
> EDITH: But I am.

There is another grinding rasp.

> BRANSON: Not quite, m'lady.
> EDITH: It doesn't seem to want to go.
> BRANSON: I think it wants to, if you ask it properly…
> That's better. You'll be putting me out of a job.
> EDITH: Won't the call-up put you all out of your jobs?
> BRANSON: I'll cross that bridge when I come to it.

8 INT. KITCHENS/PASSAGE. DOWNTON. DAY.

William is with Mrs Patmore and Daisy.

> WILLIAM: What are you giving them to eat?
> MRS PATMORE: Not much. They know the money's for the
> hospital, so they can't expect Belshazzar's Feast.*

....

* Mrs Patmore has been established in the first series as the sort of downstairs Violet. A lot of that was due to Lesley Nicol's performance, because she's a very funny actress. At the beginning, if you go back and watch the early episodes, she's really just the cook, but she gradually develops this personality and, as a writer, when you know you've got an actor who can deliver, you give them stuff to do. Lesley has never disappointed, and so by this stage she has established who Mrs Patmore is. We begin with that same tone here, with her reference to Belshazzar's Feast.

The village dame school education that the servants would have received was narrow, but it was also quite efficient, so Mrs Patmore would have known her biblical references. The emphasis then was entirely on giving the pupils what they would need to earn their living, so they were taught to read and the lost skill of good handwriting. They would also be competent in mathematics, and the girls were instructed in the domestic chores of cooking and sewing. There was not much history and almost no science, but the Bible would definitely have figured. One of the bitter ironies in all this is that a comparison of percentages in literacy between then and now makes for depressing reading. It is a sad truth that our standards of literacy have collapsed, thanks largely to the fashions in teaching that surfaced in the 1960s and 70s. To me, this was a betrayal of generations of children, and I find the teaching establishment's refusal to accept responsibility for it uncomfortable. At any rate, it is quite legitimate that Mrs Patmore would have known about Belshazzar's Feast.

DAISY: I'll make some cheese straws. What's the matter with you?*

WILLIAM: Nothing much… My dad still won't let me enlist. His lordship's made it clear he thinks I'm a coward.

DAISY: No such thing.

WILLIAM: No, he does, and I don't blame him.

MRS PATMORE: Your father has no one but you. Of course he doesn't want you to enlist. Who can argue with him?

WILLIAM: So I stand by while the lads on the farms and in the gardens go to war. Even Thomas is at the front in the Medical Corps —

MRS PATMORE: That'll have come as a nasty shock.

WILLIAM: Oh, you can make fun of him, Mrs Patmore. But he's fighting for his King and Country and I'm not.†

MRS PATMORE: Well, I dare say you won't have long to wait.

WILLIAM: Well, I hope you're right.

MRS PATMORE: Do you? Because I don't. I hope very much that I'm wrong.

....

* Here the servants are being obliged to support the war effort, but they do support it. We haven't got any conchies in this show. I suppose I felt it would have been a bit of a cliché, to have a conscientious objector among the servants.

† When conscription arrived in early 1916, they started by only calling up unmarried young men. By June of that year, married men were included, but no fathers, and so it crept on, broadening its net. The British complete indifference to whole families being wiped out was, I am convinced, quite wrong. In America, if all but one of your sons had been killed, then the survivor was taken out of the front line, which was the plot of *Saving Private Ryan*. We never had that, which seems terrible to me, but anyway, we don't get into that here. Mr Mason knows what he's asking; in plain terms, he is asking for his son not to participate in the war.

9 INT. HALL. DOWNTON. DAY.

Clarkson, in a major's uniform, and the servants arrange the gilt chairs. Cora, Robert and Isis are with Isobel.

ISOBEL: It's kind of you to let us hold it here. They'll enjoy it so much more.

VIOLET: And you can charge so much more for the tickets.

She has crept in on them in her usual stately way.

ROBERT: Good morning, Mama. This is very early for you to be up and about.

VIOLET: War makes early risers of us all. I thought I would help with the flowers. I've asked Sharp to bring whatever he can spare.

CORA: Well, Bassett has plenty… but thank you.

With a fixed smile she goes, leaving Robert and Violet alone.

VIOLET: You don't mind my taking over the flowers, do you? Cora's flowers always look more suited to a first communion in southern Italy.

ROBERT: So, what do you think?

VIOLET: I think it looks like a music hall in Southend. Well, what else have you planned for tonight's revels?

ROBERT: Anything we can think of that will raise money.

VIOLET: Hot buttered toast with a countess, at tuppence a slice?*

....

* When a series returns after a gap you want a little bit of a drum roll for the principals, and so we have this shot of Violet coming in like Vlad Dracula in her fur hat. Those things are fun to write; at least, they are in this show, because Maggie Smith is so very good at doing them. She always delivers. In a sense, Violet is a reminder that the aristocracy, in the space of not too many years, would become a branch of the performing arts, since in many cases they were going to have to turn cartwheels in order to attract the public to their houses. The fuss would begin in the 1950s with the Duke of Bedford and his safari park at Woburn, while the Marquess of Bath, not to be outdone, would install lions at Longleat.

He gives her a sharp look and she holds up her hands.

VIOLET (CONT'D): I know. War is a foreign country, and
we must all adjust accordingly.

The Major/Doctor has approached with a request.

CLARKSON: Will the new Lord Lieutenant open the
proceedings tonight? Congratulations, by the way.
ROBERT: If you want me to. What should I say? The
hospital's been promoted and the cash'll come in handy?
CLARKSON: Promotion's one word for it… The casualties
from the Somme are squeezing the system dreadfully. They
want us to double our intake.
ISOBEL: The fact is, they cannot stay with us for their
whole treatment. We just can't tie up the beds.
CLARKSON: We'll get them through the worst, then push
them off to the nearest convalescent homes, ready for the
next lot.
ROBERT: That seems rather cruel.
VIOLET: War is cruel. Horribly cruel.

....

Continued from page 14:

For us, there is nothing very strange about buying a ticket to walk round a
house and then perhaps have lunch in the former stables. But one has to
remember that for the generation who lived before us, for whom these houses
were simply their homes, it could be a very hard transition. Many of them,
after the second war particularly, would throw in the towel, preferring to live
in a rectory rather than being on show like a monkey in the zoo, which is a
sentiment that most modern people would, at the very least, understand. But
others have, happily for us, been determined to soldier on. Here, Violet gives
a hint that she will be one of the latter group and fight to the bitter end,
offering hot buttered toast with a countess, at 'tuppence a slice'.

10 INT. LIBRARY. DOWNTON. DAY.

The maids arrange the room for the evening party. Anna is still with Ethel. Mrs Hughes appears.

> ANNA: You drop the cushions on the floor to plump them up.
> ETHEL: I know.*
> MRS HUGHES: Ethel? Are you settling in?
> ETHEL: I would be. If Anna'd stop teaching me how to suck eggs. I was head housemaid in my last position.
> MRS HUGHES: You were senior housemaid, out of two, in a much smaller house.†
> ANNA: Are they to come in here tonight?
> MRS HUGHES: Only at the interval. And keep them out of the drawing room. I thought Mr Bates would've been back by now, or he could've stood guard.

She smiles at Anna, then leaves with some of the other maids.

....

* What they should have done here is drop the big seat cushions of the sofa. This was something that my wife, Emma, taught me – that you break up the density of the feathers by dropping these large, heavy cushions. Just trying to plump them up doesn't work, as they're too big. Unfortunately, they filmed it with the maids dropping the little scatter cushions, which doesn't make any sense because actually, with those, you do fluff them up by hand. I was suitably annoyed on seeing the rushes, but there was absolutely nothing we could do about it. In the end, we kept it in, because it was quite a nice observation.

† I think, if *Downton* has a sort of message about the servants, it is that being in service was a career. There was an order of seniority and it had to be respected, just as the people upstairs had to be respected. The whole set-up constituted a sort of mountain, of which the top half would be the family, and the bottom half the servants, but the butler and the housekeeper forged a path between the two groups. So Mrs Hughes, who is generally a pretty sympathetic character, and an intelligent, moral woman, has no hesitation in slapping Ethel down.

ETHEL: Who is this Mr Bates?
ANNA: His lordship's valet. He's been in London because his mother died.
ETHEL: Only everyone talks about him as if he were king.
ANNA: Do they? That's nice to hear.

Violet enters. She observes a large flower arrangement.

VIOLET: Anna, help me do battle with this monstrosity. It looks like a creature from *The Lost World*.*

She starts to pull bits out and hand them to the maid.

11 INT. CARSON'S PANTRY. DOWNTON. DAY.

Carson is cleaning silver, furiously. Mrs Hughes looks in.

MRS HUGHES: You should let William do that.
CARSON: He's got enough on his hands, getting the uniforms out of mothballs. I must remember to put Anna on alert for dinner tonight.
MRS HUGHES: You have to ease up a bit or you'll give yourself a heart attack. There's a war on. Things cannot be the same when there's a war on.
CARSON: I do not agree. Keeping up standards is the only way to show the Germans that they will not beat us in the end.

....

* Violet wants to keep up the old ways and maintain the old disciplines. But unlike the younger generation, she is aware that this will involve limiting her own personal freedoms. She is under no illusion that it will be other people making all the sacrifices. I don't ever think that Violet is either unintelligent or uninformed; she knows how the cookie crumbles. And a way of telling the audience that is to make her aware of current events – of books that have been written (such as Conan Doyle's *The Lost World*, published in 1912), of pictures that have been painted – so you feel that, in her own way, she is keeping up with what's going on, even if she just doesn't approve of quite a lot of it. This is a slightly complicated note to strike, so thank heaven we have Maggie Smith to strike it.

MRS HUGHES: Well, give me some warning the next time
we're expecting Germans at Downton and I'll see what I
can do.*

12 INT. LIBRARY. DOWNTON. DAY.

*The other servants have gone and Anna has a cloth on the floor
covered with foliage. Violet pulls out a final sprig.*

VIOLET: That's the best we can do. At least it's stopped
looking like a brush for a witch to ride home on.

*Anna is gathering up the cloth when the door opens and Isobel
comes in with Robert and Cora. She stops.*

ISOBEL: Oh. We thought we'd come in here for a little
talk.
VIOLET: Oh, well, I'm sure we won't be disturbed.

*She makes no effort to move. Anna carries out the cloth and
leaves them alone.*

ROBERT: Please.
ISOBEL: Well, the thing is, I've had a letter from
Matthew… Of course, he never tells me what he's actually
doing.

....

* A sub-theme of the story of these houses in decline is that the standards
that had been set in the old days, when you could have one man to wind the
clocks, four footmen to polish the silver and eight housemaids to clean and
re-order the rooms, just could not be maintained once the household started
to be cut down, which began in the war with the call-up. After that, you
either had older men, or just women, and later, after the war, far fewer of even
these, since there would be a widespread resistance to any kind of service as a
career. Some things could be compensated for by machinery, and we see the
arrival of toasters and Hoovers and all that stuff. But there had to be a
realisation that the way things used to be done, when they were done
'properly', was no longer possible. Carson is a classic example of someone
who will not accept that. He won't send anything up to the dining room that
isn't as clean as it would have been in 1850, and that's going to be a struggle.
Mrs Hughes, on the other hand, who is a more practical person than he is,
and who doesn't worship the way of life or the family in the way Carson does,
puts it quite simply: 'There's a war on. Things cannot be the same when
there's a war on.'

ROBERT: No. He wouldn't. But I'm glad he's all right…
I miss him.
ISOBEL: Well, that's the point. You must know he's been
here a few times since the war started.
CORA: We had heard.
VIOLET: Downton is hardly a metropolis.
ISOBEL: He wasn't being rude. He just felt it was better
to keep a wide berth.
ROBERT: Is he still determined to go back to Manchester
when it's all over?
ISOBEL: He doesn't talk much about life after the war.
None of them do. I suppose they don't want to tempt
fate. Until now, that is… He writes that he is engaged
to be married. To a Miss Lavinia Swire.*

This is a heavy moment. Violet breaks the silence.

VIOLET: Well, I suppose we all knew it would happen one
day.
ROBERT: Do you know her?
ISOBEL: Not yet. Apparently, they met when he was in
England last time. It all seems rather hurried.
ROBERT: You can't blame them for wanting to live in the
present.
ISOBEL: Anyway, he's been in London on leave and now he's
bringing her here to meet me. He'll be here tonight and
tomorrow, then he leaves on Thursday while she stays for
a bit.
CORA: So will you miss the concert?

....

* Lavinia is the Christian name of an old friend of mine in
Northamptonshire, whom I knew when I was acting at the Royal Theatre,
Northampton, the first permanent rep I went into as a player after leaving
drama school. Lavinia Dyer became den mother to the repertory company.
She had a large house in a village quite near the city and we used to race over
there after shows, drink all night and eat everything in the 'fridge. How her
husband, Rex, put up with it I cannot imagine, but he did. They are both
gone now, but I've always remained very fond of them in my memories of
that time, and so I thought I'd name a character after her. Swire comes from
the Hong Kong family. Hugo Swire, the MP, is a friend of mine, and I
borrow my friends' surnames relentlessly.

ISOBEL: Well, that's up to you. We'd all hoped that he
and Mary would sort things out between them. But if
that's not to be, then shouldn't we try to get back to
normal? Even if he's not keen to live in the village,
he's still the heir. And you're still his family.
ROBERT: I quite agree. We can't know if Matthew will
come through it… Either way, I would like to see him.
And I want to wish him luck.
CORA: The trouble is, Mary's back from London today as
well. She gets in at five o'clock.
ISOBEL: Matthew's driving down in Lavinia's car; they
won't meet on the train.
VIOLET: That's a relief.

They, and Isis, all look over to her for clarification.

VIOLET (CONT'D): I hate Greek drama, when everything
happens offstage.
CORA: But should we tell her not to come? We might still
catch her.
ROBERT: Isobel's right. We must use this engagement as a
new beginning. You bring our Lieutenant Crawley to the
concert, and stay for dinner afterwards.
ISOBEL: I was hoping you'd say that.

13   EXT.   DOWNTON.   DAY.

*Sybil is walking to the house. She's been crying. She
stops, wipes her eyes, straightens her hair and heads for
the door.*

14   INT.   HALL.   DOWNTON.   DAY.

*The space is much more organised now, with only one or two
people still working. Isobel walks through to the inner hall
as Sybil opens the door and comes in.*

ISOBEL: There you are. I'm just going home, but I'll be
back at four.

Sybil nods, but now Isobel is nearer and can see.

ISOBEL (CONT'D): Sybil? My dear, what is it?
SYBIL: Tom Bellasis has been killed. I had a letter this
morning from Imogen Bunting. She heard he was missing
and called on Lady Bellasis, but he's dead. It's been
confirmed.

ISOBEL: What a terrible thing.

SYBIL: I remember him at Imogen's ball. He made me laugh
out loud, just as her uncle was giving a speech…

The tears are coming again, as she shakes her head in sorrow.

SYBIL (CONT'D): Sometimes it feels as if all the men I
ever danced with are dead.*

Isobel takes her into her arms. But Sybil is angry.

SYBIL (CONT'D): I just feel so useless, wasting my life
while they sacrifice theirs.

ISOBEL: You've been a tremendous help with the concert.

SYBIL: No, I don't mean selling programmes or finding
prizes for the tombola. I want to do a real job, real
work.

O'Brien arrives behind the open glass door, hesitating.

ISOBEL: Well, if you're serious, what about being an
auxiliary nurse? There's a training college in York — I
know I could get you onto a course.

SYBIL: Would you, really?

ISOBEL: If you'd like me to. But —

SYBIL: What?

....

* That was actually said to me by my Great-Aunt Isie, my grandfather's eldest
sister, when we were talking about her experiences at the end of the war.
She'd had a cable saying her husband was coming home on a troop carrier, so
she got all dressed up and went down to Southampton to meet him, only to
find that he was carried off on a stretcher, dying of wounds. She took him
home and nursed him, but he died anyway, and she was then in mourning for
about a year. She had a house called Vicar's Hill in Hampshire, and she
stayed there with her little son, Russell. But at the end of the year she was
asked to a dance in London, and she thought it was time to get going, so she
went up to London and put on her dance frock. However, on entering the
ballroom she looked round and thought, just for a moment, oh God, I've
made a mistake, this is a party for women, and I'm all dressed up for a ball.
But then she saw that there was a man over there, and another over here, and
slowly she realised that these were the only men of her crowd who had
survived. That was when she told me that, at parties like the one she was
remembering, it was as if every man you'd ever danced with was dead. I
thought it was such a good line. So I used it.

ISOBEL: It may be something of a rough awakening. Are
you ready for that? Have you ever made your own bed, for
example? Or scrubbed a floor?* O'Brien? What is it?

She has noticed the maid listening behind the door.

O'BRIEN: Mr Platt's taking her ladyship and Lady Grantham
down to the village. She wondered if you'd like to go
with them.
ISOBEL: That's very kind. Thank you.

O'Brien leaves. Isobel looks at Sybil.

SYBIL: Go on. What else would I need?
ISOBEL: Well, if you're serious, what about cooking? Why
don't you ask Mrs Patmore if she could give you one or
two basic tips? She won't mind.
SYBIL: I feel pathetic saying it, but I'm not sure Mama
would approve.
ISOBEL: I'd never encourage disobedience, my dear. But,
when you get to York, it might be useful to know a little
more than nothing.

15 INT. CORA'S BEDROOM. DOWNTON. DAY.

O'Brien is helping Cora into a hat and coat.

O'BRIEN: They want to use her as a maid of all work at
the hospital. I suppose it's cheaper when Lady Sybil can
live here for nothing. But it doesn't seem quite right,
somehow. To take advantage.
CORA: No, it does not.

....

* One has to remember that this was all pretty extraordinary for these girls;
an awakening, really. Up until then, the most shocking thing they'd ever seen
was the death of a fox at the end of a hunt. There's a very good memoir by
Vera Brittain, *Testament of Youth*, about her time as an auxiliary nurse, and at
the beginning they were trained in very gentle arts. The idea was they'd write
letters for soldiers, read to them and hold their hands. But by the end she
said that, short of actually going to bed with them, she had performed every
intimate physical service that one could imagine. It was an incredible
transition. Because of the numbers of casualties, these girls, who were
supposed to be protected from anything too horrid, were helping with
amputations within days or weeks of their arrival.

O'BRIEN: I hear the young men that are being brought in now are very disfigured.
CORA: How terrible.
O'BRIEN: Limbs missing and faces blown apart, and Lady Sybil's been nurtured so very gently… And what types would she be working with? Still, you'll know what's best to do.
CORA: Yes. I certainly will.*

Coat and hat on, she picks up her gloves with real purpose.

END OF ACT ONE

ACT TWO

16   INT.   SERVANTS' HALL.   DOWNTON.   DAY.

Anna's cleaning jewellery. William sews a button on a shirt. Daisy is shelling peas. Ethel files her nails. Branson is reading a newspaper. William mutters a loud 'ouch'.

ANNA: You should wear a thimble.
WILLIAM: Of course. Yes. I should be sewing shirts with a dainty thimble.
BRANSON: What's up? As if I didn't know.
DAISY: Leave him alone.
BRANSON: You'll not catch me fighting for the English King.

O'Brien comes in, and so does Mrs Patmore, wiping her hands.

MRS PATMORE: Where's the batter for the pancakes?
DAISY: It's in the cold larder.
ETHEL: Are we having pancakes tonight?
O'BRIEN: Are we 'eck as like.
MRS PATMORE: Upstairs dinner. Crêpes Suzettes.

....

* Cora's worry about it, which O'Brien of course attempts to stoke, was shared by a lot of mothers at that time. What were their blessed daughters getting into?

ETHEL: Ooh. I've always wanted to try those. Could you save me some? If they don't finish them all.

This impertinence silences the rest of the room.

MRS PATMORE: Save you some Crêpes Suzettes?
ETHEL: If you don't mind. What are we having?
MRS PATMORE: Lamb stew and semolina.
ETHEL: Do you eat a lot of stews?
MRS PATMORE: Don't you fancy that, dear?
ETHEL: Not all the time.
MRS PATMORE: Oh, I see. Would you like to sleep in her ladyship's bedroom while you're at it?
ETHEL: I wouldn't mind. I hate sharing a room. I didn't in my last place.
ANNA: There were only two maids and a cook.
ETHEL: I'm just saying.
MRS PATMORE: And I'll 'just say' if you don't look out!

She storms out. O'Brien stares at Ethel. She speaks softly.

O'BRIEN: You've got a cheek, on your first day.
ETHEL: I don't see why. I want the best. And I'm not ashamed to admit it.
O'BRIEN: And you think we don't?
ETHEL: I think it's hard to change at your age. I don't blame you, but I suppose, in the end, I want to be more than just a servant.

17 EXT. VICTORIA. DAY.

Cora, Violet and Isobel are riding in the open Victoria.

CORA: I'm sorry, but if Doctor Clarkson needs free labour, I'd prefer him not to find it in my nursery.
ISOBEL: But Sybil isn't in the nursery.
VIOLET: No, and in case you hadn't noticed, she hasn't been there for some time.
CORA: You know what I mean.
VIOLET: No, not really. You can't pretend it's not respectable. When every day we're treated to pictures of queens and princesses in Red Cross uniform ladling soup down the throat of some unfortunate.
CORA: But Sybil won't be ladling soup. She'll have to witness unimaginable horrors. When she's an innocent.
ISOBEL: Her innocence will protect her.

VIOLET: For once, I agree with Cousin Isobel. Sybil must be allowed to do her bit like everyone else.*

18   EXT.   CRAWLEY HOUSE.   DOWNTON VILLAGE.   DAY.

Isobel climbs down as Molesley comes out to greet her.

VIOLET: What do you think about Robert's new appointment? Can they really mean to drag him off to the front?
CORA: I shouldn't have thought so, but no doubt we'll find out soon.
VIOLET: I'm starting to feel as if we're in an army camp and I'll be called any moment for drill.
CORA: How relentless it all is. What about you, Molesley? Are you ready for the call, if it comes?
MOLESLEY: It won't be coming for me, m'lady.

The ladies look to him for an explanation.

MOLESLEY (CONT'D): I had a letter from the War Office. They say I'm not suitable for service.
CORA: Why not?
MOLESLEY: I really couldn't say, m'lady.
ISOBEL: As you can imagine, Molesley's father is beside himself with joy.
VIOLET: God moves in a mysterious way, His wonders to perform.†

....

* Violet, again, comes out for me on the right side on this issue. She believes in the role of the aristocracy – there's no point in thinking she questions it, because she doesn't – but she believes in the aristocracy militant, meaning that they must do their duty. There is no social reason for Sybil not to do this job, since half the female royalty of Europe was being photographed in nurses' uniforms. The fact that it's unpleasant is no excuse for Sybil to be kept away. Once again, the exchange gives another character pointer as to how Violet thinks.

† In the days before conscription, from the start of the war until early 1916, a medical discharge was not that hard to get, because if you didn't want to enlist, you didn't enlist. Even when people realised that conscription was inevitable, you could write in with your own pungent reasons as to why so-and-so was unfit for duty, and when conscription was first brought in many excuses were accepted. The second war was much tougher.

CORA: I suppose they'll come for Branson and William next. What will poor William's father do? And how on earth will Carson manage then?

But Violet doesn't comment on this. She smiles and walks away as Pratt closes the door and remounts the box.

19 EXT. RAILWAY STATION. DOWNTON VILLAGE. DAY.

Branson watches as the passengers climb down from the train. Mary gets out of a first-class carriage and Bates leaves a third-class one with a bag. He stops to catch his breath.

MARY: Bates? No one told me you were on this train.
BATES: They didn't know, m'lady.
MARY: We'll give you a lift to the house.*

A porter arrives with Mary's cases and gives them to Branson, and they leave.

20 EXT. DOWNTON. EVE.

The car drives towards the magnificent great house. Anna and William stand by the front door. The vehicle draws to a halt. William starts to unstrap the cases with Anna, who is amazed as Bates gets out. Branson holds the door for Mary.

ANNA: Why didn't you say you were coming?
BATES: I didn't know 'til today.
MARY: Anna, I borrowed a case from Lady Rosamund. I bought some things while I was in London.
ANNA: Very good, m'lady.†

Her eyes follow Bates as he walks away to the side entrance.

....

* Someone told me that Mary would never have given Bates a lift home from the station. But of course she would, and it would not have been unusual. I am not saying they would have cuddled up on the back seat; the servant would sit in front with the chauffeur, the family member in the back. Why wouldn't this have happened? That's what is so odd about studying this kind of life, the often distorted way these things are perceived through modern eyes.

† Here we re-establish Mary's relationship with Anna. They're perfectly friendly, but Mary's first instruction is about the case. It's all quite businesslike.

21 INT. KITCHEN. DOWNTON. DAY.

Mrs Patmore is rather taken aback.

    MRS PATMORE: But what does her ladyship say?
    SYBIL: Well, it would be our secret. A surprise. You
    don't mind, do you?
    MRS PATMORE: It's not that I mind, m'lady —
    SYBIL: And I only need the basics. How to boil an egg,
    how to make tea.
    MRS PATMORE: Don't you know how to make tea?
    SYBIL: Not really.*

*There is a burst of giggles. Daisy and a couple of the
kitchen maids are laughing. Sybil turns to them.*

    SYBIL (CONT'D): You're right. It is a joke. But when I
    start my course, I don't want to be a joke. Will you
    help me?
    DAISY: 'Course we will. Won't we?
    MRS PATMORE: If you say so. Let's get started. Do you
    know how to fill a kettle?
    SYBIL: Everyone knows that.

*She takes the kettle and holds it under the tap, turning it
on far too hard. The spray soaks her.*

    MRS PATMORE: Not everyone, apparently.

22 INT. ROBERT'S DRESSING ROOM. DOWNTON. EVE.

Bates is dressing Robert in white tie.

    BATES: So will you go to the front?
    ROBERT: I imagine so. Eventually. But don't worry.
    You're quite safe.

....

* Sybil's instruction in cooking I took from an aunt of my own, who felt that
not knowing how to cook at all was faintly ridiculous. In her case, her
mother, my great-grandmother, was fine with the idea, but the cook objected
and she refused to act as teacher. She thought it was wrong and would
disturb things.

BATES: In that case, there's something I'd like your
opinion on, m'lord… Would you ever consider allowing me
to remain in my post if I were —
ROBERT: Yes?
BATES: Married. If I were married.
ROBERT: Good heavens. What brought this on?
BATES: You see, I had a bit of a shock when I was in
London.
ROBERT: Go on.
BATES: I always thought my mother rented her house. She
never said any different… But it seems now she owned it.
And she's left it to me.
ROBERT: But that's good news, surely?
BATES: It's extraordinary news, among people like us.
She had savings, too. And I've got all of it.
ROBERT: Enough to make Anna an honest woman?
BATES: She's an honest woman now.
ROBERT: Of course she is. Forgive me. I was just being
flippant.

He feels a little awkward after his bad joke.

ROBERT (CONT'D): Well, we could give you one of the
cottages. Move things round a bit, so you're near the
house.
BATES: Would you do that?
ROBERT: I don't see why not. When's the happy day?
BATES: Not yet. There's something else. And you should
know it because it may colour your answer. I have a
wife. A living wife. So there's the matter of a divorce
to finalise.

This is an enormous confession. Robert absorbs it slowly.

ROBERT: Hmm. To start with, I suggest we leave that bit
out of our account to Lady Grantham.
BATES: With your lordship's permission, I won't say
anything to anyone until it's all settled. I just wanted
to know the lay of the land.
ROBERT: I cannot approve of divorce, Bates, but we won't
fall out over it. You have not made your decision
lightly so I will say no more than that. Tell me when it
is settled, and we'll consider the options then.*

23 INT. KITCHEN PASSAGE/SERVANTS' HALL. DOWNTON.
NIGHT.

Anna is walking downstairs carrying some linen when Mrs Hughes sees her. She gives her a box with a slit in the top.

MRS HUGHES: We don't need tickets, but it'd be nice if those who go made a contribution. I won't have time for it, but take this as a start.

She gives Anna a shilling. Anna puts it into the box, which she carries into the servants' hall. Daisy follows her.

BATES (V.O.): When can I talk to you?

She spins round, laughing at the way he's made her jump.

ANNA: After the concert. Outside. In the courtyard. There's bound to be a gap before they start dinner.

They go as William comes in. He picks up the box.

DAISY: Anna's collecting for the hospital. Are you going up for the concert?
WILLIAM: Maybe. Can I sit with you?
DAISY: Don't be daft. We've got a dinner to make. I've not got time for concerts.
WILLIAM: I've had a letter from my dad. He won't change his mind. He says he can live with it if I get called up as there's nothing we can do. But if I enlist and anything happens, he'll never get over it.
DAISY: He loves you.
WILLIAM: He may love me, but he doesn't own me, and he's not being fair.

....

*This was a sadder cut for me. I don't suggest we were wrong to take it out in the greater scheme of things, but I was sorry to lose Robert's disapproval of divorce, because while divorce was not unknown among the upper classes by this time, it had required an Act of Parliament until pretty late in the nineteenth century and it was still a very Big Thing. It was the First World War that altered matters, but nevertheless it was slow. Even when I was grown-up and going to Ascot, you still couldn't get into the Royal Enclosure if you were divorced. That must be hard for some younger people to believe now, but it was true, and in my own time.

24 INT. MARY'S BEDROOM. DOWNTON. NIGHT.

Anna is dressing Mary. The other girls and Cora are there.

SYBIL: Glad to be back?

MARY: I'm never sure. When I'm in London, I long for Yorkshire, and when I'm here, I ache to hear my heels clicking on the pavement… I'd forgotten about this nightmare concert. Why didn't you warn me? I'd have come back tomorrow.

EDITH: But you'd have missed Matthew.

Mary looks at her mother for clarification.

CORA: I was going to tell you. Matthew's on leave and he's in the village, so Papa and I thought it would be a good time to mend our fences. He's coming tonight, with Isobel.

EDITH: And his fiancée.

MARY: What?

CORA: Edith, I don't know how helpful you are being.

SYBIL: Matthew's engaged. He's brought her to Downton to meet his mother.

Mary has nothing if not iron self-control.

MARY: Well, how marvellous.

SYBIL: You don't mind?

MARY: Why should I? We're not going to marry, but I don't want him to spend the rest of his life in a cave.

CORA: Exactly what Papa and I feel. Please try to be happy for him.

MARY: Of course I'm happy. Good luck to him. Anyway, there's someone I want you all to meet… Have you ever come across Richard Carlisle?*

....

* Mary hates to be pitied, and the idea that people would feel sorry for her because she has no one to call her own, while Matthew has a fiancée, would be completely unacceptable. As a result, she takes someone she's met, whom she quite likes even if she's not mad about him, and immediately elevates him to the position of suitor. The fact remains that if someone had come in and said, 'Matthew's here on his own, Mary, and he's dying to see you,' we would not have heard about Richard Carlisle, then or ever. As for his name, I think I was reading *The Eustace Diamonds* at the moment of writing this bit, and Trollope has his characters all breaking their journey at Carlisle and staying in a hotel, where the diamonds are stolen.

She examines her face carefully in the glass, but she is well aware that this is a piece of very interesting news.

EDITH: Sir Richard Carlisle? The one with all those horrid newspapers?
MARY: We met at Cliveden.*
EDITH: But how old is he?
MARY: Old enough not to ask stupid questions. Anyway, I can't wait for you to know him. If only Papa hadn't closed down the shoot.
CORA: Most people have stopped shooting now that the war's on. But I'm sure Papa would be happy to have Sir Richard to come and stay.
EDITH: Are you? I shouldn't have thought he was Papa's type at all.

She heads for the door. Cora and Sybil stand.

CORA: Sybil? What have you done with your hands? They're quite red.
SYBIL: Nothing… I was painting, and I used turpentine to clean them.
CORA: You should wear gloves. Coming?
MARY: I'll be with you in one minute!

She smiles brightly as they file out and close the door. Mary looks through the reflection at the silent, sympathetic maid.

ANNA: Are you all right, m'lady?
MARY: Oh, Anna.

Her face crumples into her hands and she sobs her heart out.

END OF ACT TWO

....

*The home by the Thames of William Waldorf Astor, 1st Viscount Astor and Anglophile American millionaire, who abandoned his native country and came to live in England, which he thought more suited to gentlemen. His eldest son married Nancy Langhorne, who as Nancy Astor became the first woman to take her seat in the House of Commons in 1919. Cliveden would remain in the Astor family until the 1960s.

ACT THREE

25 INT. HALL. DOWNTON. NIGHT.

The hall is packed. A small orchestra is tuning up. The Granthams are sitting in the front row. The inner front door opens and Matthew Crawley enters with Isobel and a young woman. He stops for a moment, to take in his surroundings.

LAVINIA: It's pretty grand.*
MATTHEW: You'd better get used to it. It'll be your home one day.
LAVINIA: I'm not sure 'home' would ever be quite the word to describe it.

But Robert is advancing up the aisle with a broad grin.

ROBERT: My dear fellow, welcome back. It's so very good to see you.

Behind him, Mary has moved up to greet Matthew. His eyes find hers, but he turns to the woman with him.

MATTHEW: May I present Miss Lavinia Swire?
LAVINIA: How do you do, Lord Grantham.
ROBERT: How do you do, Miss Swire.

Further down, Violet and Cora look from their seats.

VIOLET: So that's Mary's replacement… Well, I suppose looks aren't everything.

....

* Lavinia comes from Matthew's background; by which I mean she is not the child of a landowner, but of a rich businessman. So it's not a bad match on paper, but the point I wanted to make is that Matthew, having been very bruised by Mary, feels the need to retreat into his comfort zone, i.e. the intellectual, well educated, upper middle class, affluent, comfortable, but not hidebound and controlled by the rules that govern the landed aristocracy. In short, he does not share the Crawleys' priorities. I didn't want Lavinia to be the bad guy. I didn't want her to be unpleasant because, in a way, that would make it all much easier for Mary. The fact that she's clearly a perfectly nice girl makes it harder for Violet and Mary to dislike her, which they want to do, of course.

CORA: I think she seems rather sweet. And I'm afraid
meeting us all together must be very intimidating.
VIOLET: I do hope so.

Now Mary is with Lavinia and Matthew.

MARY: Hello, Miss Swire. I'm Mary Crawley.
LAVINIA: Of course you are. I mean… I've been longing
to meet you, because I've heard so much about you from
Matthew… That is…

She is in a hopeless fluster.

MARY: Nice things, I hope.
MATTHEW: What else would she hear from me?

*Lavinia is escorted away by Robert and Isobel. They face
each other, the ex-lovers, the eyes of the hall upon them.*

MARY: I can't say. It's been such a long time. Who
knows what you think of me now?
MATTHEW: I think I'm very glad to see you looking so
well.

At first she's silent. Then she laughs, holding out her hand.

MARY: All right. You win. We are at peace again.*

Robert is waiting, and so they sit.

ROBERT: My lords, ladies and gentlemen, it is with great
pleasure…

....

* One of the things I always enjoy about the English, of all classes, is that
until recently we gave no marks to people who felt the need to demonstrate
their emotions in public. In fact, quite the reverse; we always thought it was a
sign of a good and controlled personality that they could more or less hear of
the death of their mother and immediately go inside and give a lunch party. I
admire it still, I confess to that. Like many of my generation, I think a little
bit of emotion every now and then is all the more effective when it's rare.
We're not permanently sobbing and chucking ourselves into people's graves.
Here we have Mary playing what we suspect is a difficult moment, but very
pleasantly. She is a lady.

26 INT. CARSON'S PANTRY. DOWNTON. NIGHT.

Carson is filling two claret jugs. Mrs Hughes looks in.

MRS HUGHES: Have you found something nice?
CARSON: Why, particularly?
MRS HUGHES: As a welcome home. For Mr Matthew.

Carson emits a grunt in reply.

MRS HUGHES (CONT'D): What's the matter? I thought you'd come round to him.
CARSON: The last time he was here, he hadn't broken Lady Mary's heart.
MRS HUGHES: Lady Mary broke her own heart. That's if she has a heart to break.
CARSON: I don't think we're ever going to see eye to eye on this, Mrs Hughes.
MRS HUGHES: She refused him when she thought he'd have nothing. And when he was heir again she wanted him back.
CARSON: I thought caution was a virtue.
MRS HUGHES: Caution may be. Self-interest is not. Perhaps Miss Swire is a gentler person.
CARSON: If you ask me, this 'Miss Swire', who, it may interest you to know, is not to be found in *Burke's Peerage* or *Burke's Landed Gentry*, has an eye to the main chance.
MRS HUGHES: That's not snobbish, I suppose?
CARSON: I like to see things done properly, Mrs Hughes. And I won't apologise for that. Now, if you'll excuse me...*

He picks up the claret jugs and leaves her to her thoughts.

....

* This is a demonstration of Carson's absolute hostility to Matthew, because the young man has broken the heart of his beloved Mary. Carson's loyalties are pretty simple, but they go deep. He's never had a child and, in his head, Mary has become his daughter, whether or not he is aware of it. In his view, nobody should marry into this house who is not in *Burke's Peerage* or *Burke's Landed Gentry*, and he doesn't mind who knows it, whereas Robert never comments on Lavinia's birth. She seems a nice girl and knows how to behave and, for him, that's enough, given that he suspects Mary of having driven Matthew away. Violet, of course, is more judgemental and, like Carson, entirely partial.

27 INT. HALL. DOWNTON. NIGHT.

The orchestra is sawing away at Tales from the Vienna Woods.*
Lavinia feels someone's eyes on her. She looks up and it is
Mary who smiles pleasantly. As the musicians get ready for
the next item, two women walk down the aisle, looking about.
They hand out white feathers to youngish men not in uniform.
One of the girls holds out a feather to William.

> FIRST YOUNG WOMAN: Here.
> WILLIAM: What is it?
> FIRST YOUNG WOMAN: A white feather, of course.†
> SECOND YOUNG WOMAN: Coward.

William has taken the feather without thinking and now he
stares at it. Robert has stood. He walks towards them.

> ROBERT: Stop this at once! This is neither the time nor
> the place!
> SECOND YOUNG WOMAN: These people should be aware that
> there are cowards among them.

....

* I wanted *Tales from the Vienna Woods*, by Johann Strauss II, because of the irony of the orchestra playing Austrian music as a war-effort fundraiser. It's a very slight joke for anyone who was prepared to pick it up.

† In August 1914, Admiral Charles FitzGerald founded the Order of the White Feather, which aimed to shame men into enlisting. Women would present them with a white feather, denoting cowardice, if they were not wearing a uniform – a horrible and smug business, really, which ought to have made them all ashamed, although in fact the campaign was very effective and spread throughout several other nations in the Empire, so much so that it started to cause problems for the Government when public servants came under pressure to enlist. This prompted the Home Secretary to issue employees in state industries with lapel badges reading 'King and Country' to indicate that they, too, were serving the war effort.

Of course, the white feather has become rather a cliché now, but I think it's a useful shorthand for showing how completely ignorant many of the population were about the conditions at the front, and what they were asking these men to do. On the other hand, you need a very strong imperative in order for people to enlist, and if they'd known what they were getting into, a lot of them wouldn't have. So, one mustn't make the mistake of thinking these things are ever easy to judge correctly. You're always trying to balance the different elements.

ROBERT: Will you please leave! You are the cowards here, not they! Leader, will you continue.

The orchestra strikes up again and the women go. As they do, they pass Branson in the doorway, and hand him one.

BRANSON: I'm in a uniform.
FIRST YOUNG WOMAN: Wrong kind.

*Branson only laughs. He doesn't care.**

28 INT. DINING ROOM. DOWNTON. NIGHT.

William is serving with a very long face. The others are all there, Lavinia on Robert's right.

CORA: That was horrid, William. I hope you won't let it upset you.
WILLIAM: No, your ladyship.
ROBERT: Why are these women so unkind?
EDITH: Of course it is horrid, but when heroes are giving their lives every day, it's hard to watch healthy young men doing nothing.

Carson glances at William, who looks more depressed than ever.

ISOBEL: By the way, Sybil, very good news. They do have a vacancy. It's very short notice, because someone's dropped out. You'd need to be ready to start on Friday.
ROBERT: May I ask what this is about?
SYBIL: Cousin Isobel has got me a place on a nursing course in York. I want to work at the hospital.
CORA: We don't have to talk about it now.

Clearly, she still does not approve.

....

* I was quite keen to separate Branson from the war effort early on, because he's an Irishman and he does not support the British Government or the war. Rather than starting him with a protest, it seemed more fun to begin with him making a joke, because he doesn't care whether they want to give him a white feather or not. Part of being humiliated is to give people the power to humiliate you. And if you don't give them that power, then you are not humiliated. And here we have William, who does give these cruel young women that power and is humiliated, and Branson, who doesn't.

29 EXT. KITCHEN COURTYARD. DOWNTON. NIGHT.

Anna is with Bates.

BATES: She just turned up at my mother's house. Not long before she died.
ANNA: So what does it mean?
BATES: I think it means, at long last, I'm able to get a divorce.

She stares at him in silence for a moment before she speaks.

ANNA: Mr Bates, is this a proposal?
BATES: If that's what you want to call it. And you might start calling me John.
ANNA: Why are you sure she'll do it now when she's refused for so long?
BATES: Mother left me some money, much more than I thought. Vera's a greedy woman. She won't refuse what I can offer her.
ANNA: Will we have to leave Downton?
BATES: Not until we want to. I've spoken to his lordship and he'll find a cottage for us, near the house.
ANNA: You told him you want to marry me?
BATES: I did.
ANNA: Before you spoke to me?
BATES: You don't mind, do you?
ANNA: Of course I mind! In fact, I'd give you a smack if I didn't want to kiss you so much I could burst!

And so, at last, Anna and Bates enjoy their on-screen kiss.

30 INT. SERVERY. DOWNTON. NIGHT.

Carson enters from the dining room with a heavy tray. He is sweating, almost panting, with the effort. Daisy comes in with a covered dish on a silver tray. William is there.

DAISY: Crêpes Suzettes. And there's just enough. Mrs Patmore's making some more so they can have seconds, but there's only one each now.
WILLIAM: Shall I carry them, Mr Carson? Or shall I take the extra sauce?
CARSON: Give him the sauce.

He is gone again, on his manic, driven way.

WILLIAM: I don't know how he's going to manage when I've gone.
DAISY: Well, you've not gone yet.

31 INT. DINING ROOM. DOWNTON. NIGHT.

Carson carries the dish to the table. William follows.

EDITH: Branson says I'm ready for the road.
ROBERT: That's not what he told me.

Carson has arrived at Lavinia's left and removes the cover.

LAVINIA: How delicious. I love these.

She helps herself to one and then hesitates. She whispers.

LAVINIA (CONT'D): Do I dare?

Carson gives her a warm smile. She takes another.

ROBERT: Where did you and Matthew meet?
LAVINIA: Oh, in London. My father works in London so I've always lived there. But I love the country, too.
VIOLET: Of course you do.
LAVINIA: Daddy's a solicitor, like Matthew.
VIOLET: My, my. You're very well placed if you're ever in trouble with the law.

Robert speaks across the table to Matthew.

ROBERT: Did I tell you I've been given a Colonelcy in the North Riding Volunteers? So I'm properly in the Army again.
MATTHEW: Congratulations.

Robert is questioned about this by Violet. Matthew turns to Mary.

MATTHEW: He won't go with them, will he? When they're called to the front?
MARY: I hope not, but he seems to think so… What's it been like?
MATTHEW: Do you know, the thing is… I just can't talk about it.

But he can't not think of it, and his mind drifts away for a moment. Which Mary understands at once.

MARY: Have you missed us?

MATTHEW: What do you think?

MARY: So, might you give up the idea of Manchester and come back to Downton instead? When the war's over?

MATTHEW: Not Downton, I'm afraid, but maybe London. Swire wants me to join his chambers. Lavinia's his only child, and he doesn't want to lose her.

MARY: So you'll be his Crown Prince, as well as ours.

At the other end of the table, Carson is by Sybil.

CARSON: I'm very sorry, m'lady.

ROBERT: What's happened?

SYBIL: We've run out of pudding, but I don't care.

CORA: I fear one of you has been greedy.

She has assumed a daughter is at fault, but…

LAVINIA: It's me… I'm afraid I took two.

SYBIL: Honestly, it couldn't matter less.

*But Lavinia sees Violet raising her eyebrows at Robert.**

MATTHEW: I hope it's all right. Our coming here tonight. Mother was insistent.

MARY: Papa was every bit as keen.

MATTHEW: You don't mind my bringing Lavinia?

....

* I wanted this sequence to demonstrate a plot by Carson to make Lavinia look bad, as he tried to trick her into taking more than her share of the pancakes in order to show the family that she didn't know how to behave. Unfortunately, we couldn't persuade Jim Carter that Carson would be this nasty and so it didn't look, in the rushes, as if Lavinia had done anything wrong. Because of this, the whole story didn't work and it all had to be cut. I thought it a shame as it was one of the strands that happens above and below stairs, ending with the dog eating the last pancake in Scene 35, which now comes slightly out of left field. It was a lesson to me. You may write it, but it doesn't mean they'll do it. Looking back, I should have taken the trouble to explain the whole narrative to Jim, so it was my fault really. I wanted Cora's line, 'I fear one of you has been greedy,' to wrong-foot Lavinia publicly, giving them all that slight feeling that someone is coming into the family who doesn't know the rules, when the audience would understand it hadn't been her fault. A *Downton* moment. At any rate, that's what it was supposed to be. That said, all you want is for actors to take possession of their characters, and that Jim has most certainly done.

MARY: On the contrary, I'm glad. Glad to see you happy.
MATTHEW: What about you? Are you happy?
MARY: I think I'm about to be happy. Does that count?
MATTHEW: It does if you mean it.
MARY: You'll be the first to know.
MATTHEW: So we've both been lucky.
MARY: That's it. Happy and lucky.

She looks into his eyes, wishing she were telling the truth.

END OF ACT THREE

ACT FOUR

32 INT. SERVANTS' HALL. DOWNTON. NIGHT.

O'Brien comes in. She listens from the door.

DAISY: What are you reading?
ETHEL: *Photoplay*. About Mabel Normand. She was nothing
when she started, you know. Her father was a carpenter
and they'd no money. None at all. And now she's a
shining film star. It just shows. It can happen...*
O'BRIEN: Ethel, I've a message for you. From her ladyship.

This is rather a surprise to everybody. Ethel looks at her.

O'BRIEN (CONT'D): You're to go up and see her now.
ETHEL: What? Where?
O'BRIEN: In the drawing room, of course. They're all in
the drawing room.

....

* In this scene, we are laying the groundwork for the fact that Ethel thinks
the life she's been born to isn't good enough for her. Why shouldn't she be a
film star like Mabel Normand? Which, of course, is a sentiment I entirely
endorse. Here we will have a situation where she does get in trouble with the
Major, and she should have been more careful and less trusting. But, at the
same time, I agree with her that she has every right to dream. Maybe she
won't be a film star, but why shouldn't she go out and get a job and live a life,
and not have to be standing around handing someone their food? Ethel, I'm
on your side.

ETHEL: But what have I done wrong?

O'BRIEN: Nothing. Quite the reverse. She's very pleased with the way you've begun and she wants to thank you.

ETHEL: Now?

O'BRIEN: Yes, now. She's asked for you. How much longer are you going to keep her waiting?

Ethel looks round, then hurries away. The rest are silent. Until the hall boys, and all of them, explode with laughter.

33   INT.   DRAWING ROOM.   DOWNTON.   NIGHT.

Violet is with Cora on a sofa. They are watching Lavinia.

CORA: What do you think of my successor?

VIOLET: She's not my idea of a countess. But he's not my idea of an earl.

She shrugs. Mary and Edith are with Lavinia.

LAVINIA: I don't know much about life in the country. But I do understand how the law works, so I believe I can be helpful to Matthew there.

EDITH: But you'll be immensely helpful. Don't you think so, Mary?

MARY: Of course.

The door has opened and Ethel enters. Carson assumes that she is bringing him a message, but instead she addresses Cora.

ETHEL: Beg pardon, m'lady, for keeping you waiting.

CORA: What?

ETHEL: I'm ever so grateful for your appreciation and I want you to know that it's a privilege to work here.

The whole room is now silent, bemused by this bizarre exchange. Cora turns to the butler to help her.

CARSON: Ethel, what are you doing in here?

ETHEL: Her ladyship sent for me.

CARSON: And who gave you this message?

ETHEL: Miss O'Brien. She said I wasn't to keep her ladyship waiting.

CARSON: You may go back downstairs now, thank you, Ethel.

ETHEL: Right… Thank you, m'lady.

She bobs and retreats to the door. There is a silence.

VIOLET: Well. Do we think she's mad? Ill? Or working for the Russians?*
CORA: I'm afraid O'Brien has been playing a trick. Don't punish the girl.
CARSON: The girl is not the one I'd like to punish, your ladyship.

Isobel is sitting on a sofa with Sybil.

ISOBEL: How are you getting on?
SYBIL: Hmm. I've had one lesson and I can make tea and I think I can boil an egg. But that's about it, so far.
ISOBEL: Well done. Getting a boiled egg right is no easy matter.

34 EXT. DOWNTON. NIGHT.

Branson is by the car as Isobel and Lavinia are seen into the back seat by Robert. Matthew is walking towards it with Mary.

MATTHEW: She has plenty of time to learn. Cousin Robert will be in charge here for many years. Lavinia will be a lawyer's wife far longer than she'll be a countess. That's if I get through the war in one piece.
MARY: Of course you will. Don't even think like that… How long are you staying in the village?

....

* What we've lost now is the sense that, long before the Bolsheviks arrived, the tsarist regime was also seen as a dark power, a curtailer of liberty. The 1905 revolution, with the creation of a kind of parliament in the Duma, had altered things slightly, but nevertheless, much as we in the Seventies suspected everyone of 'working for the Russians', at the turn of the last century people had a very similar reaction to them. Funnily, and almost paradoxically, at the same time the Russians of the day had a similar role to their modern counterparts; that is, as a group of the super-rich who arrive in London and buy everything. Today, they buy all the nice houses, and go to Cartier and buy diamonds for their mistresses, and in just this way the grand dukes would arrive in the South of France and spend, spend, spend, losing more money at the casino than anyone else. So, you have the sinister element of the Cold War, as well as the money-spending plutocrat of the modern day; both of which were present in the British feelings about the Russians a century ago.

MATTHEW: Just tomorrow. I take the six o'clock train on Thursday.

MARY: And then you'll be in France.

MATTHEW: Wherever I'm going, I'm so pleased that we're friends again.

Does Lavinia look a little anxious as she waits for him?

35   INT.   SERVANTS' HALL.   DOWNTON.   DAY.

A new day. The servants eat breakfast. Mrs Patmore is there.

ETHEL: I still don't understand why it was funny. To make me look a fool. You weren't even there to enjoy it.

O'BRIEN: Oh, don't worry. We enjoyed it all right, from down here.

CARSON: Miss O'Brien, her ladyship has asked me to take the incident no further. Don't tempt me to disobey.

O'Brien looks down. Carson decides on a new tack.

CARSON (CONT'D): Did I see Lady Sybil in the kitchen yesterday?

MRS PATMORE: She wants to learn some cooking.

DAISY: She says she's going to train to be a nurse, so she needs to know how to cook and clean and everything.

CARSON: Has she told her ladyship about this?

DAISY: It's supposed to be a surprise.

MRS HUGHES: Mr Carson, it speaks well of Lady Sybil that she wants to help the wounded. Let's not give her away.*

ETHEL: Why shouldn't she learn how to cook and scrub? She may need it when the war's over. Things are changing. For her lot and us, and when they do I mean to make the most of it.

Mrs Patmore snorts, and Ethel stares at her, defiantly.

ETHEL (CONT'D): I take it they ate all the pancakes last night, then?

MRS PATMORE: They did.

....

* Mrs Hughes, for me, is always a voice of justice. She isn't in love with the social system they operate under, but she is essentially a fair person. When one of the Crawley girls does something that seems admirable, she's perfectly happy to stick up for her.

We follow Mrs Patmore to the kitchen, where she sees Isis.

MRS PATMORE (CONT'D): Here.

She puts a last pancake down. The dog eats it.

36   INT.   CORA'S BEDROOM.   DOWNTON.   DAY.

Mid morning and Cora is finishing dressing with O'Brien when Robert arrives. O'Brien retreats to tidy things on the bed.

CORA: You look very bouncy.
ROBERT: I am bouncy. I've been asked to a dinner to meet my brother officers.
CORA: When and where?
ROBERT: Friday. In the mess at Richmond.
CORA: I wish I could be as happy about it as you are.
ROBERT: It's not exactly that I'm happy, my dear, but I felt before… almost as if I were a liar. How could I criticise others for not enlisting when I was dodging the war myself?
CORA: You offered your services to your regiment the day after war broke out. What more could you do?

But he's aware of O'Brien listening, so he wants to end this.

ROBERT: Yes, well… I'll see you later. Branson'll be waiting for me.

He leaves and O'Brien returns to the dressing table.

CORA: Tell me he won't have to go.
O'BRIEN: It's very hard for you, m'lady.
CORA: What can I do? I suppose men must fight and women must weep.
O'BRIEN: It seems to me that women must weep whatever men choose to get up to.

37   INT.   DRAWING ROOM.   CRAWLEY HOUSE.   DAY.

Clarkson is with Isobel as Molesley clears away tea.

ISOBEL: What are we aiming at?
CLARKSON: They'd like us to take a hundred wounded men. Three times the number the hospital was built for.
ISOBEL: Well, that settles it. We'll have to convert the second day room.
CLARKSON: So, there's to be no convalescence at all?

ISOBEL: I'm afraid not. Once they can stand, they must go.
CLARKSON: If only there was somewhere nearer than Farley Hall. I can't get there more than twice a week at the most.

Molesley leaves, carrying a large, full tray of tea things.

CLARKSON (CONT'D): Should he be doing that?
ISOBEL: Why not?
CLARKSON: I only meant with his condition.
ISOBEL: What condition is that?
CLARKSON: His lungs. Old Lady Grantham told me he's had a lot of trouble with his lungs.
ISOBEL: And why did she tell you that, particularly?
CLARKSON: She wanted me to write to the War Office. She was anxious to spare him the humiliation of being refused on medical grounds.

There is a dawning suspicion in Isobel.

ISOBEL: And who else did she wish you to take under your protection?
CLARKSON: Only one other and not long ago. William Mason. The footman at the big house. He has a bad skin condition, apparently, and hates people to know. She wanted to spare him the physical examination.
ISOBEL: I'm sure she did.

38 INT. KITCHENS. DOWNTON. DAY.

Sybil is struggling valiantly at the stove, stirring some sauce. Mrs Patmore walks past her, looking over her shoulder.

MRS PATMORE: What in Wonderland do you call that?

Sybil turns, and Mrs Patmore remembers who she is.*

* Mrs Patmore is initially talking as she would talk to her helpers in her own kitchen. I felt it was unbelievable that she would immediately be transformed into a deferential servant, because what one has to remember is that the kitchen staff on the whole did not deal with the family. The cook, of course, spoke to the mistress of the house about the menus. But cooks didn't serve, they didn't wait at table, they didn't dress in a uniform or livery. In fact, cooks were notoriously difficult to deal with.

MRS PATMORE (CONT'D): I mean, I do not fully understand what you are trying to do, m'lady.

SYBIL: I knew it wasn't supposed to look like this.

MRS PATMORE: No, m'lady. I would go so far as to say there is no food on the earth that is supposed to look like that!

She goes as Daisy arrives. They stare at the mess in the pan.

SYBIL: Why does everything go so lumpy?

DAISY: Tell you what. Chuck it out and we'll start again.

39   INT. SERVANTS' HALL. DOWNTON. NIGHT.

Anna and Bates are alone in the room, planning their future.

ANNA: I don't think we should sell your mother's house. Not yet.

BATES: We could rent it out. Then we can save. When I've some time off, I'll go up to London and get it ready.

ANNA: Maybe I can come with you. We could do it together.

BATES: I've got an idea that a bit later on, if we want to…

He breaks off, slightly embarrassed. She takes his hand.

ANNA: If we want to start a family.

BATES: I thought, when the time is right, we might sell, and we could buy a small hotel, just a little one, maybe near here. Then we could work together and have the children with us. What is it?

She cannot answer him for a second. Her eyes are filling.

ANNA: Nothing. It's just that, in my whole life, I never thought I could be as happy as I am at this moment.

But Ethel's arrival prevents the flood gates opening. *

40 EXT. DOWNTON VILLAGE/STATION. SIX O'CLOCK IN
THE MORNING.

*Matthew is walking through the village towards the station.
He pauses to watch a milkman flirting with a housemaid. It is
all so far from war. When he emerges onto the platform, Mary
is waiting for him. He's puzzled as to quite what this
means.*

> MARY: Don't worry. I haven't come to undo your good work
> of the other night.
> MATTHEW: You must have been up before the servants.
> MARY: They were rather surprised to see me… I wanted to
> give you this.

*She brings something from her bag and holds it out. He takes
it. It's a very small, very battered, old toy rabbit.*

> MARY (CONT'D): It's my lucky charm. I've had it always.
> So you must promise to bring it back… without a scratch.
> MATTHEW: Won't you need it?
> MARY: Not as much as you. So look after it. Please.†
> MATTHEW: I'll try not to be a hero, if that's what you're
> afraid of.
> MARY: Just come back, safe and sound. Did you have a
> happy time yesterday?
> MATTHEW: I showed Lavinia the places I like most. To
> give her a few memories.

....

* I always find this scene very touching actually, when I watch it, because the
actors play it so well. I felt it was important, before everything goes wrong,
to establish an image of what life could be for the Bateses if they had a bit of
luck. The divorce going through, their getting married, starting a little hotel:
what could be nicer than that? The point is, you've got to give the characters
a bit of happiness every now and again for their sorrow to resonate.

† I had a bit of a battle initially with Mary's lucky charm, I remember,
because it photographed incredibly clean. In the script, it started out as a
rabbit, and then someone thought a rabbit was too girly. I had an old rabbit,
which I based the idea on, and I would have gladly lent it to them, but they
said, 'No, we really want a dog.' And I thought, well, I can't really just say,
'No, you've got to have a rabbit,' so we got the dog. But when we watched the
rushes it looked too new to be a child-chewed toy of many years' standing, so
it was dusted over by the special-effects lab to age it up a bit. But I thought it
worked very well, and indeed it reappears later in the story.

Of course this is exactly the point.

> MATTHEW (CONT'D): Mary, if I don't come back —
> MARY: But —
> MATTHEW: No. If I don't, then do remember how very glad
> I am that we made up when we had the chance. I mean it.
> You send me off to war a happy man.

He smiles at her as he prepares to ask a favour.

> MATTHEW (CONT'D): Will you do something for me? Will you
> look after Mother, if anything happens?
> MARY: Of course we will, but it won't.
> MATTHEW: And Lavinia? She's young and she'll find someone
> else — I hope she does, anyway — but until she does…

She is saved from answering by the whistle of an engine.

> MATTHEW (CONT'D): That's my train.

They take each other's hands. She kisses his cheek.

> MARY: Goodbye, then. And *such* good luck.
> MATTHEW: Goodbye, Mary. And God bless you.*

....

* This scene at the railway station is one of my favourites in the whole show so far, because it is all about things that they are not saying out loud. Mary is trying to contain the fact that her love for Matthew is completely undimmed. And one has to remember that even though she didn't dump him at the end of the first series and he dumped her, nevertheless she provoked him, which was the biggest mistake of her life. Now, she's not prepared to make a direct appeal, both because of her pride and her upbringing. She just can't say, 'Would it make a difference if I told you I loved you?' But, given that he may die, she can't let an ordinary goodbye at the end of an evening serve as the last time they see each other this side of the grave, which it might have had to if she hadn't come to see him off. Especially now that they're talking again. So, she is emotionally obliged to walk down to the station and say goodbye, whatever it costs her. I think Dan Stevens and Michelle Dockery both play the scene terribly well, and the whole business of Matthew asking Mary to look after Lavinia is handled brilliantly by them. In one way it is a big ask, obviously, but in another way we should understand that he needs to feel that if this poor girl is not even widowed – if he's killed before they're married – then he must try to see that she will have powerful friends to support her through it and be on her side.

A second later, she is alone. The train moves off. A woman, Vera, in her thirties, has got down onto the platform. She passes Mary and heads for the village.

41 INT. KITCHENS. DOWNTON. DAY.

Sybil is at the stove. Mrs Patmore is inspecting her work.

MRS PATMORE: Well, well, m'lady. Not bad. Not bad at all. You have come on. I wasn't sure you had the aptitude. But I was wrong. And I'm glad to admit it.
SYBIL: Mrs Patmore, might I make something for Mama? As a surprise, when I tell her what I've been doing.
MRS PATMORE: Why don't you bake her a cake?
SYBIL: But could I?
MRS PATMORE: Oh, I think so. As long as you do what I tell you and we don't try anything too fancy.

There is a small triumph in this, which Sybil shares with Daisy. She notices Branson watching her from the doorway.

SYBIL: You see, Branson? I'm not completely useless.
BRANSON: I never said you were, m'lady.

42 INT. KITCHEN PASSAGE/SERVANTS' HALL. DOWNTON. DAY.

Anna is walking along the kitchen passage. As she draws near the door to the servants' hall, she can hear voices.

VERA (V.O.): Lady Mary was very much a part of the story, I assure you.
ETHEL: But how do you know?
VERA (V.O.): Well, you see, I worked for Lady Flintshire —

Anna walks in to find Ethel with the woman we saw leaving the station. She's not bad-looking, but she has a hard face.

ANNA: Ethel? I hope you've offered our visitor some tea?
ETHEL: I'll go and ask Daisy.

She stands and walks out down the passage. Anna follows.

ANNA: What is the first law of service? We do not discuss the business of this house with strangers!
ETHEL: But she's not a stranger. She's Mr Bates's wife.

Anna is completely winded by the words. This is Vera Bates. *

ETHEL (CONT'D): Has anyone told him she's here?

43 INT. SERVANTS' HALL. DOWNTON. DAY.

Anna is with Vera, who looks at her coldly.

VERA: So you're Anna.
ANNA: I am.
VERA: You're the one who went to call on my late,
lamented mother-in-law.
ANNA: Yes, I did.
VERA: I know you did.

They lock eyes, as Ethel returns with Bates.

BATES: I'm sorry to keep you waiting, Vera. I was up in
the attics, sorting out some cupboards.
VERA: Don't worry. I've been having a nice time here
with Ethel and Miss Smith.

They are evenly matched, these two. Mrs Hughes now enters.

MRS HUGHES: Mr Bates, Ethel told me about your visitor,
so I've had the tea put in my sitting room. I thought
you might take Mrs Bates in there.
BATES: That's very thoughtful.
VERA: It is. But then you're all so kind. I'm beginning
to understand why my Batesy's got so spoiled.

Her voice is like nails down a blackboard.

....

* We were extremely lucky to get Maria Doyle Kennedy, who is a very, very strong actress. One of the difficulties when you have a character who everyone has talked about forever is that, when they do finally appear, they cannot be disappointing. And Maria managed this without difficulty. Her Vera is bitter and dominant, and yet you could believe that she must have been attractive when she was young; attractive and strong and not cowed or shy or any of those things, and perhaps rather glorious in her way. But all of that has turned into rage and hurt and a desire for revenge. I thought she was very powerful in the two scenes. Originally, we did have a little break, but then, in the edit, they made it continuous and, if anything, she was more powerful still. I would work with Maria again not long after this, in a four-part version of the story of the *Titanic*. She and Toby Jones played a married couple in Second Class – my favourite of the different narratives of that show.

44 INT. HALL. DOWNTON. DAY.

Carson approaches Cora.

CARSON: I'm sorry to trouble you, m'lady.
CORA: What is it, Carson?
CARSON: Something's been going on and I don't feel quite easy that you've not been made aware of it.
CORA: Goodness. What is this dark secret?
CARSON: Lady Sybil has spent the last two days in the kitchens.
CORA: What?
CARSON: She asked Mrs Patmore for some cooking lessons. Because of this nursing course she's going on.
CORA: I wondered where she'd been hiding. But why didn't she mention it?

45 INT. KITCHEN PASSAGE. DOWNTON. DAY.

Carson and Cora are at the internal passage window. In the kitchen beyond, the kitchen maids have gathered round. They are all in a state of nerves, as Sybil is about to take the cake out of the oven. Mrs Patmore's still in charge.

MRS PATMORE: Now steady. Even the most experienced cook in the world can burn themselves if they're not careful.
SYBIL: But do you think it's ready?
MRS PATMORE: I know it's ready.
DAISY: Go on. You don't want to spoil it.

Beyond the window, Carson whispers to Cora.

CARSON: It seems she's made a cake for your ladyship, as a surprise. But I'm uneasy with surprises at the best of times. And I wonder if the whole exercise is entirely appropriate.

Sybil turns the cake out with a flourish and steps back.

SYBIL: Da-dah!

The cake is perfect. All the girls start to clap and laugh and cheer and gather round her, as they admire her handiwork.

CARSON: I'm not comfortable with this, m'lady, not comfortable at all.

But Cora is seeing her daughter anew, independent, rubbing along with the others, laughing and chatting.

CORA: They're just girls, Carson. Just young girls. All on the brink of the rest of their lives.

The butler is puzzled by her response. She explains.

CORA (CONT'D): I was worried about Lady Sybil. But now I'm not worried any more. So, if you'll excuse me, I'll just tiptoe upstairs.
CARSON: So you don't mind, m'lady?
CORA: No. I do not mind. And I'm very grateful to you.

She starts to leave, then she stops and whispers.

CORA (CONT'D): And Carson, the cake will be a surprise, whether you approve or not. So please don't give me away.

END OF ACT FOUR

ACT FIVE

46 INT. MRS HUGHES'S SITTING ROOM. DOWNTON.
DAY.

Vera pours milk into two cups. Bates stands by the window.

VERA: Sit down.
BATES: I don't want to sit down.
VERA: Suit yourself.

She pours out the tea and sits back to drink it.

BATES: Look, I'm not saying it's all your fault for how things were between us, but I couldn't go back to that. I'll take the blame. I'll go to some hotel in Malton with a tart. So why hold on?
VERA: Because I've tried it on my own and I don't like it. You've got money now. We'll be comfortable.
BATES: You're out of your mind! What makes you think that I'd ever let it happen?
VERA: You went to prison for me once…

Vera takes a delicious sip of tea.

VERA (CONT'D): I must say this is very good. Does Lord Grantham have his own blend?
BATES: Is that all?
VERA: Not quite. You see, if you don't come back to me, I'm going to the newspapers with a cracking story. And I'd like to bet the Granthams won't survive it.
BATES: Oh? And what nonsense is this?
VERA: The nonsense I heard when I used your name to get a job with Lady Flintshire. His lordship's cousin.
BATES: I know who Lady Flintshire is.
VERA: Well, when I arrived, her maid asked if it was true about Lady Mary Crawley and the Turkish diplomat… They thought I'd know, you see, being your wife.
BATES: I hope you told them you knew nothing about it.
VERA: As if. I said: 'Why don't you tell me what you think you know, and I'll tell you if it's true?'

She gives Bates a triumphant smile.

VERA (CONT'D): Goodness me, wasn't my patience rewarded? The public's bored with the war, you see. They like gossip, and a diplomat dying in the bed of an earl's unmarried daughter… Well, that takes the ticket for the Tale of the Year.
BATES: It's a pack of lies.
VERA: I assume that's loyalty, and not ignorance? Because, you see, I heard Lady Mary needed her maid to help carry him. And, yes, you've guessed it, your precious Anna's going to figure in the story, too. Not to worry too much. It isn't a criminal offence, is it? Just a social one.

For a moment Bates is still, then he lurches towards her, his hand raised to strike her. He sounds like an animal at bay.

BATES: You bitch!

But she holds her cup and her nerve, and smiles up at him.

VERA: Please. Be my guest. But then you must excuse me while I run into town and have it photographed.

Bates sinks back against the wall. He is in despair.

BATES: What do you want from me?

VERA: Firstly, hand in your notice. Tonight. I'll put
up at the pub in the village.
BATES: What reason do I give?
VERA: You don't need a reason. Just tell them that
you're going. And then tomorrow we head back to London.
We'll stay in your mother's house for the time being,
'til we get ourselves sorted.

*But as she talks, the camera drifts to a grating in the wall,
dissolving through that wall, to find Mrs Hughes listening.*

VERA (V.O.) (CONT'D): And in case you're wondering:
whatever my future plans may be, they all involve you.

47 INT. KITCHEN PASSAGE. DOWNTON. NIGHT.

*Bates is carrying some pyjamas. He reaches the bottom of the
stairs and stops, thinking. Mrs Hughes sees him.*

MRS HUGHES: Mr Bates? Are you all right?
BATES: Oh, yes.

*Of course Mrs Hughes knows his troubles, but she can't say
so.*

MRS HUGHES: Because there are plenty of people here who'd
like to help you if they could. That's if you need help…
You're very highly valued in this house, Mr Bates. By
all of us.

He looks at her for a moment, this kind woman.

BATES: Thank you, Mrs Hughes. If that is true, then it
will be a great comfort in the days to come.

And he sets off up the stairs.

48 INT. ROBERT'S DRESSING ROOM. DOWNTON. NIGHT.

Robert is getting out of evening dress. He's in a fury.

ROBERT: What d'you mean? You can't suddenly jump ship
like a sailor on a spree!
BATES: I'm very sorry, m'lord —
ROBERT: So you bloody well should be! What about Anna?
What does she say to this change of plan?
BATES: I haven't spoken to her yet.
ROBERT: Well, don't you think you should?

Robert feels he got this man entirely wrong, and it hurts.

ROBERT (CONT'D): Bates, when you first came here I fought
to keep you. Everyone was against me, everyone, from her
ladyship to Carson! They thought I was mad! But I said
to them: 'After all that we've been through together,
Bates and I, I owe him my loyalty!'
BATES: I appreciate that, m'lord, but —
ROBERT: But what? But loyalty doesn't matter to you?
BATES: It does matter, m'lord —
ROBERT: Not enough to make you change your mind! Not
even enough to make you stay until I've found a
replacement!
BATES: I can't.
ROBERT: You won't take any more money off me! You leave
empty-handed!
BATES: I don't want money, m'lord.

But this was cheap, and now Robert feels ashamed.

ROBERT: I'm sorry, Bates. That was a low shot. Of
course you can have whatever is owing to you.

Neither man adds to this. Robert has gone from angry to sad.

ROBERT (CONT'D): I thought we were friends, that's all.
I thought we had crossed the great divide, successfully…
Well, well. I've had my say. It's your life. But
you've disappointed me, Bates. I cannot remember being
more disappointed in any man.

49 EXT. KITCHEN COURTYARD. DOWNTON. NIGHT.

Anna is with Bates.

ANNA: I don't believe it! You say my life is over and
your wife will collect you first thing and that's it?
Have you mentioned this to anyone else?
BATES: Only Mr Carson and Mrs Hughes. The others can
find out when I've gone.

Something is troubling her beyond everything else.

ANNA: I know you've not told me the real reason.
BATES: You're wrong. Vera has reminded me that I'm a
married man, that I must give my vows another chance, I
had no right to involve you in my life.

ANNA: Yes, but you see that's just what I don't agree with. You had every right. You had the right of a suffering prisoner fighting for freedom. But I know you. You're doing something gallant here. Making a sacrifice for my honour. But I don't want you to.

She seizes him with both hands, staring into his face.

ANNA (CONT'D): I don't care. Don't you understand? I don't care what people say. I'd live in sin with you! I would! I'd rather stand naked in the full light of day on top of Nelson's column than let you go!*

She is crying now, but so is he. He can only shake his head.

BATES: I can't…
ANNA: If she's threatening to ruin me, then let her! It's nothing to me! The only ruin that I recognise is to be without you!

He reaches up to stroke her cheek.

BATES: Forget me, and be happy. Please.
ANNA: I couldn't. Not ever.
BATES: You should and you must. I am nothing.

He walks into the house without a backward look.†

....

* When Anna offers to live in sin with him, for a young woman in 1916 it would have been an *enormously* significant choice. The price she would pay, if he took her up on it, would be to lose not just her respectability, but all her friends, as well as the support of her family. She would henceforth be an outcast from the world that she'd known. So it is a tremendous sacrifice that she offers, and Bates knows this, which of course makes it all the worse for him, because it is another reminder of how much they love each other. But anyway, he has to give her up, because he cannot ruin her and plunge her family into disgrace. His choice of action is the only honourable one open to him.

† I think Anna is unreasonable about Vera's desire to have Bates back, as all people in love are unreasonable about the previous partner of the object of their love. She is not inclined to see Vera's side at all, and we don't dislike her for that, but I believe we should be aware that she's not prepared to give Vera any sort of hearing, even though Vera is, after all, Bates's wife. In Season One, we did discover from Bates's mother that, actually, Vera did have a very tough time.

50   INT.   SERVANTS' HALL.   DOWNTON.   NIGHT.

Daisy comes into the dark, empty room and turns on the lights.   William is sitting there, alone.

DAISY: William?   I thought everyone had gone up.   I'm just looking for that magazine Ethel were reading…

She retrieves it.   Still, he doesn't move.   She chatters on.

DAISY (CONT'D): I hope you've noticed I'm not scared of electricity any more.   Well, not much.   I couldn't touch a switch when it were only upstairs.   But I've got used to it now.

He does not speak and she goes to sit by him.

DAISY (CONT'D): I hate to see you like this.
WILLIAM: Even though I'm a dirty coward?
DAISY: You are not.   Not to me.
WILLIAM: But why don't I enlist?   I could.   I know I promised my dad, but he's not my owner, he's not the law.   Am I frightened?   Is that it?   Honestly?
DAISY: Don't be so hard on yourself.   No one wants to go to war.   Oh, I wish you'd cheer up.   Please.   I'd do anything to cheer you up.
WILLIAM: Like what?

She thinks for a moment, and then makes a decision.

DAISY: Like this.

She leans across and kisses him gently on the mouth.   This does succeed in pulling him out of his black reverie.   But…

WILLIAM: You just feel sorry for me.
DAISY: William, I've kissed you.   You've wanted me to long enough.   Well, now I have.   Enjoy it.

WILLIAM: Does this mean you'll be my girl, Daisy? 'Cos if you were my girl, I know I could tackle anything.

But Daisy is not at all sure she was right to get into this.*

51   INT.   MATTHEW'S DUG-OUT.   THE SOMME.   FRANCE.
      DAY.

Matthew is unpacking in his dug-out.

MATTHEW: But we were supposed to be at rest for ten days at least.
SERGEANT: The orders arrived this morning, sir. The King's Own were hit bad. So they're out and we're in.

Matthew has placed a picture of Lavinia on a makeshift desk, along with Mary's rabbit. An explosion shakes everything.

SERGEANT (CONT'D): They've been shelling the trench since we got here.
MATTHEW: Is anybody hurt?
SERGEANT: Rankin's dead and Kent, and Corporal Wright was hit. Thank God the stretcher bearers were there.
MATTHEW: Let's see what the damage is now.

Standing, he grabs his steel helmet and, after a moment of hesitation, Mary's rabbit, which he stuffs in his pocket.

....

* This comes from a story told by my mother. At some point in the early Thirties, she'd gone out for dinner with a man whom she liked but wasn't really attracted to. Unfortunately, he was absolutely mad about her and sobbing with love. At the end of the evening he brought her home, and he wanted to kiss her goodnight. She gave him a kiss, which in those days was not quite the tongue job that it is now, but nevertheless she did, and then she went inside. In their house, the room that overlooked the front was my grandfather's library. He had been looking out of the window and he'd seen this exchange, and so he gave her a great telling-off. My mother thought this was absolutely outrageous. According to her, she said to her father: 'That was a poor man whom I won't go out with again, but who is terribly in love with me. When I tell him it's the end, it's going to be absolutely ghastly for him. The very least I could do is give him a kiss to remember.' And I thought, I'm going to use that.

52 EXT. TRENCH AT THE SOMME. FRANCE. DAY.

*Matthew walks down the crowded trench, past the carnage of mud and blood and groaning men. He comes to where stretcher bearers are loading a body. There is a familiar screech…**

    DAVIS: Look out!

They dive for cover as a shell hits the trench and buries them in mud and debris. All is still, then men start to fight their way out. Matthew's head appears, as his neighbour shakes himself loose. He is one of the stretcher bearers. Matthew's eyes begin to focus on him…

    MATTHEW: Thomas? It is Thomas, isn't it?
    THOMAS: Corporal Barrow now, Mr Crawley. Lieutenant Crawley, that is.

And it is. Thomas, the former first footman.

    MATTHEW: You'll never guess where I've just been.

They are certainly a long way from Downton.

53 INT. ANNA AND ETHEL'S BEDROOM. DAY.

Anna is at the window, tears streaming down her face. Below, a taxicab waits as Bates, supervised by Vera, straps his case on the back. He looks up at the façade, but Anna shrinks back. Then he climbs in after his wife. The vehicle drives off.

54 INT. SYBIL'S BEDROOM. DOWNTON. DAY.

The remains of a sponge cake fill the screen.

    MARY (V.O.): I bet you cheated and Mrs Patmore made it.

....

* For these men, one of the frightful and almost surreal parts of being in the Army was that two or three days' travelling took them not just from one place to another, but effectively from one planet to another. They would go back to England on a short leave, and there they would visit a show and have dinner at the Savoy, and then return home to their mother's house in Belgrave Square, or, further down the social ladder, they would go back to farms or shops or cottages to stay with their parents in some country village. And then, after a very few days, they would find themselves back in this mess of blood and mud and death. That was the point we were making here.

But she is laughing. The room is full. Violet is watching, while Cora, Edith and Mary help Sybil and Mrs Hughes to pack.*

> VIOLET: Where's Anna?
> MRS HUGHES: She's not very well today, your ladyship. I've taken over for the time being.
> VIOLET: Oh, that's so kind of you. Just make sure Lady Sybil packs things she can get in and out of without a maid.

The three sisters and their mother bring clothes from chests and wardrobes to the case on the bed. They crisscross each other, as Sybil keeps taking things out they've put in.

> SYBIL: I don't need that. I'd never wear it.
> EDITH: But you must have something decent. Suppose you're invited to dinner?
> SYBIL: I know this is hard for you to grasp, but I'm not there to go out to dinner. I'm there to learn.
> MARY: Take one. Just in case.

She herself folds up a simple evening dress and packs it.

> EDITH: We'll miss you.
> SYBIL: Don't be silly. It's only two months and I'll come home if I can.
> EDITH: Why don't I drive you?
> VIOLET: She's taking enough chance with her life as it is.
> EDITH: Oh, Granny.
> VIOLET: What is this driving mania?
> EDITH: It'll be useful. They won't let a healthy man drive us around for much longer. And if Sybil can be a nurse, why can't I be a chauffeur?

....

* It is a big moment for Sybil, not just because she's going off to nurse, but because she's leaving home. This was made all the more unusual because most of these women, up to that point in history, had only left home to get married. And when they didn't leave to get married, on the whole they didn't leave. But this was war, for the women as well as the men, and I wanted to reinforce Violet's attitude that, as far as she's concerned, Sybil is not doing anything that a well-bred young woman should not do *in extremis*, if it's called for.

MARY: So it's nothing to do with getting poor old
Strallan back?
EDITH: I won't take that from you.
VIOLET: I hope it is. Sir Anthony Strallan may not be
much, but what choice will Edith have by the time the
war's over?
CORA: It's such a pity he was too shy to speak out. I
was so sure he'd propose at that garden party, but then
he just seemed to run away.

Mary and Edith exchange a look. Violet stands.

VIOLET: Well, I shall leave you. I've been summoned by
Cousin Isobel for tea. Goodbye, Sybil, and good luck
with it all.
SYBIL: Thank you for being such a sport.
VIOLET: It's a big step you're taking, dear, but war
deals out strange tasks. Remember your Great-Aunt
Roberta.
MARY: What about her?
VIOLET: She loaded the guns at Lucknow.*
CORA: I'll come with you. I'll tell William to fetch the
bags.

She looks at her youngest daughter.

CORA (CONT'D): The first of you to leave the nest.

But then her eyes fill and she hurries out after Violet.

EDITH: Poor Mama. She always feels these things so
dreadfully.

....

* A classic case of these women of the Empire showing their mettle came
during the Indian mutiny, if one may still call it such, at the siege at
Lucknow, when the residency of Sir Henry Lawrence, Administrator of the
State of Oudh, was surrounded by rebel forces. The British women trapped
there, who had never done much more than order dinner for twelve and ring
for Nanny, were suddenly loading guns and crawling on their hands and
knees, taking ammunition to the men who were firing. At Lucknow most of
them managed to get out alive. But others, like the women and children
taken prisoner at Cawnpore, were less fortunate. I just thought the incident
would give us a nice reminder of Violet's values.

MARY: That's her American blood.*

SYBIL: I'm so glad we've settled everything with Cousin Matthew. Aren't you, Mary?

MARY: Oh, please stop treading on eggshells. I've other fish to fry.

Edith snorts, which Mary deliberately misunderstands.

MARY (CONT'D): Why, Edith, are you jealous?

EDITH: If your fish is Richard Carlisle, I'm not jealous; I'm embarrassed.

MRS HUGHES: And I'm finished. I think that's everything.

There is a knock on the door and William enters.

WILLIAM: Are you ready, m'lady?

She smiles and he takes up the cases.

55   EXT/INT.   DOWNTON/CAR.   DAY.

The three sisters, watched over by Cora, have a last embrace and then Sybil runs into the car. Branson shuts the door, climbs in and drives off. The girls go inside, but Cora stays there, watching. From inside the car, we see Sybil look back at the solitary figure of her mother against the huge house.

56   INT.   DRAWING ROOM.   CRAWLEY HOUSE.   DAY.

Violet is with Isobel, Clarkson and Molesley.

VIOLET: I make no apology. It would be a terrible thing if poor old Mr Molesley's son were killed. Wouldn't it, Molesley?

....

* Mary often likes to make the point that her mother is American, but that she, Mary, is not. Personally, I think having children who are a different nationality to you is a big challenge. If you marry a man from the Lebanon, and you have his children, you will find that your children, who grow up out there, will have all sorts of different beliefs and traditions from your own. It doesn't matter how often you remind them that you are English or American, they are essentially Lebanese, and at some point you must either fight that or accept it. Cora is American, but she has English children. Elizabeth McGovern has a great understanding of this, because she has also married an Englishman, and she also has English children. She says there are moments when their viewpoint is completely different from what hers would have been at their age.

But before he can do more than open his mouth…

ISOBEL: I'm sure it would, but –
VIOLET: And then I heard William's father would be left
on his own if anything happened to the boy. And what
would become of Carson if the last of his staff were
to go?
ISOBEL: That's not the point!
VIOLET: I think it is the point. Surely you can
recognise these are special cases? Do you want Molesley
to die?
ISOBEL: Of course I don't!
VIOLET: Well.
ISOBEL: I don't want my own son to die, either! But this
is a war! And we must be in it together! High and low,
rich and poor! There can be no 'special cases', because
every man at the front is a special case to someone!
CLARKSON: Mrs Crawley is right. I understand your
motives, Lady Grantham, and I do not criticise them. But
I shall write to the Ministry at once correcting the
misinformation. Good day. I'll see myself out.

It is clear he is angry. He goes, leaving an awkward trio.

ISOBEL: Molesley, you understand why I said what I did?
MOLESLEY: Indeed, I do, ma'am.
ISOBEL: You won't be called up at once. Not while there
are younger men to be taken.
VIOLET: But they'll get you in the end, Molesley. And
you can blame Mrs Crawley when they do!*

END OF ACT FIVE

....

* Violet, naturally, defends her attempts to save William on the grounds that
he is an only son. It would be a terrible thing were he to be killed. I don't
blame her at all for trying to spare William's father pain, and I rather agree
with her, anyway, but nor do I blame Isobel for trying to undo it. For Isobel,
it isn't right that some men should be taken and others spared, when it would
be hideous for anyone to lose their son, whoever they are. So, it's a *Downton*
argument, really, when most of us are sort of on both sides.

ACT SIX

57 INT. CARSON'S PANTRY. DOWNTON. DAY.

MRS HUGHES (V.O.): I wish you'd stop working for one
minute. At least put the light on, or you'll strain your
eyes.

*Carson looks up from his accounts. She is standing in the
doorway. He switches on the lamp on his desk.*

CARSON: It's getting dark so early now. Has she gone?
MRS HUGHES: She has. So, we've lost Mr Bates and Lady
Sybil in one day.
CARSON: I can't believe it. I suppose I'll have to look
after his lordship now, on top of everything else.
MRS HUGHES: And I don't want any jokes about broomsticks
and sweeping the floor.

Which makes him laugh a little. Then he sighs.

CARSON: His lordship's got his regimental dinner in
Richmond tonight. That means he'll be in the full fig.
MRS HUGHES: You'll manage.
CARSON: You know, when Mr Bates first came to this house,
I thought he could never do the work. But now, I can't
imagine the place without him. Did you see this coming?
Because I didn't.
MRS HUGHES: I have a confession… I let them have their
tea in my sitting room.
CARSON: That was nice of you.
MRS HUGHES: It was quite nice. But I had my reasons.
There's a grating on the wall, which means you can hear
what's being said in the room.
CARSON: You've never told me that before.

She raises her eyebrows slightly to acknowledge this.

CARSON (CONT'D): If I was a gentleman, I wouldn't want to
know.
MRS HUGHES: But you're not.
CARSON: Fortunately.

He gets up and closes the door.

58 EXT. COLLEGE OF NURSING. YORK. DAY.

The college is attached to a hospital. In the background, men — some on crutches, some in wheelchairs — are tended by nurses. Sybil waits for Branson to unload her two cases.

BRANSON: Now, where should we go?
SYBIL: No. I'll take them. I'm a working nurse now. It'll be tough enough to be taken seriously without a chauffeur carrying in my luggage.

There is a strange moment, as they just stand there.

SYBIL (CONT'D): …Be hard to let you go. My last link with home.
BRANSON: Not as hard as it is for me.

Too late, she realises what her words have invited.

SYBIL: Branson —
BRANSON: I know I shouldn't say it, but I can't keep it in any longer.
SYBIL: I wish you would.
BRANSON: I've told myself and told myself you're too far above me, but things are changing. When the war's over, the world won't be the same place as it was when it started.
SYBIL: I agree, but —
BRANSON: I watched you in that kitchen. You're not like the others. You were working with those girls. There was no gulf between you.
SYBIL: That's true —
BRANSON: All right, I'm a driver now, but I won't always be. I'm clever in my way, and a hard worker. And I'll make something of myself, I promise.
SYBIL: I know you will.
BRANSON: Then bet on me. And if your family casts you off, it won't be forever. They'll come round, and until they do, I promise to devote every waking minute to your happiness.

He stops. Sybil's response is not what he'd prayed for.

SYBIL: I'm terribly flattered —
BRANSON: Don't say that!
SYBIL: Why not?

BRANSON: Because 'flattered' is a word posh people use when they're getting ready to say no.*

There is an awkward moment. He's right, of course.

SYBIL: That sounds more like you.
BRANSON: What do you mean?
SYBIL: Well, you're hardly an admirer of the British aristocracy.

She is trying to lighten matters, but she has misjudged him.

BRANSON: Please don't make fun of me.
SYBIL: No.
BRANSON: It's cost me all I've got to say these things.

But she cannot give him what he wants. He snaps awake.

BRANSON (CONT'D): Right. I'll go. I'll hand in my notice and I won't be there when you get back.
SYBIL: No, don't do that.
BRANSON: I must. They won't let me stay, when they've heard what I've said.
SYBIL: They won't hear. Not from me.

59 EXT. TRENCHES. SOMME. FRANCE. DAY.

There is fighting going on, with explosions, near and distant. Thomas is struggling with one end of a stretcher.

THOMAS: Bloody hell. There must be more to life than this.

....

* I think that it would be modern and silly to imagine that, however liberal Sybil is, and however open to new ideas, she would immediately overcome the prejudice of a lifetime and embrace the chauffeur. She has to get to that point slowly, and we will watch her arriving there. Part of this process will be achieved by her working as a nurse, alongside Thomas and others like him. Again, I thought Allen Leech and Jessica Brown Findlay played all this very, very well. In fact, it amused me to write the exchange about her being 'flattered' by his compliment, because I've seen it used often in my life as a device for saying no. 'Alas, we can't, but it's terribly flattering to be asked,' and so on. 'Flattered' is a word posh people do indeed use when they're getting ready to say no, as Branson says. But there we are: she can't come across quite yet.

A shell explodes, throwing them down into the filth.

STRETCHER BEARER: Are you all right, Corporal?
THOMAS: I think so… yes. More or less.

They get up, but the wounded man is lying half-buried in mud.

THOMAS (CONT'D): My God.
STRETCHER BEARER: They wouldn't believe it, back home
where I come from. I thought, Medical Corps — not much
danger there. How wrong can one man be?

*The stretcher bearer takes out some cigarettes. He offers one
to Thomas's trembling hand, lighting that one first, then his
own as he talks.*

STRETCHER BEARER (CONT'D): I think it comes down to luck.
If the bullet's got your name on it, there's nothing you
can do. If not, then thank God you were lucky —

*As he finishes the last word, a sniper sends a bullet straight
through his head, from ear to ear. He stands, blank, for a
second and then crumples. Thomas is frozen with shock as,
around him, men take cover. He is breathing heavily when a
medical officer turns to him and instructs him to load up the
bodies. He looks at Thomas.*

MEDICAL OFFICER: Come on, Corporal Barrow. Anyone would
think you were losing your enthusiasm.
THOMAS: Never that, sir. Never that.
MEDICAL OFFICER: You heard him. He was unlucky.

*Grimly, Thomas picks up the load, pushing through the chaotic
trench, past men groaning from wounds. As he goes, he
mutters:*

THOMAS: Maybe. But in my book, you make your own bloody
luck.

60   INT.   OFFICERS' MESS OF THE LONDON SCOTTISH.
           YORKSHIRE.   NIGHT.

The table looks splendid, gleaming with regimental silver and gold. Robert is in full mess kit, talking to a General.

ROBERT: I cannot tell you how pleased I am to be here tonight, sir.
GENERAL: We're very pleased to have you here, Grantham.

Robert smiles at him. He would love this man to understand.

ROBERT: You see, just to know I'm with you all, to sense that I belong here… Well, it's as simple as this: I no longer feel like a fraud.

61   EXT.   HOSPITAL.   DOWNTON VILLAGE.   NIGHT.

Clarkson closes the door and walks across the small garden towards the road, when Molesley steps out of the shadows.

CLARKSON: Mr Molesley? What are you doing here?
MOLESLEY: I was waiting to see you, Doctor.
CLARKSON: How can I help?
MOLESLEY: It's just, I was wondering whether you'd written that letter. The one you spoke of this afternoon.
CLARKSON: To the War Office?

Molesley nods, licking his lips. He is very nervous.

CLARKSON (CONT'D): Not yet. I was planning to do it in the morning. I'm sorry you were involved in all that. I should have checked with you first, before I interfered.
MOLESLEY: Well, that's just it. You see, I think if you had checked with me, you'd have found exactly what Lady Grantham described.
CLARKSON: I don't quite —
MOLESLEY: That I have trouble with my lungs. I get so breathless sometimes, and I've noticed it's getting worse…

At last, Clarkson is beginning to grasp what is being asked.

MOLESLEY (CONT'D): They haven't written to William yet, the Ministry I mean, but they have discharged me. Won't it just make extra work for them to have to fail me all over again?*

Clarkson looks at him. Molesley is holding his breath.

CLARKSON: Very well. I shall correct my statement as regards William, but make no mention of you.
MOLESLEY: Thank you, Doctor.
CLARKSON: It's all right. But Molesley —

Molesley turns back, his face half in shadow.

CLARKSON (CONT'D): I hope you will help the war effort in other ways.

He may have helped a coward dodge the draft, but he cannot resist a slight snort of amusement as Molesley slips away.

....

* One of the reasons we started in 1916 was to begin the show with the start of conscription. Otherwise, we couldn't send men to the front who didn't want to go. That was why I tried to save William's line, in Act One, Scene 4, when he says, 'When they brought conscription in, I thought I'd be called up straight away.' One element I'm afraid we did lose is that conscription didn't operate for the first two years of the war, which I don't think most people are aware of. If we'd started earlier, it would not have been believable that Branson, for example, would enlist. But, as a young and single man, he would certainly have been called up right away. As for William, his promise to his father would have been meaningless unless conscription had not yet come in. Thomas, of course, enlisted early in the Medical Corps because he thought conscription would come in straight away, which he was wrong about. He also thought the Medical Corps would keep him out of trouble, and he was wrong about that, too. He imagined he'd be in a lovely field hospital, behind the lines, bringing people a cup of water. This is not what would have happened, and the Medical Corps was, in fact, a very, very brave part of the fighting force, but he didn't realise that. Anyway, by this stage of the episode, we have placed Thomas back in the show and at the front.

62 INT. OFFICERS' MESS OF THE LONDON SCOTTISH.
YORKSHIRE. NIGHT.

The dinner is over and they are smoking cigars. Officers are standing and talking. Robert leans back in his chair.

ROBERT: I know the Germans thought the submarines would scare everyone off, but they seem to have had the reverse effect.
GENERAL: Quite right. It's too early to crow, but it looks as if America will come in at last.*
ROBERT: When might the regiment be wanted, sir? The talk at dinner suggested it might be soon.
GENERAL: Oh, pretty soon, I'd say.
ROBERT: Well, I'm as ready now as I'll ever be.
GENERAL: For what?
ROBERT: To go to France. With the regiment.
GENERAL: Why would you do that?
ROBERT: Because I'm their Colonel, of course. There must be some use for me over there.

For a moment the General is still. Then he laughs.

GENERAL: Oh, my dear fellow. We're not as heartless as that! The position is only an honorary one. Nobody expects you to go to war.
ROBERT: An honorary one?
GENERAL: We thought it'd cheer things up a bit, to have the Lord Lieutenant at our table. And so it does. We're very glad to welcome you here.
ROBERT: I see.
GENERAL: But we old codgers have our work cut out for us keeping spirits high at home. Someone must.
ROBERT: Indeed, sir.

....

* We were very lucky to get Jeremy Clyde to play the General, because again, in a scene like this, which is essentially a two-hander, you must feel that the actor playing the other part alongside Hugh Bonneville could be a running character. There is nothing in this very well-acted exchange to tell the audience that we're not going to see the General for the next two series. Jeremy is an unusual actor. His mother was a Wellesley, and thus a descendant of the great Duke of Wellington, and Jeremy has completely got Wellington's nose. If you look at him in profile, he is the Iron Duke to the life.

GENERAL: Is that Taxi Cavendish over there? I must catch
him before I go.*

63 INT. MRS HUGHES'S SITTING ROOM. DOWNTON.
NIGHT.

Carson looks in to find Mrs Hughes.

CARSON: I'm whacked. When I've finished his lordship, I
think I'll turn in. How's Anna?
MRS HUGHES: Sobbing her heart out.
CARSON: Would the truth help her? Tell her he's still in
love with her and she'll never let go of the dream.
MRS HUGHES: Mr Bates won't change his mind?
CARSON: He can't. Not without making this house a
scandal across the country.
MRS HUGHES: That's all you care about! Keeping the
creepy Crawleys out of trouble!
CARSON: Certainly it's what I care about. And you should
care about it, too!

His stern tone does bring her back to her senses.

CARSON (CONT'D): Mr Bates has behaved like a man of
honour. Would you undo his sacrifice and render it void?
MRS HUGHES: I suppose not.
CARSON: Go to Anna. Give her what comfort you can. But
do not tell her.

....

*Taxi was the nickname of a friend of my father's. I've forgotten his surname,
otherwise I would have used it. He was a very senior diplomat, an
ambassador to somewhere quite important. But when he was a little boy, he
and his brothers and sisters used to play a game in the nursery where they
were all vehicles; he was the taxi, and it stuck. I always feel that nicknames
can be used by the upper classes to exclude outsiders, because you can very
quickly get to know someone too well to call them Lady Bateman, but not
well enough to call them Sausage. So there's a sort of Gaza Strip between
these two methods of address, and you're stuck calling them Louise or some
name which nobody who knows them uses. Of course, they don't, as a rule,
see any of this. For them, the nicknames are a reminder of their happy
nursery days. So they will still say, 'Yum, yum, lovely grub…' and 'We'd
better go, or we'll get stick,' or they will quote Nanny to each other. It's like
living in an eighty-year childhood.

64   INT.   CORA'S BEDROOM.   DOWNTON.   NIGHT.

O'Brien is getting Cora ready for bed.

O'BRIEN: So Lady Sybil got off all right in the end.   I'm
afraid we have to admit she knows what she wants.
CORA: Yes, she certainly does.
O'BRIEN: I don't s'pose the war will leave any of us
alone by the time it's done.   I'd a letter from Thomas
the other day.   He writes that when he thinks about how
things used to be, it seems like a dream.   It's not much
more than two years ago, but he says it might as well be
a century.
CORA: So you hear from Thomas.   Is he well?   Please give
him my regards.
O'BRIEN: He's well enough, m'lady.   But I don't think
he'd mind coming home.
CORA: Oh, how I wish he could, O'Brien.   How I wish they
all could.

65   INT.   ROBERT'S DRESSING ROOM.   DOWNTON.   NIGHT.

Carson has finished making Robert ready for the night.

ROBERT: Would it help if William took over again?
CARSON: I can manage for the time being.
ROBERT: Of course if Bates hadn't been so bloody selfish,
he would have let us plan for his departure properly.

Carson does not respond to this for a moment.   Then:

CARSON: Your lordship…   I have information that I have no
proper claim to…
ROBERT: Well?   What is it?
CARSON: Well, if your lordship can assure me that you
will keep it to yourself —
ROBERT: I promise, Carson.   You can drop the last veil.
CARSON: Well, I feel it only right to tell you that
Mr Bates's leaving was not selfish.   Quite the reverse.
ROBERT: It felt selfish to me.   As for the wretched Anna,
bedizened with dishonest promises —
CARSON: Mr Bates left because, had he not done so, his
wife was planning to engulf this house in scandal.
ROBERT: Scandal?   What scandal?

CARSON: The point is, m'lord, Mrs Bates would have made Downton notorious. The price of her silence was her husband's return.

ROBERT: But I must know what story she was planning to tell.

CARSON: I'm sorry, m'lord, I could not speak of it without injuring you and betraying myself.

Robert looks at him. Carson is not going to budge.

ROBERT: But you are saying that Bates fell on his sword to protect the reputation of my family?

Robert is horrified at his own treatment of his valet.

ROBERT (CONT'D): I must write to him at once. I can't leave it for a moment. If you'll kindly give me his address —

CARSON: M'lord, I cannot. We shouldn't know these things. It won't help him to find that we do. You promised.

ROBERT: Thank you, Carson, there's no need to frown at me like a nursery governess. I know what I said.

66   INT.   HALL/DINING ROOM/SERVANTS' STAIRCASE. DOWNTON. NIGHT.

Crossing the hall, Carson sees a light in the dining room. Ethel is on her knees, with a torch and a duster.

CARSON: Ethel? What are you doing?

ETHEL: Seeing to the plugs for the night.

CARSON: What?

ETHEL: Polishing the electric plugs and checking them for vapours.

CARSON: And why are you doing this?

She looks at him, puzzled by his ignorance.

ETHEL: Because you were too busy. She said you usually did it, but could I manage it tonight.

CARSON: And 'she', I take it, would be Miss O'Brien?

The penny drops for Ethel.

CARSON (CONT'D): Go to bed, Ethel. And next time she gives you an order, ask me first.*

67   INT.   CORA'S BEDROOM.   DOWNTON.   NIGHT.

Robert is taking off his dressing gown in silence.

CORA: Is anything the matter?
ROBERT: Nothing. Except that today has shown me I'm not only a worthless man, but also a bad-tempered and ungrateful one.
CORA: Well, we all know that.

She smiles, but she sees that he was not quite joking.

CORA (CONT'D): Can I help?

He shakes his head, taking her hand and kissing it.

CORA (CONT'D): I wonder how Sybil is feeling.
ROBERT: The war's reaching its long fingers into Downton and scattering our chicks. But I'm glad we've made peace with Matthew.

....

* I had a great-great-aunt who figures in several of these stories. Her name was Lady Sydenham and she lived in a house called Lamberhurst Priory in Kent, and she terrified the living daylights out of both my parents. She had a thing about electricity, that it leaked damaging vapours into the house during the night – Violet complains in the first series about electricity's terrible 'vapours' – and one of the things she insisted on was that all the plugs were stopped up every evening. A maid went round and took the plugs out, then put in stoppers to prevent the electricity leaking into the room and poisoning the atmosphere. I am perfectly serious. Anyway, it was a short step from the Tales of Aunt Phyllis to having Ethel polishing the electric plugs and checking them for vapours, which is how that came about. This aunt also had a horror of smoking. She used to say to my mother, who dreaded these visits (she was my father's aunt): 'I hope you don't smoke, dear.' And my mother would protest how horrible it was as a habit and how she detested it, when in fact she smoked like a chimney. So she used to go up into the attic after Aunt Phyllis had gone to bed, into the head housemaid's room, and they'd smoke together, puffing out of a window over the gardens. This particular maid was movie mad, and she had her walls covered in pictures from *Photoplay* and the other film magazines, all of which added up to the character Emily Watson played in *Gosford Park*.

CORA: I agree. Let us give thanks to Sir Richard Carlisle for distracting Mary at just the right moment. By the way, she wants him to come and stay. So we can all meet him.

Robert looks at his wife. He's not attracted by the prospect.

ROBERT: She wants us to invite a hawker of newspaper scandal to stay as a guest in this house? It's lucky I have a sense of irony. Which reminds me, do you know about a story…
CORA: What story?
ROBERT: Never mind. Goodnight.

And he turns out the light by his bed.

68   INT.   KITCHEN PASSAGE/SERVANTS' HALL.   DOWNTON. NIGHT.

Carson walks down the kitchen passage. He looks in at the door and sees O'Brien alone there, cleaning some combs.

CARSON: I have sent Ethel to bed.
O'BRIEN: Oh, yes, Mr Carson?
CARSON: You are on the edge of an abyss, Miss O'Brien. One false step and you will fall. Do I make myself clear?
O'BRIEN: Very. Goodnight, Mr Carson.
CARSON: Goodnight, Miss O'Brien.

He goes on about his business.*

....

* I always think it's helpful for the audience to know the extent to which the characters are deceiving each other, or to what extent they are aware of each other's foibles. This scene was one of the only moments in the series where we absolutely understand that Carson knows what O'Brien is up to. So when we had to cut it, I did think it was a bit of a loss.

69   INT.   ATTIC PASSAGE.   DOWNTON.   NIGHT.

Anna, red-eyed with weeping, is walking down the passage.
She reaches her room and pushes the door open.   Ethel is
already there, crying into her handkerchief.   Anna shuts
the door.

> ANNA: Not you, too.   What's the matter?
> ETHEL: Why ask?   You don't care.

She wipes her eyes and stands to get undressed.

> ANNA: Oh, Ethel.   Perhaps if you stopped going on about
> all the marvellous things you're going to do when you
> leave service.
> ETHEL: But you've got to have dreams.   Don't you have any
> dreams?
> ANNA: Of course I do.   Big dreams…   It's just that I know
> now they won't be coming true.

But she's not unfriendly.   In fact, she feels sorry for
Ethel.

> ETHEL: Has Mr Bates really left?
> ANNA: I'm afraid so.
> ETHEL: And he won't be back?
> ANNA: Doesn't look like it.
> ETHEL: It's very sudden.   You don't think he was in any
> trouble, do you?
> ANNA: No.   He's done nothing wrong.   He's gone because he
> thought it was the right thing to do.   I don't know why.
> But I do know that.

70   INT.   MARY'S BEDROOM.   DOWNTON.   NIGHT.

Edith pushes open the door and stops dead.   Mary is praying
by her bed.   At the sight of her sister, Mary jumps to her
feet.

> MARY: What do you want?
> EDITH: I think I left my book in here.

Mary looks round, finds the book and hands it over.

> MARY: Is that all?
> EDITH: You were praying.
> MARY: Don't be ridiculous.
> EDITH: You were praying.   What were you praying for?

Mary walks to the door and opens it.

MARY: Please go. I'm tired.

Edith leaves. Mary returns to her bed and kneels, reaching for the picture she pushed quickly under the pillow. It is of Matthew. She bends her head.

MARY (CONT'D): Dear Lord, I don't pretend to have much credit with you. I'm not even sure that you're there. But if you are, and if I've ever done anything good, I beg you to keep him safe.*

71 INT/EXT. FIRST AID POST. FRANCE. NIGHT.

Matthew is walking past the stretcher bearer post when he sees Thomas sitting, drinking tea.

MATTHEW: You look very comfortable there, Corporal.

Thomas jumps to his feet and salutes. Then…

THOMAS: Would you like some, sir? We've got condensed milk and sugar.
MATTHEW: I won't ask how you managed that.

They both laugh as Thomas hands him a cup.

THOMAS: Go on, sir.

Matthew takes the proffered cup and sips it. They sit.

MATTHEW: That's nectar… Are you sure you can spare it?
THOMAS: Gladly, if we can talk about the old days and forget about all this for a minute or two.
MATTHEW: I wonder if we'll go back to the way things were, when the war is over. What do you think?
THOMAS: To be honest, I doubt it.
MATTHEW: 'How you gonna keep 'em down on the farm, after they've seen Paree?'

....

* Edith discovers Mary at prayer, which, of course, she cannot resist teasing her about. It is a very Mary prayer, with her apology to God for not even being sure there's anyone there. She's reached that point, which I think people do reach, when they think, well, where's the harm? If there is no God, I've got nothing to lose. Because the truth is, she can't do anything to make Matthew safe, other than pray.

THOMAS: We haven't seen much of Paris, worse luck, but we have seen the world's bigger than Downton.

MATTHEW: Strange to think I was there so recently. It feels like a million years ago. Do you ever hear from anyone?

THOMAS: Oh, yes. Miss O'Brien keeps me informed. Lady Edith's driving. Lady Sybil's training as a nurse. Miss O'Brien tells me the hospital's busier than ever, with the wounded coming in. Is that true?

MATTHEW: Certainly is. They had a concert when I was there, to raise extra funds.

THOMAS: I'm curious, sir. Do you think I could ever get a transfer, back to the hospital? Seeing as it's war work?

MATTHEW: Well, you'd have to be sent home from the front first. And then you might have to pull a few strings…

He drains his cup and stands, returning it to Thomas.

MATTHEW (CONT'D): Thank you for that. Thank you, very much.

THOMAS: What would my mother say? Me entertaining the future Earl of Grantham to tea.

MATTHEW: War has a way of distinguishing between the things that matter, and the things that don't.*

....

* This meeting between Thomas and Matthew in the trenches is important for me, because the war broke down many of the social barriers. Proximity, to an extent, demystified the other classes, when before the war people had lived very much among their own kind. There is a famous quote from some army officer watching his troops bathing in a river, saying: 'I didn't know their skin was so white.' Even where there was no hostility, there was still distance. After the war, that would change, and it would keep changing as the century wore on. Clearly, whatever people at the BBC may say, we are still divided by class, but I think today we share a consciousness of the realities of life, which I don't believe we did before the First World War. I always remember my mother saying that at the end of the Second World War you were suddenly aware of whether or not the maids' rooms were pretty, and if they were nicely done. Whereas before the war, while she got on well with servants, she never really troubled herself about their lives. The war changed her for the better in that respect and she never went back. This process is what we're seeing here, as Matthew and Thomas sit together in a muddy ditch full of blood. Why shouldn't they have a cup of tea? What do those petty distinctions matter?

He touches his cap in salute and walks off. Thomas watches him go. He has come to a resolution. He starts to walk away.

    SOLDIER: Where are you going?
    THOMAS: Never you mind.

The noise of guns is constant, if distant, as Thomas walks along. At last he stops and checks to see if anyone is looking, then he lights a match and holds it above the edge of the trench. A shot rings out. Thomas clutches his hand with a cry, as blood spouts out. He falls, and whispers.

    THOMAS (CONT'D): Thank you — thank you for my deliverance.

He clutches his bleeding hand. He is in agony, but overjoyed.*

END OF EPISODE ONE

....

* This kind of injury was called a Blighty, because it was a wound that took you back to England. A Blighty was not, I think I'm right in saying, necessarily an artificially received wound, as Thomas's is here. Some men did do this sort of thing deliberately and got shot through the hand or broke their foot with a hammer, but this was very rare, and the wounds were usually received legitimately in combat. Of course, if you received a wound that disqualified you from service, but left you essentially whole, then clearly, for the men and their families, this was a huge bonus, and that was a Blighty.

The lighted match in the trenches gave rise to the superstition against lighting a third cigarette from the same match, which is still with us. There was truth in it, because when you lit a match, the Germans could see the light. But if you just lit one cigarette and blew it out, it was too short a moment for them to do anything about it. However, by the time you'd lit three cigarettes, they could take aim and fire – and a match was always an invitation to fire, because it had to mean there was a man standing there. Here, Thomas holds a match up to light his own hand as the target. But again, I don't want to pretend that lots of people did this sort of thing, because I think what is always astonishing about any history of the First World War is how brave the vast majority of the men were. All ages, all types; they were as brave as lions. But, of course, we need Thomas to come back to Downton to carry on being nasty.

EPISODE TWO

ACT ONE

1A EXT. DOWNTON. DAY.

A postman cycles up to the house.

1B INT. ROBERT'S DRESSING ROOM. DOWNTON. DAY.

Henry Lang, Robert's new valet, lays out clothes.

1C INT. PANTRY. DOWNTON. DAY.

William is working. A hall boy enters carrying a letter.

HALL BOY: Letter for you, William.

2 INT. HALL/DRAWING ROOM. DOWNTON. DAY.

April 1917. Amid the flurry of the maids opening the house, Carson is seeing to the logs for the fire. Mrs Hughes walks up to him, unobserved.

MRS HUGHES: Why on earth are you doing that?
CARSON: Someone's got to.
MRS HUGHES: Yes, indeed they do, and that someone is William or one of the maids. You're making work for yourself, Mr Carson, and I've no sympathy with that.
CARSON: I'm not asking for sympathy.

He walks off. But of course she does sympathise.

3 INT. ROBERT'S DRESSING ROOM. DOWNTON. DAY.

Watched by Isis, Robert is with Lang, who helps him into a uniform jacket. Lang is diffident and now he hangs back, nervously. Robert looks in the glass.

ROBERT: What is it? What's the matter?
LANG: I don't think it should be…
ROBERT: What? For heaven's sake, man, if something's wrong, put it right!

Lang steps forward and adjusts a strap.

ROBERT (CONT'D): I'm sorry, Lang, I don't mean to snap.

LANG: Nothing to worry about, m'lord.

ROBERT: You've been in the trenches. I have not. I have no right to criticise.

LANG: I'm not a soldier now.

ROBERT: You've been invalided out. That is perfectly honourable.

LANG: Is it? I know people look at me and wonder why I'm not in uniform.

ROBERT: Then you refer them to me, and I'll give them a piece of my mind.

4 INT. KITCHEN. DOWNTON. DAY.

Mrs Patmore is studying a letter in silence.

DAISY: A penny for your thoughts.

MRS PATMORE: They're worth a great deal more than that, thank you very much.

She puts the letter away as William appears, grinning.

DAISY: What is it?

WILLIAM: My papers. They've come. I've been called up.

MRS PATMORE: You never have!

DAISY: What does it mean?

WILLIAM: I'm to report for my medical next Wednesday, and once I'm through that I go to Richmond for training.

DAISY: And then… you go to war?

WILLIAM: With any luck. I'll be beggared if it's over before I get there.

MRS PATMORE: Well, if they'd listen to me, it'd be over by teatime.

With a sad shake of her head, she walks off to the larder.

WILLIAM: Daisy, I wonder… would you give me a picture to take with me?

DAISY: I haven't got one.

WILLIAM: Then have one taken. On your afternoon off. Please.

Mrs Patmore has returned with some onions.

MRS PATMORE: That's enough. Let her get on with her work.

William goes, still brimming with excitement.

MRS PATMORE (CONT'D): Poor lad. Little does he know…
DAISY: He wants me to get my picture taken.
MRS PATMORE: Does he, indeed? And will you?
DAISY: I don't know. I just don't know.

Daisy is troubled by the spot she's got herself into.

5 INT. CORA'S BEDROOM. DOWNTON. DAY.

O'Brien is dressing Cora.

CORA: How is Thomas coming along? I wish he could be treated at our hospital, here.
O'BRIEN: Well, it's only for officers…
CORA: Of course.
O'BRIEN: Although, ideally, he'd love to be transferred there. To work.
CORA: He won't be sent back to the front?
O'BRIEN: Not with his hand the way it is.
CORA: It's such a pity he isn't under Doctor Clarkson. We might have been able to influence him a bit.
O'BRIEN: I should hope so. Why, without this family and the money you've spent, his precious hospital wouldn't exist at all.
CORA: Perhaps I'll ask his advice. You never know. Thomas is in the Royal Infirmary in Leicester, isn't he?
O'BRIEN: I was sure you'd have a good idea of what to do for the best.

6 INT. DUG-OUT. TRENCHES. SOMME. NORTHERN FRANCE. DAY.

Davis is cleaning, as Matthew reads a telegram.

MATTHEW: Fancy a tour in England, Davis?
DAVIS: I assume you're having me on, sir.
MATTHEW: Not at all. General Sir Herbert Strutt has asked for my transfer to be his ADC. He's touring England to boost recruitment and he's remembered that I know Manchester and Yorkshire pretty well. It'll mean a couple of months at home and a promotion to Captain. I can't object to that.*

DAVIS: So you're glad?

MATTHEW: It's an odd business. I should be glad, of course…

DAVIS: But?

MATTHEW: I feel like a worried father, leaving the men to a new officer.

DAVIS: Orders are orders, sir. They'll understand.

MATTHEW: Probably rather better than I do.

7 INT. LIBRARY. DOWNTON. DAY.

Robert is at his desk. Cora is sitting on a sofa, reading letters. Carson is there with William.

CORA: Have you told your father?

WILLIAM: I've not had a chance yet, m'lady.

CORA: Don't write. Go and see him. So you can tell him yourself.

WILLIAM: I've only got a few days before the medical, m'lady.

CORA: Then go and tell your father. You don't mind, do you, Carson?

CARSON: We must manage with no footmen at all from next Wednesday. It'll be no different if we start now.

ROBERT: And you've always got Lang.

CORA: We wish you every good fortune. Don't we, darling?

Robert stands to shake William's hand.

....

* I didn't want Matthew going back and forth to the trenches as easily as if he was toddling down to Southend. We really needed him to be in England for two episodes, without returning to France, so he gets put onto the staff of General Strutt, the name of a chap I was at school with, to achieve it. This happened, in fact – officers being seconded to recruitment duties or whatever – there was nothing unusual about that. They would tour the areas where they were trying their hardest to attract volunteers, as well as the training camps for men who had enlisted, and they generally kept people's spirits up about the eventual outcome of the war. The idea was that if these new recruits could talk to soldiers who had actually been at the front, then the experienced officers would be able to dispel some of their apprehension. Otherwise, there was a fear that there would be a kind of mythological swallowing of you when you went to the front, that you would never be seen again. This is why the work that Matthew and Strutt are doing was important.

ROBERT: We certainly do. Good luck, William.
WILLIAM: Thank you, m'lord.

William and Carson go.

ROBERT: So both my footmen have gone to the war, while I cut ribbons and make speeches.
CORA: And keep people's spirits up, which is very important.
ROBERT: By God, I envy them, though. I envy their self-respect, and I envy their ability to sleep at night.

8   INT. SERVANTS' HALL. DOWNTON. DAY.

Lang is cleaning some medals and Ethel is reading when O'Brien comes in with a box of buttons to sort.

O'BRIEN: Mr Carson doesn't like the smell of cleaning materials in the servants' hall. Not just before luncheon.

Lang nods and starts to tidy up the things.

ETHEL: Go on, Miss O'Brien. We don't want to be unfriendly, do we?
O'BRIEN: You obviously don't.

But she sees that Lang's hands are shaking and he is finding it difficult to get the top back on the jar of spirits.

O'BRIEN (CONT'D): Never mind. Finish it now you've started, but don't blame me if Mr Carson takes a bite out of you.

As Lang looks up to thank her, Molesley comes in.

MOLESLEY: Hello, Mr Lang. Everything all right?
LANG: Why do you say that?
MOLESLEY: No reason. I only meant I hope you're enjoying yourself. I know I would be, in your shoes.
O'BRIEN: You never tried for the job, did you?
MOLESLEY: I hav'na got the chance. I'd no sooner heard that Mr Bates was gone than he arrived.

Molesley's jealousy of Lang is slightly uncomfortable.

O'BRIEN: What brings you here, Mr Molesley?
MOLESLEY: I was wondering if Anna was anywhere around.
ETHEL: I could find her if you like.

MOLESLEY: No, no, no… just give her this. We were
talking about it the other day, and I came across a copy.
In Ripon.

He hands over the book and retreats. Ethel picks it up.

ETHEL: *Elizabeth and Her German Garden*. Whatever's that
about?
O'BRIEN: It's about an invitation to talk some more,
that's what.*

9   EXT.   HOSPITAL.   DOWNTON VILLAGE.   DAY.

*Cora walks past the hospital sign. She is overtaken by
Branson, who opens the door for her. She goes inside.*

10   INT.   HOSPITAL.   DOWNTON VILLAGE.   DAY.

*Branson comes in after Cora. The place is a hive of
activity. Isobel and Sybil are there. Sybil is in a nurse's
uniform.*

CORA: Is Doctor Clarkson anywhere about?
SYBIL: He's in his consulting room.
CORA: Will you be home for dinner tonight? Granny's
coming.
SYBIL: Oh, Mama. Of course not.

Cora nods philosophically and leaves.

BRANSON: You're busy, then?
SYBIL: We're preparing for a big intake from Arras. If
only they'd tell us when they're coming.
ISOBEL: Sybil, Lieutenant Courtenay is asking for you.

....

* *Elizabeth and Her German Garden* was a tremendously popular book that
was first published in 1898, and which led to the beginning of a writing
career for an English woman, Elizabeth von Arnim, who had married a
German aristocrat and lived in Germany. Because in German society it still
was not acceptable for a noblewoman to have her name on the spine of a
novel, all her books were published as being 'by the author of *Elizabeth and
Her German Garden*'. She wrote: 'All needlework and dressmaking is of the
devil, designed to keep women from study.' Not surprisingly, it was very
much an iconic book of the period, as it chimed with what so many women
were thinking.

Sybil walks over to the bed of a young man. His eyes are bandaged. He is blind. She is affectionately impatient.

SYBIL: What is it this time?

COURTENAY: Could I have some water?

SYBIL: Of course. But really, anyone would have helped you with that.

COURTENAY: Not as well as you.

SYBIL: Lieutenant, I'm glad you're better, but I can assure you every nurse here knows her job as well as I do.

COURTENAY: Maybe, but none of the rest of them smell as sweet.

This makes her laugh, which Branson, still by the door, sees.

11 EXT. HOSPITAL. DOWNTON VILLAGE. DAY.

Cora's interview with Doctor Clarkson is not as she had imagined it.

CORA: Goodbye, Doctor Clarkson.

CLARKSON: Lady Grantham, I'd love to help but it's not within my power to hook men from hither and thither as I please.

CORA: That's not at all what I was asking.

CLARKSON: Forgive me, but I thought you were saying that you wanted Corporal Barrow to come and work here, when he's fully recovered?

CORA: I think it a credit to him that he wants to continue to serve in this way, after he's been wounded.

CLARKSON: Well, that's as maybe. But it's not for me to decide what happens next.

12 INT. HOSPITAL. DOWNTON VILLAGE. EVE.

Sybil is by Courtenay's bed.

SYBIL: You must be comfortable now. I've remade it three times.

COURTENAY: How soon can you make it again?

She laughs and walks off, but Isobel has been watching.

ISOBEL: We want to encourage him to feel less of an invalid.

SYBIL: But he's blind.

ISOBEL: Blind, but not ill. His wounds are healed. It's
time he moved on.
SYBIL: I don't think he's ready.
ISOBEL: My dear, you know very well every bed will be at
a premium when the new casualties arrive.

13 INT. SERVERY. DOWNTON. NIGHT.

Anna has come in and found Carson trying to pull the cork out
of a bottle. He is red-faced and sinks back in exhaustion.

ANNA: Mr Carson? Are you quite well?
CARSON: Oh, leave me alone!

He almost slops the wine into a decanter and rushes out.

14 INT. DINING ROOM. DOWNTON. NIGHT.

Carson pours wine from the decanter. Violet glances at him.

VIOLET: Oh, are you all right, Carson?
CARSON: Of course! That is, I'm perfectly all right,
your ladyship, thank you.
EDITH: Cousin Isobel says Matthew's coming home in a
fortnight. He's touring England with some general.
ROBERT: We'll have a dinner when he's here.
MARY: I was going to ask Richard Carlisle about then.
For Saturday to Monday.*
EDITH: That's the first we've heard of it.
MARY: Nonsense. Mama knows. Don't you?
CORA: Certainly.

But her look to Mary tells us this is not true.

VIOLET: Be careful, Mary. Sir Richard mustn't think
you're after him.
EDITH: Isn't that the truth?

....

* The word 'weekend', out of which Maggie Smith and *Downton* have had
such fun, was still considered a little bit common. It implied a holiday from a
working week, which had not applied to most of the upper classes – at least to
the heads of those families – before the war, and even if things were changing,
a lot of them didn't want to admit it. You can trace the word coming into use
in the Thirties, when slang was creeping in more. As always, the young
would say it before their older relations.

VIOLET: The truth is neither here nor there. It's the look of the thing that matters. Ask Rosamund. It'll take the edge off it.
ROBERT: That'd be nice. Like before the war.
CORA: How can we manage a great pre-war house party without a single footman?
VIOLET: Rosamund is not a house party. She's blood.

Edith has something she's been longing to say.

EDITH: I saw Mrs Drake when I went into the village… The wife of John Drake? Who has Longfield Farm?
ROBERT: Oh? What did she have to say?
EDITH: Apparently, their final able-bodied farmhand has been called up. They need a man to drive the tractor.
ROBERT: Hasn't Drake recovered from his illness? I thought he was better.
EDITH: No, he is. He's much, much better. But he doesn't drive.

None of them know where this story is going.

EDITH (CONT'D): So I told her I could do it.
CORA: What?
EDITH: I said I could drive the tractor.
VIOLET: Edith, you are a lady, not Toad of Toad Hall.*
EDITH: Well, I'm doing it.

15   INT.   CORA'S BEDROOM.   DOWNTON.   NIGHT.

O'Brien is tidying up at the end of the day.

O'BRIEN: When you think of what he's taken from this family! You ask one tiny favour and that's all the answer you get! I think it's a liberty.

Robert enters in his dressing gown. O'Brien goes.

ROBERT: What's she on about now?
CORA: She thinks we've been treated rather shabbily by Doctor Clarkson.
ROBERT: Old Clarkson? Why?

....

* As we all know, Kenneth Grahame's novel was published in 1908 as *The Wind in the Willows*, but the character of Toad rapidly gained currency after A. A. Milne titled his dramatisation of the book *Toad of Toad Hall.*

CORA: There was just something I thought he might take a more sympathetic view of. But it doesn't matter.

16 EXT. DRAKES' FARM. DAY.

Edith bicycles along a track and into a farmyard.

17 INT. DRAKES' FARMHOUSE. DAY.

John Drake and his wife are puzzled.

EDITH: Don't look so bewildered. It's simple. I will drive the tractor.
MRS DRAKE: But can you do that?
EDITH: Absolutely. Can you hitch up the plough or whatever it is I'm dragging?
DRAKE: Of course.
EDITH: When would you like me to start?
MRS DRAKE: Well, I'd better get you something to wear, then.*

18 INT. KITCHEN. DOWNTON. DAY.

Mrs Patmore is laying pastry over a funnel as Anna comes in.

ANNA: Oh, I like a bit of life in the house, but I just hope Mr Carson doesn't spontaneously combust.

Mrs Patmore isn't listening. She takes out a letter.

MRS PATMORE: I had a letter yesterday…
ANNA: Yes?
MRS PATMORE: It's my sister's boy… He's with the Lancashire Fusiliers… Only, he's gone missing. 'Missing, presumed dead', they call it.
ANNA: Oh, no. How did it happen?
MRS PATMORE: That's just it. They can't find out. How it happened, why it happened, whether we can be sure it did happen or he isn't lying prisoner somewhere.
ANNA: Why not ask his lordship? He'll have friends in the War Office; they can dig something up.

....

*This is the return of the Drakes. I thought they were very good in the first series, when John Drake almost died from dropsy, and I knew that the actors would like to come back. When I realised we needed a tenant farmer on the estate for this storyline, I thought, well, we've got one already set up.

MRS PATMORE: Oh, I don't like to bother him.
ANNA: Why not? He's got broad shoulders.

19 INT. DRAWING ROOM. DOWNTON. DAY.

Isobel is with Robert and Cora as Isis snoozes.

ISOBEL: Oh, very, very good news! He's been made a
captain and he's going to be away from the front for two
or three months at least! He's got a few days before he
begins his tour of the army camps, so he's bringing
Lavinia to see me.
CORA: Then we'll expect you all for dinner. By the way,
Mary's made me invite the newspaper man, Sir Richard
Carlisle. He'll be here.
ISOBEL: I don't think I'll tell Matthew. He might chuck.
ROBERT: They'll have to rub along, sooner or later.

20 INT. SERVANTS' HALL. DOWNTON. DAY.

Lang is doing some invisible mending on a tweed coat.

ETHEL: That's ever so fine, Mr Lang. However can you
make those big hands do such delicate work?
LANG: I hadn't thought about it.
ETHEL: I expect there's no end to the things they could
manage.
O'BRIEN: Giving you a slap for a start.

But O'Brien is curious and she comes to inspect.

O'BRIEN (CONT'D): That is good. Very good. I like to
see a proper skill. These days, blokes think they can
be a valet if they can smile and tie a shoelace. But
there's an art to it, and I can tell you've got it.
LANG: My mother taught me. She was a lady's maid,
like you.
O'BRIEN: Well, she knew what she was about.

Carson leans in.

CARSON: Oh, Mr Lang, as you know, Sir Richard Carlisle
arrives later and the Crawleys are coming for dinner
tonight. I really can't have maids in the dining room
for such a party, so I'd be grateful if you'd help me and
play the footman.
LANG: Me? Wait at table?

CARSON: It's not ideal, but I'm afraid I've no choice.
The footmen's liveries are in a cupboard just past Mrs
Hughes's sitting room. You should find one to fit you.

He leaves, in a nervous frenzy. Lang is frozen with fear.

21   INT. LIBRARY. DOWNTON. DAY.

Mrs Patmore is with Robert.

ROBERT: I'm not sure what I can do, but I'm happy to try.
What's his name?
MRS PATMORE: Archie — that is, Archibald Philpotts. He
was in the Lancashire Fusiliers. They think he was in
northern France.
ROBERT: You realise the most likely outcome is that he
has indeed been killed?
MRS PATMORE: I understand, m'lord. But we'd rather know
the worst than wonder.*

22   INT. KITCHEN PASSAGE. DOWNTON. DAY.

*Anna is walking down the passage, carrying an evening skirt.
She stops. Molesley is by the servants' staircase.*

MOLESLEY: Ah!
ANNA: Ah, hello, Mr Molesley. What are you doing here?

....

* This is about the paternalistic role of the aristocracy, which was in many
ways a reality. At that time, the country was still, by and large, run by the
upper middle classes, with the upper classes as the display in the shop
window. It meant that, at one remove, these people could normally pull a
string to find out something in practically any area of the country or
department of public life. Now that's rather gone, because aristocrats, as a
class I mean, are not in charge of much any more. The point being that they
formed a comparatively compact group, while the middle classes, who are in
charge now, are a much, much larger mass of people, and they do not all
know each other. So, the days when you could ring someone up and say:
'Fruity, old boy, do you know anyone at the Health Ministry?' were really
finished by the end of the Sixties. But in 1916 that system was still in
operation, and so for Mrs Patmore to appeal to Robert to find something out
is not at all stupid. It would be very easy for him, whereas it would be very
difficult for her.

MOLESLEY: I asked inside, and they said you were over at the laundry.

ANNA: Lady Mary wants to wear this tonight. I wasn't sure it was done.

MOLESLEY: I was really wondering if you'd had a chance to read that book.

ANNA: You only gave it to me yesterday.

MOLESLEY: Of course, of course. But when you have read it, I hope we can exchange our views.

ANNA: That'd be nice. Perhaps we might bring some of the others in. We could have a sort of reading club.

MOLESLEY: We could do that. Or we could talk about it together. Just we two.

O'Brien walks past, up the stairs, carrying some linen.

ANNA: Heavens. It's later than I thought. I must get on.

She hurries up after the other maid. He watches her go.

23   INT.   CORA'S BEDROOM.   DOWNTON.   DAY.

Cora is at her glass with O'Brien when Robert looks in.

ROBERT: I'm off to change, but I wanted you to know I sent a note down to Clarkson, which should do the trick.

CORA: What did you say?

ROBERT: Only that I gathered you'd asked a favour and, given that the estate shoulders the hospital costs, it did seem a little unfair if we weren't allowed a few perks.

CORA: Quite right. Thank you, darling.

He goes. O'Brien nods to her mistress in the glass.

O'BRIEN: Well done, m'lady. If you don't stand up for your rights in this world, people'll walk all over you.*

END OF ACT ONE

ACT TWO

24 EXT. DRAKES' FARM. DAY.

A sheepdog watches as Drake ties a chain around a sawn-off stump of an apple tree. The other end is fastened to a tractor, which Edith is driving.

> EDITH: Ready?
> DRAKE: Ready!
> EDITH: Come on, damn you!

She slams it into gear and forces it forward. The trunk is torn up by the roots. She stops.

> EDITH (CONT'D): Victory!
> DRAKE: Ho-oh! Yes!

She climbs down. Drake is pouring some cider from a covered jug. He gives her a tin mug and pours one for himself.

....

* Every now and then, I think it is important to demonstrate the sense of entitlement that is one of the things that divides the upper classes from the rest of the community. And it is at the root of their power, then and now. I am not, as it happens, a fan of the Eleven Plus exam, as it seems to throw children onto the scrapheap before they've had a chance, but that said, the grammar schools in many ways allowed people who had come from ordinary backgrounds to acquire a sense of entitlement that empowered them to compete with the born privileged on an even ground. By the time a grammar school leaver went to university, they could not be put down by someone from Eton or Harrow or anywhere else, and there was no reason why they should not get to the top of any profession. But the comprehensives have been less successful in inculcating this sense of entitlement and, as a result, the middle classes have retaken a great many of those areas of employment where the working class made serious inroads thirty or forty years ago.

It is difficult to challenge, because entitlement becomes, in many cases, a self-fulfilling prophecy. There are families where the children go to public school, on to university and into great jobs, even though their lineage is no great shakes and there's no real money. In fact, they will achieve the way of life they were used to as babies, all because of their sense of entitlement. Here, Cora, who may be a liberal, who may be American, still thinks the doctor should have done what he was told because he's a doctor and she's a countess, and there's no question about that.

DRAKE: To the victor the spoils.

EDITH: Did you plant that tree?

DRAKE: Steady on. It must be forty years old.

EDITH: It's not a flattering light.

Which makes him laugh.

DRAKE: My father planted it. But you have to be tough
with fruit trees and not let them outstay their welcome.

EDITH: Farming needs a kind of toughness, doesn't it?
There's room for sentiment, but not sentimentality.

DRAKE: Beautifully put, if I may say so, m'lady. You
should be a writer.

EDITH: Thank you.

Edith blushes, as Mrs Drake walks towards them with a bundle.

MRS DRAKE: How are you getting on?

DRAKE: Very well, I think.

MRS DRAKE: And it's not too hard for you?

EDITH: Not at all.

DRAKE: She's stronger than she looks.

MRS DRAKE: I've brought you something to eat, m'lady,
though I'm afraid it's not what you're used to. *[To the
dog]* Eh, it's not for you.

DRAKE: They say hunger's the best sauce.

EDITH: And I'm starving!

*She laughs, flopping down by the ploughman's lunch and
fondling the dog, which Drake sees and loves her for.*

24A   EXT.   DOWNTON.   DAY.

A man in uniform walks towards the great house.

25   EXT.   KITCHEN COURTYARD.   DOWNTON.   DAY.

O'Brien walks out to find Thomas smoking and smiling.

O'BRIEN: So it is you. Ethel thought I must have a
soldier fancy man.

THOMAS: Is she the new maid?

O'BRIEN: Yes. She's a soppy sort… So, tell me. Was
Doctor Clarkson thrilled to have your services?

THOMAS: It's Major Clarkson now, but yes. I don't know
how you did it.

O'BRIEN: What about your Blighty?

As an answer he pulls off his glove. It is horrific.

O'BRIEN (CONT'D): My God.
THOMAS: It's not so bad. And it lived up to its name and got me home.

He puts on his glove again.

O'BRIEN: You'd better come inside.

26 INT. SERVANTS' HALL. DOWNTON. DAY.

Some of the other servants watch the new arrival warily.

THOMAS: Where's William?
DAISY: Training for the Army.
THOMAS: I thought he might have died for love of you.
DAISY: Don't be nasty. Not as soon as you're back.
THOMAS: Imagine Carson without a footman! Like a ringmaster without a pony.
MRS HUGHES (V.O.): We'll have none of your cheek, thank you, Thomas.
THOMAS: I'm very sorry, Mrs Hughes, but I'm not a servant any more. I take my orders from Major Clarkson. Who's this?

He has seen Ethel eyeing him.

O'BRIEN: Ethel. The new maid. I told you.
ETHEL: When I saw you out there, I didn't realise I was dealing with an ex-footman.
THOMAS: I'm the one that got away.
ETHEL: Gives hope to us all.

She smiles, which Thomas rather enjoys. Carson looks in.

CARSON: Ethel, get ready to help with the luggage.
They're nearly back with Sir Richard.
O'BRIEN: We've got a visitor, Mr Carson.
CARSON: I've seen him.

He goes. Thomas looks round this room he knows so well.

THOMAS: Where's Mr Bates?
O'BRIEN: Gone. Replaced by Mr Lang.
THOMAS: So not all the changes were bad.

He punctuates this with a glance at Anna.

27 EXT. DOWNTON. DAY.

Sir Richard Carlisle shakes hands with Cora (without a glove). Rosamund Painswick is there. So are Robert and Mary. *

> CARLISLE: Hello.
> CORA: We're so pleased to have you here, Sir Richard.
> CARLISLE: Lady Grantham.
> ROBERT: Welcome.
> CARLISLE: Thank you.
> CORA: I hope the train wasn't too tiring?
> ROSAMUND (V.O.): Hello, Mary.
> CARLISLE: Not a bit, no. I got a lot done.
> MARY: Hello, Aunt Rosamund.

Rosamund kisses Mary and then Robert.

> ROSAMUND: Brother, dear.
> ROBERT: How are you?
> CORA: Lovely to see you, Rosamund.

The others have gone in and Mary is alone with her aunt.

> MARY: He's nice, isn't he?
> ROSAMUND: To be honest, he spent the entire journey reading his own papers. But I'm sure I'll love him dearly, if he'll ever look up from the page.

They go inside. Ethel, a valet and a lady's maid are taking some suitcases in, leaving Branson unstrapping the rest.

> ETHEL: Come with me. I'll show you the rooms. And, as if you didn't know, theirs are a lot nicer than yours.

She leads the way to the rear, as Cora hurries out.

....

* The stage direction, 'without a glove', seems rather bizarre, but it comes from an incident during the first series that drove me mad. When Mary's potential suitor, the Duke of Crowborough, arrived, he shook hands with Cora with his glove still on his hand, which no gentleman in those days would ever have done. It was one of those learning moments when I am made to realise that I am now officially an old fart, and much of what I thought was general knowledge has in fact vanished forever. Unfortunately, we did not have a tighter shot, meaning we could not cut it so as to lose the hand from vision. So, as you can see here, by the time we got to Richard Carlisle's arrival in the second series, I wasn't taking any chances.

CORA: Branson, when you've finished unloading, run down
to the hospital and remind Lady Sybil that we expect her
here for dinner. And tell her I mean it. Really,
they're working her like a packhorse in a mine!
BRANSON: I think she enjoys it, though.

This is impertinent. Cora's voice is firmer.

CORA: Please tell her to come home in time to change.

28   INT.   HOSPITAL.   DOWNTON VILLAGE.   DAY.

Sybil is indignant with Branson, under the eye of Isobel.
Some of the other nurses glance at the chauffeur and giggle.

SYBIL: I can't possibly come! Really, Mama is
incorrigible!
ISOBEL: It's not poor Branson's fault.
SYBIL: But what is the point of Mama's soirées? What are
they for?*

....

* Sybil being caught in the middle, trying to live in two worlds at once, comes
from my own experience. When I left drama school in 1973 to become an
actor, my career choice wasn't so much considered silly as completely mad.
People would say, 'You should come shooting,' and I'd say, 'No, I'm working,
I'm filming something.' They'd say, 'Can't you get out of it?' And I'd say (a)
'No,' and (b) 'I haven't the slightest desire to get out of it.' After all, it
practically killed me getting into it. And I suppose, looking back, I think
that if you move out of your old world to take up an alien occupation, your
challenge is to synthesise the two parts of your existence.

For me, when I was starting out as an actor – and I often suggest this,
actually, to young actors – I found it easier to avoid my old pals until my
career brought me back into London in a West End show. Of course, when I
was in a play at the Comedy Theatre, then suddenly my choice ceased to be
quite so mad, and it became fun. My friends from the old days would come
and see the show, and we'd all go out for dinner, and everything would be
lovely. But during those years at the beginning – about five years, really, if
you include drama school – I hardly saw any of them, because I knew I would
be facing a negative force, and it was tough enough without that. This is
what we're dealing with here. Cora doesn't accept that Sybil has, in a sense,
ceased to be Lady Sybil Crawley, a daughter of the house, and has become a
nurse at the local hospital. She wants to keep pulling her back into her old
life, whereas Isobel understands Sybil's dilemma much more clearly.

ISOBEL: Well, I'm going up for dinner tonight and I'm glad. Is that wrong?

Sybil has been defeated. Thomas comes into the hospital.

ISOBEL (CONT'D): Thomas, you can cover for Nurse Crawley, can't you?
THOMAS: I can.
BRANSON: So you're back, then, safe and sound.
THOMAS: That's not how I'd put it, with my hand the way it is. But yes, Major Clarkson's found me a place. And I'm grateful.
SYBIL: Can you give Lieutenant Courtenay his pills? Tell him I've had to go.
THOMAS: 'Course I can. I'd be glad to.

She gives Thomas the pills and walks off. He goes to Courtenay's bed and puts the pills in his hand.

THOMAS (CONT'D): She's had to —
COURTENAY: I heard. Do you know her well?
THOMAS: Who?
COURTENAY: You know who.
THOMAS: Yes and no. I was a footman at her home before I joined the Medical Corps. Lady Sybil must have been about fifteen when I first arrived.
COURTENAY: 'Lady' Sybil? She's very grand, then?
THOMAS: No. Not in herself.
COURTENAY: Is she as pretty as she sounds?
THOMAS: I suppose so. Quite pretty, yes.
COURTENAY: Don't worry. I know that's all over for me now.

29   INT. MRS HUGHES'S SITTING ROOM. DOWNTON. EVE.

Mrs Hughes is at her desk when Anna comes in.

MRS HUGHES: Is everything under control?
ANNA: Mr Lang seems a bit nervous…
MRS HUGHES: Stage fright. But what about you?
ANNA: Oh, I'm a trooper. And we can't complain, can we? Not when you think what's going on in France.
MRS HUGHES: Still, a broken heart can be as painful as a broken limb.

ANNA: Don't feel sorry for me, Mrs Hughes. I'm not. I know what real love is, and there aren't many who can say that. I'm one of the lucky ones.
MRS HUGHES: If you say so.

30   INT. DRAWING ROOM. DOWNTON. NIGHT.

The party, all dressed for dinner, is in the drawing room.

CARLISLE: So the fashion for cocktails before dinner hasn't reached Yorkshire?*
MARY: I could get Carson to make you one, but I won't guarantee the result.
CARSON: Mrs Crawley, Captain Crawley and Miss Swire.

Robert walks forward to Matthew where Mary joins them.

ROBERT: Ah! Isobel. *[To Matthew]* Well now, still in one piece, thank God.
MATTHEW: Touch wood.
ROBERT: I never stop touching it.

As Matthew shakes Robert's hand, his eyes find Mary's.

MARY: Do you know Sir Richard Carlisle? My cousin, Captain Crawley.
CARLISLE: How do you do?†
ROBERT: And his fiancée, Miss Swire.
CARLISLE: I know Miss Swire. Her uncle and I are old friends.
LAVINIA: Well, old acquaintances, anyway.

....

* London was beginning to move forward into what would eventually become the culture of the Twenties. Nightclubs and cocktails and jazz, and all sorts of other things, were happening, but of course these developments hadn't reached the North Riding of Yorkshire. You often, in period shows, see people drinking before dinner, but it's wrong. The practice was very twentieth century. They drank after dinner – in the eighteenth century, they drank enough to launch a battleship – but you didn't drink before you went into the dining room.

† We were very fortunate to get Iain Glen to play Carlisle, a genuinely heavyweight actor, who did it extremely well. Here we start our references to the Marconi story with a frisson of discomfort between him and Lavinia, that's all. We don't give any more information until later.

Rosamund is with Sybil.

SYBIL: What do you think Mary sees in him?
ROSAMUND: Besides the money, you mean?
SYBIL: It must be more than that.
ROSAMUND: For you. Not necessarily for her.

Matthew and Robert have drifted off.

ROBERT: What's General Strutt like?
MATTHEW: You know. Rather important, but nice enough underneath. And brave. He got the DSO in South Africa.
ROBERT: Is there any chance it might be permanent, that we can count you out of danger? It would be such a relief.
MATTHEW: I wouldn't want that, I'm afraid. He's promised to get me back to France when he's done with me… How's your new appointment with the North Ridings working out?
ROBERT: Oh, that. It seems I won't be going to the front after all. I made a mistake. It wasn't serious. They only wanted a mascot.

Before Matthew can sympathise, Robert has turned away.
Cora's heard this, but she says nothing. Violet is with
Carlisle.

VIOLET: Mary tells me you're in newspapers?
CARLISLE: Well, I own a few.
VIOLET: Oh, that must be quite a responsibility at a time like this… You know, in a war. When it's so important to keep people's spirits up.
CARLISLE: Lady Grantham, my responsibility is to my investors. I need to keep my readership up. I leave the public's spirits to government propaganda.*

Mary arrives to join them.

MARY: So, now you've met Granny. I warn you, she has very strong opinions.
VIOLET: You need have no fear where that's concerned, my dear. We are more than evenly matched.

31   INT. DINING ROOM/SERVERY. DOWNTON. NIGHT.

Carson, in a frenzy, checks and loads a tray with Daisy and Anna. Lang is there, looking uncomfortable in livery.

CARSON: Where are the spoons for this?
DAISY: Just here.
CARSON: Oh, my God, I've forgotten the sauce!
ANNA: Mr Lang's bringing the sauce. And the Melba toast.
CARSON: Right. Right. Good.

But he is red-faced and breathless as he sets off.

ANNA: Now, Mr Lang, are you ready?
LANG: I think so… It's always the left? And not ladies first?
ANNA: No. Just follow Mr Carson. Start with old Lady Grantham, then his lordship, then just go on round. You must have done this before?
LANG: Not since the war started.

He takes a deep breath and hurries out. Anna looks at Daisy.

....

* Carlisle is not based on a particular newspaper proprietor of the period. He is not Northcliffe, not Beaverbrook, not Camrose. Rather, he is one of a generic type that arrived in London society at that time, just as Cora is a surviving member of a social type that arrived in England in the 1880s and 1890s. As a general rule, the giant newspaper kings were still, like the newly rich at the end of the nineteenth century, keen to imitate the manners and the lifestyle of the old aristocracy. After the First World War, many of the new rich were rich in a different way. They would have enormous flats in London and, later still, apartments in New York, and helicopters and private planes, but they didn't necessarily want 20,000 acres of Yorkshire any more. But the newspaper proprietors did. They wanted hereditary titles, too – and most of them acquired them – and great palaces, the difference being that they didn't need the estates to be self-supportive, because they had huge external incomes. As a result, and paradoxically, their houses were run in a way that few genuine aristocrats could afford. Toffs were beginning to trim down a bit and adjust to the new financial realities, but the press kings went straight back into the age of the high Victorian. An immediate result of this was that they achieved prominence in society in record time, because if there's one thing the British upper classes like, it is to be allowed to live as their forebears lived, even for a weekend or ten days on a yacht, with no cost to themselves.

DAISY: I don't think I ever knew that. Why isn't it just
ladies first? Wouldn't it be more polite?
ANNA: That's the way it's done on the continent. And we
don't like foreign ways here.*

*Carson comes to Violet. She is sitting one away from Lavinia,
with Matthew between them. Violet is on Robert's right.*

VIOLET: I gather your footman, Thomas, has returned to
the village.
ROBERT: Crikey. Where did you see him?
VIOLET: At the hospital. It seems he's working there.
ROBERT: I wonder how he wangled that.

*Violet helps herself during this, from Carson's mousse and
Lang's sauce. Carson has now progressed to Robert, but Lang
has forgotten and leapfrogs him to Rosamund. Carson hisses.*

CARSON: No, no, no. Get — get back behind me!

This slightly alarms Robert, who is next to Rosamund.

ROBERT: What do you make of our plutocrat?
ROSAMUND: He's an opportunity. Mary needs a position and
preferably a powerful one. He can provide it.
ROBERT: You don't think she'd be happier with a more
traditional set-up?
ROSAMUND: Will she have the option?†

....

* One of the things – this is personal, and nothing more than that – that
drives me absolutely mad is the supposition in hotels and restaurants that it is
correct to serve the ladies first at a table, when this is a completely continental
practice and not British at all. The server should start with the woman on
the right of the host, or if you have two people in waiting, with the hostess
and the woman on the right of the host, and then work their way round the
table, man, woman, man, woman, man, woman. This makes for a much
smoother and more elegant flow.

† Rosamund has quite a harsh view of the world, although she would simply
say that she knows how the world works. She isn't merciless. Like her
mother, her great agenda is to avoid scandal at all costs. And so, if something
has happened that is potentially scandalous, she will do everything she can to
contain it. But she is a realist. When she says that Mary needs a position
and that Carlisle could provide it, she knows that Mary has 'blotted her
copybook' and cannot hope for the kind of great marriage she might once
have aspired to.

During this, with Carson whispering and hissing, Lang panics and races back to offer the sauce to Rosamund...

ROSAMUND (CONT'D): Thank you, but I already have some.
CARSON: Give that to me!

Holding the mousse tray, he seizes the sauce with the other hand but tips it into Edith's lap. She jumps up with a cry.

CARSON (CONT'D): I do apologise, m'lady! Mr Lang! Mr Lang! Get a clo—

Suddenly, he stops, clutching his chest. Both trays fall with a hideous clatter as he staggers back against the wall.

CORA: Carson. Carson! What's the matter?
MARY: Now, Carson, it's all right. Everything will be fine.

The party, except for Violet, is already standing as Matthew comes round to help. Sybil and Isobel approach.

ISOBEL: Edith, go with Branson and fetch Major Clarkson. I'll telephone and explain what's happened.
EDITH: Well, what about my dress?
CORA: Edith, we'll get you a coat. Come.
MARY: Sybil will know what to do until the doctor comes.

Violet glances across to Carlisle.

VIOLET: You'll find there's never a dull moment in this house.

Cora returns to settle her remaining guests at the table. Anna, Mary, Sybil, Carson and Matthew are at the serving end of the dining room. Mrs Hughes comes through the door with Ethel. Daisy and O'Brien hover behind her.

MATTHEW: Lady Sybil and I will take him upstairs. If Mrs Hughes will show us the way, please...
MARY: I can help.
SYBIL: No, let me. I know what I'm doing.
CARSON: I'm sure that's not necessary, m'lady.
SYBIL: It's not 'm'lady' now, Carson. It's Nurse Crawley.

The three pass through the door. The others follow gradually.

MRS HUGHES: Mr Lang. Mr Lang! Anna, Ethel, I must trust
the dinner to you.
ETHEL: I'd say the first course is a thing of the past.
MRS HUGHES: Then clear and lay the hot plates. Daisy, you
fetch the beef and the rest of it. And, Anna, you'll have
to serve the wine. Mr Lang, you can clear up the mess.

Lang is dawdling at the back, in a daze. He shakes his head.

O'BRIEN: I'll do that.
MRS HUGHES: There's no need.
O'BRIEN: I don't mind.*
MRS HUGHES: I thank you. Mr Lang, you'd better go
downstairs.

*They go about their tasks. Mrs Hughes is alone in the
servery. Alone at the table, Violet has never moved.*

32 EXT. DOWNTON. NIGHT.

Robert is seeing them all off. Branson is by the car.

ROBERT: It's rather a squash. You two go, and Branson
can come back for Matthew and Miss Swire.
LAVINIA: No, we'll walk. We'd like to.

Violet and Isobel have climbed in. The door shuts.

VIOLET: Well, they seem quite happy. I'll say that much.
ISOBEL: What did you make of Matthew's replacement?
VIOLET: Perhaps he'll improve on acquaintance.

33 INT. CORA'S BEDROOM. DOWNTON. NIGHT.

Cora and Robert are in bed. He is reading.

ROBERT: Well, Clarkson's seen him. It's definitely not a
heart attack, but he does need rest.

....

* This is the one generous act O'Brien does, I think, in three series, offering
to clean up Mr Lang's mess, because she is touched by Lang. And, in a way,
we know she is doing it for her dead brother. I like to think that this is a
Downton theme, that nobody is all bad. But also, this transference was a part
of wartime thinking. Women would nurse strangers as a way of helping their
brother at the front; they would work in munitions factories to help their
absent husbands to victory. Many wrote about it, and very moving these
accounts are, too.

CORA: He's working much too hard. For a start, he's just
got to let the maids serve in the dining room.
ROBERT: Quite right. There is a war. Even Carson has to
make sacrifices.
CORA: Poor Carson. Don't make him start working again
before he's ready.
ROBERT: I won't make him do anything.
CORA: Poor Lang! He looked like a rabbit in front of a
snake.
ROBERT: I don't understand it. He seemed so solid when I
met him, even taciturn; now he's a bundle of nerves.
CORA: I heard what you said to Matthew about the regiment.
ROBERT: Everyone else knows what a fool I made of myself.
Why shouldn't he?
CORA: I don't think you're a fool. Isn't that enough?
ROBERT: No. Maybe it should be, but it isn't. I'm
afraid it just isn't.

He switches off the light.

END OF ACT TWO

ACT THREE

34   INT.   LIVERY CUPBOARD.   DOWNTON.   NIGHT.

*O'Brien sees Lang standing, holding his livery on a coat
hanger, but he is quite stationary, staring. At the sound of
her voice, he turns a frightened face to her.*

O'BRIEN: Are you all right, Mr Lang? You're not, are
you? I've seen shell shock before, you know. I had a
brother with it. A favourite brother, as it happens.
And I was his favourite, too… They sent him back, and
he's dead now. *

....

* This was quite an important strand for me, because it allows O'Brien to
have some back story, and to hint at the circumstances that made her what
she is. Suddenly, you get a slightly different vision of her, as someone who's
survived toughness and neglect. O'Brien, of course, has spotted Lang's shell
shock earlier than anyone else.

LANG: They won't send me back. I'm a goner as far as they're concerned.
O'BRIEN: You shouldn't be working yet.
LANG: I must work. I don't know what I'd do, else.
I have to work.

There is a noise and Mrs Hughes appears.

MRS HUGHES: Mr Lang? I thought you'd gone up.
O'BRIEN: He wanted to hang up the livery before it got creased.
MRS HUGHES: Well, we can discuss the dinner another time.
I'll say goodnight.
O'BRIEN: Goodnight, Mrs Hughes.
LANG: Goodnight.

35 INT. CARSON'S BEDROOM. DOWNTON. NIGHT.

Carson is in bed. There is a knock and Mary appears.

MARY: May I come in?
CARSON: That's very kind of you, m'lady, but do you think you should?
MARY: Let's hope my reputation will survive it. And rest easy. Please.

He's tried to sit bolt upright. She takes a chair to the bed.

MARY (CONT'D): I gather it isn't too serious.
CARSON: Ah, I've been very stupid, m'lady. I let myself get flustered. I regard that as highly unprofessional.
It won't happen again.
MARY: You mustn't be too hard on yourself.
CARSON: I was particularly sorry to spoil things for Sir Richard, knowing he was a guest of yours.
MARY: Don't be. I think he found it all quite exciting.
CARSON: Will we be seeing a lot of him?
MARY: I don't know. Maybe.
CARSON: And Captain Crawley? Is he happy with the changes, so to speak?

They share a look. Mary knows that Carson loves her.

CARSON (CONT'D): May I give you one piece of advice, m'lady? Tell him what's in your heart. If you still

love him, let him know. Then, even if he's killed — and
he may be — you won't be sorry. But if you don't tell
him, you could regret it all your life long.*
MARY: And what about Miss Swire?
CARSON: Miss Swire? As if any man in his right mind
could prefer Miss Swire to you.

He looks up as Mrs Hughes comes in with some medicine.

MRS HUGHES: Oh, I'm so sorry, m'lady. I didn't know you
were in here.
MARY: I was just going… Carson's been boosting my
confidence.

She smiles at the butler and leaves the room.

MRS HUGHES: That's something I'd never have thought she
was short of.

Carson makes no comment, but takes the glass like a man.

36   INT. HOSPITAL. DOWNTON VILLAGE. DAY.

*Thomas sits talking to Lieutenant Courtenay, whose eyes are
bandaged.*

THOMAS: What about you, sir? What did you do before the
war started?
COURTENAY: I was up at Oxford. But I only ever planned
to farm. Farm and shoot and hunt and fish, and
everything I'll never do again.
THOMAS: You don't know that, sir. We've had cases of gas
blindness wearing off.

....

*This is where Carson gives Mary real advice, and, from him, because she knows he loves her, she takes it. He doesn't criticise her as he does later – in the fourth series, he is actually quite stern with her, and she has considerably more difficulty accepting his harsh words – but as long as the advice is not critical, which it isn't here, she will allow him an intimacy that she wouldn't allow any of the others. I am always sorry that the nature of making a series means that child characters who are members of the running cast are almost impossible to achieve. I mind this because the relationship between a child of a great house and the servants was quite, quite different from that of their parents. They knew the servants in a way their parents did not. All I can do here is hint at that intimacy, through Mary and Carson.

COURTENAY: Rare cases. And much sooner than this. It doesn't help me to be lied to, you know. I'm finished, and I'd rather face it than dodge it.
THOMAS: I'd better go.

37 EXT. WOODS AROUND DOWNTON. DAY.

Robert, Cora, Carlisle and Mary are walking in their tweeds. They've dropped into two couples. Robert and Cora are ahead.

ROBERT: Where's Rosamund?
CORA: She's with your Mama. Trying to talk her into the idea of Sir Richard.
ROBERT: You don't sound very enthusiastic.
CORA: Are you?

With a glance, he moves on. We drop back to the others.

CARLISLE: Can we stop for a minute?
MARY: Don't tell me you're tired.
CARLISLE: I'm not tired. I'm hot. This tweed is too thick.
MARY: It looks more suited to shooting than walking.
CARLISLE: I had it made for the weekend. I didn't know there was a difference.
MARY: It doesn't matter.
CARLISLE: That's like the rich who say that money doesn't matter. It matters enough when you haven't got it.

But he laughs. He doesn't really feel embarrassed at all.

MARY: I know you don't care about our silly rules. You're always very clear on that score.*

....

* Carlisle is conscious that he is coming up against a set of rules that he is not cognisant of. But where, I think, he shows strength is in saying that he means to learn how to do things properly. As he says, he is sure Mary could help him, but he is not ashamed of being a self-made man; he is proud of it. In a sense, I feel, at the end of this scene, we like Carlisle more than we did before, because he doesn't care about getting the tweed wrong. Next time he'll get it right, and anyway the distinction between a tweed for walking or for shooting is, of course, for him classic toff nonsense. Although, if you think about it, when you're shooting you stand still for hours, and of course you need to be warmer than when you're walking, so there is a logic in it.

CARLISLE: You make me sound rude and I hope I'm not that.
I have my own rules and I care about them.
MARY: Such as?
CARLISLE: I believe that a man who thinks he belongs at
the top of the tree should climb it as far as he can.
MARY: I agree.
CARLISLE: I'm not a Boer.* I mean to learn how to do
things properly and I'm sure you could help me a lot.
But I'm not ashamed of being what they call a self-made
man. I'm proud of it.
MARY: Is the point of all this to test me in some way?
CARLISLE: Maybe. Are you shocked by my bold and modern
values?
MARY: Oh, Sir Richard, you flatter yourself. It takes a
good deal more than that to shock me.

She walks on, and he follows her with admiring eyes.†

38   INT. DRAWING ROOM. DOWER HOUSE. DAY.

Violet is with Rosamund.

ROSAMUND: But Mama, who do you imagine is out there with
more to offer?
VIOLET: I am not a romantic —
ROSAMUND: I should hope not.
VIOLET: But even I will concede that the heart does not
exist solely for the purpose of pumping blood.
ROSAMUND: That is charming, especially from you, but Mary
seems to have blotted her copybook in some way…

If she hopes for Violet to comment, she is disappointed.

ROSAMUND (CONT'D): So she needs a suitable marriage that
will mend her fences.
VIOLET: But how do we know Carlisle is suitable? I mean,
who is he? Who'd ever heard of him before the war?

....

* I was sorry about this cut.

† Mary is not above controlling Carlisle by making him feel she's doing him a
favour, and you see her play notes on that several times. But what he is saying
here is, 'You're not in control of me. You can help me get the right tweed, but
you're not in control of me.' We like him for that.

ROSAMUND: Sir Richard is powerful and rich, and well on the way to a peerage. Of course, he may not be all that one would wish, but Mary can soon smooth off the rough edges.

VIOLET: Well, you should know.

ROSAMUND: What do you mean by that? Marmaduke was a gentleman.

VIOLET: Marmaduke was the grandson of a manufacturer.

ROSAMUND: His mother was the daughter of a baronet.

VIOLET: Maybe. But they were no great threat to the Plantagenets.

ROSAMUND: The point is, I made up for any social deficiencies and he provided me with a position. It was a good exchange and it worked well.*

But Violet is staring out of the window, distracted.

VIOLET: How can Matthew have chosen that little blonde 'piece'?

ROSAMUND: You speak so eloquently of the human heart, Mama. You must be aware of its vagaries.

....

* I quite like this putting of Rosamund in her place. But one has to remember that marrying for money and overlooking certain unsatisfactory details had been going on since the Conquest, long before the aristocracy went into crisis, and particularly in Britain.

Years ago, my father was being inducted into the top tier of the Knights of Malta. To get into it, all four of your grandparents had to come from arms-bearing families, and although my father fulfilled this qualification, he observed to the chap running the whole thing that it didn't seem very much to ask. To his surprise, the answer was that, on the continent, every new knight must have sixteen great-great-grandparents all of whom must have borne arms. When my father asked why that wasn't the condition in Britain, the reply was that none of the English would qualify. Even the Queen hasn't got that.

We have always married money, or power, or land, and if the price was to overlook failings of birth then so be it. This exchange is just a reminder of that. Rosamund, in a sense, is defending Mary's choice of Carlisle, because she made a similar choice herself, with Marmaduke Painswick. We are told his grandfather amassed his cash as a manufacturer, so the money is new, but not brand new. The son of the manufacturer was then able to marry the

39 INT. HOSPITAL. DOWNTON VILLAGE. DAY.

Thomas is opening a letter as he sits by Courtenay's bed.

THOMAS: It's from your father. 'Dear Edward, Please overcome your stubbornness and allow us to visit. There are decisions we should be facing as a family, not least about your future. Things cannot be as they were and, whatever you may think, Jack has your best interests at heart —'

COURTENAY: Stop.

THOMAS: Who's Jack?

COURTENAY: My younger brother. He means to replace me. It's what he's always wanted.

THOMAS: Yes. Well…

COURTENAY: I'm sorry. I mustn't bore you.

Thomas starts to walk away. Then he turns and comes back.

THOMAS: Don't let them walk all over you. You've got to fight your corner.

COURTENAY: What with?

THOMAS: Your brain! You're not a victim. Don't let them make you into one!

COURTENAY: You know, when you talk like that I almost believe you.

THOMAS: You should believe me! All my life they've pushed me around just because I'm different —

....

Continued from page 112:

daughter of a baronet, and Marmaduke, their son, married the daughter of an earl. The truth is, many toffs nowadays, who are baronets or the fourth Lord Whatever, come from precisely these manufacturing and banking Victorians – family fortunes that were made in the imperial economy. We had an enormous empire to supply, and supplying it generated these vast fortunes. In my opinion, this constant absorbing of new and successful blood is what kept the British aristocracy strong and politically relevant for a century longer than their continental counterparts.

Rosamund and Marmaduke did not have children. In the original publicity document I think there were two, but we came to the conclusion that she was much more use as a character if the Crawleys were essentially her main family. In that case, the Crawley girls would become her surrogate daughters, and that's what we have played.

COURTENAY: How? Why are you different?

THOMAS: Never mind. Look. I don't know if you're going to see again or not. But I do know you have to fight back.*

Courtenay reaches for Thomas's hand and squeezes it.

40 EXT. DOWNTON. DAY.

Rosamund is walking up the drive. She hears raised voices.

LAVINIA (V.O.): How dare you threaten me!

CARLISLE (V.O.): How dare I? Oh, I assure you, I dare a great deal more than that!

Rosamund, fascinated, approaches and peers through the laurels. Carlisle seems to have Lavinia's wrist in his grasp.

LAVINIA: But you can't! You wouldn't!

CARLISLE: I didn't say I would. I was merely reminding you it was in my power.

Rosamund walks forward, with a gentle cough.

CARLISLE (CONT'D): Lady Painswick.

ROSAMUND: Lady Rosamund.

CARLISLE: I'm sorry. I'll get these things sorted out before too long.

ROSAMUND: It's not important.

CARLISLE: Miss Swire and I were just talking about old times.

ROSAMUND: Happy old times, I hope.

She stares at Lavinia, who is clearly upset. No one speaks.

ROSAMUND (CONT'D): Will you forgive me? I want to write some letters before dinner.

She walks off, leaving the others standing in silence.†

....

* For anyone, going blind would be a very, very difficult test, but if you were a sporting countryman, there would be nothing left at all, and that's what Courtenay has to deal with. Actually, I'm very interested in the plight of blind men and women. I chair the RNIB Talking Books Appeal, and this story was a way of reminding the audience what blind people have to put up with.

41 EXT. DRAKES' FARMYARD. DAY.

Drake is forking hay in a hay barn. He piles it into a trailer, hitched to the back of the tractor.

DRAKE: Let's have a rest. We've earned it.

He walks over to a shelf and takes two bottles of ginger beer, then sits in the hay. Edith follows and takes a bottle.

DRAKE (CONT'D): I should have gone in for a glass. I don't suppose you can drink out of a bottle, can you, m'lady?

EDITH: I wish you'd call me Edith. And of course I can drink from the bottle… Would you like me to teach you to drive?

DRAKE: Not much. 'Cos then you wouldn't come here no more. Although that wouldn't matter to you.

EDITH: Why do you say that?

DRAKE: You're pretty and clever and fine. You're from a different world.

MRS DRAKE (V.O.): Is something wrong?

She is walking across the yard from the farmhouse.

DRAKE: No. We're just having a break.

MRS DRAKE: 'Cos you want to get into town to fetch the bone meal, and be back in time to feed the cows before it's dark.

EDITH: They could always have a midnight feast.

She laughs and so does Drake. Mrs Drake does not.

....

† Rosamund does not know why these two are arguing, but what she does realise is that, to some extent, they are not being honest, that there is a concealed truth here, which she doesn't like. Nor is she above putting Carlisle in his place. So when he calls her Lady Painswick, she corrects him – Lady Rosamund is her correct title as the daughter of an earl. Nowadays, of course, no one seems to know the difference between Lord Smith and Lord John Smith. But, then again, why should they?

42   EXT. HOSPITAL GROUNDS. DOWNTON VILLAGE. DAY.

Courtenay is walking with the aid of a stick. Tapping the ground, he moves between Thomas and Sybil.

THOMAS: That's it. That's right, sir. If you move the stick fast enough, you don't have to slacken your pace.
SYBIL: And check the width of the space as well as any possible obstruction.

Clarkson is watching from the door. He steps forward.

CLARKSON: Lieutenant Courtenay, well done. You're making good progress —
COURTENAY: Thanks to my saviours, sir.
CLARKSON: So you'll be pleased to hear that we're all agreed that it's time for you to continue your treatment elsewhere.
COURTENAY: What?
CLARKSON: At Farley Hall. You're not ill any more. All you need is time to adjust to your condition, and the staff at Farley can help with that.
COURTENAY: But sir, these two are helping me here.
CLARKSON: Nurse Crawley and Corporal Barrow are not trained in specialist care —
COURTENAY: Please, don't send me away. Not yet.
THOMAS: Sir, surely we —

Clarkson silences him with a look. He's not having this.

CLARKSON: Lieutenant, you must know that every one of our beds is needed for the injured and dying from Arras.

Courtenay is silent. Clarkson turns to Thomas.

CLARKSON (CONT'D): Corporal, I'll see you in my office.

43 INT. CLARKSON'S OFFICE. HOSPITAL. DOWNTON VILLAGE. DAY.

Thomas is in front of the desk, facing an irate Clarkson.

CLARKSON: I cannot have my decisions challenged in that way!

THOMAS: No, sir, but —

CLARKSON: There are no 'buts', Corporal! You may have been transferred here on the wishes of Lady Grantham, but her protection is not limitless.

THOMAS: Sir, I only meant to say that Lieutenant Courtenay is depressed —

CLARKSON: I will not leave wounded soldiers freezing or sweating under a canvas because one junior officer is depressed.

There is a knock at the door and it opens on Sybil.

CLARKSON (CONT'D): Yes?

SYBIL: I thought you may want to know what I think.

CLARKSON: Why should I? Nurse Crawley, I may not be your social superior in a Mayfair ballroom, but in this hospital I have the deciding voice. Please help him prepare his belongings. He leaves first thing in the morning.*

....

* By this stage, Thomas is essentially in love with Courtenay, and Clarkson, of course, is in a very difficult situation. You've got to see his point of view in this story, that you couldn't accommodate every patient who didn't want to move on. If you did, the whole system would clog up, and you'd have a log jam. It may have been hard for them, but how hard was it for the men at the front? I don't think we should see any of these positions as being heartless. And here, again, we're up against entitlement. I think Sybil feels – although she wouldn't agree with me – that she's not just a nurse; she's also Lady Sybil Crawley of Downton Abbey. It may be subconscious, but she expects that when she has given her opinion on the matter it will be obeyed. Clarkson's response, that in this hospital he is the deciding voice, is an important learning curve for her.

44 INT. CARSON'S BEDROOM. DOWNTON. NIGHT.

Carson is propped up in bed. Mrs Hughes sits on a chair.

MRS HUGHES: Anna and Ethel will wait at the table and I
will supervise. What's wrong with that?
CARSON: Nothing. Except that it's how a chartered
accountant would have his dinner served.
MRS HUGHES: I can think of worse insults.
CARSON: If you say so… But I don't want Lang allowed
anywhere near it.*

He looks to the sky imploringly.

CARSON (CONT'D): Oh, Mr Bates, where are you when we need
you? Can you bring me the wine ledgers and I'll make a
selection?
MRS HUGHES: His lordship's already done that. Just try
to rest.
CARSON: To rest or to feel redundant?
MRS HUGHES: Both, if it'll slow you down for a minute and
a half. The world does not turn on the style of a dinner.
CARSON: My world does.

45 INT. MARY'S BEDROOM. DOWNTON. NIGHT.

Mary and Rosamund are alone together.

ROSAMUND: How does he know Miss Swire?
MARY: What?

....

* The great distinction in assessing a household in modern times was whether
or not there were menservants. At the turn of the last century, any
moderately prosperous middle-class clerk would probably have a woman
helping his wife with the cooking, and a maid serving. I remember a very old
cousin of mine telling me that before coming to their rather dilapidated
house their nanny, who'd been in a frightfully grand house before then, came
down the drive for the interview and said to herself, 'If a butler or a footman
opens the door I'll take the job, but if it's opened by a maid I'll go home.'
Mercifully for the family, they had this ancient butler, who could hardly
stand, and he just used to open the door and more or less nothing else, so she
stayed. But that was the great marker. As usual, Carson feels all this more
than his employers. For him, to see Lord Grantham being served by two
maids would be an atrocity. Naturally, Robert couldn't care less. There's a
war on.

ROSAMUND: Miss Swire. They were in the garden when I came back from Mama's.
MARY: I suppose they met in London.

There is a knock and Anna looks round the door.

ANNA: Would you like me to come back later, m'lady?
ROSAMUND: No. Come in. I was just leaving.

She leaves. Mary stands for Anna to start undoing her dress.

MARY: How's Carson getting on?
ANNA: Oh, much better, m'lady. Mrs Hughes is having a job keeping him in bed.
MARY: He gave me some advice last night.
ANNA: Oh yes? Was it good advice?
MARY: It was about honesty. He thinks I should say what I really feel.
ANNA: Sounds a bit wild for Mr Carson.
MARY: But do you think he's right?
ANNA: Well, they do say honesty's the best policy. And I think you regret being honest less often than you regret telling lies.

Mary looks at her maid. This, of course, is true.

46 INT. HOSPITAL. DOWNTON VILLAGE. DAY.

It is early morning. A young nurse draws the curtains as the patients are waking. She is walking past Courtenay's bed when something catches her attention. She walks over to him and touches his cheek. She looks down. There is a pool of blood on the floor. She gasps and pulls back the bedclothes. In one hand the dead man holds a cut-throat razor; both wrists have stained the sheets with blood.

47 INT. PASSAGE. HOSPITAL. DOWNTON VILLAGE. DAY.

Sybil walks away. She does not notice Thomas standing alone, in the shadows. He is weeping.

48 INT. CLARKSON'S OFFICE. HOSPITAL. DOWNTON
VILLAGE. DAY.

*Sybil is with Isobel and Clarkson. She is profoundly
shocked.*

CLARKSON: He must have smuggled a razor into his bed.
There was nothing to be done.
SYBIL: It's because we ordered him to go.
ISOBEL: We don't know that.
CLARKSON: This is a tragedy. I don't deny it. But I
cannot see what other course was open to me. We have no
room for men to convalesce here, and Farley is the
nearest house I can send them to.
ISOBEL: There is a solution. And it's staring us in the
face. Downton Abbey.

The words electrify and inspire the other two.

CLARKSON: Would they ever allow it? Or even consider it?
SYBIL: I think they would. After this, I think they can
be made to.

49 EXT. RAILWAY STATION. DOWNTON VILLAGE. DAY.

*Branson is carrying some cases down the platform with
Carlisle's valet, while Carlisle and Mary stand nearby.*

MARY: I seem to spend my life waving goodbye from this
platform.
CARLISLE: I suppose you know why I wanted you to come and
see me off today?
MARY: To buy you some humbugs to eat on the journey?
CARLISLE: That. And other things.
MARY: But Sir Richard, you don't have to —
CARLISLE: Richard, please.

Mary is not quite sure she feels like playing this scene.

CARLISLE (CONT'D): You see, I want you to marry me.
MARY: Why?
CARLISLE: Because I think very highly of you.
MARY: Very highly? Goodness.
CARLISLE: I mean it. I think we'd do well together. We could be a good team.
MARY: Now, that sounds better. But I can't help thinking that tradition demands a little mention of love.

A train is pulling in. People climb in and out of it.

CARLISLE: Oh, I can talk about love and moon and June and all the rest of it, if you wish. But we're more than that. We're strong and sharp, and we could build something worth having, you and I, if you'll let us.
MARY: Your proposal is improving by leaps and bounds.

The whistle blows, but Carlisle won't be hurried. Mary smiles.

MARY (CONT'D): You must give me some time, but I promise to think about it. Properly.
CARLISLE: I'm counting on it.

He walks to the door where his valet waits with the guard. *

MARY: Branson, you can deliver Mama's mercy package and go back. I have an errand in the village.

50 EXT. HOSPITAL. DOWNTON VILLAGE. DAY.

Branson walks up to the hospital with a basket on his arm, as a number of wounded men are being carried in on stretchers.

51 INT. HOSPITAL. DOWNTON VILLAGE. DAY.

The scene is chaotic. Clarkson and Isobel are directing the stretcher bearers.

ISOBEL: Right to the other end, off you go.

....

* Quite deliberately we play the railway scene between Mary and Carlisle as a direct parallel to the scene between Mary and Matthew in Episode One.

Nurses, including Sybil, try to get the men into beds.
Screens are wheeled round to protect their modesty, but it's
still a muddle. Branson approaches Sybil with his basket.

> BRANSON: Her ladyship had Mrs Patmore make this up for
> you. So you could eat something during the day.
> SYBIL: Oh, I won't have time, but thank you.
> BRANSON: Are they from Arras?
> SYBIL: We'll be full after the first week of fighting…

She has been crying, and this speech takes her to the edge.

> BRANSON: What's the matter?
> SYBIL: This morning, they… Oh, it's just that it's all
> such a waste.

She is thinking of Courtenay, but she has no time for that
now. She walks off briskly to get beds ready. Branson
follows as Matthew comes in with Davis, and walks over to his
mother.

> ISOBEL: No, bring them to the other side. Oh, Matthew,
> I'm afraid I'm very busy. As you can see.
> MATTHEW: Yes, I just want to help. I can't be in the
> village and not help.
> ISOBEL: Feel free. But don't get in anyone's way.

As Matthew and Davis start to carry, Branson is with Sybil.

> BRANSON: Is it what you thought it would be?

She hesitates for a moment, thinking over his words.

> SYBIL: No. No, it's more savage and more cruel than I
> could have imagined… But I feel useful for the first
> time in my life. And that must be a good thing.
> Matthew? Are you busy?
> MATTHEW: No, of course not.

He lifts a man onto a bed. The invalid tries to salute him.

> MATTHEW (CONT'D): Never mind that, now. And remember,
> you are quite safe here.

He strides off to join Davis in lifting another wounded man, while Branson helps Sybil at another bed.

SYBIL: Please try to rest. You'll be attended to in a moment.

BRANSON: So you wouldn't go back to your life before the war?

SYBIL: Oh, no. No, I can never go back to that again.

And she vanishes into the mass of soldiers, as Branson looks on. He has heard what he wanted to hear. *

END OF ACT THREE

....

* In a workplace drama like this, you need certain areas where people can talk informally; the easiest one concerns the lady's maid and the employer's wife, the valet and the employer, because you're alone with them in a bedroom or a dressing room getting dressed. Of course they'd chat, everyone did. But apart from these obvious moments, you need to find other common ground. The hospital was useful dramatically for that. And here, Sybil makes this very telling comment to Branson, that she doesn't want to go back to the life she was leading before the war, which inevitably gives him hope, because the sacrifice he was asking her to make, of her grand life, she has already made in her heart, without its being connected to his proposal. This scene is taking them onto a level playing field. Now Branson has to win her hand, and make her fall in love with him, but he doesn't any more have to factor in that she's used to living as the daughter of a rich nobleman. She won't worry about that any more, and so he doesn't have to.

ACT FOUR

52 EXT. CRAWLEY HOUSE. DOWNTON VILLAGE. DAY.

Mary walks in through the gates. As she approaches the front door, she sees Lavinia sitting on a bench, crying.

    MARY: Lavinia? What's the matter?

Lavinia just shakes her head and wipes her eyes quickly.

    LAVINIA: Are you looking for Matthew?
    MARY: I was. But it's not important.*

Lavinia starts to cry again and Mary sits next to her.

    MARY (CONT'D): Tell me what it is. Please.
    LAVINIA: He has to go a day early. Tomorrow morning, in fact.
    MARY: Only to meet his General, surely? Not back to France.
    LAVINIA: But he must go back one day, and I can't stop thinking about what I'd do if anything happened to him.
    MARY: I know he'll be all right.
    LAVINIA: No, you don't. None of us do. We say that sort of thing, but we don't know… If he died, I don't think I could go on living.
    MATTHEW (V.O.): What's doing?

There he is, as handsome as ever.

    LAVINIA: Excuse me.

....

* Mary had made up her mind to tell Matthew that she was in love with him, and then she finds Lavinia crying, because she loves Matthew so much. It is a key *Downton* moment, really, because Mary, who is comparatively selfish, is not sufficiently selfish to ignore Lavinia's suffering and speak the words that she had intended. She looks at this weeping young girl and she feels sorry for her. This was why it was very important that Lavinia should not be an unpleasant person, but would instead be sweet and innocent and blameless. The point is that the audience, in one way, is dying for Mary to say it, and in another, they feel sorry for Lavinia, which is exactly what we want. 'You've had a wasted journey,' he says. 'Not at all,' Mary counters. 'I needed an excuse for a walk.' So, she has decided not to say it after all.

Lavinia shakes her head in an apology and runs inside.

MARY: Lavinia's a bit upset.
MATTHEW: She's awfully cut up that I have to go early.
But it's only to Coventry, which doesn't sound too
dangerous. If you're looking for Mother, she's at the
hospital. I've just come from there. I can't tell you
what it's like…

*He is lost in it, then he remembers himself, shaking his
head.*

MATTHEW (CONT'D): Forgive me. That's not very useful to
anyone.
MARY: Actually, it's you I came to see.
MATTHEW: Oh? How can I help?
LAVINIA: Mary! Can you stay for luncheon?

*She is in the doorway, eager and young and lovely and very
touching. Mary looks at her and makes a decision.*

MARY: I can't. But thank you.

Lavinia goes back inside and Mary turns once more to Matthew.

MATTHEW: So, what was your mission?
MARY: Just to say… we hope you're still coming for dinner
tonight?
MATTHEW: Certainly we are. Why wouldn't we?
MARY: Sure? It'll be your last evening.
MATTHEW: Why? Don't you want me?
MARY: Of course I want you. Very much.
MATTHEW: I'm sorry you've had a wasted journey.
MARY: Not at all. I needed an excuse for a walk. I'll
see you at eight.

She turns and strides away from the love of her life.

53   INT. KITCHEN PASSAGE. DOWNTON. NIGHT.

Anna comes along to find Molesley waiting there.

ANNA: Ethel said you wanted me.
MOLESLEY: No, no, I just need a word with you.
ANNA: If it's about that book, I'm afraid —
MOLESLEY: No. No, it's not about the book.
ANNA: What is it, then?

MOLESLEY: I understand that Mr Bates has gone for good.
ANNA: Yes. I believe that's true.
MOLESLEY: So I was hoping we might be able to see a little more of each other.

She realises that, this time, she can't get out of it.

ANNA: Mr Molesley, I take this as a real compliment.
MOLESLEY: But it's not going to happen.
ANNA: No… You see, if you had a child and that child was taken from you, if the child was sent to the moon, there'd never be one day when they were out of your thoughts, nor one moment when you weren't praying for their welfare. Even if you knew you'd never see them again.
MOLESLEY: And that's you and Mr Bates.
ANNA: That's me and Mr Bates. But thank you.

She squeezes his arm, then goes, leaving Molesley alone.

54 EXT. DRAKES' FARMYARD. NIGHT.

Drake is unloading some fencing from the trailer.

DRAKE: I've kept you too long. You'd better get back, or they'll come looking for you.
EDITH: We've done a lot, haven't we?
DRAKE: We have. I'll be forced to invent some tasks, or there'll be no need for you to come much more.
EDITH: Then start inventing. Please.

He has put down the fencing and now he walks over to her.

DRAKE: I will. Because I'd hate it if you were to stay away.
EDITH: So would I. I'd absolutely hate it.

He is in front of her now. They stare at each other for a moment and then, as he moves forward, so does she. They kiss.

DRAKE: I can't believe I've done that.
EDITH: I'm awfully glad you did.
DRAKE: You'll have me thrown in the Tower.
EDITH: Only if they give me the key.

In the shadows, across the yard, Mrs Drake is watching. *

55 INT. KITCHEN. DOWNTON. NIGHT.

Robert, splendid in white tie, looks in from the doorway.

MRS PATMORE: Daisy, how many times must I tell you? Fold
it in, don't slap it! You're making a cake, not beating
a carpet! Oh, I'm sorry, your lordship, I didn't see you
there —
ROBERT: That's quite all right, Mrs Patmore. I wonder,
is there somewhere we could have a word?

Mrs Patmore wipes her hands. She is bewildered.

MRS PATMORE: Er…
MRS HUGHES: Why not go into my sitting room?

56 INT. MRS HUGHES'S SITTING ROOM. DOWNTON.
          NIGHT.

Robert and the cook are alone. She waits in nervous silence.

ROBERT: Please sit. I do have some news of your nephew.
I telephoned the War Office and they've just come back to
me. But I'm afraid it's not good news.
MRS PATMORE: I knew he was dead all along. I said so to
my sister. I said, 'Kate,' I said, 'he's gone and you'll
have to face —'
ROBERT: Mrs Patmore, it's worse than that.
MRS PATMORE: What can be worse than being dead?
ROBERT: Private Philpotts was shot for cowardice on the
seventeenth of February.

....

* I don't think either of them expect it to go any further than a kiss. In my mind,
what they're doing is just acknowledging the fact that they have been attracted
to each other. Edith certainly isn't going to run away with a married tenant
farmer, and nor is he likely to elope with the daughter of the big house. But
living in the shadow of Mary and Sybil, Edith is never the one who's considered
beautiful. She is never thought to be marvellous or clever or talented, all of
which qualities Drake gives her. That is very powerful for her. His admiration
allows Edith to see herself, not as a great beauty or a brilliant wit, but, for the
first time, as having real potential. He lets her feel that she really does have
something to offer, and that means a lot, because she knows now that if and
when she meets the right man, she will possess these qualities for him.

MRS PATMORE: Oh, my God.
ROBERT: This explains why the regiment was reluctant to supply information.

He walks to the door, past the stricken woman.

ROBERT (CONT'D): Mrs Hughes, can you come in please? Mrs Patmore has had some bad news. Her nephew has been killed.

Mrs Hughes takes the cook in her arms.

MRS HUGHES: Oh, he never has.
MRS PATMORE: And that's not all —
ROBERT: It is all, Mrs Patmore. Let us make sure it is all. Your sister needs to know no more than this. We cannot know the truth. We should not judge. And now I'll leave you.*

57   INT.   DRAWING ROOM.   DOWNTON.   NIGHT.

The women are sitting after dinner.

VIOLET: I think it's a ridiculous idea!
SYBIL: Why?
VIOLET: Because this is a house, not a hospital! It's not equipped!

....

* Being shot for cowardice was actually very rare. We make a big thing of it now, and there is a special memorial in Staffordshire, the National Arboretum, with an area commemorating men who were shot for desertion and cowardice. In a way, it is astonishing how few there are – 306, I think – given that it was four years of the bloodiest war anyone had ever seen, involving millions upon millions of men. Nevertheless, we are a more forgiving generation, and we feel that, in many cases, they were suffering from shock and loss of nerve, so they were ill rather than cowardly. However, by having such a disciplined imperative, by making it almost impossible to give in and run for it, these men were able to fight and win the war. If they had been understanding of every man who deserted his post, would the results have been the same? We like to treat it as if it's a simple issue, but I don't think this is right. In fact, I'm sure it's extremely complicated. And if ever we were fighting a war on that scale, which I hope passionately we never are again, we would probably find it very hard to be sympathetic and yet hold the line. Of course, Robert wants to keep it private, because he knows the shame that was attendant on it.

MARY: But, Granny, a convalescent home is where people rest and recuperate.

VIOLET: But if there are relapses, what then? Amputation in the dining room? Resuscitation in the pantry?

CORA: It would certainly be the most tremendous disturbance. If you knew how chaotic things are as it is…

ISOBEL: But when there's so much good can be done —

VIOLET: I forbid it! To have strange men prodding and prying around the house, to say nothing of pocketing the spoons! It's out of the question!

CORA: I hesitate to remind you, but this is my house now, Robert's and mine. And we will make the decision.

VIOLET: Oh, I see. So now I'm an outsider who need not be consulted?

CORA: Since you put it like that, yes.

58   INT. DINING ROOM. DOWNTON. NIGHT.

Robert and Matthew are drinking port.

MATTHEW: I still think it's an honour.

ROBERT: Is it? To dress up like some fool in an *opéra bouffe?* I'm a chocolate soldier, ridiculous even to myself.

MATTHEW: And have you provided no comfort, when war has claimed the loved ones of the people around you?

Robert is silent, which allows the point.

MATTHEW (CONT'D): There. Don't talk as if your task here has no value.

ROBERT: What was it like at the hospital today?

MATTHEW: At the front, the men pray to be spared, of course. But if that's not to be, they pray for a bullet that kills them cleanly… For too many of them today, that prayer had not been answered.

59   INT. KITCHEN. DOWNTON. NIGHT.

Mrs Patmore, Daisy and the maids are cooking the servants' dinner.

MRS PATMORE: We'll eat in about twenty minutes.

WILLIAM (V.O.): Good. And would you have any to spare for a poor traveller?

He is in the doorway, in uniform.

DAISY: William! I don't believe it!
WILLIAM: Pinch me. I am your dream come true.
DAISY: You're like a real soldier.
WILLIAM: I am a real soldier, thank you very much. Now, come and give me a kiss.
MRS PATMORE: Ooh, we'll have none of that!
WILLIAM: Won't you let a Tommy kiss his sweetheart, Mrs Patmore, when he's off to fight the Hun?
DAISY: Have you finished your training?
WILLIAM: Not yet. But it won't be long now.
MRS PATMORE: Well, on the eve of departure, we'll see. But right now, put her down.

*Mrs Patmore has watched all this with tears in her eyes.**

60 INT. SERVANTS' HALL. DOWNTON. NIGHT.

The table is laid for supper. Lang is in there, reading, and Anna, but no one else, as William walks in. She stands.

ANNA: William! What a treat to see you, and how smart you look. Welcome.
WILLIAM: Thanks.
ANNA: Supper won't be long. I'm just going up to clear the dining room.
WILLIAM: Shall I help?
ANNA: 'Course not. You're in the Army now.

With a laugh, she leaves them alone. Lang looks up.

LANG: So, still full of the joys of warfare?
WILLIAM: I'm not sorry to be part of it, Mr Lang, and I can't pretend I am.
LANG: Oh, yes, you're part of it. Like a metal cog is part of a factory, and a grain of sand is part of the beach.

....

* We put in this scene, the return of William as a soldier, proud as punch of his uniform, quite deliberately after the scene in the hospital, so the audience would have a clearer idea of what he was getting into. William is an innocent about warfare, as so many of them were. But Mrs Patmore, of course, is not deceived. Her nephew has just been shot and she is full of tears.

WILLIAM: It's all right, Mr Lang. I understand. And I'm
not saying I'm important or owt like that. But I believe
in this war. I believe in what we're fighting for, and I
want to do my bit.
LANG: Then God help you.

61 INT. DRAWING ROOM. DOWNTON. NIGHT.

Matthew and Robert have joined them and Matthew is with Mary.
They glance across to an animated Edith talking to Lavinia.

MATTHEW: Edith seems jolly tonight.
MARY: She's found her métier. Farm labouring.
MATTHEW: Don't be so tough on her.
MARY: That's like asking the fox to spare the chicken.
MATTHEW: What about you? Last time you told me good news
was imminent.
MARY: Would you be happy, if it were?
MATTHEW: Of course. I've found someone now, and I want
you to do the same.

62 INT. SERVANTS' HALL/KITCHEN. DOWNTON. NIGHT.

William is recounting his tales to the table.

WILLIAM: 'If you'd taken another minute to make up your
mind, sir, we'd all have marched over the cliff!' And
I'll tell you something else as well —

As they are laughing, Daisy collects some dishes and brings
them back to the kitchen, where Mrs Patmore is tidying.

MRS PATMORE: William's got more to say than a
parliamentary candidate. What's the matter?
DAISY: I know it's my fault, but I wish I hadn't let him
think that we're… like sweethearts, because we're not.
Not by my reckoning, anyway.
MRS PATMORE: Too late for second thoughts now, Missy.
You don't have to marry him when it comes to it, but you
can't let him go to war with a broken heart, or he won't
come back.

63 INT. MARY'S BEDROOM. DOWNTON. NIGHT.

Anna is plaiting Mary's hair for the night.

MARY: What a time we've had. Poor Sir Richard must have thought he'd come to the mad house.
ANNA: I don't expect it'll put him off.

She catches Mary's eye for a moment.

MARY: I'm going to accept him.

But Anna does not comment. She just goes on plaiting.

MARY (CONT'D): Do you think I should?
ANNA: That's not for me to say. If you love him more than anyone in the world then of course you should.
MARY: It's not as simple as that.
ANNA: Oh? It is for me, but then I'm not your ladyship.
MARY: Did you love Bates more than anyone else in the world?
ANNA: I did. I do. I'll never love again like I love him. Never.
MARY: Well, there you are, then. One day you'll meet someone else and you'll marry. Perhaps it will be second best, but it doesn't mean you can't have a life.
ANNA: I think it does for me.

And she ties a ribbon into a bow to finish the plait.*

....

* Anna's moral position is higher than Mary's here. Anna is prepared to be alone for the rest of her life if Bates never comes back. Mary, on the other hand, is not prepared to be on her own forever if Matthew never returns. But, to be honest, I'm on Mary's side. I think Anna is throwing away her life. So, in one sense, in terms of romantic fiction, we're supposed to approve of Anna's abnegation and sacrifice, but in reality I approve of Mary's getting her act together and being determined to make another life. So, in the *Downton* way, I hope the audience is divided.

64 INT. DINING ROOM. DOWNTON. DAY.

Robert, Mary and Edith are eating breakfast. Carson is there.

ROBERT: Are you sure you should be doing this, Carson? We've managed very well with Mrs Hughes.
CARSON: Quite sure, m'lord. And breakfast is not a taxing assignment.

Robert shares this with the girls, as he opens a letter.

ROBERT: Edith, this is a message for you. Mrs Drake writes that they've decided to hire a man, so they won't be needing you any more.

Edith's cheerful mood is wiped away, as if by a magic cloth.

EDITH: Is that all she says?
ROBERT: Well, she's very grateful. Here we are: she says she and Drake send their thanks to you for giving up so much of your valuable time.

Edith is silent in her misery. Robert smiles at her.

ROBERT (CONT'D): I expect it's rather a relief.
EDITH: Oh, I wouldn't say that. Not entirely.

Which is all she will trust herself to reveal.

ROBERT: Has Lady Sybil gone already?
CARSON: She had a tray at half past six.
ROBERT: She would. Carson, have they told you we're to be turned into a hospital?
MARY: A convalescent home. I'm afraid we've all bullied you into the whole thing. I hope you're not dreading it too much.
ROBERT: Not dreading it exactly, but it's a brave new world we're headed for, no doubt about that. We must try to meet it with as much grace as we can muster…

END OF EPISODE TWO

EPISODE THREE

ACT ONE*

1 INT. DRAWING ROOM. DOWNTON. DAY.

July 1917.† Sybil, in a nurse's uniform, moves beds with
Edith. Cora, Branson, Anna and Ethel are with them, as well
as Doctor Clarkson, Isobel and some orderlies from the
hospital.

ANNA: Should we give them some more space between the
beds?
EDITH: Well, we could give them —
ISOBEL: Not much. I'm determined to defend the library
as a recreation room.
CORA: Where are we to sit?
ISOBEL: We can screen off the small library.
CORA: Is that all?
EDITH: I suppose we still —
ISOBEL: Or we could leave you the boudoir. I wanted to
put the intermediaries in there, but we don't have to.
CORA: How kind.

....

* The family have come to the conclusion that it's time Downton played its part in the war, with the different members manifesting greater or lesser enthusiasm. Sybil, of course, is very keen, Robert rather less so, and most of the others fall somewhere in between. It's rather like filming. People think they want you to film in their house, but when it actually starts they can't believe the disruption. And really what they wanted was for you to give them an enormous cheque so they can mend the roof, but not actually to displace anything. That is the point of this storyline, that when you make these commitments, for the best possible motives, so often you haven't really negotiated what it will do to your life. In this case, obviously, Violet has a clearer idea of what is going to happen, in the way of general disruption, than her son or any of the rest of them.

† As for the date, we were driven by the knowledge that we wanted to have a couple of episodes after the war, so that the series would take this group of men and women through the fighting and out the other side. We didn't want to have Armistice Day at the end of Episode Eight, because we needed a sense of life going on, once the war was over, rather than making it too final.

Isobel chooses not to react. Sybil is troubled.

> SYBIL: Why will we only have officers? Surely all
> wounded men need to convalesce?*
> CLARKSON: The hospital is for officers, and the whole
> idea is to have a complementary convalescent home.
> SYBIL: Of course. But I don't know if we can make that
> an absolute rule.
> ISOBEL: If the world were logical, I would rather agree
> with you.
> VIOLET (V.O.): Which comes as no surprise.

Violet is being shown in by Carson. She looks round.

> ISOBEL: You would not, I imagine.
> VIOLET: You imagine right. What these men will need is
> rest and relaxation. Will that be achieved by mixing
> ranks and putting everyone on edge?†

She turns and walks out before Isobel can reply.

....

* We had to make it clear that the hospital was for officers, and therefore Downton Abbey would be a convalescent home for officers. You must allow for modern sensibilities, and so we have Sybil, who is, I think believably, the voice of modern reason, saying how ridiculous it is that all the men don't convalesce together; how absurd to maintain the class divide, even when it comes to the war wounded, which I think is a fair enough point. Nevertheless, it is important for us to reflect the values of that time. Even today, there is a belief that too much familiarity makes it hard to take people's orders seriously. And usually, whether it's bosses in factories, or officers, or people running a house, if there is too much informality it can be difficult to make the whole operation run smoothly. At any rate, that was certainly the thinking in the War Office then. The officers had to be preserved as a kind of separate human group in order to be taken seriously by their men. I suspect there was probably something in it, whatever we may tell ourselves now.

† I don't think Violet would have been unusual in believing that it was impossible to relax with people of a different rank. There was then a feeling – and probably there is now, more than one admits – that people are more relaxed among their own tribe. Isobel, naturally, takes the intellectual, middle-ground position. Part of this story is about the way any change of situation can empower people, and if you want to be in control of it – and personally I don't think we're very much in control of anything – you have to

2 INT. HALL. DOWNTON. DAY.

This is a hive of activity. Anna, Ethel, the hall boys, the other maids and some nurses are carrying bedding in, and furniture out, of the rooms. Sybil catches up with Violet.

SYBIL: Granny, different ranks can relax together. It has been known.
VIOLET: Oh, don't look at me. I'm very good at mixing. We always danced the first waltz at the Servants' Ball, didn't we, Carson?
CARSON: It was an honour, m'lady.
VIOLET: But it's a lot to ask when people aren't at their best. I'm searching for Lady Mary, Carson. Will you tell her I'm in the library?

Carson walks away past Edith, who has just come out.

ISOBEL: Don't loiter, Edith. There's plenty to be done.
EDITH: Of course, but I'm not quite sure what's —

But Isobel has gone and Edith is talking to herself.

3 INT. SERVANTS' HALL. DOWNTON. DAY.

The servants have finished lunch. Daisy is clearing away.

ANNA: I'm going down to the village this afternoon, if anyone wants anything.
MRS HUGHES: Some stamps would be kind. I'll get you the money.
CARSON: I'd like to thank you all for your work this morning.
ETHEL: It's so strange to see the rooms converted into dormitories.
ANNA: But good. It was wrong for our life to chug along as if the war were only happening to other people.

....

Continued from page 137:

be aware of that. But Cora and Robert are not really prepared for how Isobel, inevitably, as a trained nurse, the widow of a doctor and the daughter of another doctor, will carry an authority in the world that is now moving into Downton. So she is bound to assume a leadership role, which is a direct challenge to Cora's position as the mistress of the household. All of that, obviously, was quite deliberate on our part.

DAISY: How will it be, though? Are we all working for
Mrs Crawley now?
O'BRIEN: We are not.
CARSON: I'm sure the chain of command will be sorted out
soon.
O'BRIEN: Or there'll be blood on the stairs.
CARSON: Thank you, Miss O'Brien.*

4 INT. LIBRARY. DOWNTON. DAY.

Violet is with Mary.

VIOLET: But what do you think it meant?
MARY: Really, Granny. Lavinia Swire knows Richard
Carlisle. So what? One knows lots of people in London.
VIOLET: I don't know many people who'd threaten me behind
the laurels.
MARY: Aunt Rosamund said herself she didn't know what to
make of it.
VIOLET: I still think it's a peculiar way for a gentleman
to speak to a lady.
MARY: At least you think him a gentleman.
VIOLET: The point is, do you think he's a gentleman?
MARY: I'm not sure it matters much to me.†
VIOLET: Well, I'm going up to London to stay with
Rosamund for a day or two. I think we'll have Lavinia
for tea.
MARY: You sound as if you're going to gobble her up.
VIOLET: If only we could.

....

*The chain of command for the servants was an important element that
many of these houses had to deal with, because during the war, when the
house was used differently, outside people came in and confused it. It was
something that had to be negotiated, and even Carson is not prepared to be
quite definite. We have established that, for as long as the war lasts, we will
be in this strange territory, where Downton Abbey will be a public rather
than a private house.

† Because this slight hiccough has arisen with Lavinia Swire and Richard
Carlisle, which is not part of Mary's plan, her instinct is always to dismiss it.
My own feeling about that, and I suppose in a way I use Mary to demonstrate
it, is that self-knowledge, or at any rate knowledge, is the key to achievement.
And when you ignore facts, particularly about yourself, then you open
yourself up to the possibility of failure. We toy with that notion here.

5 EXT. DOWNTON VILLAGE. DAY.

Isobel Crawley is walking along when Anna hails her. She carries a shopping basket, but it is still empty.

> ANNA: Mrs Crawley, can I trouble you? I'd like to help when the wounded come, and since you're running things —
> ISOBEL: It's not quite decided, but I think I will have the role of supervisor, yes. There really isn't anyone else who can be spared from the hospital.
> ANNA: So, what do you think?
> ISOBEL: We can't have enough help. But we mustn't steal all your free time.
> ANNA: I don't want free time, ma'am. Not at the moment… Now, I've some errands to run and I must get to the Post Office before it shuts.

Suddenly we cut back, across the village green. We are watching them chatting through someone else's eyes.

6 INT. KITCHEN. DOWNTON. DAY.

Mrs Patmore is preparing dinner. Carson is there, carrying a couple of letters. He's given one to Daisy, who's reading it.

> MRS PATMORE: But where are they going to eat?
> CARSON: I understand from Mrs Crawley that they'll share the dining room with the officers who are almost well.
> MRS PATMORE: So am I running a canteen now?*

Daisy gives a slight laugh, which distracts them. She speaks.

> DAISY: William says he's got time off between the end of his training and going overseas.
> MRS HUGHES: He'll be with his father, surely?
> DAISY: He's going home first, but he wants to come here for his last night.

....

* It is not quite fair to hire people for one job, and then blithely promise them for another without ever checking properly, although heaven knows it goes on. If you said to Cora, 'You do realise you've made an enormous amount of work for your servants,' she would be horrified, because, after all, other people are coming in from the village to help, aren't they? 'Yes, they are, m'lady, but it doesn't alter the fact that there's a lot more to do for all of them.'

MRS HUGHES: You wouldn't mind that, would you, Mr Carson?
CARSON: Certainly not. I'd be glad to wish him luck on his way.

Branson enters the kitchen. Carson hands him a letter.

CARSON (CONT'D): Ah, for you, Mr Branson.

The butler and housekeeper go.

DAISY: Why do you think he's coming here?
MRS PATMORE: To see us all and say goodbye. What's wrong with that?
DAISY: But suppose it's something more. Suppose he's got plans.
MRS PATMORE: Well, you have to deal with that when it happens. And mind you deal fair. Now go and grate that suet before I grow old and die.

7   EXT. DOWNTON VILLAGE. DAY.

Anna comes out of a shop with a full basket. Heading for the Post Office, she spies a familiar figure. She whispers.

ANNA: Mr Bates?

But when she hurries over, whoever it was has gone.

8   INT. DRAWING ROOM. DOWNTON. DAY.

Cora is with Mary, Edith and Sybil, who is making one of the beds.

CORA: Who'll be in charge?
EDITH: Cousin Isobel thinks it'll be her. She said so to Anna.
MARY: All I know is that she'll drive us mad before the end.

Cora looks at her. She does not trust herself to comment.

CORA: I'm going up to change.
SYBIL: I just want to finish this.

Cora and Mary leave.

EDITH: Aren't you going to the hospital?
SYBIL: Not yet. I'm on a night shift. I'll walk down after dinner. And please don't start lecturing me.

EDITH: I won't. The truth is I envy you.

SYBIL: Do you ever miss helping out on the Drakes' farm?

EDITH: That's a funny question. Why?

SYBIL: No reason. It's just you seemed to have such a…
purpose there. It suited you.

EDITH: It did suit me. I enjoyed it.

SYBIL: If you see that, then turn this new adventure into
something good.

EDITH: How? I feel like a spare part.

SYBIL: Trust me. You have a talent that none of the rest
of us have. Just find out what it is, and use it. It's
doing nothing that's the enemy.*

9 INT. CORA'S BEDROOM. DOWNTON. SUMMER EVENING.

Cora is being fastened into an evening dress.

CORA: I think he's made it too tight. I know it's
supposed to be a hobble skirt, but I can't even hobble.

O'BRIEN: They say women must suffer to be beautiful.

CORA: Well, women must suffer, anyway.

O'BRIEN: The truth is, m'lady, Mrs Crawley has forgotten
this is your house. And we need a friend in charge of
the day-to-day management. Because if Mrs Crawley gets
one of her toadies in to run things, she'll have her nose
in every pie before you can say 'Jack Robinson'.

CORA: But who…?

O'BRIEN: What about Thomas, m'lady? He's hospital
trained and he's always had a soft spot for Downton.

CORA: Thomas, the footman? Managing Downton Abbey?

O'BRIEN: But he's not a footman now, is he? He's a
corporal, with real battle experience as a medic.

CORA: Could Doctor Clarkson spare him?

O'BRIEN: Well, I suppose he'll have to spare somebody.†

....

* Edith has been, to a certain extent, blown around by fate, and now we start
to leak the fact that helping on the farm has given her a taste for being useful,
for going to bed feeling she's tired and has done something worthwhile with
her day. This will lead on to greater things for Edith eventually, and Sybil is
right to be encouraging.

10   INT.   ROBERT'S DRESSING ROOM.   DOWNTON.   SUMMER
                        EVENING.

Lang is helping Robert into evening dress.

  ROBERT: We'll see some rough sights. The wounded aren't
  always very pretty.

Lang concentrates on his work. He doesn't need reminding.

  ROBERT (CONT'D): But maybe to show no fear or horror in
  the face of their suffering is a kind of patriotic duty
  in itself. That's what I feel, anyway.

Lang is fumbling with the cufflinks.

  ROBERT (CONT'D): But it may be a difficult reminder for
  you. Which I quite understand.

This makes Lang's hands shake even more. He drops the link.

  11   INT.   MARY'S BEDROOM.   DOWNTON.   SUMMER
                        EVENING.

Anna is about to wave Mary's hair with a new iron.

  MARY: Ready?
  ANNA: I think so. Although I wouldn't have minded a bit
  of training.
  MARY: Don't be so faint-hearted. Mr Suter swears by
  them, and everyone goes to him now.

....

† Thomas's war has enabled this, because he's now a trained nurse. He's been
in the Medical Corps, and he's working in the hospital, again largely through
O'Brien's manipulation of Cora. And she hasn't stopped yet. What she
means to prey on is Cora's growing irritation that the whole business of
making the house over to be a convalescent home is getting away from her
control. O'Brien is a pretty good psychoanalyst. She knows that is Cora's
weak spot.

Anna starts to create a series of Marcel waves. *

MARY (CONT'D): Are you all right? You seem a bit preoccupied.
ANNA: I had a… No, never mind.
MARY: What?
ANNA: It was this afternoon. In the village. I thought I saw Mr Bates.
MARY: Bates? Isn't he in London?
ANNA: I might have been wrong. I walked over to where he was standing and there was no sign of him. But…
MARY: Do you know his address in London?
ANNA: As long as he's still there. Why?
MARY: I'll telephone Sir Richard and ask him to look into it.†

....

* That very distinctive look of the Marcel wave lasted for fifteen or twenty years, from something like 1915 to 1934 or thereabouts, when smoother hairstyles crept in. As we know, by the Forties it was those big curls and so on. But I think, funnily enough, those hot tongs that were used to produce a curl in the hair were part of the liberation of women. The long hair of the Edwardian women that needed constant brushing and combing and putting up and taking down seemed increasingly unsuitable for the lives they were living. Even for working-class women, it was on the whole not accepted for them to cut their hair, so hair became, in a way, a sign of bondage, as it is in some other cultures to this day. Long hair is a statement, both of femininity, but also of impracticality, which renders its wearers less suited to any task outside the home. In the Forties, they actually had to get the film star Veronica Lake to cut her hair, because so many women were imitating her and their hair was getting caught in the machines. So she cut off her long, seductive locks, and with them, I'm afraid, her career. But, anyway, what I liked about Anna using the Marcel waver was (a) it was distinctively period, (b) it was another advance technologically and (c) it was part of the changing role of women. Fussing with a Marcel waving machine is rather tedious, I should imagine, but in those days it was a more liberated look, because once you had done it you put a comb through your hair and you were off. That freedom is what it was for, really.

† The point here was really to remind the audience that the sort of omniscience of modern communication was coming. The telegram, the newspaper and the telephone had already begun that kind of universal information gathering that Mary takes advantage of. Here was one of the ways that the upper classes kept everything effectively under their control.

ANNA: But what would he know?

MARY: He works in newspapers — a world of spies, tip-offs and private investigators. I promise you, he can find out whatever he likes.

ANNA: All right, then. If you think he can help.

MARY: Good. I'll ring him tonight.

She steps back. It looks quite good.

MARY (CONT'D): Not bad. But try and fit in a bit of practice. We've plenty of time to get it right before there's anyone to see me who matters.

12 EXT. LADY ROSAMUND'S HOUSE. BELGRAVE SQUARE. DAY.

The cold sunlight illuminates the white-stuccoed mansion.

13 INT. LADY ROSAMUND'S DRAWING ROOM. DAY.

Violet and Rosamund are having tea with Lavinia Swire.

LAVINIA: I only know Sir Richard because he is, or was, a friend of my father's, and of my uncle, Jonathan Swire.

ROSAMUND: The Liberal minister?

LAVINIA: That's it. But I'm afraid they've fallen out…

ROSAMUND: Ah.

LAVINIA: This room is so pretty. Has the house always been the Painswicks' London home?

VIOLET: There's no 'always' about the Painswicks, my dear. They were invented from scratch by my son-in-law's grandfather.

ROSAMUND: We bought the house when we were married.

....

Continued from page 144:

Within that world, at one remove, everyone knew everyone. But if you go below that world, in the old days, there was no intercommunication network in the same way. So it was rather like a sort of KGB, although rather better dressed, who were all in touch. The information network has changed that now. It has given the power of knowledge to a much wider group and shifted the balance. People still ring each other and ask, 'Whom do we know at such-and-such a university?' 'How can we get my son into banking?' 'Thingummy needs some work experience in fashion.' And everyone pulls strings. But now this string-pulling is open to a far wider section of the community.

LAVINIA: You make Mr Painswick sound rather a rough diamond, Lady Grantham.
ROSAMUND: Marmaduke wasn't a rough diamond, was he, Mama?
VIOLET: No. He was just cut and polished comparatively recently.*

14 EXT. STABLE YARD. DOWNTON. DAY.

Branson is cleaning the car. Sybil is watching him.

SYBIL: Carson's told Papa you've been called up.
BRANSON: There's no need to look so serious.
SYBIL: You'd think me pretty heartless if I didn't.
BRANSON: I'm not going to fight.
SYBIL: You'll have to.
BRANSON: I will not. I'm going to be a 'conscientious objector'.
SYBIL: You can't.
BRANSON: Watch me.
SYBIL: They'll put you in prison.

....

* This scene demonstrates the tribalism of these families, that however much they disagree, when their interest is threatened, usually they will line up shoulder to shoulder. Which is one of the reasons that can make them quite difficult to marry into, because – and I wouldn't say this is true of every family, but I think it's true of a lot of them – you're always slightly the second banana, as the wife or husband of a true-blood member. The real club consists of the born members, and while a new arrival can eventually earn their stripes to a certain extent, nevertheless for a young spouse marrying in, I think it can be pretty tough.

Violet here cannot resist the dig about Rosamund having married Marmaduke, but I think it's important to realise that the late Victorians were a much more socially mobile society than people often think. Our taste for oppression means that we like to represent the world before the Second World War as being cruel and closed. If you were born into the top tier, fine, and if you weren't, you'd had it. In fact, this was not true from the middle of the nineteenth century onwards, because the imperial economy, with its tremendously expanding markets, meant that new families were coming in all the time.

I felt that it was more interesting to give Rosamund this slightly broader approach, that she has made the decision to marry a very rich man who is reasonably born (her mother-in-law was the daughter of a baronet, we're told), although this upwardly mobile line did not then continue, because Rosamund had no children. Nevertheless, I think it gives her a better position to advise Mary. She's not simply living in the old world, but also the new, which Violet senses.

BRANSON: I'd rather prison than the Dardanelles.
SYBIL: When will you tell them?
BRANSON: In my own good time.
SYBIL: I don't understand.
BRANSON: I'll go to the medical and report for duty. And
when on parade, I'll march out front and I'll shout it
loud and clear. And if that doesn't make the newspapers,
then I'm a monkey's uncle.

He laughs at the thought, but she does not.

SYBIL: But you'll have a record for the rest of your life.
BRANSON: At least I'll have a life.* Come on. You're not
telling me you think this war is right?

....

* One of our main storylines now gathers momentum, with Sybil actually interested in Branson enough to want him not to get into trouble or be wounded, and we also have the laying of Branson's plot, that he is going to resign from the Army while on parade, intent that it'll be in all the newspapers. I think it's actually debatable, because in those days you could control the newspapers rather more than you can now, but nevertheless he probably could have got it into some anti-war publications, and so he wants to make a public renunciation.

I quite admire Branson for this, I have to say. He's got his point to make; he doesn't think Ireland should be dragged into a European war, he doesn't feel they owe it to the British, and rather than just twist his ankle he feels he should make a statement that would certainly end up with a prison sentence. That, for me, marks him out as more than just a moaner; he is a doer, and a proactive rebel, which I like.

Sybil, I think, represents the other view. In fact, historically, in this period, the suffragette movement split into two. The main body said suffragettes should cooperate with the war effort and resume their fight at the end of the war, something for which, obviously, the Government was very appreciative, and that was, in their account, one of the reasons that women were given the vote in 1919. But some suffragettes, the militant ones, said, 'No, this is our chance, and now we must deliver.' It was rather like some unions who wanted to strike at the beginning of both wars, because the country was vulnerable. I personally find it rather heartening that, in 1914 and 1939, the trouble-makers were in the minority. The majority of workers, who I'm perfectly sure had legitimate complaints, were prepared, for the good of the country, to put them to one side until the war was settled. I like them for that, and I like Sybil for making the same choice here, which she emphatically does. So she and Branson are not on the same side over the war.

SYBIL: I don't know. But I know we must stick together, now more than ever. All our differences, of class or fortune or even politics, don't matter now. We have to come through this and we can't let people feel the sacrifice was for nothing.
BRANSON: Well, it was.

15 INT. KITCHEN PASSAGE. DOWNTON. NIGHT.

Lang drops a shirt, then socks. Picking them up defeats him.

MRS PATMORE: Cheer up. It's not as bad as that.
LANG: I'm fine. I'm just finishing off.

But still he does not move. She walks up to him.

MRS PATMORE: What's the matter, Mr Lang? Tell me. I won't bite.
LANG: I sometimes feel I'm the only one who knows what's going on over there. You all wander round ironing clothes and cleaning boots and choosing what's for dinner, while over the Channel men are killed and maimed and blown to pieces.
MRS PATMORE: We know more than you think. The war hasn't left us alone; it hasn't left me alone, however it may look.
LANG: Have you any idea how scared they are? How scared they all are?
MRS PATMORE: I lost my nephew, my sister's boy. He was shot…

She makes the decision to take someone into her confidence.

MRS PATMORE (CONT'D): For cowardice. That's what they said, but I knew him and he'd never have done such a thing if he hadn't been half out of his mind with fear.
LANG: Don't blame him. It was him, but it could have been me. It could have been any of us.*

....

* There was a largely unspoken but universal complicity not to let the people at home really know what was going on at the front and what the war was actually like. They would never talk about it. They would come home, and have dinner at The Ritz, and go to the Embassy to dance, and they'd never

16 EXT. KITCHEN COURTYARD. DOWNTON. DAY.

Thomas is with O'Brien.

THOMAS: Suppose I don't want to come back?

O'BRIEN: To be in charge? Telling Mr Carson what to do?

THOMAS: Why? What's in it for you?

O'BRIEN: Charming. I bet you say that to all the girls…
All right. It's to stop Mrs Crawley bossing her ladyship
about. She behaves as if she owns the place.

THOMAS: You've changed your tune. When I were last here
you'd have given money to see her ladyship eat dirt.

O'BRIEN: Well, like you say, I've changed my tune.
People do.

THOMAS: Not without a reason.

O'BRIEN: I've got my reasons.

THOMAS: You've also got her ladyship wrapped round your
little finger.

O'BRIEN: Maybe. That's my business. But I'll not hurt
her, and I'll not let anyone else hurt her, neither.
That's all I've got to say.†

Continued from page 148:

say, 'Yes, a man's leg was blown off in front of me, and my friend died in the ditch but it was a whole night before we could get him out,' and so on. As a result, I think people at home had rather a romanticised vision for quite long into the war as to what was actually going on. That changed gradually, but there's no doubt these men were a very brave generation. They swallowed it, and there were many, many men who fought in the First World War who would never talk about it, ever, and in my childhood and youth I met several. I'm sure some of them, a great many of them, paid with their nerves. But it is their bravery that strikes me. Lang is unusual, because he doesn't conceal the horrors that he has lived through. This is a sign of his shell shock and, of course, it renders him uncomfortable to be with. Unfortunately for her, Mrs Patmore makes the mistake of confiding in him about her nephew. But I feel that, if such a thing had happened, it would never be very far from her frontal lobe, so we can understand why she tells him.

† Here we have O'Brien's explicit reason, in as much as she's ever explicit, for why she is now protective of Cora. She caused the accident that killed Cora's baby, and while no one's ever going to know that apart from Thomas, she does now feel she owes her employer something. Again, it's all to do with my habit of shifting characters. Just when you think they're all bad, they're not quite, so you have to adjust your opinion. Which is what I like.

THOMAS: You're a queer one, and no mistake.
O'BRIEN: So will you come if I can fix it?
THOMAS: Why not? I like the idea of giving orders to old
Carson.

17 INT. LIBRARY. DOWNTON. EVE.

The family listen to Clarkson and Isobel.

VIOLET: I go away for five minutes and everything's
settled!
ROBERT: Nothing's settled! For a start, which rooms will
we live in?
ISOBEL: The small library. And the boudoir.
CORA: If Cousin Isobel can find somewhere else for the
'intermediaries'.
VIOLET: There's always the boot room. I'm sure you'll
have use of that!
ROBERT: And where are we supposed to eat?
ISOBEL: You can share the dining room with those officers —
ROBERT: No.
ISOBEL: We all have to make sacrifices —
ROBERT: No!*

....

* Isobel is trying to fight for the boudoir, which becomes the first tug of war
between her and Cora. I wanted the family to have the use of the small
library, because at Highclere the large library and the small library are only
separated by a columned arch. So I knew that if we allocated that room to
them, partitioned off with a screen, then they wouldn't actually be very
disconnected from the public occupancy of the house, which would be better
for the drama. In these arrangements, certainly when it comes to the use of
the dining room, Isobel and Clarkson run up against Robert, and in this I
was keen to demonstrate a cultural detail, that the whole set-up of a country
house to a large extent turns on eating. Robert feels that if he cannot even
lunch and dine alone with his family, then this will be a real dent in his life.
He wouldn't, obviously, put any of this into words, but nevertheless he fights
his corner, and for the first time Isobel finds herself seriously challenged.
Happily, Clarkson is less combative. He does not see the matter as a test of
strength, as Isobel does. So he is able to come up with an acceptable solution.
    Isobel has never had a sufficiently moral reason to fight the family before,
but she does actually disagree with them about all sorts of things. They've
been nice to her, and until now she hasn't wanted to pick a fight. But a fight

CLARKSON: Then we'll have tables set up in the great hall for the mobile officers and for the nurses. And Lady Grantham, I know you'll be happy about one decision. Lady Grantham asked that the house management might be put into the hands of Corporal Barrow... Your former footman. Thomas.

ROBERT: Thomas? In charge of Downton?

CORA: No, that's what I thought at first. But he isn't a footman now. He's a soldier. He's worked in medicine.

CLARKSON: The point is, someone has to run the place who's had medical training —

ISOBEL: But I really feel —

ROBERT: The men won't accept the authority of a corporal.

CLARKSON: I've thought of that. I told my commanding officer that Lady Grantham had asked for Corporal Barrow and he's prepared to have him raised to the rank of acting sergeant.

ROBERT: But can you spare him?

CLARKSON: We can. I have gone to some trouble to do so. 'Sergeant' Barrow will manage the daily running of Downton and I shall be in overall charge.

ROBERT: But you have the hospital. Aren't we missing a tier? Surely there should be someone here permanently who is under you, but over Thomas?†

....

Continued from page 150:

has come, and so she is subconsciously rechannelling all her feelings about this silly, spoiled, over-privileged family, whereas Clarkson is in a completely different position. He has a good relationship with the Crawleys, on the whole. There are many local doctors who have less cooperative great families to deal with, and he considers himself reasonably lucky, so he is not about to make trouble. In other words, they each have a different agenda.

† Cora thinks that by suggesting Thomas she is doing this for herself, but of course, in fact, she is being used by O'Brien. I am always interested in the techniques of clever manipulators.

Isobel would volunteer herself, but —

CLARKSON: That's correct. And I will make a decision before long. Until then, I do assure you, Corporal Barrow is very efficient.
VIOLET: I say good. If someone's to manage things let it be our creature.
ISOBEL: Why? Are you planning to divide his loyalties?
VIOLET: I wouldn't say I was planning it.

END OF ACT ONE

ACT TWO

18 INT. ROBERT'S DRESSING ROOM. DOWNTON. NIGHT.

Robert's cufflinks are inserted by Lang. Carson is with them.

CARSON: William has asked to stay here, m'lord. Just for a night. On his way to active duty in France.

This flusters Lang, who is having difficulty with the link.

ROBERT: Good. I should like to see him.
CARSON: I don't suppose there's any way we can keep him from harm? Him being an only child, and all. We'd hate for anything to happen.

This puts the lid on it for Lang, who is shaking even more.

ROBERT: Thank you, Lang. I can do the rest.

The nervous valet gathers up some linen and drops it.

LANG: Very sorry, m'lord.

He scrambles out. Robert exchanges a glance with Carson.

CARSON: To get back to the notion of Thomas as the manager of Downton —
ROBERT: He won't be a manager in that sense. But her ladyship fixed it all with Clarkson, and she was so pleased I didn't know what to say.

CARSON: 'I cannot have him working here because he is a thief'?
ROBERT: You know she's ignorant of Thomas's crimes. We agreed at the time that would be best… And anyway, is it honourable in us to hold Thomas's sins against him when he has been wounded in the service of the King?*

Carson almost emits a hurrumph.

CARSON: And who is to be in charge over Thomas?
ROBERT: You mean under Doctor Clarkson? Well, we asked today, but he hasn't decided.
CARSON: So we just make it up as we go along?
ROBERT: Unless you've got a better idea.

19 INT. MRS HUGHES'S ROOM/SERVANTS' HALL. DOWNTON. NIGHT.

Mrs Hughes is with Carson.

MRS HUGHES: It's all very well to talk about 'division of labour', Mr Carson, but how will it work? The nurses may do some of the cleaning, but not the basics, and who is to organise the extra loads for the laundry maids, if not me? And where do the nurses go when they're off duty?
CARSON: I thought about the housemaids' sitting room. Nobody uses it now.
MRS HUGHES: They can't climb four flights of stairs every time they want a cup of tea. You're not thinking, Mr Carson. Nobody's thinking.

Anna appears at the door.

....

* Thomas as House Manager is pretty hard for all of them to swallow, and here Robert and Carson discuss the facts about him that Cora does not know. In my morality, Robert has got himself into this fix by feeling that he needs to treat Cora as the little woman who can't be trusted. I think he is being paid out for infantilising her, just as he is later paid out for infantilising Mary. When anyone infantilises those around them in order to remain in control of events, it is, in my experience, usually a bad idea.

ANNA: Dinner's ready.*

They go to the servants' hall.   The others stand and they all sit as a hall boy brings the food to Carson's left.

O'BRIEN: Are you still here, Mr Branson?
CARSON: Stay and have something to eat.†
ETHEL: Mr Branson's been telling us the news from Russia.

....

* Here we have a section that's gone. I was rather sad to lose the housemaids' sitting room four flights up, because I liked the impracticality of it. There were many instances of this in real life. In my own house in Dorset – which is by no means Highclere, but nevertheless had an indoor staff in the old days – there was a servants' hall for eating, which was on the ground floor and is, in fact, now the kitchen. But the servants' sitting room was in the attic, up two flights of stairs. Clearly, it was more or less impossible to get there until you had finished your labours for the day. But nobody, neither the family nor whoever first allocated its purpose, would have thought in those terms. At Highclere, they put in a chapel with a family gallery, which also proved too far to be practicable, and it was abandoned and converted into an ironing room, principally for visiting maids and valets, later in the nineteenth century. It's an interesting room with lockers round it for the clothes of guests, and we have used it a couple of times for luggage – all of which is slightly at odds with its architectural magnificence, a vivid reminder that nobody will travel further to reach a room than it is worth.

† It is true that the chauffeur didn't eat with the other servants, but I cheat a bit with Branson, because I want him there, and I always feel that, if I cheat, then someone must make a point of it. So we have O'Brien complaining about him, or Carson inviting him, because we cannot have Branson simply sitting down to eat as of right. On the whole, chauffeurs lived in the former coachmen's lodgings, usually either a flat or a cottage near the stables. The thinking was that a coachman had to be near his horses and the chauffeur would want to be near his cars, since both were considered to be in need of constant care and grooming. From this, it became the custom for the chauffeur to live in a separate place. They didn't mind it, because it was far easier to be married and have children as a chauffeur than it was for more or less any living-in servant. You do get instances of the married butler, but a married footman, for instance, was very rare. It didn't matter terribly, because it was a young man's job. But with a lot of the positions, most of all for the women, it was extremely difficult to combine marriage and work. So, while some things were a source of irritation, like the housekeeper having the keys to the store cupboard, for the chauffeur to live separately was not one of them. It was, to some degree, liberation.

CARSON: What news is that?

BRANSON: Kerensky's been made Prime Minister, but he won't go far enough for me. Have you read Lenin's April Theses? He denounces the bourgeoisie along with the Tsar. He wants a people's revolution, and that's what I'm waiting for. It won't be long now.

CARSON: And what's happened to the Tsar?

BRANSON: Imprisoned. In the Alexander Palace. With all his family.

MRS PATMORE: Oh, what a dreadful thing.

BRANSON: They won't hurt them. Why would they?

ANNA: To make an example?

BRANSON: Give them some credit. This is a new dawn, a new age of government. No one wants to start it with the murder of a bunch of young girls.*

LANG: You don't know that. Nobody knows who'll get killed when these things start. Look at her nephew. Shot for cowardice. Who'd have guessed that when he was saying hello to the neighbours? Or kissing his mother goodnight?

DAISY (V.O.): Can you look at the crumble? I think it should come out, but it's five minutes earlier than you said —

She arrives and stops. Mrs Patmore sobs and runs out.

LANG: I'm sorry. I never thought —

MRS HUGHES: Then you should think, Mr Lang. You're not the only member of the walking wounded in this house.

....

*This talk about the Russian Revolution is very *Downton*-esque, in that they don't have any privileged information. They discuss big events, but only from what they've learned in the newspaper, which I think is more real than having Kerensky arrive for lunch. Branson represents what was the general opinion at that time among the soft Left – that is, not revolutionary communists and terrorists, but the ordinary, intellectual, thinking Left – that the revolution in Russia was, on the whole, a good thing that would lift the yoke from an oppressed population. He ridicules the idea that the imperial family was in any kind of danger, and this was quite usual. In fact, though it seems heartless to say it, many people would have understood the execution of the Tsar, to a degree, but it was the murder of his wife and children that proved a wake-up call. As Lang says, quite correctly, nobody knows who'll get killed when these things start.

20 INT. HALL. DOWNTON. DAY.

A figure with a suitcase, webbing and backpack comes through the door. Thomas. A maid glances at him as Carson arrives.

CARSON: Why are you coming in this way?
THOMAS: I'm the manager here now, Mr Carson. Or had you forgotten?
CARSON: No, I had not forgotten. And will you be moving into your old room? Or should we prepare a guest bedroom?
THOMAS: I'll sleep in my old room, thanks. So, are we ready for the big invasion? 'Cos they'll be here at teatime.
CARSON: We'll have to be ready, won't we, Thomas?
THOMAS: We will, Mr Carson. And it's Sergeant Barrow now.
CARSON: 'Acting' Sergeant, I believe.*

20A INT. LIBRARY. DOWNTON. DAY.

Robert looks around his library in dismay and sees a ping pong table and servants bringing in chairs and screening off one half of the room.

21 INT/EXT. HALL/FRONT ENTRANCE. DOWNTON. DAY.

Cora looks at the transformed scene around her. She is joined by Robert, Edith and Sybil and they walk to the front door to meet the arriving soldiers. An ambulance is there. Stretchers of men are being carried in. Other men, bandaged or on sticks, make their way inside.†

....

* Carson is immediately and deliberately challenged by Thomas when the latter chooses to demonstrate his new role by entering the house through the front door. This is because Thomas believes, in the words of my grandmother, that he means to start in the way he'll go on. But by demoting him to 'Acting Sergeant', Carson also shows that he is not giving in without a struggle. So much of the narrative in this sort of show is about tension, and all the time you're trying to create legitimate reasons for it in the house, because if there's no tension and everyone's having a lovely time, there's really nothing to watch.

22 INT. HALL. DOWNTON. DAY.

Isobel is trying to impose order, with Clarkson, Sybil, Edith and Thomas, as well as several nurses and maids.

> THOMAS: Major Bryant, you're in the Armada Bedroom. Do you mind the stairs?
> BRYANT: It depends what I find at the top.‡

Lang is observing from the shadows. In a corner, O'Brien, Ethel and Anna stand watching.

> ETHEL: He's handsome.
> O'BRIEN: Handsome and off limits.
> ETHEL: It'll be nice to have the house full of men.
> ANNA: Full of officers. Officers aren't men. Not where we're concerned.
> ETHEL: Speak for yourself.

....

† This was a marvellous shot, in the best traditions of *A Touch of Evil* or *The Player*, where the director, Andy Goddard, wants to make a dramatic moment as the walking wounded arrive, thereby transforming Downton Abbey into a different place with different uses. He starts it in the hall, following Robert out to the front and walking him round the busy ambulance, then he picks up whoever's going back into the house, travelling inside again and back to the hall, with a little bit of dialogue on the way. A lovely piece of work, and brilliantly judged.

‡ Most viewers who speak fluent television will understand at once that Bryant is going to have a role to play. One of the interesting things for me about war is the way it breaks down social barriers, as new and different alliances form. We've already seen this when Matthew had tea with Thomas in the trenches. I don't believe this is a flight of fancy. When you're rolling bandages with someone's cook, you chat and you make friends, and this sort of thing would prove helpful after the war. The truth is, we have to an extent reverted to a relationship between employers and employees that is more medieval, when they would all – workers and employers alike – eat in the same hall, and there was a recognition that everyone had their own worthwhile part to play. I don't mean that in those days they called each other by their Christian names, as we do now, but there was less of a barrier, less division, between the classes in 1450 than there was in 1850. To a great extent, we've gone back to that, and I think the two wars played a role in making that change. Hurrah.

ANNA: I speak for you, too, if you know what's good for
you.*
ISOBEL: Now, don't stand clogging up the doorways.
There's a lot to be done.
CORA: Can we be sure that they're all —
ISOBEL: Please. I'm very busy here. Thomas! Take the
kitchen helpers downstairs and introduce them to
Mrs Patmore!
O'BRIEN: Rather you than me.

Matthew enters. He taps Isobel's shoulder. She spins round.

ISOBEL: I'm very sorry but I'm — Matthew! What in the
world are you doing here?
MATTHEW: Well, we start our tour of Yorkshire and
Lancashire tomorrow, and General Strutt knew you lived up
here, so he's given me a few hours off.
ISOBEL: But what a lovely, lovely surprise.
MRS HUGHES: Mrs Crawley, how can we separate the
hospital's linen from our own?

Isobel needs to deal with this, but…

MATTHEW: You go. We'll talk later.

He opens a door for Mary with a tray of carafes.

23   INT.   DRAWING ROOM.   DOWNTON.   DAY.

*Beds line the walls and men in uniform lie or sit on them.
Sybil is in there, helping Edith to distribute rugs.*

EDITH: As soon as I've done this, I'll take your orders
for books.

Mary puts out the carafes. Matthew starts to help her.

....

* The difference between them is that, essentially, Ethel doesn't accept the
rules and Anna does. Although Anna is a sympathetic and important
character in the show, I rather agree with Ethel here. I know that if I were
her, and I had been born with absolutely nothing going for me, I wouldn't
accept it. I would have been one of the ones who complained and pushed at
the door. So anyone who tries to move out of their preordained sphere, as far
as I'm concerned, has my vote. But, of course, there are dangers in this, as we
shall see.

MATTHEW: I hadn't cast you as Florence Nightingale.
MARY: We can't leave all the moral high ground to Sybil.
She might get lonely there... How are you? I know I
mustn't ask what you're doing.
MATTHEW: You can ask what I'm doing in Downton. We've
finished in the Midlands and tomorrow we start on the
camps in the northern counties.
MARY: *Pour encourager les autres.*
MATTHEW: Precisely.
MARY: Will we see something of you?
MATTHEW: I think my General ought to come here. It's
exactly the sort of thing people like to read about.
Supporting our boys at the front.

Before Mary can answer, Isobel sticks her head in.

ISOBEL: Sybil, come. Edith can do that.

Sybil obeys. Matthew raises his eyebrows at Mary.

MATTHEW: Dear Mother. She does love a bit of authority.
I suppose she's driving Cousin Cora mad?
MARY: No names, no pack drill.*

24 INT. HALL. DOWNTON. DAY.

*Mary and Matthew walk back through the chaotic gathering.
They pass Lang in the shadows. He is trembling with terror.*

....

* Matthew has an imperative to get things onto a friendly level with Mary.
My own feeling is that, while they are both aware this isn't quite happening
yet, nevertheless they choose to play it as if it is, which I think is truthful.
We also have Mary beginning to find herself a job to do, and Edith. In fact,
we see all the sisters adjusting to the world at war. Before this point, Sybil
was committed to the war effort, but now all of them are. Of course, Edith
finds her new role very rewarding more or less from day one. For the first
time in her life, she is useful. But Mary's position is more neutral. These
men have fought in the war, and she is happy to do what she can to make
things easier for them, but when it's over, she won't miss it. For her, it's just
the task of the day.

25 INT. MEDICAL OFFICER'S HEADQUARTERS. RICHMOND. DAY.

An army doctor places a stethoscope on Branson's naked chest.

DOCTOR: Breathe in. And out. I'm surprised they didn't get to you before now.
BRANSON: Some people have all the luck, sir.
DOCTOR: You can get dressed.
BRANSON: Shall I report for duty in Richmond?
DOCTOR: You'll be told what to do.*

26 INT. SMALL LIBRARY. DOWNTON. DAY.

Cora is writing when Mrs Hughes enters.

MRS HUGHES: I'm sorry to bother your ladyship.
CORA: It's no bother. Come in.
MRS HUGHES: You managed to save this room, then.
CORA: By fighting Mrs Crawley tooth and nail.
MRS HUGHES: That's just it, m'lady. Mrs Crawley is downstairs now, giving orders to the servants, and —
CORA: She's what?
MRS HUGHES: She's arranging work rosters, but I must be included in these decisions if they're to make any sense.
CORA: Of course you must.

Cora has risen from her chair with a fighting face.

CORA (CONT'D): And so, very definitely, must I.†

....

* I felt it was useful to see Branson's medical, partly as a reminder that the Army was being made up of these perfectly ordinary men who had all sorts of different roles in civilian life, but who were suddenly put through medicals and dressed in uniforms and sent off to the front. And also because it will play an important part in Branson's story. I didn't want it just to be reported.

† I was sorry about the loss of this scene, because it showed that Mrs Hughes was on Cora's side, as opposed to Isobel's, which I thought was quite important. But, again, one can't keep everything.

27 INT. SERVANTS' HALL. DOWNTON. DAY.

Isobel has most of the staff captive. Thomas is with them.

THOMAS: But I must supervise the medical staff —
ISOBEL: Overseen by me. And Carson, I'm relying on you
to make sure that that is so —

Carson cannot answer before Cora sweeps in. She is furious.

CORA: What's going on?
ISOBEL: I was arranging the household duties. Where they
overlap with the duties of the nursing staff.
CORA: Shall we continue this upstairs?
ISOBEL: Well, I've made some charts and —

They stand. Who will blink first? The answer is Isobel.

ISOBEL (CONT'D): Of course.*

The two women leave. Ethel looks at Thomas.

ETHEL: Did you say you were the manager? Or the referee?

Thomas chuckles, as O'Brien whispers in his ear.

O'BRIEN: You can see what we're up against.
THOMAS: Don't worry. We'll find a solution.
O'BRIEN: As far as I'm concerned, it's drowning, gas or
the rope.

28 INT. SMALL LIBRARY. DOWNTON. DAY.

Cora is there with Robert, Isobel and Clarkson.

CORA: Of course I'm upset! You take over every room in
the house, you bark at me like a sergeant major and you
give orders to my servants!
ROBERT: Cora, I'm sure Cousin —

....

* That Isobel is now fighting for her power against Thomas inevitably means
that Thomas will make common cause with Cora and O'Brien. Gradually
the battle against Isobel's control is beginning to broaden and solidify. And
now we finally have Cora breaking out and being furious. I think all of this
was well laid by the actresses concerned. And it's good for Cora to be tough.
She's so accepting most of the time, but now she's reached her limit, and do
we blame her?

The door opens and Mary walks in with an envelope.

MARY: Oh, I'm sorry. Are you in the middle of something?
CLARKSON: We're discussing the arrangements.
MARY: Oh, good. Because we've had a letter from Evelyn
Napier. He's in a hospital in Middlesbrough, and he's
heard that we're a convalescent home now, and wonders if
he can come here once he's released.*
CORA: I hope he's not badly wounded.
MARY: He calls it a 'nasty scratch', but it could mean
his arm's been blown off. You know what they're like.
ROBERT: Don't be so macabre.
CORA: Of course he can come here.
CLARKSON: Well, now. Just a minute.
ISOBEL: There's no question of him coming here.
CORA: What?
ISOBEL: The Middlesbrough General will have their own
arrangements for where their patients convalesce.
CLARKSON: I'm afraid Mrs Crawley is right. Downton must
function as part of the official system or it cannot
function at all.
ROBERT: Now, I think perhaps I should make one thing
clear. Downton is our house and our home, and we will
welcome in it any friends or relations we choose. And if
you do not care to accept that condition, then I suggest
you give orders for the nurses and the patients and the
beds and the rest of it to be packed up and shipped out,
at once!

*The shock of this is enough to silence the room. Cora smiles
at Isobel, who is glowering. Clarkson knows when he is
beaten.*

....

* This reference to Evelyn Napier refers back to a character we're familiar
with from the first series. It always irritates me when characters leave a series
and are never referred to again. It's rather like *Watership Down*, when they
will never talk about a rabbit who's gone missing. Apart from anything else, I
don't think it's believable. Because we all talk about people we know but
don't see, and we refer to them. Hopefully, when viewers hear Evelyn's name,
they will think, oh, yes, I remember him.

CLARKSON: Thank you, Lord Grantham, for making your position so clear.
ISOBEL: Oh, just one more thing. The dog. What should we do to stop Isis getting into the patients' rooms?
ROBERT: I can answer that. Absolutely nothing!*
ISOBEL: Ah.

29 INT. INNER HALL. DOWNTON. NIGHT.

Anna is standing at a cupboard, rolling laundered bandages. Mary picks one up and starts to roll it.

MARY: Peace at last.
ANNA: We'll settle in. Once we get used to it. Any news from Sir Richard?
MARY: Not yet, but we won't have long to wait.
ANNA: I can leave this, m'lady, if you want to go to bed.
MARY: There's no hurry. Though I do think you should be downstairs. Reading or talking or something. You can't work every hour God sends.
ANNA: I want to. I want to be tired out. I don't want time to myself.
MARY: Do you miss him very much?
ANNA: I can't think of anything but him. It's as if I were mad or ill… I suppose that's what love is. A kind of illness. And when you've got it, there's just nothing else.
MARY: I know.

Their eyes are full as they continue their work in silence.

....

* The dog that played Pharoah in the first series used to drive Hugh Bonneville absolutely mad, because it did nothing it was asked. We have all heard the instruction never to act with children or animals, and many people think this is because they are bound to steal the scene. But it isn't that. It's because when a child or an animal gets it right, then that will be the take they use. It doesn't matter what sort of performance the adult actor has given. So, when you're working with them, you have to be at the top of your game for every single take, because you don't know when the dog is finally going to wag its tail, or the child is finally going to smile, or whatever it is they want. That can be very exhausting, knowing that they've got to use the one where the dog was good.

30 INT. SERVANTS' HALL. DOWNTON. DAY.

Daisy is clearing breakfast away. Carson distributes letters.

CARSON: When anyone sees Mr Branson, can they tell him there's a letter here? From the War Office.
O'BRIEN: So he's off to fight the Hun.
DAISY: Don't make light of it.
ANNA: I agree.
LANG: He doesn't know what's coming. He can't know what's coming.
CARSON: I'm not sure how helpful that is as a line of enquiry, Mr Lang.

Lang would protest, but the bells begin to ring.

O'BRIEN: Saved by the bell.

31 INT. CORA'S BEDROOM. DOWNTON. DAY.

O'Brien removes Cora's tray. Cora is reading a letter.

CORA: Captain Crawley wants to bring his General to inspect us. He thinks we're an example to our neighbours.
O'BRIEN: That's nice.
CORA: It is nice. And flattering. We must put on our best bib and tucker. I just hope Mrs Crawley allows me a look-in with the arrangements.
O'BRIEN: Oh, don't worry about that, m'lady. Thomas has got matters in hand.

END OF ACT TWO

ACT THREE

32 INT. MARY'S BEDROOM. DOWNTON. DAY.

Anna and Ethel are making the bed when Mary comes in.

MARY: Anna, there you are. Ethel, could you leave us for a moment?

Ethel goes out of the room and closes the door.

MARY (CONT'D): That was Sir Richard on the telephone. It might have been Bates you saw in the village.
ANNA: Really?
MARY: He's working up here at a pub. The Red Lion in Kirkbymoorside.
ANNA: That's odd. Mr Bates in a pub?
MARY: The question's what'll you do with the information now you've got it?

33   INT.   PASSAGE/ARMADA ROOM.   DOWNTON.   DAY.

Ethel is outside an open door. Inside, Thomas is with Bryant.

THOMAS: We can narrow this sling, sir, for more arm movement. And I'll ask Major Clarkson to reduce the pills.
BRYANT: Killjoy.

They are both distracted by a little laugh from Ethel.

THOMAS: Ethel? What are you doing there?
ETHEL: Lady Mary wanted a word with Anna. I'm waiting 'til they've finished.
BRYANT: And in the meantime, she's come to cheer me up, haven't you?
THOMAS: I hope not.
ETHEL: 'Course not.

But she giggles, and catches Bryant's eye as she goes.

33A   INT.   LIBRARY.   DOWNTON.   DAY.

Robert sits reading a newspaper in the screened-off section of the library, but the sound of men playing ping pong on the other side of the screen distracts him. A ping pong ball eventually comes flying over the top of the screen.

34 EXT. DOWNTON. DAY.

Branson is by the car. Sybil helps a patient in a wheelchair.

> SYBIL: Are you waiting for Papa? Do you want me to go and find him?
> BRANSON: They've turned me down.

She is taken aback by his tone. He explains his own anger.

> BRANSON (CONT'D): The Army. The sawbones failed me.
> SYBIL: Why?
> BRANSON: Apparently, I have a heart murmur. Or to be more precise…

He pulls a crumpled piece of paper out of his pocket.

> BRANSON (CONT'D): 'A mitral valve prolapse is causing a pansystolic murmur.'*
> SYBIL: I don't know what to say. Is it dangerous?
> BRANSON: Only if you're planning to humiliate the British Army… I suppose you're glad.
> SYBIL: You're not going to be killed and you're not going to prison. Of course I'm glad.
> BRANSON: Don't count your chickens. If I don't get them one way, I'll get them another.
> SYBIL: Why do you have to be so angry all the time? I know we weren't exactly at our best in Ireland —
> BRANSON: Not at your best? Not at your best!

He takes a moment to recover his equilibrium.

> BRANSON (CONT'D): I lost a cousin in the Easter Rising last year.
> SYBIL: You never said.

....

* I was in the voting lobby in the House of Lords when one of the peers (a very senior doctor) leaned over and said that, actually, this terminology, 'pansystolic murmur', wasn't reached until later in the century. The condition existed, and it was recognised, but it would not have been described in that way. So this is what they call a genuine mistake. Of course, there are no new medical conditions, or very few; it is only their discovery and nomenclature that is new. But my doctor friend, who originally provided the condition, was correct: it would have kept him out of the Army, even though the terminology would have been different.

BRANSON: Well, I'm saying it now. Shall I tell you what
happened? He played no part in the fighting, my cousin
Bill. He thought the Volunteers were fools. But he was
walking down North King Street one day and an English
soldier saw him and shot him dead. Just like that.
They'd orders to take no prisoners, you see.
SYBIL: How terrible.
BRANSON: His brother went down to look for him that night
and he found the body in a pile, in a yard behind the
local dispensary. When they asked why he was killed, the
officer said 'because he was probably a rebel'. So don't
say you were 'not at your best'!
ROBERT: Sorry to keep you waiting, but we're going to
have to step on it.*

*He walks across the gravel and climbs in. Branson closes the
door. The car drives away.*

....

* I was sad about the trimming here. The incident in North King Street in
Dublin, when people were shot for just walking along, is completely true, and
the bodies were indeed piled up behind the local dispensary. These are the
kind of details that most people don't know, but which nevertheless stand up
to inspection. And the reply, that he was 'probably a rebel', is also true.

My own connection in this is a family one. My great-grandmother's
uncle, in other words my great-great-grandmother's brother, was a man
called Lord Hemphill who was Solicitor General for Ireland. He was also a
supporter of Parnell and passionately pro home rule. In fact, when his sister
married my great-great-grandfather, the latter was disinherited, because his
family was equally passionately anti home rule. So it was quite a hot topic for
us, even in my childhood, and as a result we were firmly taught as children
that this was when the British missed their chance to move into the future, in
partnership with a newly conceived Ireland, which should have been given
dominion status and full home rule in the 1880s. We were told that it was a
great mistake that to some extent we're still paying for. This was unusual,
because the kind of family I come from is not generally pro Irish
independence and pro Dublin – or they weren't then. When I was young,
most people like us were always against the IRA, and, of course, I am against
terrorism – I think attacks on innocent people are a terrible thing – but I do
understand the impulse for independence. I do understand that our tenure
in Ireland, and our insistence on the Protestant religion, and all the rest of
that stuff, was nonsense. So, in a way, I did grow up on the other side of the
fence from the side that most people might expect.

35 INT. LIBRARY. DOWNTON. DAY.

Edith is taking book orders.

EDITH: I'm not sure about Marryat. I know we've got lots of G. A. Henty. And I haven't forgotten about your tobacco, Captain Ames. Just as soon as I can get into the village.

36 EXT. DOWNTON. DAY.

Nearby, Ethel tidies the rug over the knees of Major Bryant.

ETHEL: There. Now, you're sure you're quite comfortable?
BRYANT: I'm not sure at all. I think a bit of it might have come loose.

She smiles and tucks it in more tightly around his thighs.

ETHEL: Is that better?
BRYANT: Much. But I may need some more tucking, very soon.
ETHEL: Well, no one tucks better than I do.
MRS HUGHES (V.O.): Ethel!

The maid looks up and sees the housekeeper glaring at her.

MRS HUGHES: Go back inside, please. There are still more bedrooms to be done.

Ethel scurries away. Bryant looks after her with a smile.
Mrs Hughes meets his look, but she does not smile back.

37 INT. DRAWING ROOM. DOWER HOUSE. DAY.

Violet is alone with Mary.

VIOLET: Rosamund's going to find out. She knows some of those feeble-minded cretins on the Liberal front bench.*
MARY: Poor Lavinia. I feel sorry for her.
VIOLET: She's an obstacle to your happiness, dear, and must be removed. When it's done you can feel as sorry as you wish.
MARY: But even if Matthew does break it off with her, why should he propose to me again?
VIOLET: With your permission, dear, I'll take my fences one at a time.

38   INT.   ANNA AND ETHEL'S BEDROOM.   DOWNTON.
              NIGHT.

Ethel is in bed.   Anna stands before the mirror.

ETHEL: Any plans for your afternoon off?

Anna smiles, but says nothing.

ETHEL (CONT'D): Major Bryant wants me to go to the
pictures in York with him, when he's allowed out.   But
you'll say that's stupid.
ANNA: Not stupid.   Insane.
ETHEL: He really likes me, though.   He says he wants to
get to know me better.
ANNA: Has he told you how he's planning to achieve it?
ETHEL: Spoil sport…   What are you up to?
ANNA: Just practising with these for Lady Mary.   I
promised her I would.

She is applying the Marcel waving tongs to her own hair.

39   EXT.   THE RED LION.   KIRKBYMOORSIDE.   DAY.

*A bus stops in the village street and Anna climbs down, with
a new, attractive hairstyle.   She walks towards the pub.*

....

* I always like giving Violet's opinions on the Liberals, who were entering
their last few years as major players. Violet's hatred of Lloyd George is
emblematic of that class's hatred of him. In fact, when under Lord Rosebery
the Liberals had started death duties; Liberalism had come out as an enemy
of property. What they didn't realise, although people said it at the time, was
essentially that they had signed their own death warrants, because the
socialists were much more convincing as enemies of property, and enemies of
hereditary and traditional rights. By alienating the benevolent privileged,
the Liberals had lost their appeal and their core support. Within five years of
this change of direction, they would lose the election in 1922 and never
regain power.

In the event, Maggie Smith called them idiots instead of cretins, but this
may have been her instinctive good taste, as 'cretin' is now really a medical
term and so perhaps inappropriate as a term of insult.

40 INT. THE RED LION. KIRKBYMOORSIDE. DAY.

John Bates is serving a customer behind the bar.

> BATES: That's one and eight, altogether.
> ANNA (V.O.): Might I have a glass of cider?

Bates looks up and there she is. The love of his life.

> BATES: I don't know if I've dreaded this moment or longed
> for it.
> ANNA: Well, either way, it's happened.

41 INT. DRAWING ROOM. DOWER HOUSE. DAY.

Mary is with Violet and Rosamund.

> ROSAMUND: I'm glad I'm in time for tomorrow's state
> visit. I gather Lavinia will be there. We must seize
> the opportunity to challenge her.
> MARY: I don't really see on what basis.
> ROSAMUND: She stole secrets from her uncle, Jonathan
> Swire, and gave them to Carlisle to publish. Swire told
> me.
> MARY: And the papers showed that half the Cabinet were
> trying to get rich by buying shares before a government
> contract was announced. Would you rather we were kept in
> ignorance?
> ROSAMUND: It wasn't Lavinia's business to make it public.
> Without her, the Marconi Scandal would never have
> happened.*
> MARY: The politicians broke the law. Lavinia did nothing
> wrong.

....

* I wanted something real for Lavinia and Carlisle to have been involved in, rather than a fictional story. I'm sure many of the audience thought the Marconi Scandal of 1912 was completely made up, but it wasn't. There was absolutely no doubt that Asquith, the Prime Minister, Lloyd George and several senior figures in the Government were completely guilty of what would now be called insider trading, which, even if it wasn't illegal as it is today, was certainly absolutely improper. Yet they survived it, which seems almost shocking. If there was a similar scandal now – and we think people survive anything these days – I don't know if they would really have got away with it, a straight piece of profiteering from secret government policy.

ROSAMUND: She drags the Chancellor of the Exchequer's honour through the mud, and you say it's nothing!
MARY: It was only Lloyd George.
VIOLET: But why did she betray her uncle to Sir Richard in the first place?
ROSAMUND: Because they were lovers.

It rather annoys Violet to have her punchline stolen.

VIOLET: Exactly.
ROSAMUND: And now it's down to you to save Matthew from the clutches of a scheming harlot!
VIOLET: Really, Rosamund. There's no need to be so gleeful. You sound like Robespierre, lopping off the head of Marie Antoinette.

42   INT.   THE RED LION.   KIRKBYMOORSIDE.   DAY.

Bates and Anna are sitting at a table.

BATES: It was me. I knew you used to go to the village on a Wednesday and I so longed for a glimpse of you.
ANNA: But why are you up here at all? And why didn't you tell me?
BATES: Because I want to get things settled first. You see, I've discovered that Vera's been… unfaithful to me. I've got proof.
ANNA: We can't criticise her for that.
BATES: No. But it means I can divorce her. I've had to leave the house to prove that it has broken the marriage. So I came up here, to be nearer you.
ANNA: But what if she fights it?
BATES: She can't. For her to divorce me, she'd need something beyond adultery, cruelty or suchlike. But for a husband, adultery is enough.
ANNA: That's not very fair to women.
BATES: I don't care about fairness, I care about you. The point is, I can get rid of her. If she goes quietly, I will give her money and plenty of it. If not, she leaves empty-handed.
ANNA: And when will this be?
BATES: I need to get her to accept it, first. She's made threats about selling stuff to the papers.
ANNA: What stuff?

BATES: Don't worry. They won't offer what I will…
You've changed your hair.
ANNA: I was trying out Lady Mary's new curling iron.
What do you think?
BATES: I think I would love you, however, whatever,
whenever.
ANNA: We don't have to wait, you know. If you want me to
throw up everything and come with you, I will. Gladly.
BATES: I can't marry you yet, not legally, and I won't
break the law.
ANNA: It's not against the law to take a mistress,
Mr Bates.

Moved by this, he holds her hand. But he shakes his head.

BATES: That's not right for you. I know you, Anna Smith,
and I love you, and that is not the right path for you.
But it won't be long now.*

....

*The injustice of the divorce laws at that time is interesting. A man could divorce a woman for adultery, but a woman could not divorce a man for adultery. It had to be adultery and cruelty, or at any rate adultery and something else, which seems so unfair, and here Anna is allowed to point this out. The enormity of Anna's offering to become Bates's mistress they both played very well. It is always quite hard when a character has to do something in a play or in a film that in the context of the time was enormous, but in our own day would not be considered even unusual. You wonder if the audience is going to get it, but I think they did.

I remember in *Gosford Park*, there was a moment when the maid, Elsie (played by Emily Watson), who was waiting at table, suddenly defended Sir William to his wife, in front of all their guests. Then she realises what she's done, as the whole table falls silent and one of the men starts giggling, so she runs out of the dining room knowing she has lost her job, which she has. At the time, the producers were nervous as to whether the audience would understand that she shouldn't have spoken while serving at dinner. They wanted the butler to instruct her not to talk, and other hopeless suggestions, which Robert Altman, the director, ignored. But in the end, it seemed to work in the cinema. Similarly, here, I hope we understand that for a completely respectable young woman to offer to become someone's mistress and live in sin was an enormous thing, an enormous gift. Equally, it's something that Bates cannot accept, because he knows that's not who she is, and he loves her. For Anna to be happy, he has to marry her – a morality we no longer subscribe to as a society.

43 EXT. KITCHEN COURTYARD. DOWNTON. DAY.

O'Brien is watching Branson as he tinkers with the car.

O'BRIEN: So you're not going to war, then?
BRANSON: Apparently not… Is it true about Mr Crawley
bringing a famous general here?
O'BRIEN: Captain Crawley, but yes. Why?
BRANSON: No reason…

44 INT. SMALL LIBRARY. DOWNTON. NIGHT.

Carson's with Robert, Cora, Isobel, Mary, Edith and Clarkson.

ROBERT: If they arrive at five we'll walk him round the
wards, then show him the recovering men at play. And
after that, a fairly grand dinner. I'll tell them to
bring mess kit.
CARSON: That is my challenge, m'lord. How to make the
dinner sufficiently grand with no footmen in the house.
ROBERT: Plenty of people give dinners without footmen.
CARSON: Not people who entertain Sir Herbert Strutt, hero
of the Somme.
ISOBEL: I'm sure he'll have seen worse things at the
front than a dinner with no footmen.
CORA: Carson only wants to show the General proper
respect. We will not criticise him for that.
CLARKSON: Indeed we will not. But I think Lord
Grantham's plan is a good one, with or without a footman.
CORA: Matthew writes that Miss Swire is coming down from
London for it.
ISOBEL: Really? He never said so to me.
CORA: Does he need your permission?

Isobel pointedly ignores this.

ISOBEL: I think I should go round with him.
CLARKSON: You and Lady Grantham will both come with us.
ISOBEL: But won't he want to talk about treatments?
CLARKSON: The treatments and the house.

45 EXT. THE RED LION. KIRKBYMOORSIDE. DAY.

Bates and Anna are waiting by the bus stop.

ANNA: Come back to Downton. They'd love to see you and
the new valet's an odd cove. I doubt he'll stay.

BATES: His lordship won't have me back. We parted on bad
terms. And I don't want to see the others until it's all
resolved. Then I can greet them with an invitation to
our wedding.

He kisses her hand as a pledge, and helps her aboard the bus.

46   INT.   HALL/BEDROOM.   DOWNTON.   NIGHT.

*Edith crosses the dark hall. A door is open and she looks in
to check before shutting it. She hears a whispered 'Miss!'
and walks over to a bed. An officer is lying there.*

EDITH: It's Captain Smiley, isn't it? We haven't met
yet, but I'm Edith Crawley, and tomorrow I can show you
where everything is.
SMILEY: It's just that I'd like to write a letter. To my
parents.
EDITH: Of course. There's paper and envelopes in the
library.
SMILEY: No. You see, I've not written before because I
didn't want to worry my mother with the different
handwriting…

*Edith is bewildered until he takes his left arm out of the
bedclothes. He has no hand. Edith looks at him, puzzled.*

SMILEY (CONT'D): I'm left-handed. How's that for luck?
EDITH: I'm surprised your school didn't force you to use
the right.
SMILEY: My mother wouldn't let them, but now I wish they
had… I've asked the others and they say you're the one
to help me.*

....

* This scene is really about Edith's redemption, and I was extremely pleased
with it. The actor playing Captain Smiley, Tom Feary-Campbell, was left-
handed – and he had no left hand. For this role, we were keen to find an
actor who was genuinely disabled, so it would not look like computer
trickery. Originally, in the script, it was Smiley's right hand that was missing,
because the scene was about writing, but we did all the auditions and Tom
was so much the best actor that I just rewrote the scene to be about a man
who was left-handed. The bonus of this was that we could have the reference
to his not being forced to use his right hand at school, just as a reminder to
the audience that this would have been quite ordinary at that time for any
left-handed child.

EDITH: Of course I will. I'd be happy to.
SMILEY: That's what they said. If you can just find a
way to tell her…
EDITH: We'll both find a way. Together. I promise.

47 INT. CARSON'S PANTRY. DOWNTON. NIGHT.

Carson is standing at the silver cupboard. Branson arrives.

BRANSON: Mr Carson, might I have a word?
CARSON: I'm busy with this dinner tomorrow night —
BRANSON: Well, that's just it. I don't expect you'll be
using Mr Lang. Not after last time.
CARSON: I will not.
BRANSON: So I wondered if I might be any help. I've
waited at table before.
CARSON: Do you mean it? I know I've no right to ask it
of a chauffeur.
BRANSON: We have to keep up the honour of Downton, don't
we?
CARSON: I'm very grateful, Mr Branson. I'll not hide it.
Very grateful indeed. You know where to find a livery?
BRANSON: I do.
CARSON: And I gather you won't be leaving us after all?
BRANSON: Who knows what the future will bring?

He turns away. His face is a mask of nervous resolve.

48 INT. MEN'S ATTICS/LANG'S BEDROOM. DOWNTON.
NIGHT.

*The passage is dark, but we can hear a man's voice shouting.
Doors open. A befuddled Thomas comes out, then a hall boy
appears and finally Mr Carson, in a dressing gown.*

CARSON: What's going on?
THOMAS: It's Mr Lang.

*The shouts are turning into screams. We can hear a noise on
the women's side of the door and now it opens. Mrs Hughes is
there, with Anna and Ethel and O'Brien hovering behind her.*

MRS HUGHES: What in heaven's name is happening?

Carson opens Lang's door. He is writhing and screaming.

CARSON: Mr Lang. Mr Lang! Wake up!

LANG: I can't do it! I can't do it!

CARSON: You're having a bad dream, Mr Lang!

LANG: It's the soldiers, Mr Carson, it's the soldiers, but I can't. I can't go back, no matter what they —

CARSON: No one's asking you to go back, Mr Lang.

THOMAS: No. Just to put a sock in it.

At last Lang is awake. Now O'Brien pushes past the others.

O'BRIEN: Don't worry, Mr Lang. You've had a bad dream, that's all.

LANG: Is it a dream…? Thank God. Oh, thank God. Thank God.

O'BRIEN: You're all right. Let's get you back into bed.

LANG: I'm sorry.

O'BRIEN: It's all right, Mr Lang. You're all right.

She shoos the others out and shuts the door, speaking softly.

O'BRIEN (CONT'D): Is it any wonder? When he's been to hell and back?*

49   EXT. DOWNTON. DAY.

The General, with Matthew, has arrived. The house has turned out to greet him: nurses, family, servants (no kitchen staff).†

MATTHEW: My cousin, Lord Grantham.

GENERAL SIR HERBERT STRUTT: This is very kind of you, Lord Grantham.

ROBERT: Welcome.

MATTHEW: Lady Grantham, and this is Major Clarkson who runs our hospital here.

....

* With Lang we were trying to build up that only too familiar situation where you gradually realise that someone is incapable of the job they're doing, but you don't dislike them at all. It's not a question of their not trying, or being lazy, or anything else. It's just that they cannot fulfil the function that they have been employed for. For me, this is nice and complicated emotionally, because you wish them well, but you know it can't go on. Which is what Carson feels here.

ISOBEL: And I am Captain Crawley's mother, and will accompany you on your tour and explain the different levels of care we practise here.
CLARKSON: Lady Grantham and Mrs Crawley will both accompany us as we go around, sir.
GENERAL SIR HERBERT STRUTT: Makes a nice change from the craggy-faced warriors I'm usually surrounded by.
CORA: We'd like to think that were true. Please come this way.
MATTHEW: Poor Mother. She longs to hold all the reins.

He says this to Mary, who smiles. The General turns.

GENERAL SIR HERBERT STRUTT: Crawley!

Both Matthew and Robert spin round at the command.

MATTHEW: I should go, if only to keep our respective mothers apart.

The General goes in, flirting with Cora. Isobel stumps along behind. Thomas has caught at Clarkson's elbow.

....

† We were fortunate in getting Julian Wadham to play the General. In this kind of scene, one of the problems of casting a supporting role who is an officer is to find an actor who has sufficient authority for you to believe that they would be the senior officer present. In other words, you need very good actors. For this, it helps if the show in question is recognised as being respectable and good, because then people will be happy to accept a part in it. Coincidentally, Julian Wadham was at my school.

One of the supporting officers is our technical advisor, Alastair Bruce, and he runs everything on the set. He tells the actors what fork to use, and the costume department what uniforms they should be in, and so on. I know him because he is a childhood friend of my wife's, and we first worked together in the mid-1990s on a BBC version of *The Prince and the Pauper*. I needed an expert on heraldry and Alastair is an expert on everything. He was also wonderfully helpful on *The Young Victoria*, before he came to organise *Downton*. As part of all this, he has gradually played more and more roles, so he's now been Violet's butler, the General's aide-de-camp, a gun out shooting, a stalker, I think, up in Scotland, he's been a footman, he's been every kind of character. So we feel now we could probably cut together The Alastair Bruce Show. Anyway, he was a career soldier and is now with the TAs, so he was absolutely invaluable during this series, for picking up mistakes.

THOMAS: I'm afraid Mrs Crawley's none too pleased to play second fiddle, sir.

CLARKSON: Well, I hope she doesn't spoil things.

THOMAS: Well, that's just what I've been meaning to talk to you about, sir. You see, I'm trying to run a tight ship here, but Mrs Crawley insists on…

Thomas finds O'Brien and winks. He's off to put the knife in. Lavinia is on the edge of the group, which starts to go in. Catching Mary's eye, Rosamund nods sharply at Lavinia.

LAVINIA: What's the matter with your aunt?

MARY: We should follow them in, or Mama will say we're unsupportive.

LAVINIA: Tell me what it is. Please.

MARY: All right…

50 INT. KITCHEN. DOWNTON. SUMMER EVENING.

Daisy and Mrs Patmore are working.

DAISY: I know he's going to propose.

MRS PATMORE: Well, then you're going to accept. Did you get that picture taken?

DAISY: I did, yes. But…

MRS PATMORE: Fetch it. Because if you think I'm going to stand by and watch that boy's dreams stamped in the dust, you've got another thing coming. You can take back your promise when the war's over, and not before!

DAISY: But it's a lie!

MRS PATMORE: Don't make him give up when he's off to face the guns. You'd never forgive yourself if owt happened.

51 EXT. DOWNTON. DAY.

Mary and Lavinia are walking into the house.

MARY: Do you remember when Aunt Rosamund found you and Richard Carlisle together in the garden?

LAVINIA: I knew I'd hear more about that.

MARY: She thought he was threatening you… And now she's decided that you were behind the Marconi Share Scandal. In 1912. The Chancellor and other ministers were involved, including your uncle.

LAVINIA: I remember the Marconi Scandal.

MARY: No. Let's forget it. It's absurd…

LAVINIA: But Lady Rosamund is right. I did steal the evidence for Sir Richard to print. I did start the scandal.
MARY: The trouble is Aunt Rosamund can't understand why you would do such a thing unless you and Sir Richard were…
LAVINIA: Were lovers.
CORA (V.O.): Mary? You must come. I don't want the General to think us rude.

She's in the doorway. Mary nods and walks to her in a daze.

52   INT.   DRAWING ROOM.   DOWNTON.   DAY.

The General, Matthew and the family survey the room. Men lie on their beds or stand next to them. Edith is working away.

MATTHEW: The ground-floor rooms are for those men who need the most care, sir.
GENERAL SIR HERBERT STRUTT: Yes, of course.
CAPTAIN SMILEY: General Strutt, sir.

Captain Smiley gives a sign to the General, who goes over.

GENERAL SIR HERBERT STRUTT: Oh, right, yes. Tell me about this officer.
ISOBEL: Who is that man? I hope he's not complaining.
EDITH: Oh, no. That's Captain Smiley. He hasn't an unkind bone in his body.
MARY: How do you know?

The General has moved on to another bed. He calls to Matthew.

GENERAL SIR HERBERT STRUTT: Matthew! Listen to this!
MATTHEW: Everything all right, sir?
CORA: What on earth's that about?
EDITH: Oh, don't worry. Major Holmes can be a little waspish, but he wouldn't want to get us into trouble.
CORA: How do you know so much about a pack of strangers?
EDITH: They're not strangers to me.
GENERAL SIR HERBERT STRUTT: This is all very impressive, Lady Grantham. The nurses and your own staff are to be congratulated.
CORA: I believe they are.

53 INT. SERVANTS' HALL. DOWNTON. DAY.

William is with the maids, Daisy, Mrs Patmore and Mrs Hughes.

WILLIAM: I wouldn't say I was scared. I'm nervous — of
course I am — but not scared. I think I'm ready.

He glances up to see tears running down Mrs Patmore's cheeks.

MRS PATMORE: Don't mind me. Only I'm thinking of what
your dear mother would say.
WILLIAM: Well, I wish she was here to see me off.
MRS PATMORE: Oh, she'd be so proud. Why, when we waved
off our Archie, I remember —

But she breaks off. They are all silenced by this. Then…

MRS HUGHES: What do you remember, Mrs Patmore? I'll tell
you. You remember a fine young man who enlisted before
he had to and who gave his life for his country. Because
he'd be alive and well today if he hadn't chosen to go to
war.
DAISY: She's right.

Mrs Patmore is very moved by their forgiveness. She nods.

MRS PATMORE: Happen she is… Come on, Daisy. Back to the
grindstone.

William's expression tells us he has a sentence unsaid.

MRS PATMORE (CONT'D): What is it?
WILLIAM: I just want a word with Daisy.
DAISY: I'm needed in the kitchen.

She hurries past Mrs Patmore, but the cook does not help.

MRS PATMORE: There's plenty of time later on.

54 INT. SMALL LIBRARY/LIBRARY. DOWNTON. SUMMER EVENING.

*The company is dressed for dinner. Matthew, Doctor Clarkson,
the General and Robert are now in mess kit.*

ROBERT: You must be enjoying your respite from the front.
MATTHEW: Actually, I'm struggling a bit. I've just lost
my soldier servant and I haven't managed to replace him
yet.

Mary is with Rosamund and Violet. They look over to Lavinia.

> ROSAMUND: So, when will you tell Matthew?
> CARSON (V.O.): Dinner is served, m'lady.
> ROSAMUND: Don't waste the opportunity!

She stalks off towards the door, with the others.

> MARY: Why must she be so savage? It's my broken heart.
> And it was her advice that wrecked it in the first place.
> VIOLET: Classic Rosamund. She's never more righteous
> than when she's in the wrong. Come on.

END OF ACT THREE

ACT FOUR

55 INT. KITCHEN PASSAGE. DOWNTON. SUMMER EVENING.

Branson carries a soup tureen. Mrs Hughes walks along.

> MRS HUGHES: Everything all right, Mr Branson?
> BRANSON: I think so, Mrs Hughes.

56 INT. SYBIL'S BEDROOM. DOWNTON. SUMMER EVENING.

*Anna carries in some clothes. She puts them away in a
drawer. Then she sees that a folded note has blown off the
dressing table. On it is written: 'Lady Sybil' and, on the
back, 'Forgive me'. She unfolds it, scans the writing and
runs out.*

56A INT. CORRIDOR. DOWNTON. SUMMER EVENING.

Anna runs down the corridor.

56B INT. CORRIDOR/DINING ROOM. DOWNTON. SUMMER
                        EVENING.

Branson approaches the dining room.

56C INT. STAIRCASE. DOWNTON. SUMMER EVENING.

Anna races down the stairs.

57 INT. DINING ROOM. DOWNTON. SUMMER EVENING.

We start on the soup tureen, like a Hitchcock glass of milk.
Branson is carrying it towards the sideboard.

58 INT. MRS HUGHES'S SITTING ROOM. DOWNTON.
                    SUMMER EVENING.

Mrs Hughes is sitting at her desk when Anna bursts in.

ANNA: Where's Mr Branson?
MRS HUGHES: He's just taken up the soup. Why?
ANNA: Read that!
MRS HUGHES: 'They'll have arrested me by now, but I'm not
sorry. The bastard had it coming to him.'

Mrs Hughes stares at her in horror. They hurtle away.

59 INT. SERVERY. DOWNTON. SUMMER EVENING.

The women race in. Carson is there with two decanters of
white wine. He is about to go into the dining room.

CARSON: What in God's name?
MRS HUGHES: Read this! Where is he now?

Carson has skimmed the letter. He starts.

CARSON: Oh, my God! He's going to kill the General!
Anna, come with me!

60 INT. DINING ROOM. DOWNTON. SUMMER EVENING.

Carson and Anna slide out of the door. Branson's back is turned at the sideboard. They sneak up on him.

> ROBERT: I'm sorry to hear about your servant. He seemed a nice fellow.

Branson picks up the tureen, but Carson is too quick for him. He takes one elbow as Anna snatches the tureen away.

> BRANSON: No!
> CARSON: Yes!

They have only hissed these words as they march him down the room. Mary notices something is going on. The others do not.

> MATTHEW: Yes, it was pneumonia, not a bullet. He'll be okay, but he won't be back, and he's a damn hard act to follow.
> GENERAL SIR HERBERT STRUTT: I don't envy you. A decent servant can change your war. I know.

Mary catches Anna's eye, but the latter just shakes her head.

61 INT. SERVERY. DOWNTON. SUMMER EVENING.

They collapse through the door.

> CARSON: Get downstairs! Now!

62 INT. KITCHEN STAIRS/PASSAGE/KITCHEN. DOWNTON.
        SUMMER EVENING.

They push him down, Anna carrying the tureen. Mrs Hughes waits at the bottom with the kitchen maids and Mrs Patmore.

> BRANSON: All right, all right! There's no need to be so rough.
> CARSON: There's every need! To stop a murder!

The kitchen maids scream, but this brings him up short.

> BRANSON: Murder! What do you mean, 'murder'?
> ANNA: You were going to assassinate the General!

More screams from the maids. More indignation from Branson.

BRANSON: Kill the General? I was not! I was going to throw that lot all over him!

Anna lifts the lid. It's full of a black, slimy mixture.

ANNA: Ugh. What is it?
BRANSON: Oil and ink and a bit of a cowpat, all mixed with sour milk. He'd have needed a bath right enough, but not a coffin.*

Wrinkling her nose, Anna tips the black, foul-smelling mess into the sink. Daisy arrives with a saucepan.

DAISY: I thought you'd taken the soup up, but you left it in the pantry.

Mrs Hughes pulls a tureen from a shelf, hissing at Branson.

MRS HUGHES: We'll use this. It's not been heated but the hell with that! And we'll decide what happens to you later!
CARSON: Never mind later! What about now? How do we keep this dinner going?
WILLIAM: I'll serve, Mr Carson. I don't mind. And who knows when I'll have the chance again?

63 INT. DINING ROOM. DOWNTON. SUMMER EVENING.

William enters with the soup and goes to the sideboard. Anna brings in the plates and retires. Robert signals to Carson.

ROBERT: What was going on with the soup? It came, it went…
CARSON: Nothing to worry about, m'lord… Branson was taken ill, so William volunteered to be footman one last time. You don't mind, do you?

....

* The treatment of the soup tureen was actually copied from the glass of milk in Hitchcock's *Suspicion*. That famous shot, when the milk sort of glows as Cary Grant carries it, supposedly containing poison, towards the bedroom of his innocent wife, Joan Fontaine, is lodged in my brain as a Great Movie Moment. Apparently, it was achieved by having a light bulb concealed in the milk, and we half-copied it in *Gosford Park*, when Ryan Phillippe carries a glass of milk to Kristin Scott Thomas's bedroom. His purpose in that film, however, is definitely *not* murder… Anyway, that was the inspiration for Branson's tureen in this episode.

ROBERT: Not a bit. It's very kind of him. Our footman, William, is leaving us tomorrow to join his regiment. That's why he's not in livery.

He has raised his voice so the General may hear.

GENERAL SIR HERBERT STRUTT: You are a credit to this house and this country, young man. There is no livery so becoming as a uniform.
WILLIAM: Sir.

Carson serves out the soup and William carries the double plate to each of the diners. He passes Matthew and Violet.

MATTHEW: Lady Rosamund, Mary, all of you, have been so kind to Lavinia.
VIOLET: Well, naturally, we're all curious to know more of Miss Swire, if she is to reign over Downton as queen.
MATTHEW: Dear me. I hope you haven't unearthed anything too fearful.

He smiles at his own joke. Violet's response is unexpected.

VIOLET: You must ask Mary.

The General addresses Clarkson across the table.

GENERAL SIR HERBERT STRUTT: One thing I'm still not quite clear about. Who precisely is in charge of Downton when you're not here?

This immediately fascinates most of the women at the table.

CLARKSON: I've given it some thought, sir, and it seems to be only fair that Mrs Crawley and Lady Grantham should share that responsibility.

He smiles at the two women named. Isobel is almost choking in fury and defeat, but for Cora it is a real victory. In the pantry, Thomas and O'Brien are listening. They enjoy the success of their plotting with suppressed glee.

GENERAL SIR HERBERT STRUTT: Capital. Well said. The fact is I have been more than gratified by my visit here today, and I thank Captain Crawley for arranging it.
ROBERT: Hear, hear!

GENERAL SIR HERBERT STRUTT: You are all to be praised for your response to our national crisis. But I've been talking and I've been listening, and I feel there is one among you whose generosity is in danger of going unremarked.

They all look as if they might be singled out for praise.

GENERAL SIR HERBERT STRUTT (CONT'D): It seems the daily cares and needs of the patients are being dealt with, quietly and efficiently, by Lady Edith. Or that's what the officers tell me. So, let us raise our glasses and drink her health.
ROBERT: Edith?
ALL: Edith!

64 INT. SMALL LIBRARY. DOWNTON. SUMMER EVENING.

The ladies are alone. Lavinia is with Mary.

LAVINIA: We were never lovers. Not ever.
MARY: You don't have to explain anything. Not to me.
LAVINIA: But I want to. You see, my father owed Sir Richard Carlisle a lot of money. Enough to bankrupt him.
MARY: And Sir Richard offered to waive the debt if you gave him the evidence of the ministers' guilt?
LAVINIA: Papa was terrified, and I knew I could get into my uncle's office and find the proof.

Suddenly she laughs softly to herself.

MARY: What is it?
LAVINIA: He threatened to tell you all about it and now I've told you anyway. My uncle was guilty. They all were. Sir Richard didn't make it up.
MARY: I believe you.
LAVINIA: But that's not why I did it. It was entirely to save Papa from ruin.

65 INT. KITCHEN. DOWNTON. SUMMER EVENING.

William is with Daisy. Mrs Patmore is listening.

WILLIAM: Have you got that picture for me?
DAISY: I might have.

She brings it out of her pocket. He takes it.

WILLIAM: Because you know what I'm going to ask you… So, will you?
DAISY: William, you're not sure. You can't be sure.
WILLIAM: I am sure.
MRS PATMORE: So is she. Aren't you, Daisy? Isn't this just what you told me you hoped would happen? It's like a fairy story.
DAISY: Very like.
WILLIAM: Is she right, Daisy? Are we engaged? Because if we are, I know I can tackle whatever may come!
DAISY: Go on, then.*

And they embrace. But while William's eyes are closed, Daisy is staring at Mrs Patmore. They part as Mrs Hughes arrives.

MRS HUGHES: William? Do you want to go up top? The General's leaving and Mr Carson likes a full complement. No, Daisy. Not you. The war has not changed everything.

66 INT. SMALL LIBRARY. DOWNTON. SUMMER EVENING.

Matthew comes in. Mary is standing with Rosamund nearby.

MATTHEW: The General's just about to leave. I'm afraid he doesn't have time to come in here.
MARY: I hope it's all been a success.

He smiles, but something is troubling him.

MATTHEW: Cousin Violet said you had something to say about Lavinia. What is it?

....

* In those distant days, being engaged to someone did not mean you were sleeping with them, and so one must put Daisy's acceptance of William's proposal into that context. To become engaged, all the time knowing that you were probably going to break it off, did not mean you would be sexually compromised. Because normally it just wouldn't have happened. It was, as they say, a different time.

MARY: I haven't the slightest idea.

MATTHEW: Oh, what a relief. She was hinting you had uncovered some horrid stain.

MARY: The only evidence I've uncovered is that she's a charming person.

MATTHEW: What a testimonial.*

MARY: The truth is we're very much alike, so naturally I think she's perfect. We all do. Don't we, Aunt Rosamund?

ROSAMUND: Quite perfect.

67 EXT. DOWNTON. SUMMER EVENING.

They're milling about. Robert approaches Matthew.

ROBERT: Is there any chance you might take our footman, William, for your servant? The footman who was serving at dinner. I can pull some strings, get him transferred to your lot.

MATTHEW: If you'd like me to, of course. I can't promise to keep him safe.†

ROBERT: I know. But he'd have someone looking out for him. Oh, my God…

Behind them, Lang appears to be crying. Robert hurries over.

ROBERT (CONT'D): Lang? Are you all right, old chap?

Lang collapses into Robert's chest, sobbing. Carson runs up.

ROBERT (CONT'D): Come, come, man. Things can't be as bad as all that… Carson?

CARSON: Mr Lang, what's happened?

LANG: The Generals and all these officers. I don't have to go back with them, do I? Because I can't, sir! I can't!

CARSON: The General's looking for you, m'lord.

....

* I think we wanted to make the whole thing as difficult for Mary as possible, and if you like the person your beloved has run off with, it's much harder than if you can demonise them.

† Having soldiers moved around from regiment to regiment so that they could become your servants was not unusual. Someone in the press wrote that this could never have happened, but they were talking complete nonsense. It was done all the time.

He's right. The General is by the car. He hasn't noticed anything. Robert hurries back and shakes his hand. Strutt climbs into the car. Matthew is with Lavinia.

MATTHEW: If I don't see you again before I have to go back, be safe… *[To Mary]* You, too.

He kisses Lavinia's hand and climbs in. As the car pulls away, Mary puts her arm around the weeping younger woman. Some of the officers have come outside and Bryant is chatting to Ethel. Mrs Hughes is watching. The group breaks up.

MRS HUGHES: Ethel? Will you come here for a moment, please?

The maid approaches and Mrs Hughes speaks in a hiss.

MRS HUGHES (CONT'D): I hope I won't have to tell you off again. Because this is the third time. And in my book, the third time is the last!
ETHEL: If Major Bryant talks to me, I can't stay silent.
MRS HUGHES: No. But you can stay away from Major Bryant!

By now, O'Brien has taken charge of Lang.

O'BRIEN: Don't worry. You're not going anywhere you don't want to go.
LANG: They can't make me go back.
O'BRIEN: Do you know what? I think it's time you had a bit of a rest, Mr Lang. After that, we can see what's what.

She takes the unresisting man away as Robert comes over.

ROBERT: How is he?
CARSON: I'm sorry about that, m'lord. I believe he had a bad time at the front, poor fellow.
ROBERT: No apologies, Carson. I have not served at the front, but I know what they've been through. There's no need to apologise to me.

68 INT. SERVANTS' HALL. DOWNTON. NIGHT.

Thomas and some of the servants are drinking tea.

ETHEL: What will they do with him?

ANNA: That's for Mr Carson and his lordship to decide. Mind you don't speak of it. And don't judge him.

ETHEL: I don't judge him badly. He's not afraid to break the chains of the past and face a new world, is he? I think Mr Branson's a free spirit.

THOMAS: You'd better watch yourself, or you'll be flying free with him.

O'BRIEN: I wonder if Mr Carson's going to tell his lordship.

As she speaks, she doesn't see Carson approaching.

O'BRIEN (CONT'D): Because if he does, Branson must be sacked and it's bound to get out. And who's running this house where a traitor is able to threaten a General? Mr Carson, that's who.

CARSON (V.O.): Did I hear my name?

O'BRIEN: We were just saying that you'll know how to manage Mr Branson's misbehaviour. So the house won't suffer and all of us with it.

69 INT. BEDROOM PASSAGE. DOWNTON. NIGHT.

Mary is at her door when Edith turns the corner.

EDITH: I heard you giving Lavinia your blessing before we went out.

Mary gives her sister a cool look, but decides to answer her.

MARY: Whatever may be wrong with my life is not her fault.

EDITH: It isn't like you to be altruistic.

MARY: The General may have praised you, dear, but you don't need to use long words.

EDITH: I know what you're going through.

MARY: That's more like it.

70 INT. CARSON'S PANTRY. DOWNTON. NIGHT.

Carson has filled two glasses. He hands one to Mrs Hughes.

CARSON: Here. We've earned it.

MRS HUGHES: Ah. So, what will you do with him?

CARSON: Branson or Lang?

MRS HUGHES: Not Mr Lang. He isn't well, but he's not a bad man —

CARSON: Oh, not at all. But he doesn't belong at Downton.

MRS HUGHES: I meant Mr Branson.

CARSON: Hm. It's a delicate business, Mrs Hughes. Would we really be right to tell the police and cause a furore and bring riot down on our heads? And all because he wanted to pour a pot of slop over a man's head?

MRS HUGHES: From your phrasing, I gather the answer you want from me is no?

CARSON: Would it help, Mrs Hughes? That's all I'm asking. Would it help?

71 INT. SERVANTS' HALL. DOWNTON. NIGHT.

Daisy comes in with Mrs Patmore and William.

ETHEL: Where's Mr Branson?

ANNA: Mr Carson sent him back to his cottage to stew in his own juice. Will we see you in the morning, William? To wish you luck?

WILLIAM: Oh, yes. But I've got something I'd like to say now. If you don't mind.

DAISY: Don't. Not yet.

WILLIAM: They must know sooner or later. Daisy and I are going to be married.

ETHEL: You never are! When?

DAISY: After the war.

She glances at Mrs Patmore as she says it.

WILLIAM: I'm not sure I can wait that long.

Ethel is next to Anna. She whispers.

ETHEL: Aren't you jealous?

ANNA: No, I'm not jealous. But I'm happy for them, if it's what they want.

Anna glances at Daisy, who catches her eye. It troubles her.

72 INT. PASSAGE/LANG'S BEDROOM. DOWNTON. NIGHT.

A hall boy is going to bed. Carson stops outside Lang's door, knocks and goes in. Inside, Lang is packing his suitcase.

CARSON: I see what I had planned to say is already superfluous, Mr Lang. You got there before me.
LANG: I've let you down, Mr Carson, and for that I'm sorry.
CARSON: We let you down. You weren't suited for work, and I should have spotted that. You will have two months' wages, and please tell us how you get on. And when you're ready for work again you may rely on a good report from me.
LANG: That's kind. Thank you.
CARSON: But, Mr Lang, if I were you… I'd steer clear of serving at table.

73 INT. CORA'S BEDROOM. DOWNTON. NIGHT.

Cora is in bed as Robert climbs in.

CORA: How did you manage?
ROBERT: Carson came up. He says Lang must go and he's gone to tell him. We'll make it as easy as we can.
CORA: It was nice of William to serve tonight. He didn't have to.
ROBERT: I'm going to arrange for him to be Matthew's servant. With any luck it'll keep him out of trouble.
CORA: Matthew and Mary looked so natural together. Did you notice? Talking and laughing… But I suppose Lavinia's a nice girl…
ROBERT: We've dreamed a dream, my dear, but now it's over. The world was in a dream before the war, but now it's woken up and said goodbye to it. And so must we.

He kisses her and turns out the light.

END OF EPISODE THREE

EPISODE FOUR

ACT ONE

1 INT. HALL. DOWNTON. DAY.

1918. The hall is busy as maids, nurses and orderlies pass through. Edith comes in, carrying post, and sees Mary on the stairs.

EDITH: Mary, the men are arranging the concert now and they are so anxious for us both to be in it, or there'll be no girls at all. Please say you will.
MARY: Do I have to?
CORA: Yes, you do.

She strides along as Isobel also comes into the hall.

CORA (CONT'D): Keeping their spirits up is an important part of the cure, and it's so very little to ask.
ISOBEL: What's going on?
EDITH: The men are putting on a concert.
ISOBEL: Can I help?
CORA: Edith has it under control.
EDITH: I do, if Mary's willing.
MARY: Oh, all right. One song and that's your lot. What about music?

We follow them towards the door of the library as they talk.

EDITH: I'll play. Mama won't move the grand, so they've brought the upright from the nursery. I'll just hand these out and we can practise.*
MARY: Not now. I'm off to the Dower House. Granny has sent for me.
EDITH: Then we'll do it this afternoon. Oh, and they've asked for 'If You Were the Only Girl in the World'.
MARY: You cannot be serious.
EDITH: They all want it.

....

* I was sorry we had to lose the line 'Mama won't move the grand, so they've brought the upright from the nursery,' because I was always brought up on the fact that uprights were essentially for practice and for governesses, and the only real piano that could be seen in a drawing room was a grand piano. But there are graver issues.

MARY: Why don't I just sing 'Oh, Mr Porter!' and have done with it?

She leaves by the front door, and Edith goes into the big library. We return to the others.

ISOBEL: What time is Doctor Clarkson's round?
CORA: It's already happened.
ISOBEL: Without me? Why? I'm not very late.
CORA: We didn't see the need to wait. Mrs Hughes, I need to steal you for a minute. I have to check the linen books.
ISOBEL: But I went over them last week —
MRS HUGHES: Very good, m'lady. I'll get started.
ISOBEL: Surely I can —
CORA: Anna, can you tell Mrs Patmore it'd be easier for me to go through the menus this afternoon?
ANNA: Of course, your ladyship.
ISOBEL: Cousin Cora —
CORA: Please. Can it wait? I've a mountain to get through.

The maids and Cora go about their business, leaving Isobel alone in the crowd.

2   INT.   LIBRARY.   DOWNTON.   DAY.

This is now a recreation room, with ping pong and card tables, where men are playing. An upright piano has been brought in and a soldier is playing 'Chopsticks', while Edith hands out the letters.

EDITH: There's a parcel for you. There's a little one for you. This looks as if it's been opened, but it hasn't.

She notices the maid, Ethel, laughing with Major Bryant.

EDITH (CONT'D): Ethel? Have you nothing to do?

The maid blushes and hurries away.

BRYANT: I was keeping her talking. You mustn't blame her.
EDITH: I don't.

3 INT. SERVANTS' HALL. DOWNTON. DAY.

Carson is also handing out letters. He gives one to Thomas.

> CARSON: Should this go with the upstairs post? Since
> you're not on my staff.
> THOMAS: No, I'm not. So perhaps it should.

Carson moves on. Anna comes in as Thomas talks to O'Brien.

> O'BRIEN: Anything interesting?
> THOMAS: It's just from an old mate who I —

He breaks off from the letter and leans in to whisper.

> THOMAS (CONT'D): See you in the courtyard.

He stands and moves off. After a moment, so does she.

> ANNA: I suppose we are sure they're not working for the
> Germans?

Which makes the others laugh. Mrs Patmore arrives.

> MRS PATMORE: Daisy? Where's that marjoram?
> DAISY: Mr Brocket never brought it in.
> MRS PATMORE: Well, go and fetch some, then. It's only in
> the corner of the yard.

4 EXT. GARDEN. DOWER HOUSE. DAY.

> MARY: What a lovely day.

Mary is with Violet, who is pursuing a point.

> VIOLET: Are you quite sure about Lavinia?
> MARY: She wasn't Sir Richard's mistress. She gave him
> the evidence to settle a debt of… someone she loved.
> VIOLET: And this is your beau, is it? A man who lends
> money, then uses it to blackmail the recipient?
> MARY: He needed the proof to publish the story. Even I
> can see that. He lives in a tough world.
> VIOLET: And will you be joining him there?

Mary decides to tell the truth to her grandmother.

> MARY: Richard Carlisle is powerful. He's rich and
> getting richer. He wants to buy a proper house, you
> know, with an estate. He says after the war the market
> will be flooded and we can take our pick.

VIOLET: Oh, and you can dance on the grave of the fallen
family.
MARY: They will fall, lots of them; some won't rise
again. But I don't intend to be among them.*
VIOLET: That leaves Matthew.
MARY: That's done now, Granny. Finished. It's time to
move forward.†
VIOLET: There aren't many who can make me feel soft-
hearted. But you do.

They stroll along for a moment.

VIOLET (CONT'D): It's this awful war that's spoiled
everything. You and Edith should be married by now, to
normal men leading normal lives.
MARY: Normal for you. Not for everyone.
VIOLET: I suppose Edith's still mooning after poor old
Anthony Strallan.

....

* Violet wants a reason to dislike Carlisle, because she dislikes the idea of
him, so she's actually looking for a moral justification for her hostility. But
here we have a conversation that represents quite an important strand of
thought for many of these people in that period. Both Violet and Mary
know they are about to witness a considerable set-back for the upper class,
and neither of them is pretending otherwise. Their honesty is why we like
them.

† Mary's decision that she doesn't want to go down with the ship – in other
words, she wants to keep going – was inspired, I suppose, by the marriage of
Lady Patricia Herbert, the daughter of the Earl of Pembroke, who in 1928
married the 3rd Viscount Hambledon, heir to the W. H. Smith fortune,
despite, I have been told, a certain amount of family opposition. The
comparison is not quite accurate, since Lord Hambledon's mother had been a
daughter of the Earl of Arran, but he still wasn't the 26th Earl of anything,
and the money was pretty new. I believe they were happy. As a result of this
marriage, the new Lady Hambledon went on living that pre-war life, very
securely, right through the Twenties and Thirties, and so on, when it had
ended for so many of her contemporaries. Of course Violet would prefer
Mary to marry the 26th Earl and stumble along like everyone else, but it's
not what Mary is after. The irony being that it is the Violet in Mary that is
not accepting defeat, so it's all, hopefully, quite complicated.

MARY: I hear he's in the thick of it in France. So
either death will claim him. Or Edith. I know which I'd
prefer.
VIOLET: What about Sybil? Does she have anyone in her
sights?
MARY: Not that I know of.
VIOLET: Nobody? I hoped there was some well-born swain
sending letters from the field of glory… I'm going in.
It's getting cold.
MARY: I ought to go back.
VIOLET: Are you sure she has no chap in mind? How odd.
I had an endless series of crushes at her age.
MARY: I don't think so.
VIOLET: Not even some man she doesn't care to mention?
MARY: What do you mean?
VIOLET: Well, war breaks down barriers, and when
peacetime re-erects them it's very easy to find oneself
on the wrong side.
MARY: Really, Granny. How can you say that I'm too
worldly, but Sybil's not worldly enough? You cannot be
so contrary.
VIOLET: I'm a woman, Mary. I can be as contrary as I
choose.

5 INT. KITCHEN. DOWNTON. DAY.

Isobel is with Mrs Patmore. Mrs Hughes hears them.

ISOBEL: But I don't understand. The patients are always
served their luncheon at half past twelve.
MRS PATMORE: Well, today they'll be served at one.
MRS HUGHES: Is this something I can help with?
ISOBEL: Mrs Patmore seems to be disobeying my
instructions and I can't get to the reason why.
MRS HUGHES: If you mean the patients' new lunchtime, her
ladyship felt that it made the staff luncheon
unreasonably early. She moved it so that they could eat
at noon.
ISOBEL: But that will interfere with the nurses' shifts.
MRS HUGHES: Oh no, she's altered those, too.
ISOBEL: Has she, indeed? Well, we'll see about that.

She stalks off. Mrs Patmore and Mrs Hughes exchange a look.

MRS HUGHES: It was always a question of 'when'.

6 INT. BOUDOIR. DOWNTON. DAY.*

Cora is writing when Isobel looks round the door.

> ISOBEL: May I have a word?
> CORA: Can it wait?
> ISOBEL: No, it cannot wait.

She shuts the door firmly. She is furious.

> ISOBEL (CONT'D): I've just come from downstairs where I
> learned that my timetable has been wantonly disregarded —
> CORA: If you mean the new lunchtime, the wretched
> servants were having to eat at eleven and then starve
> until their tea at six, so I felt —†
> ISOBEL: I have also discovered that you've torn up the
> nurses' timetable.
> CORA: I haven't torn up anything —
> ISOBEL: Of course, it would be foolish to accuse you of
> being unprofessional, since you've never had a profession
> in your life —

....

* The set designer of *Downton*, Donal Woods, is one of the most brilliant members of the team. He has also been working on the show all the way through, from the very beginning. He has imagined the whole concept from scratch, and he is probably the most talented designer I have ever worked with. That said (and meant), for this scene in the boudoir, someone on his team found the most extraordinary, not to say eccentric, draped screens I have ever seen. I can only suppose they were concealing something that could not be looked upon by the eyes of 1918. But, quite honestly, I've been in that room many times, and I cannot imagine what it could have been that frightened them so. Perhaps they were following a visual reference – a 1917 photograph of the boudoir of Tilly Losch, or the private sitting room of the Marchioness of Milford Haven… But whatever the reason, I find them so odd that I can't really focus on anything else. In all of Isobel's shots, she's standing in front of these weird draperies, as if she were in a tent on some medieval battlefield.

† She calls the servants 'wretched' because she feels that their needs are being ignored to an absurd degree. She's not a revolutionary, and like a great many employers, it wouldn't have been that she woke up in the middle of the night worrying about the housemaids, but there was a sort of reasonableness that people like Robert and Cora thought had to be observed to make life decent for everyone. For her, to force the servants to have lunch at eleven is just unreasonable.

CORA: Now, just a minute!

ISOBEL: You may think that you have the right to ordain the universe, but in this field —

CORA: No, not in this field. In this house, yes! I do have the right! Given me by Doctor Clarkson and by the law of the land! This is my house! And I am in charge right alongside you. And if you would stop your bullying —

ISOBEL: That's enough! I will not listen to this. If I am not appreciated here I will seek some other place where I will make a difference.

CORA: Good.

ISOBEL: I mean it. I cannot operate where I am not valued. You must see that.

CORA: Certainly.

ISOBEL: I shall go. I will.

CORA: Perhaps it would be best.

ISOBEL: I repeat: I mean it.

CORA: I'm sure you do. And so do I.

Isobel has misjudged the situation. *

7 INT. HALL. DOWNTON. DAY.

Edith is crossing the hall when she sees the housekeeper.

EDITH: Mrs Hughes, I wonder if I might have a word. I'm sure there's nothing to be concerned about…

MRS HUGHES: But?

EDITH: When I was in the library this morning, I saw what looked very much like flirting going on, between Major Bryant —

MRS HUGHES: And Ethel?

EDITH: I don't think she started it, but you know how it is. They're all so handsome in their uniforms and aching

....

* My mother always used to say, very firmly, 'Never make a threat that you're not prepared to carry out,' and this is a good motto when you're bringing up children, as every parent knows. You must never say, 'You won't be allowed to watch the film,' unless you are prepared for the tantrums and shenanigans that will come when the film is cancelled. Because the moment you weaken and give in, from that day forth your word is nothing. Here, Isobel has made the mistake of uttering a threat that she has no desire to carry out. But, of course, Cora picks up on it.

for female company, and I worry that the maids are easy prey.

MRS HUGHES: Thank you, m'lady. Forewarned is forearmed.

8 EXT. STABLE COURTYARD. DOWNTON. DAY.

Sybil is talking to Branson as he mends the car.

SYBIL: Why did you promise Carson not to stage any more protests? When you wouldn't promise me?

BRANSON: I had my reasons.

SYBIL: But you won't be content to stay at Downton forever, will you? Tinkering away at an engine instead of fighting for freedom? I thought you'd join the rising in Dublin last Easter.

BRANSON: I might have, if it hadn't been put down in six short bloody weeks. But don't fret. The real fight for Ireland will come after the war, and I'll be ready for it.

Mary, unseen by them, has entered the yard. She cannot hear them, but she can see the intensity with which they talk.

BRANSON (CONT'D): The truth is, I'll stay at Downton until you want to run away with me.

SYBIL: Don't be ridiculous.

BRANSON: You're too scared to admit it, but you're in love with me.

MARY: Branson, could you take me into Ripon at three?

She is walking across towards them. She looks at Sybil.

MARY (CONT'D): I'm getting some things for Mama. Is there anything you want?

SYBIL: Nothing you can find in Ripon.

9 INT. CLARKSON'S OFFICE. HOSPITAL. DOWNTON VILLAGE. DAY.

Isobel is with a rather weary Clarkson.

CLARKSON: Well, it is her house.

ISOBEL: Does that mean she's suddenly received a medical training?

CLARKSON: No —

ISOBEL: Or are you like everyone else in thinking that because she's a countess, she has acquired universal knowledge by divine intervention?

CLARKSON: Mrs Crawley, convalescent homes are not about medical training. They are far more to do with good food, fresh air and clean sheets.
ISOBEL: Do you know what I think? I think you'd like me to push off and let Lady Grantham run the place with Thomas. You feel it'd be easier.

She stares, waiting for him to deny this. He says nothing.

ISOBEL (CONT'D): Very well. I've had a letter from a cousin in Paris who is working in the Wounded and Missing Enquiry Department. They've opened a branch in northern France under the aegis of the Red Cross. I shall offer them my services.
CLARKSON: That's… that's very drastic.
ISOBEL: I have to go where I am useful. And that place, I'm afraid, is no longer Downton Abbey.
CLARKSON: You'll be missed.
ISOBEL: By you, possibly. I hope so, anyway. But not, I think, by Lady Grantham.*

10 INT. LIBRARY/HALL. DOWNTON. DAY.

Mary is finishing 'If You Were the Only Girl in the World'. There's some applause. Edith at the piano looks unconvinced.

EDITH: I wish we had a man.
MARY: Amen.
EDITH: It would sound so much richer. But all the volunteers are spoken for.

....

* Penelope Wilton was cast in a play in London, which she very much wanted to do. And my own feeling – and, of course, it's really my sympathy with actors, because I still tend to consider myself an actor – is that people are more likely to stay longer with a show if you accommodate them as much as you possibly can. So, we bit on the bullet and decided to let it happen. We had already started on the rivalry between Isobel and Cora, so we had laid the foundations of why she would leave. We just had to let it boil up and then she could flounce off to France and be in the play. Of course, we couldn't cover the whole run, but this fictional trip to France allowed her to rehearse and open in it. After that, she had to combine the two jobs, which I think is a tough brief, filming by day and in the theatre at night. But Penelope managed to be a success in both. Well done her.

She starts to help Bryant unpack his conjuring tricks. Mary leaves. As she crosses the hall, Robert appears with Isis.

ROBERT: How's it going?

MARY: All right, I suppose, if you don't mind singers who can't sing and actors who can't act.

ROBERT: It helps to keep their spirits up.

MARY: So they say, although I can't think why.

ROBERT: I had a letter this morning, from Sir Richard Carlisle.

MARY: Oh?

ROBERT: He tells me he proposed when he was staying here. He apologises for not asking my permission, but he's asking it now. Have you decided? Is that why he's written?

MARY: No. But I have made the decision.

ROBERT: Which is?

MARY: I think I should take him.

ROBERT: Do you really, my darling? I wish I could believe in your motives.

MARY: Why? What were your motives when you married Mama?

This is a blow below the belt.

ROBERT: Your mother has made me very happy.

MARY: Perhaps Sir Richard will make me very happy.

ROBERT: What about Matthew?

MARY: Not you, too. Poor Matthew. What must he do to persuade you he's in love with Lavinia? Open his chest and carve her name on his heart?

ROBERT: Write to him. Tell him of your plans with Carlisle. You owe him that.

MARY: I don't think I 'owe' him anything, but I'll write to him, if you like.*

....

* Robert is reluctant to give up on Matthew for several reasons. One, he doesn't really want Carlisle as a son-in-law. He thinks him brash and vulgar and unsympathetic. Two, he certainly does want Matthew as a son-in-law, because he would like his own bloodline to remain at the heart of the Grantham dynasty. And three, he knows his daughter, Mary, who is a great one for bringing down the portcullis. But I think where Hugh Bonneville is very clever is that he can play all of those elements at once, which is what you get good actors for.

11   INT.   SMALL LIBRARY.   DOWNTON.   DAY.

Cora is reading.   Sybil, in her uniform, comes in from the main library, round the screen, and looks out of the window.

SYBIL: Where's Branson going with an empty car?
CORA: He's taking Isobel to the station.
SYBIL: She's really leaving, then?
CORA: Apparently.   She thinks she can do more good in France than here.
SYBIL: You sound as if you agree with her.
CORA: We needed a rest from each other.
SYBIL: It's nice of you to send the car.
CORA: Your father thought it politic.
SYBIL: Then it was nice of him.

Her eyes are on the car and her thoughts are on the driver.

12   EXT.   CRAWLEY HOUSE.   DOWNTON VILLAGE.   DAY.

Branson is loading a suitcase onto the car.   Isobel is with Molesley and Mrs Bird.

ISOBEL: I'll try to send you an address, but you can always get me through the Red Cross.
MOLESLEY: Very good, ma'am.
ISOBEL: And I'll try to contact Captain Crawley, explain to him what's happened.   If he does get leave, he'll probably come to me or stay in London, but if I miss him and he turns up here, I know you'll look after him.
MRS BIRD: Of course I will, ma'am.
ISOBEL: Cook what he likes, not what's good for him.
MRS BIRD: You don't know when you'll be back?
ISOBEL: I don't think one 'knows' anything in wartime. I'll try to give you warning.   But in the meantime, look after yourselves.   Now, I mustn't miss my train.

She climbs into the car.   Branson gets in and drives off.

MOLESLEY: So, what now?

13   INT.   SYBIL'S BEDROOM.   DOWNTON.   NIGHT.

Anna is leaving, when the door opens.   Mary enters.

MARY: Ah, Anna said you were honouring us with your presence at dinner.

SYBIL: It's easier here than the hospital. I can always
get changed back into my uniform if I need to.*

She smiles at Anna who closes the door. They are alone.

MARY: What were you talking to Branson about when I came
into the yard?
SYBIL: Nothing.
MARY: Then why were you there?
SYBIL: Why were you there?
MARY: Because I was ordering the motor. That is why one
talks to chauffeurs, isn't it? To plan journeys by road?
SYBIL: He is a person. He can discuss other things.
MARY: I'm sure he can. But not with you.
SYBIL: What do you want from me? Am I to see if Sir
Richard Carlisle has a younger brother? One who's even
richer than he is?
MARY: Darling, what's the matter with you? I'm on your
side.
SYBIL: Then be on my side!†

END OF ACT ONE

....

* I didn't want to have to keep going to the hospital every time we wanted to
see Sybil. So, we have now transferred her, as a trained nurse, to the
management of Downton, which gives her a slight edge over the other
members of the family in this set-up.

† Here we have a very clear illustration that Mary is not insensitive, but she
doesn't understand why people limit their lives. And I must say, in that, she
speaks for me. I don't often understand when people make a choice that is
going to limit their lives and their horizons tremendously. I'm not always,
God knows, right about it, but when people marry husbands and wives who
are never going to be able to meet the demands of what their lives could be –
which these days, to be honest, is much more to do with temperament and
personality and, above all, energy than rank – I don't get it. You see people
marrying those who are possessive, and unsocial, and challenged, and insecure,
and even unpleasant, and you just think, can't you see that this is a ball and
chain you're dragging down the aisle? In this instance, Mary doesn't dislike
Branson on any level, but, by marrying the chauffeur, Sybil is excluding a
million possibilities from her own future. Now, I happen to think Sybil is one
of those people – and they're extremely rare – who can make that sort of choice
and not regret it. But I don't blame Mary for failing to see that straight away.

ACT TWO

14 INT. MATTHEW'S DUG-OUT. NORTHERN FRANCE.
                    DAY.

Matthew is reading a letter from Mary.

MARY (V.O.): 'So there we have it. I look forward to
introducing the two of you, just as soon as you are next
at home. Which naturally I trust will be very soon
indeed. Please be glad for me, as I will always be for
you. Your affectionate cousin, Mary.'

Matthew is putting on his overcoat. William is there.

MATTHEW: We don't need anyone with us. The Sergeant
knows what we're doing.
WILLIAM: But what are we patrolling for?
MATTHEW: You've been taking those logic pills again.
This is the Army, Mason. We're going on a patrol because
we're going on a patrol.

*He sets the letter down. He looks at his desk, at Lavinia's
picture and Mary's rabbit, which he pockets.*

WILLIAM: Has Mary set a date yet for the wedding?
MATTHEW: She doesn't say. I think she's hoping the war
will be over soon, and they can set a date then.
WILLIAM: She could have waited and told you when she saw
you.
MATTHEW: I don't think she knows I'm due back. Did you
warn Daisy, or will it be a surprise?
WILLIAM: No, I've told her we're coming to Downton first.
Then I'll visit my dad and go back to see her for a day
at the end.
MATTHEW: Just think. Fresh Yorkshire air, followed by
London and Miss Swire.
WILLIAM: All right for some, sir.
MATTHEW: You'd never swap, though, would you?
WILLIAM: No, I'd never swap.

*As William talks, he takes out two torches and gives one to
Matthew, who puts it in his coat pocket.*

MATTHEW: We'll take them, but we should be back long
before it's dark.

15   EXT.   KITCHEN COURTYARD.   DOWNTON.   DAY.

O'Brien and Thomas are smoking as they discuss the letter.

O'BRIEN: Bates in a pub? I can't see that. I think your
pal's mistaken.
THOMAS: He met him here twice before the war. Listen:
'I said to him, "Hello, Mr Bates," and he walked off, and
wouldn't serve me after.'

Even O'Brien can see this is quite convincing. She thinks.

O'BRIEN: Next thing you know, we'll have Anna running
across the county and dragging him back by his stick.
THOMAS: I'm surprised he isn't here of his own accord,
with his lordship having no valet since the loony went.
O'BRIEN: Don't speak ill of Mr Lang.
THOMAS: You're a funny one. Talk about sweet and sour.
Better get back.

They walk inside, revealing Daisy, gathering her herbs.

16   INT.   HALL.   CRAWLEY HOUSE.   DOWNTON VILLAGE.
DAY.

*Molesley is hanging coats on the coat hooks. He stands back
to admire the effect, then changes two over. Then sighs.*

17   INT.   KITCHEN.   CRAWLEY HOUSE.   DOWNTON
VILLAGE.   DAY.

Mrs Bird is drinking tea when Molesley comes in.

MRS BIRD: Want a cup?
MOLESLEY: Not really.
MRS BIRD: What were you doing?
MOLESLEY: Let me see. I've tidied the study twice and
I've rearranged the coats in the hall. I might check his
clothes for moth. What about you?
MRS BIRD: We've cleaned everything three times over and
I've sent Beth into the village for some eggs to pickle.
Though the mistress doesn't really like them.

MOLESLEY: Well, she never eats properly, anyway. Not on her own. A butler can't do much with supper on a tray.*

They are surprised by a knock at the open outside door. A ragged individual, leaning on a crutch, stands there.

VISITOR: Beg pardon for troubling you, only the door was open.
MOLESLEY: But the front gate was not.
VISITOR: No.
MRS BIRD: What do you want?
VISITOR: Have you got any spare food?
MRS BIRD: 'Spare food'? What's that when it's at home?

The visitor nods, resignedly, and starts to move off.

MOLESLEY: Hang on, hang on, wait. You from round here? What's your name?
VISITOR: Ted Wurkett. Not far. I used to work on the farms, but, er, not any more.
MOLESLEY: You get that in the war?
VISITOR: Don't pity me. I'm one of the lucky ones.
MRS BIRD: I might have something for you.

She puts a pan on the hob while she looks in the cupboards.†

....

* Kevin Doyle has developed Molesley as a character tremendously well, and I love writing stories for him. He has created an Eeyore figure, who just assumes that bad luck is stalking him. And as with most people who believe they're unlucky, it becomes a self-fulfilling prophecy. By contrast, Mrs Bird is entirely in the centre of her own world. She doesn't seek a particularly different life, she accepts that this is what's happened to her, whereas with Molesley you always feel he has the soul of a poet, trapped inside the body of a beleaguered servant.

† In every area of the country, there were beggars. One of the great problems of war is not just that people get killed; it is also that people are wounded but not killed. And this is a reminder. Here is someone who, we are encouraged to assume, was an able agricultural worker, but who has now lost his ability to support himself, through no fault of his own. What was the country going to do with all these people who were not desk workers? It isn't a grim show, but this is a *Downton* reminder that there would be an enormous number of similarly placed men after the war.

18   EXT.   NO-MAN'S-LAND.   NORTHERN FRANCE.   DAWN.

Matthew and William are lying on the ground, listening.
Someone nearby is talking German. William whispers.

   WILLIAM: How long do we wait, sir?

Before Matthew speaks there's a cry in German and a gunshot.
They attempt to retreat through the woods but soon realise
they are surrounded. They run as multiple shots ring out
after them.

19   EXT.   DOWNTON.   DAY.

It's a new day at Downton and Molesley is walking towards it.

20   INT.   ROBERT'S DRESSING ROOM.   DOWNTON.   DAY.

Carson brushes a suit; when he looks up, Molesley is there.

   CARSON: Hello, Mr Molesley.
   MOLESLEY: They told me you were up here. I hope you
   don't mind my bothering you.
   CARSON: Not a bit. What can I do for you?
   MOLESLEY: Well, actually, Mr Carson, I've been thinking
   there might be something I could do for you.
   CARSON: Hm?
   MOLESLEY: That brushing, for instance.

He walks forward, takes the brush and starts to work.

   MOLESLEY (CONT'D): I don't like having nothing to do,
   what with Captain Crawley away at the war and his mother
   in France alongside him. And then his lordship's without
   a valet and your plate is piled so high…
   CARSON: I am quite occupied, it's true.
   MOLESLEY: So I thought I'd look in and give you a hand.
   Brushing. Mending. Cleaning shoes. Whatever's needed.
   CARSON: That's kind of you, Mr Molesley. We shall have
   to watch ourselves, or else his lordship will want to
   pinch you off Captain Crawley.

Molesley's face tells us this is exactly what he's after.

21 INT. SMALL LIBRARY. DOWNTON. DAY.

Cora is reading some papers as Robert works at the desk.

CORA: Oh, I've asked to have my luncheon on a tray from tomorrow onwards. When we're not entertaining.
ROBERT: Why?
CORA: I've too much to do and I can't down tools every day for an hour. You can eat with the girls.*
ROBERT: Have you heard from Isobel?
CORA: I'd have told you.
ROBERT: I'm sorry it had to end in an explosion.
CORA: You may be sorry, but you cannot be surprised.
ROBERT: Drop her a line. Tell her the news. Oh, and say Molesley's been working here. Brushing and whatnot.
CORA: I would, but we have no address for her. I'll write when she deigns to send us one.
ROBERT: You like her, really.

....

* I'm not on Robert's side in this. Yes, he feels neglected, and eventually he gets a bit pouty, but, like many men of his type, he is not giving his wife credit for what she's doing. I always remember my mother, sometime in the Fifties, painting a room and suddenly looking at the clock – she never wore a watch – and exclaiming: 'Oh, my God, I'm on duty in twenty minutes.' I suppose I was about seven, but I still remember how, in those twenty minutes, she cleaned herself up, got into a little cocktail frock and went downstairs, so that when my father walked in she was standing there with a jug of Martini, in a sexy dress and smelling delicious. Looking back, I don't believe he really appreciated the extent to which he was being kept in cotton wool. That was very much the thinking of her generation of women, that the husband must never see the rough bits. I know my mother felt her job was to conceal the changes that the war had brought, mainly the absence of servants (and money). She might spend half the day in the kitchen, but all that was effectively hidden from my father, so by the time he got home, there it was: a delicious dinner to be eaten by candlelight with his nice pretty wife, sitting there in her twinkling earrings and chatting away. For these women, there was an imperative to keep the flag flying, and their husbands were luckier than most of them knew. In a way, I admire it, but here I have no patience with Robert being put out. I thought as a child, and I think now, that the husband should take into account what his wife is doing to keep the show on the road. That's where, for me, Robert is in the wrong.

CORA: Maybe. But, oh, I do hate this war. Watching
Isobel glory in her own importance just made it worse.
And don't get the idea Molesley can be your new valet.
Or we'll never hear the end of it.
ROBERT: Stranger things happen at sea.

22 INT. KITCHEN PASSAGE. DOWNTON. NIGHT.

Daisy is with Mrs Hughes.

MRS HUGHES: What would you like me to do?
DAISY: I don't know quite. But he said he'd be here by
now and he's not.
MRS HUGHES: You mustn't worry about him, Daisy. Not yet.
DAISY: I'm not 'worried' like that, exactly. But this is
William. I think we should all be worried.
MRS HUGHES: Well, it's much too early to panic. Anything
might have happened. Maybe his leave was cancelled.
His plans changed. At times like these, people vanish
and turn up again in the strangest places.
DAISY: Like Mr Bates in that pub.

Mrs Hughes stares at her.

23 INT. CARSON'S PANTRY. DOWNTON. NIGHT.

Daisy is now with Carson as well as Mrs Hughes.

CARSON: Working in a public house?
DAISY: That's what he said. I thought they'd have told
you.
CARSON: It doesn't seem likely that a trained valet like
Mr Bates would be content to work in a public house.
DAISY: Well, that's what he said.
CARSON: Have you mentioned this to Anna?
DAISY: I haven't said anything to anyone. I thought you
all knew. Perhaps you should ask Thomas.
CARSON: Oh, I will ask Thomas. Don't you worry about
that, my girl.

24 INT. PASSAGE. DOWNTON. NIGHT.

Robert and Carson are interrogating Thomas.

ROBERT: Didn't it occur to you that we might be
interested to hear it?
THOMAS: Not particularly. As far as I knew, Mr Bates had
left your employment.
ROBERT: You didn't think to tell Carson?
THOMAS: I am not under Mr Carson's command now, your
lordship.

The Earl and the butler share this.

25 INT. SERVANTS' HALL. DOWNTON. NIGHT.

Several of the servants are there. O'Brien sews and Daisy
reads a paper. Mrs Patmore comes in.

MRS PATMORE: Shoo. Daisy, go to bed. Before you strain
your eyes.

As Daisy stands, Thomas arrives.

THOMAS: Thank you, Daisy, for telling Mr Carson all about
my private letter.
DAISY: I didn't know it was a secret. I'm sorry if I was
wrong.
THOMAS: There's no 'if' about it.*

Daisy hurries away, followed by Mrs Patmore.

O'BRIEN: Why answer his lordship at all?
THOMAS: What did you want me to do? Tell him to get
knotted?
O'BRIEN: He doesn't pay your wages.
THOMAS: Oh, I see. Well, I won't put you down for a
career in diplomacy, then.

....

*Thomas, of course, is furious with Daisy. In the workplace, enormous
numbers of disparate people have to live and work together, and that must
mean disagreements. In fact, whether you're working in some high
ministerial office or in a café, you have to rub along with people whom you
find unsympathetic, which is the point we're making here.

O'BRIEN: What's he after? To get Bates back?
THOMAS: If Mr Bates wanted his job back, he'd have
written for it himself.
ETHEL: Why would he want his job back?

This distracts them and they look over to her.

ETHEL (CONT'D): He's like you. He got away.
THOMAS: He's not very like me, thank you.
ETHEL: But you're both free of all the bowing and
scraping and 'Yes, m'lord' and 'No, m'lord'… I envy him.
I envy you. Because I'm ready for a new adventure, and I
don't care who hears me.
O'BRIEN: Well, you know what they say: 'Be careful what
you wish for.'

25A EXT. DOWNTON. DAY.

*Sybil is walking in the grounds, thinking about what Branson
said to her.*

BRANSON (V.O.): The truth is, I'll stay at Downton until
you want to run away with me.

26 INT. SMALL LIBRARY. DOWNTON. DAY.

Robert is with Anna, who has just appeared.

ROBERT: Ah. Good morning, Anna.
ANNA: You sent for me, m'lord?
ROBERT: I did. Come in. I have something to tell you,
but I hope I'm right. Carson didn't want you to be
troubled with it…
ANNA: Is this about Mr Bates, m'lord?
ROBERT: Yes, it is. I have no wish to upset you but it
seems he may be back in Yorkshire and working in a public
house. We don't yet know where.
ANNA: The Red Lion in Kirkbymoorside.

Which is not what he was expecting.

ROBERT: Oh. You've seen him, then?
ANNA: I have, yes, m'lord.
ROBERT: And he's well?
ANNA: He is.

There is a moment when neither knows who should speak next.

ANNA (CONT'D): He's not been back to Downton for two reasons. He's hoping to settle certain matters first, with… Mrs Bates.

ROBERT: And does he think he can?

ANNA: He believes so, m'lord.

ROBERT: Very good. And what is his second reason for avoiding us?

ANNA: He says… he parted with your lordship… on bad terms. He felt it might be… embarrassing.

ROBERT: It is for me to feel embarrassed.

27 EXT. DOWNTON VILLAGE. DAY.

Mrs Patmore is walking with Daisy.

MRS PATMORE: I had to get out of that kitchen if I'm not to be found dead under the table. It's like cooking a banquet three times a day.

DAISY: It is a lot of extra work, whatever they say. Even with the helpers —

MRS PATMORE: Don't think they lighten the load!

There's a crowd of men at Crawley House. Mrs Bird appears.

MRS PATMORE (CONT'D): Mrs Bird? What's going on?

MRS BIRD: I knew I'd be found out sooner or later. At least it's you.

MRS PATMORE: Found out doing what?

MRS BIRD: What does it look like?

MRS PATMORE: Well, I don't know what it looks like. Except some kind of soup kitchen.

MRS BIRD: You'd better come inside.*

....

* I am often criticised for the niceness of the characters, but this sort of thing went on quite a lot, and certainly my own grandmother always had a certain amount of food made ready to be given to people who banged on the door at that time. She rather broke the rules during the Second World War, though, when the Government took away all the signposts and removed all the maps in case of the German invasion. She had been put in charge of her grandchildren, so, rather than try to fight off the marauding Hun, she left a pile of maps and sandwiches on the hall table, with an instruction in German saying, 'Take what you wish, and leave us alone.' When he found out, my father hit the roof, protesting at her lack of patriotism, but she said, 'No. I had someone else's children to look after, and that changes the rules.' I do rather see her point.

28 INT. KITCHEN. CRAWLEY HOUSE. DOWNTON
VILLAGE. DAY.

Mrs Bird has a table with a large pot of stew and a basket of bread. The men are lined up from the door into the garden.

MRS BIRD: One at a time. Now, take a piece of bread —
MRS PATMORE: I'll do that. Right, Daisy, stand there, give them a bowl and a spoon.

The three women form a production line.

MRS PATMORE (CONT'D): When did all this start?
MRS BIRD: That fella turned up, asking for food. Then he came back next day with a friend and… here we are.
DAISY: What does Mrs Crawley say?
MRS BIRD: She doesn't know yet. I suppose she'll put a stop to it when she gets back from France.
MRS PATMORE: I hope not.
MRS BIRD: To be honest, Mrs Patmore, I'm not sure I can manage much longer.
MRS PATMORE: How often do you do it?
MRS BIRD: I planned to get it down to once a week. And give them only the cheapest cuts. But it is my money, and I —
MRS PATMORE: Hold it right there! If we can't feed a few soldiers in our own village, them as've taken a bullet or worse for King and Country, then I don't know what!

29 INT. LIBRARY. DOWNTON. DAY.

Edith is putting books away when Daisy comes in with a coal bucket to replenish the scuttle.

DAISY: Sorry about this, m'lady, only there's no footman to do it now.
EDITH: I don't mind. But you'd better run before Mrs Hughes sees you.
DAISY: M'lady, could I ask something? Only, William, who was in service here —
EDITH: I know William.
DAISY: Well, he's missing. That is, he was supposed to be back on leave, but he never turned up. He wrote he was coming home for a few days with Captain Crawley…

EDITH: Is William your beau?

DAISY: I wouldn't say that, no, m'lady. We're all very fond of William downstairs…

EDITH: Of course you are. Well, I'm sure it's nothing, but I'll see what I can find out.

DAISY: Thank you.

Edith puts the last books away and moves on, passing Ethel and Major Bryant.

BRYANT: I've got sixpence that says you don't mean it.

ETHEL: Then your sixpence has told you a lie.

He laughs and whispers to her.

30 INT. SMALL LIBRARY. DOWNTON. DAY.

Edith is with Robert.

ROBERT: But how do you know they didn't change their plans?

EDITH: Well of course I don't. But the poor girl seemed quite certain.

ROBERT: Just when Isobel's away and none of us know where she is. Typical.

EDITH: I suppose Matthew might have heard from Cousin Isobel and decided to meet up in France instead.

ROBERT: But that wouldn't explain why William isn't here… I'll do what I can.

31 INT. KITCHEN. DOWNTON. NIGHT.

The kitchen is crowded with Mrs Patmore's extra assistants.

MRS PATMORE: No, don't stop stirring, the butter will burn! With a pot that size, you can burn the bottom while the top is still stone cold!

She rolls her eyes at Daisy. Nearby, a woman packs some plucked and trussed chickens onto a metal store tray.

MRS PATMORE (CONT'D): You can leave those to Daisy.

She winks at Daisy who puts four chickens into a basket.

MRS PATMORE (CONT'D): That's it, Daisy. Put them in the special storage area.

The girl nods and walks off. O'Brien has been watching from the doorway. Mrs Patmore sees her standing there.

MRS PATMORE (CONT'D): What do you want?
O'BRIEN: Can I borrow some baking soda?
MRS PATMORE: Borrow? Why? Are you planning to give it back?

32 INT. DINING ROOM. DOWNTON. NIGHT.

The family is at the end of dinner. Carson and Anna attend.

CORA: I might go over to Malton tomorrow. Agatha Spenlow is madly promoting her charity fair. Do you need the motor?
ROBERT: I'm afraid I do. Can you get Pratt to take you in the other car?
CORA: It doesn't matter. I can go on Monday. But why?
ROBERT: I'm told Bates is working at a public house in Kirkbymoorside. I want to investigate.
VIOLET: I can't decide which part of that speech is the most extraordinary. Why can't someone else go?
ROBERT: Because I want to go myself.

There is the sound of the telephone in the hall. With a glance at Anna, Carson leaves. Violet turns to Sybil.

VIOLET: So, Sybil, what are you up to, dear?
SYBIL: Nothing much. Working. I don't have time to get up to anything else.
VIOLET: Only Mary and I were talking about you the other day…

She is sitting next to Sybil and speaking softly, but Mary is on Sybil's other side. She mimes: 'I've said nothing.'

SYBIL: Oh?
VIOLET: You see sometimes, in war, one can make friendships that aren't quite appropriate, and it can be awkward, you know, later on. I mean, we've all done it. I just want you to be on your guard.
SYBIL: Appropriate for whom?

VIOLET: Well, don't jump down my throat, dear. I'm only
offering friendly advice.*

Cora looks across the table to Robert.

CORA: Why do you want to see Bates? To give him his old
job back?
ROBERT: Not entirely. I mainly want to see him because
we parted badly.

Carson reappears.

CARSON: Telephone call for you, m'lord.

Robert smiles his thanks and stands.

CORA: If you did, I'm sure it's his fault.
ROBERT: No, it was mine.

*He goes. As Carson opens the door, there is a roar of
victory from somewhere across the hall.*

VIOLET: Oh, really, it's like living in a second-rate
hotel, where the guests keep arriving and no one seems to
leave.

END OF ACT TWO

....

* Violet's warning against inappropriate friendships was given to one of my
great-aunts by my great-grandmother. Naturally, I was fascinated by it. The
thinking then was that, in wartime, you will make friends with people whom
you don't necessarily want to go on with when peace comes. Naturally, my
aunt was affronted, but afterwards it made her laugh. I only recall that when
I heard things like this, I had such a sense that, shortly before my own birth
(because we were talking about 1920, and I was born only thirty years later),
the whole world must have changed into a different universe. Here, Violet is
trying to warn Sybil off, because she has a suspicion that with a young girl as
pretty as Sybil, and as lively and attractive, there must be someone in pursuit.
As far as Violet can work it out, the only reason they haven't met him has to
be because he's unsuitable, and they're not allowed to meet him; a completely
correct analysis, of course.

ACT THREE

33 INT. HALL. DOWNTON. NIGHT.

*The family walks out of the dining room into the small
library, while Robert is on the telephone. He listens.*

ROBERT: I see. Yes. Thank you for letting me know.

*Edith is last, and only she is there when he puts down the
telephone. He looks concerned.*

EDITH: Are you all right, Papa?
ROBERT: Not exactly. That was the War Office. Matthew
and William went out on a patrol a few days ago and they
haven't been seen since.
EDITH: Oh, my God.
ROBERT: Let's not fall to pieces quite yet. It happens
all the time apparently, and the men turn up in one field
hospital or another.
EDITH: But they are treating them as missing in action?
ROBERT: It's too early for that. There could be lots of
things to explain it.
EDITH: You mean they could have been taken prisoner?
ROBERT: It's possible.*
EDITH: What are you going to do?
ROBERT: There's not much I can do, until we know more.

He is thinking aloud as he now realises, and regrets.

ROBERT (CONT'D): Don't say anything to Mary. Or your
mother. Or anyone in fact. Not yet. I shouldn't really
have told you.
EDITH: What about Cousin Isobel?
ROBERT: I don't know how to contact her. And I'm not
going to sound the alarm before we know something solid…
Anyway, she's in France. She may hear before we do.

....

* Whenever anyone was missing in action, there was always a hope they'd
been taken prisoner, but it was probably an unfulfilled hope, because they
usually knew who had been captured. That is why Robert is unwilling to
offer more than faint acknowledgement of Edith's statement.

34   INT.   MRS HUGHES'S SITTING ROOM.   DOWNTON.
             NIGHT.

Mrs Hughes is with O'Brien.

   O'BRIEN: I'm not accusing her of anything, but I did
   wonder if you were aware of this 'special storage area'?
   MRS HUGHES: I dare say Mrs Patmore has her own system,
   like we all do.
   O'BRIEN: Right. Well, I'll say goodnight.
   MRS HUGHES: Goodnight.

*Mrs Hughes sees Molesley walking down the passage, outside
her door, as O'Brien slips away.*

   MRS HUGHES (CONT'D): Ah, Mr Molesley, you're very late.
   MOLESLEY: I was doing some invisible mending on one of
   his coats. I got a bit carried away, but I'm quite
   pleased with the way it turned out.
   MRS HUGHES: I don't see why you can't dress him. Until
   there's a new valet. It'd be a blessing to Mr Carson.
   MOLESLEY: I'd be happy to, if it'd help.
   MRS HUGHES: Keep this up and we won't be able to do
   without you at all.
   MOLESLEY: There's no reason why you should.

He laughs pleasantly, but his agenda is clear.

   MOLESLEY (CONT'D): Oh, er, I may be wrong, but I thought
   I saw one of the officers by the maids' staircase just
   now.

He is slightly alarmed by the hardening of her expression.

   MOLESLEY (CONT'D): I'm sure there's a perfectly
   reasonable explanation.
   MRS HUGHES: Let's hope so. Goodnight.

35   INT.   THE MAIDS' PASSAGE/ANNA AND ETHEL'S ROOM/
      HOUSEMAIDS' SITTING ROOM.   DOWNTON.   NIGHT.

*Mrs Hughes walks silently along the passage. Outside a door,
she stops, turns the knob and opens it. Anna is asleep in
one bed, but the other is empty. Mrs Hughes shuts it and
walks on. She listens at another door, quietly turns the
knob and throws the door open, switching on the light as she
does so.*

BRYANT: What the bloody —?

He stops at the sight of the housekeeper. They have made a makeshift bed on the floor of this little sitting room with blankets spread out. Ethel clutches at one to cover herself.

MRS HUGHES: Ethel! So you've found a new use for the old housemaids' sitting room.

BRYANT: We were only —

MRS HUGHES: I know precisely what you were doing, Major. I may not be a woman of the world, but I don't live in a sack.* Now, if you will kindly take your things and go downstairs.

He gets to his feet, clutching a blanket round him, and gathers his clothes awkwardly. Mrs Hughes does not help. He leaves.

MRS HUGHES (CONT'D): Ethel, you are dismissed, without notice and without a character. You will please leave before breakfast.

ETHEL: I didn't think I —

MRS HUGHES: No. And that's the problem. You never do.

....

* This is a very key line for me. These days there is always an assumption that, if you live in quite an enclosed way, you don't know anything. A monk, or a nun, for example, might live out of the world and therefore they won't know how it operates. When, in fact, you can find unworldly people at the centre of a crowded ballroom, and extremely knowledgeable and very sophisticated people living in a Trappist order. It's the same with politicians when the papers say that, because they've been to Eton, they don't know how real people live. As a rebuttal of this foolish argument, you only have to compare David Cameron to Gordon Brown. Which one of those two seems the more normal? Mrs Hughes is not shocked; she's not a maiden spinster fainting at the sight of a man's torso. She knew precisely what she would find, and she is extremely tough about it. Just as we have moments when Cora doesn't know the name of the kitchen maid, one also has to remind the audience of the rules that governed everyone in those days. However much we may love Mrs Hughes, there is no question that, in a case like this, Ethel would have been sacked on the spot.

36   INT.   KITCHEN.   CRAWLEY HOUSE.   DOWNTON
                    VILLAGE.   NIGHT.

Mrs Bird and Molesley are having a cup of tea.

MRS BIRD: And you're not nervous?
MOLESLEY: Well, I gather his lordship knows his own mind,
but I've no difficulty with that.
MRS BIRD: You'll enjoy working in a big household.
Better than staring at me night after night. What would
you say if they ask you to stay?
MOLESLEY: It would be a big step up for me. There's no
point in denying it.
MRS BIRD: Because I think they might.
MOLESLEY: Do you really, Mrs Bird?
MRS BIRD: There goes Mr Molesley. Valet to the Earl of
Grantham.
MOLESLEY: Stop it.

His glee at the prospect has shown his hand.

37   INT.   ANNA AND ETHEL'S ROOM.   DOWNTON.   DAWN.

Ethel, weeping throughout, is packing. Anna is with her.

ANNA: But why? What could you have possibly done that's
so terrible?

Ethel just shakes her head and points at the cupboard.

ETHEL: Have I taken everything of mine from there?

*Anna goes to check. There is one frock left, which she lifts
down and folds for the suitcase as she talks.*

ANNA: Would you like me to speak to her? Because I can.
I'd be glad to.
ETHEL: No. She wouldn't listen.
ANNA: She's not a bad person, Mrs Hughes. I know she can
be strict, but she's not —
ETHEL: She wouldn't listen.

38   EXT.   THE RED LION.   KIRKBYMOORSIDE.   DAY.

*The car arrives and stops, with Branson in the front and
Robert in the back. Branson gets out and opens the door.*

38A INT. THE RED LION. KIRKBYMOORSIDE. DAY.

*Bates is clearing up at the end of the day. The bell rings
as someone enters.*

BATES: We're closed.

He turns round to find that it is Robert.

39 INT. MRS HUGHES'S SITTING ROOM. DOWNTON.
DAY.

Mrs Hughes is with Anna.

ANNA: I know Ethel could be difficult, Mrs Hughes, but
she was very sorry for her mistake, whatever it was.
MRS HUGHES: I'm sure. It's cost her her job.
ANNA: But surely it can't —
MRS HUGHES: Never mind why she's gone, she's gone.
There's an end to it.

Which silences the maid.

MRS HUGHES (CONT'D): By the way, I hear Mr Bates is back
in the county. Mr Carson says you know all about it.

Anna neither confirms nor denies this.

MRS HUGHES (CONT'D): I gather his lordship has gone to
see him.
ANNA: I know. He told me he was going.
MRS HUGHES: Why in heaven's name didn't you mention any
of it to me?
ANNA: It wasn't my secret to tell.

40 INT. THE RED LION. KIRKBYMOORSIDE. DAY.

John Bates is with Robert.

ROBERT: I'm glad to hear it. But Carson said your wife
made all sorts of threats.
BATES: She won't carry them out. Not now. Since I left
Downton, I've discovered that she was… untrue to me.

Robert glances at him, but says nothing.

BATES (CONT'D): I may have been as bad in my heart, m'lord. But I've done nothing to be ashamed of. The point is, I can divorce her now, whether she likes it or not.

ROBERT: But what's to stop her blurting out her stories to the press?

BATES: If she agrees to keep silent, I will give her whatever she wants. She can't hold me now, so her choice is between poverty and plenty.

ROBERT: And what was the tale she was going to tell? Carson never made it clear.

BATES: Some silly nonsense, m'lord. I wouldn't waste your time with it. What's the news from Downton?

41 INT. SERVANTS' HALL. DOWNTON. DAY.

Most of the servants and Thomas are having tea.

MRS HUGHES: Daisy, you're not to worry about William. I spoke to his lordship earlier. He says you're not to be concerned until we know more.

DAISY: But he is missing? I mean, they don't know where he is, or Captain Crawley, do they?

MRS HUGHES: There could be a hundred explanations.

O'BRIEN: Yes, and one of them is that they're dead.

She sees Daisy's look of shock.

O'BRIEN (CONT'D): Don't mistake me, I hope very much they're not, but we ought to face the truth.

MRS HUGHES: What may be the truth. And what very well may not.

She goes to leave and meets Anna.

MRS HUGHES (CONT'D): Oh, Anna, do you think that Mr Bates will come back?

ANNA: That's for him to say.

DAISY: I hope he does. He always seems a romantic figure to me.

Anna smiles at this, but says nothing.

O'BRIEN: Does he? And how do you define romantic?

THOMAS: It's no good him thinking he can turn up here without a moment's notice and be Cock o' the Walk.

MRS HUGHES: Why is that, Thomas? Because the place is already taken?
THOMAS: I'm not making any claims.
MRS HUGHES: Well, that's a relief to us all.

42   INT.   THE RED LION.   KIRKBYMOORSIDE.   DAY.

The conversation is still in progress.

ROBERT: I hate the word 'missing'. It seems to leave so little room for optimism. I tell myself it's too early to despair, but to be honest, Bates, I don't think I can bear it.
BATES: What does her ladyship say?
ROBERT: I haven't told her yet. I haven't told any of them, except Edith, who's sworn to secrecy. I don't know why, exactly. Perhaps I don't want to make it real.

Away from the family, this is as unguarded as we've seen him.

BATES: If you'd rather not talk about it —
ROBERT: No, I want to. It's a relief. Losing Patrick was bad enough, but now the thought of Matthew gone and the future once again destroyed… More than all that, I loved him like a son… No. I love him. Let's stay in the present tense while we still can… So, will you come back with me? And help me through the Vale of Shadow?
BATES: It's not what I expected, m'lord, but I will if you want me to.
ROBERT: I misjudged you, Bates, and I abused you when we parted. I should have had more faith. I'm sorry.
BATES: God knows you've shown more faith in me than I had any right to.*

....

*This scene would qualify, in Hollywood, as a sort of mini buddy movie, where, in the narrative, you present an almost romantic arc between two heterosexual men. There was a tremendous fashion for buddy films in the late 1960s and 70s. It allows the movie-maker to put an emotional charge into the scenes, without anything funny happening in the woodshed.

43 EXT. DOWNTON VILLAGE. DAY.

Mrs Patmore and Daisy are walking along, both carrying laden baskets. Mrs Bird hurries down to take some of the load. All this has been witnessed at a distance by O'Brien.

44 INT. PASSAGE. DOWNTON. DAY.

Sybil is at the bandage cupboard, taking some out.

MARY (V.O.): Sybil?

But Sybil just goes on counting out her requirements. Mary walks over to her, but still she takes no notice.

MARY: I never said anything to Granny. Honestly.
SYBIL: Then why did she suddenly start talking about 'inappropriate friendships' out of nowhere?
MARY: She thinks you must have a beau, and if we don't know about him, then you have to be keeping him secret. It's just Granny being Granny. Don't make such a thing of it.
SYBIL: I don't deserve to be told off, not by her or by you. Nothing's happened.

Now this, of course, is an admission. Mary looks at her.

MARY: Why? What might have happened?
SYBIL: I mean it. We haven't kissed or anything. I don't think we've shaken hands. I'm not even sure if I like him like that. He says I do, but I'm still not sure.
MARY: We are talking about...?
SYBIL: Branson. Yes.
MARY: The chauffeur, Branson.
SYBIL: Oh, how disappointing of you.
MARY: I'm just trying to get it straight in my head. You and the chauffeur.
SYBIL: Oh Mary, you know I don't care about all of that.
MARY: Oh darling, darling, don't be such a baby. This isn't Fairyland. What did you think? You'd marry the chauffeur and we'd all come to tea?
SYBIL: Don't be silly. I told you, I don't even think I like him.
MARY: What has he said to you?

SYBIL: That he loves me, and he wants me to run away with
him.
MARY: Good God in heaven.
SYBIL: He's frightfully full of himself.
MARY: You don't say.
SYBIL: But I haven't encouraged him. I haven't said
anything, really.
MARY: You haven't given him away, though.
SYBIL: Will you?
MARY: I don't know. The question is, do you think he's
mad or bad?
SYBIL: Oh, mad, if he must be either. There's nothing
bad in him, Mary. He's not interested in money or who I
am. He hates people like us.
MARY: So he says. Well, I won't betray him, on one
condition. You must promise not to do anything stupid.

Sybil says nothing.

MARY (CONT'D): You must promise now. Or I'll tell Papa
tonight.
SYBIL: I promise.

Their mother comes into view. The conversation is over.

45   INT. KITCHEN PASSAGE. DOWNTON. NIGHT.

*The back door opens and Bates arrives, carrying his case. He
stands for a moment to take in the place. Mrs Hughes
appears.*

MRS HUGHES: Mr Bates. You're a sight for sore eyes.
Welcome home.
BATES: Thank you, Mrs Hughes.

At the sound of his voice, Anna comes into the passage.

ANNA: I thought it was you.
BATES: Hello.
MRS HUGHES: Come a way in, and give some substance to the
gossip of your return.

*She goes ahead of him, and as the others walk away from the
camera we see Anna delightedly rub his back and then snatch
her hand away before anyone sees.*

46 INT. SERVANTS' HALL. DOWNTON. NIGHT.

The servants have assembled to welcome Bates.

> CARSON: You'll find things a bit different from when you
> left, Mr Bates.
> BATES: Downton at war.
> CARSON: Precisely. There's some extra help in the
> kitchen, all very nice people, and the nurses, of course,
> but they live down at the hospital —
> ANNA: Except for Lady Sybil.
> THOMAS: Nurse Crawley, please.

He is standing in the doorway.

> BATES: So, we've both returned, you and I. A couple of
> bad pennies.
> THOMAS: I haven't.
> O'BRIEN: Thomas means he's not here as a servant. He
> manages the house. He's a sergeant now.
> THOMAS: I take orders from Major Clarkson. He runs this
> place on behalf of the Army Medical Corps.
> BATES: Yet another reason to pray for peace.

He looks at Daisy with sympathy.

> BATES (CONT'D): I heard about William from his lordship.
> And Captain Crawley.
> ANNA: I'm sure they're all right.
> BATES: Let's hope so.

There is an awkward silence to this. But they are
interrupted by the hurried arrival of Molesley. He carries a
long gadget.

> MOLESLEY: Sorry I'm late. Has the dressing gong rung
> yet?
> MRS HUGHES: You're not late, Mr Molesley, but you won't
> be needed, after all.
> MOLESLEY: Why not?
> CARSON: Mr Bates is back. You reminded me. I'd better
> ring it now.

Carson leaves as Molesley walks up to Bates.

> MOLESLEY: Are you staying for good?
> BATES: I'd need a crystal ball to answer that, but I'll
> stay for now. Have you been standing in for me?

MOLESLEY: I was going to. Starting tonight.
BATES: Then you'll be relieved to see me.
MOLESLEY: Oh. Tremendously.
BATES: What's that?
MOLESLEY: It's a new kind of shoehorn. I bought it for his lordship…
BATES: That's very kind of you, Mr Molesley. Thank you.

He holds out his hand and Molesley gives it up, bleakly. The gong sounds. Anna starts upstairs.

THOMAS: Daisy, fetch me some more tea.
DAISY: Thomas, I've got din—
THOMAS: Hot, this time! And it's Sergeant Barrow to you!

He is joking, really, but she scuttles away. This has been witnessed by Mrs Hughes, although O'Brien only sees Bates, who is on his way out. They exit together.

O'BRIEN: Watch yourself, Mr Bates. Thomas is in charge now, and it won't do to get on the wrong side of him.
BATES: Is there a right side?

END OF ACT THREE

ACT FOUR

47 INT. CORA'S BEDROOM. DOWNTON. NIGHT.

O'Brien is dressing Cora.

O'BRIEN: Is there any news on Captain Crawley?
CORA: Why? What news would there be?

O'Brien realises her mistress still knows nothing.

O'BRIEN: I've lost my train of thought…
CORA: Never mind. What else about Mrs Patmore?
O'BRIEN: I've nothing more to say. Beyond that I saw her with my own eyes.
CORA: I don't believe it. Why would she sell food to Mrs Bird? It makes no sense.

O'BRIEN: Well, I can't confirm the details of the arrangement. Maybe they both sell it and divide the proceeds. Either way, I felt you should know.

CORA: Have you said anything to Mrs Hughes? Or Carson?

O'BRIEN: I've tried with her, but there's none so blind as them that will not see.

CORA: I'm curious. Next time, come and fetch me.

48 EXT. STABLE COURTYARD. DOWNTON. NIGHT.

Branson's put the car away for the night. He shuts the garage door. Sybil is hovering on the edge of the courtyard.

SYBIL: So Bates is back. Papa must be pleased.

BRANSON: And Mr Carson won't be sorry… What is it?

Because she does look as if she needs to make a confession.

SYBIL: Branson, there is something you ought to know… I've told Mary.

BRANSON: I see. Well, that's me finished then, without a reference.

SYBIL: No, she's not like that. You don't know her. She wouldn't give us away.

BRANSON: But she won't encourage us.

SYBIL: No. But she won't give us away.

She is surprised, because he is smiling at her.

SYBIL (CONT'D): Why are you smiling? I thought you'd be angry.

BRANSON: Because that's the first time you've ever spoken about 'us'. If you didn't care, you would have told them months ago.

SYBIL: Oh, I see. Because I don't want you to lose your job, it must mean I'm madly in love with you.

BRANSON: Well, doesn't it?

Naturally, she knows this may be true, but…

SYBIL: You say I'm a free spirit and I hope I am. But you're asking me to give up my whole world and everyone in it.

BRANSON: And that's too high a price to pay?

SYBIL: It is a high price. I love my parents — you don't know them — and I love my sisters and my friends.

BRANSON: I'm not asking you to give them up forever.
When they come around I will welcome them with open arms.
SYBIL: And what about your people? Would they accept me?
Or would I always be the girl with the poisonous past?
The Anglican aristo? The freak?* And what about my work?
BRANSON: What work? Bringing hot drinks to a lot of
randy officers? This isn't a hospital, it's a holiday
home.

At this, Sybil recoils slightly.

BRANSON (CONT'D): Look. It comes down to whether or not
you love me. That's all. That's it. The rest is
detail.

49   EXT.   KITCHEN COURTYARD.   DOWNTON.   NIGHT.

Bates and Anna are together.   She huddles in her coat.

BATES: I've written to Vera, spelling out the case and
how she cannot win it. Then I have told her I will be
generous, if she will cooperate.
ANNA: Has she answered?
BATES: Not yet. But I don't want to harass her. There's
always a chance she'll see sense. I may go up to London.
ANNA: Will you tell her you're back in Yorkshire with me?
BATES: No. I've a friend in the Midlands who gets my
post and forwards it. I don't want her to know I'm here.
ANNA: But you're ready to give her everything? Because I
am.
BATES: Whatever it takes. I want a clean break, not an
open wound. If we can just be patient a little while
longer.

She nods and shivers.   He holds her to him, tightly.

....

* I am sorry this bit was cut, although I cannot now remember how much of
an argument I put up at the time. Not enough of one, obviously. The truth
is, it would have been very difficult for Sybil to marry into an Irish republican
family as the daughter of an English earl, and there is no doubt that some of
them would have found such a marriage impossible to accept. I also like
Sybil becoming more realistic about what she is headed for. Anyway…

BATES (CONT'D): We shouldn't be outside. It's cold.

ANNA: I'll be patient, and bear anything. Except for you to go away again.

BATES: No. That's done. You're stuck with me now. For good and proper.

50   INT. HALL/STAIRCASE. DOWNTON. NIGHT.

Mary is climbing the stairs as Edith comes into the hall.

EDITH: There's something you ought to know. Papa said not to tell you, but I don't think he's right.

Mary has stopped on the staircase.

MARY: Go on.

EDITH: Matthew's missing. At least, I'm not sure he's officially missing yet, but they don't know where he is. He was on patrol and he's just sort of… vanished. Papa hasn't told anyone. Not even Mama. I only know because I was there when he found out.

MARY: What can I do about it?

EDITH: Well… nothing. But it didn't seem right to keep you in the dark. I'm not trying to upset you. Truly.

Mary answers as she climbs on up the stairs.

MARY: For once in my life, I believe you.

But at the top, as soon as she is out of sight, she bites her hand to stop herself from crying out. *

....

* Sibling rivalry, when brothers or sisters don't get on, is very layered. If you don't like someone in normal life, then you just don't see them or have any communication, but in a family, as we all know, it's much more complicated. As a rule, in films and novels, most siblings are loving and giving towards each other, but experience tells me this is not the case all that often. Of course, those families where the siblings, even in late middle age, have to ring each other five times a day are, if anything, even more difficult to deal with than a tribe at war.

51 INT. CORRIDOR. DOWNTON. NIGHT.

Mary approaches and stares at Anna, who is waiting for her.

ANNA: They've told you, then?
MARY: Do they all know downstairs?

Anna nods.

ANNA: William's missing, too. I think everyone knows
except her ladyship.
MARY: I wish Edith had left it 'til the morning. I could
have faced it all with one more night of sleep.

52 INT. CORA'S BEDROOM. DOWNTON. NIGHT.

Robert is climbing into bed.

CORA: Can you go to the Shackletons' tomorrow on your
own? I've got a mountain of letters to get through.
ROBERT: It seems rather rude.
CORA: Don't be stuffy. I'll telephone and say I've
caught a cold.
ROBERT: I hate going to things without you.
CORA: That's sweet, but there's a war on, in case you
hadn't noticed. We can't have it all our own way.

But something in his expression prompts her next question.

CORA (CONT'D): You look very preoccupied.
ROBERT: I was just thinking about Matthew.
CORA: Has something happened to Matthew? Only O'Brien
was asking after him.

He looks at her and again decides not to trouble her.

ROBERT: Not that I know of.
CORA: How many parents and guardians are staring at the
ceiling right now, worrying about their boys?
ROBERT: That is a moving thought, but not a very
comforting one.

He turns out the light.

53 EXT. DOWNTON VILLAGE. DAY.

Cora and O'Brien hover while Mrs Patmore and Daisy, carrying baskets, go inside with Mrs Bird, past the waiting men.

O'BRIEN: See? They're queuing up to buy it.

54 INT. KITCHEN. CRAWLEY HOUSE. DOWNTON VILLAGE. DAY.

In the kitchen, Mrs Bird, Mrs Patmore, Daisy and Molesley are setting up the line, with bread, fruit and stew.

CORA: May we come in?

The others are stunned as she and O'Brien enter.

MRS PATMORE: Your ladyship… What a surprise.
CORA: O'Brien seemed to think that you and Mrs Bird were engaged in a commercial venture of some sort. So I came to see for myself.
MRS BIRD: We are not, your ladyship!
CORA: I agree that's not what it looks like.
MRS PATMORE: We feed these men once a week, and I'm not ashamed of it. I'll be back before luncheon at the big house.
CORA: I'm sure. But is it true they are fed from our kitchens?

Now, this is harder to get indignant about.

DAISY: It's only the stuff the Army gives. They are soldiers.
O'BRIEN: What did I tell you?
MRS BIRD: Mrs Patmore brings the meat here on Tuesdays, and the bread and fruit on the day we serve it.
CORA: Quite a little assembly line.
MRS PATMORE: Daisy's right. We only use the food the Army pay for. And all the men have served their country.
O'BRIEN: So, are you going to report them?
CORA: No, I'm not going to report them. Although in future, I would prefer it if you would use food paid for by the house. I don't want the Army to accuse us of mismanagement.
O'BRIEN: You mean you're going to let them get away with it?

CORA: Oh, more than that. I'm going to help them, and so are you. Molseley, if you bring that table over, I suggest we divide the food and then we can form two lines and then we'll go faster. Molesley, you'll do that for us, won't you?
MOLESLEY: Certainly, m'lady.
MRS BIRD: So you still have your uses after all.

He accepts this with resignation, as Cora finalises her plan.

CORA: O'Brien? You can manage the bread. Daisy?*
DAISY: Of course, m'lady.

Daisy throws open the doors to the first of the old soldiers.

55   INT.   DRAWING ROOM.   DOWNTON.   DAY.

Clarkson is in search of Thomas.

CLARKSON: Sergeant. One moment.

Thomas joins him. The doctor speaks softly.

....

* You will notice that, for Cora, O'Brien is O'Brien, and is never called by her first name, but Daisy is Daisy. It was all to do with rank. A lady's maid was called by her surname, housemaids, kitchen maids, almost every other female worker, was called by their Christian name. Even when a housemaid – the head housemaid, usually – maided women who were staying (but had no maid of their own), this did not change. In many houses, as in this one, the head housemaid would maid the daughters, as Anna does the girls. But she is not their lady's maid; she is the head housemaid, who maids the daughters as one of her duties. It is only when Anna is promoted to be Mary's proper lady's maid that we have all the dialogue about whether or not she should be called Bates, and they eventually decide they can't call her Bates, because Bates is already called Bates. But it is a compromise and it has to be discussed. The butler used his surname, and so did the ladies' maids. The maids and the footmen had Christian names, and the exceptions were the housekeeper and the cook, who used their surname, but with the prefix of Mrs, whether they were married or not. You may ask why this privilege was not enjoyed by ladies' maids. The answer is, I know not, but these rules were established and universal.

CLARKSON (CONT'D): I hear you're becoming mighty imperious in your manner with the staff here, Daisy in particular. Just because you're a poacher turned gamekeeper, there's no need for rudeness.
THOMAS: No, sir.
CLARKSON: So mind what I say. Carry on.

Thomas leaves, as Clarkson approaches Mrs Hughes.

CLARKSON (CONT'D): I've done as you asked, Mrs Hughes. I think Barrow's taken it on board.
MRS HUGHES: He's getting grander than Lady Mary, and that's saying something.

Cora passes by.

CLARKSON: Lady Grantham.
CORA: Hello, Doctor Clarkson.

56 INT. SERVANTS' HALL. DOWNTON. DAY.

O'Brien has put down her sewing as she commiserates.

O'BRIEN: It was Bates. I saw him watching you. He must have gone straight to the Major and sneaked on you the moment your back was turned.
THOMAS: Oh, well. Some things never change.
O'BRIEN: Don't worry. He's more vulnerable than when he was last here.
THOMAS: Why?
O'BRIEN: Because we know more. That's why.

57 INT. CORA'S BEDROOM. DOWNTON. NIGHT.

Robert is with Cora. They have changed for the evening.

CORA: Why haven't you told me 'til now?
ROBERT: I'm not sure. Perhaps I envied your ignorance.
CORA: I'm not giving up hope. Not yet.
ROBERT: Nor me, of course. But I think we should start to prepare.
CORA: Isobel doesn't know?
ROBERT: I haven't been able to reach her.
CORA: Have you said anything to Mary?
MARY (V.O.): Edith's already told me.

She is in the doorway, also changed.

    ROBERT: Has she? Well, I suppose it was too tempting to
    resist.
    MARY: Oddly enough, I don't think she was trying to make
    trouble…

Cora glances at the clock on the mantelshelf.

    CORA: We ought to go down. It's time for the concert.
    MARY: Who cares about the stupid concert?
    ROBERT: The men do, and we should, too. Because we have
    to keep going, whatever happens. We have to help each
    other to keep going.

*Cora and Robert leave. Mary is alone for a moment. She
stares at her reflection in the glass. She is in hell. She
takes a deep breath, pushes her shoulders back and follows
them out.*

      58 INT. LIBRARY. DOWNTON. NIGHT.

*A conjuring act is in progress. Major Bryant is doing tricks
with help from Edith. They are not very good. The audience
is made up of the convalescents and the staff. They are more
enthusiastic than the performance deserves.* The wheelchairs
are in the first row, with the others behind them. Clarkson*

....

* I'm afraid, for me, Major Bryant was not a very convincing conjurer, and to
be honest, I suspect we should probably have given him something else to do.
It is not at all his fault, because it is absolutely bred into your bones as an
actor that when some potential employer asks you if you can do something,
you must always say 'Yes' and then go off and try to learn it as best you can.
In their brain they think, well, I'm sure I *could* ride, if I had three lessons on
Wimbledon Common. I'm sure, if I get the job, I've got time. One director,
driven mad by actors saying they could ride when it was perfectly obvious,
when filming started, that they couldn't, said to me, 'How do I avoid this?' I
told him it was very simple. Initially, you ask, 'Can you ride?' The actor will
think for a moment, and answer, 'Yes'. Then you say, 'And are you happy
jumping?' And at that moment, the actor who wishes to see middle age will,
on the whole, reply, 'Well, no, I'm not too sure about jumping.' Now, if you
can ride, you can jump, so it's a failsafe test.

*is there and the family, including Violet, but Sybil, in her
uniform, is with the other nurses. Violet sees her and turns
to Robert, speaking under her breath.*

VIOLET: I don't know what it is about Sybil these days,
but somehow she can't even look at her watch without
making a statement.
ROBERT: I think it's a fairly benign one.
VIOLET: Cora tells me Matthew's gone missing. Is that
true?
ROBERT: There's no proof of anything yet.
VIOLET: I see. Well, I need more than that to make me
anxious.
ROBERT: I'm glad you would be anxious.
VIOLET: Of course I would be. We're used to Matthew now,
and God knows who the next heir will be. Probably a
chimney sweep from Solihull.

Branson edges over from the servants to the nurses.

BRANSON: I was harsh with you, the other night. To speak
slightingly of your work. I'd no right to do that.
SYBIL: No, you didn't.
BRANSON: It's just that when I look at you, not being
sure if you're mine, I feel I may explode.

*He is whispering under the applause, but her expression
catches Mary's attention. Edith signals to Mary it's time.*

MARY: Most of you won't know how rare it is to see my
sister, Edith, and I pulling together in a double act —
CORA: A unicorn if ever there was one.
MARY: But in wartime, we, like all of you, have more
important things to worry about. Ladies and gentlemen, I
give you the Crawley Sisters.
VIOLET: Well, now I've seen everything.

Mary joins Edith at the piano. Edith starts to play.

MARY: 'Sometimes when I feel bad and things look blue; I
wish a pal I had... say one like you; Someone within my
heart to build a throne; Someone who'd never part, to
call my own...'*

Now they both gesture to the audience and they all sing.

MARY AND AUDIENCE: 'If you were the only girl in the world and I were the only boy; Nothing else would matter in the world today; We could go on loving in the same old way…'

At that moment, there is a movement at the door and Matthew Crawley walks in, followed by William. Mary stops singing. Noticing this, the men gradually stop, too.

AUDIENCE: 'A garden of Eden just made for two; With nothing to mar our joy…'

Mary does not speak, but she murmurs under her breath.

MARY: Thank God.

There is a moment of complete silence and then Matthew, aware that he has stifled the fun, appeals to them.

MATTHEW: I'm sorry. Please forgive me. I didn't mean to interrupt anything.

Robert and Cora are on their feet.

CORA: I knew it!
ROBERT: My dear boy. My very dear boy.

Matthew catches something in Mary's expression, in all of their moods, but he wants to keep the moment light.

MATTHEW: Come on. Don't stop for me.

But the audience is still silent, absorbed in watching Mary. Then Edith starts to play again, and Matthew takes her cue, walking up to stand next to Mary.

....

* We feature the verse of the song in this scene, which you never normally hear, but which places 'If You Were the Only Girl in the World' firmly in its original period. We were lucky. Michelle Dockery has a very pretty voice, and does in fact sing – she accompanies herself on the guitar – all of which I was aware of. So, when I was writing the episode, I knew we were not going to have a problem with her singing. This is an unashamedly romantic moment, and it always makes me cry when I watch it, which tells you more about me than the show. But in war, life is reduced to its essentials, and while the danger and uncertainty bring worry and sorrow and tragedy, there are also moments of heightened emotion and romance, as most people who have been through a war will confess.

MATTHEW (CONT'D): 'I would say such wonderful things to
you…'

Mary, regaining her composure, joins him.

MARY AND MATTHEW: 'There would be such wonderful things
to do…'

And now the whole room takes up the refrain.

EVERYONE: 'If you were the only girl in the world and I
were the only boy.'

The result is applause and happiness. Edith's noted it all.

59 INT. HALL. DOWNTON. NIGHT.

*The company is milling about. Carson serves a wine cup
handed round by the servants. Mary is with Matthew and
Robert.*

MATTHEW: Somehow we got lost and then we were trapped
behind some Germans for three days. When we got out of
that we stumbled into a Field Dressing Station where we
were immediately admitted, but we weren't in any danger
so they didn't inform our unit.
ROBERT: Well, they should have jolly well told us when
you got back to base.
MATTHEW: That's army bureaucracy for you. I hope Mother
wasn't frightened.
ROBERT: I doubt she knew. Nobody knows how to get hold
of her. Do you?
MATTHEW: No. If she sent me a message, I never got it.
Then Molesley and Mrs Bird didn't even know I was
missing. So we weren't at all prepared for our
reception.
MARY: But you managed to steal the show.
MATTHEW: I hope you weren't really worried.
ROBERT: Oh, you know us. We like to be sure of our hero
at the front.
MRS HUGHES: I beg your pardon, m'lord, but the Dowager
Countess is leaving.

*Robert smiles at Matthew. As he walks away, he passes
William and pats him on the shoulder as he does so.*

MATTHEW: I want every wounded man taken down the line before it starts to get dark. We've bloody well lost enough of them for one day.

MARY: Goodbye, then. And *such* good luck.

SYBIL: But do you think it's ready?

MRS PATMORE: I know it's ready.

DAISY: Go on. You don't want to spoil it.

VERA: If you don't come back to me, I'm going to the newspapers with a cracking story. And I'd like to bet the Granthams won't survive it.

BRANSON: I've told myself and told myself you're too far above me, but things are changing.

EDITH: Don't look so bewildered. It's simple. I will drive the tractor.

SYBIL: It's more savage and more cruel than I could have imagined... But I feel useful for the first time in my life.

CARLISLE:
I know Miss Swire.
Her uncle and I are
old friends.

LAVINIA: Well,
old acquaintances,
anyway.

GENERAL
SIR HERBERT
STRUTT:
This is all very
impressive, Lady
Grantham. The
nurses and your
own staff are to
be congratulated.

DAISY: I am glad
you're all right.
Honest.

WILLIAM: You
should be. It's the
thought of you that
keeps me going.

MARY: He says you may have damaged your spine.
MATTHEW: How long will it take to repair?

DOCTOR: There's an ambulance waiting, although no one quite
knows how you managed it.
VIOLET: What exactly is the matter with him?
DOCTOR: His body's sustained too much damage. He cannot recover.

ROBERT: The ceasefire will begin at eleven o'clock on the morning of the eleventh of November.

ETHEL: They have to see him. They must see Charlie.

MATTHEW: I want to tell you all something. As you know, during this – well, I think I can say horrible – time, Lavinia has proved to be the most marvellous person...

VIOLET:
What on earth
is it?

LAVINIA:
A gramophone.

VIOLET:
I should stand
well clear when
you light the blue
touch paper.

BATES: I, John Bates,
take thee, Anna May
Smith, to be my
wedded wife.

MARY: I see
what was worrying
you. If Lavinia
had been carried
off, you wanted
to be here to stop
Matthew from
falling into my
arms on a tidal
wave of grief.

MATTHEW: I know it's a cliché, but I believe she died of a broken heart because of that kiss... And we were the ones who killed her.

O'BRIEN: Is anyone there? Is anyone there?

The girls start to laugh.

THOMAS: You must take it seriously, otherwise they'll be offended.

JUDGE:
John Bates, you have been found guilty of the charge of wilful murder. You will be taken from here to a place of execution where you will be hanged by the neck until you are dead. And may God have mercy upon your soul.

THOMAS:
What about the black bottom, m'lady?
VIOLET:
Just keep me upright and we'll try to avoid it.

MARY:
We've been on the edge of this so many times, Matthew. Please don't take me there again, unless you're sure.
MATTHEW:
I am sure.

MARY: What will you do with the rest of your leave?

MATTHEW: Well, since Mother isn't here, I think I'll run up to London and see Lavinia.

The mention of Lavinia has somehow altered things.

MATTHEW (CONT'D): I got your letter about Carlisle.

MARY: I hope you'll approve. I know you don't like him much now —

MATTHEW: I hardly know him. I'm sure I'll like him when I do. That's if he's good to you. If he's not, he'll have me to answer to.

She smiles and raises her fists like a fighter. But her gesture seems to take him somewhere else.

MARY: What's the matter? You suddenly look quite haunted.

MATTHEW: I am haunted... I only don't talk about it because it doesn't help. You see, when I'm here, I like to think it's not real. That I won't have to go back. But of course it never leaves me.

MARY: Take care of yourself. Please. It really can't be long now, and the worst thing of all is when people are... hurt, just before the end.

Near the service door, Bates is with Anna.

BATES: Who would have thought an amateur concert could be the summit of all joy? I've lived in such a fog of misery since I left you, I think I'd forgotten what happiness is.

ANNA: Me, too. But now we must get used to feeling happy. And trust it.

BATES: God, I want to.

Thomas is with O'Brien as they look at Bates and Anna.

O'BRIEN: Love's young dream, I don't think.

THOMAS: I'm not sure I care much.

O'BRIEN: You going soft in your old age?

THOMAS: I don't like him because he's a patronising bastard who sneaks behind my back, but I've got other things to worry about.

O'BRIEN: Really? That's interesting.

THOMAS: Why?

O'BRIEN: Because obviously I hold a grudge longer than you.

Daisy and Mrs Patmore are with William in the corner.

MRS PATMORE: I knew nothing bad had happened. I felt it in my waters.
WILLIAM: What about you? Did you have me boxed up and buried?
DAISY: I am glad you're all right. Honest.
WILLIAM: You should be. It's the thought of you that keeps me going.

Which makes Daisy uncomfortable. At the back of the party, a hall boy whispers something to Mrs Hughes and she slips away.

60   INT. KITCHEN PASSAGE/MRS HUGHES'S SITTING
              ROOM. NIGHT.

Mrs Hughes comes down into the deserted kitchens. *

MRS HUGHES: Hello? Hello? Who is it? Who wants me?

A figure steps out of a shadowed doorway. It is Ethel.

MRS HUGHES (CONT'D): Ethel? What on earth are you doing here?
ETHEL: I had to come, Mrs Hughes. I'm sorry to push in, but I was sitting alone until I couldn't stand it no more. You've got to help me.
MRS HUGHES: I haven't got to do anything. But what do you mean? Help with what? Is this about Major Bryant?

....

* One of the main ways in which these houses have changed in the modern day is that they are no longer full of people. When you stay in them, even in those that are still run on pretty affluent lines – and actually that happens more than it did forty years ago, because there's more money around – you may have a few nice women working in the kitchen, but seldom more than that. In the old days, these places were like factories, humming with energy. If you went down into the kitchens, there would be fifteen, twenty people walking around doing their jobs – working, talking, hurrying. At Chatsworth, dinner in the servants' hall numbered well over a hundred when all the Duke's children were staying with their families in the 1920s. So for me, anyway, there is something a little bit eerie about the silence in those halls and passages today.

Ethel nods. Mrs Hughes shakes her head angrily.

    MRS HUGHES (CONT'D): I blame myself for not stepping in
    earlier. That I will admit. How long had it been going
    on?
    ETHEL: Long enough to get me pregnant. Mrs Hughes… I'm
    going to have a baby.

Which silences the housekeeper and stops her in her tracks.

END OF EPISODE FOUR

EPISODE FIVE

ACT ONE

1 EXT. TRENCHES. DAY.

Amiens, France, 1918. Against the roar of guns and explosions, soldiers are assembled. There is a sense of apprehension as they wait.*

2 INT. DUG-OUT. TRENCHES. DAY.

Matthew stares. William is checking Matthew's uniform is correct.

MATTHEW: Am I ready?

WILLIAM: Only you can answer that, sir.

MATTHEW: They're going to chuck everything they've got at us.

WILLIAM: Then we shall have to chuck it back, won't we, sir?

MATTHEW: Quite right.

....

* Now comes the moment when we had to put our principles to the test by wounding and killing characters who were known and loved. Obviously, Gareth Neame, Liz Trubridge and I talked about this *ad infinitum*, but we did feel it wouldn't be right if no one from our running cast died. Because many, many men did die. In my own family, my grandfather died, my great-aunt's husband died, and cousins without number. One of them, Octavia Longhurst, having married the Governor of Nigeria in those dead imperial days, was torpedoed by the Germans in 1916 on her way back to England on board the SS *Appah*. She got off the ship, but the enemy then torpedoed the lifeboats and drowned the survivors, thereby rather proving the stories of the wicked Hun that nowadays we like to feel were cooked up by a hostile press. Torpedoing lifeboats is pretty bad in my book. Anyway, she died.

Since *Downton* is about an English family of a certain type, it seemed wrong to let them off scot-free. Of course, you are reluctant to kill your principals, but we knew that the one who would die had to be popular. It wouldn't be enough to introduce a character, give them seven lines and then kill them. It's like a whodunit. The killer has to be someone who was there all the time. You can't bring in a new character for the fifth act and have them turn out to be the murderer.

3 EXT. TRENCHES. DAY

Matthew addresses the men. As he does so, he strolls down the line, directing different parts of his speech to them.

MATTHEW: Now, there's no point in pretending that this is going to be easy.

He stops by one soldier, fingering his uniform.

MATTHEW (CONT'D): You've mended it. Well done.

He lifts his voice slightly.

MATTHEW (CONT'D): It's General Ludendorff's last throw of the dice and he'll throw them hard. But remember, it is the last throw. It must be.*

He stops by another soldier.

MATTHEW (CONT'D): How are you, Thompson? Have you shaken that cold?
THOMPSON: I'm all right, sir, thank you.

Which makes Matthew smile. He brings them in.

MATTHEW: Good man. We're nearly there, chaps. Just hold fast, it won't be long now.
SOLDIER: We're with you, sir.
MATTHEW: I know you are, Wakefield. I can't tell you how much lighter that makes the task. Right Sergeant. Let's go.
SERGEANT: Fix bayonets!

Matthew blows his whistle. He pulls himself over the top. William and the others follow.

4 INT. KITCHEN. DOWNTON. DAY.

Daisy is whipping some cream. Slowly, she stops, and shivers.

MRS PATMORE: Daisy? Whatever's the matter with you?
DAISY: Someone walked over me grave.

....

* It is the style of *Downton* for characters to refer to people and events and places without making a point of explaining them. We've done that always, and, for this reason, I was sorry to lose Matthew's comment on Ludendorff, the German commander, which was there to give a sense of the enemy's predicament. But we must lose some things.

4A EXT. BATTLEFIELD. DAY.

The battle is raging. Men are falling left, right and centre.

MATTHEW: Forward!

5 INT. SMALL LIBRARY. DOWNTON. DAY.

Violet, Cora and Mary are together. Carson is serving coffee.

CORA: He just wants a date for the wedding. And he'd like to make the engagement public. It doesn't seem unreasonable to me.
MARY: But why can't we just go on as we are?
VIOLET: Because only parlour maids have long engagements. Ladies say yes and get on with it.
MARY: But the war's nearly over. Everyone says so. And I don't want a wartime wedding when, if we'd waited a week, we could have just what we want.
CORA: Are you sure? Mrs Patmore tells me the rationing is getting worse.
MARY: Even if it is, I'd like to walk out of the church and know that everyone there will live forever.*

Suddenly, she trembles. The cup falls, spilling its contents.

MARY (CONT'D): I'm so sorry.
CARSON: No matter, m'lady. I'll fetch a cloth.

He goes out. The others are puzzled.

VIOLET: What happened?
MARY: I don't know. I suddenly felt terribly cold.

....

* Of all the sections cut in this episode, this is one I did regret, because (a) it's got a good line for Violet – 'only parlour maids have long engagements. Ladies say yes and get on with it' – which was more or less a direct quote from my grandmother. But also (b) it introduced the whole business of rationing, which few people realise came in towards the end of the First World War. We get into it later with Thomas trying to make money out of the black market, but it would have been nice to begin it here. In fact, rationing arrived in the last year of the war, in January 1918, and it lingered until being gradually phased out, item by item, between December 1919 and March 1921. Still, I suppose we felt that the Thomas plot would give it to us.

6 EXT. BATTLEFIELD. DAY.

Matthew is running through shot and shell. He sees a crater and dives for it. Two others are there; one of them is William.

> MATTHEW: Not much longer. One more push and then we go back.
> WILLIAM: Right, sir. I don't mind saying, I won't be sorry when this one's over.
> MATTHEW: Don't worry. We've been through so much. He won't fail us now.

But just then there is the sound of a shell. William, quick as a flash, covers Matthew with his body and throws him backwards.

> WILLIAM: Sir!

They are still falling when the shell explodes. In the thick smoke we can see that the third soldier is dead. Matthew is motionless, with William spread-eagled across him.*

7 EXT. DOWNTON. NIGHT.

The great house is quiet and at peace. But not for long. A man is running up to the front of the house. It's Molesley. He rings and hammers on the door when he gets there.

....

* Daisy and Mary's almost supernatural experiences are the kind of funny things that are difficult to explain, but do happen. Almost everyone has some similar tale, so I don't think we've gone into the realms of *The Sixth Sense*. My mother was crossing from England to Egypt in 1948 to join my father, who had been posted to the Embassy there, when my brother Rory, aged two, suddenly sat up in the middle of the night and said, 'Hello, Granddaddy.' The next day she learned that her father had died, back in London, at exactly that moment, so we must surely agree with Hamlet that 'there are more things in heaven and earth, Horatio, than are dreamed of in your philosophy'. Anyway, it is clear that something terrible has happened. To make Matthew's injuries believable, which we come to shortly, he had to fall on a hard surface, but just putting a rock behind him didn't seem to make the point. We could hardly fling him over a cliff, so, if you look carefully, you can see a hard wheel that he is blown directly onto by the force of the explosion.

8 INT. CORA'S BEDROOM. DOWNTON. NIGHT.

O'Brien, in her night clothes, is shaking Cora awake.

O'BRIEN: M'lady, m'lady, wake up.*
ROBERT: What on earth —?
O'BRIEN: You'd better come downstairs.

9 INT. SMALL LIBRARY/HALL. DOWNTON. NIGHT.

MOLESLEY: I didn't know what else to do when I saw the
telegram. I knew it was urgent, so I hope it was right.
ROBERT: Quite right. Mrs Crawley won't mind my opening
it. The main thing is, he's not dead. Not yet, anyway.

Mary is standing, hands over her mouth, white as a sheet.

SYBIL: When did it happen?
ROBERT: It looks like Monday or Tuesday.
SYBIL: Sometimes they wait to see which telegram they
should send.
ROBERT: They've patched him up. They're bringing him to
the hospital in Downton, which shows someone has their
wits about them.
CORA: When do they think he'll get here?
ROBERT: It doesn't say.
CORA: But how do we contact Isobel, how will she get
back?
ROBERT: One thing at a time. I'll ring the War Office in
the morning.
CORA: Maybe they know she's out there. Perhaps she's
with him now.
ROBERT: They wouldn't have sent a telegram here, and
she'd have rung. No, it's the usual balls — usual mess
up, I'm afraid.

....

*The lady's maid was always the one who was sent into the shared bedroom.
For some reason, it was thought acceptable that a lady's maid would see the
master of the house in his dressing gown quite often, or indeed in his
pyjamas, when she brought in the tea in the morning. But it was not
acceptable for the valet to see the mistress of the house in her nightdress.
And so, whenever they were both going to be in the room, only the maid
went in. If a message or some midnight rousing was necessary, it would
definitely have been the maid who was given the job.

At the door, Carson stands in his dressing gown.

CARSON: Beg pardon, m'lord, but we're all very anxious to know the news…
ROBERT: Yes, of course.

He strides to the door. Most of the staff is in the hall.

ROBERT (CONT'D): It appears that, a few days ago, Captain Crawley was wounded. It's serious, I'm afraid, but he's alive and on his way home, to the hospital in the village.
MRS HUGHES: Where there's life, there's hope.
DAISY: What about William? Is he all right?
ROBERT: I'll find out what I can tomorrow. I'm not sure there's much more we can do tonight.
BATES: William's father would have had a telegram if anything had happened.
EDITH: I'll drive over in the morning.

The servants are going back to bed. The family is all in the hall now and Cora, Edith and Sybil start upstairs.

MARY: Whatever you discover, tell me. Don't keep anything back.

Robert puts an arm around his daughter's shoulder.

ROBERT: I'm afraid this will put paid to wedding talk for the time being.

She takes a moment to understand his words.

MARY: What does that matter?*

10   EXT.   KITCHEN COURTYARD.   DOWNTON.   DAY.

Bates is cleaning shoes and boots. Anna comes out.

....

* Mary, being engaged to one man and in love with another, is at the very centre of her own dichotomy. The concealment of this has been possible as long as everyone was fine. But, obviously, it gets much harder for her to hide her feelings as Matthew's fortunes take a turn for the worse. In the previous episode, when Matthew was missing, she started to give herself away, and now we are going to test her to the full.

ANNA: Lady Edith's back. William was caught in it. He's gone to some hospital in Leeds. She took his father to the station.

BATES: I'm very sorry.

ANNA: We might have known. We couldn't be the only household left untouched.

BATES: Will he come through it?

ANNA: Her ladyship said it sounded bad, but we don't know more than that. Can you walk with me to the church this afternoon?

BATES: If you want me to.

ANNA: Because I'd like to say a prayer for them. For both of them. I know you don't believe in any of it —

BATES: You're quite wrong. Since I met you, I believe in everything.

11   INT.   DOCTOR CLARKSON'S OFFICE/PASSAGE.   DAY.

Violet and Edith are with Clarkson.

CLARKSON: We only cater for officers.

VIOLET: Doctor Clarkson, I am no Jacobin revolutionary. Nor do I seek to overthrow the civilised world. We just need one bed for a young man from this village.

CLARKSON: And if it were within my power, you should have it.

VIOLET: Sir, you don't understand. William's father cannot afford to leave his farm and move to Leeds.

CLARKSON: I'm very sorry. Really. But this is a military hospital, and it's not up to me to challenge the order of things.

EDITH: I'll nurse him. I'm happy to do it. It wouldn't add to your workload.

CLARKSON: If I were to break the rule for you, how many others do you think would come forward to plead for their sons? The answer is, and must be, no.*

....

* This is a typical *Downton* argument, where hopefully you're on both sides. It would be completely impossible for Clarkson to waive the rule for the big house, while refusing to accommodate everyone else, but of course Violet thinks he's being outrageous.

12   INT.   HOSPITAL PASSAGE.   DOWNTON VILLAGE.   DAY.

As Violet and Edith emerge into the passage.

VIOLET: It always happens when you give these little
people power. It goes to their heads like strong drink!

13   INT.   SERVANTS' HALL.   DOWNTON.   DAY.

Thomas is with O'Brien, at a table laid for tea.

THOMAS: I'm sorry for him. I am. I don't mind Captain
Crawley. He's a better man than most of them.
O'BRIEN: And William, too. He's not a bad lad, whatever
you say. He should've had his life ahead of him… I wish
I'd not written that letter to Bates's wife, telling her
he's back here.
THOMAS: What's that got to do with it?
O'BRIEN: I wish I'd not done it, that's all. What with
everything else going on. I know she'll come up here and
make trouble.
THOMAS: Don't blame me. It wasn't my idea.*

Daisy arrives with the tea things. Others start to drift in.

O'BRIEN: Any news?
DAISY: Only that the doctor won't let William come to the
village.
O'BRIEN: He never.
DAISY: It's for officers only, he says. So William's got
to stay among strangers in Leeds.

Mrs Patmore has arrived with a cake.

....

* I've tried to set up O'Brien as someone who is malicious and a
troublemaker, but not black-hearted through and through. And this is one
moment where she realises that her desire to make trouble for Mr Bates,
which is all it is, has made her act on it at an inappropriate time. The
household also hears from Thomas an expression of solidarity with William
in this scene, which surprises them. But it doesn't surprise me, because I
think in war your fundamental solidarities come to the fore. I always
remember my mother saying that when you were in the bomb shelters you
were all in it together, in a way that was quite novel, really, and quite moving,
too.

MRS PATMORE: And his poor father staying there with him, spending money he's not got and travelling miles to do it.
DAISY: It's not right.
THOMAS: No, it bloody well isn't.

The others are rather surprised by this intervention.

THOMAS (CONT'D): Well, I'm a working-class lad and so is he, and I get fed up seeing how our lot always get shafted.*

14 INT. SMALL LIBRARY. DOWNTON. DAY.

Robert is with Cora.

ROBERT: They say they'll get her onto a boat when they can.
CORA: But does she even know yet?
ROBERT: They think so, but they're not sure. And Matthew's already in England. He must have been mid-Channel when the telegram was sent.
CORA: Then he'll be here today?
ROBERT: Today or tonight… The story is that William saved him. Apparently he threw himself across Matthew just as it went off. He sheltered him from the force of the blast.

....

* The village hospital is for officers, just as Downton Abbey is an officers' convalescent home. This is no more than the truth. As we have observed before, there was an absolute divide between the officers and the men, enforced because of the philosophy that the private soldiers needed to see every officer as someone slightly separate in order to follow their commands. This is not because all the officers were public school boys. By 1917 that would be quite untrue, since a great many men had been promoted from the ranks into being officers. But no sooner were they promoted than they were immediately absorbed into the officer culture, quite deliberately. This led to that inter-war and post-war phenomenon of the ex-Army 'temporary gentlemen', so called as a rather nasty play on their former rank as 'temporary officers' – the golf club secretary, or the forgotten major in a Terence Rattigan play, who'd be dressed in a blazer with shiny buttons and sporting a Jimmy Edwards moustache. In time, he would become an iconic English social type, and, for me anyway, is possessed of a considerable poignancy.

CORA: All the more reason for him to be treated here. If only Doctor Clarkson would see reason.

ROBERT: He just won't. Everyone's tried. No, we shall have to come at it from a different direction.

15   INT. MARY'S BEDROOM. DOWNTON. DAY.

Mary is putting together some books and some sewing.

MARY: I thought I'd take some things down to the hospital. Then I can wait and sit with him when he arrives.

ROBERT: But we don't know when that'll be.

MARY: It doesn't matter. I can make myself useful while I'm waiting. I've read somewhere that it's very important not to leave them alone when they're first wounded, so no sign goes unnoticed. They can't spare a nurse to watch over every man, so that's what I can do.

ROBERT: Your mother's written to Lavinia.

MARY: Good. Yes. I'm glad someone's thought of that. She must stay here and not be at Isobel's by herself.

Robert is very moved by this proof of his daughter's love. He stares at her. But he cannot find the right thing to say.

MARY (CONT'D): What?

ROBERT: Nothing.*

....

* Of course, Mary simply wants to be with Matthew. She's in love with him. But she can't say that, not to her father, and not to herself, so she has to give a sensible reason for why she's going to the hospital. She may even believe that's why she's going, but her father, of course, knows better. His saying that Cora has written to Lavinia is to remind Mary of the real situation, which is that Matthew is engaged to someone else. I don't think it's unloving; what he wants is to spare her, to prevent her going in over her head and finding herself in a very difficult situation. He wants to protect her from herself, really. I thought Hugh Bonneville played this scene very well.

16 INT. CHURCH. DOWNTON VILLAGE. DAY.

Bates and Anna are alone in a pew.

BATES: You should've had a church wedding.

ANNA: Don't be silly.

BATES: No, I mean it. You in a white dress, me looking like a fool, and little girls with flowers in their hair. You ought to have had that.

ANNA: I'd rather have the right man than the right wedding. Besides, my God's more understanding than the vicar's. He doesn't hold it against you when you try to do your best.*

BATES: Well, it won't be long now.

ANNA: How long?

BATES: Hard to say, but don't worry. The Decree Nisi means we're safe. The Decree Absolute's only a formality. I'm just sorry it cost so much.

ANNA: She could've had my shoes and the shirt off my back, if it would only make her go away for good.

BATES: She's gone now.

ANNA: I suppose I could feel guilty in my happiness, knowing the troubles they're all facing back at home. But in another way, it only makes me more grateful. Let's pray. Even if you don't believe, let's pray together.

And as we watch from the back of the empty church, we see them kneeling, side by side.

....

* This trim saddened me as, by losing Anna's line, we lost their philosophical difference. The truth is that Anna is a Christian, while Bates is an atheist, and, for me, her dialogue was an expression of what she was bringing into his life that had been missing before. Not simply religion in the traditional sense, but the belief in something more, the idea of something beyond. He has been so miserable that he's shuttered his life, and she is prising open the windows.

But before we all burst into tears, I should perhaps note the many times when we were all in agreement about what should go and what should stay. That is the norm in fact, I am happy to say.

17 INT. KITCHEN. DOWNTON. DAY.

Daisy is with Mrs Patmore.

MRS PATMORE: Don't worry. The old lady'll sort something
out, now she's got the bit between her teeth.
DAISY: I'm not worried. Not in that way. I feel sorry
for William, that's all.
MRS PATMORE: Well, of course you do. We all do. I
expect you're glad now, that you let him have his little
daydream.
DAISY: I'm not glad. I feel I've led him up the garden
path with all that nonsense, and I'm ashamed… I'm so
ashamed.

To Mrs Patmore's dismay, Daisy starts to cry into her apron.

MRS PATMORE: Oh. Ssh.
VERA (V.O.): Hello?

Daisy looks up with tear-stained eyes. Vera Bates is there.

MRS PATMORE: Mrs Bates, isn't it? Well, what do you
want?
VERA: Don't sound inhospitable, Mrs Patmore. When I've
only ever known a welcome in this house.

18 INT. OUTER HALL. DOWNTON. DAY.

Violet is on the telephone, watched by Edith.

VIOLET: Hello? Hello? I want to speak to the Marquess
of Flintshire. Yes, that's right. Yes, yes — the
Minister… Well, how many Marquesses of Flintshire are
there?

She turns back to Edith in exasperation.

VIOLET (CONT'D): Is this an instrument of communication
or torture?

But it seems to have done the trick.

VIOLET (CONT'D): Hello, Shrimpie? Yes, it's Aunt Violet. Yes, very well, very — yes. And Susan? Good… Good — I won't beat about the bush, dear. Whom might we know on the board of Leeds General Infirmary?*

19 INT. SERVANTS' HALL. DOWNTON. DAY.

Mrs Hughes is going through a ledger book when Thomas enters.

THOMAS: What are you doing in here? It's not like you to join the hoi polloi.
MRS HUGHES: I've lent my sitting room to Mr Bates… I don't suppose you know why Mrs Bates has chosen to pay us a visit?
THOMAS: I might do. But it wasn't my fault.
MRS HUGHES: So if it wasn't Scylla, it was presumably Charybdis.
THOMAS: You say the nicest things.

20 INT. MRS HUGHES'S SITTING ROOM. DOWNTON. DAY.

Bates and Anna sit opposite Vera.

VERA: Excuse me, it is not settled. It wasn't settled by me that you'd come back here and take up with your floozy again. As far as I recall, that was never settled.

....

* Violet is totally at ease with the idea of pulling strings. She's not embarrassed by it. Why should she be? Her kind had been governing the country for a thousand years. Naturally, they have connections at the top of anything. It may be a cousin, or someone's husband, or someone's cousin's husband. And, with some selective letter writing, she'll find out who could help. In a way, I hope we're conveying the hypocrisy of our modern response to this sort of thing. We disapprove of it, but only until it's in our own interests, or in the interests of someone we love.

Shrimpie is a real name, but in my life it belongs to a woman. The four daughters of our friends Roddy and Tessa Balfour are called Willa, Tuppy, Jubie and Shrimpie, in that classic upper-class nickname way, which I wrote about in *Snobs*. As I have said before, I have mixed feelings about the use of nicknames in adulthood, but I like all these young women, and I am very fond of their parents, so I unashamedly stole Shrimpie's name for a character who is much more fully developed in the Christmas Special at the end of Season Three.

ANNA: How did you find out he was here?

VERA: Wouldn't you like to know?

BATES: What does it matter? Just say what you want. Spit it out.

VERA: You thought you'd got the better of me. But you were wrong.

BATES: I never —

VERA: I'm going to sell my story anyway. About Lady Mary, about the Turkish gentleman, about Miss Smith, here —

ANNA: It's got nowt to do with me.

VERA: Well, that's not what I've heard.

BATES: You gave your word. I gave you the money and you gave me your word.

VERA: Well, guess what? I was lying. I signed no contract. You've no proof.

He looks carefully at this bitter, furious woman.

BATES: If I hadn't come back to Downton, back to Anna, would you have stuck to our agreement?

VERA: Well, we'll never know now, will we?

BATES: You're angry because I'm happy.

VERA: Maybe. But you won't be happy long.

She stands and gathers up her handbag.*

....

* Maria Doyle Kennedy continued to be marvellous, and layered and interesting, in her performance as Vera. When you arrive in an established series, and everyone else has had time to develop their character, and you have to join that troupe and yet not allow your work to look thinner than theirs, it is a real test that some actors pass better than others, but I thought Maria was superb. She came in at precisely the same weight as Brendan Coyle's Bates, so that you had an equal tennis match going, right from the start.

Personally, I believe that when Bates asks, 'If I hadn't come back to Downton and back to Anna, would you have stuck to our agreement?' Vera's true answer would be 'Yes'. She is angered by him; she sees him as taking her for a ride, taking her for a fool. Why should she make all the sacrifices when he is sacrificing nothing? I hope the audience sees that because, while I don't think it exactly justifies her position, you do begin to understand her point of view.

21 EXT. STABLEYARD. DOWNTON. DAY.

Sybil comes out to Branson, who is polishing the car.

SYBIL: Can you drive me to the hospital?
BRANSON: Aren't you needed here? I've already taken
Lady Mary down.
SYBIL: I know. I want to be with her when Captain Crawley
arrives. They can manage without me here for a while.
BRANSON: Is she still in love with him?
SYBIL: I don't want to talk about it.
BRANSON: Why? Because I'm the chauffeur?
SYBIL: No. Because she's my sister.
BRANSON: You're good at hiding your feelings, aren't you?
All of you. Much better than we are.
SYBIL: Perhaps. But we do have feelings. And don't make
the mistake of thinking we don't.

She climbs into the car and he closes the door.*

22 INT. KITCHEN. DOWNTON. DAY.

Daisy is working with Mrs Patmore.

DAISY: No, I'm not going.
MRS PATMORE: What do you mean, you're not going?
DAISY: What I say.
MRS PATMORE: Don't you want to see him? Don't you want
to learn how he is?
DAISY: Of course I do, but I don't want to give him any
more false hopes. I feel bad enough as it is.
MRS PATMORE: Here's a poor lad, mortally wounded maybe,
and you don't want to give him any faith to go on?
DAISY: That's not what I said. But if I go to him now,
he'll think…
MRS PATMORE: What he's every right to think.

....

* What I hope the audience senses here is that Branson's tone is changing towards Sybil, and hers is changing towards him. When Sybil says she doesn't want to talk about whether Mary is still in love with Matthew, it is not because Branson is the chauffeur, but because 'she is my sister'. She is not putting him in his place in the sense of reprimanding a servant, but putting him in his place as a social equal. From anyone, his curiosity would be impertinent. Already, as they talk about hiding feelings and the rest of it, they have moved beyond the roles of servant and mistress.

But Daisy won't budge. Mrs Hughes comes in.

MRS HUGHES: Lady Edith's in the hall. She's asking if
Daisy's ready to leave.
MRS PATMORE: Nearly ready, aren't you, dear?
DAISY: No. I'm not ready and I'm not going!

She slams down a bowl and runs out. *

    23 INT. LEEDS GENERAL INFIRMARY. DAY.

*William lies in a bed in this full ward. An elderly man sits
by him. A little way away, Edith and Violet talk to a doctor.*

VIOLET: And has Lord Flintshire's order been acted on?
DOCTOR: It has. There's an ambulance waiting, although
no one quite knows how you managed it.
VIOLET: What exactly is the matter with him?
DOCTOR: He's suffering with hypoxic decompensation due to
his pulmonary barotrauma. There'll be multi-organ
failure as his creatinine rises.
VIOLET: Was that in English?
DOCTOR: His body's sustained too much damage. He cannot
recover.†

....

* I was sorry this scene with Daisy and Mrs Patmore went, but I'm afraid we just didn't have room enough to keep it. Daisy's conundrum, which of course we play out, is that she has allowed William to think she's his girlfriend as he goes off to the war, and she's been encouraged in that by Mrs Patmore, who's poked her into it, and will therefore have to take some of the blame. This is another *Downton*-esque situation, because we don't blame Mrs Patmore. William was a young man going off to the front, and to have a girl to write to and think about would maybe make a difference and get him through it. So I don't feel anyone's in the wrong, but I do understand why Daisy feels trapped.

† The majority vote had it that this diagnosis was too arcane to play out in a drama, but I was sad to see it go, because it gave the real reason why William is dying. As it is, all you get is that he's sustained 'too much damage', which doesn't seem enough information to me. My doctor friend, Alasdair Emslie, came up with hypoxic decompensation due to pulmonary barotraumas, which, had it been articulated, would maybe have made the public aware that this is a real, if rare, condition. Actually, as I write that, I'm not sure how many people would have taken it in. I suppose I was just anxious that William should not die like Little Nell in *The Old Curiosity Shop*, without anything very specific being given as the cause.

VIOLET: But he looks so normal. Pale, of course, and weak, but not wounded.
DOCTOR: Appearances can be cruelly deceptive. The force of the blast has fatally injured his lungs.
EDITH: But if he's lived this long —
VIOLET: Would it make any difference if he stayed here or are you just making him as comfortable as can be?
DOCTOR: That's it. There's nothing more we can do for him.
VIOLET: So you agree with our plan?
DOCTOR: I don't know about you, but I'd rather die in a familiar place, surrounded by familiar faces.

Violet gives a sign to silence him as the old man arrives.

VIOLET: There you are, Mr Mason. Seems we have everything settled, and we'll be away before too long.
MASON: He'll be forced to do better, if we can just get him back to where he knows. I feel sure of it.
DOCTOR: I shouldn't —
VIOLET: I shouldn't worry too much. We'll know much more when he's rested.
MASON: I'm very grateful, m'lady. To both of you.
EDITH: Never mind that. Let's get him ready.

She takes him off, leaving Violet alone with the doctor.

VIOLET: See, sometimes, we must let the blow fall by degrees. Give him time to find the strength to face it.*

24 INT. HOSPITAL. DOWNTON VILLAGE. DAY.

Mary, in an apron, is tidying a bed. Sybil is working with her. There is a noise and Clarkson appears.

CLARKSON: Right, they're here.
SYBIL: May I stay to settle him in?

....

* Although Violet is a law unto herself, in many ways she is also a good psychoanalyst. Here, the doctor wants to tell Mr Mason that it's over, that his beloved son is dying. But Violet knows the old man has got to get there in his own time. She wants to start him off with the notion that William is very ill, and only gradually take him to the point where he can accept that the boy is going to die, which I think is a correct analysis of what's required in this situation.

CLARKSON: Very well. I'll let them know.

MARY: I want to help, too.

CLARKSON: Lady Mary, I appreciate your good intentions, but I'm concerned that Captain Crawley's condition may be very distressing for you. Might I suggest that you hang back until the nurses have tidied him up a little?

MARY: I'm not much good at hanging back, I'm afraid. I won't get in your way, I promise, but I will stay. You have volunteers, don't you? Well, that's what I am. A volunteer.

He might have argued further, but the door opens.

CLARKSON: All right. Everyone to their posts.

SYBIL: *[To Mary]* You stand there.

The stretcher bearers carry in four men. Sybil and the other nurses obviously know the drill. We hear 'Yes, this gentleman, second in.' 'Yes, doctor.' 'Number two. Nurse Crawley, here.' 'Yes, just here. Gently, gently, gently.' As a stretcher is carried past, Sybil comes over and bends down. The stretcher bearer bends to lift him. Mary steps in. Together the three of them get Matthew onto a bed.

SYBIL: *[To Mary]* Take him under his feet. Cousin Matthew? Can you hear me?

But Matthew is unconscious, his face covered in tiny cuts.

STRETCHER BEARER: He is breathing, but he's not been conscious since we've had him. They filled him full of morphine.

SYBIL: Thank you.

The man leaves as Mary sees a luggage label tied to Matthew's wrist. She reads it.

SYBIL (CONT'D): What does it say?

MARY: 'Probable spinal damage.' What does that mean?

SYBIL: It could mean anything. We'll know more in the morning.

But in fact, together, they absorb the enormity of the words.

SYBIL (CONT'D): What's this doing here?

Pinned on Matthew's coat is a bag containing Mary's rabbit.

MARY: I gave it to him, for luck. He was probably
carrying it when he fell.
SYBIL: If only it had worked.
MARY: He's alive, isn't he?
SYBIL: I should wash him. Molesley brought some pyjamas.
This bit can be grim. Sometimes we have to cut off the
clothes they've travelled in. And there's bound to be a
lot of blood.
MARY: How hot should the water be?
SYBIL: Warm more than hot. And bring some towels.

Mary nods and goes to fetch them. *

END OF ACT ONE

....

* One of the important elements here is that Mary takes orders from Sybil, because I believe that, when things get really serious, other rivalries and histories diminish. What gave me the idea for this scene was an incident years ago in Sussex, when I was driving home on a country road after a dinner party. I saw a car parked, and a woman slumped over the wheel, so I pulled over and went to find out if she was all right. 'Blub-blub-blub, I've taken pills,' said the woman; 'my husband's left me' and all the rest of it. She was clearly sinking into unconsciousness, so I hauled her out of her car and into my own, and drove into Lewes. It was about one in the morning and I had no idea where to go. That was when I saw a young man walking along the pavement. I stopped and wound the window down, and asked him where the nearest hospital was. Hearing my voice, he turned to me with a whistle, 'Oh, la-di-da,' he said, and started to imitate the way I speak. So I said, 'Look, I haven't got time for all that now, there's a woman here who's taken an overdose.' He immediately snapped back into the situation, saying: 'Oh, right. Christ. You go down here, you take the second left, and it's on your right,' and I shot off. I have often thought that it was such a good example of how people are capable of telling serious from not serious. His class war became irrelevant as soon as he realised this woman was in real trouble. Here, Mary would not normally take orders from Sybil, but in this instance Sybil knows what she's doing, and Mary does not. So she just says, 'How hot should the water be?' and so on.

ACT TWO

24A EXT/INT. DOWNTON. DAY.

Daisy watches anxiously as William is brought in on a
stretcher.

25 INT. SERVANTS' STAIRCASE. DOWNTON. DAY.

Thomas and O'Brien are together.

THOMAS: You should never have told her Bates was here.
O'BRIEN: Don't I know it? And she was even worse after
she'd seen him than before, ranting on about a scandal
that would bring the roof down on the House of Grantham.
Silly mare.
THOMAS: What scandal?
O'BRIEN: I could make a guess, but I'd rather not.
I thought she'd just come up and take a bite out of
Mr Bates. That's what it sounded like.
THOMAS: Then you should have asked more questions. You
know what they say: 'The devil is in the detail.'
O'BRIEN: Well, I'm not standing by while she brings
misery and ruin on my lady.
THOMAS: You started it.
O'BRIEN: Oh yes, you're very important, aren't you? Very
know-it-all. With all of us at your beck and call.
THOMAS: I'm sorry if you're angry, but don't take it out
on me. You did it.

26 INT. SMALL LIBRARY/HALL. DOWNTON. DAY.

Clarkson is with Robert, Violet, Cora, Edith, Carson, Thomas
and Mrs Hughes. We can hear the ping pong next door, which
means the row must be conducted in whispers and hisses.

ROBERT: But why? If one of the servants were ill, you
wouldn't turn them out of doors because they don't hold
officer rank.
CLARKSON: William is not a servant now. He is a private
soldier.
CORA: A wounded private soldier in an army convalescent
home.

CLARKSON: But he is not a convalescent. He is a dying man. So, once again, I'm expected to break the rules. Then Lady Grantham commandeers an ambulance, no doubt leaving dead and dying by the roadside to do it —
VIOLET: Well, it can go back and get them now.
CLARKSON: And who is to look after him? Because Nurse Crawley is already fully occupied —
EDITH: I am. I'm going to do it.

The irate doctor turns to the manager.

CLARKSON: Sergeant, were you told about this?
THOMAS: I was.
CLARKSON: Why didn't you send for me?
THOMAS: Because I don't see why William shouldn't come here.
CLARKSON: This is a home for officers!
CARSON: Downton is William's home, too. We all have the right to be cared for in our own home.
CORA: I agree. And that settles it.
CLARKSON: Well, I can see I'm fighting a losing battle. But it is very hard, Lady Grantham, to find myself, time and again, defending decisions to my superiors that I have not personally taken.

With a brisk nod, he marches out. Robert looks at Edith.

ROBERT: I hope you really can look after him, after all that.
EDITH: I think so. No, I'm sure I can.*

As the meeting breaks up, Cora speaks to Mrs Hughes.

....

* We toyed with the idea of putting William in the hospital, but that seemed to me to be too unrealistic. The family does control the house, even if it does not control the hospital, so there was really only one option, if they were going to take him away from Leeds and bring him home. After all, there isn't any treatment to be given other than a hot cup of tea and someone to hold his hand. We've already established that, so there would be no reason not to have him there.

CORA: Oh, Mrs Hughes, we've had a letter from Major
Bryant. He's coming back to see his old companions on
Thursday. We're all so distracted, so can you make sure
he's looked after? Give him tea or something.
MRS HUGHES: Certainly, m'lady.

27   INT.   MRS HUGHES'S SITTING ROOM.   DOWNTON.
DAY.

Mrs Hughes is busy packing a basket when Carson looks in.
She stops and stands, blocking it from his view.

CARSON: Lady Sybil telephoned. Captain Crawley's been
brought in. I thought you'd like to know.
MRS HUGHES: Thank you. How is he?
CARSON: Still alive. I think that's about as much as she
could say. Lady Mary's down there as well.
MRS HUGHES: It's not like her to get her hands dirty.

He gives her a look, but does not go on with it.

MRS HUGHES (CONT'D): Miss Swire arrives from London
tomorrow.
CARSON: Does she, indeed? Miss Swire.
MRS HUGHES: I've put her in Tankerville. It's quiet and
she'll need what sleep she can get, poor soul.
CARSON: How's William?
MRS HUGHES: They're settling him in now. I'll take
something up in a minute.
CARSON: Doctor Clarkson isn't any happier about it.
MRS HUGHES: We've a funny way of showing our gratitude in
this country.

28   INT.   MARY'S BEDROOM.   DOWNTON.   NIGHT.

Anna is getting Mary ready for bed.

MARY: Whom is she going to sell it to?
ANNA: She didn't say. Just that there was nothing we
could do to stop her. Mr Bates has given her every last
penny to keep her quiet, but she's tricked him, and now
he's got nothing left to bargain with.
MARY: Well, we both know what I must do.
ANNA: But how can you ask Sir Richard for help without
telling him the truth?

MARY: I'd rather he heard it from my lips than read it over his breakfast.

ANNA: Suppose he won't do anything? Suppose he throws you over?

MARY: That's a risk I'll have to take. I'll go up to London tomorrow afternoon. It's a request that demands to be made in person.

ANNA: What about Mr Matthew?

MARY: Captain Crawley's out of danger and Miss Swire will be here to keep him company. I think I can take some time off to save my own neck.

ANNA: They're saying downstairs that he won't walk again.

MARY: It looks like that.

ANNA: It's very hard on Miss Swire. To spend her life behind a wheelchair.

MARY: I suppose so. Although God knows there's nothing I'd rather do.

She smiles sadly, as if this were a joke. Anna looks at her.

ANNA: Don't ask Sir Richard, m'lady. Don't put yourself in his power.

MARY: Let's not pretend I have a choice.*

29 INT. WILLIAM'S ROOM. DOWNTON. NIGHT.

William sleeps. Edith is tucking him in and generally tidying up. William's father and Mrs Patmore are with her.

EDITH: Why don't you go home now, Mr Mason, and we'll see you tomorrow.

....

*The business of newspapers latching onto these things seems very topical, and since we filmed this the Leveson Inquiry and the phone-tapping scandal have only underlined that. There is something strange when the newspapers decide to attack you, as I know, because I've lived through it. They just get you in their sights, and bang. And, lest we forget, we didn't invent sensationalism. Those late-Victorian rags would print drawings of people being shot or knifed, and cheerfully blacken reputations for the sake of selling an extra copy. When Mary is caught in the grip of this culture, the only person she knows to appeal to would obviously be Richard Carlisle. As I have said, he is not modelled on a specific man, but he is an example of that kind of new newspaper baron who had entered society at the end of the nineteenth century.

MASON: Are you sure you don't mind sitting up with him?
EDITH: He won't be alone. Not for a moment, I promise.
MASON: He looks so perfect, lying there.

He is almost overcome with sorrow as he goes.

MRS PATMORE: But he does look perfect. Are you sure
they've got it right?
EDITH: I'm afraid so. If only I weren't.*

30   INT. HOSPITAL. DOWNTON VILLAGE. DAY.

*Robert and Lavinia approach the bed, which is hidden behind
screens. Robert opens the screens to see Clarkson gently
examining Matthew's spine. He is lying on his side with his
back exposed, while a nurse and Mary look on.*

CLARKSON: Can you feel that?
MATTHEW: Mm.
CLARKSON: What about that?
MATTHEW: No.
CLARKSON: And that? Hm? Nothing at all?

Mary comes out and kisses Lavinia in greeting.

LAVINIA: Do they know any more yet?
MARY: They're examining him now.
LAVINIA: So he's conscious?
MARY: Just about. We'll go in as soon as they're
finished.
ROBERT: Have they found out what happened?
MARY: They were in a crater when a shell landed near
them. The explosion threw Matthew against something
sharp; a rock, a fallen tree…
ROBERT: Go on.

....

* A wonderful actor plays Mr Mason, Paul Copley, whom I've been a big fan
of for years and years. He has that curious dimension of truth in his work
that I find very moving. I remember seeing him in something when I was
young and I thought he was going to be a star. In fact, he should have been –
a star character actor, like Richard Griffiths or Ben Kingsley. Happily, my
enthusiasm for his work was shared by our perspicacious casting director,
Jill Trevellick, so she invited him to make what would be a very significant
contribution to *Downton*.

MARY: Doctor Clarkson thinks there may be trouble with
his legs.

*Lavinia gasps and Robert puts an arm round her as Clarkson
emerges from behind the screens. He draws them away.*

CLARKSON: Not good news, I'm afraid. There appears to be
extensive crushing of the sacrum and lumbar regions.
ROBERT: What's the prognosis?
CLARKSON: It's early days, but I'd say the spinal cord
has been transected, that it is permanently damaged.
ROBERT: You mean he won't walk again?
CLARKSON: If I'm right, then no, he won't.

Lavinia bursts into tears.

CLARKSON (CONT'D): It's a shock, of course, and you must
be allowed to grieve. But I would only say that he will,
in all likelihood, regain his health. This is not the
end of his life.
MARY: Just the start of a different life.
CLARKSON: Exactly. Lord Grantham, I wonder if I might
have a word?

He takes Robert to one side. Mary stays with Lavinia.

LAVINIA: Have you got a handkerchief? I never seem to
have one in moments of crisis.
MARY: Here.
LAVINIA: Thank you.

Out of the women's hearing, Robert looks shocked.

ROBERT: You mean there can be no children?
CLARKSON: No anything, I'm afraid.
ROBERT: But isn't there a chance that might change?
CLARKSON: The sexual reflex is controlled at a lower
level of the spine to the motor function of the legs.
Once the latter is cut off, so is the former. He will
also be permanently incontinent.*

*With sorrow, Robert looks over to the young women. Lavinia
has pulled herself together. She straightens her shoulders.*

LAVINIA: Right.

*She walks forward as the nurse opens the screens. Mary would
follow, but Robert holds her back slightly.*

ROBERT: Give them a moment together.

Mary nods. She's very calm as they step back from the lovers.

MARY: What was Clarkson saying?
ROBERT: Nothing to worry you about.†

....

*The doctors in England were obliged to work with the diagnoses that had been arrived at in the field hospitals, and the business with the labels and so on is all true. A diagnosis would be made and written on a label, which would then be tied to the patient, who'd be sent to a hospital, either in France, or over the sea to England. Here, we have a situation where Matthew's spine is very, very bruised, which would render him paralysed for a period, but the doctors at the front believe the spine has been broken, and it is correct that the symptoms would be the same. All of this happened in real life. So I confess I was rather irritated when the newspapers started to suggest that we were saying his spine had been severed but somehow, miraculously, he managed to walk again. Obviously we never said any such thing, and I can only suppose that the journalists concerned were displaying their usual indifference to truth and never actually checked what had happened in the show. There were, in fact, several instances where doctors at the front, working under the most severe and difficult conditions, did mistake extreme spinal bruising for transection. I'm not pretending it was terribly common, but it certainly happened. And what Clarkson doesn't want to do is to suggest that it might be bruising when the likelihood had to be that the spine was severed. He felt it would be cruel to give Matthew false hope, and I'm with him on that one.

This is where Mary has to deal with the fact that Matthew is going to be crippled, and we are fairly explicit that there will be no more sexual activity for him. You do see dramas where the suggestion is that men can be paralysed, but still be sexually active. This is not true; certainly it was not true during the First World War, and we try to make that clear. Of course, this being *Downton*, we don't draw diagrams.

† Part of this kind of drama is deliberately putting people into a situation where the audience will know more about what the characters are going through than the other characters will. So, you engineer uncomfortable meetings, and then you let the audience fill in the detail. That's what we do here, when Lavinia arrives. Robert has nothing against Lavinia, and he and Mary treat her as the fiancée uncomplicated, when the audience knows it's not as simple as that.

Matthew watches Lavinia approach and lifts his hand to greet her.

MATTHEW: My darling.

31 EXT. COUNTRY TOWN. DAY.

Mrs Hughes gets off a bus with two covered baskets. She walks down a side street of this strange town. She arrives at a very humble cottage and knocks. Ethel opens the door.

32 INT. ETHEL'S COTTAGE. DAY.

Ethel is unpacking the baskets, while Mrs Hughes bends over a little baby in his makeshift cot.

MRS HUGHES: If he could only see the child.*
ETHEL: He won't. I've written again and again. I've offered to bring him to any place he wants.
MRS HUGHES: I wasn't going to tell you this, but he's coming on a visit this week. To see his old pals.
ETHEL: Help me, Mrs Hughes. Let me come to Downton and show him the baby.
MRS HUGHES: Most certainly not. I won't allow that.
ETHEL: Then ask him to meet me. I know he'd listen to you. I'll give you a letter. One more can't hurt. Make him read it in front of you —
MRS HUGHES: I'll do no such thing.

....

*The Ethel story was useful to me, because I like to remind people that not everyone was living at Downton's level of comfort, even as a servant; that, in this world, there were many levels beneath the protected Downton life, as there are today. The majority had a tough deal, and some had a very tough deal indeed. Also, what's important for quite a few stories is to remind the generation under thirty-five that sexual freedom risked pregnancy, and, in those days, an unwanted pregnancy ruined lives. Modern young producers tend to believe that there was always lots of sexual activity between unmarried people but they just hid it, when this is quite untrue, because there was too much at stake. Obviously, there were people who slept together, and there were illegitimate children – Ethel's son is one of them – but, on the whole, the abyss that opened beneath your feet if you got pregnant when you were unmarried, in any class, was bottomless. And you need the audience to know that in order for them to understand some of the other characters' reactions. But of course we also wanted a plot that gave us a bit of a rest from the war.

ETHEL: But please.

MRS HUGHES: He'd say it was none of my business, and he'd be right. Besides, don't think I approve of what you've done, because I don't.

ETHEL: Haven't you ever made a mistake?

MRS HUGHES: Not on this scale, no, I have not. Sorry to disappoint you.

ETHEL: So you won't do anything?

MRS HUGHES: I'm feeding you out of the house. Quite wrongly, I might add. I've a good mind to stop that.

ETHEL: Now I'm the one who's sorry.

Mrs Hughes starts to tidy up the baskets…

MRS HUGHES: I'll take the letter and see that he gets it. But that's all I'll do.

33   INT.   BEDROOM PASSAGE.   DOWNTON.   DAY.

Mrs Patmore is almost dragging Daisy.   They come to a halt.

MRS PATMORE: Now, go in.

DAISY: I don't know what to say.

MRS PATMORE: It doesn't matter. He's dying. Just say nice, warm, comforting things. Make him feel loved. You don't have to be Shakespeare.

DAISY: But —

Mrs Patmore has opened the door and pushed her inside.

34   INT.   WILLIAM'S ROOM.   DOWNTON.   DAY.

Edith is with William, who's awake but weak, as Daisy comes in.

WILLIAM: Here she is. Come over here, where I can see you.

She sits by the bed and takes his hand.

WILLIAM (CONT'D): By 'eck, it were worth it, if I get to hold your hand.

DAISY: Don't be daft.

WILLIAM: I've never slept in a room as big as this. Where are we?

EDITH: At the end of the south gallery. Now, take this.

WILLIAM: Any news of Captain Crawley?

Edith gives Daisy a quick glance as she takes back the spoon.

EDITH: He's doing much better. Thanks to you. We're all so grateful.

This cheers William and he gives a smile to Daisy.

WILLIAM: Dad'll be here in a bit. Can you stay for a minute?
DAISY: I ought to go down… It's not fair on Mrs Patmore.
EDITH: She won't mind.
WILLIAM: Because… I did want to ask you something…
Daisy, would you ever marry me now? And not wait for the end of the war, like we said?
EDITH: You mustn't worry about all that for the moment now, William. You're here for rest, not excitement.
DAISY: That's right. There's no need to worry about it now. First, let's get you better.
WILLIAM: But would you think about it?
DAISY: I must go. They'll be sending out a search party soon.

She stands and hurries to the door, then looks back.

DAISY (CONT'D): Just rest.*

35 INT. MRS HUGHES'S SITTING ROOM. DOWNTON. DAY.

Mrs Hughes is with a woman, Jane Moorsum, in her thirties.

MRS HUGHES: It would be very unusual.
JANE: I know that. Of course it would. But I believe I could make it work.
MRS HUGHES: And if your child were ill?
JANE: My mother knows what she's doing. She's brought up five of her own.
MRS HUGHES: Even so…

....

* Now we have the proposal that Daisy has dreaded, and what makes it worse is that nobody's in any doubt that William is dying. So, for Daisy, there isn't really any reason not to take this lie to the finishing line. But she is torn, honourably torn, I would say, between the desire to make him happy at the last, and the need for there to be truth between them before he dies. Should she go on with the lie and be kind? Or should she let him die, knowing the truth and miserable?

JANE: And they're only in the village.

MRS HUGHES: I'll discuss it with Mr Carson. There's nothing wrong with your references, but of course they are from before you were married.

JANE: I'm a good worker. And I must earn.

36 INT. HOSPITAL. DOWNTON VILLAGE. DAY.

Matthew is asleep. Mary is with him.

MARY (V.O.): Matthew? Matthew?

He opens his eyes.

MATTHEW: Hello.

MARY: Are you feeling a bit less groggy?

MATTHEW: A bit. Where's Lavinia?

MARY: She's gone back to unpack. She came straight here from the station. She'll take over this afternoon. I have to go up to London.

MATTHEW: How's William? You know he tried to save me?

MARY: He isn't too good, I'm afraid.

He nods, accepting this.

MATTHEW: Any sign of Mother?

MARY: Not yet, but I'm sure she's making her way back by now.

MATTHEW: Has the doctor said anything else?

MARY: Oh, this and that. You've taken quite a hammering.

MATTHEW: I certainly have.

For a moment, he looks puzzled.

MATTHEW (CONT'D): I've still got this funny thing with my legs. I can't seem to move them. Or feel them, now that I think about it. Did Clarkson mention what that might be?

MARY: Why don't we wait for Lavinia, and then we can all talk about it?

MATTHEW: Tell me.

MARY: And you've not even been here for twenty-four hours. Nothing will have settled down yet.

MATTHEW: Tell me.

She can't get out of it. So she is quite straightforward.

MARY: He says you may have damaged your spine.

MATTHEW: How long will it take to repair?
MARY: We can't expect them to put timings on that sort of thing.
MATTHEW: But he did say it would get better?
MARY: He says the first task is to rebuild your health, and that's what we have to concentrate on.

Of course he understands what she is saying.

MATTHEW: I see.
MARY: And he says there was no reason why you should not have a perfectly full and normal life.
MATTHEW: Just not a very mobile one.

They stare at each other for a moment.

MARY: Would you like some tea? I would.

She stands. As she goes, he speaks. His eyes are full.

MATTHEW: Thank you for telling me. I know I'm blubbing, but I mean it. I'd much rather know. Thank you.
MARY: Blub all you like. And then, when Lavinia's here, you can make plans.

She walks away briskly. Tears are pouring down her cheeks.

END OF ACT TWO

ACT THREE

37 INT. LIBRARY. DOWNTON. DAY.

Mrs Hughes approaches Bryant, who is with a group of invalids.

BRYANT: What was going on through there? It sounded as if Doctor Clarkson was getting it in the neck.
MRS HUGHES: I'm sure it was nothing.

Bryant rolls his eyes and they all laugh.

MRS HUGHES (CONT'D): Major, might I have a word?

This is a surprise to all of them, but Bryant rises politely.

BRYANT: What is it?
MRS HUGHES: I have something for you.

They are standing apart and speaking softly. He smiles, but when he sees the writing he doesn't take the envelope.

BRYANT: Thank you.
MRS HUGHES: I wish you would read it.
BRYANT: Do you know who wrote it?
MRS HUGHES: Yes. I do. And I know how anxious she is for an answer.
BRYANT: With due respect, I don't believe it's any of your concern.

She steps in closer and lowers her voice even further.

MRS HUGHES: If you'd only — if you'd only see the child. He's a lovely wee chap —
BRYANT: Mrs Hughes, the last thing I'd wish to be is rude, but in this case I really must be left to my own devices. Now, I'll say goodbye. It's time I was making tracks.

She is forced to accept this. She can do no more.

MRS HUGHES: Goodbye, then, Major.*

38   INT. CORA'S BEDROOM. DOWNTON. NIGHT.

O'Brien is getting Cora ready for bed.

O'BRIEN: She's a thoroughly nasty woman and I can't think why Mr Bates married her in the first place.
CORA: But what did her threat consist of?
O'BRIEN: Only that she's got hold of some story and she's planning to publish it in the newspapers.
CORA: What story?
O'BRIEN: I think it was… something about Lady Mary. Will that be all, m'lady?

....

* Major Bryant, in a way, is rather a heartless character, but on the other hand, I'm afraid the world is full of heartless men who sleep with women and then don't want to hear from them again. It is really only his later death that makes the predicament of the child interesting.

Of course O'Brien knows much more than she is saying. Cora's veins run with ice. Robert enters, in a dressing gown.

CORA: Thank you, O'Brien. I can manage now.

The maid leaves.

CORA (CONT'D): Robert, did Mary say why she had to go to London all of a sudden?
ROBERT: I gather it was something she wanted to discuss with Carlisle… I ought to try and start calling him Richard. He keeps asking me to.
CORA: She didn't say what?
ROBERT: Nope. But she seemed to think it was urgent. Wedding stuff?
CORA: Is there any more news on Isobel?
ROBERT: She's on her way back. They're just waiting for a boat to put her on. At least she knows he's safe and… She knows everything…

His voice cracks slightly and she looks at him.

ROBERT (CONT'D): I can't really talk about him yet, or I'll start to cry.
CORA: He's alive, Robert. He'll be healthy in every other way —
ROBERT: Not, I'm afraid, in every other way. Clarkson says… there can never be any children.
CORA: Oh, no… How tragic.

He is too upset to elaborate.

CORA (CONT'D): So maybe Mary will be better off in the long run.
ROBERT: Don't ever say that to her. Or anything like it.

39 INT. SIR RICHARD CARLISLE'S OFFICE. LONDON.
DAY.*

Mary is with Carlisle in this grand, important room. There is a silence between them as he reviews what he has heard.

CARLISLE: Who'd have thought it? The cold and careful Lady Mary Crawley. Well, we know better now… I'm surprised you haven't given me some extenuating circumstances.
MARY: I have none. I was foolish and I was paid out for my folly.
CARLISLE: And when I've saved you, if I can, do you still expect me to marry you? Knowing this?
MARY: That's not for me to say.
CARLISLE: Things have changed a bit, though, haven't they? Of course we both know that, if we marry, people, your people, will think you've conferred a great blessing on me. My house will welcome the finest in the land, my children will carry noble blood in their veins.

She looks at him. They are quite well matched, these two.

CARLISLE (CONT'D): But that won't be the whole story, will it? Not any more.

Mary stands. Her manner is, if anything, more severe.

MARY: Sir Richard, if you think it pains me to ask this favour, you'd be right. But I have no choice if I am not to be an object of ridicule and pity. If you wish to break off our understanding, I'll accept your decision. After all, it's never been announced. We may dissolve it with the minimum of discomfort.

....

* When I saw the edit of this scene, after Special Effects had completed the view from the window, I had a problem with Carlisle's office, because it looked across a roofscape – to tell us, I suppose, that we were in London. But, while a modern senior newspaper executive might have his office on the fortieth floor, it would have been most unlikely in the pre-highrise 1910s and 1920s. On the whole, they would have been in very grand rooms on the first floor, looking out over other grand façades across the road. I tried to have it changed, so that Carlisle was looking across to some very important-looking buildings on the other side of a wide thoroughfare, but for some reason it was more complicated than that. I forget why. I'm afraid I still feel that a 1910s press baron in the attic is not what is commonly known as believable.

CARLISLE: Forgive me. I don't mean to offend you. I am simply paying you the compliment of being honest. You know, in many ways, if I can manage to bring it off, this will mean we come to the marriage on slightly more equal terms. I think that pleases me.

She has lowered herself and she knows it, but...

MARY: So you'll do it.
CARLISLE: I'll try to do it, yes.
MARY: You must act fast.
CARLISLE: I'll send a car for her as soon as you've left. I have the address from the favour before this one.

She holds his glance, then nods and goes to the door. *

MARY: Please let me know what it costs. I'll find a way to reimburse you.
CARLISLE: Never mind that. As my future wife, you're entitled to be in my debt.

40   INT.   SMALL LIBRARY.   DOWNTON.   DAY.

Carson is with Robert.

CARSON: We've a bit of a conundrum, m'lord. As you may know, we're short of a housemaid...

....

* This scene alters the relationship between Richard Carlisle and Mary, because it changes the terms of their deal. Up until now, Carlisle has known that Mary was attracted to him because he's very rich, and very powerful, and she is bringing to the marriage her noble birth and her social position. He will enter a level of society, and more importantly his children will be born into a level of society, that he would not have been able to reach without her help. In a sense, Mary is the giver, because she could probably get another rich man to marry her if she didn't marry Carlisle. But the revelation of her past and the fact that she is not undamaged goods means that, in a sense, he is now doing her a favour by going ahead with the arrangement, making it a much more equal exchange. When the series went out, the audience on the whole decided Carlisle was a villain, but I don't agree. He's quite straightforward, and he always tells the truth with Mary. Nor is he in the least ashamed of his own origins. All of that, to me anyway, makes him quite an attractive fellow. Added to which, he is very successful, so he can't be a fool.

ROBERT: I suspect this is something for her ladyship.

CARSON: Her ladyship is very busy and I wanted your opinion. We've had an application from a local woman, Jane Moorsum. But she is married and she has a child, a son.

ROBERT: So she wants to work part-time?

CARSON: Not exactly. She wants to leave him with her mother in the village. And visit him when she has time off.

ROBERT: But surely her husband should —

CARSON: She is a widow, m'lord. The late Mr Moorsum died on the Somme. There's no other earner, so she has to look for work. I said I would ask you.

ROBERT: Well, if Mrs Hughes agrees, I think we must do what we can for the widows of our defenders.

CARSON: Very good, your lordship.

As he leaves, Cora comes in to look for a paper on the desk.

CORA: What was that?

ROBERT: We're taking on a new maid.

CORA: He should have talked to me, not you.

ROBERT: They thought you were too busy to be bothered with it.

CORA: Well, I am busy and that reminds me: I can't come with you to the Townsends. You'll have to make some excuse.*

ROBERT: But we gave them the date.

CORA: I'm sorry. I can't help it. We've got a big intake next week and I have to be clear where we're putting them all. You'll think of something. Ah.

She's found what she was looking for. Robert is alone again.

41   INT.   KITCHEN.   DOWNTON.   DAY.

Mrs Patmore is with Daisy, speaking softly in the corner while the other kitchen workers move around them.

DAISY: You always said I wouldn't have to marry him when it came to it.

....

* I spelt Townsend without an H, so there could be no mistake in the pronunciation, but in real life the name is spelt with an H, i.e. Townshend, or it is with this family, who are neighbours of ours in Dorset. They were very kind to us when we first arrived there, and they are friends to this day.

MRS PATMORE: Daisy, he's dying. What difference does it make?
DAISY: All the more reason. I can't lie to him at the end. Don't make me be false to a dying man.
MRS PATMORE: What matters now is the poor lad knows some peace and some happiness before he goes.
DAISY: I can't.*

42 INT. HOSPITAL. DOWNTON VILLAGE. DAY.

Matthew is with Lavinia.

LAVINIA: What? Why would I have second thoughts? Don't be ridiculous.
MATTHEW: But there's another part to this.
LAVINIA: What part? I don't care if you can't walk. You must think me very feeble if you believe that would make a difference.
MATTHEW: I know it wouldn't, and I love you so much for saying it. But there is something else, which may not have occurred to you. Something which I only learned today.

She waits, nervous but determined.

MATTHEW (CONT'D): The thing is, we could never be… This is very difficult… We can never be properly married.
LAVINIA: What? Of course we can be married.
MATTHEW: Not properly. There would be no chance of children…

This is a shock to her, which she had not expected.

LAVINIA: Oh. I see.
MATTHEW: That's why I have to let you go.
LAVINIA: But that… side of things. It's not important to me. I promise.
MATTHEW: My darling, it's not important now. But it will be and it should be. I couldn't possibly be responsible for stealing away the life you ought to have.

....

* This is another classic *Downton*-ism, because we understand both why Daisy is uncomfortable letting him die in a lie, but at the same time we understand Mrs Patmore's thinking. She is only trying to give William some comfort before his death.

LAVINIA: I won't leave you. I know you think I'm weak
and I don't know what I'm taking on.
MATTHEW: How could you? For God's sake, I'll be wearing
nappies 'til I die.
LAVINIA: I'm not saying it'll be easy for either of us.
But just because a life isn't easy doesn't mean it isn't
right.
MATTHEW: Your father would hate me and I wouldn't blame
him.
LAVINIA: You leave my father to me.
MATTHEW: I won't fight with you. But I won't steal away
your life. Go home. Think of me as dead; remember me as
I was.*

....

* This is an emblematic scene, hopefully reminding the audience that a hell of
a lot of young men, and women, too, had to go through this kind of thing.
We like them both, because they are striving to be unselfish. Lavinia says it
doesn't matter that Matthew can never be a proper husband, while he says it
does matter, and he can't marry her. He is right, of course, and I hope I
would have the strength to do the same, but the point is, they are both
behaving honourably.

I had an aunt – well, a cousin of my grandfather's – whom I knew very
well as an old lady. I was extremely fond of her, but I was always haunted by
her story. She had been engaged to a man before the war, but he was severely
shell shocked and had a complete mental collapse. He went mad, really.
What was terrible to me was that both his and her family told her that she
would be letting the side down if she didn't go through with the marriage,
and that it was unpatriotic, and unfair to the poor boys at the front, even to
think of getting out of it. So she married him, under extreme pressure – all of
which I heard from her sister, not from her – and then he was killed about
two years later, so it was over fairly quickly. But the months of her marriage
were of such horror that she never looked at another man, never had a child,
never had anything. I always thought it was incredibly insensitive and
irresponsible of both families not to understand. I think that still, even
though there was a rather poignant postscript. When she died, I was
presented with the handbag she'd taken into hospital, and in it were her
purse, her keys, one or two other things, and a photograph of her husband.
So I suppose that, once he was dead, she was able to remember the man he'd
been before the war, the man she'd loved, and to forget the changeling. But
how tragic.

43 INT. GARAGE. DOWNTON. DAY.

Branson is reading a newspaper when Sybil appears.

SYBIL: Mary's telephoned. She'll be on a late train. It gets in at eleven.

BRANSON: All right. How's William?

SYBIL: It's so sad. Edith's taking care of him, but there's nothing to be done. We're waiting, really. What with that, and Matthew… What is it?

BRANSON: They shot the Tsar. And all of his family.

SYBIL: The children, too? How terrible.

BRANSON: I'm sorry. I'll not deny it. I never thought they'd do it. But sometimes the future needs terrible sacrifices. You thought that, once.

SYBIL: If you mean my politics, you know we've agreed to put that to one side until the war is won.

BRANSON: Your lot did, but Sylvia Pankhurst was all for fighting on.*

SYBIL: Oh, don't badger me, please.

BRANSON: Sometimes a hard sacrifice must be made for a future that's worth having. That's all I'm saying.

She knows only too well what he means.

SYBIL: If only it could be simpler.

BRANSON: Well, it can't be simple, but it can be real. That's up to you.

For a moment it is almost as if she might kiss him. But then she turns and walks away.

44 INT. SIR RICHARD CARLISLE'S OFFICE. LONDON. DAY.

Vera Bates is with Carlisle. She is determined not to be taken for a fool, so she is very strong in her manner.

CARLISLE: You understand it would have to be exclusive? I couldn't have you peddling different versions of the story to my competitors?

....

* Here we refer to the split in the suffragette movement, with Mrs Pankhurst saying one thing, and her daughter Sylvia saying another. I am always glad that most of the movement agreed to get behind the war effort, even if the others did not.

VERA: Of course I understand. But I can't help it if
they pick it up once you've published it.
CARLISLE: Indeed you can't. No more can I. But I would
control the timing... You'd have to sign a binding
contract to that effect. Today.
VERA: I expected that.
CARLISLE: And I warn you, I am unforgiving when anyone
breaks a contract with me. One word out of place and
you'd find yourself in court.
VERA: I expected that, too. But I'm curious: how did you
hear about me?
CARLISLE: I know everything that goes on in this city.
VERA: And what's the hurry?
CARLISLE: I'm a newspaper man. When I hear of something
good, I have to make sure of it straight away. I'm sorry
if I rushed you.
VERA: That's all right.
CARLISLE: You must dislike the Crawleys very much to want
to subject them to trial by scandal.
VERA: My husband works for them. We're not on good
terms.

He stands, holding out his hand.

CARLISLE: We have a deal, then.*

END OF ACT THREE

....

* Where we were very lucky with this story is that, by casting Iain Glen and
Maria Doyle Kennedy, we were in no danger of having any drop in energy.
They have the same energy, the same watchability, in their performances as if
you were watching two of the running characters you've followed in the series
from the beginning. That is entirely down to their both being very talented
actors. There's no mystery to it.

ACT FOUR

45 INT. KITCHEN/PASSAGE. DOWNTON. NIGHT.

Mrs Hughes arrives with a tray, which she gives to Daisy.

MRS PATMORE: How is he?

MRS HUGHES: His father's with him now and he seems to understand the situation.

MRS PATMORE: Poor man.

MRS HUGHES: Daisy, William's asking to see you.

DAISY: I can't go. Don't make me go.

MRS PATMORE: Do you care so little for him?

DAISY: It's not that. I'm very fond of William and I'm very sad. But I've led him on and led him on and made him think things that aren't true.

MRS PATMORE: But he wanted them to be true. He was happy to think they were true.

DAISY: That doesn't make it all right.

MRS HUGHES: Shall I tell him you won't come?

Faced with this, Daisy knows she must go. We follow Mrs Hughes out into the passage. She passes Anna and Bates.

BATES: He ought to know. It's bad enough that I've kept it a secret so long.

ANNA: Wait until Lady Mary gets back.

BATES: It's not right to keep him in ignorance about his own daughter.

ANNA: And is it right to break his heart?

46 INT. WILLIAM'S ROOM. DOWNTON. NIGHT.

Daisy comes in. William is with his father. He sees her.

WILLIAM: Will you leave us a moment, Dad?

The older man nods and retreats.

DAISY: There's no need to make him leave.

WILLIAM: There is a need. Come here.

Reluctantly, she takes a chair. He reaches for her hand.

WILLIAM (CONT'D): You know I'm dying?

DAISY: You don't —

WILLIAM: I'm dying, Daisy. I'm not going to make it and I don't have long… That's why you've got to marry me.

DAISY: What?

WILLIAM: No, listen. You'll be my widow. A war widow with a pension and rights. You'll be looked after. It won't be much, but I'll know you've got something to fall back on. Let me do that for you. Please.

DAISY: I can't. It would be dishonest. Almost like cheating.

WILLIAM: But it's not cheating. We love each other, don't we? We'd have married if I'd got through it, and spent our whole lives together. Where's the dishonesty in that?

Daisy catches Edith's eye in the corner. What can she say?*

47   INT.   BEDROOM PASSAGE.   DOWNTON.   NIGHT.

Daisy comes out of the door. Mr Mason is waiting there.

MASON: He's asked you, hasn't he? I knew he would. You'll do it, won't you?

DAISY: I don't think he should be bothering about it now.

MASON: What else should he be bothered with? You're the most important thing on earth to him, Daisy. You wouldn't disappoint him, would you?

DAISY: Suppose the vicar won't do it? He may want to wait 'til William's well enough to go to church.

MASON: But that time's not coming, is it?

It breaks his heart to say it. Daisy does not reply.

....

* A very important element, I believe, in the success of *Downton* is that we give equal weight to the running characters. But part of that is giving emotional stories to both groups, family and servants, that are equally complicated. We don't, I hope, ever suggest that the emotional stories of the servants are any less involving or easier to resolve than the upstairs ones. This episode is an example of that. The two big emotional stories of the week concern Mary dealing with the idea that Matthew will be permanently disabled, and Daisy having to deal with William's proposal. The audience must watch these two played out in parallel, giving them both the same attention. Now Mr Mason has arrived, and his job is to get Daisy to do what his son wants.

MASON (CONT'D): And don't worry about the vicar. I walked over to old Lady Grantham's on my way here. She'll sort it out.

48 INT. HALL/STAIRCASE. DOWNTON. NIGHT.

Carson lets Mary in as Robert comes into the hall.

ROBERT: There you are. What a marathon. Did you get it said? Whatever it was you went up for?
MARY: Oh, yes.
ROBERT: Why was it so urgent?
MARY: It wasn't. Well, it was in a way… D'you know, I think I'll go straight to my room. I'm absolutely dead.
CARSON: I'll send Anna up, m'lady. She can bring a tray in case you're hungry.
MARY: I'm fine. I ate on the train.
CARSON: No, you ought to have something. Just in case.

He leaves them alone. She starts to walk to the staircase.

ROBERT: I wish he coddled me half as much as he coddles you… Did you hear about the Tsar?
MARY: Every newsboy was shouting it all over London. Sometimes it feels as if the whole world is closing down.
ROBERT: Maybe our world is.
MARY: How's Matthew?
ROBERT: No change to report. Lavinia was with him for most of the day.
MARY: And William?
ROBERT: Bad. Clarkson says it won't be much longer.
MARY: So he's talking to you again.
ROBERT: Just about… Apparently William wants to marry the little kitchen maid. Before…
MARY: Why?
ROBERT: Well, it seems they were going to get married after the war. He says he wants her to be looked after.
MARY: I hope the Government does look after the war widows, but I rather doubt it… Poor William.
ROBERT: I'm not at all sure Mr Travis will allow it. You know what a fusspot he is. Granny says she'll talk to him tomorrow.
MARY: Well, I know who my money's on. Goodnight.

She walks up the last bit of the staircase and along the passage, when she hears weeping. She stops outside a door.

49 INT. LAVINIA'S BEDROOM. DOWNTON. NIGHT.

Lavinia is sitting up in bed, in tears. She looks up when Mary comes in. She tries to cover for herself.

MARY: Lavinia?

LAVINIA: You're back. How did you get on?

MARY: All right, I think. How about you?

LAVINIA: Matthew's told me to go home. He says he won't see me again. He feels he has to 'set me free', as he put it. I've tried to tell him I don't care, but he won't listen.

MARY: Then you must keep telling him.

LAVINIA: Yes, but you see, it isn't just not walking… Today he told me we could never be lovers, because all that's gone as well. I didn't realise. It's probably obvious to anyone with a brain, but I didn't realise.

MARY: No. No. Nor did I.

LAVINIA: And he feels it would be a crime to tie me down — to tie down any woman — to the life of a childless nun. He thinks I'd hate him in the end.

She breaks off. Mary is quite still and silent.

LAVINIA (CONT'D): I'm sorry if I've shocked you. But there's no one else I could talk to about it, and when you came in —

MARY: I'm not shocked. I'm just stunned, and desperately sad. Are you sure it wouldn't make a difference?

LAVINIA: Not to me. I'll die if I can't be with him.

MARY: No, I see that. I do see.*

....

* Mary is obliged to comfort Lavinia, which is quite deliberate. As I have said elsewhere, it was important to me that Mary should not have any excuse to dislike Lavinia, and nor should the public. Maybe she isn't as interesting a woman as Mary. We never feel that Matthew is wrong to be more in love with Mary (which he always is), but Lavinia is a kind and generous woman who really loves him, and that makes it all more complicated.

50 INT. DINING ROOM. DOWNTON. DAY.

Robert is at breakfast, reading a paper, with Edith and Mary.

ROBERT: Good God almighty!

EDITH: What is it?

ROBERT: 'The engagement is announced between Lady Mary
Josephine Crawley, eldest daughter of the Earl and
Countess of Grantham, and Sir Richard Carlisle, son of
Mr and the late Mrs Mark Carlisle of Bryanston Square,
London.' Is this why you went to see him? Why didn't you
say it'd be in today's paper?*

MARY: I didn't know.

ROBERT: Well, surely he asked your permission?

MARY: I don't think asking permission is his strongest
suit.

ROBERT: That's very high-handed. You can't let him get
away with it.

EDITH: Well, it's done now.

Carson is hovering.

ROBERT: What is it?

CARSON: William's wedding, m'lord — If it can be arranged
for this afternoon, the indoor staff would like to
attend.

ROBERT: We don't yet know if Mr Travis will agree to do
it.

CARSON: I'm afraid he has very little time to make up his
mind.

ROBERT: Of course.

CARSON: Will there be anyone from the family?

MARY: Sybil's on duty, and I'm going down to the hospital
after lunch, I'm afraid. I've promised now.

EDITH: I'll be there. I'm going up now.

CARSON: Very good, m'lady.

....

* For this announcement we had to fix what Richard Carlisle's background
was, and we decided he should come from the aspirant middle class, where he
would have absorbed their work ethic. I originally put his parents into
Bryanston Square, in London, but Iain Glen is clearly Scottish, and why
would they have come south? Carlisle wasn't Scottish in the original script,
hence Bryanston Square, but once Iain had been cast, then it became
Morningside, in Edinburgh, which seemed about right.

He goes. Edith looks at the others.

EDITH: Let's pray Granny bends the vicar to her will.

51 EXT. DOWER HOUSE. DAY.

A vicar in late middle age approaches the steps.

52 INT. DRAWING ROOM. DOWER HOUSE. DAY.

Violet and her visitor are enjoying a cup of coffee.

VIOLET: I seem to remember reading somewhere that God is
love.
THE REVEREND MR TRAVIS: God may be love, Lady Grantham,
but love does not conquer all. The Church has its rules
and we neglect them at our peril.
VIOLET: Surely the Church is sturdier than that? Rock in
Strength Upon a Rock?*
THE REVEREND MR TRAVIS: That's all very well. But this
boy is *in extremis*. How can we know that these are his
true wishes? Maybe the kitchen maid somehow hopes to
catch at an advantage?
VIOLET: And what advantage would that be?
THE REVEREND MR TRAVIS: I don't know. Some widow's dole
given by a grateful nation?
VIOLET: Mr Travis, can I remind you William Mason has
served our family well. At the last he saved the life,
if not the health, of my son's heir. Now he wishes,
before he dies, to marry his sweetheart.
THE REVEREND MR TRAVIS: Yes, but —
VIOLET: You cannot imagine that we would allow you to
prevent this happening in case his widow claimed her dole.
THE REVEREND MR TRAVIS: No, but —

....

*This is a line from a hymn, which is a favourite of mine. 'Who Is She Who
Stands Triumphant?' And the second line is 'Rock in Strength, Upon a
Rock'. The eponymous 'She' of the title is, of course, the Christian Church.
I remember singing it during a camping holiday in France when three of us
were jammed into a small army surplus tent. We had been hit by a
tremendous thunderstorm and had, literally, to hold onto the tent poles to
stop the whole thing from blowing away. We sang the hymn, very loudly, to
keep our spirits up, and we did survive, even though we were drenched to the
skin.

VIOLET: I have had an interest in this boy. I tried and
failed to save him from conscription, but I will certainly
attend his wedding. Is that an argument in its favour?
THE REVEREND MR TRAVIS: Of course, but —
VIOLET: Finally, I would point out your living is in
Lord Grantham's gift, your house is on Lord Grantham's
land and the very flowers in your church are from
Lord Grantham's garden. I hope it is not vulgar in me to
suggest that you find some way to overcome your scruples.

*Even the Reverend Mr Travis knows when he is beaten.**

53 INT. ETHEL'S COTTAGE. DAY.

Mrs Hughes attempts to comfort the crying woman.

MRS HUGHES: But you can't have expected much more? Not
when those letters all went unanswered.
ETHEL: I don't know what I expected, but you can't help
hoping.
MRS HUGHES: Have you found any work?
ETHEL: A bit of scrubbing. There aren't many places I
can take the baby.
MRS HUGHES: What do you tell them?
ETHEL: That my husband died at the front.
MRS HUGHES: It's funny. We have a new maid, Jane, who
really is a war widow, with a child, and we respect her
for it. But then, we believe her story.

....

* Michael Cochrane, who plays Travis, is a marvellous actor, but he never
really has enough to do in *Downton*. On the other hand, the Reverend Mr
Travis pops up every so often, so I hope that, even though he's better than the
part, it pays the VAT and gives him the odd nice day out in Oxfordshire. It
means a lot to us that, when Travis is going to have another wigging from
Maggie Smith or perform some service reluctantly for the family, Michael is
more than equal to the task. Travis has to deal with the Crawleys because his
living, like many livings then, would have been controlled by the Lord
Grantham of the day, which our generation would probably find rather
inappropriate. In fact, there are still livings that are allotted, even if these
days they're in the minority, and most families have made theirs over to the
Church to deal with. But under the *ancien régime*, people like Violet were
usually untroubled by the responsibility. They accepted the role God had
given them, and they thought they were the right people to do it. So, telling
this Minister of the Lord what his moral duty is doesn't trouble her one bit.

Which doesn't make things any better for Ethel.

54 INT.   SIR RICHARD CARLISLE'S OFFICE.   LONDON.
    DAY.

Vera is in a fury.   She flourishes a newspaper.

> SECRETARY: Mrs Bates, I really must insist —
> VERA: You tricked me! Well? Aren't you going to deny
> it?
> CARLISLE: Certainly not. I tricked you to protect my
> fiancée's good name.
> VERA: That's one word for her. I can think of a few
> others.
> CARLISLE: You'd better not speak them aloud if you know
> what's good for you.
> VERA: I don't want your money! I don't want that
> contract!
> CARLISLE: It's too late for that. And I warn you: if I
> so much as read her name in anything but the Court
> Circular, I shall hound you and ruin you and have you
> locked up! Is that clear?

This man is terrifying and even Vera is cowed.

> VERA: It doesn't end here, you know. Not for John Bates.
> Lady Mary might have got away, what do I care? But he
> won't. You tell him. If I go down, I'm taking him with
> me!
> CARLISLE: That's entirely your own affair.

*She stares at him for a furious moment, then storms out. He
smiles and picks up the telephone on his desk.*

> CARLISLE (CONT'D): Find Lady Mary Crawley for me.*

....

* In drama, people must have reasons for doing what they do. Now, that's not
true of everything one does in real life – sometimes there is no cogent reason
for our behaviour, particularly when we look back on episodes in our youth –
but drama requires a logic not always supplied by truth. It felt believable to
me that Vera would abandon her attempts to ruin Mary once Carlisle had
made it clear that, if she tried, she would ruin herself into the bargain. She
doesn't, after all, care about Mary. The only person she wants to see smashed
in pieces is Bates.

55 INT. SMALL LIBRARY. DOWNTON. DAY.

Robert is working when the door opens and Jane Moorsum comes in backwards, carrying two cleaning boxes.

> JANE: Where do we start?
> ROBERT: You tell me.

She spins round and stares at him in horror.

> JANE: Oh, your lordship, I — I do apologise. I thought Mrs Hughes said we were to clean in here.
> ROBERT: You must be the new maid.
> JANE: I am. Jane. And it's very kind of you and her ladyship to take me on.
> ROBERT: Not a bit. We all owe your late husband a great debt.
> JANE: Thank you.

This response has taken her by surprise and her eyes fill. Mrs Hughes appears in the doorway.

> MRS HUGHES: M'lord, there's a telephone call — Jane? Whatever are you doing? You're wanted in the drawing room, not the library, to clean it while the men are out of it.

Jane leaves, taking the cleaning boxes.*

> MRS HUGHES (CONT'D): She's very willing, but she's not quite there yet. I am sorry.
> ROBERT: Oh, don't be. What about that call?

Without his knowing it, his eyes follow the retreating maid.

> MRS HUGHES: For Lady Mary. They're waiting now.
> ROBERT: You might just catch her if you hurry. She's on her way to the hospital.

....

* I like the way that Mrs Hughes's reactions and thoughts are complicated. She's not a worshipper of the Granthams or the aristocratic system, as we've said before, but nevertheless she is quite a disciplinarian, and she doesn't like to walk in and find Jane, the housemaid, chatting to Robert. This isn't because a maid shouldn't talk to a Lord, it's not that; it's much more that this is not how a proper house is run, which Jane ought to know.

The housekeeper starts to move.

ROBERT (CONT'D): What about the melancholy wedding?
I gather it's settled.
MRS HUGHES: It is. We're holding it at four.

56 INT. HALL. DOWNTON. DAY.

Mary is just leaving when her mother appears.

CORA: Are you off to the hospital, dear?
MARY: I am.
CORA: I just wondered if you had any success in London…?
MARY: The announcement should have told you that I did.
Richard would never be willing to weather a scandal.
CORA: So the story's gone away? We won't hear any more
of it?
MARY: That would be a bold prediction, Mama, but I think
it's gone away for the time being, yes.
CORA: Thank the Lord.

57 INT. SERVANTS' HALL. DOWNTON. DAY.

*Daisy is dressed in her best, but miserable. Carson comes in
with a beautiful little posy of flowers.*

CARSON: His lordship asked Mr Bassett to bring these in
for you.
ANNA: Oh, how lovely. Here, Daisy, sit down.

*She takes a couple of small blooms out and starts to arrange
them in Daisy's hair. Mrs Patmore comes in, also in her
best.*

DAISY: I shouldn't be doing this. It's just a lie. You
know it is.
MRS PATMORE: You're doing it out of the goodness of your
heart.
DAISY: The falseness of my heart, more like.

At the other end, Thomas is whispering with O'Brien.

O'BRIEN: She's not quite the blooming bride.
THOMAS: I don't think it's the same when you're marrying
a corpse.
O'BRIEN: Are you going?

THOMAS: Why not? I wouldn't mind shaking William's hand before he goes.
O'BRIEN: Is that sentiment or superstition, in case he haunts you?

Anna pulls Daisy to her feet again as Mrs Hughes comes in.

MRS HUGHES: You look lovely, dear. Just to say the vicar is ready for us.
CARSON: Let's go up, then.

Daisy takes Carson's arm like a daughter, leading the way out.

58   INT.   MONTAGE.   THE WEDDING.   DOWNTON.   DAY.*

Mr Travis conducts the ceremony as the camera drifts over the faces.

THE REVEREND MR TRAVIS: Dearly beloved, we are gathered together here in the sight of God and to the face of this congregation to join together this man and this woman in holy matrimony, which is an honourable estate instituted of God in the time of man's innocency, signifying unto us the mystical union…

The servants, Violet, Edith… Some of them, including Carson, are in tears; some just pray. William looks at Daisy.

THE REVEREND MR TRAVIS: …If any man can show any just cause why they may not lawfully be joined together, let him now speak or else hereafter forever hold his peace. Have you the ring?

William's father hands over the ring and William places it on Daisy's finger. At the back, Violet, as straight as a ramrod, sits with Edith. Violet dabs her eyes discreetly. But when Edith squeezes her arm in sympathy, she whispers back:

....

* I didn't agree with the bed being covered in flowers – I felt it was sentimental, because it was a death bed as well as a wedding. But nobody else has ever objected, so I suspect I may be wrong about this. Certainly they all played the scene very well.

VIOLET: I have a cold.*

THE REVEREND MR TRAVIS: You may now kiss the bride.

William is too weak to lift his head from the pillow. Daisy bends to kiss him. He manages a feeble signature. Blessings are made.

59   INT.   HOSPITAL.   DOWNTON VILLAGE.   NIGHT.

Mary is with Matthew.

MATTHEW: She's better off in London.

MARY: If you say so.

MATTHEW: Do you know why I sent her away? The disgusting details as well as the pathetic ones?

MARY: I think so.

MATTHEW: Then you'll know I couldn't marry her. Not now. I couldn't marry any woman. I'd feel like a murderer.

MARY: And if they should just want to be with you? On any terms?

MATTHEW: No one sane would want to be with me as I am now. Including me… Oh God, I think I'm going to be sick.

MARY: Don't worry.

Mary seizes a bowl from the table nearby; as he throws up, she strokes the back of his head gently.

MARY (CONT'D): It's all right. It's perfectly all right.

MATTHEW: I think that's it.

He leans back as Mary wipes his mouth. He laughs.

....

*This moment was inspired by two stories of similar behaviour; one came from a cousin of Emma's, Simon Toynbee, who went to a funeral of someone he was very fond of and when he came out he was snuffling a bit, and he had a tear running down his cheek. His aunt, who was Emma's rather terrifying grandmother, Lady Broome, took one look at him, opened her handbag and brought out a handkerchief, saying, 'Here you are. I assume you have a cold.' When I heard the story, I thought at once that I would use it. The English upper classes have never festooned themselves with public emotion and, in those days even more than now, crying at a funeral was considered definitively middle class.

MARY: What is it?

MATTHEW: I was just thinking. It seems such a short time
ago since I turned you down. And now look at me. An
impotent cripple, stinking of sick. What a reversal.
You have to admit it's quite funny.*

*There is a slight movement across the ward. Isobel, in
travelling clothes, is standing in the shadows, watching.*

MARY: All I'll admit is that you're here, and you've
survived the war. That's enough for now.

*With a smile, she carries the bowl away. On the other side
of the room, she encounters Isobel.*

MARY (CONT'D): You're back. That is good news. He'll be
so pleased.

ISOBEL: You've become quite a nurse since I last saw you.

MARY: Oh, no. It's nothing. Sybil's the nurse in this
family.

She walks on as Isobel looks after her.

ISOBEL: It is the very opposite of nothing.

Then she goes towards Matthew's bed. He looks up.

MATTHEW: Mother? Is that you?

....

* Matthew's being sick was shot from behind and, when I looked at it, I was afraid we'd rather missed a trick. Originally, I had wanted the image to be much more, in modern parlance, *in your face*. This was really because I'm always interested in how, when people you love are very ill, all sorts of things become possible for you that in the normal way of things would be completely *im*possible. You can perform the most extraordinary, intimate and even disgusting tasks without really thinking about it. That is the power of love. I wanted Matthew's vomiting to be revolting, so that he would be ashamed, while Mary couldn't care less. Perhaps the director was afraid that the viewers might have been put off their pudding. And indeed they might have been. But anyway, that was supposed to be the message of the scene: the power of love.

60 INT. STAIRCASE AND GALLERY. DOWNTON. NIGHT.

Mary climbs the stairs wearily. As she reaches the landing, she sees Bates come out of Robert's dressing room.

  MARY: Bates, what's happened? How's William?
  BATES: He's nearly there, m'lady.
  MARY: I'm so sorry.

She turns away, but then remembers.

  MARY (CONT'D): Actually, Bates, I'm glad I've caught you.
  Sir Richard Carlisle telephoned me earlier. He says he's
  paid Mrs Bates for her story. She cannot speak of it now
  without risking prison.
  BATES: She won't do that.
  MARY: So I hope we can all forget it.
  BATES: It's forgotten already, m'lady.
  MARY: Thank you…

She hesitates.

  MARY (CONT'D): I'm afraid she was very angry when she
  knew she had been silenced.
  BATES: I can imagine.
  MARY: He says she made threats against you. 'If I go
  down, I'll take him with me.' That sort of thing. I'm
  sure she didn't mean it.
  BATES: Are you, m'lady?
  MARY: Well, you'd know better than I. Goodnight Bates.

As she goes, a door opens and Anna appears with a tray.

  ANNA: Lady Mary's back.
  BATES: I've just seen her. She says it's worked.
  Sir Richard has put a gag on Vera.
  ANNA: Thank God. So everything in our garden is rosy
  again?
  BATES: I hope so. I certainly hope so.

But he does not believe it. As they go their separate ways, Mrs Patmore enters the passage and heads for William's room.

61 INT. WILLIAM'S ROOM. DOWNTON. NIGHT.

Inside, Daisy sits on one side of the bed, holding William's hand, while Mr Mason is on the other. Mrs Patmore comes in.

MRS PATMORE: You must be so tired, my lamb. Why not let me take over for a while and go and lie down?
DAISY: No, thank you, Mrs Patmore. I'll stay with him. I won't leave him now. Not while he needs me.

But as she turns back to the face on the pillow, Mason speaks quite gently.

MASON: He doesn't need you no more, Daisy. He doesn't need none of us no more.

It is true. William is dead.

END OF EPISODE FIVE

EPISODE SIX

ACT ONE*

1 EXT. DOWNTON. DAY.

1918. Mary is pushing Matthew along the terrace in a wheelchair.

> MARY: I shall have muscles like Jack Johnson if I'm not careful.†
> MATTHEW: I'm strong enough to wheel myself.
> MARY: I'll be the judge of that.

She rests for a moment and Matthew looks round.

> MATTHEW: I keep thinking of William. How he should be here. Not exactly instead of me, but… sacrifice should be rewarded. He was the brave one.
> MARY: You were both brave. And I don't think we can say 'should' about things that happen in war. It just happens, and we should live with it.

....

* For this episode, we have a slight time jump. We don't have any ruling as to how much time has passed between episodes, or between series, for that matter. We do what we like, to be honest. We might, for example, begin a series four or six months later, so we can avoid funerals, and the initial stages of getting over someone's death. I say this because I always feel it is after about six months that you start getting back into gear. We return to this topic at a later date.

† I don't really understand why Michelle Dockery said 'arms' instead of 'muscles', which I originally wrote, but anyway that story comes from an experience of my grandparents – my mother's parents – who were once at an incredibly boring dinner party. Afterwards, they were sitting in the drawing room with this woman who was banging on about going to North Africa to get away for the winter, and she pulled up her sleeve and said, 'Just look at the colour I picked up,' and she pushed her arm under my grandmother's nose. At that moment, my grandfather, who was sitting next to his wife, suddenly woke up, saw the arm and shouted, 'By Jove! Jack Johnson!' because Johnson was a heavyweight boxer at that time. Of course, the woman was mortally offended, but the story always made me laugh, so I put it in as a memento of him.

2 INT. SMALL LIBRARY. DOWNTON. DAY.

Carlisle watches them from the window. Robert is with him.
Carlisle asks his question under his breath.

CARLISLE: Ought I to be jealous?

ROBERT: You won't ever have to be jealous.

He is aware of Edith reading. Now he raises his voice.

ROBERT (CONT'D): I'm sorry. What were we talking about?

CARLISLE: I was asking about Haxby Park. I'm taking Mary
over there tomorrow.*

EDITH: Our Haxby Park? Why? Are the Russells selling?

CARLISLE: Not officially. But I'm told they're open to
offers.

ROBERT: Sad. The Russells and the Crawleys have been
neighbours for centuries.

CARLISLE: They're not living there any more.

....

* For this sort of thing, I stare at maps of Yorkshire, and I try to avoid any place name that might land me in the soup, because I was caught out on *Titanic*. I wanted to call someone the Earl of Manton, and I put 'the Earl of Manton' into Google and clicked 'Search', and there was nothing, so I thought, well, good, that's safe. But in fact there was a *Lord* Manton. He just wasn't an earl. I should have known this actually, because his sister married a chap I was at school with, and you'd think that would have rung a bell, but it didn't. Anyway, sometime later I found myself at his house, where he was hosting, very charmingly, the wedding of a mutual friend. When we were alone, I said, 'Look, I'm most frightfully sorry, but I have actually put a couple into a series about the *Titanic* and they're called the Earl and Countess of Manton. They're terribly nice, you needn't be afraid that they're horrible, but I expect it will be a bit irritating.' In fact, he and his wife couldn't have been nicer, although, when the show aired, his mother was rather annoyed. So, now, when I want to invent someone, I type in 'the Earl of', 'the Duke of', 'Lord...' And it's only when I've drawn a blank on every possible alternative that I dare to put it into the script. With Haxby, I remember I found the village, and then I put in Haxby Park and Haxby House and Haxby Grove, and Haxby everything, until we knew we were safe. But, having said that, when this is printed there'll probably be a flood of letters.

ROBERT: It'll be strange for Mary. She's been going to that house ever since she was a little girl in a party dress.*

EDITH: We all have.

CARLISLE: There's nowhere better near Downton.

ROBERT: Well, Haxby's nice enough and very grand, of course. The shooting's good, or could be with a little money spent judiciously.

CARLISLE: I intend to spend a lot.

ROBERT: I'm not sure how comfortable it is.

CARLISLE: Well, it'll be comfortable when I'm finished with it. Central heating, modern kitchens, bathrooms with every bedroom. It's all possible.

ROBERT: Sounds more like a hotel.†

Carson opens the door. Clarkson is behind him.

CARSON: Major Clarkson.

CLARKSON: Good morning, Lord Grantham, Lady Edith, sir. We've had a request. A Canadian Major has asked to come here because of a family link with the house. We've taken officers from his regiment before, but I wanted to be sure you'd no objection.

For some reason, this interests Edith.

....

* That really came from a memory – I've never forgotten this – of a very old friend of mine. She was, in fact, the Countess of Gosford, and she was the person I named *Gosford Park* after. A wonderful, very interesting woman, Francesca Gosford was a great patroness of my youth. She told me a story about a party that someone had given for her, in a London park or a garden, or at any rate somewhere open. Suddenly, through the guests came this woman – a tramp, really – dressed in rags, with a dirty raincoat tied with string and a battered old hat. Anyway, she walked up, with everyone shrinking back slightly, and she said, 'Hello, Francesca, I hope you don't mind my coming.' To which Francesca replied that she was sorry, but she didn't remember who this woman was. So the new arrival gave her name, and she said, 'You used to come to my parties when I was a little girl.' And then Francesca remembered. That was the extraordinary thing. She could remember going to a great country house, to parties given for a spoiled, pretty little rich girl, and there was this dirty bag lady, sleeping in the doorway of the Underground. How time changes things. Anyway, that was a slight trigger for Robert's speech.

EDITH: What's his name?
CLARKSON: Gordon. Patrick Gordon. He was with Princess
Patricia's Canadian Light Infantry at Passchendaele.
Caught in a blast and burned rather badly, I believe.
ROBERT: Ah, poor fellow. Well, he's perfectly welcome.
I'm not aware of how we are connected, but you never
know.
CLARKSON: Sir.
EDITH: How strange he should be Patrick.
ROBERT: Yes. Yes, I suppose it is.

3 INT. SERVANTS' HALL. DOWNTON. DAY.

Anna, Bates, Jane and O'Brien are performing various tasks.

JANE: I've never worked in a house where a valet and a
housemaid were wed.
ANNA: It'll be unusual, I agree.
O'BRIEN: I hope it doesn't break us up. Having you two
set apart in a home of your own, all special. While the
rest of us muddle on for ourselves.
ANNA: You sound as if you're jealous.
O'BRIEN: Oh, I'm not jealous. I just don't want it to
spoil things.
BATES: Why? Because we've all been such pals until now?

....

† This line was inspired by a remark of my stepmother's father, who was
letting his house in Rutland, and he was halfway through arranging the
contract with an American woman when she said, 'Oh, and I'll put in a
bathroom for every bedroom,' and he immediately cancelled the whole thing.
Naturally, his wife was furious, because she was half-American and she loved
the idea of all these new bathrooms, so she asked why he'd done it. He
replied: 'I didn't want it turned into a ghastly hotel.' Another instance I
remember from my school days. I was in French Literature class with a chap
called Fenwick when he remarked that he'd 'just had a letter from my father,
and he's bought a new house for us in the country. He says it's got eight
bedrooms and six bathrooms.' Now, in those days, this was really wild;
practically no one had more than two for the family in that sort of house.
And I said, 'Wow, that's amazing.' And he said, 'I suppose so, but he's taking
three of them out.'

Daisy has brought some tea things. She sets them down and leaves without a word. The others exchange glances.

ANNA: Give her time.

4 INT. DRAWING ROOM. CRAWLEY HOUSE. DAY.

Isobel's having tea with Violet and Cora, served by Molesley. During the scene he clears it all away onto a tray.

CORA: Matthew's making such progress.
ISOBEL: I think so. But are we doing enough for him, for all of them, when it comes to rehabilitation? They're going to have to face a very different world after the war.
CORA: I agree, but they'll all be leaving Downton soon.
ISOBEL: Leaving?
CORA: Well, Turkey's about to capitulate and Robert says Vittorio Veneto will finish Austria.* So it's only a matter of weeks, even days, before it's over. We wouldn't send anyone home too soon, of course, but sometime in the New Year we will have our house back.
ISOBEL: So you want it just to be a private house again?
VIOLET: Well, shouldn't she? Or would you like to abolish private houses?
ISOBEL: Well, that life of changing clothes, and killing things and eating them… Do you really want it again? Wouldn't you rather Downton was useful?
CORA: But the house is useful. We provide employment, and —
ISOBEL: Oh, please, let me look into keeping it open as a centre of recovery. I could run it. The house could be so much more than it was before.
VIOLET: What about you, Molesley? Are you looking forward to this brave new world of Mrs Crawley's imaginings?
MOLESLEY: I'm glad of my job, m'lady, and I should very much like to hold onto it, with Mrs Crawley's permission.

He has opened the door and now he leaves. Isobel laughs.

....

* This is a real battle, one of the last in fact, which did take Austria out of the war, and that's why I used it. By this point, the whole thing was beginning to shut down.

ISOBEL: Servants are always far more conservative than
their employers. Everyone knows that.
VIOLET: Then I must be the exception that proves the
rule.*

5 INT. MRS HUGHES'S SITTING ROOM. DOWNTON. DAY.

*Mrs Hughes is packing food into a basket when she is
disturbed by Carson holding an envelope.*

CARSON: What do you think this means? 'I would be
grateful if you could come to my room when you have rung
the dressing gong. Richard Carlisle.'
MRS HUGHES: He wants you to check his tails.
CARSON: You don't like him much, do you?
MRS HUGHES: I think he's a hard man. But then she's a
hard woman, so I suppose they deserve each other.

His look admonishes her. Then he notices the basket.

CARSON: Who's that for?
MRS HUGHES: Oh. You know. One of my causes.

6 INT. DRAWING ROOM. DOWNTON. DAY.

Edith watches as the new arrival is settled in. He looks up.

EDITH: Hello. My name's Edith Craw—
GORDON: Lady Edith Crawley, I know. Second daughter of
the house.

....

* The end of any war is always an opportunity for great change, whether one
approves of it or not. This is why all regimes dread war, because when peace
comes the public will want to feel that something is different. They've given
up their lives, and often their sons (and daughters, these days), and they want
to know that something has changed. That has to be bad news for a
monarchy, but it also means change at a more domestic level. There was a lot
of feeling, in many families, that they couldn't just go back to an Edwardian
way of life. Not least because a great many of them, from the 1880s onwards,
didn't have enough money to live as they had been living.

The young, particularly, had survived four years of war, and they wanted a
new life, not just to return to changing their clothes all day and observing the
rules. This was true of many older people, too, and as a result certain houses
were turned over to other uses. We go on with this idea in the next series.
Violet, of course, decides it is her job to put Isobel off.

There is something strange in this. She starts again.

> EDITH: In charge of non-medical welfare. So whatever you need in the way of errands run or books to read, then I'm your man.

The man gestures at the bandages half covering his face.

> GORDON: Thank you. I hope this doesn't put you off.
> EDITH: I can assure you, at this stage, there isn't much that puts me off.
> GORDON: Did they tell you we're related?
> EDITH: Er, yes. But I'm afraid I'm not much good at family history, although Papa's found an aunt in 1860 who married a Gordon. Perhaps that's a clue.
> GORDON: No. That isn't it.
> EDITH: Well, as I say, I'm hopeless.
> GORDON: I thought you'd recognise my voice, but of course I sound Canadian now.

This is really odd. She was going, but she stops.

> EDITH: You mean we've met before?
> GORDON: It was a long time ago.

Sybil comes in.

> SYBIL: Edith, I need you.
> EDITH: Funnily enough, you do seem… When was it, exactly?
> GORDON: Perhaps it'll come back to you.*

....

*The Gordon plot, and Edith's falling for it, begins here, and she is the one he targets. Does he choose her using that curious instinct that all true bullies have? Because bullies have a nose for a victim. They will smell out the people who will accept their bullying. I think this is why it is so incredibly difficult to be the victim of a bully, because you half hate yourself for having been chosen. I speak as one who knows. It is an incredibly complicated situation. I feel very strongly that we must all take a stand against bullying. And this exchange, 'We've met before,' and so on, is a kind of bullying.

7 INT. KITCHENS. DOWNTON. DAY.

Daisy and Mrs Patmore are preparing vegetables. Daisy wears a black band round her left arm. Jane has a pamphlet.

> JANE: It just explains what you're entitled to.
> DAISY: That's kind, but let's face it, I'm not a widow, am I? Not really.
> JANE: Of course you are.
> DAISY: No, I'm not. How long was I married? Six hours? Seven? I shouldn't have taken his name, except it were what he wanted.
> JANE: Well, I'll leave it with you…

She walks away. The other two are alone.

> MRS PATMORE: Daisy, it wouldn't please William if you don't take what's owing. He wanted you to be looked after —
> DAISY: Because he thought I loved him, when I didn't. And I'm not going to use his name to steal now!
> MRS PATMORE: I only meant —
> DAISY: No! You made me a liar while he was alive. You made me swear dishonest oaths as he lay dying. You'll not make me be false to his memory!

Mrs Patmore doesn't try again.

8 INT. ROBERT'S DRESSING ROOM. DOWNTON. NIGHT.

Robert is being dressed for dinner by Bates.

> ROBERT: So the war's going to end, and I will never have been in it.
> BATES: Haven't we all been in the war in our different ways?
> ROBERT: You sound like her ladyship.
> BATES: Then I agree with her, m'lord.
> ROBERT: How about your war? Yours and Anna's?
> BATES: We're winning, I think. But like the Allies, it's taking its time. Which I don't quite understand.
> ROBERT: Perhaps we'll all come into port together: Europe, America and you.
> BATES: I very much hope so, m'lord.

9 INT. CARLISLE'S ROOM. DOWNTON. DAY.

There is a knock and Carson comes in to find Carlisle being
dressed by his valet. He only has his tails left to put on.

    CARLISLE: You can leave me, Brooks.
    BROOKS: Yes, sir.
    CARSON: Mr Bates said you wanted to see me, sir.

The valet picks up the linen and goes.

    CARLISLE: Ah, yes. I asked you up here because I want to
    offer you a job.
    CARSON: I have a job, sir.
    CARLISLE: Yes, of course you do. I'm sure you enjoy it.
    I don't mean to suggest I am offering a better one.

Carson acknowledges that this is a little more polite.
Carlisle takes the tail coat, but Carson relieves him of it
and holds it open.

    CARLISLE (CONT'D): Thank you. Although it would mean a
    considerable increase in salary.

Carson mentally withdraws his momentary sense of approval.

    CARLISLE (CONT'D): Lady Mary and I intend to buy a home
    near Downton. It's a long way from London, but I've made
    enough money to please myself these days. I know she
    holds you in high regard; I believe she would very much
    appreciate your help when she first sets up house as a
    bride.
    CARSON: You mean you wish me to leave Downton Abbey and
    transfer…?
    CARLISLE: Tomorrow we go to see Haxby Park. If we buy
    it, we'll take on the whole 12,000 acres.*

This time Carlisle is determined on a vocal response…

    CARSON: No doubt, you will discover many interesting
    walks to enjoy.
    CARLISLE: Of course it's run down, but there's nothing
    wrong with it that money can't fix… So? What do you
    think?
    CARSON: One thing I must ask: is Lady Mary aware that you
    have approached me?
    CARLISLE: Not yet. I wanted to surprise her.

CARSON: I could not discuss it with his lordship before I
knew her wishes. And I must discuss it with him before I
could give you an answer.
CARLISLE: She thinks highly of you, Carson. I hope I
won't be taking on a rival.
CARSON: I await Lady Mary's instruction.

He goes, leaving Carlisle feeling rather flat.†

....

* For me, this is a key moment. We begin a theme here that we play on
through the third and fourth series. It is charting the beginning of the
decline of these families. After the war, although this way of life did survive –
more, in fact, than many people think – nevertheless the writing was on the
wall for those who could read it. Despite most of the upper classes going on
in the old way until the Second World War, albeit on a reduced scale, there
were families that threw in the towel even at this point. In the early
Twenties, when Lloyd George removed the agricultural grant, with no
warning at all, for food-producing estates, that proved a breaking point for
many. What made it more difficult for them was that you could still sell an
estate as a capital gain, which would be tax free, while the alternative was to
continue farming it with erratic returns and severe income tax, which had
risen steeply. Predictably, weighing a lovely lump of tax-free capital against
struggling on with a house where the estate wasn't really paying its way any
more proved too great a temptation for quite a lot of people. And at the same
time, the new rich were buying these estates, because they still represented
the way of life with the highest status, so there was a transition going on. We
used Haxby to mark this. The Russells have been neighbours for centuries,
but only Carlisle can afford to live there.

† My father had some cousins in Yorkshire who famously poached a butler
and a cook. Normally, with a couple, one of them is great and the other less
great, but in this instance an absolutely fantastic butler was married to an
equally fantastic cook. They were working for a family, and, I blush to say it,
these relatives of mine found out what they were paid, offered them more and
poached them. The county rightly thought this was totally reprehensible,
but they wouldn't ever address how ghastly it had been. I adored them, but
they wouldn't face their own guilt. I suppose it must have been tempting to
offer an extra fiver and, in so doing, transform your life, but it still wouldn't
do. It's a good *Downton* moment, though, because again they're all torn.

10 INT. HALL. DOWNTON. NIGHT.

Robert, Cora and Violet walk away from the drawing room from where we can hear chatter. They reach the outer hall.

> VIOLET: I don't dislike him. I just don't like him, which is quite different.
> ROBERT: Did he talk about Haxby? He's got ghastly plans for the place. Of course, Cora doesn't agree.
> CORA: I'm an American. I don't share your English hatred of comfort.*
> ROBERT: Downton's comfortable enough for me. I can't wait to have it back.
> CORA: That's if Cousin Isobel allows it. She turned up today with a hideous list of projects that stretched to 1920 and beyond.
> VIOLET: Well, surely you can put her off?
> CORA: I don't know how, once the bit's between her teeth.
> VIOLET: Well, change the bridle. Find a cause that needs her more than Downton.
> CORA: She's such a martyr.
> VIOLET: Then we must tempt her with a more enticing scaffold.

Anna steps forward with her cloak as Carson opens the door.

11 INT. SERVANTS' HALL. DOWNTON. NIGHT.

It is after dinner. Daisy is clearing the last of it away.

> BATES: We're safe. We've got the Decree Nisi. I'm sure it's all right —
> ANNA: Except you're not sure.
> O'BRIEN: Not sure about what?

....

* Here we have Robert and Violet talking about how frightful Carlisle is going to make Haxby, and Cora disagreeing. That is my childhood. I can always remember, when we moved into our house in Sussex in 1959, my mother carpeting her bathroom and saying to my father, 'I don't care how common it is, I don't like cold feet.' This was very daring of her because, in those days, the well-bred bathroom had horrible linoleum, and was preferably at the end of a long and draughty passage. The whole business of having it open off your bedroom, and be carpeted and warm and just for you, was still to come for most people, and was considered to be quite ghastly.

Jane is mending lace on a frame near where Thomas is sitting.

JANE: What about you, Sergeant? Have you started planning for after the war?
THOMAS: Not really. Not yet.
MRS PATMORE: I know what you should be doing. I know what we should all be doing.
THOMAS: Oh, yeah? What's that?
MRS PATMORE: Hoarding. It may be wrong, but this rationing is starting to bite. Even with everyone's books, I'd a battle to get enough sugar for this week.
THOMAS: But where would I find a supplier?
MRS PATMORE: You're a clever fellow. You're always telling us so, any road.
THOMAS: Are you suggesting the black market, Mrs Patmore? I'm shocked.
MRS PATMORE: Oh, I doubt that very much.

For this last exchange they have dropped their voices.
Carson is drinking his tea when Mrs Hughes comes back in.

MRS HUGHES: You're quiet this evening, Mr Carson. What did Sir Richard want?
CARSON: I think he wanted to take advantage of my good nature.

12 INT. MARY'S BEDROOM. DOWNTON. NIGHT.

Anna is helping Mary undress.

ANNA: So Mary Pickford has this operation and then she can walk again. After three years. It was so beautiful.
MARY: Why is it called *Stella Maris*?
ANNA: I don't know. But the point is that you should never give up hope. That's what Conway Tearle said. At least, that's what the card said.
MARY: Yes, but it's just a film, isn't it?*

....

* *Stella Maris* was a real film. The fact that it was all about operations and walking again seemed very appropriate, so I was pleased to have found it. Of course, you always have to weigh the relative importance of what is cut and what is kept, but I was sad when it had to go. I've always admired Mary Pickford. At the beginning, the early film-makers didn't let anyone know the names of the actors, because they didn't want the actors to think they could charge more. But when they saw that the public would follow certain players

She sits wearily down at her dressing table as Cora enters.

CORA: I've ordered a hamper for tomorrow, so there's no
need to find a hotel.
MARY: Why? We can easily get there and back in time for
luncheon.
CORA: Richard told me he wants to make a day of it. I
think that's nice. And before you can be rude to me, I'm
going to say goodnight.

She has gone, leaving the other two alone.

MARY: She's afraid I still want Matthew, with all his
limitations.
ANNA: And do you, m'lady?
MARY: Only when I'm honest.

13   EXT.   KITCHEN COURTYARD.   DOWNTON.   NIGHT.

The back door opens and Mrs Hughes emerges, carrying two full
bags.   A figure comes out of the shadows.   It is Ethel.

MRS HUGHES: I'm sorry I couldn't get down this week but
we've had a houseful. Who's looking after the baby?
ETHEL: Oh, my neighbour. And she's lent me her bike, so
I can get back.
MRS HUGHES: Ah, well, you'd best be off. I'll be over in
a few days if I can manage.

Ethel hooks the bags onto the handlebars as Mrs Hughes
watches.

14   INT.   BACK DOOR.   KITCHEN PASSAGE.   DOWNTON.
                       NIGHT.

Mrs Hughes comes in, shuts the door and turns to find herself
face to face with Carson.

....

Continued from page 317:

to the box office, they decided to take advantage of it. Initially, she wasn't
allowed to have a name, so they called her the girl with the curls. The
distributors would put a card outside the cinema – 'featuring the girl with the
curls' – and the crowds would pour in. Finally, she was allowed a name, and
she became the first proper film star.

ACT TWO

15 INT. STAIRCASE/MAIN HALL. DOWNTON. DAY.

A new day. Robert is with Cora.

> CORA: I can't, darling. I've got too much work. We're
> losing two of the nurses and I must rearrange the roster.
> ROBERT: But if Mary's out with Carlisle and Edith's going
> to Mama's, I'll be on my own. What about Sybil?
> CORA: Sybil's on duty.
> ROBERT: I wish you'd told me. I could have fixed
> something up for myself.
> CORA: You could always ask Major Clarkson to join you.
> If you really can't be on your own for one luncheon.*

But Robert doesn't want to make an issue out of it.

> ROBERT: I'll manage. And now I want to say hello to the
> new chap.

....

* Cora has found a role that is much more in keeping with her own
upbringing than just being an English lady sitting on a sofa. She is truer to
her real self here. But I'm afraid that, by paying Robert less attention, Cora
opens up the field for the pretty housemaid. I'm not justifying it, but men are
pretty feeble in that way. They're just not very good at resisting temptation.
I think the difference is – I'm not sure if it's true now, but it was still true
when I was young – that, for any sexual encounter, the man had to make all
the running. As a man, you were always trying to find out who was going to
say yes in the end, and whom it was worth lavishing dinner on, and all that
stuff. As a result, when it was offered on a plate, it was more than you could
do to say no. It wasn't offered very often – certainly not to me – but it is
being offered here and, to make matters worse, Robert is feeling neglected by
his wife. I like Robert, who is based on my father – although he's not actually
as clever as my father – but, like many such men, he takes it for granted that
he's the centre of the picture, and when that is threatened he doesn't like it
much.

16 INT. LIBRARY. DOWNTON. DAY.

Robert comes in to find Mary, Matthew and Edith with Gordon.

ROBERT: Major Gordon, how do you do? Edith tells me you
don't think we're related through my Great-Aunt Anne?
GORDON: We're a bit closer than that.
MATTHEW: It's odd we don't know about it.

Robert stares at Matthew. The door opens. It is Richard.

CARLISLE: The car's ready. We should be off.
EDITH: Is this your house-hunting?
CARLISLE: It is.

He walks away and Mary follows him.

ROBERT: I'd better get on. I hope they make you
comfortable.

As he goes, Matthew looks up and Robert bends down.

MATTHEW: Did I say something wrong?
ROBERT: Only that the poor chap's link to us is obviously
illegitimate, and you put him right on the spot.
MATTHEW: Oh, crikey.

17 INT. EMPTY ROOM. HAXBY PARK. YORKSHIRE.
DAY.

MARY: It's so empty. I didn't know they'd gone.
CARLISLE: They've given up.
MARY: You can't blame them. When Billy was killed, it
knocked the stuffing out of them completely.

She stares at the huge building.

MARY (CONT'D): What'll we do about furniture and pictures
and everything?
CARLISLE: What does anyone do? Buy it, I presume.
MARY: Your lot buys it. My lot inherits it… We ought to
be getting back.
CARLISLE: Why? What's at Downton that needs your
attention so urgently?

*She looks at him and says nothing. They both know the
answer.*

CARLISLE (CONT'D): So, shall we rescue it? Shall we give
the house another chapter?
MARY: Well, I suppose one has to live somewhere.*

18   INT. SMALL LIBRARY. DOWNTON. DAY.

Cora is at her desk. Carson and Mrs Hughes are with her.

CORA: You're telling me we've been feeding Ethel for some
time?
MRS HUGHES: We have, m'lady. Well, supplementing her
food. I didn't think you'd mind, what with the baby and
all, but Mr Carson suggested you'd like to be informed,
all the same.
CORA: Carson is right, Mrs Hughes.

This is a reprimand, which both the others recognise.

CORA (CONT'D): Really, what with Mrs Bird's old soldiers
and now this, I'm beginning to feel we're feeding half of
Europe.
MRS HUGHES: But the girl was our employee, and while she
was in the wrong —
CARSON: Indeed, she was! Men will always be men, but for
any young woman to let her judgement so desert her —
CORA: She's not the first girl to be taken in by a
uniform. And don't worry, Carson. The baby will ensure
she pays the price. Has she tried to get the father to
assume some responsibility?
MRS HUGHES: She's tried and failed, I'm afraid.

....

* I wasn't sure they were right in choosing a house with a very similar gallery
going round a double-height hall, like Highclere. I know, if I had been
choosing the location, I would have picked one that was very different from
Highclere, so you didn't get essentially the same image of looking across from
one gallery to another. The other thing I had a problem with was the carpet,
which is fitted on the landing, and it would have been a runner. But I'm
being picky. I'm sure they had sound logistical reasons for choosing it. The
house was clearly very big, which was all that was needed. I like Mary's line
at the end, 'I suppose one has to live somewhere.' But the point of the scene
is that, to Carlisle, buying this house is a statement. To Mary, it's just the
sort of house one lives in. In my head, Mary is choosing, quite deliberately,
someone who can afford to provide the same way of life she has always
known, whatever the future may bring.

CORA: I wonder, if I were to write to Major Bryant, inviting him to visit us again, maybe Lord Grantham can prevail on his good nature.
MRS HUGHES: I'm not sure he's got one to prevail on.*

19 INT. KITCHEN STAIRCASE. DOWNTON. DAY.

Carson and Mrs Hughes come downstairs. She is quite sharp.

MRS HUGHES: Satisfied?
CARSON: I feel sorry for Ethel, but I cannot condone her inability to pronounce a simple two-letter word: 'No.'

He looks at his watch.

CARSON (CONT'D): The wine delivery should have been here by twelve. Get me out of the dining room when they come.
MRS HUGHES: Serve the main course and let Jane finish. He won't mind.

20 INT. DRAWING ROOM. DOWER HOUSE. DAY.

Violet is with Edith.

EDITH: I feel rather guilty. I've left poor Papa to eat luncheon alone.
VIOLET: Why? What's your mother doing?
EDITH: She always has a tray at her desk these days. She says she's too busy to waste time. The trouble is, they keep reducing the staff, but they send the same number of invalids.
VIOLET: Beware enthusiasm, my dear. And remember, if you marry, include your spouse, whenever you can.
EDITH: You don't believe in spending time apart, then?

....

* We cut Cora's line in this scene about Mrs Bird's soldiers, but later I wondered if it was right, because without it Cora becomes too generous. If she had been allowed to be a little bit caustic, she would have been a more normal person, objecting to the fact that food was flowing out of her kitchen. That said, the main reason for this scene is to show that Cora is in alliance with Mrs Hughes about the unfortunate Ethel's seduction by Bryant, which they make clear. Whereas for Carson, Ethel could always have said no, and so now she must take her punishment. The women are both more inclined to sympathise with Ethel, which is the side I'm on, in fact.

VIOLET: Certainly not. The devil makes work for idle husbands.

She opens a pretty folder full of papers and letters.

VIOLET (CONT'D): Now, I've done some research, but I want your opinion: which of these would tempt Cousin Isobel the most? Diseased children, refugees or women who'll lose their jobs to returning soldiers?
EDITH: You are clever. I should think each one is almost irresistible.

The butler appears to announce luncheon.

21 INT. DINING ROOM. DOWNTON. DAY.

Robert is alone with Isis. Jane brings in the pudding.

ROBERT: Has Carson abandoned me?
JANE: He's dealing with a wine delivery, m'lord. Shall I fetch him?
ROBERT: No, no. I dare say we'll manage… I hope you're happy here, and that your family arrangements are not proving too complicated.
JANE: Your lordship has a good memory.
ROBERT: All our lives are lived around our children. How old is your son?
JANE: Twelve, m'lord.
ROBERT: Is he at the local school?
JANE: He is. But he's trying for a scholarship to Ripon Grammar.
ROBERT: Ah. Is that a realistic prospect?
JANE: I think so. He has a real talent for mathematics, and his teachers believe it's worth a try.
ROBERT: Well done, him. I'm impressed.
JANE: Since the Education Act, they have to give a quarter of the places to scholarship boys from the public elementaries, so why not Freddie?
ROBERT: Why not, indeed? Perhaps I can put in a word.

JANE: I'm sure I should say he wants to do it all by himself, but — but I'm not proud, so if you can say anything, m'lord, then for heaven's sake do.*†

She laughs as she says this, and so does he.

CARSON (V.O.): Jane? Have you finished in here?

He is by the servery door. She nods and hurries out.

CARSON: I hope she wasn't talking out of turn, m'lord.
ROBERT: Not at all. It was my fault. I asked the questions.

But he knows that Carson disapproves strongly.‡

22 INT. KITCHENS. DOWNTON. DAY.

Mrs Patmore and Daisy are working when Jane arrives.

JANE: There's a meeting this afternoon in Ripon. War Widows Rights and so on —
DAISY: I could never get time off.
MRS PATMORE: You can have time off, if you like.
DAISY: I don't like.
JANE: Well, if you're sure.

....

* This is what I always feel when people ask me, 'Would you have a word?' It's not that I think my word's going to make any difference, but it's not going to hurt, and so why not?

† This is also an example of where you write a line to make something clear to an audience, in this case that Jane is beginning to find Robert attractive. It is deliberately worded to take her slightly over the line that divides employer and servant. But, in the event, although I like the line and I was glad it stayed in, it was completely unnecessary, because Clare Calbraith's performance had already made it perfectly clear that she finds him attractive and nice. A good actor's skill will always obviate some of the dialogue.

‡ Carson doesn't like the fact that he walks into the dining room and finds a conversation going on. He wouldn't mind at all if he walked in and heard Robert asking for some sugar, but the idea that they're chatting about Ripon Grammar School offends his sense of what's right.

She turns to go, then she stops.

> JANE (CONT'D): He's nice, Lord Grantham, isn't he?
> MRS PATMORE: He is. Very nice. A very considerate man.
> JANE: That's good to know.

She goes. Mrs Patmore and Daisy exchange a quick glance.

23 INT. ETHEL'S COTTAGE. DAY.

Ethel is excited by what she has just heard.

> ETHEL: But surely, if his lordship asks him, he must do something?
> MRS HUGHES: Why? What difference will it make? We're not in the fourteenth century.
> ETHEL: But when he hears that Lord Grantham knows what he's done —
> MRS HUGHES: What's he done? That all young men aren't anxious to do, behind the bicycle sheds every night?
> ETHEL: Then what am I going to do? If Major Bryant doesn't come round?
> MRS HUGHES: Who knows? Go to a big city. Invent a past… You've broken the rules, my girl, and it's no good pretending they're easily mended.

24 INT. SERVANTS' HALL. DOWNTON. DAY.

The servants are having tea when Carson looks in.

> CARSON: Mr Bates? There's a telephone call for you. It's your lawyer.

This sends a frisson through the company. Bates stands.

> ANNA: Shall I come with you?

He nods and they leave together. Carson is about to go, but —

> THOMAS: Lady Mary was looking for you.
> CARSON: When was this?
> THOMAS: When she got back from her outing.
> CARSON: And were you going to keep it a secret all day?

He walks out. The others enjoy this. O'Brien winks at Thomas.

> O'BRIEN: I'm going to fetch me button box.

INT. DRAWING ROOM. DOWNTON. DAY.

Major Gordon is lying on his bed, reading. Edith comes in.

EDITH: Any letters to post?

Gordon shakes his head, but before she turns away…

GORDON: Look, I know I've changed and not for the better, but even so… Do you really still not recognise me?
EDITH: I know. Why am I being so silly?
GORDON: It's funny, isn't it? I came here all the time when I was growing up.
EDITH: You were here? At Downton? You're not saying you're…
GORDON: Patrick. Yes, I am. That's exactly what I'm saying. I've just been hoping you'd realise, without my having to spell it out.
EDITH: But Patrick's…
GORDON: Dead? Drowned on the *Titanic*? Of course, this must be very hard for you…

END OF ACT TWO

ACT THREE

26 INT. CARSON'S PANTRY. DOWNTON. DAY.

Bates is on the telephone, with Anna listening.

BATES: No, I'm not saying it's a lie. But it wasn't a payment… Well, I suppose it was, but I never thought — Collusion…? But how long can they hold it up…? That's ridiculous! No, I'm sorry. Of course I'm not saying it's your fault. It's mine, it's all mine… Yes… Thank you. Goodbye.

He puts back the receiver.

BATES (CONT'D): She's only gone and told the judge that I paid her to agree to a divorce.
ANNA: I suppose you did, didn't you?

BATES: Yes, I bloody well did!

ANNA: So what does it mean?

BATES: Because we withheld it from the Court, it means the judge can withdraw the Decree Nisi… It means I'm not divorced after all. And above all, it means I am a stupid, stupid, stupid man!

ANNA: This won't change a thing. We are going to be together, whether she wants it or not. If we have to leave here, if we have to leave the country, we are going to be together.*

The camera drops back to find O'Brien listening outside.

27 INT. DRAWING ROOM. DOWNTON. DAY.

Edith and Major Gordon are still talking.

GORDON: I was on the *Titanic*. That much is true. But I was pulled out of the water by Fifth Officer Lowe, the only one of them to come back — at least that's what they said later. When I properly came round, they misidentified me as Canadian and shipped me up to Montreal.

Edith is close enough now to sit on the bed. She is in shock.

EDITH: I don't understand. Why didn't you just tell them who you were?

....

* I had to ask Fiona Shackleton about this. She's a very senior divorce lawyer, who's a friend of ours, and is, indeed, in the Lords with me. I told her that everything about the divorce was agreed, and Bates has got the Decree Nisi, so how could I make it go wrong? Fiona was extremely helpful, and got a second opinion as to how a divorce could be spoilt, and how and why a judge would withdraw it under the rules of those days. One answer was if there was any reason for the judge to suspect collusion. That is, if money had been paid from one divorcing party to the other, and it was enough for the judge to withdraw the Decree Nisi and cancel the Decree Absolute. We wanted Bates to think his divorce was unstoppable, that all he had to do was to wait, but in fact it could still be stopped. This story is what Fiona and her friend came up with.

GORDON: Because I couldn't remember. I don't know if it
was the blow to the head or the shock or the cold, but I
had no memory. It was wiped blank. As far as I knew I
was Canadian.
EDITH: So, what happened?
GORDON: Well, I had no reason to go back to England
so, in the end, I took my name from a gin bottle
and got a job in a bank. Then, in 1914, I joined
Princess Pat's Infantry.*
EDITH: And what changed?
GORDON: I was caught in a big explosion at Passchendaele.
When I woke up, it all came back. Suddenly I knew who I
was. I began to call myself Patrick again.
EDITH: Why not your whole name? And why didn't you send
a message at once?
GORDON: I nearly did. And then I heard that Downton was
an officers' convalescent home. I thought that if I came
here and you knew me, the hard part would be over.
EDITH: But we didn't know you.
GORDON: Precisely.
EDITH: I must talk to Papa. We've Matthew, the new heir,
to think about.
GORDON: Ah. The new heir. Yes. This will be very
difficult for him, of course.

....

* Princess Patricia of Connaught was a daughter of the Duke of Connaught, a younger son of Queen Victoria. Her sister married the Crown Prince of Sweden, and Patricia was the first choice of King Alfonso of Spain, so she could have been a queen, but she was quite an independent soul and instead fell in love with the younger son of the Earl of Dalhousie. She insisted on marrying him, and the deal was that she should exchange her royal rank for that of a duke's daughter. So she ceased to be Her Royal Highness Princess Patricia of Connaught and became first Lady Patricia Saxe-Coburg-Gotha, and then, after her marriage, Lady Patricia Ramsay. Her original name only survives in this Canadian troop, Princess Patricia's Light Infantry.

I am told that her arrangement was the model for the offer made to Princess Margaret. You often see in the papers that the Princess was forbidden to marry Group Captain Townsend, but I don't believe this is necessarily so. I may be wrong, but I think, instead of being forbidden, she was told that, if she married him, she would have to surrender her royal rank and become Lady Margaret Townsend. For whatever reason, guided, I'm sure, by her sense of duty to the Crown, she did not consider this acceptable.

EDITH: It must be so hard for you, what with Mary getting married...
GORDON: Did I love her very much?
EDITH: Well, I'm the wrong person to ask.
GORDON: Because you were the one who really loved me, you mean?
EDITH: I never thought Patrick knew.
GORDON: Well, he did... I do.

Edith stares at him. She is totally convinced. *

28 EXT. DOWNTON. DAY.

Mary is wheeling Matthew's chair along.

MARY: It's big. The staircase is prettier than the one here, but mainly it's just big.
MATTHEW: Can we stop? I'd much rather see your face when we talk.

They do. She sits on a bench facing him.

MATTHEW (CONT'D): So will he buy it?
MARY: Probably. He says he wants to steal Carson to come and run it for us.
MATTHEW: I don't envy you telling your Papa.

....

* Gordon's account of the *Titanic* sinking is all true. Fifth Officer Lowe was the only officer to go back, but he miscalculated and waited too long. The famous Molly Brown got into a terrific fight with the seaman in charge of her boat, because he wouldn't go back, and the women couldn't make him. Lowe was a brave man, but in order for his rescue mission to make sense he had to empty one boat, and that took time. The trouble was they were terrified of being swamped, of 1,500 people trying to get on board. As a result, there were only about six survivors pulled out of the water, and of those, one died at once.

Funnily enough, by this time I had been asked to write *Titanic* for ITV, so I had become a *Titanic* expert. It is an extraordinary story, actually, an extraordinary, extraordinary story. It sounds rather an odd thing to say, but it is also a very heartening one, because they were so unbelievably brave. The modern historian is usually a miserabilist and is only happy when reporting how badly everyone behaved, but if he tries this with the *Titanic* he will be disappointed. I'm not saying nobody behaved badly, but very few did. And in all three classes, there were so many examples of staggering courage.

MARY: Suppose Carson won't do it?

MATTHEW: Since he would open his veins for you, I don't think there's much doubt.

She is amused by this. She looks at him steadily.

MARY: I don't have to marry him, you know.

MATTHEW: Yes, you do. If I thought for a moment that I was an argument against your marriage, I should jump into the nearest river.

MARY: And how would you manage that without my help?

MATTHEW: Well, I'd get you to push me in.

Which makes them both laugh. Sort of.

MATTHEW (CONT'D): Seriously, I can only relax because I know that you have a real life coming. If I ever felt I was putting that in jeopardy, I'd go away and never see you again.

MARY: You don't mean that.

MATTHEW: But I do. I am the cat that walks by himself and all places are alike to me. I have nothing to give and nothing to share. And if you were not engaged to be married, I wouldn't let you anywhere near me.

29 INT. SMALL LIBRARY. DOWNTON. DAY.

Carlisle is watching Mary and Matthew, who are still talking. This time Cora is the only other person in the room.

CARLISLE: You'd think he was in Mary's sole charge.

CORA: They do spend a lot of time together, it's true.

CARLISLE: I worry it'll mean a big adjustment for him. When we marry.

CORA: I don't believe Matthew has any desire to stop her marrying, Richard. Quite the contrary.

CARLISLE: Maybe. But is she as convinced as he is that they have no future?

CORA: What are you saying?

CARLISLE: I suppose I'm asking whether you want Mary to have children. Because, if you do, isn't it time for Lavinia Swire to come back into his life?*

30 EXT. STABLEYARD. DOWNTON. DAY.

Sybil walks over to where Branson is working under a car.

SYBIL (V.O.): I wish I knew how an engine worked.

He pulls himself out. His shirt is open at the neck and he is marked with oil. He looks rough and strong as he stands.

BRANSON: I can teach you if you like.
SYBIL: That's Edith's territory.
BRANSON: I thought you were avoiding me.
SYBIL: Of course not.
BRANSON: But you haven't come up with an answer yet, have you?
SYBIL: Not yet, I'm afraid. I know you want to play your part in Ireland's troubles and I respect that, but I just can't think about it all until the war is over. It won't be long now, so will you wait?
BRANSON: I'd wait forever.
SYBIL: I'm not asking for forever. Just a few more weeks.

31 EXT. KITCHEN COURTYARD. DOWNTON. EVE.

O'Brien is having a smoke when Thomas appears.

O'BRIEN: You look very purposeful.
THOMAS: I am. You know, old Ma Patmore's not as mad as I thought.
O'BRIEN: Why do you say that?
THOMAS: I've made some enquiries and she's right.
There's a big demand for rationed food if I can find it.

....

* I always like to write those scenes, when the topic of conversation isn't really what they're talking about. And here, what they're really discussing is whether or not Mary will stay in love with Matthew, even though Carlisle can offer her what Matthew never can, i.e. children. That's the issue. So they decide to involve Lavinia to get things back on track. Cora's quite cynical in supporting this plan, because she feels her daughter will be happier if she does not contract a childless marriage with a man in a wheelchair. That seems believable. I don't think it makes her heartless. But the fact is, mothers are tough when it comes to protecting their children's future. She doesn't want her daughter to sacrifice her life. That doesn't make her a bad person, to me.

O'BRIEN: And can you?

THOMAS: Maybe. I've been given a name… I'll have to come up with the money, though. They're only interested in selling in bulk.

O'BRIEN: And can you find the money?

THOMAS: I think so. I've a bit put by. God knows I've worked long enough for it. And I could borrow some.

O'BRIEN: It's a risk, though, isn't it?

THOMAS: You've got to speculate to accumulate. Hadn't you heard?

O'BRIEN: No. But I know the one about neither a borrower nor a lender be.

32   INT. ROBERT'S DRESSING ROOM. DOWNTON. NIGHT.

Robert is putting on a dinner jacket and a black tie.

ROBERT: What do you think? All the chaps are wearing them in London. Only for informal evenings, of course.

BATES: I'm not sure you'll get much use out of it when the war's over.

ROBERT: Maybe not. But I can wear it when her ladyship and I are on our own.*

But when he looks at his valet, Bates is staring into nothing.

ROBERT (CONT'D): You're very preoccupied tonight.

....

* The dinner jacket is another minor subplot. When it came in, it was to allow men to be completely informal in the evening, and Violet detests it. We've broken our own rules once or twice – not deliberately, really, but because there's always so much going on – but what we try to do is to put all the men into white tie when Violet is coming for dinner. But when she's not, and it's not a dinner party, then it's black tie, certainly by the time the series has reached the early Twenties. Of course, once or twice the men wear black tie in front of Violet for a reason, because a guest hasn't brought his white tie, or whatever, and Violet hates it.

There is that wonderful quote, when Duff Cooper was talking to his brother-in-law, the Duke of Rutland, who was a very formal character. He said, 'Don't you ever wear black tie?' And the Duke thought for a moment. 'Maybe,' he said. 'If I'm dining alone with the Duchess in her bedroom.' We use black tie to show that the world is changing and becoming a more modern place.

There is a swift knock and Edith appears.

EDITH: Papa, can I have a word?

She looks at Bates, who picks up the day's linen and goes.

ROBERT: Now? What is it?
EDITH: I think you'd better sit down.

33 INT. DINING ROOM. DOWNTON. NIGHT.

Carson is checking when Mary, dressed for dinner, comes in.

MARY: I knew you'd be in here. Making last-minute
adjustments.
CARSON: Never leave anything to chance, m'lady. That's
my motto.
MARY: Mine too, really. Sometimes I wish it wasn't… I
gather Sir Richard's asked you about coming with us, when
we're married.
CARSON: I need to hear what you think.
MARY: It's a terrific idea. If anyone can keep me out of
trouble, it's you.
CARSON: What about his lordship?
MARY: Of course he'll kill me, but I'm sure he'll
understand.
CARSON: Will you be poaching anyone else?
MARY: I'd love to take Anna, but she won't leave Bates,
and Mrs Hughes'd never come, so I think it's just you.
CARSON: Well, I'll give you my answer when you've spoken
to his lordship. It'll be a huge wrench for me to leave
Downton.
MARY: But you'll say yes?
CARSON: After you've spoken to his lordship.

34 INT. DRAWING ROOM. DOWNTON. NIGHT.

There are only two men in here now. They are in their beds.
Gordon looks up as Robert approaches. He speaks softly.

ROBERT: Major Gordon, Edith has given me an account of
your conversation.
GORDON: She said she would.
ROBERT: I wish you'd spoken to me first. Obviously, I
need time to consider what you've said.

GORDON: Well, I can offer little proof, except that I know things only the real Patrick would know. I was never 'finger printed' or anything.
ROBERT: Presumably you understand that people would be seriously affected should your story be true.
GORDON: You mean Cousin Matthew.
ROBERT: It would be very hard on Matthew.
GORDON: Of course it would, but Robert —

He has taken an envelope. Robert flinches at the familiarity.

GORDON (CONT'D): I mean Lord Grantham, if you'd prefer it.
ROBERT: I would. Until we know more.
GORDON: When I was in hospital I had my story written down, so you can have it checked, as far as that's possible.
ROBERT: Thank you. I'll send it to my lawyers in London, and I'll break the news to the family tomorrow.

Gordon makes a gesture, sealing his lips by holding up his index finger, as if telling a child to 'Sssh!' Robert stares.

ROBERT (CONT'D): Where did you learn to do that?
GORDON: Do what?
ROBERT: Never mind.

He turns away and walks towards the door.

GORDON: Am I really a stranger? Do you not recognise me at all? It feels very odd to be talking so formally.
ROBERT: The whole situation is certainly odd. That I freely admit.*

....

* I wanted it to be unclear as to whether Gordon was telling the truth or not. I think he probably isn't, but he must have known Patrick to pick up his mannerisms, like the little thing that he does with his finger. This is why we establish that he may have worked with Patrick. Hopefully, all this just plants a slight doubt, allowing Robert to walk into the room assuming he's a fraud, but by the time he leaves his position in the whole matter has slightly changed.

35 EXT. DOWER HOUSE. DAY.

A new day. Isobel is with Violet.

VIOLET: The war may be at an end, but the upheaval is
only beginning.

ISOBEL: Oh, how right you are. That is why Downton Abbey
still has such an important role to play.

VIOLET: Dear me, there's so much to be done. When you
think of all the children laid up with disease —

ISOBEL: But they're making such advances now, aren't
they? Now, could we talk about the lecture programme for
Downton?

VIOLET: If we must, we must. If only I wasn't haunted by
those women whose jobs will be snatched from them when
the boys come home.

ISOBEL: But we have to find work for our heroes, don't
we? That must be our priority, however hard that might
sound.

VIOLET: As you say… And what about those wretched
refugees? What will become of them?

This is her last throw.

ISOBEL: Ah, now you've struck a chord.

VIOLET: Have I, really? Oh, thank heaven.

ISOBEL: What do you mean?

VIOLET: Hmm? Nothing, only the thought of those poor men
and women, flung across Europe, far from their homelands,
and so much in need of your help.

ISOBEL: My help? Why do you say that?

VIOLET: Well, you know they've established a resettling
bureau up here? No one could bring more to it than you.

ISOBEL: But if I'm running Downton —

VIOLET: When it comes to helping refugees, your
experience in the Wounded and Missing Enquiry Department
renders your value beyond price. One of the organisers
said those words.

ISOBEL: Which organiser?

VIOLET: I forget.

ISOBEL: But what about running Downton? I can't do both.

VIOLET: Well, I suppose you must decide what is more
important: exercise classes and lectures on pottery, or
helping men and women build a new life.

Isobel stands.

ISOBEL: I must go. But I will think about it. Are you coming to Cousin Robert's dinner tonight?
VIOLET: Are you?
ISOBEL: I didn't feel I could say no. He sent a note this morning and it was most insistent. What's it about?
VIOLET: I have no idea, but we'll talk there. We're onto something for you, and we mustn't let the iron grow cold.
ISOBEL: Thank you.*

36 INT. ROBERT'S DRESSING ROOM. DOWNTON. NIGHT.

Bates has dressed Robert in white tie. Mary is there.

ROBERT: You know there is nothing more ill-bred than to steal other people's servants?
MARY: But you're not 'other people', and Carson brought me up.
ROBERT: What does he say?
MARY: That he won't do anything without your permission.
ROBERT: Which, of course, is so cunning. How can I refuse a man who says that?

Bates helps him on with his tail coat.

ROBERT (CONT'D): What do you say, Bates?
BATES: I say Mr Carson must have the last word on where he lives and works.
ROBERT: You're ganging up on me.

But of course he has given in. Mary kisses his cheek.

MARY: You're a darling and I love you. Now, what's this dinner all about?

Her question entirely alters the mood in the room. He sighs.

ROBERT: I'd forgotten it for a moment.
MARY: Won't you tell me?
ROBERT: You'll find out.

....

* In a sense, Isobel is a cause addict, as some people are, certainly today. They need to feel they're doing good all the time, and they will become incredibly indignant about practically anything, at the drop of a hat. Isobel does suffer from that a bit.

37   INT. SERVANTS' HALL. DOWNTON. NIGHT.

The servants are assembling to eat. Carson comes in.

CARSON: Right. Can someone tell Mrs Patmore we're ready?
O'BRIEN: Aren't you serving them coffee?
CARSON: Not tonight.
THOMAS: What's different about tonight?
CARSON: His lordship wishes to be alone with the family.
MRS HUGHES: Why is that?
CARSON: I am surprised at you, Mrs Hughes. Jane, when
they've gone to bed, can you please check the boudoir?
JANE: Of course, Mr Carson.

She is at the other end with Anna and Bates.

JANE (CONT'D): I thought they were in a funny mood at
dinner, didn't you?
BATES: How 'funny'?
JANE: Difficult to say, only his lordship seemed very
cast down.

38   INT. SMALL LIBRARY. DOWNTON. NIGHT.

*They are crowded into the room — Violet, the Granthams, their
daughters, Isobel, Matthew, Carlisle — all in evening dress.*

ROBERT: I'm sorry if it's a bit of a crush; I didn't want
to be overheard.
VIOLET: Are we talking financial ruin or criminal
investigation?
ROBERT: Neither. I'll get straight to the point. We
have a patient who has been badly burned who goes by the
name of Patrick Gordon, but he claims to be Patrick
Crawley.
ISOBEL: But I thought he was dead. Didn't he drown on
the *Titanic*?
ROBERT: Well, of course it is what we all thought. Until
now.
EDITH: They never found a body.
MARY: They never found lots of bodies.
CARLISLE: I'm so sorry, but I'm not quite on top of this.
Who's Patrick Crawley?
MATTHEW: The man who would displace me as heir. If he's
alive, then I am no longer the future Earl of Grantham.

This flattens the room. And enrages Mary.

MARY: It's ridiculous! How can it be true? Where's he been hiding for the last six years?

EDITH: In Canada, suffering from amnesia.

ROBERT: He does have a story that would explain it. I'm not quite sure about how to test the facts.

EDITH: He knows all sorts of things that only Patrick, or someone very close to him, would know.

MARY: What a stupid thing to say! Any fortune teller at a fair comes up with a dozen details he couldn't possibly know!

CORA: There's no need to be angry. This young man is either Patrick or he's not. There must be a way to find out. Is he like Patrick to look at?

MARY: He isn't like anything to look at!

SYBIL: How unkind.

ROBERT: I've sent his account up to George Murray in London to ask for his advice.

MARY: But what a waste of time and money!

EDITH: What's the matter? We were all so fond of Patrick. You were going to marry him, for heaven's sake. Aren't you glad if he's survived?

CARLISLE: Dear me. Should I be worried?

MARY: Certainly not! This man is a fake and an impostor! And I think it's a cruel trick to play, when Matthew's been through so much!

She is starting to cry, which has, of course, given her away.

MATTHEW: My dear, don't be too quick to decide. You never know. This might be a blessing in disguise.

ISOBEL: What do you mean?

MATTHEW: Well, he seems a nice enough chap. He's not very pretty, of course, but he can walk round the estate on his own two legs, and sire a string of sons to continue the line. All in all, I'd say that's a great improvement on the current situation… Sybil, could I prevail on you to take me back to my room?

SYBIL: Of course.

She goes to the chair and wheels him out. Carlisle opens and shuts the door, leaving the others in silence.*

END OF ACT THREE

ACT FOUR

39   INT.   CORA'S BEDROOM.   DOWNTON.   NIGHT.

Cora is with O'Brien when Mrs Hughes knocks and enters.

CORA: Ah, Mrs Hughes, we've had a letter in the evening
post which rather slipped my mind. From Major Bryant's
father replying to my letter to his son. He must have
found it hard to write for it seems the Major has been
killed. In the Battle of Vittoria Veneto.
MRS HUGHES: How sad. I'm sorry to hear it.
CORA: I know. And right at the end. But there we are.
I'm afraid it's the end of our story, too.
O'BRIEN: What story is that, m'lady?

....

* I'm always interested by the way some people feel facts can be adjusted to suit their own prejudices or desires. Very often in my business you get a situation where people want someone to be very talented, because they're the sort of person who ought to be talented, they fit in and they have the right opinions, and so on, while they may not want someone else to be talented, because they're wrong for the industry. They're wrong philosophically or politically, or whatever. But, unfortunately for them, the first of these is not talented, and the second is, and that's just a fact. Similarly, here, Mary is not interested in the possibility that this man might really be Patrick, their cousin. This is because she doesn't want to hear that Matthew is not the heir. He's had so much to put up with that it's unacceptable to her that he should now have his future taken away. She is unable to grasp that whatever Matthew's been through is irrelevant – either Gordon is the real Patrick or he is not. Mary hides behind her own questions until Cora has to intervene. That's what the scene is examining; how, if people dislike someone, then they can and will invent reasons for disliking them to justify their feelings. But the reason comes after the fact.

CORA: A friend of Mrs Hughes knew the Major. Can you relay the news?
MRS HUGHES: Of course. Will that be all?
CORA: Yes. Thank you.

Mrs Hughes goes. O'Brien works on.

O'BRIEN: Is that the Major Bryant that Ethel always thought so handsome?
CORA: Too handsome for anyone's good.

40   INT.   SMALL LIBRARY.   DOWNTON.   NIGHT.

The room is in darkness when Jane opens the door. She turns on a light and there is Robert, sitting alone.

JANE: I beg your pardon, your lordship. I thought everyone had gone up.
ROBERT: Not yet.
JANE: Is there anything I can fetch you?
ROBERT: Nothing that would help… I must lose two people who are dear to me. I don't relish the prospect.
JANE: It's always difficult when the first child marries.
ROBERT: Correction. Three.

He stands. He has no intention of explaining.

ROBERT (CONT'D): Never mind me. Good night.

41   INT.   CARSON'S PANTRY.   DOWNTON.   NIGHT.

Mrs Hughes opens the door. Carson is reading. He looks up.

CARSON: What was it?
MRS HUGHES: She wanted to tell me that Major Bryant has been killed.
CARSON: Well, well. So that's that.
MRS HUGHES: I suppose. Although it doesn't make much sense. They send them here and we nurse them and nurse them and coax them back together. All so they can go back to the front and be blown into a million pieces.
CARSON: That's war, Mrs Hughes.
MRS HUGHES: That's waste, Mr Carson.

42 EXT. GARDENS. DOWNTON. DAY.

The next day. Major Gordon is walking with Edith.

EDITH: Not a shock exactly, but obviously it was a tremendous surprise.

GORDON: So what happens next?

EDITH: Papa has sent your statement up to his solicitor. What is it?

GORDON: I was only thinking how lovely it is to be here again.

EDITH: Do you remember this place?

GORDON: Of course I do.

EDITH: How we used to hide over there?

GORDON: I remember. Wasn't there a governess none of you liked?*

* The German governess comes from my own great-aunt, Isie. My great-grandmother was widowed in 1893, when her husband was killed in a carriage accident – something you don't expect outside the pages of *Tom Jones* – and she was quite young, thirty-nine or forty, with six children. The girls were educated at home, which wasn't unusual then, and every summer an extra governess would arrive, who spoke only French, or only German, or only Italian, to force these languages into their heads. Of all the women, the German governess was a complete failure; they all absolutely detested her. The French governess, however, was a tremendous success.

There were two boys, Peregrine, who was my great-uncle, and Harry, my grandfather, and I remember Aunt Isie telling me that she and her sisters were all bewildered by Mademoiselle, because the brothers were always getting her to go off with them, and 'We never knew what they were up to.' History does not relate what they *were* up to, but the story is a reminder of that slightly odd tradition of home education, which is how pretty well all of these girls were taught – certainly the Crawley girls of Downton – at least before the First World War.

Another story from Isie places them firmly in that period of the late nineteenth century, before the end of the Old World. There were four girls, Isie, Lorna, Phyllis and Ierne, and when they were fairly young they were made to follow their governess round the garden. When she stopped, they had to stop, too, and start a conversation with the tree or the bush they were standing next to, sometimes in English, sometimes in the foreign languages they had been drilled in. This was so that, in future, when they lived happy and benign lives in large houses at the end of long drives, they would always be at ease socially. And it didn't matter if they were giving away prizes or opening a school or launching a ship; that was how they would do it… Another planet.

EDITH: Fräulein Kelder.

GORDON: That's it. Fräulein Kelder. What fun we used to make of her!

EDITH: Do you know, I do recognise you now.

GORDON: Do you? You haven't changed at all. Not a jot… God knows I have.

EDITH: That's not important.

GORDON: Edith, if you really mean it, do you think, once it's all settled, we might talk again?

He takes her hand. His own is scarred, but it grips hers.

43 INT. ETHEL'S COTTAGE. DAY.

Ethel is weeping, as Mrs Hughes comforts the baby.

ETHEL: But if they've read her ladyship's letter, won't his parents know?

MRS HUGHES: I don't think so. She only wrote to invite him to pay a visit. She thought the subject of the baby would come better face to face.

ETHEL: Could I write to them?

MRS HUGHES: You could try, but where's your proof? With him dead, you've no evidence at all.*

ETHEL: Then I'm ruined.

MRS HUGHES: You were ruined already, my girl, so don't let's go overboard.

ETHEL: How's that new maid getting on? The widow with the little boy?

MRS HUGHES: Very well, thank you. Why?

ETHEL: Just thinking. Why everyone wants to help her, to feed her, to find her work, because her son's father is dead. But so is the father of my son. Where's the difference?

....

* Now we get to the next act of the Ethel story, which is the death of the Major. I always have a special sympathy for people whose sons or husbands were killed towards the end of a war. I mean, it shouldn't really make any difference, logically, when they died, but somehow it does, and the very end is even worse than their being killed right at the beginning. It breaks my heart. Anyway, that is Major Bryant's fate, not that it's the end of the story.

MRS HUGHES: The difference is Jane is a respectable married woman that some man chose to be his wife.
ETHEL: Is that enough?
MRS HUGHES: It is in the real world.

But she looks at this despairing soul and takes pity.

MRS HUGHES (CONT'D): Maybe it's a good thing. You can put him out of your mind. There's no help coming from that quarter, you know it now, so you must build a new life for yourself and little Charlie.
ETHEL: And that's 'good'?
MRS HUGHES: It's always good when you give up flogging a dead horse.

44   INT.   HALL.   DOWNTON.   NIGHT.

Carson is ringing the gong, when Carlisle appears.

CARLISLE: Carson, I wonder if I could be put on the London train at nine o'clock tomorrow morning.
CARSON: His lordship's valet is catching that one. Would you object to his riding in the front with the chauffeur?
CARLISLE: Not at all. Meanwhile, have you given my proposition any thought?
CARSON: A great deal, Sir Richard.
CARLISLE: I'll be back on the night of the tenth. Perhaps you can let me have your answer then?
MARY (V.O.): Answer to what?

She is walking towards the staircase.

CARLISLE: As to whether Carson will be Captain of our ship.

Mary looks back at the butler as she starts up the stairs.

MARY: With you at the helm, there's much more chance of a smooth crossing.

45   INT.   ROBERT'S DRESSING ROOM.   NIGHT.

Bates is with Robert, who is dressing for dinner.

BATES: Your lordship, I need to go to London tomorrow. I've spoken to Mr Carson and he has no objection.
ROBERT: Please say this concerns property and not the former Mrs Bates.

BATES: I only wish she was 'the former', or better still, 'the late'.

ROBERT: Indeed. I hope you're not planning anything foolish. We've seen enough of what she can do when she's angry.

BATES: I have to reason with her. I have no other choice. She's found a reason to delay things again. No, not delay. She's found a way to ruin things.

ROBERT: Be sensible, Bates. Above all, do not lose your temper.

45A INT. ETHEL'S COTTAGE. NIGHT.

Ethel is alone, cradling her child and sobbing.

46 INT. SERVANTS' HALL. DOWNTON. NIGHT.

The servants are having tea.

CARSON: A German republic? Nah, I don't think so, Mr Branson. The Kaiser will go, I grant you, and maybe the Crown Prince, too, but there'll be a regency, mark my words. Monarchy is the lifeblood of Europe.

BRANSON: Sorry, Mr Carson, but I think you'll find the kings and emperors have had their day. If President Wilson has anything to say about it.*

At the other end of the table, Bates is with Anna.

....

* At the time, it must have been incredibly difficult for people to imagine what President Wilson was determined on, which was the republicanisation of Europe. I am a monarchist, a constitutional monarchist, but a monarchist *quand même*, and I think that Wilson's insistence on republics was disastrous for Europe. It's unfashionable to say so now, and people have moved on, but he didn't understand that creating a vacuum in Germany was bound to lead to the rise of a demagogue, which it did in the shape of Hitler, and in Austria, too. He simply didn't grasp what he was risking. The American republic has managed to generate sufficient charisma to survive. The US Presidency and the concept of the First Family have always had a glamour from the early days, which took the place of a monarchical presence in their society. But very few European republics – with the possible exception of the French – have managed the same. Few, outside their countries, could name the President of Portugal or Poland or Romania or even Austria, which once

BATES: I'll have to go to London.

ANNA: But what will you say to her that you haven't said already?

BATES: I don't know, but I know that staying here won't make any difference.

O'BRIEN: You're always going up and down to London these days, Mr Bates.

BATES: I have business in London.

O'BRIEN: Oh, yes? Well, judging by your expression, your business doesn't seem to be prospering.

ANNA: The trick of business is to mind your own.

They are interrupted by the arrival of Robert. They stand.

ROBERT: I'm sorry to disturb you, but I've just heard news from the War Office and I thought you'd all like to know… that the war is over!

There is a burst of spontaneous applause.

ROBERT (CONT'D): The ceasefire will begin at eleven o'clock on the morning of the eleventh of November.

MRS PATMORE: Why can't it begin now?

THOMAS: The eleventh of the eleventh seems pretty tidy to me.

ROBERT: We will mark the moment in the Great Hall and I expect all of you, including the kitchen staff and hall boys, everyone, to be there. And Carson —

....

Continued from page 344:

dominated the globe. But Wilson was fixed in this position, and he insisted on connecting post-war aid with the downfall of the thrones. Before the war ended, it was generally thought that Crown Princess Cecile would be made Regent of Germany. She was popular and she could have presided until her sons were old enough to take over, but it was not done, and Hitler was the result.

For me, the point is that none of this was inevitable, and I always take any opportunity to point out that history is not inevitable. When I was young, the subject was always taught as if there was some inexorable Marxist march, and you couldn't get out of the way. But it's all nonsense. Everything that happens turns on slight accidents, an unfortunate personality, or the fact that it was raining, or someone was late for an appointment.

He draws to one side with the butler. The staff rejoice and hug each other and pour drinks and propose a toast:

ALL: To peace!

ROBERT: Lady Mary has spoken to me. You are free to make your choice of whether you leave or stay.

CARSON: M'lord, this is not easy for me. I had always expected to serve out my time here and lie at the end in the Downton churchyard.

ROBERT: But you feel Lady Mary needs you.

CARSON: I feel I must go where I can be most useful. I hope you understand.

ROBERT: I understand. You will not be easy to replace, but… I wish you well, Carson, whatever you decide. Now, hadn't you better ring the gong?

47   INT. DRAWING ROOM. CRAWLEY HOUSE. DAY.

Molesley is serving tea to Violet, Cora and Isobel, who is awkward. She has something to get off her chest.

CORA: Your seedcake is so much better than Mrs Patmore's. I wonder if Mrs Bird could give her some tips.

ISOBEL: I'll ask her… The truth is, Cora, there is a reason for inviting you here today and I very much fear I'm going to be a great disappointment to you.

CORA: Oh?

ISOBEL: Cousin Violet is in part to blame.

VIOLET: Yes, I usually am.

ISOBEL: It was she who drew my attention to the plight of the war refugees. This area, like every other, must play its part in resettling them.

CORA: Of course.

ISOBEL: And I am forced to concede that I do have skills and experience, after my war work, that make me uniquely qualified to help.

VIOLET: Who could doubt it?

ISOBEL: I feel very guilty since I chivvied you, and now I'm jumping ship. But I can't run Downton as well.

CORA: You must go where you can make a difference.

ISOBEL: Well, this is what I think. But I hope you will consider keeping the house open, without me.

CORA: I must be honest with you. It was your idea, not ours, so I doubt very much we'll go on with it now. But what does that matter when one thinks of the work you'll be doing? Don't you agree, Mama?

VIOLET: I — I cannot find the words to say how I feel. What do you think, Molesley?

MOLESLEY: Sometimes Fate knows best, m'lady.

VIOLET: I couldn't put it better, myself.

48 INT. THE MOTOR CAR. DAY.

Isobel steps back. The car pulls away.

CORA: There really is something for her to do?

VIOLET: Absolutely. It's all set up. I had to promise to be a patron, but it seemed a small price to pay.

CORA: I know it was for Robert and the girls, but I thank you, without irony, from the bottom of my heart.

VIOLET: And I accept your thanks, my dear, with no trace of irony, either.

They drive on, unusually at peace.

49 INT. LIBRARY. DOWNTON. NIGHT.

Edith is with Patrick Gordon.

EDITH: Lawyers take forever to answer anything. So they can charge more.

GORDON: But the others don't believe me, do they? Not like you.

EDITH: I think they want to be certain.

GORDON: But how can they ever be? If the lawyer casts even the slightest doubt, won't that give them the excuse to cut me out and stay with Matthew? If only one of them recognised me.

EDITH: They will do, soon. I know it.

GORDON: No, they won't. They've forgotten me.

He shoves the table in frustration.

GORDON (CONT'D): I'm a stranger to them now!

EDITH: Well, you're not a stranger to me.

50 INT. SERVANTS' HALL. DOWNTON. NIGHT.

It is late. The servants have finished dinner.

O'BRIEN: I wouldn't be Vera Bates. He left here at dawn
with a face like thunder. I wonder if she knows what
she's started.
THOMAS: If I were you, I'd keep out of it.
ANNA: Wise words.

She has come in, followed by Jane who sits next to Daisy.

MRS PATMORE: How did you get on?
JANE: Yeah, it was interesting… Daisy, I wish you'd let
me tell you about it.
DAISY: There's no point.
O'BRIEN: No point in what?
DAISY: Jane keeps making out I'm a war widow. But I'm
not, am I? You all know that. I married William on his
death bed. That don't count.
ANNA: Of course it counts.
DAISY: I don't think so. And I wasn't good to him. He
thought I loved him, but I didn't. I don't think I did.
Not like he loved me. I should never have married him in
the first place, only he were — dying and… We all liked
him so much, didn't we? All of us?

She looks round at her fellow workers.

MRS PATMORE: Everyone liked William.
CARSON: He was a fine lad.
DAISY: He was, wasn't he? Good-natured and kind and
sunny to have around, and it didn't feel right not to
make him happy when it seemed like such a little thing.
Only now I don't think it was little. I think it was
big. And I shouldn't have done it.
MRS HUGHES: Marrying him was a great kindness —
DAISY: No! It wasn't kind. It was wrong. And I
shouldn't have done it!

*She runs out, bumping into Bates in the doorway. In their
shock, it is a moment before they register the new arrival.*

MRS HUGHES: Mr Bates? How did you get here?
BATES: I walked from the station.
CARSON: You should have said; we'd have sent someone to
meet you.

BATES: I was glad of the walk. I was glad of the air.

He's bruised. Anna approaches, drawing him into the passage.

ANNA: I never thought you'd be back tonight. How was it?
BATES: Worse than you can possibly imagine.

She goes to touch the bruise on his face, but he gently brushes her hand away.

ANNA: What's —?

51 INT. SMALL LIBRARY. DOWNTON. DAY.

All the family are in there. Robert is talking.

MARY: I assume that whatever Mr Murray has told you means the man is a fake. You can't have asked Matthew to be here unless you know that.
ROBERT: It's very complicated. Lowe was the only officer to go back to the site of the wreck. He did pull some people out of the sea and it seems one of the men was unidentified.
EDITH: There!
ROBERT: One of the reports has him dying before they reached the *Carpathia*.
MARY: Precisely.
ROBERT: Another witness says the man did get to New York alive, but there's no clear record of his name.
EDITH: Which could be Patrick Crawley.
ROBERT: There's more. There was a Peter Gordon, who worked with Patrick at Martin's Bank.* Now, he emigrated to Montreal in 1913.
VIOLET: Yes, and when his face was blown away he decided every cloud has a silver lining. He was perfectly placed to impersonate his dead friend. I mean, no doubt they shared confidences, so he just brushed them up, and put himself forward for a major inheritance.

....

* I cannot now remember why Hugh Bonneville altered the place where Major Gordon and the real Patrick had worked together. It became the Foreign Office, whereas I had it as Martin's Bank, which I should have thought quite as smart as the Foreign Office, but there must have been some reason for the change.

MARY: Granny's right. All he needed was a survivor from
the *Titanic* who was unaccounted for, and he found one.
EDITH: But the *Titanic* story bears out Patrick's version
in every way!
MARY: The man in the boat was dead.
EDITH: Not according to the other witness.
CORA: What do you think?
ROBERT: I don't know what to think.
MARY: How can you even hesitate?
EDITH: But Mary, you haven't heard the things he
remembers —
MARY: I don't need to. 'I remember how we played, and
your pony and your birthday, and how we hid in the garden
from the nasty governess.'

This is so like what he did say that Edith is silenced.

MARY (CONT'D): What other memories would you have of a
childhood spent here?
ROBERT: Murray will continue to investigate so, Edith,
can we be polite to the man, but nothing more? The end
of the war should make it easier to unearth the evidence.
That is all for the time being.
CORA: How strange it is. You pray and hope and hope and
pray and then, quite suddenly, the war is over.
ROBERT: I thought Carlisle was going to come back for our
ceremony tomorrow. But he never sent a train time.
MARY: He's driving up. He'll be here in time for dinner
tonight.

They have risen to go. Robert is with Matthew.

ROBERT: I'm sorry I can't be more decisive.
MATTHEW: Don't be. I meant what I said the other day.
It will take a man who is more than I am now to follow
you. So, don't think about me.
ROBERT: My dear chap, how can you say that? I never
think about anything else.

52 EXT. FOLLY. DOWNTON. DAY.

Edith is in the folly with Major Gordon.

EDITH: Tomorrow, when we all assemble to hear the clock
strike, I'm going to introduce you properly to Mama.

GORDON: But what do they make of this Peter Gordon
character they've uncovered? Do they think that's who
I am?
EDITH: Do you remember him?
GORDON: Very well. Peter and I were good friends. Very
good friends.
EDITH: Did you know he'd moved to Canada?
GORDON: How could I? When I'd forgotten who I was until
two months ago?
EDITH: Of course.
GORDON: So what will they do now?
EDITH: Track him down, I imagine. Find out what happened
to him.
GORDON: Suppose he joined the Princess Pat Light
Infantry?
EDITH: I don't understand. What are you saying? Why
would he?

Gordon looks at Edith quite tenderly.

GORDON: You're very sweet, you know. So sweet you made
me think that all things were possible. But perhaps the
lesson is, you can't go back.
EDITH: You're tired and I don't blame you. But you're
not to give up. I won't let you. We'll find this Peter
Gordon. I know we will.
GORDON: Yes. I expect you will.
EDITH: And then won't we show them?*

....

*Trevor White was very good as Gordon. He brought a curiously touching
quality to his whole performance, layered in with his bully-boy scheming and
manipulation of Edith, which also deepens into something different. In
other words, he did good and interesting work for us. I was especially
impressed by his breakdown in Scene 49. This was written to be in the
library, but was played in the hall among all the men at their refectory tables,
which was better. In fact, I am probably questioned about when he is coming
back more than people ask about almost any other character. I may resolve
the story one day. I am tempted.

One of Emma's and my charities is called Changing Faces. It's for people
who are severely facially disfigured, either by birth or after an accident, or as
the consequence of an operation. It is led by an extraordinarily charismatic
chap called James Partridge, whom we both admire enormously. One of
their fundraisings was a *Downton* evening, with Michelle Dockery and

53 INT. CARSON'S PANTRY. DOWNTON. NIGHT.

Carson is reviewing the wine books. Mrs Hughes arrives.

MRS HUGHES: They'll be going in to dinner in a minute.

He nods and stands, but glances back at the pages.

CARSON: We've built a good cellar here, you know. I'm not saying it's legendary, but it's nothing to be ashamed of.

She knows well enough what this means.

MRS HUGHES: You've made your mind up, then?
CARSON: I think so. Yes, I think I have. But with a heavy heart, Mrs Hughes.
MRS HUGHES: And just when we thought we were getting back to normal.
CARSON: Don't tell me you'll miss me.
MRS HUGHES: I will, Mr Carson. Very much. And it costs me nothing to say it.
CARSON: Thank you. That means a lot to me.

54 INT. DINING ROOM. DOWNTON. NIGHT.

Dinner is over. Cora and her daughters are there. Robert, in black tie, stands. He glances at Matthew in his wheelchair.

ROBERT: Shall we go through with the ladies? And let them get in here?
MATTHEW: Of course.
CORA: I wonder what happened to Richard.
MARY: He'll have started late, and —

....

Continued from page 351:

Trevor White as the celebrities. Guests were interested to meet the actor who had played a disfigured character, who was nevertheless a principal in the narrative, with a romantic sub-plot. Apparently, this does not usually happen, which makes me slightly ashamed of my profession. I'm always very moved, actually, when I go to the Changing Faces events, because I look around at these really rather marvellous men and women, and I just think: what on earth am I complaining about?

But there is a noise. Carson goes to investigate but Richard Carlisle comes in. They are all standing now.

CARLISLE: Oh, I do apologise, Lady Grantham. We got stuck in Royston and a cart had overturned in Baldock.*
CORA: Hello, my dear, how lovely to see you.

For a moment, the others are puzzled. But then Lavinia appears from behind Carlisle and steps into the room.

LAVINIA: Are you sure? Sir Richard said you were expecting me, but are you?

Robert has been looking at Cora, but now he smiles.

ROBERT: Of course we are.
CORA: Can you take Matthew into the small library? Are you hungry? We've finished, but Mrs Hughes can easily put something on a tray. Carson?

Carson nods and retreats to the servery door.

....

* Royston and Baldock refer to the days of my youth, when I was at Ampleforth College in Yorkshire, a part of my very Catholic education. In those days, there was no M1, and you had to drive up on the A1, which, before all the motorway stretches and bypasses, was essentially the old carriageway made good. On this journey, you passed through Royston and Baldock, and my parents always used to stop for lunch in one or the other. One time, I missed a term at school, as I'd been in a car crash. I had cracked my skull – which explains a lot – and I was kept at home for the summer term. Ill-advisedly, my parents decided to take me with them when they drove up for what was known as 'Exhibition', to visit my brothers. I remember I slept in my house, St Bede's, and I've never enjoyed anything so much, because I knew I was going home at the end of it, on Monday. Of course, all the other boys in the dormitory were jealous and furious, but my father felt he'd paid for the whole term, and he was damned if he was going to pay my hotel bill on top of it, so I could jolly well sleep in the school. I don't think he realised the extent of the naughtiness he was inviting, but it is a happy memory even now, including the drive through Royston and Baldock.

55 INT. SMALL LIBRARY. DOWNTON. NIGHT.

Lavinia pushes Matthew's chair in through the door.

MATTHEW: Nothing's changed.
LAVINIA: But you see, it has. Because I've changed.
When I was last here, I was so bowled over that I let you
send me away. But not this time. I love you. I'm going
to look after you. That's all there is to it.
MATTHEW: And if I refuse?
LAVINIA: I'm sorry but I mean it. You won't frighten me
away, whatever you do.

56 INT. DINING ROOM. DOWNTON. NIGHT.

Robert and Cora are alone in the room.

CORA: Before you scold me, it's no good pretending Mary
is not a good deal too attached to Matthew.
ROBERT: So you summon Lavinia? To be sacrificed like
some latter-day Iphigenia, doomed to push his chair
through all eternity?
CORA: Robert, it's quite simple. Do you want Mary's
marriage to be a success? Do you want grandchildren?
ROBERT: Sometimes, Cora, you can be curiously unfeeling.*

57 INT. HALL. DOWNTON. NIGHT.

*Mary has come out of the dining room with Carlisle. They are
overtaken by Sybil and Edith, who all follow Matthew and
Lavinia into the small library. As soon as Mary and Carlisle
are alone, it is clear that Mary is very angry.*

MARY: Suppose he doesn't want her back? Have you thought
of that?
CARLISLE: He needs someone to look after him.

....

* Cora and Robert are fighting it out. Robert feels, and there is justice in his
viewpoint, that there is no moral reason why Lavinia should be sacrificed on the
altar of Matthew any more than Mary, but that's not Cora's way of thinking.
As I have pointed out before now, Cora is a mother and Mary is her child. As
far as she's concerned, her daughter is the one to be saved. She doesn't dislike
Lavinia, in fact she likes her, but if Lavinia has got to be sacrificed to save Mary
from a wasted and childless life, then tough. I do not know that I speak for all
mothers in this rather blinkered approach, but I certainly speak for my own.

MARY: Yes, but —
CARLISLE: And you'll be too busy with our new life, won't you?
MARY: Look, I know you're used to having your own way —
CARLISLE: Yes, I am. And I'll say something now I hope I won't have to repeat. If you think you can jilt me, or in some way set me aside, I tell you now you have given me the power to destroy you and don't think I won't use it. I want to be a good husband and for you to be happy. But don't ever cross me. Do you understand? Never. Absolutely never.*

58 INT. HALL. DOWNTON. NIGHT.

Cora stalks out of the dining room. Mary and Carlisle are still in the hall, Mary still stunned by Carlisle's words.

CORA: I expect you love birds would like to be alone. I don't think there's anyone in the smoking room.

She moves on as the 'love birds' stare at each other.

END OF ACT FOUR

....

* When Carlisle reveals his nasty side, I don't believe it comes as a great surprise. We've always known there was something pretty rough about him underneath, and he was never going to be pushed around by Mary. Unfortunately for her, by telling him her secret Mary has empowered him. Even if she told him to publish, it wouldn't quite restore the power balance between them to the position they were in before, because Mary is a different person in his eyes, and her own. These things – romances, scandals – change you. I suppose that's what I'm writing about here.

ACT FIVE

59 INT. DRAWING ROOM. DOWNTON. DAY.

Edith comes in, but Gordon's bed is stripped, his table cleared. Sybil is there.

EDITH: What's happened to Major Gordon?

SYBIL: He's gone.

EDITH: But he can't have. When?

SYBIL: After breakfast. We couldn't very well stop him.
The war's over… He left this for you.

She takes an envelope from her pocket and hands it to Edith.

SYBIL (CONT'D): What does it say?

EDITH: 'It was too difficult. I'm sorry. P. Gordon.'

SYBIL: P for Patrick or P for Peter?

EDITH: I know what you think, but I don't accept it. We
drove him away. His own family drove our cousin away.

SYBIL: But you believed in him, whoever he was. And
that's worth something.

60 INT. HALL. DOWNTON. DAY.

*The entire household has been assembled by Carson. A clock
has been placed on a table at the front. The family arrives.*

ROBERT: Are we all ready?

He turns to the company.

ROBERT (CONT'D): I think, while the clock strikes, we
should all make a silent prayer, to mark the finish of
this terrible war, and what that means for each and every
one of us. Let us remember the sacrifices that have been
made and the men who will never come back, and give them
our thanks.

*They have only a moment to wait. The clock starts to strike
eleven and we range over all the faces: Carson, Thomas,
O'Brien, Matthew, Violet, Robert, Cora, the sisters, the hall
boys and kitchen maids, Clarkson, Isobel… Some, like Daisy or
Jane or Mrs Patmore, have tears rolling down their cheeks,
some murmur their prayers softly, some are silent. It's over.*

ROBERT (CONT'D): Thank you, everyone. Remember, this is not just the end of a long war, but it is the dawn of a new age. God bless you all.

Across the hall, Lavinia is struggling with Matthew's chair.

BATES: Let me help you with that.
LAVINIA: Can you get him back to his room? I'll open the door.

She runs ahead a little. Bates starts to push, then…

MATTHEW: My God.
BATES: Is something wrong, sir?
MATTHEW: No. Nothing… Bates, if I felt…
BATES: If you felt what, sir?
MATTHEW: It doesn't matter. Not yet. Not until I feel it again.

*With this cryptic uttering, he sits back.**

61 EXT. FRONT DOOR. DOWNTON. DAY.

Robert is there with Carson.

CARSON: I thought that was very dignified. Very calming. Thank you, m'lord.
ROBERT: I don't suppose you're having any doubts about leaving?
CARSON: I'm afraid not, m'lord.
ROBERT: Well, I can't say I'm not sorry.
CARSON: I won't go until we've found a proper replacement.
ROBERT: Whoever we find won't replace you.

62 INT. HALL. DOWNTON. DAY.

Edith crosses the hall and rushes out through the front door. Mary is on the stairs. Robert comes out of the library.

ROBERT: Have they told you Major Gordon's gone? Packed up his duds and left, first thing this morning.
MARY: No wonder Edith looked so upset.
ROBERT: I suppose he was the other chap.
MARY: Papa, he was just a fraud. A common or garden fraud.

....

*This is really to tell the audience not to give up on Matthew.

ROBERT: I wish I could be as sure of anything as you are of everything.
MARY: Mr Murray will find the proof. You'll see.
ROBERT: I hope so... What puzzles me is why would anyone put themselves through all that?
MARY: To be Earl of Grantham, of course.
ROBERT: They should try it from the inside.

63 EXT. FOLLY. DOWNTON. DAY.

In the gardens Edith sits weeping, holding the letter.

64 INT. SERVANTS' HALL. DOWNTON. DAY.

Daisy is laying the table for lunch.

JANE: Knowing it's over somehow makes me think of Harry all the more. I s'pose it's the same with William.
DAISY: I suppose it is, yes.
MRS PATMORE: We all think of William, bless him.

To her dismay, Daisy finds she is crying. She hurries out.

JANE: You know there'd be none of this if she hadn't loved him?
MRS PATMORE: Of course I do. But I wish she did.

Carson enters.

CARSON: Mr Bates. Telegram for you.

He hands it over and Bates opens it. He reads it, then walks out of the room, giving it to Anna as he goes. She looks down.

THOMAS: What was that about?
ANNA: His wife's dead. Someone found her early this morning.

64A   INT.   VERA BATES'S HOUSE.   DAY.

*Vera Bates lies dead on the floor.**

END OF EPISODE SIX

....

* And now, as a last *bonne bouche*, we kill off Vera Bates, and end with her
lying stretched out, dead, on the kitchen floor. Initially, I wasn't sure about
this idea as an episode finish, but I think it works. At the time, I thought we
should have ended on Anna's line, with a lingering shot of her and Bates, as
they absorbed the information that would probably ruin their lives. But the
consensus went against me, and the general vote was for having Vera lying on
the floor, dead. Looking back, I think I was wrong and they were right.

EPISODE SEVEN

ACT ONE*

1 EXT. DOWNTON. DAY.

1919. An army lorry is driving away from the front of the house. Edith watches from the doorway.

2 INT. HALL. DOWNTON. DAY.

Mrs Hughes joins Edith.

> EDITH: That's the last of the equipment gone.
> MRS HUGHES: Which means the drawing room can go back to normal.
> EDITH: I'll help.
> MRS HUGHES: Oh, there's no need for that, m'lady. We can manage.

Edith smiles. She is rather sorry they can manage.

> MRS HUGHES (CONT'D): So there's only Captain Crawley left. Captain Crawley. Mr Crawley. What do we call him now?
> EDITH: Mr, I think. It's not quite right to go on with army titles when you're not a regular.†
> MRS HUGHES: So, when will he be going home?
> EDITH: The trouble is, Crawley House is all stairs…

....

* We began the series in 1916, because we felt we could say what we wanted to say about the war in the first six episodes, and we definitely wanted to use the end of the series and the Christmas Special to take the audience into the post-war world. I suspect that many in the audience had assumed that when we got to the end of the war that would be the end of the series, but not so.

We knew we wanted to explore the changes and adjustments that these families were going to have to go through, a theme which became the subtext for the rest of the series and beyond. That was the thinking, so we wanted to have two episodes after the Armistice had happened, and then a break before the Christmas Special. One always has to remember, though, that in America there is no break between the series and the Special. It is simply the final episode of the Season, so it needs to be constructed to play either as the end of a series, or as a stand-alone, which is a bit complicated, though one must never make one's work sound more demanding than it is.

3 INT. DRAWING ROOM. DOWNTON. DAY.

Cora is reading when Robert looks in.

ROBERT: I'm walking down to the village. I want to have
a word with Travis.
CORA: You know that Richard will be here any moment.
ROBERT: That's why I'm telling you. Give him my excuses.
I'll see him at dinner.
CORA: Is there any news on the Bates situation?
ROBERT: Not that I'm aware of.
CORA: So you still want to keep him on?
ROBERT: Cora, Bates's wife has committed suicide. It's
very sad, of course, but not, when I last looked, a
reason to sack him.‡

....

† I do not question the decision to cut this exchange, but I regret losing the
information about military titles, because I think it's something that many
people don't know. In the First World War the officer class originally came
from the upper or the upper-middle classes, as they always had done. But a
lot of these men were killed, and by halfway through the war promotion from
the ranks had become more normal. It was quite a tough job for those new
officers, because they needed to convince their own men that they were
indeed real officers. They had that extra burden to negotiate. They weren't
members of the club; they'd come from a different background. So they were
caught in a kind of limbo.

As I have said before now, these men became an English type, celebrated
in the plays of Terence Rattigan – viz. the character of the Major in *Separate
Tables*. Field Marshal Haig, in particular, tried to help them after the war,
but in the end they just had to muddle through and make the best of it. They
were, in a way, casualties of war. The sea had receded and left them stranded
on the beach. It wasn't very dissimilar from the Eurasians in India, who were,
I think, very badly treated when the British left. They'd had a key role to
play, running the railways, managing the nation's transport, but then,
suddenly, the new India wasn't interested in them, and nor were we. The fate
of the ex-officers, promoted from the ranks, was much the same, played out
in a minor key. I sympathise with and pity both groups, and I admire what
was, in many cases, tremendous gallantry against the odds.

‡ At the beginning of every episode, we remind the audience of various
strands we intend to advance that week with a couple of references. It's a
standard technique, really, but the great thing is never to assume that they
will remember every detail of an earlier episode, because they won't.

His manner's curt to say the least. Cora changes the subject.

CORA: They've taken the rest of the beds.
ROBERT: So that's the finish of it.
CORA: Not quite. We still have Matthew. And I wanted to ask you, isn't it time he went home?
ROBERT: I see. You want to throw him out.
CORA: Robert, I want him to learn to be as independent as he can. And I want Mary to get on with her life. What's wrong with that?

Her words make him look at her more carefully.

ROBERT: Is there something you're not telling me?
CORA: What do you mean?
ROBERT: About Mary. And Matthew. Some element you haven't told me?
CORA: Of course not. You're being silly.
ROBERT: If thinking that trying to protect Mary with a ring of steel is silly, then yes, I am very silly.

He goes, leaving Cora to digest his words.*

....

* In the *Downton* way, Robert and Cora both have a point in their disagreement about sending Matthew home. As we know, Cora does not want her daughter to be desperately in love with a man who is incapable of fathering any children or living a normal life. In one way, she is not being fair, but in another, how many mothers out there would criticise her for it? Robert, meanwhile, feels there is something dishonourable in dumping Matthew. He is very fond of him, and, of course, vastly prefers him to Richard Carlisle, who is the very antithesis of everything he admires.

But, for me, by taking that position, Robert is making a classic mistake of his own class. In fact, their resentment of new people joining the club is illogical and self-defeating. The English aristocracy survived for as long as it did as an important and politically powerful class because there was a way for new people to join, as opposed to some of the tighter nobilities on the continent of Europe, where the doors were shut, particularly after the monarchies fell. As a result, they became weaker and weaker, and more and more irrelevant. I stand in a completely different position from Robert in this context, not just about Carlisle, but about the phenomenon of the New Man, which I think was a very important element of the Twenties and Thirties, and bought the aristocracy extra time. For me, the greatest threat to the survival of the aristocracy today is that they have locked the gates, and no one new may now join.

4 INT. LIBRARY. DOWNTON. DAY.

Matthew sits in his wheelchair. Lavinia is with him while Edith is sorting books. Carson has brought in the tea.

MATTHEW: You shouldn't be doing that.

CARSON: Let us hope the end of the war brings the return of the footman, Mr Crawley.

LAVINIA: Do you think they will return?

CARSON: I certainly hope so.

MATTHEW: I'm sure Sir Richard can buy you a dozen when you get to Haxby.*

....

* There were people at all levels of society who wanted everything to go back to the way it was. But there was also a different group who thought things *would* revert to the way they used to be, not necessarily because they wanted it, but because that was what was going to happen.

This was the anomaly, if that's the right word, of the 1920s, which I wanted to explore. I remember talking to a great-aunt about it. She was in her forties by the time the Twenties began, and so grown up, but not old. She said that the thing was, at the very beginning, it was quite difficult to see what had changed, or whether it was all going to go back to how it had been, because various elements, like footmen and butlers, did reappear. Not in every house – some families were strapped for cash after the loss of the agricultural subsidies and when income tax went up – but, nevertheless, on a lot of estates, the young men returned and went back into service, and it was only later in the decade that you started to realise that in fact things had changed, not only for economic reasons, but because there'd been a shift in thinking.

The American song 'How You Gonna Keep 'em Down on the Farm After They've Seen Paree?' really exemplified a lot of what was going on. These men had travelled, they'd been all over Europe. Before the war they might never even have left their own county, but now they'd been everywhere. Then the movies and the radio and modern music were all telling people that there was a world out there, and maybe you don't want to be the village cobbler, maybe you've got something else in you. That attitude really took root after the First World War, and it was never controlled again. In the end, these strands would all build into the modern philosophy: you can be what you want, you can do what you like. Of course, such things don't happen overnight, but this was the beginning of the 'Me Generation', as we call it now.

Mary comes in.

> MARY: Carson, do you know if Branson's left for the station?
>
> CARSON: I think so, m'lady, but I can go and check. Or I can get Mr Pratt to take you in the other motor —
>
> MARY: Don't bother. It doesn't matter.

Carson leaves. Mary pours herself a cup of tea.

> MARY (CONT'D): What's the betting he's missed the train? Edith, what are you doing?
>
> EDITH: Trying to sort out the books. The novels have got into such a mess.
>
> MARY: I should have thought you'd be glad of the chance to put your feet up.
>
> EDITH: You'd think so, wouldn't you?

5 EXT. PARK. DOWNTON. DAY.

Robert is strolling through the park. He stops for a moment and looks at the house that dominates his life. He sighs, but then, ahead of him, he sees Jane. She has dropped her bag and some apples are rolling about. He walks over.

> ROBERT: Let me.
>
> JANE: Oh, no, m'lord. I can manage… The handle broke.

Robert pays no attention and collects some itinerant fruit.

> ROBERT: Aren't we feeding you?
>
> JANE: They're from my mother's apple store. She always loads me up.
>
> ROBERT: How's your boy doing? Uh, Freddie?

She is flattered he has remembered the name.

> JANE: Yes, Freddie. He's doing very well.
>
> ROBERT: I wrote to the headmaster of Ripon Grammar. I said to look out for him.
>
> JANE: That's — that's so kind, m'lord.
>
> ROBERT: I hope it works. I don't really see why it should, but you never know.

He looks at her. For a moment, it seems he might kiss her. *

ROBERT (CONT'D): I suppose you miss your husband very much?
JANE: Of course. But I have Freddie, and when you think of what some families have gone through...
ROBERT: I know. Almost thirty dead on this estate alone. And the Elcots down at Longway lost three out of four sons; Mrs Carter's only boy was killed a month before the end of the war. Poor William. And then there's Matthew...

He sighs. †

ROBERT (CONT'D): Do you ever wonder what it was all for?

....

* Robert has been tempted by this nice, pretty woman and she is tempted, too. I never thought she wanted to ensnare him. Jane is a perfectly nice character, but she's lost her husband and she's lonely, and Robert's lonely because Cora's busy elsewhere, and there you have it.

We also see an expression of Robert's thinking, which is interesting because it is typical of his kind. When Jane asks for help to get her son into Ripon Grammar, he does it. But he feels he has to say, 'I hope it works. I don't really see why it should, but you never know.' Now, of course he is well aware that if he, the Earl of Grantham, writes to the head of the local grammar school and asks him to look out for a particular boy, then, unless he does it every week, and as long as he keeps his recommendations to a manageable level, the headmaster is very unlikely to ignore him, because the school may want some treat from the Downton estate, or they may need some money. Which is the key to the old system. It worked, as long as everyone trod gently. The moment they trod with heavy feet, it ceased to work.

† I was very pleased we were able to keep this in. I had worried that it would be a casualty of the edit, but the truth is, an estate the size of Downton, because of the death rate of the war, would have lost quite a few, and the village would have suffered as well. We wanted to remind people that one of the curious things about the war was that, at the end of it, everyone knew an enormous number of people whose sons and husbands were dead. It was a phenomenon shared by all classes; nobody had been spared. And for a while the world was a haunted sepulchre, until a new generation came up, who'd only been in their teens at the end of the war. But for a few years it must have felt very, very strange.

There is the noise of a car arriving. In front of the house, Branson holds the door of the car for Sir Richard Carlisle.

JANE: I'd better go in, m'lord.

She hurries away towards the kitchen court. He watches her before turning away and walking over to Carlisle.

CARLISLE: The train was late.
ROBERT: Welcome to the new world.
CARLISLE: When a war is over, the first emotion is relief, the second disappointment.
ROBERT: How sad. But how true… Come in and have some tea.

6 INT. SERVANTS' HALL. DOWNTON. NIGHT.

The servants are having their tea.

ANNA: Will you miss the extra staff, Mrs Patmore?
MRS PATMORE: Not really. When push comes to shove, I'd rather do it myself. Though God knows what I'm to feed them on. There's nothing out there to be had. Oh well. The Lord tempers the wind to the shorn lamb.*
DAISY: What about you, Thomas? How much longer will you stay?
THOMAS: Well, now the last of the invalids have gone, I suppose I'm finished. I'll report to Major Clarkson, but he won't be taking anyone on.
ANNA: I suppose the hospital will revert to the way it was, before the war.
DAISY: Where will you go?
THOMAS: What's it to you?

....

* Food shortages and rationing at the end of the First World War weren't like rationing in the Second World War, which started pretty early on. In the 1940s, the Government knew there would be shortages and they prepared people for it and limited supplies. At the end of the First World War, when they started running out of everything, it was a surprise to most of the population. And actually, I didn't even know there was rationing in the first war, so it was also a surprise to me.

Daisy gives up on him, but O'Brien is curious.

O'BRIEN: Where will you go?

She looks at him. He winks. He lowers his voice. So does she.

THOMAS: I'll tell you where I'm going. Into business. It's all set up.
O'BRIEN: Do you mean black market business?
THOMAS: Don't look so surprised. I've found a dealer, and as soon as I make the payment I'll have the supplies.
O'BRIEN: Where will you keep them?
THOMAS: I've got a shed in the village, and I'll get a banger to deliver the stuff. I'll be well fixed as soon as word gets out. You heard her. There are shortages all round.
O'BRIEN: Isn't it dangerous?
THOMAS: I don't think so. I don't think the police are bothered about rationing, now the war's over. It won't last forever, but by the time it's done I should have enough to go into business properly.*
O'BRIEN: So that's your future settled as a plutocrat. In the meantime, have you found somewhere to live?
THOMAS: Not yet, but there's no hurry. I'm sure they won't object if I stop here for a week or two.
O'BRIEN: I shouldn't bet on it.

The gong sounds and the ladies' maids and Bates all stand.

....

* What's important about Thomas is that he represents those people who didn't want to go back into service. He feels he's too good for service, that there's more in him than waiting at table, and I don't disagree with him. I think he is a classic case of someone who, in the nineteenth century, probably would have gone through the whole thing without too much trouble, but now the door is open, he thinks there's more to life than what he was doing before the war. We know his plan will be defeated, because nobody wants to lose him from the series, but nevertheless he stands for people who had a perfectly legitimate grievance and tried to change things. Naturally, we don't approve of his chosen route out, the black market, but we do sympathise with his desire to escape.

7   INT.   ROBERT'S DRESSING ROOM.   DOWNTON.   NIGHT.

Bates is helping Robert into white tie.

> BATES: I nearly put out the new dinner jacket, m'lord,
> but then Mr Carson said the Dowager was dining here.*
> ROBERT: Quite right. Mustn't frighten the horses… By
> the way, her ladyship was asking if there was any more
> news about Mrs Bates.
> BATES: I don't think so, m'lord. They'd like to know why
> she did it, but I don't suppose we ever shall.
> ROBERT: You'd think she'd leave a note.
> BATES: Perhaps it was a spur-of-the-moment decision.
> ROBERT: But it can't have been, can it? Wouldn't she
> have to get hold of the stuff?

Bates is increasingly uncomfortable, which Robert now sees.

> ROBERT (CONT'D): Please forgive me. I was thinking
> aloud. We'll drop the subject.

....

* As we saw in the previous episode, the dinner jacket was beginning to be worn for informal dinners, although on the whole they avoid wearing it when the Dowager's coming, because she hates it, seeing in it a sign that everything is cracking up, which, of course, is a completely accurate observation. Eventually they become less careful, and by the fourth series they do sometimes wear it when Violet is there. She continues to make rather caustic remarks, however.

The dinner jacket really started in America, as a sort of costume for all-men dinners and then completely informal dinners. They were called tuxedos, because they were invented by a man who lived in Tuxedo Park, a very swanky rich man's village outside New York. The legend is that he had the tails cut off his coat, or perhaps he simply ordered a new jacket to be made without tails.

The Prince of Wales saw an American friend wearing one, borrowed it and had his tailor copy it. He would wear it for informal nights, and later he would go out to nightclubs in a dinner jacket, which was considered very wild. But, with his launch, society started to take up this suspicious garment. Initially it was considered halfway between correct clothing and dining in a dressing gown, but it gained ground. It was certainly more comfortable, especially when the shirt eventually softened. That hasn't happened yet, of course. They are still in stiff shirts here.

8 INT. BEDROOM PASSAGES/CARLISLE'S ROOM. DOWNTON. NIGHT.

Anna comes out of Mary's bedroom, carrying some things.

CARLISLE (V.O.): Anna. It is Anna, isn't it?
ANNA: Yes, sir.

He is standing in an open doorway. She waits to hear.

CARLISLE: I want to ask a favour of you.
ANNA: Of me, Sir Richard?
CARLISLE: You. I've been waiting for you. I wonder if you could step into my room for a moment?

She does not want to, but she doesn't see what she can do. Rather nervously, she walks inside and he closes the door.

CARLISLE (CONT'D): You attend Lady Mary and her sisters, don't you? In addition to your other duties?
ANNA: I do, sir. Yes.
CARLISLE: You must be kept very busy. I hope it's worth your while.

Naturally, she is silent at this impertinence.

CARLISLE (CONT'D): Because I would be very willing to increase your stipend —
ANNA: If this is about coming with Lady Mary when you marry, it's very good of you, sir, but you see, my fiancé, Mr Bates, works here and I don't think I —
CARLISLE: No, it's not that. Although it's a pity. Lady Mary's very fond of you.
ANNA: That's kind.

They stand. She is puzzled. What else could it be?

CARLISLE: You see, I'm anxious to make Lady Mary happy.
ANNA: Of course you are, sir.
CARLISLE: And to that end, I feel I need to know a great deal more about her than I do. Our customs are so strange in this country. A couple is hardly allowed a moment alone together before they walk down the aisle.
ANNA: I'm not sure I understand, sir.
CARLISLE: I'd like to know more about her interests: where she goes, whom she sees, what she says to them —
ANNA: Excuse me, sir. Do you mean you want me to give you a report of Lady Mary's actions?

CARLISLE: It'll be extra work, but I'm happy to pay.

ANNA: I'm sure. But I'm afraid I wouldn't have the time. Thank you, sir.

CARLISLE: It's your choice, of course.

She takes this as a dismissal and goes to the door.

CARLISLE (CONT'D): I'd be grateful if you didn't mention this to Lady Mary. I wouldn't want her to think I was checking up on her

She leaves without another word.

END OF ACT ONE

....

* Carlisle entirely misjudges the relationship between a servant and their employers, but I'm not sure Anna's loyalty was true in every case. One has to remember that, by the end of the Old World, and throughout the nineteenth century, one of the key positions for spies was to place them as personal servants. If they could get a spying lady's maid into a politician's house, or a spying valet, the thinking was that they would pick up an enormous amount of information, because their guard would be down when they were undressing. It was particularly the lady's maid and the valet – even more than a butler – who were considered the best leaks.

I'm not suggesting that Carlisle is breaking some fundamental tenet, but when the relationship between the servant and master worked, or, for that matter, works, there is a degree of trust that a professional servant would not wish to break. And here, Anna's instinct instantly rebels against the notion that she is being offered money to spy. I felt Joanne Froggatt played this scene very well, because she managed somehow to make even his invitation to step into his bedroom feel tremendously uncomfortable and out of order. Which it would have been.

ACT TWO

9 INT. DRAWING ROOM. DOWNTON. NIGHT.

The family is there, having coffee after dinner.

ROBERT: I nearly came down in a dinner jacket tonight.

VIOLET: Really? Well, why not a dressing gown? Or better still, pyjamas?

ROBERT: That's why I didn't.

ISOBEL: I like the new fashions. Shorter skirts, looser cuts. The old clothes were all very well if one spent the day on a chaise longue, but if one wants to get anything done, the new clothes are much better.

VIOLET: I'll stick to the chaise longue.

SYBIL: But Granny, you don't really want things to go back to the way they were, surely?

VIOLET: Of course I do, and as quickly as possible.

SYBIL: What about you, Papa?

ROBERT: Before the war, I believed my life had value. I suppose I should like to feel that again.

There is a melancholy in this that makes them uncomfortable.

MARY: Have you seen the boys' haircuts the women are wearing in Paris?

MATTHEW: I hope you won't try that.

Naturally, this sends a faint frisson through the company.

MARY: I might.

LAVINIA: I'm not sure how feminine it is.

MARY: I'm not sure how feminine I am.

CARLISLE: Very, I'm glad to say.*

....

*The whole business of dress and government is something that hasn't really been explored and analysed much, but nevertheless it seems to me to be key. One of the basic facts about government in the old days was that people in power looked as if they were the right people to be in power. To this end, you had tremendous displays of splendour. Louis XIV of France, who'd emerged from a savage civil war, had such horrible memories of it that he was determined to strengthen the monarchy and never risk it again. One of his methods was to drive the Court around the country to show off these splendid, glorious people who ought to be in power.

He's fighting back. Cora decides to change the subject.

CORA: Carson, I keep forgetting to tell Mrs Hughes we've
had a letter from Major Bryant's mother. She and her
husband are in Yorkshire on Friday and she wants to pay
us a visit.
ROBERT: Why?

....

Continued from page 373:

Women played a big part in the politics of display. Louis would pack them into open carriages and order them to dress in their best and display their jewels. You can imagine the roads, the mud and the dust of 1690s France, but he was completely without mercy. He would ride through the towns, followed by his diamond-studded Court, proclaiming through them that the reins of government were in the right hands. At Versailles, he would receive, standing at the top of the ambassadors' staircase, with his glittering Court all around, wearing new clothes and new gems and under orders to shine.

As late as the 1890s, when the Shah of Iran arrived in Great Britain, people like the Marchioness of Londonderry and the Duchess of Devonshire would be ordered to entertain him. In fact, the aristocracy became a shop window, a great exhibition, to show the splendour and the money and the style of these people. But when democracy came, one result would be that the new ruling class ceased to look like a ruling class. The trouble was that the old system meant dressing very uncomfortably in order to look superb, in corsets and uniforms and stiff collars and top hats, under the Indian sun as much as anywhere else. There's a letter from Lady Curzon in Calcutta, saying that she can hardly do up the buttons of her evening frock because her fingers are so slippery with sweat, but she never thinks to abandon the formal costume and wear a cotton shift. Then it all changed. It is quite interesting, the moment when the upper classes – and it really came about in the Twenties – decided it wasn't so important any more to look different from everyone else. This was a key moment in their loss of control.

Here, Isobel is essentially democratic – not ludicrously so, but she believes in a more open and equal society, and she doesn't agree with the system that keeps people like the Crawleys on top. They are discussing the shorter haircut and, of course, it was a tremendous step forward for women, who were going into the workplace in a serious way. If you have hair to your waist that takes an hour to put up, you are not a serious worker, but the new woman could just put a comb through her bob and get going. The modern world had begun.

CORA: The last time they saw him alive it was here.
I can understand.
CARSON: Will they be staying, m'lady?
CORA: No, but we'll give them luncheon. That way, they
can talk about the Major with all of us who knew him.
VIOLET: That let's me out, thank heaven.

10   INT.   GARAGE.   STABLEYARD.   DOWNTON.   NIGHT.

Branson is working when Sybil comes in.

BRANSON: You look very fine.
SYBIL: Everything I own is from my Season before the war.
I'm trying to wear them out… Where have you been all
day?
BRANSON: Nowhere. I've just been busy.
SYBIL: I envy you. I feel so flat after the rush and
bustle of the last two years. They were sighing for the
old days at dinner, but all I could do was think about
how much more I want from life now than I did then.
BRANSON: Does this mean that you've made up your mind, at
last?
SYBIL: Not quite, but almost.

She reaches up and strokes his cheek.

11   INT.   CARSON'S PANTRY.   DOWNTON.   NIGHT.

Carson is sitting with Mrs Hughes, drinking tea.

CARSON: What do you mean, how did she say it? Mr and Mrs
Bryant are coming for luncheon on Friday. That's it.

But the way Mrs Hughes nods means that isn't quite it.

MRS HUGHES: How are things over at Haxby?
CARSON: Pretty good. Building materials are in short
supply, but Sir Richard knows how to get around that.
MRS HUGHES: I bet he does.
CARSON: You should see some of the gadgets in the
kitchens. And the bathrooms. Oh, goodness me. They're
like something out of a film with Theda Bara.
MRS HUGHES: I'm surprised you know who Theda Bara is.
CARSON: Oh, I get about, Mrs Hughes. I get about.

She puts down her cup.

MRS HUGHES: But will you be happy there? That's what I
want to be sure of.

He looks at her and nods.

CARSON: If you're asking whether I'll regret leaving
Downton, I will regret it every minute of every day.
I thought I would die here and haunt it ever after.
MRS HUGHES: Well, then.
CARSON: You see, I think I can help her. In those early
years when it's important to get it right. And if I can
help her, then I must.
MRS HUGHES: I wish I could understand. To me, Lady Mary
is an uppity minx who's the author of her own
misfortunes.
CARSON: You didn't know her when she was a child, Mrs
Hughes. She was a guinea a minute then. I remember
once, she came in here, she can't have been more than
four or five years old. She said: 'Mr Carson, I've
decided to run away and I wonder if I might take some of
the silver to sell.'

He laughs at his own memory.

CARSON (CONT'D): 'Well,' I said, 'that could be awkward
for his lordship. Suppose I give you sixpence to spend
in the village instead?' 'Very well,' says she, 'but you
must be sure to charge me interest.'
MRS HUGHES: And did you?
CARSON: She gave me a kiss in full payment.
MRS HUGHES: Then she had the better bargain.
CARSON: Oh, I wouldn't say that.*

There is a tentative knock. Anna is standing there.

ANNA: There you are, Mrs Hughes. They said you were in
here. Might I have a word?
MRS HUGHES: Of course. Shall we go to my room?
ANNA: There's no reason Mr Carson shouldn't hear it. In
fact, I think he probably should… You see, I've had a
request from Sir Richard that you ought to know about…

12   INT.   MATTHEW'S BEDROOM.   DOWNTON.   NIGHT.

In a ground-floor room, Bates buttons Matthew's pyjamas.

MATTHEW: When the nurses left, I should have asked
Molesley to come and help me.
BATES: I don't mind, sir. Are you ready?

Bates lifts him, and swings him from the chair to the bed.

MATTHEW: You've done this before.

Bates chuckles. He lifts Matthew's legs and tidies the bed.

MATTHEW (CONT'D): Bates, can I ask you something? If I
started to feel a… tingling in my legs, what do you think
that might mean?
BATES: Have you told Doctor Clarkson?
MATTHEW: Yes. He says it's an illusion. A memory of a
tingling or something. But, I mean, I do know my back is
broken. I understand that I won't recover, but I do keep
feeling it. Or I think I do.

Bates considers this for a moment.

BATES: Well, it isn't a good idea to long for things that
can never be.
MATTHEW: No.

....

* This sequence when Carson describes Mary as a child was originally filmed
for the first series, but we ran out of time in the episode, and it was taken out.
I fought for its remounting, as I felt it was quite important to know that
Mary had won the butler's heart as a child, and so he would always see the
child in her, as opposed to a new servant, who would only have seen a
haughty young woman who is conscious of her position. So they reshot it,
and I put the case for it to stay in the edit, because for me it was a key
moment of Carson's back story. Happily, the others agreed. I have said
before, I'm always sorry it is not really practical to develop a relationship
between the children of the family and the servants, which in reality was a
very significant part of this set-up. I am constantly receiving letters from old
people talking about being given piggy-back rides by favoured footmen and
secret treats by the cook. Alas, the problem of ageing child characters has, so
far, defeated us, so this story, of the love between Carson and Mary, is the
closest we can come to suggesting that side of Downton life.

BATES: But, then again, life's a funny business. I
should wait and see. If something is changing, it will
make itself known. Now, will that be all?
MATTHEW: Yes, thank you… Bates, please don't tell
anyone. I couldn't bear it if Miss Swire or Mother or…
or anyone started to hope.
BATES: I won't say a thing. Good night, sir.*

12A EXT. DOWNTON VILLAGE. DAY.

Mrs Hughes walks through the village and boards a bus.

13 INT. ETHEL'S COTTAGE. DAY.

Mrs Hughes is with Ethel.

MRS HUGHES: I don't know why I'm doing this. I must be
out of my mind.
ETHEL: Because you know it's my last chance.
MRS HUGHES: Well, that's true. They won't be back. Not
after this trip.
ETHEL: So what should I do?
MRS HUGHES: Come to the house. But stay outside in the
game larder. I'll leave some food there and a blanket,
and then I'll try and find a moment alone with Mrs Bryant
and tell her about little Charlie. And then, if she asks
— only if she asks, mind you — I'll bring her out to see
the child.
ETHEL: What about him?
MRS HUGHES: If either of them are in the least
interested, it'll be the mother.

....

* I was attacked for this in the newspapers, and yet it's all medically based. In
the case of severe spinal bruising, the returning sensation starts with faint
tingling. But the difficulty of tingling is how to read it. If you have a leg
amputated, for instance, you can still feel pain in the leg, even though there's no
leg, because the nerves mislead you. And many men would have felt tingling,
even though their back was broken and they would never walk again. Matthew
is aware of all this, and so I agree with his not telling anyone, just as I agree
with Clarkson's thinking it would have been wrong at the beginning to give
him false hope. For Matthew to tell his mother or Lavinia that he's feeling
tingling in his legs would start up a whole colony of rabbits that would be very
difficult to get back in their holes. So, I'm entirely on Matthew's side over that.

ETHEL: And do you think she'll help me?

MRS HUGHES: She might.

ETHEL: Suppose she won't see him?

MRS HUGHES: Then you're no worse off than you are already...
Look, I shouldn't be doing it. So if you're not keen,
then for heaven's sake let's forget all about it.

ETHEL: No. I'll be there. I promise.

*But Mrs Hughes already regrets what she has instigated.**

14 INT. DRAWING ROOM. DOWNTON. DAY.

The room is normal again. Edith and Sybil are replacing the
photographs and things on the chimneypiece.

EDITH: Where does this go? I've forgotten.

SYBIL: On here, I think... Doesn't it feel odd to have the
rooms back?

EDITH: And only us to sit in them. I suppose we'll get
used to it.

SYBIL: I don't want to get used to it.

EDITH: What do you mean?

SYBIL: I know what it is to work now. To have a full
day. To be tired in a good way. I don't want to start
dress fittings, or paying calls, or standing behind the
guns.

EDITH: But how does one escape all that?

SYBIL: I think I've found a way to escape.

EDITH: Nothing too drastic, I hope.

SYBIL: It is drastic. There's no going back once I've
done it. But that's what I want. No going back.

....

* Mrs Hughes was the right character for this, because although she's very
organised and very straightforward, she's also a rebel against the system,
albeit in a very minor way. So it's not at all out of character for her to attempt
to help Ethel. Later, when it's clear it's not going to work, then the
managerial side of her character kicks in, because she does not believe in
disorder and chaos. I thought I had seen a game larder at Highclere, which is
why I set the scene in one. A lot of country houses had these often very
pretty outside larders for shot birds to hang in the open air, protected from
marauding foxes and the like by mesh or grills, and many of them have
survived. But not, apparently, the one at Highclere, if it ever existed.
Anyway, we did the best we could.

EDITH: I don't want to go back, either.

SYBIL: Then don't. You're far nicer than you were before
the war, you know.

Edith thinks for a moment about her busy times.

EDITH: Sybil, do you ever think about Major Gordon?

SYBIL: Not really, no.

EDITH: So you're absolutely sure he wasn't Patrick?

SYBIL: Don't be silly. We know he wasn't. But you're
not to worry. You will find your mission, and next time
it'll be the right one.*

15 EXT. DOWNTON VILLAGE. DAY.

*Thomas and O'Brien, in her coat and hat, are outside a large
shed, hidden in a side street. He opens the padlock.
Inside, the space is crammed with tins and bags and barrels
and jars.*

O'BRIEN: Where did you get it all?

THOMAS: I told you. This bloke from Leeds.

O'BRIEN: Where did he get it?

THOMAS: Some's army surplus, some's from America. And
Ireland… Everywhere. He's got contacts all over.
That's what I'm paying him for.

O'BRIEN: How much have you paid him?

THOMAS: A lot. But I'm not worried. I've taken nothing
perishable. This lot'll last for months. I'll be sold
out long before any of it's gone off.

O'BRIEN: Starting with Mrs Patmore…†

....

* The war has altered Edith and Sybil, and the question is: what are they
going to do with their lives now? Sybil is much more convinced by her own
alteration, so she's quite happy to engage with the fact that she's going to live
a completely different life from the one she probably would have lived if the
war had never happened. Edith isn't quite ready for that, but she has become
nicer, my theory being that, when you feel you are useful and doing
something worthwhile, with the soldiers genuinely appreciating your efforts,
it brings out the best in you. But the exchange was designed to make the
audience aware that Edith is now in search of a purpose.

16 INT. BOUDOIR. DOWNTON. DAY.

Mary is with Carson. She is obviously upset.

MARY: But Carson, if you're abandoning me, I think I deserve to know the reason why.

CARSON: I do not believe that Sir Richard and I would work well together.

MARY: But there must be more to it than that. You knew what Sir Richard was like. We were to educate him, together, you and I. Wasn't that the plan?

After an agonising silence, Carson decides on the truth.

CARSON: Sir Richard offered Anna a sum of money to report your activities to him. Whom you saw, what you said…

MARY: He wanted her to spy on me?

CARSON: Naturally he used a different word.

MARY: Naturally. And she refused.

CARSON: She refused and she reported the offer to Mrs Hughes and me.

MARY: Well, I wish she'd come to me first. So you mean you'd be uncomfortable? Working for a spymaster?

He does not answer. She shakes her head bitterly.

MARY (CONT'D): How disappointing of you. And I always thought you were fond of me.

....

† I got the idea for this story from the first time I was made aware of the black market. This was some years ago when I was in Russia filming the first episode of *Sharpe*, with Sean Bean. Where we were, in the town of Simferopol, there was a lot of caviar for sale, which you could buy quite cheaply in the shops, perfectly legitimately, and indeed I got quite a lot of it before I was done. But there were also people in the market place selling it for almost nothing. Their patter was that it had fallen off the back of a lorry and so on, when in fact it was old stock, long past its sell-by date, that they'd stolen from dustbins after it had been thrown out, and it was dry and quite inedible. The truth is, the moment you're dealing with expensive or rare food that goes off and is liable to end up in a rubbish bin, still in its original tins or packaging, you will find that this sort of thing goes on. Thomas's story was born of that.

Carson opens his mouth to reply, but Carlisle enters.

> CARLISLE: Ah, there you are. What about a quick walk before dinner?
>
> MARY: We ought to get changed first. We're terribly late as it is.
>
> CARSON: Will that be all, m'lady?
>
> MARY: Yes, Carson. Thank you. I think that will be all… Carson has decided not to come with us to Haxby.
>
> CARLISLE: Oh. I'm sorry. Is there anything I can say to change your mind?
>
> CARSON: I'm afraid not, sir.

With a crisp nod, he goes, leaving her in a thwarted fury, but he overhears:

> CARLISLE: What a shame.
>
> MARY: Not really. Butlers will be two a penny now they're all back from the war.*

17 INT. SERVERY. DOWNTON. DAY.

A door opens and Robert comes in. Jane is working there.

> ROBERT: I gather Carson was looking for me.
>
> JANE: Shall I go and find him, m'lord?
>
> ROBERT: It's all right. Tell him I'll be in the dressing room.

He looks around. Jane catches his glance.

> ROBERT (CONT'D): Has he done the red wine yet?
>
> JANE: It's over here, m'lord.

Two full decanters stand, without their stoppers. There are two empty bottles. Robert picks one up, sniffs it and nods.

....

* Although Mary is shocked about Carlisle's offering Anna money, she's not yet prepared to change her plans, which is classic Mary, really. She needs to weigh up where she stands in it all before she makes a decision. It is the thinking that lost her Matthew in the first place. Most of all, here, she's angry with Carson, who has, to her, blown Carlisle's lapse all out of proportion. When she says, 'Butlers will be two a penny, now they're all back from the war,' she is trying to hurt his feelings, and this is because she thought she could always do what she wanted with Carson, but now he's let her down. The audience is obviously on Carson's side. Or they should be.

ROBERT: Ah, I'm pleased. It's a new one on me. I had
some at a dinner in London and ordered it… Carson
thought we might try it tonight.
JANE: It's important to try new things…
ROBERT: Well, I'd better go up.

But they continue to stare at each other.

JANE: You made me sad yesterday. Wondering what the war
was for.
ROBERT: Oh, don't listen to me. I'm a foolish man who's
lost his way, and I don't quite know how to find it
again.

*Suddenly, he takes her in his arms and kisses her, then steps
back, amazed.*

ROBERT (CONT'D): I'm terribly sorry. I can't think what
came over me.

She says nothing, but the incident has clearly stunned her.

ROBERT (CONT'D): Please try to forgive me.

*He hurries away, but is still within earshot when she does
speak, gently.*

JANE: I do forgive you…*

18   INT.   KITCHEN PASSAGE.   DOWNTON.   DAY.

Carson is walking along when Jane comes downstairs.

JANE: Oh, Mr Carson. His lordship said you were looking
for him.

....

* Robert's kissing Jane is not a big surprise to the audience, even if it is quite a
surprise to the characters. But this stuff did go on, for both sexes, though
some people are reluctant to believe it. I remember a distinguished peer
saying that he had really enjoyed *Gosford Park*, but one thing he didn't believe
was that Lady Sylvia would ever have had a relationship with a servant. A
gentleman might sleep with a governess or a maid, but a lady would never do
the equivalent. I was rather touched by this, because, of course, lots of
aristocratic women had entanglements with servants over the centuries,
including Queen Elizabeth I's cousin, who went off with her groom. In fact,
the handsome footman became quite an iconic type in a certain kind of
fiction.

CARSON: And?

JANE: And, well, I was to say that you'd find him in the dressing room.

CARSON: What's the matter with you?

JANE: Nothing.

But she looks somehow pink and disturbed. As she hurries away, Anna appears with a tray. Carson signals to her.

CARSON: Anna, you should know that, as a consequence of what you told me, I have decided not to go from here —

ANNA: Because of what I said?

CARSON: But I would rather you kept the reason to yourself.

ANNA: Of course, Mr Carson.

END OF ACT TWO

ACT THREE

19 INT. SERVANTS' HALL. DOWNTON. DAY.

Anna comes into the servants' hall, where Bates is working on a waistcoat with some chalk. He looks up as she sits down and starts to set out the kit to clean jewellery.

ANNA: What are you doing?

BATES: I'm not sure. I thought this was oil, but the chalk's not moving it.

ANNA: It might be fruit. You could try milk if you can wash it after.*

He nods. But he seems preoccupied as she glances at him.

ANNA (CONT'D): Are you all right?

BATES: Now you ask, there is —

....

* I'm sorry that exchange went, because I always like to remind people of the old solutions, but clearly it was less important than preserving the narrative. Before Dabitoff and its modern descendants, there were various ways you got marks out. Here, these suggestions were taken from a book of household hints, published some time in the 1880s.

O'Brien comes in. She notices he has clammed up.

O'BRIEN: I'm sorry. Have I interrupted something?
ANNA: No, no.

She turns to Bates, who mouths 'Later'.

20   INT. DRESSING ROOM. DOWNTON. DAY.

Robert, in black tie, is with Carson. Isis is on the floor.*

CARSON: I wrestled with it, m'lord. I don't mind admitting. And I wanted to be there to help Lady Mary, and —
ROBERT: And protect her from Sir Richard.
CARSON: Well, I wouldn't quite put it like that, but yes, I suppose. Only…
ROBERT: Only you felt you couldn't work for a man who would offer a bribe?
CARSON: That is correct, m'lord. He was asking Anna to spy on her mistress.
ROBERT: Are you quite sure you won't regret it? I know how fond you are of Lady Mary.
CARSON: But I couldn't work for a man that I don't respect. And I certainly couldn't have left Downton for him.
ROBERT: I shall take that as a compliment. For myself and for my house.

21   INT. MARY'S BEDROOM. DOWNTON. NIGHT.

Mary is with Anna, who is finishing dressing her.

MARY: I still don't see why you didn't tell me first.
ANNA: I'm sorry, m'lady, but I didn't want to add to your troubles.
MARY: Well, you have done, whether you wanted to or not.

This is harsh.

....

* I have to keep mentioning Isis in the stage directions, otherwise there is a tendency for her to get left out, because she slows up the filming. Emma gets really cross with me if the dog's not in quite a bit of the episode, so I have these two forces pulling me in opposite directions.

22 INT. LIBRARY. DOWNTON. NIGHT.

Matthew, in his chair, and Lavinia are dressed for dinner.

MATTHEW: Nobody's down yet.

LAVINIA: They won't be long.

She looks across at a table with a tray loaded with plates.

LAVINIA (CONT'D): Oh, look. They've cleared the tea but forgotten to take that tray. They must have been distracted.

MATTHEW: Ring the bell.

LAVINIA: I'll do it. They'll be busy getting dinner ready.

She stands and picks up the tray.

MATTHEW: It's too heavy for you.

LAVINIA: No, it's not. I'll just take it to the dining room. Someone will be in there.

But she looks round at him as she says this and now she trips on the rug and starts to fall towards the burning fire.

MATTHEW: Look out!

She drops the tray with a crash and continues to fall, but she catches at the mantelshelf and manages to save herself.

LAVINIA: Heavens, that was a near thing.

She has brought her eyes up to Matthew. She stops.

LAVINIA (CONT'D): My God.

He is as stunned as she is. He is standing.*

....

* This sequence was quite cleverly done with a stunt woman. If you look at it carefully, you can see there's a double for Lavinia doing the actual stumbling and the fall. It is a side of filming I always enjoy. When my son Peregrine was a little boy he used to say, 'Slow it down, slow it down, Daddy, I want to see where James Bond turns into the double.' So I would rewind and play it more slowly and he'd say, 'It's James Bond, it's James Bond, *it's the double!*' The danger of this is that children of the industry have a completely different relationship with film narrative, and inevitably he'd bring his friends home from school and enthusiastically show them some special effect that was completely unsuitable, and they'd all be terrified out of their wits.

23   INT. HALL/STAIRCASE/LIBRARY. DOWNTON. NIGHT.

As Mary appears, Robert is running downstairs with Lavinia.
The others come out of their bedrooms and follow him.

    ROBERT: Mary! Girls! Cora! Come at once!

As he gets to the hall, the others appear.

    CORA: Robert? Wait!

But he does not wait.

    ROBERT: Everyone, come at once!
    MARY: What is it? What's happened?
    ROBERT: Come and see this!

As Sybil and Edith also hurry down, he has run into the
library, and now they follow him, to find Matthew in his
chair, which is a slight let-down.

    ROBERT: Is it true? Is it true what Lavinia says?

Matthew nods. Very carefully, he hoists himself up and is
once more standing. Mary starts to cry.

    MARY: I can't believe it!
    CORA: It's so wonderful.
    SYBIL: It is, but don't tire yourself out. Sit down now
    and we'll send for Doctor Clarkson.
    ROBERT: She's right. Edith, go with Branson. Get
    Clarkson, but fetch Mama and Cousin Isobel as well. I
    don't care what they're doing. Tell them to come now!

He is also nearly weeping as he wrings Matthew's hand.

    ROBERT (CONT'D): Oh, my dear chap. I cannot begin to
    tell you what this means to me —
    MATTHEW: It's pretty good news for me, too.

Which makes them laugh and cry at the same time. But by now
Carlisle has joined them. He stands back, as ever opaque.

24   INT. LIBRARY. DOWNTON. NIGHT.

They are all gathered as Clarkson speaks.

    CLARKSON: There is only one possible explanation. It
    starts with my own mistake. Every indication told me
    that the spine was transected, which would have been
    incurable.

ROBERT: But when Sir John Coates came to see Matthew, he
agreed with you.

But this is an awkward point. Clarkson takes a deep breath.

CLARKSON: Well, he didn't. Not entirely. He thought
that it could conceivably be a case of spinal shock…
That is, intense bruising. Which was sufficiently severe
to impede the leg mechanism…
MARY: But which would heal?
LAVINIA: Why didn't you tell us?
CLARKSON: Because I didn't agree with him, and I didn't
want to raise Captain Crawley's hopes to no purpose.
MATTHEW: I understand and I don't blame you.
CLARKSON: You must take it slowly. Rome wasn't built in
a day.
MATTHEW: I know.
CLARKSON: And I'm afraid you will carry a bruise on your
spine for the rest of your life —
MATTHEW: But I will have a life.
CLARKSON: Yes. I think we can say that. You will have a
normal life. And it won't be long in coming.

He is greeted by joy and relief. Isobel kneels by the chair.

ISOBEL: My darling boy. My darling boy.*

....

* When Matthew stood, I was attacked in the newspapers. They clearly
wanted to believe we had dramatised a physical impossibility, because it
meant they could legitimately criticise the show, which during the second
series was quite a strong item on their agenda. If Matthew had broken his
back and severed his spinal cord, they shrilled, he could not possibly recover.
Naturally, the answer to this is: of course not. But, if they had bothered
actually to watch the show, instead of looking for darts to throw, they would
have seen that their analysis was not at all what we were saying. We make it
clear that the issue, from the start, is whether Matthew's spine is bruised or
severed, and the London specialist, Sir John Coates, had actually diagnosed
it as a possible case of spinal shock, but Doctor Clarkson did not wish to raise
Matthew's hopes. The glee with which the papers greet a genuine mistake is
sad enough, but when, as here, they deliberately pretend that the show is
wrong when it is not, it can be really depressing.

In fact, the problem here is not that Matthew's story was impossible,
which it was not, but that David Robb, who plays Clarkson, has to persuade
us that he is a competent doctor when the plot requires him to misdiagnose

*She is weeping along with most of the others. Carson arrives
at the door. He catches Robert's eye.*

    CARSON: Excuse me, m'lord. But Mrs Hughes is wondering
    what she should do about dinner.

Robert claps his hands to quiet them.

    ROBERT: You'll all stay for dinner, won't you?
    CLARKSON: Well, I'm afraid I'm not dressed.
    ROBERT: Oh, never mind that. Who cares about that? What
    about you, Mama?
    VIOLET: Oh, certainly. All this unbridled joy has given
    me quite an appetite.

25 INT. KITCHEN PASSAGE. DOWNTON. NIGHT.

*There is a lot of chatter and laughter from the servants'
hall. Anna comes out and almost runs into Bates.*

....

Continued from page 388:

more or less everything. So we were quite careful in the third series, when we
got to Sybil's death, to make sure that he was the one who got it right, when
the other doctor got it wrong.

Anyway, now we realise that Matthew is going to recover. Dramatically, I
cannot lie, it was important that Matthew would once again be able to
function as a fully active character, because it would have been too limiting in
narrative terms to keep him in a wheelchair forever, and a big problem if he
was permanently unable to father a child. This last detail would not
necessarily be true in 2013 – there are many treatments now that can be tried
– but in the 1920s it certainly was true. And so we would have had no baby,
which would have brought everything to a bit of a full stop. Also, in terms of
the story, Mary, who is intensely practical, was in the process of negotiating a
deal with herself, in order to marry Carlisle and have a normal life. Which
the audience would not have wanted. My own belief is that, if Matthew had
remained in a wheelchair, she would have married Carlisle. Whether that is
shocking for the fans, I don't know, but she just doesn't strike me as an
Iphigenia figure, tethering herself to a rock and staying there forever,
uncomplaining. Lavinia, on the other hand, is prepared to sacrifice her life to
Matthew and ignore the sexual side of things. But I don't think Mary would
have done that. Either way, once Matthew was well again, then it was gloves
off, and the business facing Mary was to get him back.

ANNA: There you are. I wondered what had happened to you. It's wonderful news, isn't it?
BATES: Wonderful… Are you busy?
ANNA: I'm just going up to help in the dining room. Why?
BATES: It'll keep.
ANNA: No. Tell me. I've got time.
BATES: It's just something his lordship said recently, I can't get it out of my mind. How Vera must have bought the poison, and taken it home.

This comes from left field. She tries to respond adequately.

ANNA: Yes. I suppose she must. And it's — it's a terrible thing to think of —
BATES: But she didn't. I did.
ANNA: What?
BATES: Months ago, before I left. Vera said we needed rat poison and I bought it. It was arsenic, and I've been thinking: that's what she must have taken. We used a bit of it, but the rest was in the cellar.
ANNA: Have you told the police?
BATES: No. The shop was quite a distance. How would they make the connection?
ANNA: Tell them. If you don't and they find out, it'll look bad.
BATES: But wouldn't I be asking for trouble?
ANNA: You're asking for trouble if you stay silent.
CARSON (V.O.): Anna, we're starting.
ANNA: Sorry, Mr Carson.

She hurries up the stairs. *

....

* Anna's instinct is, for me, significant, and her belief that by not telling the police about the poison Bates will make everything worse turns out to be true. I have a theory that, in life, the easy way out so often turns out to be the difficult way, in the long term. It's rather like when people try to appease someone who's impossible and, by appeasing them, they only make matters worse. You see people living with a partner, or working with someone, and constantly appeasing them, but in the end they create a situation that is untenable. Whereas if they had just said at the very beginning, 'Look, you've got the wrong guy, I'm not going to put up with this,' then maybe things would have improved. And if they didn't improve, if the impossible partner walked out and brought it to an end, they would still be better off.

26 INT. DINING ROOM. DOWNTON. NIGHT.

They are all at dinner, waited on by Carson and Anna.

VIOLET: Tell me, how are things progressing at Haxby?
CARLISLE: Quite well. I've put in a condition so the
builders are fined for every day they go over.
VIOLET: Does that make for a happy atmosphere?
CARLISLE: I want it done. They can be happy in their own
time.
VIOLET: Why the rush?
CARLISLE: I like everything I own to be finished and
ready to sell.
VIOLET: But you're not thinking of selling Haxby, surely?
CARLISLE: Depends. We'll have to see if it suits us to
be so close to Downton.

*Violet follows his gaze to where Matthew is chatting to
Lavinia. Mary, on Matthew's other side, is watching him.*

MATTHEW: I'm getting tired, so I'm going to sneak off to
bed in a minute —
ISOBEL: You must.
MATTHEW: But before I do, I want to tell you all
something. As you know, during this — well, I think I
can say horrible — time, Lavinia has proved to be the
most marvellous person…

He turns to her amid murmurs of 'hear, hear'.

MATTHEW (CONT'D): I never thought we would marry, for all
sorts of reasons, but she wouldn't accept that, and so
now I am very pleased to say that she's been proved
right.

Mary has stopped everything and is just staring at him.

MATTHEW (CONT'D): Lavinia and I will get married —
ROBERT: Oh my dear fellow.
ISOBEL: Isn't it wonderful?
MATTHEW: Just as soon as I'm well enough to walk down the
aisle. Doctor Clarkson can help us with when.
CLARKSON: Not long now.
MATTHEW: And she feels we ought to marry here, at
Downton. To bury forever the memories of what I hope has
been the darkest period of my life.
ROBERT: Of course!

LAVINIA: Are you sure? I know it should be at my home in London, but we've been through so much here —
ROBERT: We'd be delighted.

There are smiles and chatter, but Violet is looking at Mary.

VIOLET: Bravo! Excellent news. Mary! Isn't that excellent news?

Her sharp tone forces Mary to pull herself together.

MARY: Just excellent.*

27 INT. GARAGE. STABLEYARD. DOWNTON. NIGHT.

Branson is reading a pamphlet by oil light. Sybil appears, her shimmering evening dress in contrast to his shirtsleeves.

BRANSON: You're very late. Won't they worry?
SYBIL: They're all so excited, they won't care where I am.
BRANSON: I'm pleased. I like Mr Matthew.
SYBIL: He announced at dinner that he wants to get married at Downton… Somehow, it made me feel more than ever that the war is really over and it's time to move forward.

Her tone thrills and frightens him. He stands.

BRANSON: Do you mean you've made your decision?
SYBIL: Yes. And my answer is… that I'm ready to travel and you are my ticket. To get away from this house, away from this life!
BRANSON: Me?
SYBIL: No. Uncle Tom Cobley.

....

* Obviously, some viewers complained that it would have been wrong for them to marry at Downton, but I don't agree. When the bride lives in an ordinary, although affluent, street in Belgravia, and the groom is the heir to an estate, to place the wedding at the man's great house is not terribly unusual. Indeed, some friends of ours did it quite recently, so there was nothing untruthful about it. Mary, of course, is absolutely livid, because from the moment that Matthew stood up she has decided she's going to get him in the end. So this jolly plan is a real blow.

BRANSON: I'm sorry. But I've waited so long for those words, I can't believe I'm hearing them… You won't mind burning your bridges?
SYBIL: Mind? Fetch me the matches!

She laughs, as he takes her in his arms.

SYBIL (CONT'D): Yes, you can kiss me, but that is all until everything is settled.
BRANSON: For now, God knows it's enough that I can kiss you.

Which he does. Passionately.*

28 INT. CORA'S BEDROOM. DOWNTON. NIGHT.

Robert is getting into bed with Cora.

ROBERT: What a day. I can't stop smiling.
CORA: No. But another time, please ask me before you agree to host a wedding.
ROBERT: What?
CORA: I'm fond of Matthew, of course, but you do realise this means Mary's marriage will be delayed?
ROBERT: I can't help that.
CORA: Mary is our first priority, Robert. And just because Matthew's been lame —
ROBERT: Matthew's been lame! Can you hear the words coming out of your mouth? Can you hear how stupid and selfish they are? Because I can.

She's shocked, but before she can react he turns out the lamp.

END OF ACT THREE

....

* I felt it was important to make the audience understand that Sybil and Branson may be progressive, but they are still children of their own time. It always slightly annoys me when characters in period drama, in order to make them sympathetic, are given modern attitudes and modern choices. The fact is, Sybil's sexual morality would be as shared by her left-wing sisterhood as by her right-wing cousinage, because, in those pre-pill days, this was a woman's greatest citadel and greatest loss when it was stormed. Given all this, it would be completely unbelievable for her suddenly to say, 'Good on you. Chocks away.'

ACT FOUR

29 EXT. KITCHEN COURTYARD. DOWNTON. DAY.

*Mrs Hughes is putting a folded blanket, some sandwiches
wrapped in greasepaper and a thermos into the game larder.
She turns and walks towards the house when Carson comes out.*

> CARSON: What are you up to?
> MRS HUGHES: I was going to inspect the laundry, but I
> thought I'd leave it for now.*

She wants to take the conversation in a new direction.

> MRS HUGHES (CONT'D): Did you mean it when you said you'd
> changed your mind about going?
> CARSON: After what Anna said? Could you work for a man
> like that?
> MRS HUGHES: Everyone will be so pleased.
> CARSON: Not everyone…

30 INT. KITCHEN. DOWNTON. DAY.

Thomas and O'Brien are with Mrs Patmore and Daisy.

> MRS PATMORE: Don't bother me with it now. I've enough
> on, trying to make a luncheon that looks worth eating.

....

* One thing that has always made me nervous is the Downton laundry.
There are no laundry maids, there is no head laundress, in short there's no
laundry, all of which there obviously would have been. But we decided at the
start we simply could not service another whole mini-staff dramatically.
Where it's not untruthful is that the laundry maids were considered pretty
rough. They were the female equivalent of agricultural workers at a great
house and they were usually village women who did not have to refine their
ways, since they absolutely never came into contact with their employers, and
they both lived and worked quite separately. In many houses, the laundry
was in a separate building, but even if it was connected it would be at the end
of some wing in one of the courtyards and the staff would come and go
independently. Quite often, they didn't live in, they simply lived locally, but
still it does worry me, and so, every now and then, I make a character say that
they're just going over to the laundry, or that so-and-so is in the sewing
room, next to the laundry, and, almost without exception, it's cut.

THOMAS: But that's what I'm saying. Everything's in short supply now.

MRS PATMORE: Short supply? No supply, more like! Oh, talk about making a silk purse out of a sow's ear. I wish we had a sow's ear. It'd be better than this brisket.

O'BRIEN: That's just it. Thomas has come by some groceries and such, and he's prepared to let them go for the right price.

MRS PATMORE: Oh, he's prepared to let them go, is he? And how did he come by them? That's what I'd like to know.

THOMAS: Well, they're not stolen, in case you're worried.

MRS PATMORE: Oh, I'm not worried. You're the one who should be worried.

But she thinks for a moment.

MRS PATMORE (CONT'D): Tell you what. I'm making a wedding cake now, for Mr Crawley. I'll finish it early and feed it with brandy. So if I give you a list of ingredients, can you get them?

THOMAS: I can.

MRS PATMORE: And then we'll see. Now, will you leave me and let me get on with this travesty.*

31   EXT/INT.   DOWNTON.   DAY.

The Bryants have arrived. Their gleaming car, with a chauffeur at attention, tells us they're prosperous, moneyed Midlands people. But they are not quite top drawer. Carson is there. He's puzzled to find Mrs Hughes by the entrance.

CARSON: Why are you here?

She ignores him, looking over at Mrs Bryant, who is with Cora.

ROBERT: Mr Bryant, Mrs Bryant, welcome.

MRS BRYANT: We're so pleased to be here. This is so kind of you, Lady Grantham.

....

* I feel that only the pressure to produce a decent wedding cake for Matthew would induce someone like Mrs Patmore, who is generally honest, to break her own rules and get the material from Thomas. Given the situation and the war shortages, I did think this was believable.

MR BRYANT: It is kind, but we ought to make it clear we can't stay long. I wasn't sure we had time to come at all.
CORA: Luncheon is quite ready.
MR BRYANT: We must eat and run, I'm afraid. We have to be at Maryport by six.

They walk inside, into the front hall, followed by the two servants.

ROBERT: We're all so terribly sorry about the reason you're here.
MRS BRYANT: If we could see Charles's room…
MRS HUGHES: Shall I take Mrs Bryant up?
CORA: No, I'll do it.
ROBERT: We'll all do it. My cousin, Mrs Crawley, who looked after Major Bryant, and my daughters, who nursed him, will join us for luncheon.
MRS BRYANT: How thoughtful.
MR BRYANT: But we can't be long. I've told our chauffeur he's to stay in the car.
MRS HUGHES: Will I take him something to eat?
MR BRYANT: Leave him be. He's quite happy.

He is a discourteous man, which the others have absorbed.

ROBERT: Now, please come and see where Major Bryant lived while he was with us…*

....

* Kevin R. McNally, who plays Mr Bryant, is the husband of Phyllis Logan, our Mrs Hughes. So we had this husband and wife team in various scenes, although, of course, playing on opposite sides, which was quite fun. I'm not entirely hostile to Mr Bryant, who is self-made, successful and rich. I think it would be wrong to read any hostility from me into it. Clearly, Mrs Bryant is a much nicer person, both more sympathetic and less judgemental, but Bryant has come a long way in the world; he put a lot of effort and, I think, love, into his son, and it's all come to a tragic nothing. So, I believe one has to take a slightly more open view of him.

In this scene, I am guilty of being rather snobbish in making Mr Bryant thoughtless about his own chauffeur, and of course I am comparing him to the terribly considerate Cora and Robert. In real life, I am fully aware that whether employers are thoughtful or not has absolutely nothing to do with their social origins and everything to do with their personality, so I apologise for slipping into something of a cliché.

32 EXT. KITCHEN COURTYARD. DOWNTON. DAY.

Ethel is sitting in the game larder, holding her boy. She has the rug round them both. Mrs Hughes approaches.

MRS HUGHES: I'm afraid it's not going to work.

ETHEL: Why?

MRS HUGHES: They're in the dining room now, and they're getting straight into the car when they've finished. I tried to speak to her on her own, but there was never the right moment.

She strokes the cheek of the infant.

MRS HUGHES (CONT'D): Your granddaddy is a bit of a bully.

ETHEL: But I must see them. I've come all this way.

MRS HUGHES: Of course it's a disappointment —

ETHEL: You said yourself there wouldn't be another chance.

MRS HUGHES: We can't know that. Maybe you should write to them, after all. You've nothing to lose.

ETHEL: No. No, they have to see him. They must see Charlie.

MRS HUGHES: Well, maybe they will, sometime in the future. I hope so. You'd better go now.

33 INT. KITCHEN. DOWNTON. DAY.

Daisy is with Mrs Patmore.

DAISY: Can I ask you something?

MRS PATMORE: Will it work if I say no?

DAISY: This wedding cake. Can I make it?

MRS PATMORE: You wouldn't know how to start.

DAISY: But you could tell me. And if I make it early, then you could make another if it's no good.

MRS PATMORE: Hmm... If I say yes, will you do as you're told?

They are interrupted by the arrival of Mrs Hughes.

MRS HUGHES: Daisy, there's a wretched chauffeur at the front who's not allowed to get out of the car, so can you make him a sandwich and take him up a bottle of pop?

DAISY: We've some ham and — what was that?

They turn just as Ethel runs through towards the stairs.

MRS HUGHES: Oh, my God.

She races after her. Mrs Patmore is amazed.

DAISY: Who was that?
MRS PATMORE: Wasn't that Ethel? Did you see what she was
carrying?
DAISY: No.
MRS PATMORE: Then just let's leave it like that.

34 INT. DINING ROOM. DOWNTON. DAY.

The Crawleys and the Bryants are having lunch.

MRS BRYANT: I'm afraid Downton will be a place of
pilgrimage for a while.
CORA: We're glad to be, if we can help to bring some
peace of mind.
MR BRYANT: There's no point in wallowing in it. What
good does it do?*

*Before anyone can comment, there is a scuffle in the servery
and Ethel runs in, followed by Anna. Carson looks aghast.*

ETHEL (V.O): Leave me alone!
MRS HUGHES (V.O.): Ethel!
ANNA: I tried to stop her —
ROBERT: What on earth?

Cora has jumped to her feet, as Mrs Hughes hurries in.

CORA: Ethel! I know what this is. Mrs Hughes, I don't
think it's quite the right —
ETHEL: I'm stopping. Until I've had my say… This is
Charlie. Your grandson. He's almost a year old.

Mrs Bryant starts, but Bryant stands, speaking sharply.

....

* I remember talking to an old lady once, whose childhood home, like
Downton, had been used for convalescent officers during the first war, and
she recalled that, after the fighting was over, the families of inmates who had
died would come back in pilgrimage. Her parents had found it very
upsetting but totally understandable, because it would have been during a
period of convalescence that their families visited, and often it was the last
time these men and women saw their sons alive. For the owners of the
houses, it was an extra post-war service that was expected of them.

MR BRYANT: What proof have you?

This is so unexpected that it silences everyone.

ETHEL: What?

MR BRYANT: I say what proof have you? If my son was the father of this boy, where is your proof? Have you any letters? Any signed statement?

ETHEL: Why would there be letters? We were in the same house.

MRS HUGHES: I think she is telling the truth.

MR BRYANT: I'm not interested in 'think'. I want proof that my son acknowledged paternity of this boy. If what you say is true, then he would have known of the boy's existence for months before he… before he was killed.

ETHEL: Yes. He knew.

MR BRYANT: So? What did he do about it?

ETHEL: Nothing. He did nothing.

MR BRYANT: Thank you. That's the proof I was looking for. If Charles was the father, he would never have shirked his responsibilities. Never.

ETHEL: Well, he did.

MR BRYANT: I won't listen to any more slander. Now, will you please go, and take that boy with you, whoever he is. You are upsetting Mrs Bryant.

MRS BRYANT: Well, I would like —

MR BRYANT: I say you are upsetting Mrs Bryant. Lord Grantham, are you going to stand by while this woman holds us to ransom?

ROBERT: This isn't doing much good.

MRS HUGHES: Ethel, you'd better come with me. Come on.

She ushers the young woman out. Mr Bryant looks round.

MR BRYANT: She thinks we're a soft touch. They hear of a dead officer with some money behind them, and suddenly there's a baby on every corner.

ISOBEL: But if she's telling the truth —

MR BRYANT: If Charles had fathered that boy, he would have told us. No, I'd say she's done her homework and discovered he was an only child. She thinks we'd be ripe for the plucking.

MRS BRYANT: You knew her. Was she one of the nurses when he was here?

CORA: She was a housemaid.

CARLISLE: Were you aware?
MARY: No.

Isobel is next to Mrs Bryant. She speaks quite gently.

ISOBEL: No one told me Major Bryant was your only son.
MRS BRYANT: That's right. Just Charles. We wanted more,
but it didn't happen.
ISOBEL: Matthew is my only son, and he nearly died.
I think I know a little of what you're going through.

Mrs Bryant glances at Matthew. Her voice is wistful.

MRS BRYANT: He seems such a nice young man —

Mr Bryant is uneasy at his wife's intimacy with Isobel.

MR BRYANT: Well, I think that's cast rather a shadow over
the proceedings, so I don't see any point in prolonging
it. Daphne, come on, we're leaving.

Mrs Bryant looks at Isobel with a sad smile.

MRS BRYANT: He's afraid of his own grief. That's why he
behaves as he does. He's terrified of his own grief.*

....

* My mother, when I was young, always used to say that it was better to be gullible than suspicious, and there is something about suspicious people who always assume they're being tricked or gulled in some way that is unattractive. Mr Bryant is just such a person, and here we have his suspicious instinct kicking in. I don't know what Kevin McNally decided for this scene when he was playing the part. In my own head, Bryant doesn't engage with the boy yet; he doesn't really think he is his grandson. All he can see is a woman who wants him to write a cheque, and it takes time for him to look beyond that, whereas his wife, of course, sees her grandchild from the moment Ethel comes into the dining room.

We have some fun here with Bryant's indignant, parental pride. As it happens, we know that Major Bryant was a thoughtless and shallow flirt, but I'm always amused by parents over-estimating the qualities of their children, which lots of people are guilty of. I like the moment, too, when Bryant accuses Ethel of 'upsetting Mrs Bryant'. He, of course, is perfectly happy to upset Mrs Bryant as much as he likes, but he needs an accusation to hide behind. And all through this exchange, Mrs Bryant wants to know the truth. Isobel understands the situation better than the rest. 'No one told me Major Bryant was your only son. Matthew is my only son, and he nearly died.' Of course, when I wrote that line, I didn't know what was coming. Oh, God.

35 INT. SERVANTS' HALL. DOWNTON. DAY.

Ethel is weeping. Anna and some of the others are with her.
The astonished faces show they have just learned the truth.

    ETHEL: If that's what he's like, I don't want his help!
    I don't want it!
    O'BRIEN: I doubt you'll have the option… You're a dark
    horse. How did you keep it a secret all this time?
    ANNA: Maybe when he's thought about it he'll feel
    differently, you never know.
    CARSON: Anna! Will you kindly go upstairs and help in
    the dining room!

He stands in the doorway. Anna hurries away.

    CARSON (CONT'D): Ethel! Please take the child and leave.
    How did you get here?
    ETHEL: I caught the bus and walked up from the village.
    CARSON: Then can you reverse the process as quickly as
    possible?
    BATES: She's very badly shaken, Mr Carson. She's lost
    everything.

His appeal is passionate enough to move Carson.

    CARSON: Are you all right for the fare?
    ETHEL: Yes, thank you.

Her eye lights on an unfamiliar face.

    ETHEL (CONT'D): You're the new maid, aren't you? The
    widow with the son.
    JANE: I am, yes.
    ETHEL: Thought so.

....

Continued from page 400:

Bryant storms out, leaving it to his wife to give the true analysis: 'He's afraid of his own grief.' Certainly, this is often true of Englishmen, but I'm sure all over the world there are men who see emotions essentially as weakness, and so when they feel them they're taken unawares. They are genuinely astonished to find that they are in love, that they are tremendously unhappy, whatever it may be, because they see such things as unmanly. So they put emotion from them for a time, until it becomes unmanageable, and that is what has happened to Bryant here.

Before she can elaborate, Mrs Hughes arrives with a basket of food. She sees Carson.

MRS HUGHES: Here we are. Just to tide her over.
CARSON: I'll see you later, Mrs Hughes.*

35A EXT. DOWNTON. DAY.

The Bryants' car drives off, leaving Robert standing outside the house.

36 INT. LIBRARY. DOWNTON. DAY.

The party, minus the Bryants, are served coffee by Carson.

MARY: He's their only grandchild. There can never be another.
CARLISLE: Even if Ethel is telling the truth —
CORA: I believe she is.
CARLISLE: Even so, there's no legal reality to it. The child is her bastard and has no claim on them.

The word sends a tremor through the room. Carson shudders.†

....

* I was sorry when we had to cut the Jane/Ethel exchange, because, for me, humankind is full of ironies and this illustrates one of them. Here we have Jane and Ethel in exactly the same situation – the fathers of their children were killed in the war and these two little boys are much of an age – but one, Jane, has done it all according to society's rules, the other has not. So a support mechanism comes into play for Jane, while there is no support for Ethel. I suppose I wanted that one moment where they see each other face to face to underline this difference, but anyway it was elbowed to make room for more important information.

† It seems right to remind the younger generation particularly about laws and situations that were quite different until fairly recently. At that time, an illegitimate child was entirely the mother's responsibility, and had no claim on the father whatever. With this story, it was important for the audience to grasp that Ethel might persuade the Bryants to take some responsibility for her child, but she couldn't command it. She couldn't go to the police and say, 'Their son was my boy's dad and I need an income,' which you could now. In those days, even if the child was the spitting image of the father, it still didn't mean anything in terms of the law.

ROBERT: Steady on, sir. The ladies have had enough shocks for one day.

CARLISLE: I just don't see the point in pretending something can be done, when it can't.

MATTHEW: What about you, Mother? Can't one of your refugee charities help?

ISOBEL: But she's not a refugee, and we have more claims on our funding than we can possibly meet.

MARY: The truth is, Ethel's made her choice and now she's stuck with it.

LAVINIA: That seems a little hard.

MARY: Does it? Aren't all of us stuck with the choices we make?

37   INT. CARSON'S PANTRY. DOWNTON. DAY.

Carson is with Mrs Hughes. The door is closed.

MRS HUGHES: Yes, I knew she was coming, but that was not how we arranged it.

CARSON: But why let her come here at all? You must have known you risked embarrassing her ladyship.

MRS HUGHES: Now, this is where we differ. Her ladyship's embarrassment and a child's life do not seem to me to weigh equal in the balance!

CARSON: Will you apologise to her?

MRS HUGHES: If you insist, I will apologise for Ethel's behaviour, yes.

CARSON: But you won't mean it.

MRS HUGHES: Not really, no. But I suppose making apologies you don't mean is part of a servant's lot.

She goes, leaving him unclear as to who won. *

....

* I'm sorry that Carson didn't tell off Mrs Hughes in the final edit, because I felt it was a good illustration of their different views regarding the family. I may find a place for something similar further down the line.

38   INT. KITCHEN. DOWNTON. DAY.

Thomas and O'Brien are with Mrs Patmore and Daisy. The table is covered with bags and tins.

MRS PATMORE: Candied peel? Well, well. I never thought you'd find that.

THOMAS: I hope you're pleased, Mrs Patmore.

DAISY: 'Course she is. Aren't you? There's stuff here we haven't seen since before the war. I can't wait to get started.

MRS PATMORE: I won't ask where you got it from, because I don't want to know.

THOMAS: I keep saying. There's nothing wrong. So what I'd like to know is —

O'BRIEN: When will he get paid?

MRS PATMORE: When I'm satisfied.

O'BRIEN: And when will that be, oh Mighty One?

MRS PATMORE: When Daisy's baked the cake and I'm pleased with it. He understands. He knows this is just the sprat to catch the mackerel.

She walks off as the dressing gong sounds.

39   INT. MATTHEW'S BEDROOM. DOWNTON. NIGHT.

Bates is dressing Matthew, who stands as he puts on his tail coat and then is helped back into the chair.

MATTHEW: I really ought to walk to the library.

BATES: No need to rush it, sir. You're getting better every day.

There is a knock. Bates opens the door to find Violet.

VIOLET: Oh, Cousin Matthew? Are you dressed? May I come in?

MATTHEW: Please.

He half struggles to his feet but she waves him back down.

VIOLET: No, no, no. No, stay where you are.

She looks at Bates, who leaves and closes the door.

VIOLET (CONT'D): No doubt you will regard this as rather unorthodox. My pushing into a man's bedroom, uninvited.

MATTHEW: Well, um —

VIOLET: It's just, I don't want us to be disturbed.

She has sat down. Now she launches into her subject.

VIOLET (CONT'D): I'm sure you know how pleased I am that you will recover after all.

MATTHEW: Thank you.

VIOLET: Just as I am delighted that you can once more look forward to a — to a happy married life.

MATTHEW: I'm very lucky.

VIOLET: Now this may come as a surprise, but I feel I must say it all the same.

MATTHEW: Please do.

VIOLET: Mary is still in love with you.

MATTHEW: What?

This is a great surprise — at least that Violet is saying it.

VIOLET: I was watching her the other night, when you spoke of your wedding. She looked like Juliet on awakening in the tomb.

MATTHEW: Mary and I have always —

VIOLET: Of course, I suspected long ago that the flame hadn't quite gone out, but then there was no chance of your recovery and it seemed best to let her try for happiness where she could.

MATTHEW: I quite agree, and Sir Richard is —

VIOLET: Oh, now, let's not muddy the pool by discussing Sir Richard. The point is, you loved her once. Are you sure you can't love her again?

MATTHEW: Cousin Violet, please don't think I mind your speaking to me in this way. I quite admire it. But consider this: Lavinia came back, against my orders, determined to look after me for the rest of my life. Which meant that she would wash me and feed me and do things that only the most dedicated nurse would undertake, and all with no hope of children or any improvement.

VIOLET: Yes, yes, it's all very admirable. And I give her full credit.

MATTHEW: And giving her that credit, do you think it would be right for me to throw her over because I can walk? To dismiss her, because I no longer have need of her services?

VIOLET: Spoken like a man of honour, and we will not fall
out over this.
MATTHEW: But you don't agree.
VIOLET: I would just say one thing: marriage is a long
business. There's no getting out of it for our kind of
people. You may live forty, fifty years with one of
these two women. Just make sure you have selected the
right one.*

40 INT. HALL. DOWNTON. NIGHT.

*Robert comes downstairs and almost walks into Jane coming out
of the dining room. He is awkward as he nods and walks
towards the drawing room. Jane looks after him before going
through the baize door. All this is seen by Mrs Hughes, who
emerges from the shadows, as Cora comes down into the hall.*

MRS HUGHES: Your ladyship, I'm sorry about that…
interruption at luncheon.
CORA: I assume it wasn't exactly planned.
MRS HUGHES: No. Ethel was only here because I hoped
there might be a chance for Mrs Bryant to see the baby…

....

* The strangeness of Violet coming to Matthew's bedroom was quite
deliberate on my part. I wanted it to seem almost daring, an extreme
measure – but it is also a sensible one. She could have cornered him in the
drawing room for a chat, but that would have risked their being overheard,
which she avoids by button-holing him in his room. For me, the point of this
exchange is to show that Violet is good-hearted, but also practical. She
would not encourage Mary's love for Matthew if they were not both
unmarried, nor while Matthew was unable to walk or to father a child. But
all of that's been solved, so her imperative now is to stop four youngish
people making the wrong decision, and to help at least two of them to be
happy. Of course, it's true that Violet would rather see Mary as Countess of
Grantham living at Downton than as Lady Mary Carlisle living in London,
or even at Haxby. But there is more to it than that. She would like her
granddaughter and Robert's heir to live contented lives, and she has no
patience with Matthew's allowing principle to overturn their chance of this.
For Violet, reality trumps theory every time. She doesn't dislike him for
defending his vows to Lavinia, quite the contrary, but she has the experience
of the old to know that what we're talking about is half a century of lost
opportunity, and it won't be worth it.

CORA: I don't think we knew quite what we'd be dealing with in Mr Bryant.

MRS HUGHES: I hope you weren't too embarrassed.

CORA: If a little embarrassment could've helped to unite that baby with his family it would've been worth it.

MRS HUGHES: Well, that's just what I said — I mean, thank you, m'lady.

CORA: I'm only sorry it didn't work.

She walks towards the drawing-room door…

41   INT.   DRAWING ROOM.   DOWNTON.   NIGHT.

Cora enters.   The family is gathering before dinner.

EDITH: But of course we'll all help. We'd love to.

LAVINIA: It won't be a grand affair. Really not. Just local friends and family.

EDITH: Will it be April or May?

VIOLET: I should steer clear of May. 'Marry in May, rue the day.'

LAVINIA: I think it's April. Matthew should be walking normally by then.*

EDITH: Spring weddings are the prettiest of all…

On the other side of the room, Mary is with Carlisle.

CARLISLE: All this talk of weddings is making me impatient.

MARY: I don't think we can go into competition with Matthew and Lavinia, do you?

CARLISLE: After, then. In the summer. Let's settle it before I return to London. You must be looking forward to travelling again. I know I am.

MARY: Very well. The end of July. Then we can be out of England for August.

CARLISLE: You don't sound very excited.

MARY: To quote you: 'That's not who we are.'

She looks at him for a moment.   The door opens and Matthew wheels himself in.

....

* As in all her story, we're very careful to make Lavinia sweet and warm as she discusses the nuptials. Hopefully, the nicer she is, the more the audience thinks, poor girl. That's the idea, anyway.

MARY (CONT'D): Why did you try to bribe Anna?
CARLISLE: She told you, did she? I thought she'd give me away.
MARY: She didn't. Not to me. But why did you do it? Next time, if you want to know anything, just ask me.

Matthew guides the chair to the chimneypiece, then stands, holding onto it.

ROBERT: Well done.

The others in the room applaud.

CARLISLE: All right, then. I will. Once and for all, are you still in love with Matthew Crawley?
MARY: Of course not. Would I ever admit to loving a man who preferred someone else over me?

She laughs and strolls over to Edith and Lavinia.

MARY (CONT'D): Where's Sybil?
EDITH: She's not feeling well. She told Anna she wouldn't be down for dinner.

Robert has joined Carlisle. He raises his brows.

ROBERT: I suppose your wedding will follow hard behind.
CARLISLE: Don't worry. I can always help you out, if things are tight.

Robert had been quite polite. Now he becomes glacial.

ROBERT: How kind. But it won't be necessary.*

42 INT. KITCHEN PASSAGE. DOWNTON. NIGHT.

Bates is with Anna.

ANNA: What is it?
BATES: I heard from my lawyer today. Apparently, Vera wrote to a friend just before my last visit.
ANNA: Why are they telling you now?

....

* I was sorry we lost Carlisle offering Robert money to help him out. If he'd understood Robert better, he would have realised that all this offer would do would be to confirm his dislike. But the gulf between Robert and Carlisle is too wide for any bridge to span. Then again, I suspect we have already made the differences between them clear by this stage.

BATES: It was lost in the post. It was only delivered a few days ago.
ANNA: Do you know what the letter says?
BATES: They've sent me a copy.

He takes out a letter and hands it to her.

ANNA: 'John has written and he's coming here tonight. His words sound as angry as I've ever heard him, and you know how angry that is. I never thought I'd say this, but I'm afraid for my life —'

She looks up, bewildered.

ANNA (CONT'D): But what did you write to her?
BATES: Nothing like that. At least, that I can remember. I said I was coming that evening and I meant to have it out with her. I may have said she was being unreasonable, but so she was.
ANNA: Will it change anything?
BATES: Well, think about it. Before Vera's death she had taken all my money and she had wrecked the divorce. Now, as her widower, I inherit everything and we can marry whenever we like.

His words strike her with the situation afresh.

ANNA: So what are you saying? You had a motive to kill her?
BATES: Of course I had a motive. And I had the opportunity…
MRS HUGHES (V.O.): Anna, they're going in.

She is watching them. Anna nods and leaves.

MRS HUGHES: You look as if you've got the cares of the world on your shoulders.
BATES: Not the whole world, Mrs Hughes, but quite enough of it.

43   INT.   BEDROOM PASSAGE.   DOWNTON.   NIGHT.

Mary is outside Sybil's door. She knocks and turns the handle, but, to her surprise, it is locked. She knocks again.

MARY: Sybil? Sybil, I just want to say goodnight.

But there is no response. She tries the door again.

44   INT.   KITCHEN PASSAGE.   DOWNTON.   NIGHT.

Anna stops outside Mrs Hughes's door and opens it.

ANNA: Mrs Hughes, can I borrow the duplicate keys for
upstairs?
MRS HUGHES: Why?
ANNA: Lady Mary says one of the bathroom keys isn't
working. She thinks it must have got swapped.
MRS HUGHES: Oh, I'll come.
ANNA: No, no, there's no need. I'll bring them back in a
jiffy. You've done enough for one day.
MRS HUGHES: Well, that's true.

She gives the ring of labelled keys into Anna's hands.

45   INT.   SYBIL'S BEDROOM.   DOWNTON.   NIGHT.

*The door opens and Mary and Anna appear. The room is empty,
the bed made. Mary seizes the note on the dressing table.*

MARY: Oh, my God. She's eloped. She's on her way to
Gretna Green…*

46   INT.   EDITH'S BEDROOM.   DOWNTON.   NIGHT.

Edith is hurriedly fastening a day skirt.

EDITH: But if they've taken the car —
MARY: They've taken the old car. You'll have to drive
the Daimler.

Edith looks at her sister, still in evening dress.

EDITH: You'd better get changed, too.

Mary looks at Anna in her maid's outfit.

MARY: And you, if you're coming with us. Get the keys
back to Mrs Hughes and meet us in the stableyard. And
for God's sake, don't tell anyone.

....

* The elopement came from a real story I heard at a dinner party in
Derbyshire. An earl's daughter, the great-aunt of my table companion,
eloped with the groom one night in the early 1900s and left a note for her
parents. In the event, the father took off after them and brought her back,
and what happened subsequently I could not tell you. Anyway, as I listened,
I thought, yes, that's rather good.

Anna nods and hurries away.

47   INT.   CORA'S BEDROOM.   DOWNTON.   NIGHT.

Robert is in bed while Cora is sitting at her glass.

> ROBERT: What a Boer that fellow Carlisle is. Will we be
> able to stand him on a regular basis? I can't help
> wishing she'd throw him over.
> CORA: It's pointless to think like that.
> ROBERT: I don't see why. He could probably sell Haxby at
> a profit. I'm sure there's some ghastly tycoon who'd
> love what he's done with it.
> CORA: Mary is in Richard's debt. She owes him a great
> deal.
> ROBERT: What do you mean?

*Cora had been talking absent-mindedly, as she was absorbed in
her appearance. Now she realises what she has said.*

> CORA: I don't mean anything.
> ROBERT: Why is Mary in Carlisle's debt?
> CORA: Robert, the point is, it's too late to relaunch
> Matthew and Mary, if that's your plan.
> ROBERT: It was too late for that the moment you decided
> to bring Lavinia back into his life.
> CORA: I'm too tired to argue. Can we go to sleep?

48   INT.   MOTOR CAR.   GREAT NORTH ROAD.   NIGHT.

*Edith is at the wheel. Mary is next to her, with Anna
behind.*

> MARY: They must stop at some point. It won't be open
> before the morning.
> EDITH: They won't expect us to be in pursuit until
> tomorrow, so they'll stay somewhere on the road.
> ANNA: We hope.

This is not very helpful.

> EDITH: Everyone keep an eye out for the motor.

They race on.

49 INT. KITCHEN/LARDER. DOWNTON. NIGHT.

*The kitchen is empty. Daisy comes in and turns on the light,
and goes into the larder. There are three cakes, the layers
of a wedding cake, on a wire tray, with a little one next to
them. She smiles. Then Mrs Patmore arrives.*

    MRS PATMORE: Daisy? What in God's name are you doing
    down here at this hour?
    DAISY: I just wanted to check it were all right. That it
    hadn't, you know, caved in or anything.
    MRS PATMORE: Caved in? It's a cake, not a soufflé.
    DAISY: I know. But I've never made a wedding cake
    before.
    MRS PATMORE: Is that the one for tasting?
    DAISY: Yes, Mrs Patmore.
    MRS PATMORE: Well, bring it out. We'll give it a try.

*Daisy emerges with the little cake. They sit and Mrs Patmore
cuts two slices. They each take a mouthful. And spit it
out.*

    MRS PATMORE (CONT'D): Ugh! What in God's name do you
    call this?
    DAISY: I don't know… I did everything that you said.
    I promise.
    MRS PATMORE: But didn't you taste the mixture?

Daisy shakes her head in misery.

    MRS PATMORE (CONT'D): Oh, well, then I'm afraid it's time
    to look at Thomas's ingredients.

*She storms into the larder again, reaching for a jar labelled
'Flour'. She sticks in her finger and licks it.*

    MRS PATMORE (CONT'D): Pah! It's two-thirds plaster dust.
    Where's the peel?

*Daisy brings down a pot. Mrs Patmore tastes and spits it
out.*

    MRS PATMORE (CONT'D): Ugh! Well, this were old when Adam
    were a boy.

She turns to the weeping Daisy.

    MRS PATMORE (CONT'D): So, Thomas was happy to 'let it
    go', was he? Well, it won't go anywhere near me in

future! Chuck the whole bally lot out and we'll have to think again…

50 INT. MOTOR CAR. GREAT NORTH ROAD. NIGHT.

The three are still watching, when…

ANNA: Isn't that the car?

Edith slows down.

51 INT. PUBLIC HOUSE. GREAT NORTH ROAD. NIGHT.

The three young women face a tired man in a dressing gown.

INNKEEPER: It's too late. We're not open.
MARY: We don't want a room. We've an urgent message for two of your guests. It's a matter of life and death. Literally.
INNKEEPER: Which guests?

52 INT. SYBIL'S ROOM. PUBLIC HOUSE. NIGHT.

The door bursts open and they run in. Sybil turns on the light. She is on the bed, fully dressed, and Branson, also dressed, is sitting in a chair. He jumps up.

BRANSON: How did you find us? How did you know?
MARY: Never mind that. At least nothing's happened, thank God.

By now Sybil is standing.

SYBIL: What do you mean, nothing's happened? I've decided to marry Tom and your coming after me won't change that.
EDITH: This isn't the way.
MARY: She's right. Of course Mama and Papa will hate it —
BRANSON: Why should they?
MARY: Oh, pipe down. Sybil, can't you let them get used to the idea? Take your stand and refuse to budge, but allow them time. That way, you won't have to break up the family.
SYBIL: They would never give permission.
MARY: You don't need permission. You're twenty-one. But you do need their forgiveness, if you're not to start your new life under a black shadow.

Sybil is weakening. She sees the logic of what Mary's saying.

> BRANSON: Don't listen. She's pretending to be reasonable
> to get you home again.
> MARY: Even if I am, even if I think this is mad, I know
> it would be better to do it in broad daylight than to
> sneak off like a thief in the night.

Sybil turns to Branson. She does need his permission.

> BRANSON: Go back with them, then. If you think they can
> make you happier than I will.
> SYBIL: Am I so weak you believe I can be talked out of
> giving my heart in five minutes flat? But Mary's right.
> I don't like deceit, and our parents don't deserve it.
> So I'll go back with them. But, believe it or not, I
> will stay true to you.

*She picks up her case, which Anna takes off her. They go.
Edith follows and Branson and Mary are alone.*

> BRANSON: I'll return the car in the morning.

Mary nods and starts for the door.

> BRANSON (CONT'D): You're confident you can bring her
> round, aren't you?
> MARY: Fairly. I'll certainly try. Do you want some
> money? For the room?

Branson stares at her, the class enemy who has defeated him.

> BRANSON: No, thank you, m'lady. I can pay my own way.*

....

* Mary's behaviour to Branson is not unreasonable, certainly not in the
context of the world as it was then. Initially, she thinks the relationship is an
absurd idea, and it doesn't occur to her to consider it in any light other than
as a mad scheme that they have to rescue Sybil from. But later, once it's
happened, she is not prepared to quarrel with her sister, so she thinks the
only sensible course is for them all to get used to the idea and make friends
with the chauffeur/suitor. In my experience, this is true of most sensible
people when dealing with the prospect of a marriage within their family that
they consider to be mad. They will fight against it, almost to the death, but
once it's happened they will try to put all that behind them and get on with it.
The problem comes when the bride or groom whom no one wanted cannot
forgive the initial lack of welcome.

ACT FIVE

53 INT. SERVANTS' STAIRCASE. DOWNTON. THE DARK
BEFORE DAWN.

They are by the servants' stairs. Sybil takes her case.

    SYBIL: Go to bed.
    ANNA: I'm supposed to be up in an hour.
    SYBIL: Get Jane to say you're ill.

Mary turns to Sybil.

    MARY: You're all right. You can just go on pretending to
    be ill and have a day in bed.
    ANNA: You'd better go up the main stair, in case you meet
    Daisy coming down.

They part. Anna hurries upstairs.

    SYBIL: I suppose I should thank you, and I do in a way,
    but you won't persuade me to give him up.
    EDITH: I can't talk about it any more tonight.
    MARY: At least that's something we can all agree on.

*Silently, they push through the door into the main hall.**

54 INT. DINING ROOM. DOWNTON. DAY.

Robert is at breakfast, with Carson, when Cora looks in.

    CORA: Where are the girls?
    ROBERT: I suppose Sybil's still ill, and the others just
    haven't appeared.

....

* This scene had to go, but it was rather a charming moment when they all
peeled off to go to their different rooms. The four of them have come in by
the servants' entrance and therefore climbed the servants' stairs, because they
have all been in this adventure together. It would have been the only time we
ever saw Mary on the service staircase. But we always have too much, and it
just wasn't important enough to survive the cut.

CORA: I hope they're not coming down with anything. The stories of this 'Spanish 'flu' are too awful.
ROBERT: No, it's nothing of the sort. Why are you up so early?
CORA: I'm meeting Isobel. She wants me to help with her refugees.
ROBERT: I thought the whole point of Mama arranging that was to keep her out of your hair.
CORA: I know. But now the soldiers are gone, I do have a lot of time on my hands, and maybe I can be useful.
ROBERT: Why is it different from before the war?
CORA: I don't know exactly. It just is. Maybe the war's changed me. I guess it's changed everybody.
ROBERT: Not me.
CORA: Don't be too sure. If I'm not back before luncheon, don't wait.

She goes. Carson picks up the chafing dish with a cloth.

CARSON: I'll take this down to keep it hot, m'lord.

As he goes out through the servery, Jane enters from the other door. There is an oddness here. Robert looks at her.

JANE: I wanted to catch you alone.
ROBERT: Oh?
JANE: Yes. You see, I think you might be happier if I tendered my resignation.
ROBERT: What?
JANE: I'd hate you to be uncomfortable in your own house and —
ROBERT: I won't hear of it.
JANE: But I know —
ROBERT: You will not be deprived of your livelihood because I behaved in an ungentlemanly manner. The fault was entirely mine. You will not pay the price.

There's a noise. She slips out of the door as Carson appears. His eyes take in the retreating figure. Robert says nothing.

54A INT. SHED. DOWNTON VILLAGE. DAY.

Thomas enters and goes on the rampage. In a fury, he begins cutting open bags of flour, pulling things off shelves and destroying everything in sight before collapsing to the floor.

55 INT. DRAWING ROOM. CRAWLEY HOUSE. DAY.

Lavinia is embroidering and Matthew is reading as Isobel comes in. She is holding Mary's little toy rabbit.

ISOBEL: Is this yours? Molesley found it in your dressing room.

Matthew looks up. He doesn't know what to say.

ISOBEL (CONT'D): It's not one of your old toys, is it? Because I don't recognise it.
MATTHEW: No. It was given to me. As a charm, I think. To take to the front.
ISOBEL: Well, you're home and safe now. Shall I put it in the barrel for the village children?
MATTHEW: No.

He has spoken quite sharply and Lavinia looks up.

MATTHEW (CONT'D): You never know. It might be bad luck not to keep it.

And he takes the toy and puts it in his pocket.

ISOBEL: Luncheon will be ready soon.*

56 INT. SHED. DOWNTON VILLAGE. DAY.

Jars are tipped up and spilled, bags cut into, boxes half empty. In the middle stands Thomas, covered in flour. O'Brien is with him.

THOMAS: It's all rubbish! It's all bloody rubbish!
O'BRIEN: Can't you ask for your money back?
THOMAS: Oh yes. 'Course I can ask. And a fat lot of good that'll do!
O'BRIEN: You must challenge him.
THOMAS: How? I only ever met him in a pub. I wouldn't know where to find him.

....

* Once more we have the toy dog, which looks good here, even if I am still nostalgic for my original rabbit. I don't know why I didn't just lend them the real rabbit it was based on – my own very scruffy and much-loved toy – as that might have persuaded them. It was stupid of me, really. Anyway, the dog plays its part well enough. The moment Matthew tells Isobel not to give away the toy, we know he hasn't let go of Mary.

O'BRIEN: But surely, you —
THOMAS: Don't you understand, woman? I've been tricked!
I've been had! I've been taken for the fool that I am!

His eyes are full now, and she is moved by his plight.

O'BRIEN: How much did he get from you?
THOMAS: Every penny I had! And then some!
O'BRIEN: What are you going to do now?
THOMAS: I don't know. I don't bloody know.*

He starts to weep as she takes him into her arms for comfort.

END OF EPISODE SEVEN

....

* This is a good *Downton* finish, I feel, because it's dramatic and harsh, but it also probably means that Thomas won't be leaving the series, because he's got no money.

EPISODE EIGHT

ACT ONE

1   INT. HALL. DOWNTON. DAY.

*1919. The hall boys are clearing the hall of furniture and rolling up the big rug. Cora supervises with Mary, Lavinia, Isobel and Mrs Hughes. Matthew, walking with a stick, is with them.**

CORA: We can put the presents in the drawing room, against the window.

MRS HUGHES: Very good, m'lady.

ISOBEL: I suppose we do have to display all the presents? It can look rather greedy.†

LAVINIA: I can't bear the disruption we seem to have brought down on your heads.

CORA: Don't be silly.

Mary is talking to Matthew.

MARY: How are you feeling?

MATTHEW: Just wish I could get rid of this damn stick — I'm sorry.

MARY: Don't be. If anyone has a right to swear, it's you.

LAVINIA: Don't bully yourself. Think of where we were a few months ago and smile.

MARY: I quite agree.

MATTHEW: But I want to make it up and down that aisle without assistance.

....

* It is always quite traumatic to roll up the big rug in the hall at Highclere, and we very much need permission from the Carnarvons to do it. The result of this is that we strive not to overplay our hand and roll it up lightly, on the slightest excuse, but there are certain functions we just have to take it up for, and obviously Matthew's wedding was one of them.

† Wedding present displays have gone now, but they lasted well into my childhood, when you would walk into a drawing room, as part of the reception, and there were all the presents – silver and china and jewels, and so on – laid out with their cards, so you could see who gave what. It seems rather a vulgar idea now, but it wasn't in the least unusual.

LAVINIA: Up, yes. You'll have me to lean on when you're coming down.

MARY: And you still have three full days of practice. So never say die.

ISOBEL: My goodness, is that the time? I must be getting back. Cousin Cora and I are helping with the new batch of refugees at four.

LAVINIA: I'll go with you.

MATTHEW: She's just sucking up, Mother.

LAVINIA: Any bride who doesn't suck up to her husband's mother is a fool.

2 INT. CARSON'S PANTRY. DOWNTON. DAY.

Mrs Hughes is at the door carrying a letter.

MRS HUGHES: Can I bother you? Mrs Bryant has written a letter I did not expect. She says her husband wants to see the baby. They both do.

CARSON: Isn't that what you hoped?

MRS HUGHES: Yes and no. Remember what he was like the last time. I don't want to build up Ethel's hopes again.

CARSON: Ethel's not important. It's the boy's chances you have to look to.

MRS HUGHES: I believe you're right. Though we come at it by different routes.*

3 INT. MARY'S BEDROOM. DOWNTON. EVE.

Edith and Sybil are dressed for dinner. Anna is tending Mary.

MARY: But why announce it tonight all of a sudden?

SYBIL: He's got a job on a newspaper. He heard today. It's a real chance.

....

* I felt that the Bryants' wanting to see the baby, once they'd considered matters, was truthful. Mr Bryant's initial response to Ethel's news would believably be anger, but it feels real that the moment they really absorbed that there was a baby, that they could still have descendants even though their only child was dead, they would reconsider – or rather, he would. Mrs Bryant was open to the boy from the start. You can imagine them talking about it all the way home in the car.

EDITH: You're not just trying to bury it under all the fuss of the wedding?

SYBIL: Certainly not. It's because of the offer. Tom has to decide right now.

MARY: Maybe he does, but you don't. Let him go to Dublin and then you can use the calm to consider.

EDITH: Mary doesn't want you to be trapped before you're completely sure.

SYBIL: But I am sure! How many times do I have to say it? Anna, tell them.

ANNA: Lady Mary's right. It's a very big thing to give up your whole world.

MARY: Thank you. Listen to her if you won't listen to me.

SYBIL: But I'm not giving up my world. If they want to give me up, that's their affair. I'm perfectly happy to carry on being friends with everyone.

MARY: Married to the chauffeur.

SYBIL: Yes. Anyway, he's a journalist now, which sounds better for Granny. We're going to tell Papa tonight.

EDITH: We? You mean you and Branson?

SYBIL: He's coming in after dinner.

EDITH: But what will Papa do?

MARY: I imagine he'll call the police.*

4 INT. KITCHEN PASSAGE. DOWNTON. EVE.

Anna is coming downstairs when Mrs Hughes sees her.

MRS HUGHES: Anna, can you lay another place at the dinner table? The Dowager's here. They forgot she was coming.

ANNA: Old Lady Grantham's here tonight?

MRS HUGHES: Yes. Why?

ANNA: No reason. I'll go and do it now.

....

* Mary, of course, was hoping the whole thing would die away, but it's not going to happen.

5 INT. DINING ROOM. DOWNTON. EVE.

Anna is serving the pudding with Jane, supervised by Carson.

VIOLET: What is there for refugees in the North Riding of
Yorkshire?
EDITH: The chance to build a new life.
VIOLET: But why here, if they're used to Vladivostok or
Peru?
CORA: They're mainly from central Europe, which has been
laid waste by the war. They're here to start again.
VIOLET: Won't they be lonely so far from home?
LAVINIA: But they're safe. And safety's worth a little
loneliness.

*During this, Sybil has signed to Anna, and when the latter
bends down to hold the pudding plate Sybil whispers:*

SYBIL: Find him and tell him not to come in. Tell him
Granny's here.

Anna nods. Jane holds a dish for Robert. He smiles at her.

ROBERT: Thank you.
CORA: Tomorrow we must settle the flowers with Bassett.
VIOLET: Specify the detail. The last thing we want is
his creative streak.

6 INT. CARSON'S PANTRY. DOWNTON. DAY.

Carson is with Thomas.

CARSON: Downton is not a hostel.
THOMAS: No, Mr Carson.
CARSON: And you made such a point of not being a servant
any more. Our ears are ringing with it.
THOMAS: The trouble is… I'm a little out of pocket at
the moment.
CARSON: I cannot say that I'm sympathetic. When you
dabble in the black market —
THOMAS: I just need some more time, Mr Carson…
CARSON: How long is it since the last patient left,
Sergeant? You are trespassing on our generosity.
THOMAS: I'll try to make myself useful.
CARSON: Just find somewhere to go.

7 INT. SERVANTS' HALL. DOWNTON. EVE.

Anna comes in and scans the table. Bates looks up.

ANNA: Is Mr Branson here?
BATES: I haven't seen him. What should I say if I do?
ANNA: I'll be upstairs clearing. Tell him to come and
find me. It's important.

She hurries away. Bates looks at the other servants.

BATES: Very mysterious.
O'BRIEN: But then you love a mystery, don't you,
Mr Bates?

8 EXT. DOWNTON. EVE.

Branson is turning into the kitchen courtyard, but he stops.

BRANSON: No, dammit. This time, you're going through the
front door.

9 INT. DINING ROOM. DOWNTON. EVE.

Anna and Jane are finishing clearing the table.

ANNA: You look very chipper.
JANE: I am. I heard this afternoon my son's got into
Ripon Grammar… Oh, Lady Edith's forgotten her shawl.
ANNA: Put it at the bottom of the stairs.

Jane vanishes for a moment and then returns.

JANE: Whyever is Mr Branson in the hall?
ANNA: Mr Branson —?

She hurries out to see Branson opening the drawing-room door.

10 INT. DRAWING ROOM. DOWNTON. EVE.

They all have coffee. Carson is serving drinks.

EDITH: Lavinia's coming first thing. We can't decide
anything without her.

During this, Branson has walked in. Now Robert notices him.

ROBERT: Yes?

BRANSON: I'm here.

ROBERT: So I can see.

There is a strange pause. Sybil stands and goes to him.

SYBIL: I don't think this is such a good idea. We mustn't worry Granny…

BRANSON: You've asked me to come and I've come.

VIOLET: Would someone please tell me what is going on? Or have we all stepped through the looking glass?

BRANSON: Your grandmother has as much right to know as anybody else.

VIOLET: Why don't I find that reassuring?*

11 INT. KITCHEN. DOWNTON. EVE.

Mrs Patmore is with Daisy.

MRS PATMORE: How much longer is Mr Carson going to be? This is why it's never worth trying to make food interesting in the servants' hall… You're very quiet this evening.

DAISY: I've had a letter. Off Mr Mason. William's dad.

MRS PATMORE: Oh, yes? What does he want?

DAISY: To see me.

MRS PATMORE: Oh, there's nothing very wonderful in that. You're his daughter-in-law. Why shouldn't he see you?

DAISY: I wish it were as simple.

MRS PATMORE: Well, I think it is, but I'll not reopen the wound. Oh, Mr Carson, where can you be?

....

* Branson is wearing rather an awkward and inappropriate outfit, a sort of tweed coat. This was a brilliant touch on the part of our costume designer, Susannah Buxton, who is a true genius in this department. And Allen Leech's performance is wonderfully judged, too – slightly awkward, slightly defensive, and then, with Sybil's support, comes a gradual relaxation. Of course, when Violet asks whether they have all stepped through the looking glass, she demonstrates that she knows what's going on. She hopes she's wrong, but she knows she isn't, really.

12 INT. DRAWING ROOM. DOWNTON. EVE.

They are all completely stunned, including Carson. Robert is standing and, at this moment, interrogating Mary.

ROBERT: What do you mean, you knew?

MARY: I hoped it would blow over. I didn't want to split the family when Sybil might still wake up.

ROBERT: And all the time, you've been driving me about, bowing and scraping, and seducing my daughter behind my back?

BRANSON: I don't bow and scrape, and I've not seduced anyone. Give your daughter some credit for knowing her own mind.

ROBERT: How dare you speak to me in that tone? You will leave at once!

SYBIL: Oh, Papa —

ROBERT: This is a folly, a ridiculous, juvenile madness —

VIOLET: Sybil, what do you have in mind?

ROBERT: Mama, this is hardly —

VIOLET: No. She must have something in mind, otherwise she wouldn't have summoned him here tonight.

Somehow this calms them all down a little.

SYBIL: Thank you, Granny. Yes, we do have a plan. Tom's got a job on a paper. I'll stay until after the wedding — I don't want to steal their thunder — but after that I'll go to Dublin.

CORA: To live with him? Unmarried?

SYBIL: I'll live with his mother while the banns are read. And then we'll be married, and I'll get a job as a nurse.

VIOLET: What does your mother make of this?

BRANSON: If you must know, she thinks we're very foolish.

VIOLET: Oh, so at least we have something in common.

ROBERT: I won't allow it! I will not allow my daughter to throw away her life!

SYBIL: You can posture all you like, Papa, it won't make any difference.

ROBERT: Oh, yes, it will.

SYBIL: How? I don't want any money, and you can hardly lock me up until I die. I'll say goodnight, but I can promise you one thing: tomorrow morning, nothing will have changed. Tom?

Branson nods and they leave together. The door closes.

> CORA: She's right about one thing: we can't lock her up until she dies.
> VIOLET: Worse luck.*

END OF ACT ONE

ACT TWO

13   INT.   CORA'S BEDROOM.   DOWNTON.   DAY.

A new day. O'Brien is dressing Cora.

> O'BRIEN: Lady Mary and Lady Edith are with Miss Swire in the drawing room.
> CORA: Of course. The flowers for the wedding. It's good to have something else to talk about. Oh —

She has started to walk when she feels unsteady.

> O'BRIEN: Your ladyship?
> CORA: I felt a little dizzy… It's gone now. I'll just sit for a moment… Tell me, how's Thomas getting on with finding a job?
> O'BRIEN: I'm afraid it's more difficult than he thought it would be.
> CORA: Well, I suppose he has his army pay. That should tide him over.

O'Brien makes no comment.

....

* I thought they did all this very well. When Branson denies that he either bows or scrapes, when he says, quite rightly, that he has not seduced anyone, then not just Robert but everyone in the room sees that whatever relationship they may have had with their former chauffeur is now over and done with. Branson knows, too, as he stands there in the drawing room, that he is no longer the chauffeur at Downton Abbey. That was an important moment in this story and they brought it off.

14   INT.   DRAWING ROOM.   DOWNTON.   DAY.

Lavinia is on the sofa talking to Mary and Edith.

MARY: What I can't bear is the thought of Sybil waking up
in a Dublin slum, away from everything she knows.
EDITH: Perhaps Branson will discover oil or something,
and make a fortune.
MARY: Would it wash him clean? I wonder.
LAVINIA: Well, it worked for Richard Carlisle… My God,
I'm so sorry. I don't know what came over me. Please,
please forget I said that.
MARY: We never will, of course. But it doesn't matter.*

15   INT.   ETHEL'S COTTAGE.   DAY.

Mrs Hughes is with Ethel and the baby in this dismal cottage.

ETHEL: He's not coming here. I don't want him to see
this place. I won't have him pity me.
MRS HUGHES: The question is, are you prepared to let them
into Charlie's life?
ETHEL: I suppose so. Yes.
MRS HUGHES: Good. I'll ask them to Downton for Monday,
at four. And this time, it'll be all above board.†

16   INT.   SERVANTS' HALL.   DOWNTON.   DAY.

Thomas, O'Brien, Bates, Anna and some others are there.

O'BRIEN: You can't have expected to live here free
forever.

....

* I thought it a shame that we lost Lavinia being rude about Carlisle, because
I felt it was nice for her to make a spiky and sarcastic remark. It would have
been a new colour for her. But, again, saving one line wasn't sufficient
justification for retaining the scene.

† It's important to realise that Ethel wants them to make her life easier. That
is all. In other words, at this stage, she doesn't understand what she's letting
herself in for. So often in life, you start a chain of action going, and then
bitterly regret the consequences. But in this instance her feelings will be very
complicated. In a way, there is a kind of triumph in the thought that her son
might enjoy an interesting and privileged life. But in another way, of course,
she must curse the day she ever began it, because she cannot bear the thought
of losing him.

THOMAS: I didn't expect to get booted out.
O'BRIEN: You'll have to find some work.
THOMAS: It's not that easy. Every Tom, Dick and Harry is looking for work these days and they don't all have a hand like a Jules Verne experiment.

Branson arrives in the doorway.

ANNA: Mr Branson, I know it wasn't easy last night. I'm sorry I missed you.
BRANSON: I'm not. There's been too much deceit and too many lies. That's one thing I'll grant his lordship. We should have spoken out long ago.
DAISY: Spoken out about what?
BRANSON: Ah, why not? Lady Sybil and I are getting married.

This is like an earthquake. Carson appears in the doorway.

CARSON: Have you no shame?
BRANSON: I'm sorry you feel like that, Mr Carson. You're a good man. But no, I have no shame. In fact, I have great pride in the love of that young woman. And I will strive to be worthy of it.
CARSON: I will not disgrace myself by discussing the topic, and nor will anyone else. Now, if you will go, Mr Branson, we will continue with our day. Leave an address where we may forward what is owing to you.
BRANSON: No problem there, Mr Carson. I'll be at the Grantham Arms in the village until Lady Sybil is ready to make her departure. I bid you all a good day.

He goes. The company is, in common parlance, gobsmacked.

JANE: Is it really tr—?
CARSON: Please! I have asked for silence and silence I will have!*
ANNA: Are you quite well, Mr Carson?

* Branson's greatest enemy at Downton Abbey is unquestionably Carson, who feels passionately that the former chauffeur has broken the trust between an employer and their employees. For Carson, Branson's seduction of the daughter of his employer is the ultimate, iconic betrayal in ancient literature or modern fiction, and yet that is inescapably what Branson has done, even if 'seduce' isn't quite the right word. He will remain the enemy of Carson for longer than almost anyone else in the house. I think I am right in saying that even Violet forgives him before Carson. Again, that feels truthful.

He certainly is looking rather green around the gills.

    CARSON: If I'm not, is it any wonder?

17   INT.   SYBIL'S BEDROOM. DOWNTON. DAY.

Robert is with Sybil.

    SYBIL: So you've nothing to say against Tom except that
    he's a chauffeur?
    ROBERT: Don't be such a baby. I'm not asking you to
    agree with the system. Merely to acknowledge it.
    SYBIL: But I don't acknowledge it. You want me to give
    up the man I love for a system I don't believe in.
    Where's the sense in that?

18   INT.   HALL/DRAWING ROOM. DOWNTON. DAY.

*Lavinia and Mary are trying to set up a huge gramophone when
Violet comes in. Carson straightens up.*

    VIOLET: What on earth is it?
    LAVINIA: A gramophone. Some cousins of mine have given
    it to us.
    VIOLET: I should stand well clear when you light the blue
    touch paper.*

*She walks on into the drawing room, where Edith is arranging
gleaming wedding presents on a table in the window.*

    VIOLET (CONT'D): All on your own?

Edith half shrugs as she works. Violet surveys the table.

    EDITH: I've left space at the front for jewels. I know
    Lavinia's getting something from Papa.

....

* This gramophone reappears in Season Four and, for me, it is a symbol of
the period. When you think of the Twenties, you think of the music and the
arrival of these syncopated jazz rhythms, and the gramophone meant that,
for the first time, you could have the real sound in your own home, and not
some sister trying to approximate it on the piano in the schoolroom. It may
not sound now like modern music to young ears, but at the time it was clear
that things had changed since their mothers had wept to 'After the Ball Is
Over' or laughed with *Naughty Marietta*, who wasn't that naughty, worse
luck. The gramophone marks this journey. Obviously Violet detests it.

VIOLET: And from me. Though she's so slight, a real
necklace would flatten her… What news of Sybil?
EDITH: Papa's with her now.
VIOLET: I'm afraid it'll end in tears.
EDITH: Maybe. But they won't be Sybil's.*
VIOLET: I used to think that Mary's beau was a
mésalliance, but compared to this he's practically a
Hapsburg…

Edith sighs as she unpacks the silver frames and boxes.

VIOLET (CONT'D): Don't worry. Your turn will come.
EDITH: Will it? Or am I just to be the maiden aunt?
Isn't this what they do? Arrange presents for their
prettier relations?
VIOLET: Don't be defeatist, dear. It's very middle
class. Now, I'd better go up and support your father.†

19   INT.   SYBIL'S BEDROOM.   DOWNTON.   DAY.

Robert isn't any closer to convincing his daughter.

SYBIL: Your threats are hollow, don't you see? I won't
be received in London, I won't be welcome at Court. How
do I make you understand? I couldn't care less.

There is a brisk knock and Violet enters. They stand.

....

* Edith understands what is going to happen, and we might as well all get
used to it.

† In a way, this is an American sentiment as well. The British posh and
the Americans share a feeling that you should always make it look as if
everything's going your way. Everything's well, everything's fine, everything's
great. Obviously, there is a risk of falsity to this, and it may be that the
following week you get a divorce and they foreclose on the house. But
nevertheless, for me, there is something weak about inviting sympathy and
telling people what's wrong with your life to make them pity you. Most of us
would consider the invitation to pity to be ill-bred. In fact, with American
friends, it's only when they tell you something they're worried about that you
realise you must have actually become quite close, because up to that moment
nothing could be going better than their lives. When they show you a little
weakness, it means everything has moved to a different level, emotionally.

VIOLET: I do hope I'm interrupting something.

ROBERT: I only wish you were, but I seem to be getting nowhere. Have you seen Cora?

VIOLET: Oh, she's lying down, and can we blame her? Now, Sybil dear, this sort of thing is all very well in novels, but in reality it can prove very uncomfortable. And while I am sure Branson has many virtues —

Robert glares at her, but she defends herself.

VIOLET (CONT'D): Well, no, no, he's a good driver.

SYBIL: I will not give him up.

ROBERT: Don't be rude to your grandmother.

VIOLET: No, she's not being rude. Just wrong.

SYBIL: This is my offer. I will stay one week. To avoid the impression I've run away and because I don't want to spoil Matthew's wedding. Then we will marry in Dublin, and whoever wishes to visit will be very welcome.

ROBERT: Out of the question.

SYBIL: Will you forbid Mary and Edith?

Robert would answer, but Violet raises her hand.

VIOLET: No, no, don't say anything you may have to retract.

ROBERT: Know this: there will be no more money. From here on in, your life will be very different.

SYBIL: Well, bully for that.*

20 INT. CARSON'S PANTRY. DOWNTON. DAY.

Carson looks terrible. Mrs Hughes arrives with a cup of tea.

MRS HUGHES: I thought this might tide you over —
Mr Carson! Whatever is the matter?

CARSON: Oh, I'm sure I'll be all right if I can just stay still for a moment —

MRS HUGHES: You will not stay still. Not down here. Get to bed this minute! I'll send for the doctor.

....

* I always think it's quite funny when you see someone trying to bargain with a bargaining tool that has no currency. It's like threatening a child. If you say you won't take them to some treat you've planned and they couldn't care less, then suddenly you have no power over them. Here, Robert has no power over Sybil, because she doesn't care about his threats.

CARSON: I can't. We've got the Crawleys tonight and Miss Swire, what with this business of Lady Sybil —
MRS HUGHES: I'll deal with it.
CARSON: Get Mr Molesley to help.
MRS HUGHES: There's no need.
CARSON: I mean it. The war is no longer an excuse for sloppy presentation.
MRS HUGHES: Oh, very well, I'll ask him, but only on condition you go to bed!

21 INT. DRAWING ROOM. CRAWLEY HOUSE. DAY.

Isobel and Matthew are together.

MATTHEW: Well, if they have brought Spanish 'flu, it's not your fault.*
ISOBEL: Isn't it? Mrs Dupper's new maid has got it, and the Lanes' two labourers, and I placed them all. Oh, thank you, Molesley.

The door has opened and Molesley appears with the tea tray.

MOLESLEY: I've had a message from Mrs Hughes, ma'am. Mr Carson's been taken ill and they're wondering if I could help them out tonight.
ISOBEL: There'll be no one here, so why not?
MATTHEW: Rather a challenge.
MOLESLEY: Oh, I don't know, sir. But I'm pleased to go if they need me.

He's very confident. Matthew smiles. Lavinia comes in.

MATTHEW: How did you get on?
LAVINIA: Quite well, I think. And we got Cousin Binny's gramophone going. Woosh! I do feel rather worn out.

....

* Matthew is referring to the refugees, who were being sent all round the country, often with the result that the disease spread even faster than it might have done anyway. The Spanish 'flu epidemic of 1918–19 has been almost forgotten today. After the series went out, I was so interested by how many young people thought I had exaggerated its seriousness. And when you tell them that twice as many people died of the 'flu than in the war, they are absolutely astonished. They will accept there was a bit of Spanish 'flu about – they have heard that somewhere – but not that it was a decimation. I always like it when I feel we're telling them something they didn't know.

ISOBEL: Do you want to cry off dinner?

LAVINIA: No, it's too late to chuck. I'll be all right
if I can just have a bath to recover.

22 INT. KITCHEN PASSAGE. DOWNTON. EVE.

Mrs Hughes hails Anna. She is with Molesley.

MRS HUGHES: Anna, Mr Molesley is kindly helping with
dinner tonight. When you've finished the young ladies,
can you take him through it, please?

MOLESLEY: If you've time, but honestly, I'm quite happy
to go sight unseen.

23 INT. CORA'S BEDROOM. DOWNTON. EVE.

Robert, dressed, is with Cora and O'Brien.

O'BRIEN: Are you too hot in that, m'lady? We still have
time to change.

CORA: No, I'm fine. Thank you.

But she dabs her temples, as the maid leaves.

CORA (CONT'D): So what do we do next?

ROBERT: God knows. This is what comes of spoiling her.
The mad clothes, the nursing. What were we thinking of?

CORA: That's not fair. She's a wonderful nurse. And
she's worked very hard.

ROBERT: But in the process she's forgotten who she is!

CORA: Has she, Robert? Or have we overlooked who she
really is?

ROBERT: If you're turning American on me, I'll go
downstairs.*

....

* A reminder of my beloved stepmother who, if the conversation threatened it,
would always cry: 'Now, don't let's get psychological!' It is all part of that British
horror of introspection, which has only recently lost its grip on the nation.
Robert would certainly have shared this view, and I'm not completely convinced
we have profited as much from the change as some people like to think.

24   INT.   SERVERY.   DOWNTON.   EVE.

Anna is with Molesley.

ANNA: Mr Carson likes to serve two white wines, which you should open and decant just before they eat. A light one for the hors d'oeuvres, then a heavier one with the soup. Keep that going for the fish and then change to claret, which you should really decant now. There's a pudding wine and, after that, whatever they want in the drawing room with their coffee.
MOLESLEY: Blimey. It's a wonder they make it up the stairs.
ANNA: They don't drink much of any of it. Now, let me show you the decanters. These four for the white, the jugs are for the claret; oh, and it's a peculiarity of his, but he always…

Molesley starts to realise what he has taken on.*

25   INT.   HALL.   DOWNTON.   EVE.

Mrs Hughes is with Cora, who seems hot and puzzled.

CORA: So I don't have to receive that terrible man again?
MRS HUGHES: It won't be necessary. They'll meet Ethel here, but then — should you be downstairs, m'lady?
CORA: Oh, I'm perfectly all right, thank you.

26   INT.   KITCHEN.   DOWNTON.   EVE.

Mrs Patmore is working with Daisy. Thomas is there.

THOMAS: Why Molesley? I could have done it.
MRS PATMORE: But you always make a mountain out of not being a servant.

....

* As I have said before now, it was considered second rate for an upper-middle-class household, let alone an aristocratic one, to have no male servants. This was a snobbish prejudice, but it was usually held as passionately, or more so, by the other servants as by the employers. And Carson believes very strongly that for a maid to wait at table is a stain that would not easily be eradicated. Here, the obvious solution to his illness would be for Anna to run the dinner, but that doesn't occur to him or to anyone else.

THOMAS: I'm just trying to be helpful.

MRS PATMORE: I'm afraid 'being helpful' is not something we associate you with.*

Thomas pushes off.

MRS PATMORE (CONT'D): Oh, it's wonderful what fear can do to the human spirit.

DAISY: What do you mean?

MRS PATMORE: Never mind… Daisy, did you ever answer that letter from William's dad?

DAISY: Yes.

MRS PATMORE: What did you say?

DAISY: I said I didn't see the point of meeting. That I thought it would make things worse for him, to be reminded. Where's the good in that?

Which Mrs Patmore must accept.

27 INT. SERVERY. DOWNTON. EVE.

Anna and Jane carry in food. Molesley sips from a glass.

ANNA: Are you quite right, Mr Molesley?

MOLESLEY: Yes. I just want to be absolutely sure that this is the lighter wine.

JANE: What does it matter? As long as it's white.

MOLESLEY: No. I believe in starting the way you mean to go on… I don't want to get off on the wrong foot.

He pushes through into the dining room, carrying the carafes.

....

* In putting himself forward as someone who wants to be helpful, Thomas is trying to get taken back onto the staff. This is not because he wants to be in service any more than he did at the end of the war, but because he doesn't know what else he's going to do. I suspect quite a lot of post-war servants were secretly beginning to entertain ideas of an alternative career, as many of them did start to slip away when the opportunities presented themselves.

28 INT. DINING ROOM. DOWNTON. EVE.

The family, plus Violet and the Crawleys, are at dinner.

VIOLET: I'm glad you're here, Sybil, dear. I was afraid
you'd have a tray in your room.

ROBERT: Maybe you should have done.

SYBIL: Why? I'm not eloping like a thief in the night.
I might have once, but Mary and Edith talked me out of
it.

VIOLET: Oh? The plot thickens.

ISOBEL: After all, Sybil's had enough time to think about
it —

MATTHEW: Mother! It is not for us to have an opinion.*
Mr Molesley? Are you quite well?

Molesley has slopped wine out of the glass. He is green.

MOLESLEY: I — I'm all right. Thank you, sir.

MATTHEW: I don't believe you are.

CORA: The awful truth is, I'm not quite all right, and
I'm afraid I'm going to ask you to excuse me.

She stands and so do the men.

ROBERT: I'm so sorry. Would you like us to call Doctor
Clarkson?

CORA: Not now, darling. It's too late.

ANNA: He's coming anyway, your lordship, for Mr Carson.

EDITH: I'll bring him up when he arrives.

ROBERT: I can sleep in my dressing room.

....

* It's a personal thing of mine, but I am always interested when, in a group
discussion, a subject arises that is only really the business of the couple or the
family concerned. In which case, the polite thing to do for the other
participants is to keep out of it. Someone who understands how life is lived is
always able to judge which conversations they have a right to take part in,
and which ones they have nothing to add to. In fact, if you do not develop
this instinct, you can be a very tiresome guest. Here, Matthew judges
correctly that it is not for them to start talking about whether or not Sybil
should marry Branson. Unfortunately, Isobel's judgement is less reliable.

He is by the door as he says this. Jane has heard and she catches Robert's eye. Almost reluctantly, he holds her look. *

29 INT. MRS HUGHES'S SITTING ROOM/PASSAGE. DOWNTON. EVE.

Anna comes in. Mrs Hughes is sewing.

> ANNA: Her ladyship's been taken ill. So when the doctor gets here, can you hold onto him and tell Lady Edith?
> MRS HUGHES: I thought she wasn't looking too clever.

Anna leaves and runs into Bates in the passage outside.

> ANNA: Oh, I'm glad I've got you.
> BATES: Aren't you serving?
> ANNA: They're on the main course so I can spare a moment. I've been thinking… and I have to say something that you won't agree with.

He looks at her. She takes a breath.

> ANNA (CONT'D): We're going to get married.
> BATES: Don't be silly. We can't, not now. Would I risk your being widowed by the noose?
> ANNA: You're not listening. You're going to Ripon tomorrow afternoon to take out a special licence — I don't care how much it costs — and fix a day. We'll tell no one. But this you will do.
> BATES: I can't.
> ANNA: Aren't I as strong as Lady Sybil?
> BATES: I don't doubt that.
> ANNA: Well then, if she can do it, so can we. That's what I've been thinking. I have stuck by you through thick and thin.

....

* For our own narrative purposes, in this instance, Robert decides to sleep in his dressing room. In fact, as we have already made clear, he doesn't sleep separately from his wife, as many men did then. But even for couples who slept together, a bed in a dressing room remained an essential for many years after this. And not just a bed, but a bed that was permanently made, with clean sheets. This is true, I should perhaps say, of my own life, because to have a bed that is always made up means that, if you develop a cough or someone suddenly has to stay the night, you don't have to fuss around. You've already got one extra bed in the house that is permanently ready.

BATES: Thin and thin, more like.
ANNA: Then you will grant me my deserts, please,
Mr Bates. If we have to face this, then we will face it
as husband and wife. I will not be moved to the
sidelines to watch how you fare from a distance, with no
right even to be kept informed. I will be your next of
kin, and you cannot deny me that.*

He looks into her eyes. Jane comes running down the passage.

JANE: Anna! You'd better come! Quick!

30   INT.   SERVERY.   DOWNTON.   EVE.

Molesley's slumped over the carafes of wine as they run in.

ANNA: Mr Molesley, what's happened? Haven't you taken
that in yet?
MOLESLEY: I'm not well. I'm not well at all.
JANE: First Mr Carson, then her ladyship and now him.
ANNA: Help him down to the servants' hall. The doctor
can take a look at him, too, when he gets here.

31   INT.   DINING ROOM.   DOWNTON.   EVE.

ISOBEL: And to Downton. Doctor Clarkson says he's got
ten cases already…

Anna arrives at Robert's right with the carafe. He looks up.

....

* Anna's determination to marry Bates is moving, but it also has some
resonance in the modern world, since the importance she places on being
Bates's official next of kin was one of the bases of the Civil Partnership Bill.
What people forget is that a simple request or statement was never enough to
turn someone into your next of kin, in a hospital or a prison or anywhere else.
Even if you've been someone's girlfriend or boyfriend and lived with them for
many years, this counted for nothing unless your kinship was officially
recognised and sanctioned. Anna's desire to marry is partly because of her
love and loyalty, but it's also that she doesn't want to have to deal with their
coming trials while being shut out from all deliberations. As Bates's wife, she
will have an official position from which to fight, and that's really what she's
after. Of course, until the Civil Partnership Bill, this was not an option open
to gay men and women, who often had to stand and watch as forgotten
cousins from the shires took precedence over their partner in any official
context. Thank heaven that's over.

ROBERT: Ah, I thought Molesley had joined the Temperance
League.
ANNA: I'm afraid he's been taken ill, m'lord. I am
sorry.
ROBERT: Molesley, too? Good heavens, everyone's falling
like ninepins.

Mary notices that Lavinia, who has been silent, looks grey.

MARY: Lavinia?
LAVINIA: Do you know, I'm not at all well, either. I
wonder if I could lie down for a minute.
MARY: Of course. Come to my room. They'll have lit the
fire by now.
LAVINIA: Excuse me.

Lavinia stands, again so do the men, and the two women leave.

ISOBEL: Do you think we should take her home?
MATTHEW: No, let her rest for a moment.
ISOBEL: Well, I think I should go and help.

*She stands. So do the men. She goes, leaving an empty
chair.*

VIOLET: Wasn't there a masked ball in Paris when cholera
broke out? Half the guests were dead before they left
the ballroom.
ROBERT: Thank you, Mama. That's cheered us up no end.*

END OF ACT TWO

....

* Spanish 'flu did tear through households, and often you would get several
members of the same family falling ill, as well as their staff or fellow workers.
It must have been so frightening. Violet's reference to the masked ball in
Paris is not invented. As a young man, I was fascinated by an engraving –
not, I think, by Dürer, but it was that sort of thing – of a costume ball at some
point in the fifteenth century where, during the evening, cholera struck. It
was not that it actually killed them within seconds, but it rendered them
incapable of moving, so they sank to the floor and died there. The result was
this extraordinary scene in a Paris ballroom, of people dead while still in
fancy dress. I remember the image vividly, and what Violet says here is
perfectly true.

ACT THREE

32 INT. BEDROOM PASSAGE/HALL. DOWNTON. NIGHT.

Clarkson and Mrs Hughes leave Cora's room. Robert is walking towards them.

MRS HUGHES: I'll take you to Mr Carson now. And then to
see Mr Molesley in the servants' hall.
ROBERT: Doctor Clarkson. You're kind to come. How is
she?
CLARKSON: Not too bad, I'd say. But she'll need some
nursing for a day or two.
ROBERT: Oh, don't worry about that. All our daughters
are professionals. Let's leave her to get some rest.

Now Mary and Isobel walk down the passage towards them.

MARY: Miss Swire may be another victim. But she's
sleeping now, so I don't want to disturb her.
CLARKSON: When she wakes, give her some aspirin and
cinnamon in milk and keep her here. I'll look at her in
the morning.
MARY: Why cinnamon? How can that help?
CLARKSON: It's to bring down the temperature.
ISOBEL: Tomorrow, we could try them with some salt of
quinine.
MARY: If it is the 'flu, is it serious?
CLARKSON: It's a strange strain and a cruel one.
Normally, children and the old are the most vulnerable,
but this seems to strike at young adults who should be
able to throw it off... I'd better go to Carson.*
ISOBEL: I'll come, too.

....

* For once, Clarkson diagnoses the illness correctly, and he has his work cut out. Cinnamon in milk was a period treatment to bring down the temperature; it was supposed to have some sort of coolant effect. I cannot comment on its efficacy. Clarkson's explanation of it was cut, but in a way I agree with that; I like references that seem puzzling, but when you look them up you find they're completely accurate. I was sadder to lose the curious – and true – fact that Spanish 'flu was most pernicious with young adults. This meant that many men died who had survived the war, which seems cruel even by nature's standards.

Mrs Hughes and Clarkson share a look, as she takes them by a door to the servants' staircase. Robert is left with Mary.

ROBERT: If you'll excuse me, I'll go to bed.

He kisses her and walks off. She continues on down the main stair. Matthew is alone in the hall, on the edge of the empty floor by the gramophone, leafing through records.

MARY: Where is everyone?
MATTHEW: I'm not sure. Cousin Violet's gone home.
MARY: What about you?
MATTHEW: I'm waiting for Lavinia and Mother.
MARY: Doctor Clarkson wants Lavinia to stay here. He'll see her tomorrow... I don't know this one.

She is looking through the recordings.

MATTHEW: Actually, I rather like it. I think it was in a show that flopped. *Zip Goes a Million*, or something.

He puts on the record and 'Look for the Silver Lining' starts to play. He holds out his hands, and they begin to dance. *

MARY: Can you manage without your stick?
MATTHEW: You are my stick.

They dance on for a moment.

MARY: We were a show that flopped.

....

* The treatment of 'Look for the Silver Lining', here, wasn't quite as I'd imagined it. I wanted it to start with the slightly thin sound of an actual recording from the period, and then for the tune to be taken up by a hidden orchestra until they were dancing to a lush, heart-moving treatment of this very romantic tune by Jerome Kern. But for some reason the production decision was instead to bring in a version of the Matthew and Mary theme, and only go back to 'Look for the Silver Lining' at the end. I'm afraid, for me, the two tunes jarred and the result was rather less than enchanting; in fact, the sound had a slightly unpleasant dissonance. Usually, when I see what I've written realised, it is, if anything, better than I had imagined, but in this instance I found that what should have been an incredibly romantic moment wasn't quite. But of course that was only a personal opinion. I don't remember any letters of complaint.

Her words hit the target. He looks at her. His face crumbles.

MATTHEW: Oh God, Mary.

He whispers into her ear, as close to her as a lover.

MATTHEW (CONT'D): I am so, so sorry. Do you know how sorry I am?

MARY: Don't be. It wasn't anyone's fault, or if it was, it was mine.

MATTHEW: You know Cousin Violet came to me and told me to marry you?

MARY: When was this?

MATTHEW: A while ago. When we knew I would walk again. She said marriage was a long business and if it was you that I loved then you were the one I should marry.

MARY: Classic Granny. What did you say?

MATTHEW: That I couldn't accept Lavinia's sacrifice, of her life, her children, her future, and then give her the brush-off when I was well again... Well, I couldn't, could I?

MARY: Of course not.

MATTHEW: However much I might want to.

MARY: Absolutely not.

But the admission is enough. A moment later they are kissing.

LAVINIA (V.O.): Hello?

They spring apart to see Lavinia coming down the stairs.

MATTHEW: What are you doing up?

LAVINIA: Shouldn't we be getting back?

MARY: It's decided. You're staying here. Doctor Clarkson's coming in the morning, so he can treat all of you together. You can borrow some things until Matthew brings you what you need. I'll go and organise a room.

She walks out towards the green baize door.

MATTHEW: How do you feel?

LAVINIA: Like a nuisance.

MATTHEW: You could never be that.

LAVINIA: I mean it, Matthew. Don't ever let me be a nuisance. Don't ever let me get in the way. Please.*

33 INT. SERVANTS' HALL. DOWNTON. NIGHT.

Molesley is slumped over. Clarkson is with Mrs Hughes, O'Brien and others. Clarkson talks as he goes to examine Molesley.

O'BRIEN: I'll sleep on a chair in her room.
CLARKSON: Oh, no. There's no need for that.
O'BRIEN: I don't mind. I'd like to be on hand.
MRS HUGHES: So we're quite the hospital again.
CLARKSON: You'll probably gain some more patients over the next few days. But you don't need to worry about Molesley. He'll be fine in the morning.
MRS HUGHES: Oh?
CLARKSON: Uh-huh. The others have Spanish 'flu. He's just drunk.

Molesley raises his head as if to protest, but no.†

34 INT. LAVINIA'S BEDROOM/PASSAGE. DOWNTON. NIGHT.

Anna and Jane have made the bed. Jane folds the bedcover.

ANNA: I'll fetch Miss Swire.

She leaves. Jane follows. In the passage, Bates is walking away. The door opens. Robert is there in his dressing gown.

JANE: Oh, did you want Mr Bates, m'lord?
ROBERT: I forgot to say I want to be woken early.
JANE: Well, I can tell him that… Freddie got into Ripon Grammar. So whatever you said, it worked.

....

* I thought Zoe Boyle, as Lavinia, was charming in this section, and very touching. Without the lines to express it, she nevertheless made it quite clear that she realised that once Mary was coming after Matthew, full on so to speak, it was an unequal contest. A really good piece of work.

† Kevin Doyle is a wonderful actor. He has created this extraordinary, three-dimensional, emotionally wracked loser that I now write for. His Molesley has that marvellous combination of being both hilarious and very moving – a gift to a writer.

ROBERT: Marvellous. Some good news at last.
JANE: I hate to hear you talk like that.

Somehow her words alter the tone to a more intimate one.

ROBERT: I'm sorry. That was selfish of me. To spoil
your happy moment.
JANE: You need never say sorry to me… How are you?
Really?
ROBERT: Since you ask, I'm wretched. I lost my youngest
child today, I suspect forever, and I can't see any way
round it.
JANE: I wish you knew how much I want to help. In any
way.
ROBERT: Do you?
JANE: I think you know I do.

He holds out his hand and draws her into the room.

35   INT.   CARSON'S BEDROOM.   DOWNTON.   NIGHT.

Mrs Hughes is waiting for Carson to drink the brown milk.

CARSON: I'll see if I can get up tomorrow.
MRS HUGHES: Oh, don't be foolish. You're ill, and in all
probability you're going to be a lot iller in the
morning.
CARSON: Yes, but how will you manage? And what about the
wedding?
MRS HUGHES: I'm not sure there'll even be a wedding.
But, either way, I won't burden you with it.
CARSON: Well, perhaps Mr Molesley could come on a
permanent basis? Until I'm better.
MRS HUGHES: I doubt that's the solution, Mr Carson.
Neither my patience nor his liver could stand it.

36   INT.   ROBERT'S DRESSING ROOM.   DOWNTON.   NIGHT.

Robert is kissing Jane.

ROBERT: If you only knew how much I've longed for this.
JANE: Have you, really? Because I have. I know it
should feel wrong, but it doesn't. Not to me.
ROBERT: Right or wrong, by God, it feels free. Free of
the war, free of duty, free of my life. I've lived so
long according to my duty and now I find myself
constantly wondering why —

They kiss again but there is a knock and the door is opening.

    ROBERT (CONT'D): Who is it?

*Robert pushes Jane behind the door, then opens it further and
stands there, facing Bates. His heart is pounding.*

    BATES (V.O.): I'm sorry, m'lord. We never settled the
    time you wanted to be woken.
    ROBERT: Early, I think, with everyone ill. Seven. I'll
    breakfast at half past.
    BATES: Very good, m'lord. Goodnight.

*He goes and Robert shuts the door. Jane comes to him. She
lifts her arms to embrace him again, but he holds them.*

    ROBERT: This isn't fair. I'm placing you in an
    impossible situation.
    JANE: I want to be with you. I want to make things
    easier for you. Let me.

But Robert steps back, releasing her arms. She looks at him.

    JANE (CONT'D): I see. You don't want me now.
    ROBERT: I want you with every fibre of my being. But it
    isn't fair to you, it isn't fair to anyone.
    JANE: You didn't say that a moment ago.
    ROBERT: And in that moment I have woken up. I am myself
    again. Oh, my dear, I wish I had it in me to break the
    rules and glory in it. But that isn't the man I am or
    could be. I wish I were different, I wish everything
    were different.
    JANE: I don't want you different. I like you the way you
    are.
    ROBERT: Thank you for that. I will cherish it. Truly.

*But he opens the door, looking up and down the passage. He
comes back and takes her hand. She kisses her finger and
touches his cheek, then slips out.**

    37 INT. SERVANTS' HALL. DOWNTON. DAY.

Mrs Hughes is at her wits' end. So is O'Brien.

    O'BRIEN: I'm not easy. I'm not easy at all. When will
    the doctor see her?
    MRS HUGHES: As soon as he gets here and not before.

What does his lordship say?

    O'BRIEN: I don't know. He's gone out.
    MRS HUGHES: What about Miss Swire?

A hall boy comes in coughing. He hands Mrs Hughes a letter.

    ANNA: Not too bad, I think. I'll take her up something
    on a tray in a minute.
    MRS PATMORE: And we've three kitchen maids down, so it's
    me and Daisy *contra mundi*.

By now, Mrs Hughes has glanced through the missive.

    MRS HUGHES: That's all I need.
    ANNA: What is it?
    MRS HUGHES: Never you mind. Jane, come along. No
    day-dreaming today, please.

The hall boy coughs again.

    MRS HUGHES (CONT'D): Anyone ill, will you please take
    yourself to bed! Don't stay down here and spread
    infection!

38   INT. CARSON'S BEDROOM. DOWNTON. DAY.

Carson is reading the letter. He looks terrible.

    CARSON: Why did you invite them?
    MRS HUGHES: Because I didn't see any harm in it. No one
    was ill then.
    CARSON: You must put them off.
    MRS HUGHES: But how? They're coming this afternoon. How
    can I stop them?

---

* When I first wrote this scene, I did intend to put them into bed, but when I thought about it, I felt it wasn't really truthful. With his wife dangerously ill, and with everything else swirling about him, Robert would not do that, not once he'd had time to think. And here, Bates's intervention is key, because it wakes Robert up. Once he has woken up to the fact that he's kissing a maid while the woman he loves is his wife, then he can't go on with it. Jane may be up for some action, possibly, but she's in a different situation. Her husband is dead, she's in love with Robert, and in this I'm sure she's perfectly sincere. In other words, she doesn't have the same emotional brakes to apply. But anyway, Robert wakes up, and so it's not going to happen. Jane has lost, which she is decent enough to accept.

CARSON: Well, I'm no use to you. I got up a while ago
and nearly passed out.
MRS HUGHES: I could use a dose of 'flu myself...

39   INT.   CORA'S BEDROOM.   DOWNTON.   DAY.

O'Brien tends Cora, with Edith and Mary. Mrs Hughes arrives.

MRS HUGHES: What can I bring to help?
O'BRIEN: Ice. To bring her temperature down.
MARY: Mrs Hughes, Sir Richard telephoned this morning.
He's coming down to help. I wonder if you could have
some rooms made ready for him and his valet, and tell
Mrs Patmore?
MRS HUGHES: Very good, m'lady. As long as he's here to
help.

She clearly has her own views on how this will help.*

40   EXT.   DOWNTON VILLAGE.   DAY.

Robert is walking towards the Grantham Arms.

41   INT.   BRANSON'S ROOM.   GRANTHAM ARMS.   DOWNTON
VILLAGE.   DAY.

Robert is with Branson.

BRANSON: But I don't accept that I am ruining her life,
nor that I'm cutting her off from her family. If you
want to cut her off, that's your decision.
ROBERT: But how will you look after her? How can you
hope to provide for her?
BRANSON: With respect, m'lord, you seem to think that she
can only be happy in some version of Downton Abbey. When
it's obvious that if she wanted that life, she would not
be marrying me.

....

* Mrs Hughes obviously does not believe that Sir Richard's coming will help,
and most of us can remember similar situations, when we are obliged to
accept an offer of help, but we know very little help will be forthcoming. I do
think people coming in to help when they don't help at all is the bane of all
our lives, making everything more difficult and time-wasting than it needs
to be.

Robert considers this, then reaches inside his jacket for a
large chequebook. He sits at a table and takes out his pen.

ROBERT: Very well. I'd hoped to avoid this, but I see
that I can't. How much will you take to leave us in
peace?
BRANSON: What?
ROBERT: You must have doubts. You said your own mother
thinks you foolish.
BRANSON: Yes, she does —
ROBERT: Then yield to those doubts, and take enough to
make a new life back in Ireland. I'll be generous if we
can bring this nonsense to an end.
BRANSON: I see… You know your trouble, m'lord? You're
like all of your kind. You think you have the monopoly
of honour. Doesn't it occur to you that I might believe
the best guarantee of Sybil's happiness lies with me?
ROBERT: Well, if you're not prepared to listen to reason —
BRANSON: I'm not prepared to listen to insults.
ROBERT: Then I will bid you a good day. And I want you
to leave the village.
BRANSON: Even though she'll come to me the moment I call?
Do you really want me to leave now, when I will take her
with me that same hour?*

42   INT. HALL. DOWNTON. DAY.

Robert walks in to find consternation. Isobel greets him.

ISOBEL: Ah, there you are. Doctor Clarkson's here.
Cora's not at all well. Sybil and Edith are with her.
Mary's gone to meet Sir Richard from the train —
ROBERT: What's he come for?

....

* Robert is unable to resist his own ingrained instincts, and so he assumes
that a cheque will sort it out. But I agree with Branson. It is nonsense to
believe that the upper classes have the monopoly of honour, and Robert is
letting himself down by taking this particular tack. It is just possible, if he
had put forward a reasoned argument explaining how Branson would be
taking Sybil into a life she would find difficult to deal with, that Branson
might at least have given it ear time. But once Robert had offered him
money, it meant that Branson was not going to listen to him for one more
minute, so in fact Robert's rare coarseness in this instance works against him.

ISOBEL: I gather he wants to be useful.
ROBERT: I don't see how.

Edith comes downstairs as Mrs Hughes arrives.

MRS HUGHES: M'lord, we're two more maids down. I hope
you can forgive some catch-as-catch-can in the days
ahead.
ROBERT: Which maids? Not Jane?
MRS HUGHES: No, m'lord. Not Jane.

*She registers this. No one else does. Men carry in
greenery.*

ROBERT: What are they doing?
EDITH: Decorations for the wedding. It still hasn't been
cancelled. Until it is, they have to prepare for it.*

43 INT. SERVANTS' HALL. DOWNTON. DAY.

The coughing hall boy is resting his forehead on his hands.

THOMAS: Go to bed.
HALL BOY: If I do, there'll be no one on duty.†
THOMAS: I'm on duty. Go to bed.

Mrs Hughes arrives in a fluster.

MRS HUGHES: If Anna or Jane appear, tell them to come and
help me do the room for Sir Richard. I'll be in Armada.
THOMAS: Right, I can help you with the bedroom, then I'll
sort out a room for his man and I'll serve at dinner.

....

* I liked the irony of the fact that while Lavinia may be upstairs with Spanish
'flu, they would still have to continue to pin up the greenery and prepare for
the wedding, until it had been cancelled.

† I gave the hall boy a line, and then it was cut, which must have been
maddening for him, and I am sorry. The hall boys and those maids who have
no lines take their contribution very seriously and we are lucky that they do.
In fact, they do a superb job. These parts may not have much in the way of
lines, but they are very important to the show. I can tell you that when the
supporting actors are not good, when they don't take it seriously, they can
undermine the whole thing, like a bad apple in a barrel. So I'm sorry he had
to lose the reward for his excellent work.

MRS HUGHES: But I've no money to pay you.

THOMAS: Call it rent.*

She doesn't argue, but hurries out, past the sick hall boy.

MRS HUGHES: Do what he says and go to bed.

44 INT. LAVINIA'S BEDROOM. DOWNTON. DAY.

Isobel and Matthew are with Lavinia.

ISOBEL: The awful truth is, the wedding simply cannot go ahead.

MATTHEW: Oh, don't say that.

ISOBEL: I must. Doctor Clarkson says you'll be groggy for at least a week, maybe even longer. We have to face the facts. I'd be leading you on if I said any different.

LAVINIA: What about my father?

ISOBEL: Well, Matthew can telephone him.

LAVINIA: He can't come here while everyone's ill. He has a weak chest and mustn't take the risk.†

MATTHEW: All right. Well, I suppose we've made a decision, then? To delay?

....

* Mrs Hughes has a budget when it comes to wages, and she's spent it. Every now and then, it feels right to remind the audience that this is a workplace. In fact, *Downton Abbey* is essentially a workplace drama, where we show the workplace of the servants in the early twentieth century. The point here being that, if you want people to do something, you must pay them, which some employers, then or now, can forget when they make extra demands. One of the basic questions of any drama is: why do these men and women stay? If things are so difficult, why don't they go? But with a workplace drama you have a built-in fundamental imperative to stay, because this is how they earn their living. We are just reminding the audience of those realities here.

† We didn't really have anything for an actor playing Mr Swire to do. We would need him at the funeral, of course, but we could have him played by a supporting artist for that (the man who did it was very good), and the fact remained that we didn't really want him in the mounting emotional drama. We needed it to be played out between Matthew, Lavinia and Mary, and we had no room for a sobbing Papa. So, in the end, we gave him a weak chest, and kept him away.

LAVINIA: I don't think we've got any choice.

ISOBEL: No. I'm afraid we don't.

MATTHEW: I should get started. I'll go home now for the lists. What a palaver.

Matthew and Isobel talk quietly at the door.

MATTHEW (CONT'D): Well, at least she doesn't seem too serious.

ISOBEL: No, no. I'd say she's been lucky. But I am terribly sorry about the wedding.

MATTHEW: These things are sent to try us.

45   INT.   CORA'S BEDROOM.   DOWNTON.   DAY.

Cora is feverish and delirious, covered only in a sheet.

ROBERT: Why didn't anyone tell me she was like this?

SYBIL: She took a turn for the worse about half an hour ago. Where were you?

ROBERT: Out. I went for a walk.

Sybil is in her nursing uniform. She acknowledges his look.

SYBIL: It's cleaner and safer, and some people find it comforting.

ROBERT: I'm sure they do.

O'Brien has arrived with a bowl of ice water. She starts to bathe Cora's brow gently, talking softly, as to a child.

O'BRIEN: There you are, m'lady. That's better, isn't it?

Sybil whispers to her father.

SYBIL: She's been with her all night.

ROBERT: O'Brien, you must have a rest.

O'BRIEN: Not just now, m'lord, if you don't mind. I want to see her through the worst, if I can. Now, I'll just make this cooler for you.

She goes on with her work. Robert returns to Sybil.

ROBERT: How is she? Really. Tell me the truth.

SYBIL: I can't, yet. Doctor Clarkson says we will know more in a few hours.

ROBERT: God almighty. How can this be? My whole life gone over a cliff in the course of a single day.

SYBIL: Don't give up hope, Papa. It's much too early for that.

*But her words are more alarming than comforting.**

END OF ACT THREE

ACT FOUR

46 INT. SERVANTS' HALL. DOWNTON. DAY.

Anna looks in to find Bates, who is talking to a hall boy.

BATES: Take care of that. Thank you.

The hall boy leaves.

BATES (CONT'D): How are you doing?
ANNA: I'm not sure. Her ladyship's worse.
BATES: I'm sorry.
ANNA: Jane said you wanted to see me.
BATES: It's only to say that I've done it. I've booked the registrar.
ANNA: When for?
BATES: He's had a cancellation. So it's… it's Friday afternoon.
ANNA: This Friday?
ETHEL (V.O.): Hello?

Ethel is there with Charlie, as Jane comes downstairs.

....

* My own thinking was that, by this stage, the audience would have begun to work out that if you have as many major characters as this with Spanish 'flu, one of them has had it. So, hopefully, they are asking themselves which one has drawn the short straw. I wanted them to assume it was Cora, because then Robert would be on the horns of a dilemma, having just fallen for the charms of another woman. And then they would consider the plot possibilities of our finding another wife for Robert, and maybe his having more children, maybe a son who would change everything… Anyway, all of this was quite deliberately suggested to make them think it would be Cora who was on the way out. I don't know if anyone was taken in.

ANNA: Ethel? What are you doing here?

JANE: Those Bryants have turned up again.

ETHEL: That's what.

ANNA: I'll find Mrs Hughes and come back for you.

47   INT.   DRAWING ROOM.   DOWNTON.   DAY.

Mr and Mrs Bryant sit in silence, when Mrs Hughes enters.

MRS HUGHES: I hope I haven't kept you waiting.

MRS BRYANT: No, no.

MRS HUGHES: I'm afraid we have illness in the house, so I hope you can excuse Lord and Lady Grantham.

MR BRYANT: It's not them we've come to see, is it? Is she here?

MRS HUGHES: She's just coming now. Ah.

Anna ushers in Ethel with the boy. Ethel is very torn.

MRS BRYANT: May I meet him properly?

ETHEL: Come along, Charlie… This nice lady is your… grandmother.

MRS BRYANT: Perhaps you could call me Gran?

MRS HUGHES: He's a stout little chap, isn't he?

MRS BRYANT: And so like Charles. I thought it when we were last here. I know what was said at the time, and Mr Bryant's sorry for it now, but I could see he was just like Charles.

MR BRYANT: Never mind all that. Let's get down to business.

ETHEL: Business?

MR BRYANT: That's what you want from us, isn't it? To find out what we mean to do for little Charlie in the future?

This is such good news to both Mrs Hughes and Ethel.

48   INT.   KITCHEN.   DOWNTON.   DAY.

Mrs Patmore is with O'Brien and Daisy.

DAISY: What do you mean, she might die?

O'BRIEN: She's very ill. She may die.

DAISY: I know, but… I mean, die?

O'BRIEN: What do you think happens with a fatal illness? The fairies come?

The truth is, she is very upset, which Mrs Patmore can see.

MRS PATMORE: By heaven, if anything happens to her it
won't be your fault, Miss O'Brien. I've never seen such
care.

This catches O'Brien off-guard. She has to confide.

O'BRIEN: I wish I could talk to her, that's all. But she
doesn't know me.
MRS PATMORE: I'm sure she knows how hard you've worked
for her.
O'BRIEN: It's not that. There's something I need — never
mind. Either I will or I won't.

*During this, Mrs Patmore has poured the contents of a
saucepan into a cup on a tray. O'Brien carries it away.*

MRS PATMORE: You never know people, do you? You can work
with them for twenty years, but you don't know them at
all.

49   INT. BEDROOM PASSAGE. DOWNTON. DAY.

Robert is walking along when he sees Sybil with a full tray.

ROBERT: Can you manage?
SYBIL: I'm taking these up for Carson and the hall boys.
ROBERT: I suppose you'll be leaving soon? Now the
wedding's been put back.
SYBIL: Of course I'm not leaving. Not 'til Mama is well
again. We may disagree, but I'm still your daughter.

He opens his dressing-room door. She gives a querying look.

ROBERT: I'm going to wash and change and then I'll go
back to sit with Mama.

50   INT. DRAWING ROOM. DOWNTON. DAY.

Ethel and Mrs Hughes are less pleased than they were.

ETHEL: What? You mean give him up? Never see him again?
MR BRYANT: Those are my terms.
MRS HUGHES: But would it hurt if Ethel were to care for
him in your own house? She could be his nurse.
MRS BRYANT: That might be poss—

MR BRYANT: Of course you can't be his nurse! Just think
for a minute! We mean to bring him up as a gentleman,
send him to Harrow, say, and Oxford. And all the while
his mother's down in the servants' hall? How does that
work?
ETHEL: Well, I — I could —
MR BRYANT: No, no. Don't you see? We want to raise him
as our grandson, not as a housemaid's bastard.

The word has a shocking effect on the room.

MRS HUGHES: Well, he has to know the truth sometime.
MR BRYANT: Maybe, but not for a long time. 'Til then,
his father had a wartime marriage until he died. And his
mother succumbed to Spanish 'flu.
MRS BRYANT: A lot of people have.
MRS HUGHES: We've quite a few upstairs.
MR BRYANT: And that, for many years at least, is all that
Charlie will be told.
ETHEL: So I'm just to be written out? Painted over?
Buried?
MR BRYANT: What matters is what's good for Charlie.
ETHEL: What's good for Charlie and what's good for you!

She turns to Mrs Bryant, whose eyes are full.

ETHEL (CONT'D): You've got a heart. I know you have.
You see what he's asking —
MR BRYANT: Ethel, consider this. In the world as it is,
compare the two futures: the first, as my heir, educated,
privileged, rich, able to do what he wants, to marry whom
he likes; the second, as the bastard —
MRS HUGHES: I think we've heard enough of that word for
one day.
MR BRYANT: Very well. As the nameless offshoot of a
drudge. You're his mother. Which would you choose for
him?
ETHEL: Suppose I could be his nurse and never tell him
who I am? Suppose I promise that?
MRS BRYANT: Surely —
MR BRYANT: Come on! We all know that's a promise you
could never keep.

The door opens and Anna comes in.

ANNA: I'm sorry, Mrs Hughes, we must send for the doctor
to come at once. Her ladyship's much worse.

Mrs Hughes turns to the others.

MRS HUGHES: I — I'm afraid —
MR BRYANT: You go where you're needed. We've had our
say, and you know how to reach us when you've made your
decision. Come along, Daphne.

*Mrs Bryant is with Ethel. They look at each other.**

51 INT. CORA'S BEDROOM. DOWNTON. DAY.

O'Brien sponges Cora's brow. Thomas looks round the door.

THOMAS: They've rung for the doctor. He'll be here any
moment.
O'BRIEN: Can you get some more ice if there is any?
Clean towels, new sheets. Anna can help me change them.
THOMAS: What about you? Are you all right?
O'BRIEN: Just fetch those things. Please.

Thomas nods and goes out. Cora stirs.

....

* Just as the early episodes of the Bryant story were, in part, to give us a break
from the war, so now they come as a slight relief from the 'flu. In a show like
this, you normally try to have one story that is nothing to do with whatever it
is that's concerning everyone else. Although I'm sure the Bryants are sorry
that Spanish 'flu is in the house, it doesn't really bother Mr Bryant, certainly.
He's come to see the baby, and that's all. This is constructed to be a *Downton*
moment, because in one way we dislike Mr Bryant, and we dislike the offer
he makes to Ethel. But on the other hand, is Ethel right in refusing his
proposal, because of the reality of the situation? As a matter of fact, after it
went out, some people attacked me for being sentimental in allowing Ethel
to keep the boy and throw away his chances. I was speaking in a library in
Hampstead, when a woman came up and absolutely shook me by the scruff
of the neck. I could only suggest that she wait to see the next series before
she unleashed her wrath.

A character I enjoy every time I watch this storyline is Mrs Bryant, played
by Christine Mackie, who gives a wonderfully layered performance as a
decent woman torn in different directions. Here, she is in agony, because she
doesn't want to deprive Ethel of the child, but at the same time she knows
they can give Charlie an extraordinary start in life, and raise him as their
future heir. A *Downton* dilemma is when you see both sides.

CORA: O'Brien? Is that you, O'Brien?

O'BRIEN: Yes, m'lady. It's me, m'lady.

CORA: You're so good to me. You've always been so good to me.

O'BRIEN: Not always, m'lady.

CORA: So good.

O'BRIEN: No. And the fact is, I want to ask so much for your forgiveness, because I did something once which I bitterly regret. Bitterly. And if you could only know how much —

CORA: So very good.

O'Brien is weeping, but Cora knows nothing. Robert comes in.

ROBERT: How is she?

O'BRIEN: She slept and she seemed better, then suddenly the fever came back —

ROBERT: O'Brien, thank you for the way you've looked after her. I mean it. I'm very grateful. Whatever comes.

This is a moment of reconciliation. Sybil arrives with ice.

SYBIL: I can manage here, O'Brien. You must have a rest. I insist.

O'BRIEN: There'll be plenty of time for that when we know what's happening.

Robert watches the two women. He is thinking.

52   INT.   LAVINIA'S BEDROOM.   DOWNTON.   DAY.

Matthew enters gingerly. Lavinia sits up, with Isobel.

MATTHEW: What a marathon, but I think I got them all. Everyone sends love. I've told your father I'll telegraph him as soon as it's safe for him to come.

LAVINIA: But not before…

They look at Isobel, who stands.

ISOBEL: Well, I don't think I should leave you alone. But if you don't tell…

With a smile, she goes, and Matthew pulls up a chair.

MATTHEW: I've been thinking about the date for the rematch and — What is it?

LAVINIA: If I say something, will you promise not to be cross?

MATTHEW: How can I promise anything, when I don't know what it is?

LAVINIA: I wonder if we haven't been rather lucky.

MATTHEW: I think we've both been very lucky.

LAVINIA: That we've been given a second chance.

MATTHEW: A second chance at what?

LAVINIA: To be quite, quite sure about what we're doing.

The mood has suddenly changed.

MATTHEW: Darling, what can you mean?

LAVINIA: The thing is… I might as well say it… When I came downstairs and you and Mary were dancing, I heard what you said and I saw what you did.

MATTHEW: Oh, but that was —

LAVINIA: No. It's not that I'm in a rage and a fury. In fact, I think it's noble of you to want to keep your word when things have changed. But I'm not sure it would be right for me to hold you to it.

MATTHEW: Lavinia, I can explain —

LAVINIA: No, listen. I've had lots of time to think about it. I love you very, very much, and I've wanted to marry you from the first moment I saw you. All that is true. But I didn't really know what I was taking on. It's not in me to be queen of the county. I'm a little person, an ordinary person, and when I saw you and Mary together, I thought how fine, how right you looked together.

She is crying, but she is determined to get it said.

MATTHEW: I don't want to hear this.

LAVINIA: Well, you must. Because it isn't a sudden thing. I was starting to worry, and when you were wounded I thought it was my calling to look after you and care for you. And I don't think Mary would have done that quite as well as me, really.

He is almost crying, too, by this stage. He shakes his head.

MATTHEW: No. No, not nearly as well.

LAVINIA: I do have some self-worth. Just not enough to make you marry the wrong person.

MATTHEW: What you're saying is pointless. Mary's marrying someone else.

LAVINIA: Is she? We'll see.

MATTHEW: I won't let you do this.

LAVINIA: You will, but we won't fight about it now. In fact, I'm tired. Can I rest for a bit? We'll talk later.

MATTHEW: Of course.*

53 INT. DRAWING ROOM. DOWNTON. DAY.

Mary is with Carlisle.

MARY: It's good of you to come, but I don't really see what you can do.

CARLISLE: I just thought I'd better do my bit. You say the chauffeur's gone, so I could always drive the car —

MARY: Preferably over the chauffeur.

She gives a little angry laugh.

CARLISLE: Your father's not having an easy time of it. How's Lady Grantham?

MARY: Not well. Clarkson's with her now.

CARLISLE: And Miss Swire?

MARY: Oh, she's —

She breaks off, suddenly enlightened.

MARY (CONT'D): Is that why you've come? Because I said Lavinia had been taken ill?

CARLISLE: I was coming up anyway, in a day or two. For the wedding.

....

* Lavinia, seemingly better, now realises that Matthew shouldn't marry her, because he's in love with someone else. These crushing disappointments do happen, and I think it is very tough to have to make the decision, but people who can face the truth in this, as in so many areas, benefit from it, quite as much as the person they are setting free. Actually, to insist on marrying someone who's not in love with you is a terrible template for a life, so I didn't feel Lavinia was doing the wrong thing where her happiness was concerned. To go further, I would say she was doing absolutely the right thing, for her own future as much as for his, and if things had been different she would have profited from it.

MARY: Well, she won't be getting married on Saturday,
which I suppose is what you'd like best.
CARLISLE: But she's not seriously ill?

She studies him, appraisingly.

MARY: I see what was worrying you. If Lavinia had been
carried off, you wanted to be here to stop Matthew from
falling into my arms on a tidal wave of grief.
CARLISLE: It's a tricky disease. I've already known two
people who died.*
MARY: A neighbour here died in February. Did you know
Sir Mark Sykes?

The door opens. Thomas comes in.

THOMAS: His lordship's asking for you, m'lady. Now, sir,
what can I get you in the way of tea?

54   INT. KITCHEN. DOWNTON. DAY.

Mrs Patmore and Daisy are with Mrs Hughes.

MRS HUGHES: I think we should aim at a sort of buffet
dinner. Then they can run in and out as it suits them.
I'm sorry to make extra work —
MRS PATMORE: Never mind that. At times like these, we
must all pull together.†

Mrs Hughes gives a letter to Daisy.

MRS HUGHES: Oh, this arrived in the afternoon post,
Daisy.

....

* Carlisle is absolutely right about Spanish 'flu being a tricky disease. The
horrible deception was that you seemed to be recovering, and then you
suddenly fell back. You weren't out of danger until your temperature had
come right down. That was the big imperative.

† Mrs Hughes's goal is always to run the house properly. Everyone is ill,
indeed Lady Grantham may be dying, but it doesn't alter the fact that,
somehow, she and Mrs Patmore have got to feed the people who are still in
the house. And the only realistic way of doing that is to have a buffet where
people can come in, help themselves and go, as and when they need to. So,
part of her brain is always thinking like a professional. The marker of how ill
everyone is, absurd as it may sound, must be the fact that nobody will change
their clothes for the evening.

Thomas comes in.

THOMAS: Tea for Sir Richard in the drawing room.
MRS HUGHES: Well, I'm glad to know he's here to help.
THOMAS: I can do it.
MRS HUGHES: You're very obliging, Thomas.
THOMAS: I can take some up to Mr Carson, if you'd like.

He winks and goes.

MRS PATMORE: Is that from your Mr Mason?
DAISY: He's not 'mine'.
MRS HUGHES: What does he say?
DAISY: He just says again we should talk about William.
He wants me to go to his farm.
MRS PATMORE: Oh, poor man. Will you not visit him?
DAISY: I'm not going to any farm.
MRS HUGHES: You're all he's got, Daisy.
DAISY: Well, then he's got nobody, 'cos he hasn't got me.

55 INT. MARY'S BEDROOM. DOWNTON. EVE.

Mary comes in. Anna is turning down the bed.

ANNA: Oh, I'm sorry, m'lady. I didn't think you'd want
to change tonight.
MARY: I don't. I just need a handkerchief.
ANNA: How's her ladyship?
MARY: Not good, I'm afraid… What is it?
ANNA: I don't mean to bother you, m'lady.
MARY: Go on.
ANNA: Can you keep a secret? Well, I know you can… You
see, Mr Bates and I had a plan… to get married this
coming Friday.
MARY: What?
ANNA: He's worried the police haven't finished with him…
And if he's right then I'm not going through it with no
proper place in his life.
MARY: Well, that's a very brave decision.
ANNA: Or a very stupid one. But, anyway, with her
ladyship ill now and half the servants on their backs,
and everybody working flat out —
MARY: Where is the marriage to be?
ANNA: Just in the register office in Ripon. It wouldn't
take long, but —

MARY: Go. I'll cover for you. We're all here, and you won't help Mama by changing your plans.*

The door opens and Edith appears.

EDITH: You'd better come. She's worse.

56 INT. CORA'S BEDROOM. DOWNTON. EVE.

Clarkson is with Robert, Isobel, Mary, Edith and Sybil. Cora is still being tended by the faithful O'Brien.

ISOBEL: We've given her quinine.
CLARKSON: Good. I've given her the epinephrin —
O'BRIEN: Doctor! Come quickly!

Cora is bleeding from the nose.

EDITH: Oh, no! What does that mean?
CLARKSON: It's a haemorrhage of the mucous membranes. It's not unusual —

Cora is seized by a fit of vomiting. Sybil snatches up a bowl but O'Brien takes it from her, holding Cora's head gently.

O'BRIEN: It's all right, m'lady, don't worry, don't worry a bit. Everything's going to be all right.

Robert is with Clarkson in the corner of the room.

ROBERT: Everything is clearly not all right. How bad is it?†

....

* Mary's not offended by this proposal, because for Bates and Anna to marry is quite suitable, except that Bates is in trouble. In fact, she thinks it's a brave decision, and even if it is a stupid one, as Anna says, either way it's going to happen. It's all part of Mary's universe. I suppose that's what a lot of the show is about – whether or not people are being allowed to exist within their own universe, and here, nothing is disrupting that.

† Like Martin Clunes's wonderful creation, Doc Martin, I always think blood is frightening. The moment blood appears, you think (or I do), God, what's happening? And that's exactly Robert's reaction here; he is getting more and more frightened. I was a little bit nervous about the line, 'I've given some medicine to Mrs Hughes, she'll bring it up later,' in the following scene, in case it sounded as if Mrs Hughes had taken the medicine and was about to be sick, but we seemed to get away with it.

CLARKSON: If she lasts through the night, she'll live. What about the others?
MARY: Come with me.
CLARKSON: I'll be back shortly.

57 INT. CARSON'S BEDROOM. DOWNTON. EVE.

Carson looks dishevelled as the other two come in.

CLARKSON: I've given some medicine to Mrs Hughes. She'll bring it up later.
CARSON: I gather her ladyship is not improving.
CLARKSON: Well, we'll… we'll know more tomorrow.
CARSON: And Miss Swire?
CLARKSON: Not too bad, I think. I'll go to her when I've seen the rest of the servants.

They are interrupted by Thomas arriving with a tray of tea.

CLARKSON: Ah.
THOMAS: Thank you, sir. Here we are, Mr Carson. Now, have you got everything you need? M'lady.

The butler nods and Thomas and Clarkson go. Carson looks at Mary.

CARSON: I want to thank you for coming up, m'lady.
MARY: Not at all.
CARSON: I mean it… I know I've been a disappointment to you.
MARY: Maybe. But I've relied on your support for too long to do without it entirely.
CARSON: You'll always have my support, m'lady.
MARY: And you mine. On which subject, I should be careful of Thomas.
CARSON: Oh, I don't know how we're to get rid of him, after all this.
MARY: But I doubt he'll want to stay a footman forever. So watch out.

*She shares this with Carson, who is worried.**

58 INT. DINING ROOM. DOWNTON. EVE.

Cold food is laid out. Thomas supervises. He has changed into his old footman's uniform. Edith, Matthew and Carlisle sit at the table, picking at some food. Mary enters.

MARY: You look very smart, Thomas.

THOMAS: Well, I still had the shirt, m'lady, and I found my livery in the cupboard. So I thought, why not?

Mary is helping herself. She would sit next to Matthew but…

CARLISLE: I have a place for you, here.

She goes to him. Isobel arrives and starts to help herself.

ISOBEL: How is Lavinia?

MATTHEW: All right, I think. The illness has made her rather confused…

MARY: What do you mean?

MATTHEW: Not now.

There is the sound of someone running on the stairs.

SYBIL (V.O.): Matthew! Mary!

She runs in through the door. Mary and Edith jump up.

MARY: Oh, my God! Is it Mama?

SYBIL: That's what's so… It's Lavinia!

Matthew, Edith and Isobel run out. Carlisle catches Mary.

CARLISLE: Let him go to her! Let him be with her! Surely you owe her that!

Mary stares at him, then throws his hand off and runs out.

....

* Mary breaks the rules to a certain extent by visiting Carson in his bedroom. True, she goes at other times to his sitting room; however, this is different. But I think we can accept it, because we know they have a relationship that means she can break the rules without being afraid she'll somehow put a spoke in the wheel and ruin Carson's working relationship with the family. She is completely secure in his affection, which, of course, is a great part of his appeal for her. Carlisle is the opposite. He has said he's come to help, but really he's come to make sure of Mary if Lavinia dies, and to control her, which is just what Carson never even tries. Really, Carlisle is trying to manage things that actually cannot be managed.

59 INT. LAVINIA'S BEDROOM. DOWNTON. EVE.

Lavinia tosses, murmuring, hot and sweating, in a fever.
Clarkson is with her, and Mrs Hughes, as they all arrive.

ISOBEL: What happened?
CLARKSON: This is how I found her. It's bad, I'm afraid.
Very bad. The worst.
MATTHEW: I don't understand. When I was with her, she
was talking. She was fine.
CLARKSON: It's… It's a strange disease with sudden,
savage changes. I'm terribly sorry.

Clarkson is speaking as he takes her pulse. Sybil has
removed all but the sheet, and she is sponging Lavinia's
brow.

MATTHEW: Well, what can I do? Can I talk to her?
CLARKSON: Yes, of course. Why don't you talk to her now?
It can't do any harm.

But he puts his hand on Sybil's shoulder and shakes his head.
She drops back and joins Isobel. They both know what is
happening. Matthew kneels down and takes Lavinia's hand.

MATTHEW: My darling, can you hear me?

This draws the sweating face towards him. She stares at him.
Now Robert has come in. Mary holds a finger to her lips.

MATTHEW (CONT'D): It's me. It's Matthew.
LAVINIA: Matthew? I'm so glad you're here.
MATTHEW: Of course I'm here, my darling. Where else
would I be?
LAVINIA: But you mustn't be sad, you see. You absolutely
mustn't be sad.
MATTHEW: Why would I be sad? I'm not sad. You're going
to be well again.
LAVINIA: I don't think so, my dearest one. But please no
tears. Now or ever. Isn't this better? Really?
MATTHEW: I don't understand you.
LAVINIA: You won't have to make a horrid decision… Be
happy, for my sake. Promise me. It's all I want for
you. Remember that. That's all I want…

None of the others can follow this at all.

MATTHEW: But I can't be happy. Not without you. How
could I be happy?

But, to the horror of everyone present, Lavinia is dead. *

END OF ACT FOUR

ACT FIVE

60 EXT. DOWNTON. DAY.

Matthew walks into the house. He has a black band on his arm.

61 INT. HALL. DOWNTON. DAY.

*When he enters, he finds Thomas, Jane and Anna taking down the
greenery and silver bows hung round the gallery.*

   MATTHEW: What are you doing?
   THOMAS: They were put up for the wedding, Mr Crawley.

There is a nervous silence. Robert comes out of the library.

   ROBERT: My dear chap, I cannot find the words to say how
   sorry I am.
   MATTHEW: How is Cousin Cora?
   ROBERT: Much better. Thank you.

....

* This was a good top shot. Having built the kitchens and the attics at Ealing,
which works well, we also, in order to avoid ever getting really stuck by the
programme of events at Highclere, have a bedroom that we can redecorate to
fit the bill. It is copied from the Highclere bedrooms, and it is normally
Mary's room, but we can redecorate and rearrange it as we see fit. If there's
only one little scene, we'll probably do it in a real bedroom at Highclere, and
there are a couple that we're allowed to use, but every now and then we have a
strong enough reason to alter and use the Ealing bedroom. In the first series
we redecorated it for the Turk. Here, it became Lavinia's room. The
advantage is that, by having a room constructed in a studio, you have no
ceiling and you can move the walls to suit whatever camera angle you want.
You can also make certain shots that are not possible in an architecturally real
room, and we took advantage of that here, for the top shot of Lavinia dead.

DOWNTON ABBEY · EPISODE EIGHT
469

MATTHEW: I'm glad to hear it. I came up to see if
there's anything I need to do…
ROBERT: We've taken care of all that. As you know, we
always use Grassby's.
MATTHEW: Of course.
ROBERT: Travis has suggested Monday for the funeral. To
give people time to get here. It'll be in tomorrow's
paper.
MATTHEW: That's very kind of you.
ROBERT: I know Mary wanted to see you —
MATTHEW: No.

The suddenness of his reply is a shock to them both.

MATTHEW (CONT'D): I mean, I don't really want to see
anyone. Not yet. Now I know everything's settled, I'll
go back.
ROBERT: You must decide where she's to be buried. When
you speak to her father, do ask him to stay here.
MATTHEW: Thank you. He'll be very grateful.
ROBERT: Just tell me what you want me to do and I'll
do it.*

62 INT. SERVANTS' HALL/PASSAGE. DOWNTON. DAY.

*Bates and Anna are at the end of the table. They talk
softly.*

ANNA: I still can't believe it. I mean, there she was,
young and pretty and packing her trousseau, and now we're
laying out black for her funeral.
BATES: Are you saying you want to delay? It doesn't have
to be tomorrow.
ANNA: No. No, I don't want to delay. Who knows? It
might be me next, and I'm having Mrs Bates on my
tombstone or I won't lie still in my grave.

Which makes him smile.

....

* Matthew is once more in what I call a *Downton* emotional quandary,
because in one way Lavinia's death is a release, and in another way it makes
him feel more guilty than ever. As for the great question of which member of
the cast was going to die, I think even the most pessimistic members of the
audience will have worked out that we were not going to kill two of them. So
we've now told them who's dead, and that's it. Cora will ride again.

63 INT. CARSON'S ROOM. DOWNTON. DAY.

Mrs Hughes has just given Carson his medicine.

MRS HUGHES: Are you feeling more yourself?
CARSON: A bit… I still can't get over it.
MRS HUGHES: I hope you'll not pretend you liked her now.
CARSON: I didn't want her here, Mrs Hughes, I'll admit.
But I had no objection to her being happy somewhere else.

64 INT. CORA'S BEDROOM. DOWNTON. EVE.

Cora is alone, sitting up in bed. Robert is with her.

ROBERT: A sight to gladden my heart.
CORA: Is it? I hope it is.
ROBERT: You gave us quite a fright.
CORA: They told me about Lavinia.
ROBERT: The funeral is on Monday.
CORA: I'd like to go if I can.

She holds out her hand and takes his. She looks at him.

CORA (CONT'D): We're all right, aren't we, Robert?
ROBERT: Of course we are.
CORA: Only I know I got so caught up in everything…
I think I neglected you. And if I did, I'm sorry.
ROBERT: Don't apologise to me.*

Luckily for him, O'Brien comes in with a tray.

CORA: His lordship was saying how wonderful you were
while I was ill.
O'BRIEN: No more than you're entitled to, m'lady.
CORA: I'm entitled to your work, O'Brien. No one is
entitled to devotion.
O'BRIEN: That's as may be.

She glances at Robert as she picks up a rug to fold it.

....

* We have Robert caught in a very difficult conundrum when Cora apologises
for not paying him enough attention, because he can't apologise for his own
offence without making it even worse for her. That position really comes
from my mother. When she gave her four sons any marital advice – which
was not very often – she was quite clear about this. I remember she told me
once that when we were married, if we were ever so weak and foolish as to

65   INT.   MRS HUGHES'S SITTING ROOM.   DOWNTON.
                        NIGHT.

Ethel appears at the door.

MRS HUGHES: Ethel? Whatever are you doing here at this
time of night?
ETHEL: I said I'd be back with my answer and here I am.
MRS HUGHES: You know we're a house in mourning?
ETHEL: Yes, and I'm sorry, but if anything it's made my
mind up for me. Life is short, and what's my life
without Charlie? They're not having him.
MRS HUGHES: As long as you're sure.
ETHEL: They say they can do better for him, but what's
better than his mother's love? Answer me that.
MRS HUGHES: I'll write and tell them.
ETHEL: You agree with me, though, don't you?
MRS HUGHES: My opinion has no place in this.*

66   EXT.   REGISTER OFFICE.   RIPON.   DAY.

The sun shines down on the building. Bates and Anna go in.

....

Continued from page 471:

stray, we must not try to lighten the burden of our guilt by sharing it. So we
had this tough instruction to keep silent. Normally, when people confess to
being unfaithful, they will tell you how they had to restore the truth in their
relationship, because they wanted to be honest, but according to my mother
that's not the real reason. The burden of guilt oppresses them, and so they
have to share it with their luckless wife or husband, so that they can be
forgiven. It is rather an Edwardian instruction, to keep silent when guilty,
but it was part of my own training.

* Mrs Hughes is in a difficult predicament. She thinks Ethel's making a
mistake – not an unloving mistake, but a mistake from the boy's point of view
– because, for Mrs Hughes, the world is the world, and there is no doubt that
the Bryants could give this child a start in life that would mean no activity, no
dream of achievement, would be beyond him, whereas the start in life that
Ethel can give him, as the bastard son of a sacked housemaid, is nothing. I
like Mrs Hughes, and I like her here, when she won't comfort Ethel by
agreeing with her, but she won't upset her by disagreeing.

67 INT. REGISTER OFFICE. RIPON. DAY.

They stand before the desk as the registrar conducts them through the service. Two strangers sit behind them.

    REGISTRAR: I, John Bates…
    BATES: I, John Bates…
    REGISTRAR: …take thee, Anna May Smith…
    BATES: …take thee, Anna May Smith…
    REGISTRAR: …to be my wedded wife.
    BATES: …to be my wedded wife.

The Registrar nods to Anna.

    REGISTRAR: I, Anna May Smith…
    ANNA: I, Anna May Smith…
    REGISTRAR: …take thee, John Bates…
    ANNA: …take thee, John Bates…
    REGISTRAR: …to be my wedded husband.
    ANNA: …to be my wedded husband.
    REGISTRAR: And now the ring. With this ring, I plight thee my troth…
    BATES: With this ring, I plight thee my troth…
    REGISTRAR: …as a symbol of all we have promised…
    BATES: …as a symbol of all we have promised…
    REGISTRAR: …and all that we share.
    BATES: …and all that we share.

He slips a gold ring onto Anna's finger.

    REGISTRAR: It therefore gives me great pleasure to say you are now husband and wife together.

The camera retreats from these two, husband and wife at last.*

68 INT. HALL. DOWNTON. DAY.

Edith is coming downstairs when Mary appears.

    EDITH: I can't find Anna. I want her to sort out my black for Monday.

---

* We put the audience through the wringer with Lavinia's death, and so now they have an event that they have hopefully looked forward to for a long time: the marriage of Bates and Anna. And it was very charming. I thought it was really nicely done.

MARY: I sent her into Ripon for something. I'm sorry.

EDITH: It'll keep. Mary…

She hesitates.

EDITH (CONT'D): Are you going to try again now?

CARLISLE (V.O.): Try again for what?

He has come out of the library. He stands there, smiling.

MARY: To get into last year's funeral kit. But to be honest… I doubt it would still fit.

69 INT. LIBRARY. DOWNTON. EVE.

Jane comes through the door, which unsettles Robert.

JANE: You rang, m'lord.

ROBERT: I keep forgetting Carson's ill.

JANE: Mrs Hughes says he's much better.

ROBERT: I really want Bates. He'd gone out earlier.

JANE: He's in the dressing room. He went up with your evening shirt.

ROBERT: Golly, is that the time?

He stands as if to leave. She would go, but…

ROBERT (CONT'D): Actually, can you stay a moment? I was trying to think how to contrive a meeting, and here you are… You see, Lady Grantham's illness has reminded me what I owe her…

JANE: I'm glad Lady Grantham's better. Truly. And don't worry. There's no harm done.

ROBERT: No harm done yet. We've resisted temptation once. But I wouldn't care to test myself again.

JANE: There's a compliment in there, somewhere. I'm almost packed. And I've given in my notice.

This is both a surprise and not a surprise. To them both. She smiles, as he takes an envelope out of his pocket.

ROBERT: This is the name and address of my man of business —

JANE: Why? You don't owe me anything.

ROBERT: It's not for you. It's for Freddie. Let me give him a start in life.

JANE: I'm not sure…

ROBERT: It would make me very happy.

JANE: If I thought that, then I'd take it gladly. Will you be happy? Really?
ROBERT: I have no right to be unhappy, which is almost the same.
JANE: Almost. Not quite… Can I kiss you before I go? Can I tempt you for one last time?

He hesitates. He might say no… But then he does.

ROBERT: You do tempt me. You know you do. I dare not say how much.

*She raises her hand to stroke his cheek, and slips away.**

70 INT. MARY'S BEDROOM. DOWNTON. NIGHT.

Mary is in her nightdress. Anna is brushing her hair.

MARY: The secret Mrs Bates.
ANNA: We will tell everyone, but I thought we should leave it for a while. At least until after the funeral, anyway.
MARY: You'll have to control yourselves.
ANNA: Well, we've had enough practice.

But Mary stands and walks to the door.

MARY: Come with me.

71 INT. BEDROOM PASSAGE. DOWNTON. NIGHT.

The two walk round a corner and in through another door.

....

* I had some opposition to Robert's insistence on giving Jane enough money for Freddie to have a decent start in life. But Robert Grantham is a rich man, while Jane is the widow of a private soldier and has little put by. He is very fond of her, and he knows that, for both their sakes, their relationship can't go any further. For him to give her a bit of capital – we don't specify the amount, but it's enough to make a difference – so that she can bring up her boy with some spare money, seems to me to be a perfectly decent thing to do. So, when I was criticised, I fought back for Jane's widow's mite, or whatever you might call it. But I don't think Robert would want to go on seeing her. Particularly after Cora's recovery. That was fate speaking to him, and he listened.

72 INT. BEDROOM. DOWNTON. NIGHT.

A four-poster bed has been turned down. The lamps are on.
A fire is burning. Anna turns to Mary, amazed.

MARY: Smuggle Bates in here when everyone has gone to
bed. And for heaven's sake, make sure he gets the right
room.

They giggle. Then…

ANNA: I don't know what to say, m'lady. Who did all
this?
MARY: Jane. I told her. She said it would be her
leaving present. You can stay all night. She won't
tell.
ANNA: M'lady. Thank you very, very much.*

73 INT. CARSON'S PANTRY. DOWNTON. NIGHT.

Thomas is returning silver to the cupboard. There is a cough
behind him. He turns. It is Carson, in a dressing gown.

THOMAS: Are you sure you should be up, Mr Carson?
CARSON: I wanted to check the silver before tomorrow.
THOMAS: I think I've cleaned all the pieces we might
need. We'll get everything ready the moment breakfast
is over.
CARSON: Thank you for the way you've kept it all going,
Thomas. I wish I knew how to express my gratitude.
THOMAS: You'll find a way, Mr Carson.

Carson gestures to take the keys off Thomas. Thomas hands
them over. Carson grunts and goes. Thomas then hears:

O'BRIEN: Why are you Goody Two-Shoes all of a sudden?
What's the idea? And don't say there isn't one, because
I know better.

He hesitates, then he smiles.

....

* In a sense, this incident is a piece of charming wish fulfilment. I am often
accused of this, usually wrongly, but here there may be some substance to the
accusation. Some special treats were arranged, though, for well-loved
employees, which I know first-hand. Of course, this would have been a very
big treat, but that said, why not?

THOMAS: You know me too well, Miss O'Brien. All right.
If I've got to be a servant again, I'm not going to be a
bloody footman for long. You watch while I make myself
indispensable.
O'BRIEN: And Mr Carson's getting on...?
THOMAS: Exactly.*

74 INT. MRS HUGHES'S SITTING ROOM. DOWNTON. NIGHT.

Mrs Hughes is giving an envelope to Jane.

MRS HUGHES: I think that's everything we owe.
JANE: Thank you, Mrs Hughes.
MRS HUGHES: I'm sorry you're going, Jane. You're a good
worker. I wish you well.
JANE: I'm sorry, too, Mrs Hughes. But in the end, I
think it's for the best. For everyone.

Mrs Hughes gives her a long, hard look. She knows.

MRS HUGHES: When all is said and done, my dear, you may
be right.†

75 INT. BEDROOM. DOWNTON. NIGHT.

*It is late now. The lights are out, and the naked couple in
the bed are lit by the flickering flames of the fire.*

BATES: Well, Mrs Bates, you've had your way with me.
I just hope you don't live to regret it.
ANNA: I couldn't regret it, no matter what comes. I know
only that I am now who I was meant to be.
BATES: I'm not worthy of you, that's all I know, and
they'll call me names for pulling you into my troubles.
ANNA: Maybe there won't be any trouble.
BATES: There's trouble. Or there will be if the police
find out I bought the arsenic. I know it.

* This was a cut we all agreed on very easily, because Rob James-Collier's performance is so well judged that he had made Thomas's intentions completely clear without the need for this dialogue.

† In this last line, we understand that Mrs Hughes knows, not precisely what is going on, but what might go on if Jane stays much longer. She has presumably seen a certain amount of this sort of thing, after a life in service.

But Anna is not fazed by this. Not at all.

ANNA: Mr Bates, we've waited long enough to be together,
you and I, and now that we're man and wife, can we let
that be enough, just for this one night?*

END OF ACT FIVE

ACT SIX

76 EXT. DOWNTON CEMETERY. DAY.

*The earth falls onto the coffin of Lavinia Catherine Swire.
The mourners (the regulars, including Clarkson, except for
Mrs Patmore and Thomas) are in black.*

THE REVEREND MR TRAVIS: …Earth to earth, ashes to ashes,
dust to dust, in sure and certain hope of the
resurrection to eternal life through our Lord Jesus
Christ, who shall change our vile body that it may be
like unto His glorious body, according to the mighty
working whereby He is able to subdue all things to
Himself. Amen.
ALL: Amen.

....

* Some people were rather critical about this, a bed scene in *Downton Abbey*,
but I think we can be allowed it. The *Downton* rule is, basically, when you're
not married you may lie on top of the bed with your admirer, but you won't
get under the covers without a ring on her finger. Whereas when you are
married you can be seen in bed and smiling. Actually, and perhaps unusually,
we needed special effects in this scene, because we had to take out Brendan
Coyle's inoculation scar on his arm; obviously the sight of it put him into a
different generation. You wouldn't think special effects had a role to play in a
bed scene, but they did. And so we have the Bateses' moment of happiness.
That was quite conscious on our part. We wanted them happy and fulfilled
before we then flung them back into the fire. I always think Anna senses
what's coming when she stops him talking about his troubles. In moments
like that, I never know if it's something I intended or the strength and
subtlety of the actor's performance.

They break up. Matthew and Isobel stand with an older, grief-stricken man. Robert, Edith and Violet are together.

EDITH: Why did he want her buried here?
ROBERT: He has no relatives. He feels that when he's gone…

Matthew is the only one left to look after her grave.

VIOLET: A business-like solution to what could have been a problem.
ROBERT: Be kind, Mama.
VIOLET: Since when was it an insult to call a man business-like?

The servants are walking towards the gate.

MRS HUGHES: Ah, we'd better get moving, if we're to be back there before they arrive.
ANNA: Mrs Patmore and Thomas will go ahead in the trap. They'll sort it out between them.
MRS HUGHES: Hm, I've no doubt Thomas will have everything sorted out.
CARSON: I'm sorry, Mrs Hughes, but it's no good thinking that we'll get shot of him now.
MRS HUGHES: Why doesn't that come as a surprise?

Daisy is with the others when she sees a solitary figure. He is standing by a grave on the other side. It is Mr Mason. She goes over to him and he greets her.

MASON: I've been hoping I might meet you here one day. I expect you come as often as I try to do.
DAISY: It was a funeral. Of a lady that was going to marry Mr Crawley.
MASON: I heard about that. There's nothing so wrong as when young folks die.

Daisy nods, looking at William's grave. To her discomfort, she finds she is crying, and wipes her tears away quickly.

MASON (CONT'D): Nay. You needn't hide your tears from me, love. It does me good to see how much you loved him. It does. It means he didn't die for nothing.

What can Daisy say? Meanwhile, Matthew is with Mary.

MARY: You must tell me if there's anything I can do? Anything at all?

MATTHEW: Thank you, but I don't think so.

She nods and might walk away, but he speaks again.

MATTHEW (CONT'D): That night, when we were dancing and Lavinia came downstairs... she heard, she — she saw everything.

MARY: How terrible for her. I'm so sorry.

MATTHEW: Because of what she saw, she thought we should cancel the wedding. That I belonged with you, not with her.

Mary doesn't quite grasp where this is going. He explains.

MATTHEW (CONT'D): She gave up, because of us. She said to me when she was dying, 'Isn't this better?' I know it's a cliché, but I believe she died of a broken heart because of that kiss... And we were the ones who killed her.

MARY: Oh, Matthew...

MATTHEW: We could never be happy now. Don't you see? When we destroyed Lavinia, we destroyed any chance we might have had. We're cursed, you and I, and there's nothing to be done about it. Let's be strong, Mary. Let's accept that this is the end.

MARY: Yes, of course it is... Of course it's the end. How could it not be?

Richard Carlisle approaches. He speaks to Matthew.

CARLISLE: I'm so very sorry about this.

MATTHEW: Thank you.

Carlisle turns to Mary.

CARLISLE: Can I walk you up to the house, or —?

MARY: Certainly you can. I want you to.

She takes his arm, and without a backward look they move off.* Robert is alone when he sees Sybil with Branson. He approaches them. Branson braces himself.

ROBERT: Why are you here?

BRANSON: To pay my respects to Miss Swire, and to see Sybil.

ROBERT: Lady Sybil.

SYBIL: Oh, Papa, what's the point in all that nonsense?†
ROBERT: I suppose you'll go to Dublin now. Isn't that
your plan?
SYBIL: In a day or two. Mama is well again. And I see
no reason to delay. Although I do so wish we could have
parted friends.
ROBERT: What about you? Do you want to part friends?
BRANSON: I do. Although I don't expect to.

*Robert stops walking. Most of the mourners have gone on, and
they are almost alone. He looks at his daughter.*

ROBERT: All right.
SYBIL: What?
ROBERT: Well, if I can't stop you, I see no profit in a
quarrel. You'll have a very different life from the one
you might have lived. But if you're sure it's what you
want —
SYBIL: I am.

....

* I think it was right to take out Violet's rather harsh remark at the start of
this scene. She is, after all, not an unkind woman. But the main intention
here was to show the audience that, just as they might think Mary and
Matthew have at last got to the straight now that Lavinia's out of the way,
they haven't at all. We have to make it more complicated than that. I think it
was truthful. When someone dies, and their death makes things easier, there
is always a certain amount of guilt attached, especially in a situation like this
one, when Matthew has actually been untrue in his heart to the promises he
made. It would be perfectly natural for a man in such a position to feel
crippling guilt as he stood by the side of his fiancée's grave. Inevitably, he
feels that he and Mary deserve to be punished. She understands this and, at
this point, starts to accept that she will probably end up with Carlisle.

† I had a friend who was the daughter of an earl, but who married a man
whom I think I can still call 'unlikely'. Obviously, this was in comparatively
modern times, perhaps thirty years ago, but her mother would continue to
address her letters to Lady Mary X, until one day her daughter said to her: 'I
don't mind. If that's what you want to write on the envelope, it's absolutely
fine. But that just isn't the life I'm leading. Not any more.' I remember this
because it was a hard thing for the mother to let go of. Not that she was a
snob – she wasn't at all, actually – but it was difficult for her to accept that her
daughter had moved into a different world, far away from her own. So I felt
to give Robert this attitude would be a good way of showing his resistance.

ROBERT: Then you may take my blessing with you, whatever that means.

SYBIL: Oh, Papa, it means more than anything. More than anything!

She is weeping as she hugs him. Robert turns to Branson.

ROBERT: If you mistreat her, I will personally have you torn to pieces by wild dogs.

BRANSON: I'd expect no less.

SYBIL: Will you come over for the wedding?

ROBERT: We'll see… We'll talk about that later. And there'll be some money.

He pauses, and in an admonitory tone:

ROBERT (CONT'D): But not much.

Robert proffers his hand to Branson. Branson takes it and the two men shake hands. Sybil takes Branson's hand and walks on up towards the house.

VIOLET (V.O.): So, you've given in?

She is watching him from a short distance away. He shrugs.

ROBERT: She would have gone anyway.

He looks around after the distant mourners.

ROBERT (CONT'D): And perhaps we should let Lavinia's last gift to us be a reminder of what really matters… Of course, you'll think that's soft.

VIOLET: Oh, not at all. The aristocracy has not survived by its intransigence. Oh, no, no. We must work with what we've got, to minimise the scandal.

ROBERT: But what have we got to work with?

VIOLET: Well, you'd be surprised. He's political, isn't he? And a writer? Well, I could make something out of that. And there's a family called Branson with a place not far from Cork. I believe they have a connection with the Howards. Well, surely we can hitch him onto them…?

During this they walk away from the camera, arm in arm. *

77 INT. PASSAGE/SERVANTS' HALL. DOWNTON. DAY.

The servants have returned. They take off their coats and
resume their aprons, etc. Bates and Anna walk in.
Mrs Patmore glimpses them out of the kitchen door and
hurries over.

    MRS PATMORE: Mr Bates.

He stops. But she is almost too nervous to speak.

    BATES: You all right, Mrs Patmore?
    MRS PATMORE: I'm all right, but I don't know what you'll
    be like when I've told you. There are two men waiting
    for you in the servants' hall.

He looks at Anna. Then, watched by Mrs Patmore and Daisy,
Bates and Anna walk into the servants' hall, where two men in
bowler hats and overcoats stand as they enter.

    BATES: Are you looking for me?
    POLICE OFFICER: John Bates?
    BATES: Yes.

....

* Robert dropping his resistance to the marriage feels believable to me,
because his acceptance is within limits. He is just not prepared to quarrel
with his daughter. I think most of us would do the same, eventually, however
much you might have fought your child's choice. Actually, I don't have a
problem with fighting it. Lots of people will tell you there's nothing you can
do, but I think that's nonsense. And if you don't have a relationship with
your son or daughter where you can speak your mind, then the more fool you.
But there comes a moment when most of us are not prepared to live on terms
of enmity with our own offspring, and that's what Robert has reached.

Which brings us to Violet's pragmatism, born of the same impulse to
make the best of it. I was given the idea for her plan by one of the heralds at
the College of Arms. He told me once of an old gentry family, nameless here
of course, to which a famous and senior politician had laid claim. In fact,
there was absolutely no traceable blood connection at all, but they were as
pleased by the fictional relationship as he was. So from then on, whenever
there was a family event, he would be in the front pew, even though there was
no real link whatever. I thought something similar would occur to Violet as a
solution.

POLICE OFFICER: You are under arrest on the charge of wilful murder. You are not obliged to say anything unless you desire to do so. Whatever you say will be taken down in writing and may be given in evidence against you upon your trial.
BATES: I understand.

The other policeman has brought out a set of handcuffs.

ANNA: No, no.
BATES: Please do whatever is required.

The man snaps the handcuffs on him. Bates whispers to Anna.

BATES (CONT'D): I love you.
ANNA: And I love you. For richer, for poorer, for better, for worse.

She kisses him, but she can say no more for they are taking him out. The other servants stand there, shocked, as Bates is led away.*

END OF EPISODE EIGHT

....

* It seems to me both believable and right that Bates should be placed under arrest, as all the evidence is against him, so this is not meant to be an attack on the injustice of the system. But I hope the audience found it heartbreaking after all that the lovers have gone through. I was particularly impressed by the shot of Joanne Froggatt at the end, when the camera pulls back, leaving Anna so vulnerable… You've always got to give the audience a reason for coming back next time.

CHRISTMAS SPECIAL

ACT ONE*

1 EXT/INT. MONTAGE. DAY.

*Christmas 1919. A truck drives through the woods with a huge
tree strapped on the back of it.*

*The truck pulls up in front of the house. Thomas
instructs the men to untie the tree.*

*Daisy carries buckets of coals and stops to admire the
tree until Mrs Hughes enters the hall and tells her off.*

*Mrs Hughes, Thomas, O'Brien and the maids help Mary and
Edith to decorate the tree, supervised by Carson and Robert,
who give contradictory higher/lower gestures and commands.
In a corner, Anna watches, silently.*

*Rosamund steps out of the car, kisses her nieces and
instructs her maid, Shore, who gets out of the front, to help
Thomas with the luggage.*

*Cora and O'Brien kneel on the drawing-room floor wrapping
presents together and scream when Matthew opens the door,
shooing him out.*

Carson chooses different wines.

*In the library, Violet picks up a Christmas card, looks
closely at the signature, grimaces and puts it back.†*

....

* Since we had not done one before, we felt the first Christmas Special should
be a Christmas show. The great hall at Highclere lends itself to a giant
Christmas tree, and besides, it was an opportunity to explore the rituals of a
country house Christmas, which I freely confess tended to be those of my
own childhood Christmas. Every family develops their particular
programme for the festive season and most of the Downton details – the
turkey eaten in the evening and not at lunchtime, playing 'the game' after
dinner, and other things we'll get to – have come from my family customs.
But the Crawleys also have their own traditions like everyone else.

Christmas 1919 was dictated by the narrative. Bates had been arrested for
murder at the end of Season Two, and there is a limit to how much time you can
leave between the arrest and the trial of a principal character. By featuring the
trial in the Special, it meant that we could lose all the preliminaries and jump
straight to the courtroom itself; in other words, cut the meat. We also liked
the idea of it being the end of 1919, so that the Servants' Ball could come just
after New Year, in January 1920. This would allow the audience to grasp that
the next series would take them into yet another era, leaving the war far behind.

2 INT. HALL. DOWNTON. CHRISTMAS DAY.

It is Christmas at Downton, with a huge tree in the hall, and Cora, Mary and Edith give out presents to the servants in turn. Isobel, Matthew, Rosamund and Carlisle are there. The maids are given a bolt of cloth as well as something wrapped. Mary calls out 'Anna', and Anna goes forward.

CORA: This is for you.
MARY: The usual cloth for a frock, I'm afraid, but I hope you like the other thing.
ANNA: I'm sure I will, m'lady. Thank you.‡

....

† The montage of preparations for Christmas is taken from life, as well as accounts of Christmases at various houses long ago. I'm always accused of sentimentalising these things, but inevitably these rituals of decorating the tree and everything else involved the staff as much as they did the family. And Christmas was, in many households if not in all, quite a useful bonding period between employers and employed, because there was a unifying element to the whole thing. The semi-democracy of the firm's Christmas party is, after all, still with us.

‡ The bolt of cloth was absolutely standard. Female servants were given material for a new dress, which they were expected to make up themselves. One of the tougher aspects of life in service was that the women and downstairs staff were expected to provide their own clothes, whereas employers would equip the footmen with livery. If clothing was bought for the maids, the cost would be subtracted from their wages, which I always find very harsh. But many families – including, of course, the Crawleys, because they're nice – got round it by making the bolt of cloth part of the Christmas present. Of course, it wasn't really a present, in the sense that it was material for clothes to work in, but nevertheless it didn't cost the maid anything.

It may seem to be asking a lot for them all to make their own dresses, but sewing was routinely taught as part of a village school education, where the emphasis was entirely on necessary skills to gain employment. The goal was that the boys and girls would leave able to earn their living. Indeed, the handwriting of the clerks of that period is absolutely superb compared to our own, and numeracy was a very important part of it. Beyond that, the girls were probably taught more sewing than cookery, the idea being that, on the whole, the only people who would be employed to cook were cooks, and that was quite a narrow element of the female workforce. Sewing, on the other hand, was something that would come in useful for everyone. The giving of the bolt of cloth is part of that tradition.

CORA: We all prayed for him in church this morning.

Anna smiles a little.

ROBERT: Happy Christmas, Anna.

Cora calls for Mrs Patmore, who steps forward, as Anna walks back to stand by Mrs Hughes.

CORA: I can't wait for you to open this.
MRS PATMORE: Thank you, your ladyship.
MRS HUGHES: What did her ladyship say?
ANNA: She was just being kind.
MRS HUGHES: I wish I could tell you not to worry.
ANNA: My husband's on trial for his life, Mrs Hughes.
Of course I worry.
MRS HUGHES: Well, I'm old-fashioned enough to believe
that they can't prove him guilty when he's not.
ANNA: Would you mind if I didn't join you for Christmas
luncheon?
MRS HUGHES: You have friends all around you.
ANNA: I know that. Truly. But I'd rather take a tray
up. Unless you'd like me to help in the dining room?
MRS HUGHES: No. They look after themselves at lunch on
Christmas Day, and I don't want to give them any ideas.

Robert is talking to Carson. The latter has a large book.

CARSON: *The Royal Families of Europe.* Oh, my. I shall
find this very interesting, m'lord.*
ROBERT: Good… Carson, are you quite happy about
everything?
CARSON: What, precisely, m'lord?
ROBERT: Well… Going on with Christmas and the New Year's
Day shoot and the Servants' Ball and all the rest of it,
with Bates in his lonely cell.

....

*This is my joke about Carson's being given the book, *The Royal Families of Europe*, which was published by *Burke's Peerage* and of course included all those endless families in Germany, the princes of Anhalt-Dessau and Mecklenburg-Schwerin and such like. It always makes our producer, Gareth Neame, chuckle when he sees this scene, but I am sure that Carson, and others like him, would want to be up in all the details of the continental reigning families.

CARSON: I'm as sorry as you are, m'lord. But I do not believe Mr Bates would want us to abandon the traditions of Downton because of his troubles.

Across the hall, Anna looks at her little wrapped box.

MRS HUGHES: Go on. Open it.

She does. It contains a gold brooch in the shape of a heart. She glances across at Mary, who catches her eye and nods.

3 INT. SERVANTS' HALL. DOWNTON. CHRISTMAS DAY.

The servants are nearly at the end of their lunch. We start with the younger ones, who are pulling crackers and wearing paper hats. At the other end, Mrs Hughes and Carson are not.

MRS HUGHES: I don't want to spoil their fun, but I couldn't wear a paper hat. Not with poor Mr Bates locked away.
CARSON: His lordship said much the same.

A lady's maid, Marigold Shore, who was in the hall, speaks.

SHORE: Is Mr Bates the one Lady Rosamund told me about? The murderer.
CARSON: Mr Bates has most unjustly been accused of murder. That is all.
SHORE: All? I should think that's quite enough for most people.

Anna walks in with her tray. The room falls silent.

MRS HUGHES: Did you have everything you wanted?
ANNA: Yes, thank you. I thought I'd go and make a start on the dining room.
MRS HUGHES: It's almost time to take the tea up. No rest for the wicked.

Anna leaves. Thomas looks after her.

THOMAS: Mr Carson, if things don't go right for Mr Bates, have you given any thought to his replacement?
CARSON: There will be plenty of time for that conversation after the trial.

Thomas leans back and talks to O'Brien on his other side.

THOMAS: I mean, I hope he's coming back. I do, honestly.
But the fact remains he may not be, and there's no point
in being overly sentimental.
O'BRIEN: No one would accuse you of that.

4 INT. LIBRARY. DOWNTON. CHRISTMAS DAY.

*The remains of tea, with a Christmas cake (no forks, no
napkins). Wrapping paper shows they've had their presents.* *
....

*The remains of tea with the Christmas cake, but no forks, no napkins!
Another bizarre stage direction. This is a tricky area, because obviously the
people who have dressed the set work very hard and do their research and it
must be extremely difficult to have me or Alastair Bruce, our wonderful
historical advisor, walking in and changing things, relaying the places, taking
the spoon and fork from the top and putting them down by the side, and the
rest of it. But the point is, it's not a question of wrong or right. There is no
wrong or right. It is simply what is right for this particular group. All the
different tribes that comprise English society have their own way of doing
things, and we want to get it right for the Crawleys. But in this department
you have to find a way to explain it all that is acceptable to the many men and
women working on the show. I don't believe I have always been successful
in this.

I first had forks and napkins at teatime in *Gosford Park*. I was standing by
Robert Altman behind the camera and I said, 'Oh God, sorry Bob, sorry, but
they wouldn't have forks and they wouldn't have napkins.' He was very
surprised. 'But how will they eat the cake?' I said, 'Well, they'll just break it
off with their fingers and eat it.' 'Suppose they get it all over their fingers?' I
answered that they might think of something, but they wouldn't have a
napkin. It was quite a testing moment, because it was right at the start of
filming, and I thought: either he's going to believe me, or he's going to believe
his own team who have set it all up. I think he considered both options, but
then he realised there was not much point in having me there, standing
beside him, if he wasn't going to do what I suggested. So, somewhat to my
relief I can tell you, the call went out: 'Lose the napkins, lose the forks.'

In that scene we had a wonderful bit of business, which is absolutely
correct, where Maggie Smith's character does get something on her fingers
and, without talking about it, Maggie takes her handkerchief out of her bag,
wipes her hand and puts it back. Which is exactly what my great-aunts
would have done. That is one of the things about working with Maggie; she
does have real knowledge and understanding of these people. It is very
lightly worn, but the detail in her performances is invariably correct, which is
thrilling to watch.

CARLISLE: Why do we have to help ourselves at luncheon?
ROBERT: It's a Downton tradition. They have their feast
at lunchtime, and we have ours in the evening.
CARLISLE: But why can't they have their lunch early and
then serve us, like they normally do?
MARY: Because it's Christmas Day.
CARLISLE: It's not how we'll do it at Haxby.*
VIOLET: Which I can easily believe… Oh, this is ni—
This is — What is it?

....

* Carlisle represents, in a sense, the world that is coming. As I have
explained, I'm not hostile to him. I've been accused of disliking him, but I
don't at all. His ways are not entirely compatible with the ways of the
Crawleys, but that doesn't mean I don't like him. In fact, I admire people
who have made the journey he's made, but inevitably, when you have fought
every step of the way, it beats all sentimentality out of you. Whereas the
weakness of great families like the Crawleys is that they want to be liked, as
well. So they're terribly nice, with lots of 'Oh, Nanny, you really must put
your feet up,' which is designed, although subconsciously for the most part,
to present them as warm and caring people, when in actual fact their
demands are no less stringent than those of Carlisle, and that's what we're
contrasting here.

But in real life, then or now, and whether Carlisle likes it or not, if you
want things to run smoothly it is necessary to evolve a way of doing things
that answers the needs of the family but is still acceptable to the staff. Very
few people want to be served by men and women they dislike and who dislike
them, and to work out an acceptable regime means ensuring a degree of
pleasantness all round. At Downton, the staff have a decent Christmas lunch
and the family gives them time off for it. And before anyone yells, this was
not an uncommon pattern and happened in many houses. It wasn't so much.
They may serve themselves at luncheon, but they don't clear away, and Anna
makes the point when she asks if she should go up and 'make a start on the
dining room?'

Not long ago, there was an Englishman on television in America talking
about *Downton*, because we had been nominated for an Emmy or a Golden
Globe or something, and he said that I had perpetrated a great lie on the
public. Obviously I found this very interesting. But the lie turned out to be
that I had suggested that people like the Crawleys could be likeable. In that
small vignette, you can suddenly see the extraordinary blindness that we have
been led into by twentieth-century prejudice. As if a large group of people
can be likeable or unlikeable. In fact, any dismissal of a nationality or a
generation or a class or a race is just childish, and often pernicious, nonsense.

ISOBEL: What does it look like?

VIOLET: Something for getting stones out of horses'
hooves.

ISOBEL: It's a nut cracker. We thought you'd like it.
To crack your nuts.

Across the room, Edith is talking to Robert.

EDITH: Who's coming on New Year's Day?

ROBERT: The usual guns. Us three, and some locals.
You'll know all of them.

EDITH: Have you asked Anthony Strallan?

ROBERT: I tried. In fact, I gave him three dates, but he
said no to all of them. Perhaps he's given it up.

EDITH: But he was so keen before the war.

VIOLET: Perhaps he's heard enough banging for one life.

She has joined them. She is interested by Edith's eagerness.

ROBERT: Oh, and Rosamund's forced me to invite Lord
Hepworth.

VIOLET: Really?

ROSAMUND: Well, I told him I was coming down here, and he
dropped hint after hint.

CORA: Perhaps he has nowhere to go. It can be a lonely
time of year.

Violet addresses her next remark to Robert only.

VIOLET: Jinks Hepworth, lonely?* I find that hard to
believe. Hepworth men don't go in for loneliness much.

ROBERT: How do you know him?

VIOLET: I knew his father in the late Sixties. *Mais où
sont les neiges d'antan?*†

....

* When I wrote this, I had just seen the 1944 Rita Hayworth musical *Cover
Girl*, and appearing in it was a model called Jinx Falkenburg who played
herself. She was an interesting character, really, the first supermodel, and
while her acting never generated much heat, she and her husband, the
journalist Tex McCrary, more or less pioneered the chat show, though how
grateful we should be for that is open to question. At any rate, I thought she
was worth doffing my cap to, so I used her name here. It didn't matter that
Violet was talking about a man because it's a name for either sex.

5 INT. HALL. DOWNTON. CHRISTMAS DAY.

Mary emerges from the library. Matthew is by the telephone.

MARY: Isobel told me you were telephoning for news of
Mr Swire. How is he?‡
MATTHEW: Not good. I'm catching the train first thing in
the morning. I hope I'm in time.
MARY: Is it as bad as that? I'm so sorry.

Before he can answer, Carlisle comes out of the library.

MARY (CONT'D): Matthew's going to London tomorrow.
Lavinia's father is ill.
CARLISLE: You'd better warn Robert if you'll miss the
shoot.

....

† This reaches into Violet's past, and what fascinates me is quite when this early romance would have taken place. At the start of the show, set in 1912, we needed Violet to be about seventy. This means she was born in 1842 and she would have come out in about 1860, to enjoy a few flirtations before marriage claimed her. One of the things that always fascinates me is how quick history is and how a long life goes through two or three quite distinct eras. The Violets of this world, who were seventy-eight and very much still around in 1920, would have been young women wearing vast crinolines who visited the Paris of the Second Empire and might have been presented to the Emperor Napoleon III and the Empress Eugénie. They grew up in an entirely different world and yet they were still going in the 1920s, with movies and aeroplanes – and television not far off. When a branch of my family died out last year, the house and the estate were sold and I rescued some family pictures at the auction. What interested me is that I had one ancestor, a picture of whose daughter was in the sale, who was essentially a late-Georgian figure, born in 1778. The girl in the portrait was born in 1817 and she appears as a mid-Victorian. Her child would have lived an essentially *fin-de-siècle* life, and her grandson would belong in the twentieth century. It all happens so fast.

‡ Lavinia Swire's father is really the most important of the non-characters in *Downton Abbey*. We only ever saw him once, at her funeral, and he didn't have any lines, but of course he has a massive part to play in the story. Matthew is fond of him, which is fine, and he's going up to see him, and none of that I think occasions much surprise. But of course no one knows what is coming.

MATTHEW: I'll be back by New Year's Day. He won't last that long, I'm afraid. Forgive me if I'm casting a gloom.

MARY: Don't be silly. We're all under the shadow of Bates's trial. We made a pact not to mention it on Christmas Day, but everyone's broken it.

MATTHEW: Will any of you have to testify?

MARY: Only Papa and some of the servants. But I'm going, to support Anna.

MATTHEW: Would you like me to come with you? To explain what's happening? Or will you do that?

MARY: Richard wants to get back to work the day after the shoot, don't you?

CARLISLE: Yes, I do.

Carson has arrived to sound the dressing gong.

6   INT.   KITCHEN.   DOWNTON.   CHRISTMAS NIGHT.

Daisy holds a huge silver cloche, which she has washed.*

DAISY: Shall I put this in one of the back cupboards?

MRS PATMORE: Yes. We won't be needing that for another year. Now, Thomas?

She lifts the Christmas pudding topped with holly as Thomas waits. Daisy goes to a back cupboard and is moving things around to make space when she fishes something out. It is the board of a game with letters of the alphabet in a circle and an eye in a star at the centre. O'Brien is mixing some starch nearby.

DAISY: What's this?

O'BRIEN: It's a board for planchette.

DAISY: What's that?

....

* We have had a huge silver cloche all my life. It's a family one with a crest, but the only thing that it has ever been needed for is the turkey at Christmas. So once a year, even now, this thing is removed from the back of a cupboard, cleaned with enormous difficulty, used once over the space of about two days and is then returned to the darkness for the next twelve months.

O'BRIEN: A game. Well, not quite a game. More a method
of communication.
DAISY: How?
O'BRIEN: Never mind. I'll take it, if you like.*

7 INT. DINING ROOM. DOWNTON. CHRISTMAS NIGHT.

*Carson carries in the flaming pudding. Everyone cheers.
Carson brings it to Violet's left. She plunges the spoon
in.†*

EDITH: Sybil's favourite.
VIOLET: A happy Christmas to us all.
ALL: Happy Christmas!
EDITH: Don't forget to make a wish.
ROBERT: Let's all make a wish.
MARY: A wish and a prayer.
CARLISLE: Is this about Bates again?

....

*Table turnings, mediums, séances, ectoplasm and talking to your dead husband or children all made up a very strong part of the mid-Victorian culture. Planchette, which had its origins in the 1850s, was a sanitising of the frightening territory of communicating with the deceased. If you didn't have the strength to go off to some medium in St John's Wood and watch ectoplasm bubbling around, one answer was to buy a little planchette table and ask the dead questions yourself. Its giggle-and-chill factor made it immensely popular, and it was still around in the Twenties, only gradually receding as the Second World War drew near. I had a few experiences of it in my youth at Cambridge, and it frightened the life out of me. But that is another story.

† There's a limit to how many scenes per episode we can put in the dining room, if only because they drive Jim Carter as Carson completely mad. He has to stand there for hours on end with hardly anything to say, ditto the footmen. Those men have the toughest jobs in the series, because the others are all either in the Highclere scenes, so they get most of the time spent at Ealing off, or they're in the kitchen scenes, at Ealing Studios, so they get most of the time spent at Highclere off. Only Carson and the footmen cross over all the time, and at Highclere they have these absolutely interminable dinners. But of course we couldn't miss out on Christmas night.

ROSAMUND: My new maid says the servants' hall is full of
it. How terrible it is.
MATTHEW: We mustn't lose faith. He's been wrongly
accused.
CARLISLE: I'm sure you hope so.
ISOBEL: We know so.

*Carson has taken the pudding to the sideboard and now he and
Thomas start to bring the double plates to everyone.**

CARLISLE: How has Mr Murray managed to have the trial
held in York?†
ROBERT: I don't know, but thank God he has.
CARLISLE: And he's confident?
CORA: He seems to be.
VIOLET: Lawyers are always confident before the verdict.
It's only afterwards they share their doubts.

....

* The key here is the double plates, which were used when anything was
served at the sideboard. It was all to do with the servant never touching the
plate that you're going to eat off, which is why footmen wore gloves at dinner.
The butler didn't wear gloves because he'd pour the wine and so he didn't
touch the glass, he just poured the wine into the glass, but the double plate
was used for soup. You couldn't serve yourself with soup because all the
women's dresses would have been covered in it. So soup was brought to you
but in a double plate. The servants held the under-plate, but the one you
were actually going to eat out of reached you in a state of pristine virginity.

† York was one of the big legal circuits, and obviously I needed to get the trial
to York, because if Bates was being tried in London where the crime had
occurred, then the show would be in big trouble. I asked a lawyer about it
and apparently it wasn't very difficult to get a trial moved north. In fact,
sometimes, although not in this case, trials are quite deliberately removed
from the place where they've occurred. So there's no kind of legal
requirement for you to be tried at the scene of the crime, but obviously
getting it to York does rather beg the question: how did Mr Murray manage
it? We don't know. Presumably he employed some Grantham muscle.

8 INT. SERVANTS' HALL. DOWNTON. CHRISTMAS
NIGHT.

The planchette is on the servants' hall table. There is a glass at the centre and O'Brien, Thomas and two maids have their fingers resting on it. Daisy is watching with Shore. *

O'BRIEN: Is anyone there? Is anyone there?

The girls start to laugh.

THOMAS: You must take it seriously, otherwise they'll be offended.
DAISY: What is it?
THOMAS: We're talking to the dead.
DAISY: But how? They can't talk back.
SHORE: They can. That's the whole point.
THOMAS: Come on, Daisy.
DAISY: No. I don't think it's right.
O'BRIEN: If you'll all be quiet, I'll try again. Is there anyone there?

The glass starts to move towards the letters Y. E. S.

THOMAS: Yes. Someone is there.
MRS HUGHES: What is going on?
O'BRIEN: We're just playing a game.
MRS HUGHES: A very unsuitable game, Miss O'Brien, especially on Christmas night. Please put it away at once.

O'Brien removes the glass, folds the board and stands.

MRS HUGHES (CONT'D): I'm surprised at you, Daisy.

....

* As I have implied, I always find planchette slightly scary. I never know what I believe about anything, to be perfectly honest, but when I was young and at university there was a fashion for it, which I followed, but with some cynicism. I did find it slightly alarming. People always say that someone must have been pushing the glass, but I'm not so sure. None of the friends I played it with would want to push the glass. That said, I suppose there must be other possibilities of a kind of shared illusion.

When I wrote this, I assumed the planchette board would just have letters in a circle, and they would use a glass to receive the messages, as we used to do in my youth. But they found a much more sophisticated version, so the glass was quite unnecessary.

```
DAISY: Are you sure there's nothing in it?
MRS HUGHES: Quite sure, thank you.
DAISY: Don't you believe in spirits, then?
```

This is slightly tricky. Mrs Hughes hesitates.

```
MRS HUGHES: Well, I don't believe they play board games.*
```

9   INT.   HALL.   DOWNTON.   CHRISTMAS NIGHT.

The company are playing 'the game'. Mary is miming reading.

```
EDITH: You're reading.
MARY: For heaven's sake, yes, I'm reading because it's a
book title.
ROBERT: No talking.
MARY: I know, but honestly.
```

She holds up five fingers.

```
ALL: Five words.
```

She holds up four fingers.

```
ALL: Fourth word.
```

....

* One of the things that has always interested me is the position of the Christian churches – principally the Anglicans and the Catholics – about ghosts, because they're always very strongly opposed. They don't like people believing in ghosts, and they certainly don't like people dealing with ghosts, and yet both Churches have exorcism. In other words, there is absolutely no doctrinal logic in their position. The conundrum is simple: if there is no life after death, what are we all talking about? And if there is, why is the idea of a ghost so offensive and difficult?

Since both Anglicans and Catholics are encouraged to believe in the possibility of redemption through good works, i.e. a well-spent, moral life will bring its own rewards beyond the grave, then this must mean that when your life has been spent doing bad work, you will be plunged at the very least into Purgatory or some Anglican equivalent of it. Since you would presumably be full of regret, isn't it only logical to think you might wish to revisit the scene of the follies committed in life? I've never, even as a child, been able to understand the Church's hostility to the idea of ghosts, but you find it among many devout Anglicans and Catholics. Here, Mrs Hughes is put on the spot when Daisy challenges her belief in spirits. Her reply, 'Well, I don't believe they play board games,' may get her out of the situation, but it doesn't answer the contradiction.

ISOBEL: Two syllables.
ALL: First syllable.

Violet is next to Carlisle, as the guessing continues.

CARLISLE: Do you always play charades on Christmas night?
VIOLET: This isn't charades. This is the game.
CARLISLE: What's the difference?
VIOLET: In charades you speak, in the game you are
silent. You mime.
CARLISLE: Do you enjoy these games? In which the player
must appear ridiculous?
VIOLET: Sir Richard, life is a game in which the player
must appear ridiculous.
CARLISLE: Not my life.
ISOBEL: Fall… Past… Oh, fell! Wild, fell! *The Tenant
of Wildfell Hall!*

There is a burst of applause.

CORA: Richard, your turn. Come on.
VIOLET: How soon your maxim will be tested.

Mary joins Matthew on a sofa.

MATTHEW: Well done. Who wrote it?
MARY: Anne Brontë. The one people forget.
MATTHEW: I forget all of them.

She laughs, which the others notice, including Carlisle.

CARLISLE: Mary! Concentrate!*

....

* The game was always played in the Fellowes household after dinner on
Christmas Day. It was the only game my father participated in throughout
the year, and usually someone would lose their temper. All my life, I have
struggled with the fact that television has rechristened 'the game' as
'charades', whereas charades is quite a different activity. For charades, you
make up little playlets and you speak lines. In the first playlet, you say the
first syllable of a four-syllable word and in the last one, the fifth playlet, you
have to say the whole word, so the last act is always full of masses of long
words. But of course, unlike the game, it requires writing and rehearsal and
in Victorian house parties people would spend the whole day preparing their
charade. Alas, nobody has time for that now, so charades on the whole has
been abandoned by this generation. Still, the distinction remains important
to me, so I make Violet say, 'This isn't charades, this is the game.' Inevitably,

10 INT. BATES'S CELL. YORK PRISON. CHRISTMAS
                        NIGHT.

Bates is on his bed, holding a photograph of Anna.
Somewhere, a man is singing 'Silent Night'. There are other
noises, ugly and loud, but the voice carries through. His
eyes are full. *

11 INT. ROBERT'S DRESSING ROOM. DOWNTON. BOXING
                        DAY.

It is morning. Carson is dressing Robert.

   ROBERT: Christmas over for another year.
   CARSON: M'lord, I wonder… If Mr Bates should not come
   back —
   ROBERT: I am not replacing Bates.

....

Continued from page 501:

in the edit, they asked if we really needed it, and we probably didn't, really, but I defended the line fiercely and it stayed in. I was very sorry when we cut 'Anne Brontë. The one people forget,' explaining who wrote *The Tenant of Wildfell Hall.* I always rather feel for Anne Brontë, which is why I chose her book. But, of the two, preserving Violet's corrections was more important.

   Naturally, Richard Carlisle doesn't suffer from the upper-class fantasy that the answer to everything is childhood and the recreation of childhood; the nickname culture and the playing of things one used to play, and the eating of things one used to eat, and all the jolly things one did years ago in the schoolroom, which has always been a security blanket for the posh in this country. The upper classes themselves believe it preserves an innocence at the core of their sensibilities. I don't believe that's true, but I believe that they believe it. However, Carlisle doesn't need to fantasise about his childhood or anything else. He's come up the hard way.

* It was a hard year for Brendan Coyle, because in a way he was cut out of the series, which for him became 'Bates in Prison', and apart from Joanne Froggatt, who plays Anna, he had almost no interaction with the rest of the running cast. The cell was a set, but when he went out for some exercise we were in a real prison. I think it was quite isolating for him, but he came through it and sustained the energy, which is what matters. For Jo Froggatt it was a tough season in the opposite way. She was in almost every scene in Bates's story, but she also had all her other stuff to do, both at Highclere and at Ealing Studios.

But he regrets snapping Carson's head off.

ROBERT (CONT'D): What were you going to say?
CARSON: Only that I know that Thomas is keen to be
promoted. I think we must all concede he's earned the
right to stay, and you don't, I trust, feel you need a
new butler.
ROBERT: The trouble is, being dressed and undressed is an
intimate business. We've forgiven Thomas his early sins,
I know, but I cannot imagine I would ever quite feel the
trust.
CARSON: Say no more, m'lord. I'm sure Mr Bates will be
home soon, which will settle the matter.

12   INT. KITCHEN. DOWNTON. BOXING DAY.

Daisy is arranging a cake (which is uncut) and sandwiches.

SHORE (V.O.): Did you make all that?

Daisy looks round. Shore is watching her.

DAISY: Yes. Why?
SHORE: And you're still only the kitchen maid?
DAISY: I don't know what I am.
SHORE: You could be a sous chef at least, in London.
DAISY: I don't know what a soojeff is.
SHORE: Or a cook? Maybe not in a house like this, but
you wouldn't have to go far down the ladder before they'd
snap you up.

Just then, Mrs Patmore appears.

MRS PATMORE: Daisy, find Thomas and tell him the tea's
ready to go up. Then we should get started on the
mixture for the cheese soufflés.
SHORE: Does Daisy cook the soufflés, too?
MRS PATMORE: What's it to you?

Shore does not answer, but she catches Daisy's eye.*

....

* Shore is a type who would become much more common as the century wore
on: people who no longer accepted the boundaries of the old system. Just
because they had been born to a certain position, why should they give in to it?
Why should they live it? With Shore, it all feeds into her desire to be Lady
Hepworth, which is where she plans to end up, but I sympathise with her.

13 INT. CARSON'S PANTRY. DOWNTON. BOXING DAY.

Mrs Hughes is with Carson. She holds a letter.

CARSON: Not this again. I thought we'd seen the end
of it.
MRS HUGHES: I know.
CARSON: What's the good of chasing over here for a
glimpse of the child, if they haven't changed their
terms?
MRS HUGHES: I agree. But I don't think I can refuse
without Ethel's permission. I'll see if she can look in.
CARSON: She won't want to meet them.
MRS HUGHES: I'm sure, but I feel I must ask.*

14 INT. LIBRARY. DOWNTON. BOXING DAY.

Robert looks up. Anna has come in.

ANNA: May I have a word, m'lord?

....

Continued from page 503:

One of the first things about achievement, if you want to achieve, is never
to see a glass wall separating you from those who have gained what you want.
I always say this to young writers or young actors. I tell them that when
they're sitting in the dentist's waiting room looking at pictures of the Oscars
ceremony in a thumbed version of *Hello!*, they should never forget that the
men and women in those photographs are people just like them, and in many
cases have come from very unpromising beginnings. I am old enough now
not to think everyone has to be ambitious, but if you are, then you should get
out of your own way and start believing that whatever you want is possible.
At any rate, that is what Shore believes.

* For the Special, we shot the whole of the end of the Ethel story, with the
Bryants being given the baby and all of it, but we took it out and in the end
we staged the final act in the third series. The problem was that we couldn't
make the child behave for this version. He was a nice little boy, but with
children it's always pretty unpredictable. As I've mentioned before, actors
hate working with them because when the child gets it right, that's the take
they'll use, so you, the actor, have got to be good in all the takes. We had a
different boy in the third series who was absolutely marvellous and
heartbreaking. But the situation was unusual. So we shot the whole thing
for the Special, and then we cut it out completely and got all the actors back
the following year to do it again.

He nods and waits.

ANNA (CONT'D): I've had a letter saying I can visit
Mr Bates on Monday afternoon. I'm sorry if it's not
convenient, but it's their time or no time. I've told
Mrs Hughes, but I thought you should know.
ROBERT: Please give him our best wishes.
ANNA: It means a great deal to him that you believe he's
innocent, m'lord. I know, because he writes about it.
ROBERT: I look forward to the day when we can open the
champagne.

15 EXT. DOWER HOUSE. DAY.

A car pulls up containing Sir Anthony Strallan.

16 INT. DRAWING ROOM. DOWER HOUSE. DAY.

Violet is with Edith. Tea has been set out.

EDITH: What do you mean you've invited Anthony Strallan?
I thought it was just us.
VIOLET: I sent him a note. He replied by telegram, so he
must be quite eager… Is that him now?

She goes to the window. Edith joins her.

VIOLET (CONT'D): Oh, very important. Never used to use a
chauffeur. Well, you were so disappointed that he
wouldn't come shooting.
EDITH: Oh, Granny, why didn't you warn me? I'm in all
the wrong clothes.

But the door opens, and Strallan comes in.

STRALLAN: Good afternoon, Lady Grantham. Lady Edith.
What a charming surprise. It's been far too long.
EDITH: It's so nice to see you. It's such a relief to
see any of our friends who've made it through unscathed.

She holds out her hand, but he takes it with his left hand.

STRALLAN: I'm afraid I haven't quite.

He pats his right arm, which hangs quite immobile.

STRALLAN (CONT'D): I took a bullet in the wrong place.
It seems to have knocked out my right arm.
EDITH: But not for ever, surely?

STRALLAN: Apparently.

EDITH: But how?

VIOLET: Edith —

STRALLAN: No. It's perfectly all right… You won't have heard of it, but there's a spot behind the shoulder called the brachial plexus.

EDITH: I've heard of the brachial plexus.

STRALLAN: Of course. You're all medical whizzes now, aren't you? Well, the upshot is I'm afraid the wretched thing is now no use to man or beast.

EDITH: Well, now we know why you didn't want to come shooting.

STRALLAN: Indeed.

They laugh together, as if this were somehow amusing. *

STRALLAN (CONT'D): So, how is everyone? Lady Sybil is married, I hear. Living in Ireland? How was the wedding?

VIOLET: Quiet. It was in Dublin. They didn't want a big affair.

STRALLAN: Did you all get over?

EDITH: Mary and I did. Papa, Mama and Granny…

VIOLET: We were all ill. Isn't it sad?

STRALLAN: What's he like?

....

* We wanted Strallan, to whom Edith was attracted in the first series, to be wounded in the war so that he would feel he couldn't possibly saddle a young woman with this – using his word – 'cripple', when he's too old for her, anyway. Edith was so happy nursing sick men in the war that she doesn't agree with that. But again, it's a typical *Downton* plot in that you see both their points of view. Strallan is clearly an honourable man throughout and he is motivated by a moral heart, but Edith knows what would make her happy. Anyway, we obviously had to decide just how he was wounded. We had a lot of stuff to do with him and we didn't really want something that would require special effects, like a missing arm, because it would have been both expensive and complicated. So I got hold of my doctor/advisor and asked for a serious disability that would not involve the loss of a limb, and this is what he came up with. Annoyingly, once again the true explanation of the condition, the stuff about the brachial plexus, ended up on the cutting-room floor, which undermined the truth of the situation and turned it into a sort of stage convention, but it couldn't be helped. Let's hope that when people read it in the script, they'll get it.

VIOLET: He's political.

STRALLAN: As long as he's on the right side.

He laughs merrily. So do they.

STRALLAN (CONT'D): So, does he shoot?

EDITH: I'm sure he does.

VIOLET: But I don't think pheasants.*

16A INT. YORK PRISON. DAY.

Anna is taken through into the prison.

17 INT. YORK PRISON. DAY.

Prisoners are seated at rough tables facing their visitors. Anna sits across from Bates.

ANNA: Lady Mary's coming with me. And Mr Matthew. To explain things.

BATES: I wish you'd stay away.

ANNA: Would you not come then, if I were on trial for my life?

She reaches for his hand, but a voice rings out.

WARDER: No touching!

She draws it back.

ANNA: And his lordship will be there.

BATES: Mr Murray thinks a reference from an earl will go in my favour. I'm not sure such things matter when it comes to murder.

ANNA: I think it'll help.

BATES: Because you want to think so. Anna, you must prepare for the worst.

....

* I wished to make it clear that, although Robert has given permission, he doesn't endorse Sybil's marriage. So, he and Cora and Violet did not go to the wedding. He didn't forbid the girls and they went to Dublin, meaning there is no major quarrel, but he did not go. Presumably he forbade Cora, as I think left to her own devices she would have wanted to be there. That is all to set up his response to Branson when he makes his appearance in the following series as Robert's son-in-law. In a way, these references are trailers of coming attractions. I did like the exchange, 'Does he shoot?' 'I'm sure he does.' 'But I don't think pheasants.'

She flinches, but she does not speak.

> BATES (CONT'D): I'm not saying it'll happen, but you must prepare for it. They have a strong case against me. It's mainly circumstantial, in which lies my hope, but it is strong.*
> ANNA: I know it could happen. I do. But the time to face it is after it has happened, and not before. Grant me that?

END OF ACT ONE

ACT TWO

18   EXT.   DOWNTON.   NEW YEAR'S EVE.   DAY.

Carson holds the door of the car for Lord Hepworth. He's a handsome, easy-going fellow. Cora is there with Rosamund.

> HEPWORTH: Lady Grantham. Lady Rosamund.
> CORA: Hello, Lord Hepworth. Welcome.
> HEPWORTH: Thank you.†

....

* Bates is trying to warn her that the verdict may be the worst. I have always quite deliberately left a very slight doubt as to whether or not Bates's account is the whole truth.

† When Nigel Havers agreed to play Hepworth, we knew we were in luck, because there's no one in Equity better at acting a cad. Not only do you believe he is entirely self-interested and immoral, but you also think he's terribly good fun. So you never wonder that women find him attractive or men enjoy his company, but at the same time his performance lets you know that he is bound to let them down. Nigel's work has a kind of light-heartedness that almost belongs in a different era, which was perfect for us. But it was quite difficult because he was in a play at the time and he spent half the shoot being driven overnight to get to us, and overnight to get to the play. He was very plucky about it.

After the war, many people were having to address the fact that the old life was gone. But while some in that situation will make a new life, get a job, find a flat, others simply cannot accept the changes, and among that generation

Carson is hovering. Cora looks at him.

CARSON: Will your man be coming on from the station, m'lord?
HEPWORTH: I haven't got one with me. Is that a nuisance? I'm so sorry.
CARSON: Not at all, m'lord. Thomas will take care of you while you're here.

He glances at the footman by the door, who walks forward, a trifle wearily, to start unstrapping the cases and guns.‡

HEPWORTH: Splendid.
CORA: Do come in.
HEPWORTH: Thank you.

19 INT. DRAWING ROOM. DOWNTON. NEW YEAR'S EVE. NIGHT.

Cora looks up as Robert comes in with an envelope.

ROBERT: This came for you in the evening post. It's from Sybil.
CORA: We must go up and change.

But she starts to open the envelope and read the letter.

ROBERT: So, what do you make of Rosamund's pal?
CORA: He seems agreeable enough.

....

Continued from page 508:

was a tidal wave of chancers who tried, by popping pictures and sponging off old aunts, to keep the show on the road for a few more years – or for as long as they themselves lasted, anyway, frequently leaving their children to mop up the mess. One must have some sympathy. This class had already endured the agricultural collapse of the 1880s, even before the war started, so there had been a long spiral downwards, while they tried everything – from mortgages they could not sustain to American heiresses they could not corner – to stave off ruin. Hepworth is very much part of that, as becomes clear. Of course, unlike Carlisle, Hepworth is the genuine article. He is a real toff and he knows how it all works. He's got the clothes, he's got the patter, he's got the guns and he's not going to put a foot wrong. It's only morally that he might be found wanting. Violet understands that. Even Robert has a suspicion.

‡ We have often shown how footmen would work as valets for any guests who arrived without one of their own.

ROBERT: I suspect he's in the profession of making himself agreeable.
CORA: O'Brien says Rosamund's maid speaks very highly of him and that seems a good reference to me —

But she interrupts herself with a gasp.

ROBERT: What is it?
CORA: Sybil's pregnant!
ROBERT: I see. So that's it, then. No return. She's crossed the Rubicon.
CORA: She crossed it when she married him, Robert… She says we're not to tell anyone. Not even the girls.
ROBERT: I wondered why she didn't ask to come for Christmas.
CORA: Would you have allowed it?

He glances at her, without answering. Then he sighs.

ROBERT: Well, well. So, we're to have a Fenian grandchild.
CORA: Cheer up. Come the revolution, it may be useful to have a contact on the other side.
ROBERT: Hmm.*

20 INT. KITCHEN PASSAGE. DOWNTON. NEW YEAR'S EVE. NIGHT.

Mrs Hughes speaks to Thomas as he comes downstairs.

MRS HUGHES: Thomas, has Lord Hepworth got everything he needs?
THOMAS: I think so. But why doesn't he have his own valet?
MRS HUGHES: Perhaps his servant is ill… Anyway, he's quite comfortable?
THOMAS: He certainly is. And very pleased to find he's next door to Lady Rosamund Painswick.

....

* Cora's line came from an exchange when I married. One of my greatest friends, then or now, is the actor Oliver Cotton, who was extremely political and, particularly in his younger days, very much a leading light of the Left in our profession. Anyway, for my wedding he read one of the lessons and he had to get into a morning coat, which was not his native costume. Naturally, he was photographed during the day, and I said to him later: 'Come the revolution, I will hold this picture over you, so you will get us out to safety.'

Carson joins them. Thomas goes. Carson lifts his eyebrows.

> MRS HUGHES: Don't look at me. Lady Rosamund's maid
> suggested it. I don't approve, either. But you'll say
> it's not my place to have an opinion.
> CARSON: Nor is it.*

21 INT. BEDROOM PASSAGE. DOWNTON. NEW YEAR'S
     EVE. NIGHT.

*A door opens, held by Shore, and Rosamund comes out. As she
does, the next door opens and Hepworth emerges. Both he and
Rosamund are in evening dress.*

> HEPWORTH: Oh, I say. This is very cosy, isn't it?
> ROSAMUND: What is?
> HEPWORTH: To find ourselves next door.
> ROSAMUND: I'm not certain it's quite proper to remark on
> such things.

*Her door opens again and Shore emerges, carrying some
discarded linen under a silk shawl.*

> ROSAMUND (CONT'D): You remember my maid, Shore?
> HEPWORTH: Certainly, I do. I hope they've got a jolly
> party planned downstairs.
> SHORE: Why would they have?
> HEPWORTH: Because it's New Year's Eve, of course.
> SHORE: Oh, that. I doubt it, m'lord, but I don't mind.
> I make my own fun. If that's everything, m'lady, I'll go
> down now and see you after midnight.
> HEPWORTH: Only wish I could say the same.

....

* I was sorry that we had to lose the reference here to Hepworth being put
into the bedroom next to Lady Rosamund's, because one of the things that is
shocking to our generation is that these hostesses, who were incredibly
correct in their public life, were perfectly happy to put married men and
women next door to their lovers. In many houses a husband and wife would
be given two bedrooms, but on the other side of the wife's bedroom would be
her lover, and on the other side of the husband's bedroom would be his
mistress, so it was all worked out quite carefully. If you go to these houses,
including Highclere, they frequently have intervening doors between the
bedrooms that mean you wouldn't have to go out into the passage.

Rosamund ignores this sally and Shore leaves as the others start downstairs. Hepworth flashes a smile at Rosamund.

HEPWORTH (CONT'D): Only joking.

Below, Violet is coming in. Hepworth sees her.

HEPWORTH: I wonder if she'll remember me…
ROSAMUND: Oh, she will.
HEPWORTH: Good evening, Lady Grantham. I don't suppose you remember me.
VIOLET: Of course I do. Oh, how is dear Hatton? I have such happy memories of it from the old days.*
HEPWORTH: I'm not often there, not since my mother died.
ROSAMUND: Perhaps it needs a woman's touch.
HEPWORTH: Don't we all?

He smiles at Violet.

VIOLET: How very like your father you are. It's almost as if he were standing here before me. I hope you'll come to tea and then we can talk about him.
HEPWORTH: I should love it, Lady Grantham. If they'll release me.
VIOLET: Oh, they'll release you.

The three of them have reached the drawing-room door.

22 INT. SERVANTS' HALL. DOWNTON. NEW YEAR'S
          EVE. NIGHT.

The servants are gathered. Daisy carries a tray of glasses.

SHORE: What are those for?
DAISY: We always have a glass of wine at midnight on New Year's Eve.
SHORE: Very civilised. In my last place we were expected to be upstairs and serving, New Year's Eve or not.

....

* Hatton is in fact a real house, Hatton Grange in Shropshire, the home of the Kenyon-Slaney family where I was very fortunate to be invited to stay and shoot for some years. Of all the houses I have visited in England, I think it is the one that I envied most, because it was built on a most perfect scale, incredibly pretty with two little pavilions, but without being colossal, and with miraculous plasterwork in the dining room. I absolutely love it, so I commemorate it here.

DAISY: Were you not a lady's maid, then?

Shore hesitates, but Mrs Patmore speaks instead.

MRS PATMORE: How long have you been with Lady Rosamund, Miss Shore?
SHORE: Two months.
MRS PATMORE: Oh, I see. You're quite a new girl.

At the other end of the table, O'Brien is with Thomas.

THOMAS: I can read Mr Carson's hint. His lordship doesn't trust me.
O'BRIEN: Because of the stealing, you mean?*
THOMAS: So what should I do?
O'BRIEN: Get him to trust you.
THOMAS: That's easy to say, but how?
O'BRIEN: Make him grateful. Do him a good turn. Hide something he loves, then find it and give it back.
CARSON: Miss O'Brien?

He is holding out a glass he has poured. She stands and goes to get it, at which moment Robert's dog, Isis, comes into the room. She sees Thomas looking at her and wags her tail.

23 INT. DRAWING ROOM. DOWNTON. NEW YEAR'S EVE. NIGHT.†

Robert is checking his fob watch against the clock.

ROBERT: Not long now. Does everyone have a glass?

Edith has a tray, with a couple left. She approaches.

....

* Stealing was, as I've said before, the blackest mark for a servant. It was absolutely the worst thing that a servant could be accused of. Other things could be forgiven; stealing, never.

† Now we have the same New Year's Eve scene being played out with the family. All of the moments that play in parallel are quite deliberate, because I do believe that a good many elements of our life are common to every part of our society, and I don't think it hurts to remind people of that. Our shared experience includes that slightly gauche moment on 31 December, Happy New Year. Personally, I have a horror of big New Year bashes, although I don't mind a jolly dinner party. I think just two of you sitting there in the library with a glass of eggnog is a bit sad.

EDITH: Anthony Strallan was at Granny's for tea the other day, so I know why he wouldn't shoot. He's hurt his arm.
ROSAMUND: Shame. Well, we shall try again next year.

Edith drifts off as Violet steps in, speaking softly.

VIOLET: Oh, I am sorry I started that. Now, don't encourage it. She'd spend her life as a nursemaid.

Mary is with Carlisle, who takes a glass from Edith's tray.

CARLISLE: Once again, the servants are downstairs and we're on our own.
MARY: In the whole year, we fend for ourselves at Christmas lunch and on New Year's Eve. It doesn't seem much to me.
CARLISLE: You haven't had to fight for what you've got.
MARY: Oh, do try to get past that. It makes you sound so angry all the time.

She strolls off, towards Matthew.

MARY (CONT'D): I hope London wasn't too grim.
MATTHEW: Well, I got down there in time, which is the main thing. And I was with him when he died. So he wasn't alone.
MARY: I'm so sorry, and so glad.
ROBERT: Here we go!

The clock strikes the first chime of twelve. They toast the Happy New Year (without clinking glasses).

ROBERT (CONT'D): Happy New Year!
ALL: Happy New Year!
MATTHEW: Happy New Year, Mama.
ROBERT: Happy New Year, Mama.
VIOLET: 1920. Is it to be believed? I feel as old as Methuselah.
ROBERT: But so much prettier.
VIOLET: When I think what the last ten years has brought, God knows what we're in for now.*

24 INT. BEDROOM PASSAGE. DOWNTON. NEW YEAR'S EVE. NIGHT.

Anna is walking when she sees Hepworth talking to Shore. Hepworth goes back into the room. Shore joins Anna.

SHORE: He's pushing his luck.

ANNA: How?

SHORE: He wants me to speak up for him. To Lady Rosamund.

ANNA: If I were you, I'd keep out of it.

25 EXT. DOWNTON. NEW YEAR'S DAY.

There are eight men. Nearby, seven loaders carry guns, some pairs, some single guns. Matthew has his own. Robert holds out the case of numbered spills for them to choose. Mary, Rosamund and another wife are there, all in country clothes.†

....

* This is the moment when the twentieth century really started, although I do understand that the 1910s completed the previous decade and the new one would begin in January 1921. We also have a little bit of passage acting in the following scene, with servants glimpsing various conjunctions – Shore talking to Hepworth, and so on. It is all to do with keeping several different stories going at once. In my experience, the audience always likes knowing things that the people on screen don't know. So, here, they are encouraged to start thinking there's something up.

† Once again, Alastair Bruce, our wonderful master of everything, is here as one of the guns, to keep an eye on the detail. We have them pulling numbers for their places, which I put in because I prefer it to being placed at the pegs, as some hosts do. If you've chosen a number and then you get a bad peg for a particularly wonderful drive, it's nobody's fault, which, to me, seems to be a more satisfactory way of managing it.

In this episode, we tell the audience how a day's shooting works. First, you often walk to the first drive, then, after the second or third drive, you will have a drink or some soup and, at the end of the morning, there's lunch, and so on. All of this is quite useful dramatically, because it means you can bring characters together or push them apart, but also I like to think that we have explained some of the appeal of shooting to people who are unfamiliar with it.

I know shooting gets a bad press these days, and of course it's unfashionable to say it, but we should perhaps remember that gamekeepers were the main ecologists for centuries. They were the ones who protected undergrowth, or the woodland, or the headland round a field. Far from destroying the countryside, they preserved it, but I know these things are

ROBERT: We'll walk to the first drive, then use the
wagonette after that.
HEPWORTH: Splendid. I hope you're going to stand by me.
ROSAMUND: I thought I'd chum my brother. Cora isn't
coming out until luncheon.
HEPWORTH: Well, the second drive then. You ladies will
have to distribute your charms fairly as there are only
three of you. Do you agree, Lady Mary?

Mary smiles and opens her mouth to speak, but:

CARLISLE: Lady Mary will stand by me.
MARY: Now, just —
MATTHEW: I thought you were going to stand with me for
the first drive. Isn't that what you said?
MARY: Did I? Yes, I think I did.

*She half shrugs at Carlisle, as if her hand were forced.**

26 INT. MRS HUGHES'S SITTING ROOM.   NEW YEAR'S
                                        DAY.

Mrs Hughes is with Ethel, drinking lemonade.

ETHEL: But why? What's to be gained?

....

Continued from page 515:

complicated, and it is understandably hard for the urban population to
understand that nobody enjoys the sight of fox cubs playing more than a
huntsman, and nobody enjoys a pheasant on a wing more than a shot. Of
course, after trying to put the country case, my reward was to be attacked in
the papers by some fathead criticising the leggings they were wearing. He
was, in fact, quite wrong, but more than that, I wanted to say: 'Look, you silly
man, I have given shooting to sympathetic characters. That in itself should
merit your support, if they'd come in a clown's outfit.'

* I thought the shooting scenes were incredibly well filmed, and the image of
the guns walking down the hill was one of my favourites in the whole series.
When it comes to the business of where Mary should stand, there are no
hard and fast rules. Perhaps your wife stands with you for most of it, but she
may be with someone else for a particular drive and his girlfriend may stand
with you. That is perfectly ordinary at shoots in real life and is also useful for
us dramatically, because we create a whole Matthew/Mary/Carlisle situation
out of it.

MRS HUGHES: If you ask me, nothing. I wrote to them and
I made it very clear you would not be changing your mind.
ETHEL: I suppose he wants to bully me.
MRS HUGHES: I think it highly likely. So, that's
settled. How's Charlie?
ETHEL: Very well, thank you, Mrs Hughes. My neighbour's
looking after him.
MRS HUGHES: Good.
ETHEL: Of course, I wouldn't like Mr Bryant to think I'm
afraid of him.
MRS HUGHES: Why would he think that?
ETHEL: He mustn't feel I'm scared to face him, 'cos I'm
not… No. Tell them I'll meet them if they want to hear
'no' in person. Tell them to come.

*Mrs Hughes so wishes this wasn't down to her.**

26A EXT. FARMLAND. DOWNTON. NEW YEAR'S DAY.

*The shooting party walk along together, chatting away as they
go.*

26B EXT. WOODLAND. DOWNTON. NEW YEAR'S DAY.

*Beaters make their way through the woods, striking at the
ground to raise the pheasants into the air.*

27 EXT. FARMLAND. DOWNTON. NEW YEAR'S DAY.

*Matthew is at his peg. He fires. Nothing comes down. He
takes a cartridge out of his pocket. Mary is with him.*

MARY: Why don't you have a loader? Barnard would have
found you one.
MATTHEW: I'm not very good at it. They saw double guns
and I don't want a witness.

....

*When Amy Nuttall, who plays Ethel, was told that the whole of her story
was going to be excised from the Special, her heart must have plunged. I'm
sure they said that we would reshoot it for the next series, but in those
situations you don't usually believe that they will. Because, in a way, the story
was finished. Once she had decided to keep the child, that was a conclusion,
if we had chosen to see it as such. But actually she was quite safe, because we
all felt it would have been such a false message to have sent out.

MARY: I'm a witness.

MATTHEW: Then please don't spread the word of my incompetence.

MARY: I never know which is worse: the sorrow when you hit the bird, or the shame when you miss it.

He fires again. Nothing. She smiles.

MARY (CONT'D): Thank you for intervening back there before I said something rude.

MATTHEW: He does rather beg to be teased.

MARY: The awful truth is, he's starting to get on my nerves. Still, you're not the person to burden with that.

MATTHEW: You're still going to marry him, though?

MARY: Of course. Why wouldn't I?

He glances at her, then fires again. Both barrels.

MATTHEW: I think I might have got that one.

The horn blows. Matthew breaks his gun and unloads it. They start to walk back to the other guns.

MATTHEW (CONT'D): You must promise faithfully to lie when they ask you how I did.

Mary is laughing at this when she sees Carlisle watching her. *

....

* Matthew has been brought up in Manchester and is not a particularly good shot. In this he represents me, because I am not a good shot, although I've been shooting since I was fourteen, so I have much less excuse. Happily, my son is very good, which pleases me no end. As for Matthew/Mary versus Mary/Carlisle, what Mary is hiding from is that she is naturally more relaxed with Matthew, because they are more compatible as personalities. So they can joke and chat and make each other laugh, but she doesn't really have that with Carlisle. Which, of course, Carlisle is fully aware of. It makes him angry, because he knows this kind of easy, unforced compatibility is so important in marriage. When you're in love, the romance and the sex are both much more important than anything else, but when you're married, then the fact that you're with someone with the same sense of humour is crucial. Carlisle does not suspect anything improper has taken place, but he sees the ease between them and that threatens him.

28   INT.   KITCHEN.   DOWNTON.   NEW YEAR'S DAY.

Daisy works with the others, packing hampers.

MRS PATMORE: Daisy? You've got a visitor.

Daisy looks over and Mr Mason is standing there.   He smiles.

MASON: I were visiting the grave. I thought to misself,
why not go and see her now? Take William's blessing with
me… I want you to come to the farm. Just for the day.
MRS PATMORE: Why not go and sit for a moment in the
servants' hall? We're sending out the shooting lunch.
As soon as we're finished, Daisy can bring you a cup
of tea. I'm sure Mrs Hughes won't mind, will you,
Mrs Hughes?
MRS HUGHES: Indeed, I will not. This way.

She takes the older man away with her.

DAISY: Well, he's here now, so I think I should make
things clear.
MRS PATMORE: Don't, Daisy, please. William wouldn't
thank you for it.
DAISY: He wouldn't thank me for bamboozling his old dad,
neither.

29   INT.   STRALLAN'S LIBRARY.   NEW YEAR'S DAY.

*A butler announces Edith and in she comes. Strallan is
working at his desk. He stands.*

EDITH: Now, I know you're going to say no, but I was just
passing and I suddenly thought, why don't we go for a
drive? Like we used to.
STRALLAN: But didn't I explain —?
EDITH: I don't mean you. I can drive now. I've got the
car with me.
STRALLAN: I don't think I should. I really can't spare
the time… Would you like a cup of something?
EDITH: All right. Yes, thank you, that would be nice.

She sits, as he goes to ring the bell.

STRALLAN: Is everyone well?

EDITH: Quite well.*

The butler opens the door.

STRALLAN: Lady Edith will be joining me for tea.
BUTLER: Certainly, sir.

He nods and leaves. Strallan turns back to Edith.

STRALLAN: As a matter of fact, I'm glad to have got you
to myself for a moment…
EDITH: Oh?
STRALLAN: I feel it gives me the chance to make some
things clear… I'm not sure I was that clear when we met
the other day. It's been worrying me.
EDITH: I don't understand.
STRALLAN: You see, I couldn't bear for you to think that
we might… take up together again, when of course we
can't.
EDITH: Because of what Mary said that time? Because you
know it wasn't true. She only said it to spite me.
STRALLAN: No, it's not because of that. And if you say
it wasn't true, I'm sure it wasn't.

Edith is thoroughly puzzled. He starts to explain.

STRALLAN (CONT'D): See, the thing is, I'm far too old for
you.
EDITH: I don't agree.
STRALLAN: Of course I am. And now, well, look… I'm not
a man any more, I'm a cripple. I don't need a wife, I
need a nurse. And I couldn't do that to someone as young
and as lovely as you.

....

* The following lines were cut from this point as the final running order of
scenes rendered them unusable:

EDITH: They're all in York today. That is, Papa and Mary
and Matthew are. For the trial.
STRALLAN: It's today, is it? Dear me. I wonder how
they're getting on.
EDITH: Our lawyer said it won't take more than one day,
so we'll know the worst this evening.
STRALLAN: Poor chap. You think he's innocent?
EDITH: Papa's made it an article of faith, so I wouldn't
dare question it.

EDITH: I don't accept a single word of that speech.

STRALLAN: Lady Edith —

EDITH: If you think I'm going to give up on someone who calls me lovely —

STRALLAN: I'm afraid you must.

The door opens and the butler appears with a tray. She is silenced, but the look on her face suggests it isn't over yet. *

30   INT.   SERVANTS'   HALL.   DOWNTON.   NEW YEAR'S DAY.

Mason looks up as Daisy comes in with a tray. She pours.

MASON: Oh, lovely. I'd like you to know the place he grew up. He always wanted to work with animals. Horses, really. But his mother saw him as a butler, lording it over a great house…

DAISY: He loved you both so much.

MASON: I'm only grateful his mother went first. She couldn't have borne it.

DAISY: No… But she would have had to face it, wouldn't she? Like you. We all have to face the truth, don't we?

MASON: We do, lass. Hard as it may be.

DAISY: Because I want to tell you the truth.

Mrs Patmore has drawn near to the door. She is listening.

DAISY (CONT'D): You see, William and me were friends for a long time before he started to feel something more…

MASON: Well, that's always the best way, isn't it? To know that there's friendship, as well as passion.

DAISY: Yes. But you see, I didn't…

She looks down at this sad, good man, looking up at her.

....

* For Strallan's house we used Hall Barn in Buckinghamshire, which actually had been Maggie Smith's house in the opening shot of *Gosford Park*. It was famous because George V used to shoot there as a guest of Lord Burnham, and on one particular day there was an incredible bag – something like 1,000 birds were shot in six hours. It is the only time he was ever known to have made a remark that might qualify as sensitive. Reviewing the incident some time later, he said: 'We went a little too far that day.' This is the evidence for a softer side to King George V.

DAISY (CONT'D): I didn't feel the love so soon, so I'm afraid I wasted some of the time we could have spent together.
MASON: No, you didn't, Daisy. You gave him the thrill of the chase. He talked of nothing but you from dawn 'til the cows came home. And when he saw you felt the same, well, the pleasure was all the sweeter for the waiting. I promise you.
DAISY: Good.
MASON: So when are you going to come to the farm?
DAISY: I'll let you know… Shall I get you some more hot water?

She takes the jug, walking past Mrs Patmore. She whispers.

DAISY (CONT'D): More lies.
MRS PATMORE: Were they?*

31   EXT.   WOODLAND.   DOWNTON.   NEW YEAR'S DAY.

The wood is quite dense. Mary and Carlisle walk towards a numbered peg. A horn blows.

CARLISLE: Well, that's the horn. Where's the damn loader?
MARY: Looking for your damn peg, I imagine.

He stares upward, annoyed, as some birds fly overhead.

CARLISLE: Why were you laughing with Matthew? At the end of the first drive?
MARY: I suppose he said something funny.
CARLISLE: Am I never to be free of him?
MARY: Of course not. You know how families like ours work, and he'll be head of it, one day.
CARLISLE: I might understand if you'd let me think for a solitary minute that you preferred my company to his. I have tried, Mary. Give me that. I've done everything I can to please you —

....

* We don't agree with Daisy here. We think William was entitled to die happy. I'm not a believer that honesty is always the best policy or that everything should be told. I know that is some people's credo, but it's not mine and I am entirely on Mrs Patmore's side here, thinking that nothing will be helped by the truth.

MARY: If you mean you've bought a large and rather vulgar house —

Thirty yards away, Matthew is alone by a peg. He hears shouting and follows the sound, pushing through the wood.

CARLISLE (V.O.): You cannot talk to me like that! What have I done to deserve it? What?
MATTHEW: Is something the matter?

They look round and he is standing there.

MARY: Richard's loader seems to have got lost, and this is one of the best drives. He's missing all the fun.
MATTHEW: I see.

He does see. A loader carrying two guns and a bag appears.

CARLISLE: Where the bloody hell have you been?
LOADER: Sorry, sir.
MARY: I'm afraid Sir Richard's rather anxious to begin.

Muttering apologies, the man hurriedly starts to load the first gun from his cartridge bag. Matthew nods at Mary.

MATTHEW: I'd better get back to my post.
LOADER: There you are, sir.*

....

* Carlisle takes everything seriously, and one of the hallmarks of a gentleman is that they take everything lightly. But the other side of that argument is that it explains why gentlemen are so seldom successful in competitive business and why, on the whole, they are happier with a role carved out for them as an officer or landowner or something, which will allow for their gentle and attractive manner, but will keep them safe from having to compete. Carlisle's level of achievement, by contrast, is precisely because everything is deadly serious to him, which I admire. In fact, when Carlisle says, 'I might understand if you'd let me think for a solitary minute that you preferred my company to his,' I am on Carlisle's side. He wants to marry Mary, he is prepared to swallow her murky history, but even so, she will not give him a break. For her, the fact that she's prepared to marry him should be enough. But it's not quite enough, is it?

32 INT. BARN ON THE DOWNTON ESTATE. NEW YEAR'S DAY.

The luncheon is set out in a barn, but the table is spread with a cloth and laid exactly as it would be at Downton, with Carson and Thomas serving. They are at the very end of the feed, with a large Stilton which they have eaten from. Cora and Isobel are with them.*

ISOBEL: Where's Lord Hepworth gone?
ROBERT: He wanted to change his guns, and we ought to drink up, too, or Barnard will be angry with me.
ISOBEL: Robert, Matthew is going to York for Bates's trial and, um... well, I wondered if I might come as well.
ROBERT: Of course, if you want to.
ISOBEL: Cora's told me she's not going, and I feel I just might be useful. As part of the bucking-up brigade.

....

* Shooting lunches are quite a big part of the day and there were certain rituals practised in that era, many of which are now gone. For instance, it was the only time in some houses when a footman served at table with no gloves, because they didn't wear livery and would often be in tweeds – but then again, there were some great ducal palaces where the whole thing was done like an ordinary lunch.

I remember when we first saw the shot of the beaters and loaders having their lunch outside, it was very dark. They'd had to film it at the wrong time of day, but they managed to correct it. As usual, Alastair Bruce is one of the guns at the table, making sure everything is done properly. The whole business of lunch in a barn, of taking the sacred rites to another place, but still having it served by a butler and a footman, is a curious sort of cultural anomaly that I rather enjoy. In *Gosford Park* they have lunch in a temple, which was actually far too cold. I pointed that out to Robert Altman, but he paid it no mind.

In my own life, I remember once, when I was very young, staying in a grand house. It was in the summer, and the hostess said: 'You know, it's such a lovely day I think we'll have a picnic lunch. Let's all meet here at a quarter to one.' So I got dressed in jeans and a T-shirt with Bluto on the front, and some gym shoes. I went downstairs and the whole of the rest of the house party were dressed just as they would normally. We then walked along the terrace to a Gothic summer house where luncheon had been laid with a butler and a footman to serve it, and I had to sit there in my Bluto T-shirt feeling about an inch high. After a bit, the woman on my left, Lady Someone Nice, turned to me and said: 'Of course, you're much more sensibly dressed than we are.' I loved her for that.

ROBERT: That's kind. Thank you.

ISOBEL: It's odd, isn't it? Us just chatting away here, while that poor man waits to hear his fate.

ROBERT: Please don't make me feel any worse than I do already.

At the serving table, Carson hisses at Thomas, who is piling the used plates into a hamper.

CARSON: Have we time to serve the coffee or not?

THOMAS: I'm not sure, Mr Carson. We could have used one of the maids today.

CARSON: Maids at a shooting lunch? Hardly.

Further down the table, Mary is next to Matthew.

MARY: Anna's very grateful you're coming with us.

MATTHEW: Why, I have to go to London, but I'll be back.

MARY: What are you going for?

MATTHEW: Reggie Swire's funeral. He wanted his ashes to be buried in Lavinia's grave. I'll bring them back.

MARY: What does Mr Travis say?

MATTHEW: I haven't asked him. I thought I'd do it myself one day.

MARY: Well, let me know when. I'd like to be there. If you don't mind.

MATTHEW: No, I don't mind.

Carlisle is watching all this.*

33 INT. KITCHEN. DOWNTON. NEW YEAR'S DAY. NIGHT.

Daisy takes the dirty plates out of the hampers.

SHORE: It seems hard you have to clean out the hampers, when you cooked all the food that went into them.

DAISY: It's all right.

SHORE: But you've a skill, Daisy. Let it bring you a better life. The Lord helps those who help themselves.

---

* The thing about these group scenes – the luncheons, the dinners, the drawing-room scenes, and so on – is that they always have to advance about six or seven stories at the same time, often by no more than a line. So the audience has to store it all and then put the plots together at the end.

DAISY: Do you believe that, Miss Shore?

SHORE: I know it. And call me Marigold.

34 INT. DRAWING ROOM. DOWER HOUSE. NEW YEAR'S DAY. NIGHT.

Violet is with Hepworth, in his shooting clothes, with stockinged feet below his breeches, having tea.*

VIOLET: This is very nice of you. To spare some time for a poor old woman. Won't they miss you at the tea?

HEPWORTH: I'll regain some novelty value at dinner.

VIOLET: Very well. What shall we talk about? Hatton? Shall we discuss why you never go there now? Or Loch Earle? Or what about Hepworth House in Grosvenor Square? I spent so many happy evenings there, with your father in hot pursuit.

She stares at him. At last, he nods.

HEPWORTH: I see it's time for some honesty.

VIOLET: A change is as good as a rest.

HEPWORTH: I think you know that Hatton's gone. So has Loch Earle. And Hepworth House has so many mortgages, I — I could only sell it at a loss.

VIOLET: So my spies tell me… So you want Rosamund, or rather the fortune of the late Mr Painswick, to come to the rescue?

HEPWORTH: My feelings for Lady Rosamund are sincere. I admire her immensely.

VIOLET: I do not doubt it. My only fear is that you admire her money more.

HEPWORTH: Lady Rosamund is too young to be alone. And you'll concede there are many varieties of happy marriage.

....

* When guns come in for tea, they take their muddy boots off, but they often have no replacement footwear with them and so they have their tea in stockinged feet. This is quite ordinary, even if it is one of the only times you ever see such a thing with these people, so I felt it would be rather a nice touch here. For Violet, the fact that one of the guns is in stockinged feet for tea after a shoot wouldn't mean anything, because she'd have seen it all her life. I think that's nice.

VIOLET: Maybe. But they are all based on honesty. I insist you tell the truth about your circumstances to Rosamund. After that, it's up to her.

HEPWORTH: My father was very smitten with you, you know. He often told me so.

VIOLET: He may have been. But you see, he could not afford me. And I could not afford him.*

35   INT. SERVANTS' HALL. DOWNTON. NEW YEAR'S DAY. NIGHT.

Anna is there with Shore and Thomas.

THOMAS: I see Lord Hepworth is trying to butter up the old lady.

ANNA: How do you know that?

THOMAS: He told me he'd been there for tea.

ANNA: Will Lady Rosamund take him?

SHORE: She will if I've got any say in it.

THOMAS: And have you?

SHORE: Is that clock right?

ANNA: We should get going, if you want Lady Rosamund to have a hot bath.

36   CARSON'S PANTRY. DOWNTON. NEW YEAR'S DAY. NIGHT.

Mrs Hughes has brought a letter to read.

MRS HUGHES: What do you make of this? 'If Mrs Bryant and I were to arrive early, we would like the use of a ground-floor room for an hour or so before our proposed meeting. We won't require any help from the servants. Might this be allowed?'

CARSON: Have you asked her ladyship?

MRS HUGHES: I have and she's all for saying yes. But then she'd say anything to get them out of our hair for good.

....

* I was sorry when we cut the lines about Hepworth's father, because it finished the hinted-at plot of Violet's youthful romance with old Lord Hepworth. Without Violet's explanation, we never know why she didn't go on with it. But there we are. Needs must.

CARSON: Well, we can't countermand her. Give them the drawing room. That'll disturb his lordship least.

MRS HUGHES: I'd like to know what they're planning. It won't be for Ethel's benefit, that's for sure.

37   INT. DINING ROOM. DOWNTON. NEW YEAR'S DAY. NIGHT.

Dinner is over and only the end of the fruit course and the glasses remain on the table. Everyone is already on their feet. The men are waiting for the women to leave. Hepworth speaks to Rosamund as she is on her way to the door.

HEPWORTH: When the men go through, can I steal you for a moment?

ROSAMUND: Why, particularly?

HEPWORTH: There's something I should tell you.

ROSAMUND: Something nice, I hope.

HEPWORTH: Not very nice, no. But you can make the nastiness go away.

ROSAMUND: 'Curiouser and curiouser,' said Alice.

Carlisle seems to have caught at Mary's arm as she was walking past him. He is finishing an argument.

CARLISLE: I'm only asking to set a date.

MARY: But what's the hurry?

CARLISLE: Hurry? Glaciers are fast compared to you on this, Mary. I warn you, even my patience has its limits!

The other women have gone by now and so Mary is the last of them to leave. The other men sit down again, but Robert and Matthew have overheard this angry little exchange.*

....

* This is a trick we use several times, which is the moment at the end of dinner when the ladies leave and everyone stands. The women are going into the drawing room, while the men will stay behind for a glass of port. It gives you different conjunctions of people who haven't sat next to each other at the table. Here, we have the moment of Carlisle's rage with Mary, which, if the audience is alert, will hint at the probable result. Because nobody tells Mary what to do.

38 INT. HALL. DOWNTON. NEW YEAR'S DAY. NIGHT.

Attended by Thomas, Cora, Edith and Rosamund are entering the drawing room when Mary hears Matthew call softly.

MATTHEW: Mary… Can I help?

MARY: After today, I won't insult you by asking what you mean.

MATTHEW: You don't have to marry him, you know. You don't have to marry anyone. You'll always have a home here, as long as I'm alive.

MARY: Didn't the war teach you never to make promises…? And anyway, you're wrong. I do have to marry him.

MATTHEW: But why? Not to prove you've broken with me, surely? We know where we stand. We've no need for gestures.

MARY: If I told you the reason, you would despise me. And that I really couldn't bear.

CORA: Mary! Rosamund wants to play bridge until the men come through…

MARY: Of course.

She walks away and Matthew returns to the dining room.

END OF ACT TWO

ACT THREE

39 INT. SERVANTS' HALL. DOWNTON. NEW YEAR'S DAY. NIGHT.

O'Brien has brought out the planchette board again. The servants are all gathered round. Thomas, O'Brien, Shore, a maid and a hall boy play. They speak the letters aloud. Y. O. U. A. R. E. T. O. O. F. A. T. Mrs Patmore is watching.

THOMAS: He says you're too fat.

MRS PATMORE: My Archie never said that. You're pushing the thing. Come away, Daisy. We've got work to do.

SHORE: I hope it's rewarding work, Mrs Patmore? Something to challenge our Daisy?

DAISY: Leave it alone.

She hurries off, but she's troubled. Mrs Patmore is with her.

MRS PATMORE: What did she mean? That Miss Shore?
DAISY: Nothing.

40   INT. DRAWING ROOM. DOWNTON. NEW YEAR'S DAY.
                  NIGHT.

Cora is alone, reading, when Robert comes in.

CORA: Who was telephoning so late?
ROBERT: Murray. He apologised. He's going to come here
the day before the trial. To talk it all through with
Mrs Hughes, O'Brien and me.
CORA: Why have they been chosen and not the others? What
do they know?
ROBERT: Search me. I've told Carson.
CORA: Will Mr Murray be staying?
ROBERT: No. He wants to get to York. We'll meet him
there the following day.
CORA: Oh, my dear. I hope you can be strong if it goes
against him.
ROBERT: It won't.* Where are the others?
CORA: The men are playing billiards and the girls have
gone to bed.†
ROBERT: There was an awkward moment tonight between Mary
and Carlisle. At the end of dinner. Did you notice it?
CORA: I'm sure Mary has him under control.

....

* It is time to get back to Bates's trial. But first, we must prepare the audience
to return to it, which is what we are doing here. If we now had just cut to
their arriving outside the courthouse, it would have been too sharp a
transition.

† In a large house like Downton, or the real Highclere for that matter, when a
lot of people were staying, there would have been different things happening
everywhere. For people who live in a more modest house, that is quite an
interesting concept to grasp. Most of the population might be used to having
some people talking in the kitchen, while others are watching television in a
different room, but that would be about it in terms of separate activities
under one roof. And even in that case, one group could probably still hear
the other. But in one of these palaces, during a house party, conversations,
love affairs, arguments and games would be happening in different rooms,
quite separately, all over the place, which I like to remind the audience of.

ROBERT: Does she? I look at her and all I can see is a tired woman with a tiresome husband, not a bride on the brink of heaven. I wish I could understand why she goes on with it. Do you think there's some element I might have overlooked?
CORA: Yes.

Her response has surprised both of them. She glances at him nervously.

ROBERT: Cora, if there is something and you know what it is, tell me. Please.

For a moment, she says nothing, but then she sighs.

CORA: Perhaps it's time.
ROBERT: I was hoping you'd say I was wrong.
CORA: You're not wrong. But if I do tell you, swear not to fly off the handle and try not to be too hurt…
ROBERT: Now you must tell me, because nothing could be worse than my imaginings.
CORA: Very well… Do you recall a Turkish diplomat who stayed here, before the war?
ROBERT: I think I can be relied on to remember any guest who is found dead in his bed next morning.
CORA: Well, that's the thing…

41 INT. SERVANTS' HALL. DOWNTON. DAY.

Murray is talking to O'Brien, Mrs Hughes and Carson. Robert is there.

MURRAY: I wanted to explain how it will work. You'll both have received official notification through the post.
O'BRIEN: But why have I been called? What's it to me? I know nothing.
MURRAY: Since you are summoned as a witness for the prosecution, the police would obviously disagree.
MRS HUGHES: But I'm there for the prosecution, too, when I have no doubt of Mr Bates's innocence. How can that be?
MURRAY: It'll be made clear on the day.
CARSON: Where does Anna stand in all this?
MURRAY: A wife cannot be compelled to testify against her husband.
MRS HUGHES: Well, that's a mercy, anyway.

42 INT. CARSON'S PANTRY. DOWNTON. NIGHT.

Carson looks up as Mrs Hughes comes in.

MRS HUGHES: I think I'll say goodnight. I've got a long day tomorrow.

CARSON: I don't envy you.

MRS HUGHES: I can't bear to think about it. What can they want from me?

CARSON: Just do your best, and you'll be home before you know it.

MRS HUGHES: And what news will I bring with me? That reminds me. What should we do about the Servants' Ball? It's only five days away. Can we delay it?

CARSON: But the Servants' Ball is always held on the twelfth of January, the birthday of the first Countess.

MRS HUGHES: I don't care if it's the birthday of Chu Chin Chow. This year, should we hold it back?

CARSON: The verdict will guide us to the appropriate response.*

43 INT. KITCHEN COURTYARD. DOWNTON. DAY.

The next day. O'Brien is with Thomas. They are smoking.

O'BRIEN: This is my last one. We're off in a minute.

THOMAS: Are you nervous?

O'BRIEN: Not nervous, no, but I don't want to go. Why can't I just refuse?

THOMAS: Because they'd put you in prison for contempt of court, that's why.

O'BRIEN: It seems wrong to me.

THOMAS: Do you think it'll go against him?

O'BRIEN: I think it might.

....

* I was in the chorus of a revival at Northampton Rep of *Chu Chin Chow*, and I mention it here because it had been one of the great musical successes of the First World War. I was the understudy to the Prince, who was the romantic lead. Naturally, I worked hard to keep him well. Every time he felt even slightly queasy, I'd rush off to the chemist and buy every nourishing lozenge or elixir I could find, all with my own money, to get him better. Because the last thing I wanted was to be judged on an understudy's performance.

THOMAS: So his lordship will be looking for a replacement after all.

He catches her look.

THOMAS (CONT'D): I know, I know…

44   INT.   COURTROOM.   YORK.   DAY.

Bates is in the dock. Murray sits with his barrister. Mary, in a veil, Matthew, Anna and Isobel are together in the gallery. O'Brien is in the witness box.

O'BRIEN: As far as I could make out, he was talking to his lawyer. He seemed to be blaming his wife for cancelling the divorce.
PROSECUTION LAWYER: You heard this yourself?
O'BRIEN: I wasn't eavesdropping. He was speaking loudly. But I don't think you can blame him —
PROSECUTION LAWYER: Just answer the questions, please, Miss O'Brien. When John Bates returned from London, on his final visit to Mrs Bates, did you notice anything about his appearance?
O'BRIEN: He had a scratch on his cheek, but he might have got that —
PROSECUTION LAWYER: And I believe the maid, Anna Smith, asked him how the meeting had gone.
O'BRIEN: Well, she and he were —
PROSECUTION LAWYER: And how did he answer her?
O'BRIEN: He said it had been worse than she could possibly imagine.

Anna is watching. She glances at Mary. They both know this is bad. Mrs Hughes is in the witness box now. She is in misery.

PROSECUTION LAWYER: And what did he call her?
MRS HUGHES: I shouldn't have been listening in the first place. I had no right to be there.
PROSECUTION LAWYER: But you were listening, Mrs Hughes. So please tell us what he called her when he grew angry.
MRS HUGHES: He said she was a bitch.
PROSECUTION LAWYER: Did it sound as if he threatened to strike her?

Mrs Hughes looks at Bates in the dock.

MRS HUGHES: But what people say in an argument —
PROSECUTION LAWYER: Did he threaten to strike her?

She looks at Bates again. He smiles at her and nods.

MRS HUGHES: I'm afraid he did. Yes.*

45 INT. A PASSAGE IN THE COURTHOUSE. YORK. DAY.

Murray is with Robert, Matthew, Isobel, Mary and Anna.

MURRAY: Every case looks as black as night by the time
the prosecution has finished. We've heard nothing in
Bates's defence yet.
ANNA: I can't believe Mrs Hughes would say those things.
Miss O'Brien maybe, but not Mrs Hughes.
ISOBEL: It's difficult to lie on oath. Few of us can
manage it.
MARY: She looked as if she were in hell.
ROBERT: It does sound worse than I expected.
MATTHEW: It's a great pity he didn't speak up about
buying the poison.
ANNA: I told him to. I begged him to.
MURRAY: He should have listened. The other problem is
the letter. It's written by a woman who expects an
assault.
ROBERT: Perhaps she was a neurotic, taking fright at
every shadow.
ANNA: No. Vera Bates wasn't like that.
ROBERT: Then it's down to me to convince them that this
crime is simply not in Bates's character.

....

* I had a nice letter from a member of the Lords who had been a judge and he said, 'I really enjoyed watching Bates's trial on *Downton*, because I felt all the witnesses were attempting to tell the truth and were resisting the temptation to lie.' He added that 'in a lifetime at the Bar, I have witnessed every form of lie, in every trial I've been part of, so I really enjoyed this exhibition of the truth'. I met him later and I said, 'Obviously you didn't feel our trial was very close to real life.' He said, 'No, but I wish it was like that.'

Mrs Hughes, of course, can't lie. I think that is believable in her case. She doesn't want to say any of it, but she finds that she cannot actually tell a straight lie, not when she's on oath.

Anna looks at him. She knows she's on the edge of an abyss.

ANNA: Because it's not.

46 INT. COURTROOM. YORK. DAY.

Robert is in the box.

DEFENCE LAWYER: So you have no doubt at all?
ROBERT: None whatsoever. We served in the African war
and I owe my life to John Bates, who acted to protect me
without any care for his own safety. Is this a man who
could plot to kill his wife? Absolutely not.

He thinks he has finished, but the prosecution lawyer stands.

PROSECUTION LAWYER: Lord Grantham, did John Bates ever
speak to you about his wife?
ROBERT: Not that I recall.
PROSECUTION LAWYER: Never? He never once spoke one word
of this wife who'd prevented all his dreams from coming
true?
ROBERT: Well, you know, one talks about this and that.
PROSECUTION LAWYER: Did he give you the impression he was
losing patience with Mrs Bates? Around the time she had
prevented the divorce?

Robert is really uncomfortable. He looks at Bates.

PROSECUTION LAWYER (CONT'D): Were you aware that he was
angry at what had happened?
ROBERT: I suppose so.
PROSECUTION LAWYER: Did he ask permission to travel to
London, to see her that last time?
ROBERT: I believe he did.
PROSECUTION LAWYER: And did you recommend restraint in
his dealings with his wife?
ROBERT: I don't think so.
PROSECUTION LAWYER: You are absolutely sure?
ROBERT: Well… Perhaps I may have done.
PROSECUTION LAWYER: You did, Lord Grantham. Mr Bates
has, in his interviews, stated that you prescribed
discretion. His case is that he followed your advice,
but I wonder why the defence has chosen not to refer to
this.
ROBERT: I can't tell you.

PROSECUTION LAWYER: No… And was there one statement of his that prompted you to advise him to moderate his behaviour?

Robert looks at Bates. He is in agony.

ROBERT: I can't remember. Not precisely.
PROSECUTION LAWYER: Give us an approximate.

But Robert does not reply. The judge intervenes.

JUDGE: I must urge that the witness gives an answer.

Robert glances at the gallery, where Anna and Mary sit.

ROBERT: I said I hoped his trip to London was to do with some property he owned and not to do with the former Mrs Bates.
PROSECUTION LAWYER: And how did he answer?
ROBERT: He said…
JUDGE: Lord Grantham…
ROBERT: He said: 'If only she was the former, or better still, the late.'

The court is silent.

47 INT. A PASSAGE IN THE COURTHOUSE. YORK. DAY.

They huddle together. Robert is with Mary. He talks softly.

ROBERT: I should have lied, of course I should have lied.

Mary gently shushes him, indicating Anna, but she's overheard.

ANNA: I will not believe he needs lies to save him.*

In the passage are O'Brien and Mrs Hughes. Isobel walks over.

MRS HUGHES: I don't know what to say, ma'am. They twist your words —
ISOBEL: You had to answer their questions.

....

* I am sad about this cut, as we never had Robert's moment of genuine regret that he testified against Bates, which I think we needed. At the time, I don't believe I recognised its importance, or I would have put forward a stronger argument to keep it. As it is, it feels odd that he never refers to the fact that his own testimony has led to Bates's conviction.

MRS HUGHES: I wish to God I'd never listened.

ISOBEL: Well…

O'BRIEN: I suppose Anna is very bitter… I wonder if you would tell her —

ISOBEL: I know that you're both praying for her, as I am.

MURRAY: Mrs Crawley! The jury's returned!

48 INT. COURTROOM. YORK. DAY.

The judge is reading the verdict. He looks up.

JUDGE: Are you all agreed?

FOREMAN: We are, my lord.

The judge nods to the usher.

JUDGE: The prisoner will stand.

Bates gets to his feet. In the gallery, Robert, Mary, Isobel, Matthew and Anna hold their breath. Behind them, Mrs Hughes and O'Brien wait tensely for the verdict. The foreman stands.

JUDGE (CONT'D): Do you find the prisoner to be guilty or not guilty, as charged?

FOREMAN: Guilty, my lord.

Anna lets out a scream before she can cover her mouth. Mary gasps. There is a tremendous stir. Then a silence as the judge takes up the black cap and places it on his head.

JUDGE: John Bates, you have been found guilty of the charge of wilful murder. You will be taken from here to a place of execution where you will be hanged by the neck until you are dead. And may God have mercy upon your soul.

ANNA: No, no, this is wrong! This is — This is terribly, terribly wrong!

The judge looks up towards her, but she is silent now.

JUDGE: Take him down.

Just for a moment, Bates raises his eyes to the gallery, and he calls to Anna. Then the gaolers take him away.

END OF ACT THREE

ACT FOUR

49 INT. DRAWING ROOM. DOWER HOUSE. DAY.

Violet is with Rosamund, having tea.

ROSAMUND: Did you know this Bates well?

VIOLET: No, not really. Oh, I saw him once, yes, when I went to talk to Matthew in his bedroom, just before dinner.

ROSAMUND: That sounds rather risqué.

VIOLET: Oh-ho, alas, I am beyond impropriety.

ROSAMUND: There'll be a stink in the papers.

VIOLET: Well, to be honest, I'm surprised there hasn't been one already. Perhaps Sir Richard had a hand in it.

She drinks her tea.

VIOLET (CONT'D): And while we're on the subject of unsuitable spouses…

ROSAMUND: Lord Hepworth is not unsuitable, Mama. You are unjust.

VIOLET: He's hardly the consummation devoutly to be wished. Did he tell you what I asked him to tell you?

ROSAMUND: I know he has no fortune, if that's what you mean.

VIOLET: No fortune? He's lucky not to be playing the violin in Leicester Square!

ROSAMUND: He's fond of me, Mama. I'm tired of being alone and I have money.

VIOLET: He's a fortune hunter, my dear. A pleasant one, I admit, but a fortune hunter. Still, it's your decision. So, have you made it?

ROSAMUND: Not quite. I'm going to ask Robert to get him back for the Servants' Ball.

VIOLET: Oh, will that happen? After today?

ROSAMUND: Well, he can come and stay, whether or not we feel like dancing.

50 INT. HOTEL SITTING ROOM. YORK. DAY.

Robert, Mary, Isobel, Matthew, Murray and Anna have been shown in. Both Anna and Robert are in a daze. A manager hovers in the doorway. Isobel takes over.

ISOBEL: Thank you. We don't need anything.

MARY: Do sit down, Anna.

The man goes as Anna sits, stiffly, next to Mary.

ISOBEL: You mustn't think that this is the end.

MURRAY: For the judge to pronounce the death sentence is a matter of routine —

ANNA: Routine?

MATTHEW: He means the judge had no choice. If a man is found guilty of murder he must be sentenced to death. But there are many reasons for it to be commuted. Many reasons.

ANNA: Is being innocent one of them?

MURRAY: We have to work to change the sentence to life imprisonment —

ANNA: Life imprisonment?

MATTHEW: Because it won't demand a retrial or an overthrow of the Crown's case. Once we have that, we can begin to build a challenge to the verdict.

MARY: Do you understand?

Anna has now taken control of herself. She nods.

ANNA: Yes, m'lady. I do.

ROBERT: I still can't believe it.

ISOBEL: Well, I'm afraid you must.

MATTHEW: We'll need you to write a letter to the Home Secretary, a Mr Shortt.

MURRAY: I'll leave for London at once and put it into his hand myself.

ROBERT: He's a Liberal, isn't he? Pity.

ISOBEL: He's a decent man.*

....

* Edward Shortt was Home Secretary in Lloyd George's Government from 1919. Later, he argued that the grave responsibility of recommending a reprieve or the reverse should no longer rest upon the Home Secretary's shoulders alone. The responsibility for the final decision should be shared by a commission of three: the Home Secretary, the Lord Chief Justice and the judge who presided at the trial. But he did not manage to persuade them to change the system.

MURRAY: The flaw in their case is the question of
premeditation. Even if Mr Bates had run to the cellar
for the poison and pushed it into her food, we can argue
strongly he didn't plan it.
ANNA: He didn't plan it because he didn't do it!
MATTHEW: And we'll stress the circumstantial nature of
the evidence. There may still be elements that come to
light.
ANNA: What chance do you think we have?

Matthew looks at Murray, who makes the decision to be honest.

MURRAY: It's not a good chance, Mrs Bates. But there's
still a chance…*

51 INT. SERVANTS' HALL. DOWNTON. EVE.

*The household is assembled and silent. Mrs Hughes and
O'Brien are both there. Carson comes in as Mrs Hughes is
speaking.*

MRS PATMORE: When will they be back?
MRS HUGHES: I'm not sure. They took Anna to an inn to
help her catch her breath.
DAISY: How will we ever face her?
MRS HUGHES: With kindness, I hope.
HALL BOY: When will he be hanged?

There is a beat of silence. Carson turns to the housekeeper.

....

* I was pleased with that scene, which I thought they all played very well.
Anna has to grasp that if they still try to plead Bates's innocence, he will
probably hang, but if they simply argue lack of premeditation, then he
probably won't hang, which will mean that they can get back to work and
attempt to prove him innocent. For the wife or the husband of someone who
has been wrongly convicted, this would be a very, very difficult suggestion to
accept.

I always enjoy it when Mr Murray comes up from London to advise the
family on the latest drama. He is played by a very old friend, Jonathan Coy,
and we met making a play for Granada in 1976, almost forty years ago, which
is rather frightening.

CARSON: Her ladyship wondered if you could give her an account of the day.
MRS HUGHES: Of course.

But before she leaves, she addresses the room.

MRS HUGHES (CONT'D): I'd like to say, I may have been called for the prosecution, but I do not believe in Mr Bates's guilt.
SHORE: What about you, Miss O'Brien? You're very quiet.
O'BRIEN: I'm sorry to have been part of it.

Mrs Hughes and Carson have gone. Thomas leans over.

THOMAS: There'll have to be a new valet now. Won't there?
O'BRIEN: I don't often feel selfless. But when I listen to you, I do.*

52 INT. DRAWING ROOM. DOWNTON. NIGHT.

Mrs Hughes is with Cora.

CORA: His lordship will be so upset.
MRS HUGHES: We're all upset downstairs, m'lady.
CORA: Of course you are... His lordship and Lady Mary won't want to change, so we won't either. Please ask Mrs Patmore to serve dinner twenty minutes after they arrive.
MRS HUGHES: Very good, m'lady.
CORA: When is that terrible man coming? To look at Ethel's boy?
MRS HUGHES: Saturday, m'lady. But there's no need for you to see them.
CORA: Thank heaven for that. Oh, Mrs Hughes, this is a time of grief for us. Of grief and heartbreak.

Mrs Hughes nods and goes to the door with a heavy heart.

....

* Here we see the other side of O'Brien. There are no entirely unsympathetic characters in *Downton*. But there is always a sub-text, or at least I try to suggest one. O'Brien made this trouble by sending the letter and getting Vera up to Yorkshire to confront Bates. It was all her fault, and I think it's believable that, now a man is to hang for it, she is sorry. She doesn't like Bates, but she doesn't want anyone to hang because of something she's done.

53 INT. KITCHEN. DOWNTON. NIGHT.

Daisy is working with Mrs Patmore.

DAISY: I suppose it's down to me again.

MRS PATMORE: What is?

DAISY: To produce dinner twenty minutes after they arrive, when we don't know if it's in two or ten hours' time.

MRS PATMORE: What's got into you all of a sudden?

DAISY: Nothing. I mean, I know I'm a dog's body, but —

MRS PATMORE: How can you choose today of all days to complain about your lot? I expect Mr Bates would rather be wondering how to keep a roast chicken warm than sitting in a lonely cell, facing his Maker.*

54 INT. LIBRARY. DOWNTON. NIGHT.

Robert is alone by the fire with a glass of whisky, which he sips, staring into the flames. He looks up as Mary comes in.

MARY: You've been hiding from us.

ROBERT: I couldn't do any more chatter. Are the Crawleys still here?

MARY: They went ages ago. Mama and Edith have gone up.

She sits near him.

MARY (CONT'D): I am so dreadfully, dreadfully sorry about today.

ROBERT: I know you are… How's Anna?

MARY: I sent her to bed.

ROBERT: It must all be resolved by Friday, anyway… Can I ask you something?

MARY: Of course.

ROBERT: Do you stay with Carlisle because he's threatened to expose the story of Mr Pamuk dying in your bed?

....

* Daisy's discontent has been stirred up by Shore. It is a belief of mine that there are people in this life, and quite a lot of them are politicians, who spend their life persuading everyone who'll listen that they are very unhappy with their lot. They tell their audience that they're being ill-used and mistreated and taken advantage of, and all of this stuff is coming from people who wish to control the lives of others. I hate controllers, so wherever I can attack them, I certainly do.

This is an astonishing revelation. Mary almost gasps.

MARY: When did you find out?

ROBERT: Your mother told me, when I asked why you were still with Carlisle when you were so tired of him.

MARY: How very disappointed you must be.

ROBERT: Your mama chose her moment well. She spoke at a time when it seems quite unimportant, compared to other disappointments we must face. And you're not the first Crawley to make a mistake.

MARY: To answer your question, it is partly true, but not entirely. In Mama's phrase, I am damaged goods now. Richard is, after all, prepared to marry me in spite of it, to give me a position, to give me a life.

ROBERT: And that's worth it? Even though he already sets your teeth on edge?

Mary does not try to deny this.

ROBERT (CONT'D): What about Matthew? How does he view the late Mr Pamuk?

MARY: He doesn't know.

ROBERT: So that is not what split you apart? I thought it might have been.

MARY: Oh, no… There were other reasons for that… to do with Lavinia…

ROBERT: I see. And those reasons are final?

MARY: They are final for Matthew, so, yes, they are.

Robert stands as he turns this round in his brain.

ROBERT: Here's what I think. Break with Carlisle. He may publish, but we'll be a house of scandal anyway with Bates's story. Go to America. Stay with your grandmother until the fuss dies down. You may find the New World is to your taste.

MARY: He'll keep my secret if I marry him.

ROBERT: Once, I might have thought that a good thing, but I've been through a war and a murder trial since then. To say nothing of your sister's choice of husband. I don't want my daughter to be married to a man who threatens her with ruin. I want a good man for you, a brave man. Find a cowboy in the Middle West and bring him back to shake us up a bit.

MARY: Oh, Papa!

*She jumps up and hugs him for his forgiveness.**

55 INT. CARSON'S PANTRY. DOWNTON. NIGHT.

Carson is checking the silver.

THOMAS: Have you got a minute, Mr Carson?

CARSON: Only a minute. I've to go up and attend to his lordship.

THOMAS: Well, that's the point. This news is going to change things, isn't it?

CARSON: I have every hope that Mr Bates's sentence will be commuted. His lordship is doing everything —

THOMAS: I know. And I hope he's successful, but even if he is, Mr Bates won't be coming home this weekend, will he?

CARSON: I'm afraid not.

THOMAS: So I — I wondered if you'd given any more thought to my application.

This is a little awkward.

CARSON: I'm sorry, but I have spoken to his lordship and he thinks you're more suited to your present position.

THOMAS: He doesn't trust me, does he? Because of the stealing. I knew it.

CARSON: If you knew it, then why did you pursue it?

....

* A lot of things are routinely said about posh people, that they never worry about money or that they're always rude to their servants, or whatever, and much, if not all, of it is untrue. But they do hate scandal. They hate publicity, and they hate to be in the papers, with very few exceptions. So, for Robert to suggest that it might be better for Mary to brave the scandal than to marry the wrong man is a most amazingly loving thing. And once Mary knows that her father doesn't think it's worth avoiding the bad publicity, then we realise she's not going to marry Carlisle. Within the strictures of posh behaviour, this scene is as genuinely loving as any moment in the entire show, and they play it beautifully. I was pleased with the line about the cowboy: 'Bring him back to shake us up a bit.'

56 INT. KITCHEN. DOWNTON. DAY.

Daisy is sighing as she peels potatoes.

MRS PATMORE: What is it now?

DAISY: Nothing.

MRS PATMORE: Well, it's not nothing, is it?

DAISY: I just feel taken for granted. Sometimes I think you don't notice that I'm human at all.

MRS PATMORE: Oh, so it's my fault?

DAISY: You talk to me like when I first came, but I know things now —

MRS PATMORE: Things I taught you.

DAISY: Maybe, but I learned them and I work well, but you wouldn't know it the way I'm treated. It may be wrong to complain with Mr Bates like he is, but he reminds me that life's short and I'm wasting mine.

SHORE: Please listen to her.*

She is standing in the doorway, watching.

MRS PATMORE: Have you put her up to this?

SHORE: It's what she feels.

MRS PATMORE: Daisy, you're tired. Why not get away for a day? You told Mr Mason you'd go to the farm. Go, then. Breathe the air. Have a rest.

DAISY: I couldn't. I don't think William would like it.

MRS PATMORE: Ohh!

57 EXT. CEMETERY. DOWNTON VILLAGE. DAY.

The new gravestone reads: Lavinia Catherine Swire, 1895–1919, beloved daughter of Reginald and Anne Swire, 'I will turn their mourning into joy.' Mary is walking towards the grave when she sees Matthew and Isobel standing there.

MATTHEW: You got my note. I'm so pleased.

ISOBEL: I'm going to fight off Mr Travis if he objects. He can be so difficult.

....

*They took Shore out of this scene because the actress couldn't film on that day, which was rather a shame, but that's just one of those things. Good actors tend to be busy actors and one just has to work round it. That said, there are of course many, many actors who are very good indeed but who never get that essential first lucky break.

MARY: We should be able to manage him between us.

Matthew speaks to Mary, but he does not exclude his mother.

MATTHEW: I'm so glad you're here. And I feel, somehow, we were all of us part of each other's story for a while and...
MARY: And now that story is at an end.
ISOBEL: In what way?
MARY: Well, Matthew doesn't want to live here, and I'm moving away soon.
MATTHEW: You mean to Haxby?
MARY: Wherever I go, the time we shared is over. And Lavinia was a part of that.
ISOBEL: Let's take a moment to remember her.

And the three of them bow their heads as Matthew starts.

MATTHEW: I thought we'd start with a prayer. Our Father, which art in Heaven...

58 INT. LIBRARY. DOWNTON. DAY.

Violet walks in and sits down. She hears sobbing.
Surprised, she gets up and walks round the sofa to find Daisy.
The girl is wracked with sobs as she builds the fire.

VIOLET: Oh! What on earth's the matter?

Daisy nearly jumps out of her skin.

59 EXT. DOWNTON VILLAGE. DAY.

Mary walks off. Matthew and Isobel start for Crawley House.

ISOBEL: She's still in love with you, you know?
MATTHEW: I don't think so.
ISOBEL: Well, I'm sorry, but it's as plain as the nose on your face.
MATTHEW: I thought you didn't like her for throwing me over.
ISOBEL: That's a different conversation.
MATTHEW: Mother, it has to be like this. I'm afraid I can't explain why... At least, I'm not going to.
ISOBEL: Something to do with Lavinia?
MATTHEW: Maybe.

ISOBEL: Well, you see, I think you're wrong. Lavinia wouldn't have wanted this. She was a sweet girl, a kind girl… She wouldn't have wanted you to be unhappy.
MATTHEW: You don't understand. I deserve to be unhappy. So does Mary.
ISOBEL: Nobody your age deserves that. And if you are, and you can do something about it and don't, well, the war's taught you nothing.
MATTHEW: That's your opinion.
ISOBEL: Yes. It is.

END OF ACT FOUR

ACT FIVE

60 EXT. GARDENS. DOWNTON. DAY.

Robert is walking when Carson hurries up.

CARSON: The Dowager Countess has arrived. She's waiting in the library.
ROBERT: Waiting for what?
CARSON: Well, you, I suppose, m'lord.
ROBERT: I was out here looking for Isis. You don't know where she might be?
CARSON: I haven't seen the dog, m'lord.
ROBERT: Can you ask in the servants' hall?*

....

* The clue to Isis's disappearance came at the New Year's Eve drinks, when Thomas looks at her and she wags her tail. For that moment we made quite a big thing of the shot of the dog, because we knew the plot would have to hang over for quite a long time before Thomas took action in his endeavour to be appointed Robert's valet. He has followed O'Brien's suggestion: 'Make him grateful. Do him a good turn. Hide something he loves, then find it and give it back.' And there is nothing Robert loves more than his dogs.

61 INT. LIBRARY. DOWNTON. DAY.

Violet is now seated, with Daisy standing before her.

VIOLET: But you can't have been false to him. You were his wife for only half an hour.

DAISY: It's difficult to explain, m'lady.

VIOLET: Well, try.

DAISY: I led him on. When he was wounded, I let him think that I loved him.

VIOLET: Why?

DAISY: I thought it'd cheer him up, give him something to live for.

VIOLET: And you did all this when you didn't even like him?

DAISY: No. I did like him. Very, very much. Everyone liked our William.

VIOLET: Oh, so you married him to keep his spirits up at the end?

DAISY: I suppose I did, yes.

VIOLET: Well, forgive me, but that doesn't sound unloving. To me, that sounds as if you loved him a great deal.*

The door opens and Robert comes in.

ROBERT: I'm sorry to keep you waiting, Mama, I've been outside. I was looking for —

Daisy bobs a curtsey, snatches up her bucket and hurries out.

ROBERT (CONT'D): What was she doing?

VIOLET: Mending the fire and suffering.

ROBERT: She shouldn't be here at this hour. Why isn't Thomas on duty?

VIOLET: I don't need you to tell me the world is falling

....

* I always like to bring about conjunctions involving characters who don't meet in the natural way of things. And there is no greater distance at Downton than that between the Dowager Countess and Daisy the kitchen maid. So I was looking for some legitimate reason that would allow them to share a scene. Of course, before the war, if a fire had to be mended during the day, it would be a footman's job, but this slight breakdown in the routine seemed to reflect the changes going on all around, so I felt it was reasonably believable.

about our ears... Is there any news on Bates?

ROBERT: Not yet. Murray has a meeting with the Home Secretary later today. We should know something then.

VIOLET: I'm surprised there isn't more in the papers. 'Earl's valet to swing' and so on, but I've seen hardly anything, and nothing about you.

ROBERT: I quite agree and I can't enlighten you. Is that why you're here?

VIOLET: Well, not exactly. I wanted to talk about Rosamund and Hepworth.

ROBERT: Careful. She might come in.

VIOLET: Then I shall speak quickly. I only want to know one thing: is a woman of Rosamund's age entitled to marry a fortune hunter?

ROBERT: Does she know all the facts?

VIOLET: Yes, yes, she does.

ROBERT: Then I would say yes. But, for God's sake, let's tie up the money.

VIOLET: My thoughts exactly... What is the matter, Robert?

ROBERT: Isis has gone missing. I can't think where she's got to...

62 EXT. WOODLAND. DOWNTON. DAY.

The dog is walking along through the woods, being led on a string by Thomas. He arrives at an old shed, a shelter for the keepers. He puts the dog inside and slides the bolt.

THOMAS: In you go, Isis, in you go. Good girl. Good girl.

63 INT. ROSAMUND'S BEDROOM. DOWNTON. DAY.

Rosamund is changing for dinner, helped by Shore.

ROSAMUND: Any talk of the luckless valet?

SHORE: Nothing downstairs... So, is Lord Hepworth coming for the ball?

ROSAMUND: Lady Grantham's written to ask him. But I think now I should have waited until I was back in London.

SHORE: Oh, no. He'll cheer you up, m'lady. I promise
you. Specially if the house is in mourning.
ROSAMUND: That's a comfort, I suppose.*

64 INT. YORK PRISON. DAY.

Anna is with Bates, alone, with a warder watching.

ANNA: Mr Murray's gone to London with the lawyers and
he's going to see —
BATES: Ssh.

He smiles at her, much less unhappy than she is.

BATES (CONT'D): Will you stay on at Downton?
ANNA: Who says they'll let me?
BATES: They'll let you. And you'll have some money.
Mr Murray thinks you can keep it, or most of it.

She will not comment. She just shakes her head.

BATES (CONT'D): I want you to thank his lordship for
trying to help me —
ANNA: Yes, but what he said —
BATES: He didn't want to say it. And I won't blame him
for not lying.
ANNA: He regrets not lying. I heard him say it.
BATES: Give him my best wishes for the future. And wish
all of them well. I don't want you to hold it against
Mrs Hughes or Miss O'Brien —
ANNA: If you think I can ever —
BATES: Even Miss O'Brien. We've not been friends, but
she doesn't want me here. Please forgive them. I do.†
ANNA: I'm not sorry, you know… Not a bit. I would marry
you now, if I wasn't already your wife. I would!

....

* We lost this scene between Rosamund and Shore, which was sad because I
feel that when someone is playing a lady's maid, or a valet, or a chauffeur, you
want to see them doing the job. That was the only moment when we actually
saw Shore working as Rosamund's maid, as opposed to coming out of her
room into the passage, but it wasn't one I wanted to go to the stake for.

† Needless to say, Bates forgives Robert and generally forgives everyone,
which Anna finds much harder to do than he does. But I never feel he is too
much Saint Bates to be true. There is darkness underneath. That is the
strength of Brendan Coyle's wonderful performance.

BATES: God knows, I'm not sorry, either. Maybe I should be, but no man can regret loving as I have loved you.

She can't speak, but reaches for his hand across the table.

WARDER: No touching!
BATES: For God's sake, man. You know where I am bound. How dangerous can this be?

The warder looks for a moment, then nods and turns his back. Bates stands and draws Anna to him.

BATES (CONT'D): One kiss. To take with me.

He kisses her. There is the sound of a guard outside the door and they are apart by the time the door is thrown open…*

65 INT. SERVANTS' HALL. DOWNTON. NIGHT.

O'Brien and Thomas are playing planchette when Mrs Patmore arrives. Daisy is watching and two maids are also playing.

MRS PATMORE: Still at it?
THOMAS: The secrets of the universe are boundless.
MRS PATMORE: Are they indeed?

Then she looks at Daisy and has an idea.

MRS PATMORE (CONT'D): All right. Shove over.
O'BRIEN: You've changed your tune.
MRS PATMORE: Have I? Perhaps I have. Now, let's get going. Who's out there?

She has planted her finger on the glass.

O'BRIEN: But we've already —
MRS PATMORE: Here we go.

The glass moves firmly towards W. Thomas and O'Brien seem to be struggling to control it, but now it heads for I. L. L. I. A. M.

DAISY: William? Is it really you, William?
MRS PATMORE: YES.

....

* It was a different system then and visits of this sort were supervised by a single warder, as prison officers were called. This one has a reasonably kind heart and allows them a kiss. Hopefully, as a result, eyes were streaming among the show's followers.

DAISY: Oh, my Lord! Oh, my God! William? Is it you?
What do you want?

Mrs Patmore is red-faced with effort as the glass continues to
move apparently against the wishes of O'Brien and Thomas.

MRS PATMORE: GO. TO. FARM. MAKE. DAD. HAPPY. Go to
the farm. Make Dad happy. You can't say fairer than
that.
SHORE: Is it usually so specific?
O'BRIEN: Not usually, no.
MRS PATMORE: Well, that's enough for me. Ooh, this stuff
is thirsty work.

She stands and retreats to the kitchen, followed by Daisy.
The game has broken up. O'Brien looks at Thomas.

THOMAS: That was a clear instruction.
O'BRIEN: Very clear. Mrs Patmore's stronger than she
looks.
THOMAS: Nobody's stronger than she looks…

66 INT. HALL. DOWNTON. NIGHT.

Matthew has just been admitted by Carson.

CARSON: They're in the drawing room, sir.
MATTHEW: I'm really only here to see Lady Mary, Carson.
Is there any chance of hooking her out?
CARSON: Leave it with me, sir.
ROBERT: Matthew? You should have come earlier. You
could have had dinner.

He is walking across the hall towards them, looking worried.

MATTHEW: Is something the matter?
ROBERT: My dog's gone missing. I was going to go and
look for her.
MATTHEW: We should organise a search party, ask the
menservants to join us. Then we can apply some real
method. Wouldn't you agree, Carson?

67 EXT. WOODS. DOWNTON. NIGHT.

A line of searchers with lanterns fans out across the woods,
calling. Robert leads them. Mary is with Edith further
back.

ROBERT: Isis! Come here, girl! Isis!

MARY: Poor Papa. I wonder if she's been stolen.

EDITH: What a horrid thought.

Through the trees, Thomas can glimpse the shed. He is walking alongside Carson when he stops and stares at it.

CARSON: Thomas? What's the matter with you?

THOMAS: Nothing.

He would go over to the shed... when Robert claps his hands.

ROBERT: I'm afraid we'll have to call it a night, but remember there's ten pounds for anyone who finds her tomorrow. For now, thank you all very much.

MARY: Poor Papa. It's terrible for you.

ROBERT: She may turn up. She may be trapped somewhere. We could still find her.

Carson turns to Thomas.

CARSON: Get back to the house as fast as you can and ask Mrs Patmore to heat up some soup for the searchers.

Thomas glances at the outline of the shed in the darkness.*

CARSON (CONT'D): Thomas?

THOMAS: Yes, Mr Carson.

There is nothing he can do. Mary is now walking by Matthew.

MATTHEW: Poor Robert. This is an awful time for him.

MARY: Why were you up at the house this evening? Did Papa summon you?

MATTHEW: As a matter of fact I came to see you. I wanted to find out what you meant when you said you had to marry Carlisle... and that I'd despise you if I knew the reason —

MARY: Yes. You would.

MATTHEW: Whatever it is, it cannot be enough for you to marry him.

MARY: That's what Papa said.

MATTHEW: So you told him?

---

* I think that if Thomas could have arranged to find Isis in the shed that night, he would have done it, and got the dog back inside the house. But of course he can't because he's been sent on an errand by Carson. So he's stuck with leaving it there. But he's got nothing against the poor animal, and I'm pretty sure he would have been uncomfortable about it.

MARY: Yes.

MATTHEW: And does he despise you?

MARY: He's very disappointed in me.

This is the first real clue. He looks at her.

MATTHEW: Even so. Please tell me...*

68   INT. MRS HUGHES'S SITTING ROOM. DOWNTON.
           NIGHT.

Carson is with the housekeeper. He still has his coat on.

MRS HUGHES: You'd think the good Lord would have spared him the loss of his dog. At a time like this.

CARSON: Ours not to reason why.

MRS HUGHES: When will we hear about Mr Bates?

Carson shakes his head as he takes the coat off.

MRS HUGHES (CONT'D): I don't know how they've kept it out of the papers. I suppose that'll change if it goes ahead. I can't bear to think of it. How will Anna bear it?

CARSON: As the widow of a murderer? She'll have to get used to a degree of notoriety, I'm afraid. And so will we, as the house that shelters her.

ANNA: Then let me put you out of your misery right away, Mr Carson. By handing in my notice.

She is standing in the doorway.

MRS HUGHES: You don't mean that.

....

* Matthew wants to have it out with Mary and learn her terrible secret, whatever it may be, and so we leave them to it, assuming she will tell him all. But what sets the style of *Downton* with moments like this is that the audience knows what is being said, so they don't have to hear it. It's the same with our treatment of sex in the series. The audience knows what's happening, or going to happen, but on the whole we let them imagine it, rather than see it. They will understand that the event has taken place, and they can argue about it, standing round the water cooler the following day, but they are spared the abrasive experience of actually watching it. Of course, it is slightly old-fashioned, and as a narrative style owes more to old Hollywood than modern television, but it seems to work for us.

ANNA: Yes, I do. If I stay here, I keep the story alive.
If I go away, to Scotland, say, or London, it'll die soon
enough. I'll just be one more housemaid, lost in the
crowd.
CARSON: She has a point.
MRS HUGHES: Not one that I accept.
ANNA: I mean it, Mrs Hughes. I do.

69 EXT. DOWNTON. NIGHT.

Matthew is silent. Mary watches him. He is stunned.

MARY: Say something. If it's only goodbye.
MATTHEW: Did you love him?
MARY: You mustn't try to —
MATTHEW: Because if it was love, then —
MARY: How could it be love? I didn't know him.
MATTHEW: But then why would you —?
MARY: It was lust, Matthew, or a need for excitement or
something in him that I — Oh, God, what difference does
it make? I'm Tess of the d'Urbervilles to your Angel
Clare. I have fallen. I am impure.
MATTHEW: Don't joke. Don't make it little. Not when I'm
trying to understand.

His pain does move her, and her voice softens.

MARY: Thank you for that… But the fact remains that I am
made different by it. Things have changed between us.
MATTHEW: Even so, you must not marry him.
MARY: So I must brave the storm?
MATTHEW: You're strong. A storm-braver if ever I saw
one.
MARY: I wonder. Sybil's the strong one. She really
doesn't care what people think, but I'm afraid I do…
Papa suggested I go to New York, to stay with Grandmama
to ride it out.
MATTHEW: You can find some unsuspecting millionaire.
MARY: Preferably one who doesn't read English papers.

For the first time, they both half laugh.

MATTHEW: Go or stay, you must sack Carlisle. It isn't
worth buying off a month of scandal with a lifetime of
misery. When is he due back?

MARY: Tomorrow. He and Aunt Rosamund's beau are returning for the Servants' Ball.
MATTHEW: Will that still go ahead?
MARY: Not if Bates is — Not if the worst happens. Papa hasn't faced that it probably will.
CORA: Matthew, are you coming in for some soup?

She is standing in the doorway.

MATTHEW: You're kind, but no, thank you. My work is done for tonight.

Cora goes back inside. He turns to Mary.

MATTHEW (CONT'D): You were wrong about one thing.
MARY: Only one? And what is that, pray?
MATTHEW: I never would, I never could, despise you.*

70 INT. SERVANTS' HALL. DOWNTON. NIGHT.

O'Brien and Thomas are alone.

O'BRIEN: Why didn't you just go and 'find' the poor thing there and then?
THOMAS: How? His lordship was in the way and Mr Carson sent me back with a message for Mrs Patmore.
O'BRIEN: So you're going to leave the wretched animal out all night?

....

* I like this scene because Mary doesn't try to sentimentalise what she did. She fancied a man very much and she went to bed with him. That is the beginning, middle and end of it. There's something in her, and this is why in the end you like her despite her toughness, that won't allow her to lie. She won't say: 'Oh, we fell so in love and we were married in our hearts.' She wants Matthew to see the worst of her, because if he's going to forgive her, he's got to forgive what really happened and not the version he would prefer to hear.

The reference to Tess of the D'Urbervilles and Angel Clare – i.e. the fallen woman and the saintly man – is probably lost on people who haven't read the novel, but Hardy lived almost next door to us in Dorset, and in fact he used our village church as the model for the marriage of Tess and Angel, so it felt right. It's quite an interesting church, actually, with a rood screen from Archbishop Laud's unpopular revival of many Catholic practices in the 1630s. Cromwell's army destroyed Laud's screens in all but a handful of churches in England, and our village boasts one of them.

THOMAS: What reason could I give? If I went back and found her now?

O'BRIEN: Go first thing, once you're free, and just pray nothing's happened. For your own sake.

71 INT. ATTICS. DOWNTON. NIGHT.

Anna is making her weary way to bed when she hears singing. She turns the corner and finds Shore opening her door.

SHORE: I'm sorry. I didn't mean to sound so merry.

ANNA: Why not? The whole world doesn't have to be grieving because I am.

SHORE: I wish you luck. I do. Truly.

With that, she starts to go into her bedroom.

ANNA: Why were you so merry?

SHORE: Oh… no reason, particularly.

72 INT. KITCHEN. DOWNTON. NIGHT.

The kitchen has been closed up for the night. Daisy is hanging the drying cloths by the stove.

DAISY: Do you think that was William?

MRS PATMORE: Who else could it have been? Who else would have known you'd been asked to the farm?

DAISY: That's true.

MRS PATMORE: So will you go?

DAISY: I feel I should, don't you?

MRS PATMORE: Oh, I think so.

She turns out the lights, adding under her breath:

MRS PATMORE (CONT'D): If only to spare my fingers…

END OF ACT FIVE

ACT SIX

73 EXT. DOWNTON. DAY.

A car and a van are parked outside.

74 INT. SERVANTS' HALL. DOWNTON. DAY.

Ethel looks in with her little boy.

    ETHEL: Is Mrs Hughes about?
    SHORE: I'll go and find her if you like.

She goes, leaving the two of them alone.

    ETHEL: Who's she?
    ANNA: Lady Rosamund's new maid.

Ethel remembers who she is talking to.

    ETHEL: Oh, Anna. What am I thinking of? I'm ever so
    sorry.

Anna manages a slight smile as Mrs Hughes appears.

    MRS HUGHES: There you are, Ethel. Come with me.

They go, passing Carson, who barely nods at Ethel.

    CARSON: Where's Thomas? Has anyone clapped eyes on him?
    O'BRIEN: He went out after breakfast for something. He
    won't be long.

75 EXT. WOODLAND. DOWNTON. DAY.

*Thomas approaches the hut. He unbolts and opens the door.
It is empty. He is horrified.*

76 INT. SERVANTS' STAIRCASE. DOWNTON. DAY.

Mrs Hughes and Ethel climb the stairs together.

    MRS HUGHES: Now, I don't want any rowing.
    ETHEL: No.
    MRS HUGHES: Dignity at all times.
    ETHEL: Yes.
    MRS HUGHES: I don't know why you're doing this.

ETHEL: Because I want them to see once and for all that I know my own mind. That I'm not nobody. It's important.
MRS HUGHES: Well, let's get on with it.

77   EXT.   MASON'S FARM.   DAY.

Green fields surround the peaceful farmhouse. Daisy approaches.

78   EXT.   WOODLAND.   DOWNTON.   DAY.

Thomas is fighting his way through briar and tare.

THOMAS: Isis! Good dog! Isis! Good girl.

He trips and falls into the mud.

THOMAS (CONT'D): Oh, for God's sake! Will you just bloody come, you stupid dog!

79   INT.   KITCHEN.   MASON'S FARM.   DAY.

Mason and Daisy sit at a groaning table.

DAISY: You shouldn't have gone to all this trouble. Not for me.
MASON: No? Not when you're the nearest thing to a child of mine left on earth?
DAISY: But I don't deserve it. Not when I were only married to William for a few hours. You were there. You saw it.
MASON: You may not know this, Daisy, but William had three brothers and a sister.*
DAISY: What?
MASON: All dead. At birth or not long after. I think that's one reason why William married you. So that I wouldn't be alone with all my bairns gone. Without you, I'd have no one to pray for. I think William knew that.
DAISY: Oh.

....

* We knew William was an only child, but we did not know what we learn here, that he was the sole survivor of his parents' children. Which was bad luck, but not extraordinary for that time. So maybe Mason is right and it was always William's plan that his father should adopt Daisy, at least in his heart.

MASON: So, will you be my daughter? Let me take you into
my heart, make you special? You'll have parents of your
own, of course —
DAISY: I haven't got any parents, not like that. I've
never been special to anyone.
MASON: Except William.
DAISY: That's right. I were only ever special to
William. I never thought of it like that before.
MASON: Well, now you're special to me.

80 INT. DRAWING ROOM. DOWNTON. DAY.

Mrs Hughes, Ethel and little Charlie step into a fairyland.
There is a rocking horse and soldiers and a castle and a
little pedal car and a hoop and a bicycle and sweets and…
Mr and Mrs Bryant standing at the centre of it all. Ethel is
dumbstruck, as little Charlie stumbles over to the horse.

MR BRYANT: Would you like to ride it, Charlie?

We have never seen him smile before, but now he does as he
lifts the boy and holds him on the horse. Mrs Bryant comes
over.

MRS BRYANT: Thank you for letting us come.
ETHEL: I'm only here to say that…

She tails off. Her child is playing with a teddy bear now,
which Mr Bryant manipulates to walk towards him. Charlie is
laughing and rolling about as he plays with the toys.

MR BRYANT: What did you want to say? Did you want to
tell us about the childhood he's having with you? Or
shall we talk about the one he could have with us?
MRS HUGHES: Mr Bryant, I don't think this is fair, to
Ethel or the boy —
MR BRYANT: Why is that? Because she's sure she wants to
take all this away from him? Is that why it's not fair?

Ethel is standing, dumb with misery.

MRS HUGHES: Come on. Tell them what you came to tell
them… Ethel will not be cowed by your bullying,
Mr Bryant, and no more will I.
MR BRYANT: Is she right, Ethel? Will you really prevent
the boy from enjoying his good fortune, to prove a point?

Held by Bryant, Charlie squeals with laughter as a giant jack-in-the-box jumps out at him. Ethel looks over at her happy little son and the happy man playing with him, so unlike the bully we have seen until now.

ETHEL: You're buying him really, aren't you? That's what it comes down to.

For the first time, Bryant's tone is almost gentle.

MR BRYANT: No. We're not buying him. We're showing you what he could have. What he could be.

But he longs to get back to playing with the boy, playing with the toys, being a father again.

MRS BRYANT: My dear, I know you only want the best for him. Like every mother.

Ethel stands there, tears pouring down her cheeks, looking at her son playing with this loving grandfather who can give the boy everything. She nods. She has made the decision.

81 EXT. DOWNTON. DAY.

Thomas, his clothes torn, covered in mud, almost staggers towards the house. Suddenly, the dog Isis bounds out at him.

THOMAS: Isis? Where have you bloody been, eh?

But Robert has come round the corner, after the dog.

ROBERT: What in God's name happened to you?
THOMAS: I've been looking for the dog.
ROBERT: A village child found her yesterday. Somehow the silly animal had got herself shut into one of the keepers' shelters. They took her back and claimed their reward this morning.
THOMAS: Oh… Well, that's good.

Robert is staring at Thomas.

ROBERT: Did you really get yourself into this mess looking for my dog?
THOMAS: I know how fond of her you are.
ROBERT: I'm impressed, Thomas. It's good to know there's some decency in the world at a time like this. Thank you.

THOMAS: That's all right, m'lord. The main thing is she's home and healthy.

Robert is completely revising his view of the man.*

82 EXT. DOWNTON. DAY.

The men have finished loading the last toys into the van. We glimpse the rocking horse. The Bryants' car is waiting there, too. The van drives off as the Bryants, Mrs Hughes and Ethel come outside. Mr Bryant has Charlie by the hand.

MRS BRYANT: Won't you say goodbye to the nice lady, Charlie?

Ethel kneels and kisses her son for the last time.

ETHEL: I give you my blessings for your whole life long, my darling boy. You won't remember that, or me, but they'll stay with you all the same.
MR BRYANT: Let's not make a meal of it.

After all, he is still the same man. Ethel stands and moves back.

MRS BRYANT: You go on, dear, and settle him in.

Mr Bryant takes the boy over to the car and they climb in. The motor starts. During this, Mrs Bryant turns to Ethel.

MRS BRYANT (CONT'D): I'll write to you. Make sure Mrs Hughes always has your address.
ETHEL: But he said —
MRS BRYANT: A little judicious disobedience is a key part of marriage, as I hope you find out, my dear. Write to me, too, if you wish. I always get to the post before he does.
ETHEL: But I can't see him, can I? He'll never let me see my Charlie again.

....

* The irony of this story is that Thomas's going to look for the dog changes Robert's opinion of him, when in fact he set the whole thing up, meaning to work it differently.

MRS BRYANT: Never is a long time, Ethel. Too long for me
to second guess… And we will love him, you know. Not
just for his father's sake, but for his own. So,
goodbye, my dear, and you, Mrs Hughes, and thank you.

*She joins the others in the car, which drives away, watched
by the two women.*

MRS HUGHES: You've done a hard thing, today, Ethel. The
hardest thing of all, but I think it was right.
ETHEL: Was it?
MRS HUGHES: You know it was. Until we live in a very
different world from this one. And you're young. You'll
find work. You'll have a future.

Ethel looks up at the house behind them.

ETHEL: I won't be working here, though, will I? I'm not
good enough for Downton Abbey. I'm a sinner now and I
mustn't contaminate the other maids.

The housekeeper looks at her and shakes her head.

MRS HUGHES: Ethel, Ethel… Why do you always have to push
your luck?

Still shaking her head, she goes back inside.

83   EXT.   MASON'S FARM.   DAY.

Mason is putting some fruit and flowers into a trap.

DAISY: I could walk to the station. I walked here, after
all.
MASON: I want to talk while we go.

Daisy seems to know what this will be about.

MASON (CONT'D): If you're my daughter, you must allow me
to give you advice.
DAISY: I s'pose.
MASON: Well, then, if you're not content with the way
you're treated, don't sulk and answer back. Tell them.
DAISY: They wouldn't listen.
MASON: You don't know. You haven't given them the
chance. Go to Mrs Patmore, and explain to her why you
think you're worth more than you're getting. Make your
case and put it to her.

DAISY: But Miss Shore says —
MASON: Daisy, do me a favour and stop listening to that
Miss Shore.

With that, he shakes the reins and the horse moves off. *

84   INT.   STAIRCASE/PASSAGE.   DOWNTON.   NIGHT.

*Lord Hepworth is climbing the stairs when he sees Rosamund
coming down.   He's in travelling clothes, she in evening
dress.*

ROSAMUND: Are you here?   Nobody told me.
HEPWORTH: Only just.   The train was late.   I'll have to
scramble to get changed.
ROSAMUND: I'm afraid it may be a rather gloomy visit.   No
news yet for the poor valet, I'm afraid, so the Servants'
Ball has been cancelled.
HEPWORTH: Never mind.   I'm very flattered to be asked
back on any terms.   I hope I can read something into it.
ROSAMUND: Only my desire not to lose my maid.   Shore
wouldn't stop nagging me until you were invited.   You owe
her a tip.   But I mustn't delay you.

She walks on down the staircase. †

85   INT.   MARY'S BEDROOM.   DOWNTON.   NIGHT.

Mary is dressed for dinner.   Anna puts on her shoes.

ANNA: What will you do in America?
MARY: What I do here?   Pay calls and go to dinners.   My
grandmother has houses in New York and Newport.   It'll be
dull, but not uncomfortable.

....

* In a sense, Mason is my voice in this exchange in that I agree with him that
deliberately encouraging people to feel a grudge is incredibly negative. Like
him, I believe that if you've got a legitimate complaint, then don't sulk. Just
complain to the right person.

† Hepworth's coming back is a little bit of a cheat. Would he really return to
Yorkshire for a Servants' Ball? But on the other hand, wouldn't he come back
for anything he was asked to, if he felt it was promoting his cause with
Rosamund?

ANNA: M'lady, I've been thinking... If things go badly for us... I thought I might come with you.

MARY: You mean you won't leave, after all?

ANNA: I have to leave Downton, but I don't have to leave you.

MARY: But of course you can come with me. You don't need to ask... But let's not give up hope yet.

ANNA: No, m'lady. Let's not do that.

She works on. She wants to change the subject.

86 INT. ROBERT'S DRESSING ROOM. DOWNTON. NIGHT.

Carson is dressing Robert.

CARSON: Sir Richard and Lord Hepworth are here. Their train was late.

ROBERT: I don't know what they've come for.

CARSON: You mean we won't be holding the Servants' Ball, m'lord?

ROBERT: Of course not.

He glances at himself in the glass.

ROBERT (CONT'D): I'm not sure Sir Richard will be staying after tomorrow, anyway.

He looks at Carson, almost reluctant to speak.

CARSON: M'lord?

ROBERT: I was only going to say that... if I do need a new valet, I think I'd like to give Thomas a trial.

CARSON: Really, m'lord?

ROBERT: I think I've misjudged him. There's more true kindness in him than I'd given credit for.

CARSON: Is there?

ROBERT: I think so. At any rate, let's give him a chance. Everyone deserves a chance. Even Thomas.

But he is sad.

87 INT. MARY'S BEDROOM. DOWNTON. NIGHT.

ANNA: So Sir Richard's back?

MARY: I haven't seen him yet. He and Lord Hepworth only just arrived in time to change.

ANNA: Are you ready?

MARY: I think so. I'll ask him to meet me in the boudoir after dinner. I know what I have to say to him. It's time.*

88 INT. OUTER HALL. DOWNTON. NIGHT.

Thomas has taken coats from Isobel and Matthew. He leaves.

ISOBEL: I wish you'd take my advice and fight for her, but I know you won't.
MATTHEW: I don't expect you to understand.
ISOBEL: Well, that's good, because I can't. And please don't invoke the name of that sweet, dead girl again.

She leads the way on through.

89 INT. MRS HUGHES'S SITTING ROOM. DOWNTON.
NIGHT.

Mrs Hughes is with Anna.

ANNA: I've always wanted to see America. So at least I've got a plan.
MRS HUGHES: I suppose so. I still can't be glad you'll be leaving here. But it's good news that you won't be casting off entirely.
ANNA: It's only if…

She cannot finish the sentence.

MRS HUGHES: I know.

She is on the edge of tears herself.

MRS HUGHES (CONT'D): Just so's you know, you're highly valued by all of us. Both of you. Very highly valued.

She takes the sobbing Anna into her arms and holds her.

....

* By this stage of an episode you are wrapping everything up, and the audience is aware that they've got several pay-offs to come. What's really going to happen to Bates? Because they can't believe he's actually going to hang. When is Mary going to fire Carlisle? Because they know by now she's not going to marry him. When is Rosamund going to find out about Hepworth? And so on. You encourage them in a sense of expectation.

90 INT. BOUDOIR. DOWNTON. NIGHT.

Carlisle is with Mary. He is furious.

CARLISLE: By God, Mary. What more could I have done?

MARY: Nothing. But you must see we're not well suited.
We'd never be happy.

CARLISLE: You won't be happy by the time I'm finished!
I promise you that!

MARY: Of course I'm grateful —

CARLISLE: So you should be! I buy your filthy scandal,
I keep it safe from prying eyes! And why did the papers
leave you alone over Bates? Why has there been nothing
linking him to the great Earl of Grantham? Tell me!

MARY: I suppose you stopped it.

CARLISLE: With threats, bribes, calling in favours, yes,
I stopped it!

MARY: Papa will be so thankful.

CARLISLE: You don't think it holds now, do you? You
don't think I'll save you or him for one more day?

MARY: And you wonder why we wouldn't make each other
happy?

Carlisle's shouting has covered the opening door.

MATTHEW: Mary? Are you quite all right?

CARLISLE: Oh, here he is. The man who can smile and
smile and be a villain! Is she not to be trusted even to
get rid of me without your help?

Matthew ignores him and speaks only to Mary.

MATTHEW: I heard shouting —

CARLISLE: Lavinia knew it, you know. She knew you never
loved her.

Now Matthew turns to him, enraged.

MATTHEW: Don't you dare —

CARLISLE: Oh, she said it once. It was late and she was
tired. You two were locked together in the corner of the
room and she said: 'If he could just admit the truth,
then all four of us might have a chance.'

MATTHEW: You liar!

CARLISLE: I'm not a liar. No, I am many things, but not
that. She regretted it, of course, but she said it.

MATTHEW: You bastard!

He takes a swing at Carlisle, who fights back, sending Matthew into a table, shattering a vase. The door flies open.

ROBERT: Stop this at once!

The dishevelled pair do stop and stand there awkwardly.*

ROBERT (CONT'D): I think we should all go to bed. I presume you will be leaving in the morning, Sir Richard. What time shall I order your car?

Carlisle comes up to him.

CARLISLE: How smooth you are. What a model of manners and elegance. I wonder if you will be quite so serene when the papers are full of your eldest daughter's exploits.
ROBERT: I shall do my best.

Violet appears in the doorway.

VIOLET: What on earth's the matter?
CARLISLE: I'm leaving in the morning, Lady Grantham. I doubt we'll meet again.
VIOLET: Do you promise?

Carlisle flounces off. Robert looks at Matthew.

ROBERT: I'm afraid you may have found his reference to Mary puzzling.
MATTHEW: No. She's told me all about it.
ROBERT: Then I'm glad you can still fight for her honour. I am not surprised, but I am glad. Thank you.
MATTHEW: Sorry about the vase.
VIOLET: Oh, don't be, don't be. It was a wedding present from a frightful aunt. I have hated it for half a century.

END OF ACT SIX

....

* Matthew has obviously been listening outside the door, in my head anyway. He's heard the shouting and he's come in to find out what's going on, and at last we have this very satisfactory fight between the two men, which we've been waiting for and longing for. What I liked about the fight was that both men really had a go. It became undignified and silly, in the way that fighting is always undignified and silly, and somehow that made it very real.

ACT SEVEN

91 INT. KITCHEN. DOWNTON. DAY.

Daisy, in her coat and hat, is with Mrs Patmore.

MRS PATMORE: Here's a cake to give to Mr Mason. And
enjoy your day off. You'll be working hard when you get
back.
SHORE: In other words, business as usual.

She stands there with a tray of breakfast.

MRS PATMORE: Don't you start spreading the slime of
discontent.
SHORE: If she's discontent, it's not my fault.
MRS PATMORE: Are you, Daisy? Is that what this is about?
Are you unhappy here?
DAISY: I'd best be going.

92 EXT. DOWNTON. DAY.

The car is being loaded by Carlisle's valet.

93 INT. HALL. DOWNTON. DAY.

*Carlisle, dressed for travel, is leaving. Mary appears,
hurrying down the staircase.**

MARY: Wait!
CARLISLE: After last night's exhibition, I rather hoped
to escape unobserved.
MARY: I didn't want you to go without saying goodbye.

....

* I was keen to have this moment. I didn't wish to say goodbye to Carlisle in
the library when he's lying on the floor, looking dishevelled and ridiculous.
We owed him, and Iain Glen who played him, more than that. And for me,
what he says in this scene is true. I am quite sure that Carlisle loved Mary
much more than she loved him. In fact, I suspect they would have done
pretty well together if Matthew had never existed. For this reason, and for so
many others, we were very lucky to get Iain Glen. He had the confidence not
to shrink from the hard side of the character, but he never entirely lost your
sympathy. At any rate, he never lost mine. I thought he got the whole
characterisation absolutely spot on.

CARLISLE: Well then, goodbye.

MARY: I suppose you feel I've used you, and I'm sorry if I have. I'm sorry about Haxby, about all of it.

CARLISLE: I assume this is a plea to stay my hand from punishment. But I warn you, I'd feel no guilt in exposing you. My job is to sell newspapers.

MARY: Papa has suggested I go to New York to wait it out, so I'll be all right. I just didn't want our final words to be angry ones.

He looks at her and now he is almost tender.

CARLISLE: I loved you, you know. More than you knew, and much, much more than you loved me.

MARY: Then I hope the next woman you love deserves you more than I did.

Carlisle starts towards the door.

CARLISLE: And don't worry about Haxby. I'll sell it at a profit. I usually do.

94   EXT. DOWNTON. DAY.

Carlisle emerges. He looks at this great house he will never visit again. Then he sets his face and climbs into the car.

95   INT. BEDROOM PASSAGE. DOWNTON. DAY.

Anna is walking along when she hears giggling. She rounds the corner and Shore is standing with Hepworth. They break apart and Shore joins Anna.

SHORE: He's still on at me. To press his case with the mistress.

ANNA: He's very tenacious, I must say.

SHORE: You know men.

She walks on through the door to the service staircase.

ANNA: And I know women, too…

96   EXT. DOWNTON. DAY.

A man is bicycling towards the house.

97   INT.   HALL/DRAWING ROOM.   DOWNTON.   DAY.

Carson is running towards the library.

98   INT.   LIBRARY.   DOWNTON.   DAY.

Carson bursts into the room.   Robert and Cora are working.

> CARSON: M'lord! M'lord!
> ROBERT: What in heaven's name —?
> CARSON: A telegram, m'lord.

Robert stands. He hesitates, looking at his wife.

> CORA: Open it.

He does so, scans it and looks up.

> ROBERT: Thank God. He's been reprieved. It's life
> imprisonment, but he's been reprieved.
> CORA: Go and fetch Anna.

99   INT.   LIBRARY.   DOWNTON.   DAY.

Anna is there, with Cora, Mary, Edith, Carson and Mrs Hughes.

> ROBERT: The Home Secretary finds that many details call
> into question the case for premeditation… The point is,
> he will not hang.
> ANNA: But it's still life imprisonment.*
> MARY: Don't dwell on that. Not now. It's life, not
> death. That's all we need to think about.
> ROBERT: We've a task ahead of us, it's true, but we won't
> be rescuing the reputation of a corpse. Bates will live
> and he is innocent. In time, we'll prove it and he will
> be free.
> ANNA: I must go and see him. Today. They'll let me,
> won't they?
> ROBERT: I can't believe they won't. I'll get Pratt to
> run you into York.

....

* Anna has slightly more mixed feelings about this result than the others, because her husband is facing the prospect of life imprisonment. To the *Downton* audience, that means we're going to have to prove that he didn't do it, and they are probably confident that we will manage it, but Anna doesn't have the advantage of being a television viewer. She can only see that Bates is being locked up for a crime that she, at least, is certain he did not commit.

CORA: I hope this means you can hold the Servants' Ball
after all?
CARSON: Anna?
ANNA: Of course you can. And I'll be back for it.
That's if you can get it ready in half a day.
MRS HUGHES: Just you watch us.

100   INT.   SERVANTS' HALL.   DOWNTON.   DAY.

Carson is addressing the servants.

CARSON: So that is the news. It only remains for me to
add that we will be holding the Servants' Ball tonight
after all.
THOMAS: Tonight? Are you serious?
CARSON: Mrs Hughes thinks we can manage it.

There is a good deal of relief and happiness at this.

MRS PATMORE: I never thought they'd hang an innocent man.
SHORE: He wouldn't have been the first.
O'BRIEN: Well, it's a relief. It is. I don't mind
saying it.
MRS PATMORE: But he has to stay in prison?
CARSON: Only until they prove he didn't do it.
MRS HUGHES: If you don't mind, we can worry about that
later. Right now, we have a great deal of work to do.
MRS PATMORE: And it would be on Daisy's day off.

101   INT.   YORK PRISON.   DAY.

Bates is with Anna.

ANNA: His lordship means to work with Mr Murray.
BATES: Will you stay at Downton now?
ANNA: Of course. I'm sorry to let Lady Mary down, but I
think I should. There may be some way I can help them to
overturn the conviction. I don't know what I can do, but
there may be something.
BATES: I don't deserve you.
ANNA: Because we will overturn it. I won't rest until we
have you out.
BATES: But it may take years. That's if you ever manage
it. So there's one thing I must ask.

She waits.

BATES (CONT'D): I can't have you grey-faced and in perpetual mourning. Promise me you'll make friends, have fun, live life. I need to know I'm not a drag weight. Tell me you can laugh while I'm in here.

He means it, and she answers seriously.

ANNA: I'll try. I promise.

102 INT. HALL. DOWNTON. NIGHT.

The hall is decorated for a party. A buffet of food and drink runs down one side and a small village band is tuning up.

103 INT. SERVANTS' HALL. DOWNTON. DAY.

Most of the servants, spruced up in their best, are getting ready to go up. Thomas, dressed as a valet, is with O'Brien.

THOMAS: No. I'm getting his rhythm now. I think we'll do well together.
O'BRIEN: As long as you can keep your fingers out of his cufflink box.

Anna comes in. She has taken off her apron but, unlike the others, she is in her black dress with her heart brooch.

O'BRIEN (CONT'D): Are you not coming up?
ANNA: Yes, I am. And don't worry. I'm not going to be a misery guts. I am a working woman and my husband is away. That's how I see it, and I'd be grateful if you'd all look at it like I do.
MRS HUGHES: Well, let's hope he won't be away for long.

104 INT. LIBRARY. DOWNTON. NIGHT.

Matthew comes in and finds Robert. They are in white tie.

ROBERT: Can I give you some whisky to fortify you for the coming ordeal?*

....

* I had a letter from America that interested me. It was about the snobbery in the show that was apparently demonstrated in this scene. The writer felt that Robert and Matthew should have been joyous and glad to dance with their servants, rather than dreading it. Personally, I felt that this member of the audience was missing the point. We present the family as nice people,

MATTHEW: That's very kind. Is there anyone I should
dance with, particularly?
ROBERT: Well, Cora opens it with Carson —
MATTHEW: Not Cousin Violet?
ROBERT: Not since my father died. No, Mama ought to
dance with my valet, but we let it lapse while Bates was
here. Perhaps Thomas will revive the privilege.
MATTHEW: He's certainly got the nerve.
ROBERT: Then I join in with Mrs Hughes. So perhaps it
would be nice if you were to partner O'Brien.
MATTHEW: Crikey.
ROBERT: By the way, Mary told me about Mr Swire.
I'm sorry to hear it.
MATTHEW: At least I was with him, and we'd made our
peace. I didn't deserve it. I let Lavinia down.

....

Continued from page 573:

and there are also nice people downstairs. Nevertheless, this was a working
house and the employees' job was to make the family comfortable. They are
not equal, and it is not a love-in. It was a way of life, an unjust one in many
ways, but populated here by men and women who are trying to do their best.
That doesn't make any of them saints.

In fact, I always try to drop in 'truth reminders', so Mrs Hughes will say
'Daisy says…' and Cora will ask 'Who is Daisy?' and you're reminded of the
fact that the family probably doesn't know what the kitchen maid's name is.
In just the same way, the Servants' Ball would have been a bit of a trial. Not a
horrible trial, and they're fine about it, but it is not the evening of choice for
most of the Crawleys. I felt that tone would strike a truthful note, as opposed
to a sentimental one. But I also had to face various shrieks in the papers that
such a thing, the mixing of the family and the servants at a social gathering,
would never have happened, when in fact the Servants' Ball was an annual
fixture in the vast majority of great houses, and remained so for long after
this date. There is a wonderful description of the Servants' Ball at Welbeck
where the butler leads off the dancing with the Duchess of Portland, while
the Duke partners the housekeeper, all described by one of the maids who
kept a diary. The point is, it was absolutely standard.

They filmed the party terribly well, with the intercutting of all the
different participants dancing and watching and having fun. I allowed
myself a slightly vulgar joke for Violet, when Thomas asks about the black
bottom: 'Just keep me upright and we'll try to avoid it.'

ROBERT: You were ready to marry her, Matthew. You would have kept your word. You can't be blamed for feelings beyond your control.

This makes Matthew look at him. Robert understands.

ROBERT (CONT'D): If Swire had any inkling of that, he would have respected you for it.

Cora enters.

CORA: Glug those drinks down, both of you. We have to go in.

105 INT. HALL. DOWNTON. NIGHT.

Carson is steering Cora through a stately waltz. Robert dances with Mrs Hughes. Matthew partners O'Brien. At the side, Mary stands with Violet.

VIOLET: I gather Anna isn't going to America.
MARY: No. But of course I'm glad for her.

They see Thomas coming towards them.

MARY (CONT'D): Uh-oh. Here he comes. To claim his prize.

Thomas has arrived. He gives a slight bow to Violet.

THOMAS: Your ladyship, may I have the honour of this dance?
VIOLET: Well, yes, as it is a waltz. I'm far too old for that awful foxtrot.
THOMAS: What about the black bottom, m'lady?
VIOLET: Just keep me upright and we'll try to avoid it.

In a corner of the hall, Anna hears voices.

HEPWORTH (V.O.): Come on, Marigold! They'll never notice we've gone!
SHORE (V.O.): You'll be the death of me.

She glances at the secondary staircase to see them hurrying up it. Back in the hall, Daisy and Mrs Patmore are talking.

MRS PATMORE: Daisy, I'm having trouble understanding what you mean. So, are you saying you want to leave?

DAISY: No. I don't want to leave unless I have to. But I want to move on. I think I'm more than a kitchen maid now. I want to be a proper assistant cook. I know I can be.

MRS PATMORE: Well, I've no objection, if the budget stretches to it. I'll have to ask Mrs Hughes and her ladyship.

DAISY: I'll work for it. I promise.

MRS PATMORE: Why couldn't you have spoken of this sensibly the other night, instead of going off into a pet?

DAISY: Because I took the wrong advice.*

106 INT. BEDROOM PASSAGE/HEPWORTH'S BEDROOM. DOWNTON. NIGHT.

Mary, Rosamund and Anna are walking along.

ROSAMUND: I hope this isn't a practical joke.

MARY: It is a joke in a way, I'm afraid.

They have stopped outside a door. Mary nods and Anna throws it open. Inside, Hepworth and Shore are in bed together. For a moment, he is frozen, but only for a moment.

HEPWORTH: My dear, this is — isn't what it seems.

ROSAMUND: Is there room for misinterpretation?

HEPWORTH: But I can promise —

ROSAMUND: Clearly, I have been managed and steered by an expert hand, which I now see has not been yours.

HEPWORTH: But Rosamund —

SHORE: Let her go. It's over. Don't make yourself ridiculous.

ROSAMUND: Good advice. Why not marry her? She'll more than cover any social flaws with her resourcefulness.

SHORE: Isn't that what I'm always saying, you silly old whatnot?

MARY: There are no more trains tonight, so you'll have to leave first thing.

SHORE: Oh, don't worry. We will.

The others go and shut the door behind them.

....

* That is, she listened to Shore instead of Mr Mason.

ROSAMUND: Please forgive me, but — damn!

MARY: Why? It's a lucky escape, if you ask me.

ROSAMUND: That's true, of course. I just can't stand it when Mama is proved right!*

107 INT. HALL. DOWNTON. NIGHT.

Anna comes down with the others to find Robert in the hall.

ANNA: Your lordship, may I have a word?

ROBERT: Of course. How was Bates?

ANNA: Relieved, shocked, tired, grateful.

ROBERT: I'm sure.

She goes to him.

ANNA: M'lord, I wonder if I might withdraw my resignation.

Robert is wreathed in smiles.

ROBERT: I was hoping you'd say that.

ANNA: Because we've a fight on our hands now. And I think I should be here. So we can fight it together.

ROBERT: I quite agree. Have you discussed it with Bates?

ANNA: I have, m'lord.

ROBERT: And?

ANNA: He wants me to stay.

ROBERT: Then who are we to disagree?

Matthew and Mary are on the edge of the dance floor.

MATTHEW: What about it?

MARY: Why not?

They start to waltz.

MATTHEW: How are your plans for America going?

MARY: I'll book my crossing as soon as I hear back from Grandmama.

MATTHEW: Will you be gone long?

MARY: I don't know. I'll have to see…

....

* I'm sad, actually, about the departure of Hepworth, which is probably final. I thought Nigel Havers made a very good job of him. Nobody could have done it better.

108 INT. LIBRARY. DOWNTON. NIGHT.

Robert comes in to find Cora on her own.

> CORA: Do you think we can go to bed?
> ROBERT: I expect so. I think we've done our duty.
> Mama's gone home and so has Isobel.
> CORA: And the girls?
> ROBERT: I think Edith's upstairs, and the last time I
> looked Mary was dancing with Matthew.
> CORA: Don't let's interfere with that.

Robert pours himself a drink from a decanter on a tray.

> CORA (CONT'D): I've written to Sybil. I sent her your
> love.

He accepts this, but he does not comment.

> CORA (CONT'D): I won't be kept away from my first
> grandchild, Robert.
> ROBERT: I don't know what you mean. I didn't quarrel
> with her. I gave my permission. I didn't fight it.
> CORA: But you wouldn't go to the wedding.
> ROBERT: No.
> CORA: It isn't what I wanted for her. None of it is.
> But this is what's happened, and we must accept it.

He sips his drink, looking at her.

> CORA (CONT'D): I want to go over there. And I want Sybil
> to come here.
> ROBERT: And the chauffeur?
> CORA: Him, too.

She walks over to him. He stares at her. Then he sighs.

> CORA (CONT'D): It's been a happy day, Robert. Let's end
> on a happy note.

*He puts his arm around her shoulder, which is a surrender.**

....

* Of course, here we're setting up the next series. There's a certain amount of streamers you throw out to trail the stories of the following year. Basically, you're saying to the public, we won't resolve this tonight, but if you keep watching, at some point we will. Or we'll try to.

109 INT. SERVANTS' HALL. DOWNTON. NIGHT.

Daisy comes in. O'Brien is there with the planchette board.

O'BRIEN: Tired, already?
DAISY: A bit. I was thinking about William. He always loved the ball.

There is the sound of a bell. Anna arrives.

ANNA: Miss O'Brien. Her ladyship's ready for bed.

O'Brien stands and leaves. Daisy sits idly before the board.

DAISY: I'm ever so glad Mr Bates is going to be all right.
ANNA: Well, he's alive. I think we're quite a way from 'all right'.

But she smiles as she says it.

ANNA (CONT'D): Go on.

They have both idly put their fingers on the glass and now it begins to move.

ANNA (CONT'D): Are you pushing it?
DAISY: No. Are you?

But it starts to fly towards one letter after another:
M. A. Y. T. H. E. Y. B. E. H. A. P. P. Y.

DAISY (CONT'D): That doesn't make sense.
ANNA: Yes, it does. May they be happy.

W. I. T. H. M. Y. L. O. V. E.

ANNA (CONT'D): With my love.
DAISY: What does that mean?
ANNA: I don't know. I suppose the spirit wants some couple to be happy.
DAISY: You were moving it.
ANNA: No, I wasn't. You were.*

....

* I was rather attacked at the time for actually allowing a spirit to speak through a planchette board. I don't really have any argument against the criticism, except to point out that it was Christmas, and stranger things happen at sea.

110 EXT. DOWNTON. NIGHT.

Matthew and Mary are alone.

MATTHEW: That was fun. There'll be a few thick heads in the morning.

MARY: No doubt they think it's worth it.

But Matthew has something more than this on his mind.

MATTHEW: So you're really going to America? Would Carlisle make your life a nightmare if you stayed?

MARY: I couldn't tell you. Maybe. Even if he does let me go, my story's still out there and always will be.

MATTHEW: Would you stay? If I asked you to?

MARY: Oh, Matthew. You don't mean that. You know yourself we carry more luggage than the porters at King's Cross. And what about the late Mr Pamuk? Won't he resurrect himself every time we argued?

MATTHEW: No.

MARY: You mean you've forgiven me?

MATTHEW: No. I haven't forgiven you.

MARY: Well, then.

MATTHEW: I haven't forgiven you because I don't believe you need my forgiveness. You've lived your life and I've lived mine. And now it's time we lived them together.

This speech does change things for her, but...

MARY: We've been on the edge of this so many times, Matthew. Please don't take me there again, unless you're sure.

MATTHEW: I am sure.

MARY: And your vows to the memory of Lavinia?

MATTHEW: I was wrong. I — I don't think she wants us to be sad. She was someone who never caused a moment's sorrow in her whole life.

MARY: I agree.

MATTHEW: Then will you?

MARY: You must say it properly. I won't answer unless you kneel down and everything.

Which he does.

MATTHEW: Lady Mary Crawley, will you do me the honour of becoming my wife?

MARY: How can you ask?

```
He stands and kisses her and they remain held in a tight
embrace as the camera sweeps up and away from them.*
```

THE END

....

* As we reach this blessed event, we should take a second to consider what they have been through since they met, these two, seven and a half years before. Any writer or producer of a series always dreads allowing lovers finally to come together, because once they have, there's very little left you can do with them in terms of narrative, other than making them unhappy about something else. So you keep them apart and keep them apart, but it's my belief that there comes a time when the audience thinks, oh, for Christ's sake, are they going to get together or not? I felt we had reached it, and that to spin it out any more would be wrong. Once that decision had been arrived at, naturally we wanted to make the proposal as big a moment as we possibly could.

I originally gave Mary a longer response to Matthew's proposal than the one Michelle Dockery chose to say. She answers simply 'Yes!' But perhaps she was right and the moment called for sincerity, not wit.

One thing that annoyed Gareth Neame, our producer, about the scene was that, for some reason, they had chosen to send Mary outside without a coat, even though we had snowflakes swirling all around her. So in a scene in the fourth series we have her remembering the proposal and saying: 'I was standing outside in the snow and I didn't have a coat, but I wasn't cold, because all I kept thinking was: he's going to propose,' which solves it for me. Anyway, the point is, we got there, and to mark the moment we thought we'd have the snow and the moon and the stars and the music and everything. And Matthew going down on his knees. I copied this from someone I knew who told her fiancé: 'No, you must do it properly, you must get down on your knees.' I agree with her. Men who try to get out of it by muttering, 'You know what I'm going to say,' just aren't playing cricket.

CAST LIST

Robert Bathurst	Sir Anthony Strallan
Samantha Bond	Lady Rosamund Painswick
Hugh Bonneville	Robert, Earl of Grantham
Zoe Boyle	Lavinia Swire
Jessica Brown Findlay	Lady Sybil Crawley
Michael Cochrane	Reverend Mr Travis
Paul Copley	Mr Mason
Clare Calbraith	Jane Moorsum
Timothy Carlton	Judge
Laura Carmichael	Lady Edith Crawley
Jim Carter	Mr Carson
Jeremy Clyde	General
Jonathan Coy	George Murray
Brendan Coyle	Mr Bates
Michelle Dockery	Lady Mary Crawley
Kevin Doyle	Mr Molesley
Maria Doyle Kennedy	Vera Bates
Tom Feary-Campbell	Captain Smiley
Siobhan Finneran	Miss O'Brien
Joanne Froggatt	Anna Smith
Iain Glen	Sir Richard Carlisle
Howard Gossington	Veteran
Richard Hansell	Medical Officer
Nigel Havers	Lord Hepworth
Thomas Howes	William Mason
Rob James-Collier	Thomas Barrow
Dominic Kemp	Jury Foreman
Allen Leech	Tom Branson
Phyllis Logan	Mrs Hughes
Christine Lohr	Mrs Bird
Cal MacAninch	Mr Lang

Christine Mackie	Mrs Bryant
Elizabeth McGovern	Cora, Countess of Grantham
Kevin R. McNally	Mr Bryant
Peter McNeil O'Connor	Sergeant Stevens
Sophie McShera	Daisy Robinson
Lesley Nicol	Mrs Patmore
Lachlan Nieboer	Edward Courtenay
Amy Nuttall	Ethel Parks
Fergus O'Donnell	Mr Drake
Stephen Omer	Registrar
Graham Padden	Army Doctor
Daniel Pirrie	Major Bryant
Simon Poland	Defence Lawyer
Tony Pritchard	Prison Warder
David Robb	Doctor Clarkson
Nick Sampson	Prosecution Lawyer
Cathy Sara	Mrs Drake
Anton Saunders	Police Officer
Sharon Small	Marigold Shore
Maggie Smith	Violet, Dowager Countess of Grantham
Dan Stevens	Matthew Crawley
Stephen Ventura	Davis
Julian Wadham	General Sir Herbert Strutt
Trevor White	Major Gordon
Penelope Wilton	Isobel Crawley

PRODUCTION CREDITS

Writer & Creator	Julian Fellowes
Executive Producers	Gareth Neame
	Julian Fellowes
Series Producer	Liz Trubridge
Director (Episodes 1 & 2)	Ashley Pearce
Director (Episodes 3 & 6)	Andy Goddard
Director (Episodes 4 & 5)	Brian Kelly
Director (Episodes 7 & 8)	James Strong
Director (Christmas Special)	Brian Percival
Production Designer	Donal Woods
Directors of Photography	Gavin Struthers
	David Marsh
	Nigel Willoughby
Editors	John Wilson A.C.E
	Steve Singleton
	Mike Jones
Costume Designers	Susannah Buxton
	Rosalind Ebbutt
Make-up & Hair Designer	Anne 'Nosh' Oldham
Casting Director	Jill Trevellick C.D.G
Music	John Lunn
First Assistant Directors	Phil Booth
	Howard Arundel
	Tim Riddington
Second Assistant Directors	Chris Croucher
	Sarah Hood
Third Assistant Directors	Danielle Bennett
	Tamara King
Script Supervisors	Sarah Garner
	Vicki Howe
Location Manager	Jason Wheeler

Assistant Location Manager	Mark 'Sparky' Ellis
Unit Managers	John Prendergast
	James Lucas
Line Producer	Charles Hubbard
Production Accountant	Denis Wray
Production Co-ordinator	Jonathan Houston
Assistant Production Co-ordinator	Oliver Cockerham
Assistant Accountant	Matthew Lawson
Camera Operators/Steadicam	Richard Stoddard
	Adam Gillham
Focus Pullers	Dean Thompson
	Scott Rodgers
	David Hedges
Clapper Loaders	Milos Moore
	Joanne Smith
Grips	Simon Fogg
	Bobby Williams
	David Littlejohns
	Paul Hatchman
Gaffer	Phil Brookes
Best Boy	David Staton
Supervising Art Director	Charmian Adams
Art Director	Mark Kebby
Production Buyer	Corina Floyd
Set Decorator	Judy Farr
Standby Art Director	Pippa Broadhurst
Assistant Art Director	Lucy Spofforth
Art Department Assistant	Chantelle Valentine
Sound Mixer	Chris Ashworth
Prop Master	Charlie Johnson
Dressing Props	Don Santos
Standby Props	Damian Butlin
	Andy Forrest
	Neil McAllister
	Mark Quigley
Special Effects	Mark Holt Special Effects
	James Davis
Stunt Co-ordinators	Paul Herbert
	Paul Heasman
	Andreas Petrides
	Tom Lucy
Stunt Performers	James Cox

	Kelly Dent
	Jamie Edgell
	Rob Hunt
	Ian Kay
	Will Willoughby
	Belinda McGinley
Costume Supervisors	Alison Beard
	Vicky Salway
Crowd Costume Supervisors	Sarah Touaibi
	Jason Gill
Costume Design Assistant	Joanne Mosley
Make-up & Hair Supervisors	Christine Greenwood
Make-up & Hair Artists	Elaine Browne
	Gerda Lauciute
	Polly Fehily
	Nora Robertson
Make-up & Hair Assistant	Jo Jo Dutton
Historical Advisor	Alastair Bruce
Military Advisor	Taff Gillingham
Medical Advisor	Peter Starling
Script Editors	Sam Symons
	Claire Daxter
Production Executive	Kimberley Hikaka
Business Affairs	David O'Donoghue
	Aliboo Bradbury
Unit Publicity	Milk Publicity
Post-production Supervisor	Jessica Rundle
Assistant Editors	Mike Phillips
	Andrew Melhuish
Colourist	Aidan Farrell
Online Editors	Clyde Kellet
Re-recording Mixer	Nigel Heath
Assistant Re-recording Mixer	Alex Fielding
Sound FX Editor	Adam Armitage
Dialogue Editors	Alex Sawyer
	Tom Williams
Titles	Huge Design
Visual Effects	The Senate Visual Effects

ACKNOWLEDGEMENTS

My gratitude to Gareth Neame and Liz Trubridge remains as fervent as ever. Essentially, we three make the series, and we have spent the last four years in each other's company, inhabiting the extraordinary place that *Downton Abbey* has become. We work together to shape the scripts and the episodes and, heaven knows, we have been rewarded. I am also deeply in Ion Trewin's debt for his Herculean labours in yet again turning the screenplays and my commentary into a book; and, if anything even more than last year, I salute Doctor Alasdair Emslie, whose medical knowledge was constantly employed in finding the wounds and ailments that brought our characters home from the front. Thanks, too, to Andrew Roberts, the military historian, for suggesting several stories, great and small, based on real events from the First World War, and Fiona Shackleton for her expert advice on 1920s divorce. Cathy King and Jeremy Barber are still my terrific agents, and I am happy to say that my wife, Emma, and my son, Peregrine, have lost none of their enthusiasm for rescuing me from glaring plot errors that might otherwise have engulfed us. I am very, very grateful to them all.

Immerse yourself in the world of

DOWNTON ABBEY

THE COMPLETE SCRIPTS
SEASON ONE

Available in paperback and eBook

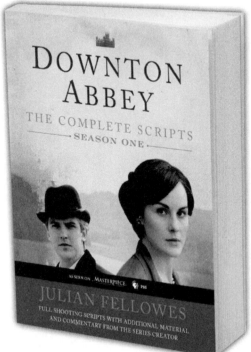

THE COMPLETE SCRIPTS
SEASON TWO

Available in paperback and eBook

Created by Oscar-winning writer Julian Fellowes, *Downton Abbey* has delighted viewers with stellar performances, ravishing sets and costumes, and above all, a gripping plot.

Each handsome volume includes the full shooting scripts as well as introductions, additional material and commentary from Julian Fellowes, and eight pages of full-color behind-the-scenes photos!

Available wherever books are sold.